## HELEN MACINNES

One of the few truly great writers in the suspense field, she wrote books that consistently hit hardcover bestseller lists and continue to sell millions of copies in paperback.

## HELEN MACINNES

Her hallmarks are sharply drawn characters, ever-twisting plots, and nailbiting suspense—the kind that keep readers glued to the pages.

## HELEN MACINNES

One of our most celebrated writers.

# *While Still We Live*

*by Helen MacInnes*

FAWCETT CREST • NEW YORK

# Contents

*Poland has not yet perished
While still we live!*

These are the opening words of the Song of the Polish Legions. It was first sung in the black year of 1797, when Poland had been divided between the three empires of Russia, Prussia, and Austria, and her exiled sons were fighting in the Legions under the gallant General Dombrowski. Thereafter, during the nineteenth century, with its incessant bloody revolts against foreign tyranny, the Song of the Legions spread secretly all over Poland, giving encouragement and hope to all those who were willing to sacrifice themselves for the future freedom of their country. Such was its power and so glorious was its history that it became the national anthem of liberated Poland; and even under new oppressors it is still sung by the Polish people, who refuse to become slaves. The noble truth of its words has been proven by history, past and present: no nation, no cause will ever die if it breeds the kind of man who is willing to sacrifice everything for it, even his life.

# While Still We Live

# CHAPTER I

## End of a Summer

THE BLINDING DIRECTNESS of the sun had gone, but its heat remained. In front of the house, the island of uncut grass baked into brown hay. The pink roses were bleached white. Only the plot of scarlet flowers still held its bright color. The heavy scent of ripening plants was in the air.

Sheila stood for a moment beside the open window. The truth was, she kept repeating to herself, she hadn't wanted to leave. There was no use in blaming her irritation on the heat; or on this last-minute packing, too long delayed; or on Uncle Matthews' latest telegram, which pinpricked her conscience every time she looked toward it and the dressing table. Even now, when she should be elbow-deep in a suitcase, she was still standing at this window, listening to the precise pattern of the Scarlatti sonata which struck clearly up from the little music room. Teresa was playing it well, today. Sheila half-smiled as she imagined the child sitting so very upright, so very serious, before the piano, while her mother, Madame Aleksander, counted silently and patiently beside her. The difficult passage was due any moment now. Sheila found herself waiting for it, and breathed with relief when it came. Madame Aleksander would be smiling, too. Teresa had managed it.

"Now," said Sheila, "I can get on with my packing." But she still stood at the window, her eyes on the driveway which entirely circled the long grass. Thick dust lay white on its rough surface. A flourish of poplars, erect and richly green against the brown harvested fields, formed the entrance gate to the house. There the driveway ended and the road to the village began. Across the road, there was nothing but plain, stretching out towards the blue sky. Here and there, the woods made thick dark patches, beside which other villages, other manor houses, sheltered. But above all, the feeling was one of space and unlimited sky. Unlimited sky ... Sheila thought suddenly of bombing planes. She turned back into the room. The smile, which had stayed on her lips since Teresa's triumph over difficult fingering, now vanished. She began to

11

pack. It was baffling how clothes seemed to multiply, merely by hanging in a wardrobe.

The music lesson was over. The house was silent. And then, downstairs in the entrance hall, the phone bell rang harshly. Sheila, by a process of ruthless jamming and forcing, had managed to close the last suitcase. She was locking it, with no small feeling of personal triumph, when Barbara's light footsteps came running up the staircase, through the square landing which was called Madame Aleksander's "sewing room," through Barbara's own bedroom, and then halted abruptly at the doorway of the guest room. Sheila finished untwisting the key before she looked up. Barbara had been waiting for this look. She came into the bedroom slowly, dramatically. Her wide eyes were larger than ever with the news she brought.

"Actually finished," Sheila said, and searched in the pocket of her blouse for a cigarette.

Barbara said, "Sheila, that was Uncle Edward phoning." She spoke in English, her voice stumbling, in its eagerness, through the foreign language.

"Was it?" Sheila was now looking for the perpetually disappearing matches.

"Sheila, you know quite well that something has happened," Barbara said reproachfully. Her face showed her disappointment: her excitement was waning in spite of itself.

Sheila relented, and laughed. "All right, Barbara. What's your news?"

"Uncle Edward."

"What about Uncle Edward?" Sheila thought of the quiet, forgetting rather than forgetful Professor Edward Korytowski, who was Madame Aleksander's brother.

"He has just phoned from Warsaw." Barbara was walking about the room now, straightening the pile of books and magazines, arranging the vase on top of the dressing table. She broke into French in order to speak more quickly. "He's worried about you, and he must be very worried to drag himself away from the Library and his books. He even suggested he was coming here to fetch you, if we didn't get you away tonight."

"But the news has been bad for weeks..." Weeks? Months, rather. Even years.

"Well, it must be worse. Uncle Edward has friends, you know, who are in the government. Before he was a professor, he was active in politics, himself. It looks as if someone has managed to get him away from his manuscript long enough to waken him up again. Certainly, he is very worried. He made me fetch Mother from the kitchen, where she had gone after the piano lesson to attend to something or other. He made me bring her to the phone when she was in the middle of preparing a sauce. And now she is so worried that she even forgot to be angry about the sauce. She is coming up to see you as soon as she can get away from the kitchen."

Sheila found it wasn't so easy after all to pretend that everything was normal. There was no use getting excited, but on the other hand there was no use disregarding Uncle Edward. He was far from being a sensationalist.

"What did Uncle Edward say, exactly?"

"To me, he said: 'Is Sheila Matthews still there? In heaven's name, why? Didn't I advise her to leave last week at the latest? If she doesn't leave tonight, I'll come down and get her and see her on that train, myself.' And then he told me to bring Mother to the phone, and grumbled about a pack of women losing all count of time."

Sheila looked towards the open window with its square of blue sky and green treetops, watched a large black bee hovering with its sleepy murmur over the window sill. Yes, one lost all count of time, all sense of urgency here. That was one of the things she had enjoyed most at Korytów.

"Is the wireless set working yet?" Sheila asked.

Barbara's pretty mouth smiled. "Stefan thinks he has found out what is wrong. Don't you hear that crackling coming from his room?"

"Peculiar noises are always coming from Stefan's room," Sheila gave an answering smile. She had a particular fondness for Barbara's fourteen-year-old brother Stefan, the great inventor. The wireless set had been having its monthly overhaul. The result, so far, had been a strong sound of frying at each turn of the dial.

The two girls heard Madame Aleksander's footsteps, now. They had halted for a moment in her sewing room, before she came through Barbara's room.

Barbara and Sheila exchanged quick glances. Madame Aleksander's footsteps told them so much. The underlying worry of the last month, with all its alarms and false reports, was now plain in their eyes.

Madame Aleksander hesitated a moment at the doorway of the guest room, as if she were tired, depressed, loath to give them the news she had brought. The fair hair, fading to platinum, was smoothly braided round the neat head. The bright blue eyes under the straight eyebrows were desperately worried. There was a droop to the corner of her mouth. And then, as she saw the girls watching her so silently, there was the beginning of a smile. It was a good effort, Sheila decided appraisingly, and offered Madame Aleksander the solitary chair.

"I'm afraid we shall have to miss our late afternoon talk, today," Madame Aleksander said. It was the custom of this house for all the members of the family to gather in Madame Aleksander's sewing room, and there, in the little white-paneled room with its polished floor and faded brown velvet chairs, with its soft green porcelain stove and its long window looking out between the front pillars of the house, they'd drink a glass of coffee and talk. There was no dearth of conversation in this house. Aunt Marta, who managed the farm lands as her sister looked after the household, would arrive from the fields or her office. Barbara would leave the books she was reading for the autumn examinations at Warsaw University. Teresa would clatter up the staircase until her mother's quiet but firm voice reduced her speed to a polite walk. Teresa had been to see her friend Wanda, the little goosegirl, or had rushed round to the stables to see her friend Felix, or had talked with her friend Kazia coming back from the market at Lowicz. (It was Teresa who brought the news of the day "My friend Wanda," or "My friend Felix," she would begin halfway up the staircase, and then would follow a rambling, breathless story. There was a new baby in the village. There was to be a wedding, but not a proper one: there would be no four days of dancing and fun, because the man had been called up for the army. The schoolteacher had come back from his holiday, and there were going to be lessons again once the harvesting was all finished. Wanda's grandmother had a pain in her back, and you could hear it creak when she bent over the cloverfield.) Last of all to arrive was Stefan, and as soon as he arrived, Aunt Marta would send him away to tidy himself. "Stefan, if you must oil the clocks, please leave the oil where it belongs. *Not* on your hands." Stefan would smile good-humoredly and obey. Sheila had guessed that the boy only made this appearance, anyway, out of politeness and a sense of duty. He wasn't interested in the discussions about crops and prices (Aunt Marta), or in the problems of housekeeping or education (his mother), or in Students' Clubs (Barbara), or in "my friend Wanda" (Teresa). But he hid his boredom well. Perhaps the fact that his two older brothers—the remaining members of the Aleksander family—were so much occupied in Warsaw made Stefan feel the responsibility of being the man of the house.

Madame Aleksander had tried to make her voice sound normal, but the attempt wasn't so successful as her smile. Perhaps she knew there were not going to be any more afternoon talks—neither today, nor tomorrow, nor any other day.

Barbara had sensed that, too. "Sheila is almost ready," she tried.

"It is unbelievable, isn't it?" Sheila said hurriedly. "I really must apologize for being such a persistent guest. I came for three weeks, and I stayed more than two months. I don't think I realized that until I looked at a calendar, today."

"It is our fault. We enjoyed your visit so much, that we have kept you too long." Madame Aleksander's English was grammatically perfect. There was a slight twist in the accent which added to the charm of her low voice. "But you will have to leave tonight, Sheila, if not for your own comfort, then certainly for your own safety. Edward is very gloomy. He has stopped all work on his book."

"Then the news *is* serious!" Barbara exclaimed.

"Be serious, yourself, Barbara." There was an edge to Madame Aleksander's usually calm voice. Barbara was chastened. When you are twenty-one, it is difficult not to make a joke, not to try to make people smile. She sat on the arm of the chair and placed her hand on her mother's shoulder. Sheila, watching them together, thought how comic it was, but in a charming way, to see such a strong family resemblance. But then, Sheila told herself with a touch of private bitterness, that was only because she herself had no family. Except Uncle Matthews, of course, and he scarcely counted: he was much too busy. There wasn't much in common between him and her—not even a nose. With the Aleksanders, it was so different. Barbara was a younger, more enthusiastic Madame Aleksander. Teresa was a miniature Barbara. Even Aunt Marta had the same wide-set blue eyes, broad brow, straight eyebrows, short nose, round chin. So had Andrew, the second oldest son, who lived in Warsaw. So had Uncle Edward. Only Stefan and Stanislaw, the eldest son, were different. Stefan was black-haired, brown-eyed, with the thin high nose of his dead father's portrait. Stanislaw was the image of his father, Sheila had heard: he was the only Aleksander whom Sheila hadn't met. He was a diplomat, married to a rich wife. And as Aunt Marta said frequently, "What between watching military attachés with one eye, and his wife's international antics with the other, it's small wonder that Stanislaw had little time to look in our direction nowadays."

Madame Aleksander broke the silence. "Well, it's all arranged. Andrew is coming here, this evening. That nice young American friend of his, Mr. Stevens, is bringing him down in his car."

Barbara's face lighted. "It will be almost a party, mother! Is Andrew coming to say good-by to Sheila? Couldn't he have seen her as she passed through Warsaw?" She was laughing as Sheila's face reddened.

"Andrew," Madame Aleksander said slowly, "is coming to say good-by to us all. He joins his regiment tonight at ten. They leave Warsaw at dawn."

When the girls didn't speak, but remained staring at her, Madame Aleksander said, "Sheila is to travel back with Mr. Stevens and Andrew to Warsaw. Uncle Edward and Mr. Stevens will see that she catches the midnight express from Warsaw."

She rose abruptly. She was once more the capable mistress of the house, her eyes on the watch which was pinned to her blouse, her mind already calculating the amounts and varieties of food and drink available at such short notice. "They'll be here at six o'clock and must leave by eight. We haven't long." She frowned, as she considered the time it would take to prepare the food. And then, brusquely, "Sheila, do see that eveything's packed. And don't place your passport at the bottom of a suitcase. Barbara, run to the village, and tell them your brother is coming. We shall need help for Maria and Zofia in the kitchen. And ask everyone to come to the house later this evening. There will be plenty to eat and drink. When you've done that, come right back, for I need your help in the storeroom and with the linen and silver."

Barbara paused as she left the room. "Shall we invite the schoolmaster to dinner?" Her voice was too casual.

"I don't think it's necessary. He was here last week." Her mother's voice was equally casual, but the straight eyebrows were straighter. As Barbara's footsteps descended the staircase, Madame Aleksander looked uncertainly at Sheila.

"Sometimes," she said unwillingly, "I worry about Barbara."

"I don't think you need to, Madame Aleksander." Sheila smiled as warmly as she could.

"You don't?" Madame Aleksander's blue eyes were searching her face.

"I really mean what I said."

There was a slight pause.

Then, "Do you like that young schoolmaster?" Madame Aleksander asked slowly.

"Yes. I like Jan Reska."

"Aunt Marta doesn't. She says he is a radical."

"I think all the nicest old men I've met were radicals when they were young."

"But it seems so odd, Sheila, to bury yourself in a little village like this if you have talent."

Sheila, watching the anxious face, thought: You yourself do a very good job of burying, Madame Aleksander. She said, "Jan Reska was a farmer's son. He hasn't been able to free himself of his love of the land. That's why he chooses to teach in a country village."

Madame Aleksander nodded. She looked as if she could understand and believe that. Suddenly she raised her hands in a quick gesture to her face. "Oh, how dreadful . . . I nearly forgot. Sheila, would you hurry after Barbara? Tell her to visit Kawka's house. His mother is very ill. I want to know how she is. And if Father Mazur is there, tell Barbara to invite him to dine with us." She paused, and then added: "Tell her to invite Jan Reska, too."

Sheila hurried down the curving staircase and through the square entrance hall. Behind her was the kitchen, the smell of spiced fruit newly bottled, Maria's voice raised in anger. Zofia's weeping followed Sheila out of doors into the warm air. As she crossed the shaded veranda, with its four white pillars rising to support the overhanging roof, and descended the shallow steps, hot to the touch of her thin shoes, she was thinking how strange it was that one servant should be so arrogant with another. Madame Aleksander ruled the kitchen with a firm hand, but she never reduced Zofia to wailing. Maria could, and frequently did.

Sheila hesitated on the sandy surface of the drive. Barbara had probably taken the short cut, past the small west wing of the house, past the stables and the duckpond. My friend Wanda was there, sitting under the shade of a willow that wept into the dark water. A yellow kerchief hid her tightly plaited hair, her bare legs were straight and wide apart before her, like a ballet girl on a Degas canvas. One of the geese hissed angrily at the running Sheila. "Boo to you," she called in English over her shoulder. Wanda looked up from her knitting, and her face crinkled. She didn't understand, but she laughed, anyway. Sheila gave the child a wave of her hand, as she passed through the line of linden trees and entered the path which edged Kawka's long, narrow stretch of land. His was the first house in the straight row of rye-thatched cottages which formed the village of Korytów.

She saw Kawka and his wife and his sister, working halfway up the field. And then, just as she was wondering if her hesitating attempts to speak Polish would be understood by them, or if they wouldn't object to hearing some German instead, she saw Barbara. And with Barbara was the schoolmaster. They were standing under one of the broad linden trees. They waved, as if they had noticed her indecision. She went forward slowly, thankful that it had been she, and not Aunt Marta, who had found them standing hand-in-hand so openly. But as she saw the numbed, helpless look in their eyes, she knew that the time for discretion was past. Time was too short. They knew it.

"Jan cannot come," Barbara replied to Sheila's message from Madame Aleksander. "He leaves within the hour. The call came this morning. Just a piece of paper handed silently into his house. That was all."

Sheila didn't know what to say. Anything seemed trite. She looked at Reska. He had the strong body, the quiet, large-boned face of a countryman. The sweat still glistened on his throat. His hands and forearms were covered with harvest dust. He had been working with Kawka. He had chosen to help on that piece of land because it lay nearest to the manor house, and he had desperately hoped to see Barbara, or Sheila, or even Teresa, to give them the news of his going.

His blue eyes were fixed on the horizon, as if he could see the German waves ready to roll over these plains. "I wonder just how many men they really have," he said softly, almost to himself. "There's been so much bluster and talk." Then he smiled as if to cheer the anxious girls, and the hard line of his high cheekbones and strong chin softened.

"If things were desperate, I'm sure the Polish armies would be fully mobilized and at the frontier now," Sheila said hopefully.

"It's a long frontier." Reska's voice was not dejected, only philosophic. "And we have been mustering the troops slowly, almost secretly. We are far from being mobilized. The democracies have asked us to give the Germans no excuse for attack, so we leave ourselves vulnerable in trying to keep the peace. Personally, I think we would have been wiser to have mobilized weeks ago. If the Germans don't find an excuse, they invent one."

Sheila suddenly felt she shouldn't be here with them. Hurriedly she said, "I'll go down to Kawka's house. Father Mazur will understand me if I talk German, won't he?"

Barbara nodded.

To Reska, Sheila spoke the Polish good-by phrases, which she had been mastering in the last few days. He bowed with unexpected grace, and gave a neat reply which embraced Poland, her allies, his good wishes for her safe journey to London, his hope to see her again in Poland once victory was won. He raised her hand, and kissed the cuff of her sleeve.

By the time she left Kawka's house, Barbara was waiting

alone for her under the linden tree. Neither of them appeared aware of the heavy tears on Barbara's cheeks. Sheila found herself staring at the western horizon as Reska had done.


## CHAPTER II

## *The Last Dinner Party*


ANDREW ALEKSANDER and Mr. Stevens had arrived. The car had driven up in a swirl of warm dust, Teresa and Stefan had rushed outside, the stable dogs had barked, the ducks and geese had added their contribution of noise from the pond. In the kitchen, women's high voices had subsided with their hurrying footsteps. Everything was ready.

In her room, Sheila pretended to make a last search through the drawers of the dressing table. She was increasingly nervous about going downstairs. She persuaded herself that she must give Andrew and his friend time to meet the family. One drawer, forgotten in its smallness, roused a vague suspicion. She crossed over to the little rosewood writing desk. She was right. She had almost left her diary. Small wonder that she had forgotten it: she hadn't entered a thing in it for weeks. In London, where she had always been so busy, she had yet managed to keep an account of what she had done each day. Here, there had never seemed to be any time for writing a diary. She smiled at that. Diaries must be for lonely people.

She opened the book, crossing over to the window to have better light to read. What had she been doing one year ago today? That was always amusing to find out. *August 30, 1938....* The Sudeten question. Enrollment in a class for voluntary nursing. An appointment with a newspaper editor, in the hope of being accepted as a very minor member of his staff.... Not a very good entry.... The Sudeten question was now solving itself in Danzig. The voluntary nursing hadn't been much of a success—why did other people not turn sick at the sight of blood? As for the newspaper job ... too many would-be correspondents, too few openings.

A movement from the clump of bushes near the American's car caught her eye. There was a glimpse of white loose sleeve, as an arm grabbed a small, tow-headed boy, and pulled him back into the thick shrubbery. There was a giggle; children's voices trying to be subdued and not succeeding; and once more the head of the boy struggling into view.

This time, he evaded the arm, and dashed towards the running-board. By standing on tiptoe, he could just see over the edge of the open car.

"Red," he squeaked excitedly over his shoulder. He stared inside once more, his small hands clutching the car's side tightly. "Leather!" he added. There was a flurry of excitement in the bushes. Yellow-topped Wanda darted forward, followed by an older girl in the wide-sleeved blouse. Then Felix appeared, charging round from the stable end of the house with a yell like a factory whistle. The children vanished. Felix, growling into his long mustache, searched in the bushes. But the birds had indeed flown. My friend Wanda's high laugh sounded from the straggling pinewoods beyond.

Sheila laughed too, and Felix looked up. He had dressed himself in his best clothes—tight, black trousers tucked into tight, high boots; a sleeveless jacket over a clean, white shirt—and he had combed his few remaining hairs into a toothy parting.

"Felix, you do look handsome," Sheila called down, and won a broad gap of a smile.

"The young lady is ready to leave?"

"Yes." Sheila heard the sound of galloping horses. They were coming from the east, but the pine woods which hid the children also blocked any clear view.

"That is sad. Everyone is going away. All the young people, once more." He stood shaking his upturned head.

The hoofbeats struck the road, and two horses swept into the driveway. Sheila held her breath. The horses reared as they were tightly reined in, stood erect on their quivering haunches for a long moment, and then dropped their forefeet slowly to the ground. A white-haired man dismounted and gave the reins over to Felix. But the dark young man in uniform still sat on his horse. He was looking up at Sheila with sufficient interest to freeze the smile on her lips into self-consciousness. She drew back half a pace. Then, with a smart salute to the tip of his smart cap, the officer vaulted lightly off his horse, threw the reins over Felix's waiting arm, and followed the older man into the house.

Sheila placed the diary on top of a suitcase. Before the mirror, she combed her fair hair, added more powder to an already perfect skin. Her brown eyes looked back at her reprimandingly. "You had no need," they said severely, "to keep staring at him."

Barbara, white-faced, sad-mouthed, interrupted her thoughts. "Sheila, aren't you ready? We are waiting. And we have other guests, too, now. Adam Wisniewski and his father have ridden over from their house. Adam's regiment is moving north, and it is stationed tonight near Lowicz. It is requisitioning more horses. Adam got leave to see his father, and they have come over here to say good-by. He's Andrew's greatest friend. Did you meet him when Andrew was in London last year? Adam passed through there on his way to the Dublin Horse Show. He rides, you know."

"So I saw."

"Mother would like me to marry Adam. Can you see any reason why I don't fall in love with him?" Barbara was half-smiling.

"None." Sheila paused. "Except that you fell in love with Jan Reska."

Barbara must have been thinking of Reska too. Her voice wasn't very steady now. "It's funny . . ." She took Sheila's arm, and together they walked slowly towards the staircase.

"What is?" Sheila asked gently.

"Falling in love. How you do it, with whom . . ." Barbara managed to control her voice better. "Mother wants to see all her children married to people she likes. Of course you knew that was why she asked you to visit us this summer? She was so eager to see you, after Andrew came home from London and talked about you most of the time."

"Oh." Sheila had wondered about that. After all, that was one of the reasons which had made her decide to accept Madame Aleksander's invitation: she had wanted to find out, too, if she were really in love with Andrew.

"You would have been just my choice for a sister-in-law," Barbara was saying. She watched Sheila's face as if hoping for a denial that Sheila wouldn't be her sister-in-law. She saw, instead, a look of embarrassment and unhappiness well mixed. In some things, Barbara thought, the British girl seemed so much older than she did—in other things, such as falling in love and recognizing it, Sheila was so much younger. It was incredible that people should be afraid of their emotions, instead of enjoying them.

"Don't worry, Sheila." Barbara's sun-tanned arm went round Sheila's shoulder. "Don't worry. Mother has other things to think about now. She is talking downstairs about leaving for Warsaw to do hospital work if war comes. She nursed in the last one, you know."

In the hall, there was the sound of many voices, even laughter.

"Is the news better?" Sheila asked, as a heavily laden Maria, followed by a twittering Zofia, bustled past the girls.

Barbara shook her head slowly. All pretense of lightheartedness was gone. Then Maria's broad back had pushed the dining room door wide open, and Madame Aleksander had seen them, was coming forward to welcome Sheila.

"You aren't shy?" she asked gently, looking at the girl's wide eyes. And Sheila immediately lost the composure she had been mustering. The faces around her were so many, so vague. Then suddenly, they focused sharply. She found herself looking into the brown eyes of the tall cavalry officer. She *would* have to pick on him, she thought angrily, and looked quickly away. She had the feeling that it wasn't quickly enough. He was smiling.

Andrew was beside her now, looking very strange and serious in his uniform. There were the introductions to be completed: Father Mazur, Pan Wisniewski, Mr. Russell Stevens, Captain Adam Wisniewski. There was a scraping of chairs. The last party in Madame Aleksander's house was about to begin. As if everyone were admitting it secretly to himself, there was a sudden restraint, a hush that continued after the priest's blessing was over.

Teresa ended it. Her eyes, round with excitement at having been included in a real grownup party, were examining the elaborately embroidered cloth, the silver vases and candlesticks.

"When did you get all this, mother?" she asked suddenly.

The men roared with laughter. The priest's serious face relaxed into a smile. Aunt Marta, looking more Roman matron than ever in her best black dress, said severely, "Teresa, they were your great-great-grandmother's. At times, they have been buried deep in the earth to save them from the Cossacks. But when it was safe to bring them out, they came out for special occasions. Tonight is a special occasion." With that, Aunt Marta turned to Pan Wisniewski and began a conversation about the requisitioning of horses, the low price of hogs, and the long summer drought. Madame Aleksander was talking with Father Mazur, their voices so low that Sheila guessed the latest news was under discussion. Captain Wisniewski was doing his best to entertain Barbara with his most recent troubles. Now and again, the captain would glance across the table to Sheila, as if including her; and then Sheila would hastily renew her conversation with Andrew on her right. The American on her left seemed to understand that Andrew had a lot to say, for he kept silent and devoted himself to the variety of food which Maria and the other women were serving. Maria's habit of entering into the conversations with a crusty comment or two seemed to amuse Mr. Stevens. His Polish, Sheila noted, was more fluent than her own efforts. His appetite was certainly better.

The pinpricks of light from the tall white candles had spread into a rich glow as the sunset faded. There was a steady flow of talk, but the animation was tense and strained. Andrew was quiet, gentle, sympathetic, but there was a hard look in his eyes whenever the subjects of present news, probable war, or Germany were introduced. So he and Sheila talked of London, of the friends he had made there last winter, when he had visited England with a Purchasing Commission for army supplies. Then Andrew spoke of her Uncle Matthews, who, he was sure, would blame him for not having made Sheila leave Poland ten days ago.

"No," Sheila said quickly, emphatically. "No, Andrew. Please don't worry about that. My uncle knows by this time that you did try to get me to leave two weeks ago, when you left Warsaw for Gdynia. He also knows me. I think . . ."

Andrew smiled at that. Sheila avoided Captain Wisniewski's very direct look.

"I must say I had rather a shock today when I got back to Warsaw and discovered you had never gone to England," Andrew admitted. "Why didn't you go when you said you would?"

"I meant to. But somehow there were so many things I still had to do. And there was a wedding in the village to which I was invited. It is strange, isn't it, how a village can catch you up in a way that a big city never touches you?"

Sheila was suddenly aware that the American was listening, too. She turned to him and smiled to excuse her neglect.

"Hello," he said very seriously. "I'm Russell Stevens. Remember me? I'm the fellow that came in with Andrew."

"I'm Sheila Matthews," she countered weakly.

"I know. I'm a friend of Andrew's." He watched the heightening color in her cheeks with matter-of-fact interest. "And how does our English friend enjoy the Polish countryside? It's all too marvelous?"

The mocking note of quotation in his voice annoyed Sheila. I am *not* an impressionable schoolgirl, she thought irritably. She glanced involuntarily across the table, and then wished she hadn't. Captain Wisniewski had given up all pretense of talking to Barbara, and was watching her quite openly. The calm scrutiny opposite, with its implied masculine confidence, had its effect. The neat little speech which she was preparing for Mr. Stevens' benefit suddenly disintegrated.

"Go on," Mr. Stevens said encouragingly. "You look very charming when you are indignant."

She checked her next words in embarrassment. At a time like this, she would only argue emotionally. Perhaps Mr.

Stevens had guessed what she was thinking, for he gave her an unexpected smile and glanced at his watch. That was the third time he had looked at it in the last half-hour.

Sheila said, "I'm sorry I am giving you all this trouble. The journey to Warsaw, I mean. But you don't have to put me on a train. I've caught midnight trains abroad, before now."

"On the eve of a war? And what a war!"

Sheila was silent.

"I'm not worrying about you, Miss Matthews. You are one of the lucky ones. You are leaving." He looked round the room. Food and wine had slackened the tense conversations. The animation was gone. A calm fatalism had taken its place.

"They've suffered more than our countries have," Sheila said slowly.

"We'll learn." The American's voice was grim. Suddenly he was alert. "What's that?"

Sheila listened tensely. So did Madame Aleksander and Barbara. But it was only the engine of a high-powered car.

"Someone to visit you, Madame Aleksander," Stevens said, more for the sake of ending the sudden silence than for anything else.

"An emergency, perhaps?" Wisniewski's strong, deep voice suggested. Both he and Andrew had risen to their feet as the brakes screeched on the driveway. Their uniforms emphasized the serious look they interchanged.

Maria entered with a short announcement. "There's a man to see the English lady."

"A gentleman to see Miss Matthews," Madame Aleksander said pointedly.

"He's a German," Maria said, equally pointedly.

For one painful moment, all eyes were fixed on Sheila's astonished face, and then suddenly, everyone had something interesting to say to each other. To Sheila, it was as embarrassing as silence would have been.

Teresa was already out of her chair. "Mother, I want to see a German."

"Stay where you are, Teresa."

"But, mother," Stefan said, his brown eyes urgent, "I'd like to see what kind of car he has. Listen, all the children are looking at it." Through the open windows, the voices of the children had indeed grown louder. Sheila, as she rose from the table, saw many people outside on the grass. The villagers were beginning to arrive. It must be nearly eight o'clock.

She excused herself with a slightly bewildered smile, and

hurried into the hall. Russell Stevens followed her along with Stefan and Teresa.

"And *don't* be long with your German friend," he warned her. "We've only ten minutes." He gave her a grin, and went outside with the children.

Maria was pointing to the music room. "He's in there," she said unceremoniously. All her friendliness was gone.

Sheila pushed aside the white paneled door. The man, who had been sitting uncomfortably on the piano stool, rose and faced her. He was a complete stranger.

Sheila widened her eyes to see better in the darkening room. The man moved to the window. She followed him there, and they stood looking at each other in the last of the evening light.

"I think there's a mistake," Sheila said in German. "I don't know you."

The man was staring at her curiously: a white-haired, square-faced man with tight lips and clever eyes.

"No, Miss Matthews," he said in English, "you don't know me. My name is Johann Hofmeyer. I have business connections with your uncle, Mr. John Matthews. He had just wired me about you."

"Then he sent you here?"

The man bowed. "He telegraphed yesterday, and gave me your address. I am at your service, Miss Matthews, to take you back to Warsaw. There is a plane to Bucharest which you could catch tonight."

Sheila's confusion left her. She was suddenly on the alert.

"My uncle doesn't have a branch of his business in Warsaw," she said.

"I am not in your uncle's business." There was a suspicion of a smile. "I have my own business. I export the finest Polish table delicacies. Your uncle's firm is a very good customer. I have been under obligations to him. So, when he telegraphs me in urgent language, then I feel impelled to do as he asks."

Sheila relented. "I am afraid I have given you unnecessary trouble. I am very sorry. But I am just on the point of leaving for Warsaw."

"And when are you leaving Warsaw?"

Sheila smiled. This man was quick. "By a train about midnight," she answered.

Mr. Hofmeyer produced a bulging pocketbook. He handed her several pieces of paper, neatly clipped together. "Your plane tickets. Give up the idea of a train, Miss Matthews. You are sure you won't come with me now?"

Sheila shook her head. "It's very kind of you, but my friends are waiting for me."

"So. Well, at least my journey here wasn't wasted. I can let your uncle know that you *are* leaving Warsaw, tonight."

Sheila was thinking, why does he keep looking at me like this? She said, "How did you know when I came into this room that I *was* Sheila Matthews?"

She couldn't fathom the man's half-smile, the suddenly guarded look on his face.

"Am I really so like my uncle?" she asked gently, and waited tensely for the reply.

"No. Not really." Then, as if he had said too much, Mr. Hofmeyer turned towards the door.

"Mr. Hofmeyer," Sheila began awkwardly, "thank you for coming here. I should think it must have been a very unpleasant journey for you, at the moment."

The man caught her meaning. "I've lived in Poland for twenty years. There are a number of Germans here, landowners and businessmen. We are accepted as Poles."

Sheila looked at the square face, white, heavy-lined. She couldn't read anything there. If the man worried about his status in Poland at this time, it wasn't evident. A blank look had spread over his features. His face had become unmemorable, undistinguished.

"Good-by, Miss Matthews. My regards to your uncle."

"Good-by."

Sheila heard his light, firm step cross the parquetry floor in the hall.

Involuntarily, she stood close to the window. There was a crowd of children in the garden. The American's tall shoulders were surrounded by a waist-high sea of sleek heads and bright clothes. He was showing them how the lights of his car switched off and on. Sheila heard the children's Oh's and Ah's of bliss. In the general clamor of thin light voices, Mr. Hofmeyer's square figure had hurried down the steps of the house. The villagers, who had been staring through the dining room windows, turned to watch him as he entered his car. As it swung into the road and gathered speed, there was the beginning of a song from the other side of the house. A woman's voice was chanting a four-lined stanza, a man's followed it with another verse, and then a slow rhythmic chorus came from the other peasants, and quickened to a crescendo. The villagers were saying good-by in their own way.

The door opened, and Madame Aleksander came in. "Sheila, they are leaving." Her voice, at last, had no disguise.

Sheila's throat tightened. "I don't know how to thank you," she began. And then as she saw Madame Aleksander's face, she said quickly with a rush of emotion and much truth, "I have loved being here ... all of you ..." Madame Aleksander embraced her quickly. There were tears on her cheeks too. Not just for this parting, Sheila knew. They were both weeping for all the partings this night. They were weeping for all the women who were weeping with them.

Aunt Marta was in the hall, calling them in her firm voice. The others were gathered there too now.

Madame Aleksander quickly dried her tears, and blew her nose. She went forward to Andrew.

Sheila, still holding the plane tickets in her hand, took the hat and gloves and coat and handbag and diary which Maria had brought downstairs.

"Everything else is in the car," Aunt Marta was saying.

Stefan said eagerly, "You will send me those airplane magazines you promised?" Sheila gave him a bear's hug and a nod. So many outstretched hands to take and hold for a brief moment, so many voices, kind, affectionate, well-wishing. Teresa's small, thin fingers wouldn't let go.

Barbara was saying, "Write me at Uncle Edward's flat. I'll be in Warsaw, if war comes."

Adam Wisniewski stood slightly apart, watching the group round Sheila and Andrew almost grimly. Sheila's eyes met his. She had a feeling he was going to speak. But Russell Stevens had taken her coat and her hat and her arm, and was leading her determinedly towards the car. "We'll be late," he was saying anxiously.

Sheila settled herself obediently in the car, but she wondered at her sudden annoyance with anyone so helpful as Mr. Stevens. It was all because of this parting, she decided. Partings were unsettling: you lost something, and you were never sure of being able to possess it again. That was it, she told herself firmly. Partings were disturbing.

She heard Adam Wisniewski's voice saying, "See you in Berlin, Andrew," and saw his arm round Andrew's shoulders. Then there were other voices—Stefan's, Teresa's. And Aunt Marta calling practical advice.

Andrew left his family.

It was over. At last. They were driving through the gate of poplars. The lighted windows, the moving heads of people crowding around the house, the four white pillars sheltering the group of upraised hands, the children's shouts, were gone. Above them was a dark sky, and the sudden coolness of a night breeze.

# CHAPTER III

## Warsaw

THE JOURNEY to Warsaw was spasmodic. Every now and again, the car pulled to the side of the wide, flat road, to let the columns of soldiers, with their rifles and blankets slung across their shoulders, go marching past. Long, boat-shaped carts, piled with supplies and equipment, lumbered along on their creaking wheels. The horses didn't like the noise of the car, and the men walking at their head helped the drivers control them. Twice a detachment of cavalry trotted past. The tilt of the men's caps reminded Sheila of Adam Wisniewski. There were army cars, too, forcing their way westwards past the moving men and rearing horses. Twenty feet away from the main road was a smaller, rougher track. Along this, groups of silent men were walking with the long easy stride of the peasant. They were going east to report for duty. Soon they, too, would be marching westwards like the soldiers they now met. Everywhere was the taste of dust, the smell of gasoline, the whinnying of horses, the jingling of harness, the roar of engines, the grinding of sudden brakes, commands, shouts, oaths, and the steady ominous rhythm of marching boots. How often Sheila had read "Mobilization is being completed. Troops are moving to the frontiers." But never had she imagined this labor and sweat, the exhaustion of tempers and bodies, the ear-rending confusion of sounds intensified by the darkness.

Once she said softly to the American, "Why don't they use the trains?"

"They are using the trains," he replied.

And once she said to Andrew, "Surely mobilization is almost complete now." It was an effort to cheer him up as much as an expression of her amazement at the numbers of men and the quantities of material which she was now seeing.

Andrew shook his head sadly. "Not yet," he answered. And Sheila, who had never pretended to know much about war, but had often agreed with loud demands for action against Nazi Germany, fell miserably silent. There was so much more to war than indignation meetings ever imagined.

After the darkness of the countryside, Warsaw's lights seemed gay and confident. Three armed policemen stopped the car for examination on the outskirts of the city. Then, it became a matter of speedy driving through the southwestern suburbs, with their broad streets, modern apartment houses, and well-spaced gardens; of skirting the busy center of the town, with its lighted shops and cafés and tramcars. They reached the River Vistula, and turned north on the new parkway at the enormous Kierbedz Bridge.

As they neared the Citadel, Andrew leaned forward to give last directions. He was standing on the running-board of the car as it slowed up at the large gateway. A bleak light above the sentry's head glared down at them. Andrew had only time to jump off, to salute them, to say something which Sheila didn't even manage to hear, and then he was hurrying past the rigid sentry. For the second time that night, Sheila felt hot tears sting her eyes. The parting had been so quick, so brisk. She hadn't meant to say good-by like this. It was callous. She felt she had been totally inadequate. The American must have felt that too. He broke the long silence of their journey, back into the center of the town again, only as they passed the Church of the Holy Cross and entered the little side street which would bring them to Professor Korytowski's flat. And then he said, rather gruffly, "What's that you have been holding in your hand all this time?"

Sheila looked down at the sheaf of papers. She had forgotten about them. She said, "Plane tickets to Bucharest," and stuffed them into her coat pocket.

"I'll phone the airport while you wash your face," Stevens said bluntly. And then he addressed the windshield, "Although it beats me how a girl can cry so much for a man she doesn't care two straws about!"

Sheila didn't answer that. She had been wondering too. Perhaps it was because she liked Andrew so much that she was sorry he was in love with her. But she couldn't tell Stevens that. He wouldn't see the logic, only the vanity, in that. It would have surprised her greatly to know what Mr. Stevens actually had decided: "Well, she's honest, at least. No false pretenses." He gave her an encouraging smile, which she hadn't quite expected, as the car halted in Czacki Street.

The outside of the house hadn't changed so much since June, when Sheila had first arrived in Warsaw and had spent a week with Barbara here. Except that the window-panes were all taped, now; and there was a large notice pasted up outside the porter's house at the gateway; and inside the gateway itself, there were buckets of sand and water. A round-faced, bald-headed porter was sitting under the solitary entrance light at the doorway to his flat. He lifted an eye from his newspaper to identify them. A radio voice was talking earnestly from an open window behind his head. There was a smell of cooking sausage. A woman's voice called, "Supper, Henryk!" before her head appeared through the window. She looked at the two newcomers curiously.

Henryk had risen slowly. He limped towards them, and peered cautiously at Sheila and Stevens as if he had bad eyesight.

"Well, it's the American gentleman," he said. "Going to visit the Professor?"

"Yes." Russell Stevens didn't wait for any further questioning. Sheila had turned her head towards the garden round which the block of apartments was built. She had no desire for anyone to see her face, stained with dust and tears, at this moment. The American seemed to understand, for he took her arm, and led her into the garden courtyard. "Inquisitive old buzzard," he said under his breath.

"He's new, isn't he? There was a younger man here in June," Sheila said.

"The younger chap is now in the navy. Henryk came last month. Usually, I don't mind him. But I guess my nerves need a good stiff drink tonight."

"Do you come here often, then?" They were following the paved path round the edge of the garden to the doorway in the courtyard which led to Professor Korytowski's staircase.

"Once a week. About. There's always a good party on Sunday nights. Just men, and a lot of talking."

The night in the city seemed warm. It hadn't the edge of the air at Korytów. But inside this courtyard, there was the sweet perfume of flowers and leaves, strangely remote from the busy streets only a hundred yards away. Sheila stepped carefully round another pail of sand at the foot of the staircase. There was still another one on the landing outside Professor Korytowski's door.

As they waited for the door to be opened, Sheila said, "You know, I have rather a strange feeling..." She ignored Stevens' grin. "I should either have gone home two weeks ago—"

"You're dead right, there."

"—or," Sheila finished, "I shouldn't go at all. Not just now, anyway."

"Just when, then?"

Sheila was thinking, what is it that he finds so funny about me? She said, "Oh, after some weeks, once the war, has settled down. After all, people stayed in Paris during the last war, and did what they could to help."

Russell Stevens looked at her in alarm. "You are leaving, tonight!" he said determinedly. "Personally, I don't care whether you go or stay. You are old enough to take care of yourself. But Andrew Aleksander happens to be a friend of mine, and he has asked me to see you leave. So leave you do. Even if it kills me, or what is more important, even if it loses me my job." He glanced at his watch, and pressed the doorbell once more.

"You have work to do?" That might explain Mr. Stevens' impatience.

"A mere detail of broadcasting at one o'clock in the morning." The voice was acid, and justifiably so. Sheila felt more of a nuisance than ever. She gave Professor Korytowski a very subdued greeting. The look of worry and strain on his face didn't ease her conscience.

The apartment had three rooms and a very small kitchen. There was the living room in which Uncle Edward ate and worked and received his students, there was his small bedroom, and there was the slightly larger one which Barbara used during the University term. Before Barbara, Andrew had occupied it, and before Andrew, Stanislaw. For Uncle Edward, foreseeing the needs of numerous relatives whom he intended to set firmly into the professions, had provided the extra bedroom as a necessary economy for the family purse. Aunt Marta alone opposed him. "Someone has got to look after the land," she had said in protest to a family of professional men; and she had registered stony disbelief when her brother replied, "By the time the children are all grown up, the State will look after that." A more effective silencing was the way in which he transferred the Korytowski house and lands to his two widowed sisters, so that they were freed of dependence on him. For himself, he had his work. The little money which he earned was sufficient for his ideas of how a man should live. Barbara had once said, "Uncle Edward thinks that a good review of one of his articles in a University publication is more important than a bank account." Now Sheila, standing in the bare "guest room," with its two couches, simple furniture (she smiled as she noticed that the most important article was a bookcase, filled with an excellent choice in novels and poetry), remembered the pride in Barbara's voice. It was easy to understand Barbara and Jan Reska when you remembered that.

Sheila searched for the jug of water standing in its basin under the table. Its coldness, splashed vigorously over her face, made her feel, as well as look, better. Outside, in the narrow hall, the American was phoning. From the living room came the sound of men's voices. She hurriedly combed the wind tangles out of her hair. ("I'm afraid we don't have much time left, Miss Matthews," Professor Korytowski had said, which was his polite paraphrase for "Hurry up. You're late.") She paused in the middle of combing her hair at the memory of Uncle Edward's way of pronouncing "Matthews." He pronounced it like every foreigner, stumbling over the impossible combination of *th*, and giving it more of the French sound of "Mathieu." Only Mr. Stevens had said it the exactly correct way. Only Mr. Stevens—and Mr. Johann Hofmeyer. Perhaps he had lived for years in England or America. Why worry about a detail like that anyway? There was more to think about at the moment.

Nevertheless, the thought of Hofmeyer prompted her to search in her coat pocket. She studied the small bundle of clipped papers, looking curiously at the tickets which would enable her to leave for Britain. But there was something else beside the tickets and the regulations on air travel. There was a sheet of paper with elaborate printing. *Kotowitz. The Old Square, Number 31.* That was the heading. Underneath was the legend: *Importer and Exporter.* Under that: *Finest Table Delicacies.* Then came very small type at the foot of the announcement, which told you that Johann Hofmeyer was the present proprietor, that enquiries would receive full and prompt attention, that the telephone number was 5-7177. The whole announcement was repeated in three other languages: German, English, French. Mr. Hofmeyer's business was an expansive one. For a moment Sheila wondered. And then she jammed all the papers back in her pocket. No doubt the advertising sheet was only included to prove Mr. Hofmeyer's identity. She would present it to Uncle Matthews as a souvenir from an obliging business connection.

In the hall, Stevens was still phoning. He was leaning on an elbow against the wall, a pencil in one hand tapping impatiently, a long-suffering look in his eyes. Someone must have spoken at last, for he suddenly stopped lounging and he was listening intently.

In the living room, the desk lamp with its pleated pink silk shade gave a soft light which left the bookcases, lining three walls in darkness. In the fourth wall was the large window, at which Professor Korytowski was nailing up, with more determination than skill, a large sheet of black cloth. From a chair beside the desk, with its periodicals and offprints and papers now neatly arranged and neglected, a small thin man with glasses, a fading hair-line and a sardonic smile was talking steadily. At the man's elbow was an ugly little box of a radio, muted so as not to interfere unduly with the conversation.

Professor Korytowski abandoned his labors, and introduced the strange man, who had risen to his feet and was watching Sheila keenly. His name was Michal Olszak.

"We've been talking of the old days, which is one of the few escapes left us from the present," Korytowski said. "Now do sit down, and we'll wait until Mr. Stevens finishes verifying the airplane time."

Sheila sat quietly, and tried to listen to a conversation which had now switched, for her benefit, to the most recent news. But she was wondering if Mr. Olszak had seen as much danger as Edward Korytowski had in the "old days." That phrase meant the Polish fight for freedom during the last war; and then the continued fight for Polish boundaries after 1919, when the rest of the world relaxed into peace and forgot Poland; and then the establishing of a liberal régime. Edward Korytowski had been in the short-lived government. He had "retired" with Paderewski and Sikorski and the other liberals. In his disappointment, he had given up politics completely. Well, if Professor Korytowski said they were talking about the old days, then he and Mr. Olszak had indeed been talking about them. So much, Sheila thought, for the strange feeling she had had, as she entered the room, that they had been talking about her. What she needed, she told herself wryly, was not two months, but two years, submerging her personality into a family like the Aleksanders. Then she'd be less of an egotist, and happier altogether.

Her thoughts and Uncle Edward's slow voice were interrupted by the American. He was still worried, but he was also excited. He began pacing the room, his hands plunged deeply into the pockets of his light-colored tweed jacket.

"I phoned the office twice," he was saying quickly. "First time, no dice. Second time, after I made calls to the airport and station, they told me a blackout is rumored. Some of the districts in the city are already dimming out. They want me to get to the broadcasting station at once, just in case. As for the plane to Bucharest, all civilian reservations are canceled for the next twelve hours. Then I tried the station. Trains are needed for the army. Those for civilians are few and far between. I reached Bill Robertson, who had been covering the station, trying to get a news story that way. Bill says it's hopeless. Stations jam-packed." He looked at Sheila and shrugged his shoulders. "So what?" he said.

Sheila's dismay left her, perhaps because she felt he expected her to be dismayed. "You'd better go to the broadcasting station," she said in a voice that was calmer than her thoughts. "I'll go to the station and wait. That's all that can be done, anyway."

"I'll go with Miss Matthews," Professor Korytowski said. "And if there isn't a train available, Miss Matthews can have Barbara's room until there is one. I think that would be better than a hotel in this emergency." He looked towards Sheila for her acceptance. She gave him a thankful smile. That was one worry gone, anyway. A few days in a hotel, and there would be little money left to get her to Britain.

Russell Stevens still stood undecided. He was obviously relieved at the quickness of their decisions, but he seemed reluctant to accept them. He looked at her for a moment. He knew determination when he saw it.

"Hurry," Sheila said. "You've wasted enough time on me already. And thank you very much for having wasted it."

There was a smile in the businesslike gray eyes as he gripped her hand in his. And then his even, sure footsteps were running down the stone stairs.

"Suitcases," Sheila called after him from the landing. "No time. Leave them with Uncle Edward." She saw Russell Stevens' upturned face, saw a wave from his hand that he understood and agreed, and then he had disappeared into the courtyard. Professor Korytowski smiled as he struggled into a thin coat, which never seemed to get properly onto his large, stooping shoulders.

"I have a nice niece, I hear," he said as Sheila came back into the room.

Sheila smiled, too. The "Uncle Edward" had slipped out so easily, so unconsciously. "I'm sorry——" she began.

"Not at all, I like it. And I'll see that your luggage is forwarded to you later. Now, I suppose we ought to leave, too. Are you sure you really want to go to the station, after Stevens' information?"

"Frankly, I don't want to go. But I've promised everyone I would leave Warsaw tonight. So I suppose, I have to try at least. Just to satisfy my conscience." She fumbled in her pocket, wondering if she should explain about Mr. Hofmeyer and the plane tickets. But Mr. Olszak turned the volume control on the wireless set, and said in his crisp voice, "Total blackout in fifteen minutes. That's the latest announcement."

He looked at Sheila, gathering up her handbag and gloves. "Perhaps you shouldn't go," he said. "Not tonight."

"I'll have to try, I'm afraid."

Mr. Olszak remained staring at the girl. "The resemblance is really very strong, in every way," he said incredulously in Polish. Sheila looked puzzled. She didn't quite understand. Perhaps she had misunderstood. She was tired, and Mr. Olszak spoke so quickly. Perhaps she had misunderstood. Certainly, Mr. Olszak was thinking of something else now. "I'll wait for the others," he said to Uncle Edward. "We'll begin without you, if necessary." He picked up a newspaper.

"If you are expecting—" Sheila began in alarm.

"Hush, child. You worry too much. Either there will be a possible train, or there won't be one. We needn't wait long at the station. I'll be back in time to see my guests."

Mr. Olszak had come over to the door, with the newspaper still in his hand, to say good-by. "I hope we may meet again, some day, when all this trouble is over." He looked as if he were expressing an impossible wish. "There is much we could talk about. Good-by, and a safe journey."

Under the row of chestnut trees in the quiet little street, Sheila was still wondering about Mr. Olszak. Uncle Edward seemed to think that something Olszak had said had depressed her.

"Don't worry," he said reassuringly. "This trouble may not last so long as Michal thinks. He is always rather too realistic, too gloomy. That's why his newspaper sells so badly. He *will* write editorials which are both true and unpleasant. He says there are two kinds of journalist. One becomes rich and powerful, and cynical of the poor. Another remains poor, and cynical of the rich and powerful."

"I think I would like to meet Mr. Olszak again, some day," said Sheila.

"He was a great friend of your—" Uncle Edward halted abruptly. He was suddenly businesslike. "There's a taxi," he said. He waved vehemently. They were standing outside the Church of the Holy Cross. Around them, on Main Street, there were tramcars and lighted restaurants and numerous cafés crowded with earnestly talking people. It seemed as if every open window concealed a wireless set, turned fully on. In June, Sheila remembered, there had been music and laughter and smiling faces on the street. Now, the lights were darkening. People were leaving the cafés. People were walking urgently.

The taxi-driver justified Professor Korytowski's extravagance. The cab reached Central Station as the last lights vanished, like the flames of candles briefly snuffed out. Uncle Edward looked up and down the darkened street, as they stood accustoming their eyes to the night. "I do believe," he said as he stared at the buildings in their new austerity, "I do believe a blackout is an improvement." And Sheila found herself almost smiling.

Inside the large, modern station, the ghastly light from

infrequent, blue-painted lamps was certainly no improvement. Masses of people stood patiently in crowded groups. Children had fallen asleep on benches against the walls; their exhausted bodies drooped pathetically. Professor Korytowski steered Sheila through the crowd of stolid faces. They were going home, these people. They belonged to the villages, and in this moment of crisis they wanted to return there, these older men and women and children. A war was threatened; the villages would have to be defended. Even years of city life had not eradicated that simple belief.

"The foreigners will be over there," Uncle Edward said, indicating the section where express trains usually left for abroad. He mixed force with polite phrases to ease a way through the crowds.

Sheila heard them before she saw them, sitting on piles of luggage or elbowing each other round the notice boards. Worry hadn't improved their tempers; their smart clothes were as jaded as their nerves.

Voices of many nations were outshouting each other.

"Ridiculous . . . I'm going back to the hotel." It was an English voice, too.

"And start this all over again, tomorrow?"

"Ridiculous . . . a few extra trains and we would all get away."

"You're darned right it's ridiculous," a third voice said. An American voice. "How do they expect to win a war if they don't have organization?"

Sheila looked at them savagely, all the more savagely because Uncle Edward was pretending not to have heard them. How did they expect a war to be won if soldiers had to walk to the frontier so that a batch of foreigners wouldn't have to wait for a free train? A Frenchman argued bitterly with an Italian. A Rumanian family quarreled loudly among themselves. A woman, who evidently believed in traveling with her jewelry, complained and complained. She had lost a hatbox. A fat, dark-haired, sallow-faced man was buttonholing every station employe he could see. It never seemed to dawn on him that these hurrying, harassed men had each his own job to do. "I'm a neutral," the fat man kept saying. "I've a neutral's rights. The Embassy told me there would be a train, tonight. Where's that train?" The only silent people, it seemed, were three young American chorus girls with immaculate hair and elaborate shoes, and a tight-lipped Englishwoman whose dull clothes spelled governess. These four had drawn together. They stood beside a worried Cook's Tour agent, and listened, with amusement and disapproval

respectively, to the unanswerable questions which bombard-
ed the unfortunate man.

Professor Korytowski had managed to attract the attention
of the Cook's Tour man. In Polish, he asked quickly if there
was to be a train, if they should wait?

The man, his thin face thinner under the wide scoop of his
official cap, nodded. "There is to be a train, specially provided." His tone said, "But why, in God's name, for such people?"

"Thank you. We shall wait, then," Professor Korytowski
replied.

Someone said behind them, "A Pole! Imagine that! When
they should be staying at home to fight!"

Sheila turned to face the elbowing woman who carried a
dog under her arm.

"Don't worry. Your dog can have my place on the train,"
she said clearly, and walked away. Professor Korytowski managed to reach her as she struggled free from the last of the
crowd.

"But there is a train, Sheila. Any minute perhaps."

Sheila, still telling herself what she could have said to the
woman, still thinking of bitter, stinging phrases now that it
was too late, looked up in silence at Professor Korytowski.

"With *these* objects?" she asked at last. The scorn in her
voice, the vehemence in her eyes left Professor Korytowski
no reply. He looked worriedly towards the notice board, but
Sheila was already walking out of the station.


CHAPTER IV

## The Old Square


SHEILA twisted once more on the narrow bed. Outside, she
heard the cool sound of water as the porter hosed the pavement. It must be nearly morning, she thought. The sound of
voices from the living room still came mumbling through the
hall, like the intermittent stirring in a hive of bees. *Can't
sleep, can't sleep,* ticked the clock on the bookcase. *Can't
sleep, can't sleep,* hissed the water against the house wall.

"Can't sleep. How can I? How can anyone?" Sheila said
bitterly to the ceiling. "If," she told herself, "you hadn't
been so very high and mighty at the station last night, if
you hadn't had so much pride that you didn't want to be
seen even dead with that crowd of hysterics, you'd now be

on a train. And soon you would be arriving in a country where it would be safe enough for your fellow-travelers to regain their good humor and elegant charm. As Mr. Stevens would say, 'So what?' All right, so what?" But the fact remained that today and tomorrow and tomorrow she would also refuse to get on a train. Well, call it pride; but she wasn't going to start scrambling to leave Warsaw. Not after the kind of scene she had witnessed at the station last night. The only trouble was money. She had stayed so much longer than she expected that she hadn't much left. She would have to write to Uncle Matthews in London, explaining her point of view: a nice, long chatty letter to keep him from worrying. He would send her some money through the Embassy.

She listened to the hoofbeats of many horses being driven through the empty streets. Now and again, there was the dull rumble of tanks and heavy trucks. At other times, there was the creaking and groaning of farm carts bringing in supplies of food. Sheila listened, and dread and fear and pity and excitement kept her staring at the ceiling. She wondered how many millions were lying awake with these same emotions, millions who had the added sorrow of parting from those they loved. (She was indeed one of the lucky ones, as Mr. Stevens had said: she hadn't a husband or a sweetheart or a son or a brother to worry over, like all those other women.) It seemed unfair of life, somehow, that other millions could sleep in peace, and need only worry about nothing more than breakfast when they awoke.

Having decided that she belonged to those who worried and stayed awake, Sheila fell deeply asleep.

When she awoke, it was early afternoon. The apartment was silent. Dressing didn't take long when the choosing of clothes was eliminated. She was filled with sudden energy. First, the suitcases; clothes. Second, the Embassy, and a wire, with a letter to follow, to Uncle Matthews: money. Third, a talk with Uncle Edward: something to do, to help while she stayed in Warsaw. How long would she be here? Looking at that question in the practical light of day and not in the emotional atmosphere of a blackout, she smiled ruefully. Uncle Matthews would have a lot to say, and Professor Korytowski, although he had been too polite last night to argue when she was so tired and unhappy, might very well find a piece of gentle advice to give her when she was rested. But they would find she was in earnest. The only thing that worried her now was that she might not be considered useful, or worse still, that she would be a positive worry and nuisance to them all.

What could she do? Nursing? If she could somehow learn to control an overturning stomach the minute a patient started being sick. She could drive a car, but she would have to learn about its insides. She could speak French passably, Polish haltingly and blunderingly, German really well. She could understand them all; especially German. Why did she have to choose that language as her best one? She wasn't a bad shot; even Uncle Matthews admitted that. But it wasn't likely that much shooting would be done in Warsaw behind the trenches. And, she was forced to admit, her shooting had been with clay-pigeons. She had never killed as much as a mouse in her life. It seemed as if all her assets for war had a "but" attached. The trouble was, her instincts and training were geared for peace. Well, she would just have to learn. That was all. She wasn't the only one.

She moved over to the window to comb her hair in the sunlight. The green fingers of the chestnut leaves were outstretched below her, shielding the pavement from the heat. In the cool-looking shadows of the opposite side of the street, a large notice was fixed to the pillar of a colonnade. It must be new, for everyone who passed would stop to read it. They stood in a small, fluctuating, yet constant, group. Each one, as he gave place to a new arrival, would detach himself quietly from the others and go his own way. And yet he was linked to the others he had left. The heads bent in deliberation, the silence, the thoughtful steps, were the link that bound them. It couldn't be war. Not yet. The skies were empty of planes. Not yet, with the skies still blue and broken only by a light wisp of cloud.

The rest of the apartment was as empty as it had sounded. It was neat and clean, so the porter's wife, who came up each day to "look after" Uncle Edward, must have finished her work. The living room had lost its disorder of chairs and smoke-filled atmosphere. Last night, she had just had time to notice that, through the half-open door, before Uncle Edward had shown her into Barbara's room. He had offered her food and something to drink, but she had refused. She hadn't been invited into the living room. She had been too tired anyway, but her glimpse of the crowd of middle-aged and oldish men gathered there had aroused her speculations. They had stopped talking as she passed through the hall, had looked out with an interest which now seemed rather strange and undeserved. There she was, imagining things again. Sheila turned impatiently away from the living room. The curtains moved in the cross-current of air as she held its door open. A sheet of paper fastened by a paper clip to the incongruous pink lampshade (probably a Christmas present from Madame Aleksander: there was a definite "woman's touch" about it) flapped, too.

Sheila smiled at Uncle Edward's idea of a prominent place

to leave a message, and her smile broadened as she read it. In large scrawling letters he had printed, "Coffee and sugar in the small cupboard to your left in the kitchen. Bread in the tin box. Butter, milk, ham in the box of wire netting near the window. Matches at side of gas oven. Will be back before six. Important!—Stevens phoned. Suitcases at his apartment at Frascati Gardens. Telephone 6-5488. A Mr. Hofmeyer phoned twice. No message." Then followed two drawings in the James Thurber technique: one shapeless figure was stuck by an angry-looking telephone, while an equally shapeless figure ("Do I look like that to him?" Sheila wondered) was stretched out on a tablelike bed, with snoring signs above its head. ("And I don't snore, either," Sheila added.)

She decided to have something to eat outside: that would save both time and Professor Korytowski's food supply. But she would phone Mr. Stevens first of all. There was no reply. And then, after some hesitation, she decided to phone Mr. Hofmeyer. It was only polite, for one thing. For another, she might be in time to stop any alarmed telegram to Uncle Matthews. She had left the business leaflet somewhere in the bedroom. She opened the phone directory instead. H. . . . HOFMEYER Adolf, HOFMEYER Bruno, HOFMEYER Helmut, HOFMEYER Sigurd . . . There was no HOFMEYER Johann. She couldn't remember the name of the firm which he owned. She had to go back into the bedroom and search for the leaflet.

Yes, his first name was Johann, all right. And his telephone number was 5-7177.

She was surprised to be answered not by a secretary or a clerk, but by Mr. Hofmeyer, himself.

"Sheila Matthews," she said.

"I'm sorry to hear your voice," Mr. Hofmeyer replied in English. His voice sounded more British over the phone than it had sounded yesterday at Korytów. "You should have left Warsaw last night."

"The plane—"

"I know. But there was a train."

"Yes, but—"

"Please leave as quickly as you can. How are you for money?"

"I have a little."

"That won't be enough. Call here, and you will find an envelope with money waiting for you. Come at once. Before four o'clock. There's a last train around seven. Good luck."

Sheila had begun to thank him, but there was no reply, only a dead silence which told her he hadn't waited for formalities. She replaced the receiver on its hook, thoughtfully. "Call here." Surely that meant the business address.

She looked at the crumpled leaflet, and on impulse searched for the name Kotowitz in the telephone book. It existed all right. The Old Square, 31. But its telephone number was not the one she had just used to find Mr. Hofmeyer. His must have been a private number, no doubt. Probably he hated the telephone as her Uncle Matthews did, and tried to discourage being phoned. She tried to visualize him as she had seen him yesterday evening. All she could remember was white hair, a squarish face, and the quick light footsteps. She realized suddenly that there had been a vague quality about him, an expressionless quality, so that it was hard to remember him. It was strange, for he hadn't impressed her as being without determination or character. The least she could have done, she thought angrily, was to have paid more attention to someone who had taken so much trouble for her. She jammed the business leaflet into her handbag, grabbed her hat and gloves—it was too warm for a coat—and hurried out of the apartment. "Before four o'clock," he had said. She hadn't much time. She ought to get to the British Embassy and let someone know she was staying in Warsaw. That was the right thing to do, she supposed. And if the Embassy wouldn't arrange to get money for her from her uncle, then she would have to fall back on Mr. Hofmeyer's generosity. In normal times, she wouldn't have had the courage to accept his offer. But this was, as Uncle Edward had said last night, a state of emergency. And her Uncle Matthews would see to it that Mr. Hofmeyer was not left out of pocket.

Her thoughts kept her company into the courtyard, past its clumps of lilac trees, through the vaultlike gateway. In the street outside, Henryk, the porter, was airing a terrier.

"Good day," he said, and burst into a long sentence. Sheila, snatched away from her plans of campaign, stared blankly at him. He wouldn't understand English, but he might be able to understand German. Many people in Poland could.

*"Bitte?"* she asked politely.

He looked at her with sudden sharpness. "Don't speak German," he said in a low voice, and turned his interest to the dog.

Neatly snubbed, Sheila thought. She had better try no more German on strangers today, even out of politeness. But as she picked her way across the heavy cobbled surface of the street, trying to avoid twisting a high heel in one of the deep cracks, she suddenly began to wonder. What was it he had said? "I don't speak German," or "Don't speak German"? But what did it matter anyway? Either a concierge couldn't talk German, or he was advising her not to speak in German. What did matter was the proclamation pasted across one of the pillars of the colonnade. She joined the small group of people round it.

General mobilization. Transport completely militarized. Horses, bicycles, cars to be commandeered. Every man on receipt of his mobilization papers was to report at his district's army headquarters within two hours. That was all. It ended with the date: "31st August, 1939."

There it was at last. There it was in the quiet, determined faces round her, in the men walking away to set their house and business in order before the two hours hung over them. Hofmeyer had said there was a "last train." There must be a special one, then, for foreigners. But there was none for these people. Sheila felt her resolve tighten: all the arguments, for and against, why and why not, which had plagued her like a cloud of persistent mosquitoes ever since her sudden decision at the station last night, were swept away for good. She wanted to say to the strained face beside her, "Look, if you can stay here, so can I." But she kept silent, edged her way out of the group, and walked towards Main Street. She wouldn't have time to eat, after all. She hadn't time to phone Stevens again. She found a *droshki*, and drove to the British Embassy.

When she arrived there, she felt helpless and unnecessary. Too many people were there. Too many men with urgent faces and decided steps were passing through the courtyard. They had serious business. She felt negligible. She hesitated for some minutes, and then entered the building. In the waiting room, there was a line of people, hurrying secretaries, busy men. This, she realized, was going to take hours. She looked at her watch and saw it was after half-past three. She left the building quickly, and no one even noticed her abrupt exit. She felt microscopic. After all, she told herself as she searched for another *droshki,* they would probably want to send her home. If they heard that she had practically no money left, then they'd ship her off as a Distressed British Subject. Somehow, a D.B.S. didn't sound so funny at this moment.

A *droshki,* its horse too thin and old to be worried about his duty to the army, was coming along the avenue. Sheila left the railings, looked up at the imposing balcony, and said good-by to the British Embassy. She would go to Mr. Hofmeyer. The *droshki* driver, an old man with his identification tag hanging at the back of his thin red neck, drove as urgently as he and the horse could manage. They were crossing the city to reach the older district in the north. In the gardens and pleasant green parks, men and women and children were digging.

They had reached the Old Square, at last. As the cab rolled over the wide expanse of cobblestones, flanked on four sides by rows of gabled houses, Sheila looked at her watch, and found she was late. She determined not to worry: nothing she could do now would make her any earlier. She looked at the houses, tall and narrow in the late Gothic manner, with their fronts newly restored to their onetime glory. In the last twenty years, they had been reclaimed from the slums into which they had degenerated under foreign rule. She wondered which house was Number 31. The broadest of the houses had four-window façades, which was the sign that some three hundred years ago, or more, princes had lived there. Those with three windows had housed nobles. Those with two had belonged to merchants. These social differences still remained in the carefully preserved façades, but the people behind the painted walls were now equal in lack of titles and of wealth. Some of the houses had long flourished as restaurants famed for this, or wine cellars famed for that. It was near one of them that the House of Kotowitz had its restrained medieval setting.

A car was standing in front of the arched doorway. The entrance led past a small but intricately carved doorway, past a flight of handsome stone stairs leading to the apartments above, and ended inside a cobbled yard with chestnut trees. Sheila, thinking how strange it was that one always went too far when one was late, retraced her steps, to the carved doorway. That seemed the only possible entrance to the ground-floor shop. With difficulty, she discerned the name of Kotowitz written in elegant but faded lettering. The door opened easily, and she was in a room, bright with sunlight from the Square. It was more like an office than a shop. There was a large table, and a girl with a ledger. She looked up and scrutinized Sheila closely.

"My name is Sheila Matthews. I believe Mr. Hofmeyer has an envelope for me."

The girl's eyes widened. "Oh, yes!" she said. Then she rose and looked towards a door in the rear of the office. "You are to wait. I'll get it."

Sheila waited. Then the rear door opened, and the girl returned. Behind her was a young man with a heavy, but pleasant, face. It had assumed a serious expression for the moment. The eyes were very businesslike. Rising young executive, Sheila thought: well-polished shoes, neat pin-stripe suiting, hat in hand, and all.

The young man was speaking. "Miss Matthews? I am sorry that the envelope has not yet arrived. Mr. Hofmeyer asked me to bring you to his house to save further delay."

Sheila looked at him uncertainly. He returned her stare too blandly, quite unaware of the puzzle in her mind. The girl had said, "I'll get it." This man said, "The envelope has not yet arrived."

"But is this not Mr. Hofmeyer's house?"

"This is his place of business," the man said patiently. He reached for the door handle. Sheila looked at the girl, standing once more behind the table. There was a cold, hostile look in the girl's eyes. Their enmity warned Sheila.

"I am sorry," she said with evident finality. She didn't move. How the dickens did you say in Polish: "I haven't much time. I have another engagement. Anyway, I don't know who on earth you are and I am not going to accompany you to any strange house"? She was deciding on the correct phrases, and was just about to try a murderous version in desperation, when the young man moved away from the door, came over to her, and took a firm grip on her arm.

She tried to shake herself free. "I have no time. I am sorry. I have no time," she said in a mixture of anger and alarm.

"I am sorry too," the man said politely, but with equal conviction. "I'm afraid you must come." He gave a nod to the girl who hurried promptly, eagerly, over to the window. She waved. Sheila remembered the waiting car.

"What *is* this, anyway?" Sheila said angrily in English. She struck herself sharply free. She was hot with temper. She ran to the door. It was already opened. Two men, as neatly dressed as the man who had gripped her arm, stood there quite placid and immovable. They were broad enough to fill the doorway. Sheila halted, let her anger cool. She had to: she needed to think very clearly.

"You must come with us," the young man was saying. He was angry. He was rubbing his arm where she had hit him, and his eyes had narrowed and didn't look at all so pleasant now.

"Why?" Sheila's voice was cold and hard. She returned his angry stare with equal vehemence.

"Security police. You may as well resign yourself. There is no choice for you but to come with us. And please don't make any scenes. There is no need ... a matter of routine." He looked sharply at Sheila. "Do you understand what I say?"

"I don't understand anything." But the word "police" had reassured her. She walked outside, shrugging off the young man's arm. The girl at the table stared after her as if Sheila were a leper. Sheila found herself firmly wedged between two large men in the car which had been standing at the entrance to Mr. Hofmeyer's place of business. She was quite

convinced by this time that she wasn't going to see Mr.
Hofmeyer's house either.


## CHAPTER V

### Interrogation

THE JOURNEY was as unpleasant as she expected. It was a
hot afternoon. The men on either side of her filled most of
the car's seat. And whenever she tried to see a landmark to
help her guess where she was being taken, the young man
who sat opposite her would watch her keenly. When she
relaxed, he watched her speculatively. He had relieved her
of her handbag unexpectedly and very neatly, as she had left
Mr. Hofmeyer's office. He now held it determinedly if incongruously under his arm. It was a relief when the car's
speed slackened, and it stopped before a large square building of modern structure. She couldn't recognize the street
when they ushered her firmly across the pavement into the
large doorway, and her heart sank still further. She tried
to believe that foreigners straying about the city had to be
counted like so many sheep. Probably the Security Police
wanted to send her home to England. Probably. But her heart
kept on sinking.

The two bodyguards, their mission accomplished, had gone.
She was left alone on a stone bench with the first young
man. She found it difficult to restrain herself from fidgeting
as she felt his eyes watching her closely. As they waited,
their backs against an impressively paneled wall, their feet
on the highly polished floor of intricate design, neither spoke.

Hurrying men, worried men, men carrying papers which
they still studied, men walking urgently from one doorway
in the long hall to another, men and only men passed by.
Most looked at her with a quick impersonal glance. Some
nodded to the silent man beside her, and gave her a second
look. There were other benches in the hall. Four other
people sat there, as silently as she did, each with a neatly
dressed, watchful man beside him. One of these people was
a woman: a middle-aged, defiant-looking creature with a face
carefully camouflaged to conceal the wrinkles, with expensive clothes cut to flatter the contours. Of the others, one
seemed a prosperous businessman, one was a hotel porter,
one was a workman with an excessively honest face. The
three men shared the woman's defiance. Sheila wondered if

they were here for the same mysterious reason which had brought her to this place. She watched their faces, and she felt still more worried. No reason seemed to link together such a varied collection of people. They certainly were not British, nor Americans, nor Frenchmen.

Sheila glanced at her watch nervously. It was almost half-past five. Ten minutes later, the man beside her rose and motioned her to enter the doorway which had just opened. The three men and one woman still sat and waited in the hall. They were getting restless now. The woman was trying hard not to cry.

The room which Sheila entered was unexpectedly simple after the impressive entrance hall. Simple and businesslike. So was the uniformed man with a dark mustache who sat at the desk, with a window behind him. On one side of him was a man in civilian clothes, seated, waiting with a note-book and an open fountain pen. On the other side of the desk stood another uniformed man, as neat and slender as a French general. An empty chair faced the desk, the three men, and the window. A series of office cabinets covered the wall on her left; to her right, there was nothing but a door leading to an adjoining room.

Sheila determined to be equally businesslike. She crossed the room quickly, sat down on the obvious chair, and looked at the man with the black mustache. He didn't seem an unreasonable man: cold, perhaps, and impersonal; but not unreasonable. She waited while he adjusted his pince-nez and a black leather folder in front of him.

He looked up suddenly at the young man who had escorted Sheila here. "Better get the Special Commissioner, if he is available," he said. "He has had much to do with the case of Margareta Koch." He transferred his look, as he pronounced the name, to Sheila.

She took a deep breath of relief, as the young man placed the handbag on the desk and went to look for the Special Commissioner. This, she told herself, was nothing else than a complete mistake. Well, it would soon be cleared up.

She said with a smile, "May I speak in English? My Polish is very weak."

"Any other language you can speak?" the man with the black mustache asked very gently.

"French, or German."

"Oh. . . . Well, we all understand German. Would you speak in the language?" But it was more of a command than a question.

Sheila began eagerly. "Am I supposed to be this Margareta Koch?"

"What makes you think that?"

"By the way you looked at me when you said her name."

The men exchanged quick glances. "And do you deny that you are Margareta Koch?"

"Of course. I am Sheila Matthews."

The man behind the desk smiled. Sheila began to feel that this wasn't going to be as easy as she had thought.

"An Englishwoman?"

"Born in England. My father was Scots."

The man with the fountain pen began writing. The man with the mustache smiled again. "Just answer these questions, please. Your name is Sheila Matthews? Spell it."

Sheila did so.

"Born where, and when?"

"In High Wycombe: a small place just outside of London. On August 7, 1916."

There was another interval for more spelling.

"Your parents?"

Sheila suddenly lost her resolve to be patient. "Is this necessary?"

"Most necessary. Your parents?"

"Both dead. My mother died in September 1916. My father, Charles Matthews, was killed in December of the same year."

"Killed? How?"

"In action."

"In France?"

"No." Sheila found that her uncle's insistence on silence over her father's death was even, at this moment, making it difficult for her to talk about it. "In Poland," she said reluctantly.

"Really?" All three men were watching her intently, now. "Just where in Poland in December 1916?"

"Here in Warsaw."

"There were no Allied troops fighting in Warsaw by December 1916. By that time, the Germans were in possession of the city."

"The Germans shot him. There's a tablet erected to his memory in the Citadel."

The man who looked like a French general said aside in Polish, "This is devilish clever."

"That can be verified," the man behind the desk continued. "You speak very calmly of your father's death."

"Well, after all, I never saw my father." And Uncle Matthews wouldn't talk about him, either. "All I can feel," Sheila added honestly, "is pride, and curiosity, and regret that I never knew him."

"Who was responsible for your education?"

"My father's only brother, John Matthews."

"Profession?"

"He is a businessman. His firm is Matheson, Walters, and Crieff. Exporters."

Her interrogator nodded. "Verify that," he said to the secretary. And then he continued, "Any other relatives?"

"None. My uncle is unmarried. My mother had two brothers, but they were killed in the war. France and Gallipoli."

"How is it that you came to visit Poland at this time?"

"I came at the end of June, on an invitation. I stayed longer than I should have."

"Why are you still here at this time?"

Sheila shrugged her shoulders. There were so many explanations to that, all little, all very personal, that it seemed useless to start listing them.

"Who invited you?"

There was a sound of the door behind her being opened, and closed; of footsteps which halted just inside the room, so that she couldn't see the newcomers. Her eyes seemed to be stuck at the desk. She couldn't look over her shoulder.

"Who invited you?" The question was sharper, this time.

"A Polish family." Sheila wondered desperately how she could keep the Aleksander name out of this stupid mess. She probably couldn't without rousing more suspicion. She told them quickly of Andrew Aleksander's visit to London last winter on a Purchasing Commission; of her visit here this summer at the invitation of Madame Aleksander; of her stay at Korytów.

"How did Aleksander come to meet you in London?"

"His aunt, Pani Marta Korytowska Madalinska, had given him a letter of introduction to my uncle. Her husband was killed by the Germans along with my father." Sheila felt more confident again. All these facts could be checked, and her story would be proved. But the next question left her gasping.

"Then why did you visit Hofmeyer's shop, today? Why did he leave money for you in an envelope? Quite a large amount?"

"Why don't you ask Mr. Hofmeyer?" Sheila said angrily. Surely she didn't have to start explaining all that, too. . . .

"Unfortunately, Mr. Hofmeyer disappeared half an hour before our men arrived to arrest him. He has been in contact with German agents. He met one of them—who has since been arrested and given us the necessary information about Hofmeyer—at Lowicz yesterday evening. Lowicz is near

Korytów. We have traced his visit to you there. Yes, you may look dismayed, Miss Koch. When we arrest him, which should happen any minute now, you may find he is less thoughtful of you than you have been of him."

"But I am not this woman Koch. I am Sheila Matthews."

"Koch used many names, sometimes English or American ones. Matthews would have been an excellent one to choose." He said to the secretary, "Now check all these main points in her story." The man rose obediently, and hurried through the communicating door.

The man who looked like a French general was watching Sheila coldly. He picked up the black leather folder: " 'Margareta Koch, age twenty-five, born at Grünwald near Munich, medium height, slender, straight fair hair, brown eyes, for three months employed by Johann Hofmeyer (Polish citizen) as secretary. Disappeared without trace on March 17, 1939. Believed to have returned secretly to Germany, and then to the United States.' Complete evidence on her undeniable guilt as an organizer of diversionist activities and of spying then follows. . . ."

"But my hair isn't straight," was all that Sheila could say with complete inadequacy.

The uniformed man waved her silent. "Forgetting about permanent waving, Miss Koch, or Miss Matthews, what course of action would we take when we heard that an envelope with money was to be delivered to someone who was to call at the business address of a man who faces charges of being a traitor? Especially when the person who called was a blonde young woman of medium height, with brown eyes? Especially when some of us believe that the rumor of Koch's departure for Germany and America was merely, a fake, to cover her continued presence in Warsaw? What would you have done in our place?"

Sheila, watching the secretary's face as he returned with a slip of paper which he handed to the man with the black mustache, watching that man reading it with interest, said slowly, "I'd arrest her, of course, in a time like this. And then I'd find out who she was. And then I'd check her story. And then I'd release her and apologize."

The slip of paper had now been passed to the French general. He read it with one eyebrow raised.

"What if," he continued still more coldly, "a London directory of business firms lists all men who have any important positions in the various firms; lists Matheson, Walters and Crieff, and all its directors; but doesn't mention a John Matthews? Or is he now an unimportant clerk, so that we can't check on his name?"

Sheila said, "But he is important." Remembering Uncle Matthews' clothes, his house, his friends, she added lamely, "At least, he had money enough."

"Have you visited his office?"

"No." Uncle Matthews didn't approve of that. "But I've phoned there, often enough, to leave a message for him. His secretary always took the message."

"For Mr. Matthews?"

"Yes. For Mr. Matthews. For Mr. John Matthews."

"I see. What if we have found the record of Charles Matthews, found that he was murdered along with Andrew Madalinski by the Germans, but that there was no mention of any child? It was known to his friends that he had a wife and a brother, who doesn't happen to be named on this report. But there is absolutely no mention of either the wife's death, or of a child."

Sheila sat very still. She could only think: he didn't know, he didn't know I even existed. . . . He didn't know.

The man was talking again. She tried to listen, but her thoughts were with her father. For him, she had never existed. If the men in this room had tried their best to find some argument to end her resistance, they couldn't have succeded more brilliantly, more cruelly. Suddenly, as her silence remained unbroken, they realized something had had an effect.

The man with the mustache pressed home the advantage. He said quickly, "If Koch, knowing that she was in danger of being discovered, and yet knowing that her work in Poland was still to be finished, wanted an excellent and safe means of returning here, what could be better than to become the daughter of a man who died for Poland some twenty odd years ago? Then she could enter a Polish family of good standing, and as their guest she could spend the summer safely and quietly until the time came for her to finish her work. And that time is now. Now, with war threatened . . ."

Sheila roused herself. She said tonelessly, "But I didn't seek out any member of a Polish family. He had a letter of introduction to my uncle. He was invited to our house."

"That will be checked."

"That's all I want." But, she wondered, would things be checked quickly in a time of national emergency? Andrew had left Warsaw with his regiment that morning. Professor Korytowski could only say that he had met her as a friend of his nephew's.

"Look here," she said in desperation. "Why don't you take me back to Mr. Hofmeyer's place? That girl at the desk told a lie when she identified me as this Koch woman. The other employees there could tell you I am a complete stranger to them all." The conviction that she had at last given them an unassailable piece of proof added confidence to the last sentence. She was almost cheerful again, as she ended the little speech.

"Either you are very innocent, or very clever," the black mustache said with a peculiar smile. "You know, or didn't you, that the present secretary whom you saw today has only been recently employed by Hofmeyer? That the rest of the staff are now discharged, or have scattered? Some are innocent. Others are in hiding. When they are found they will be shot as spies."

Sheila made her last attempt. "If I were as clever and mysterious as you think, why should I have walked into such a trap this afternoon? Surely Hofmeyer would have warned me, if I were his accomplice?"

"He would have warned you, I am sure, if there had been time. We heard the Lowicz German's confession at four o'clock, implicating Hofmeyer. When our men arrived to arrest him, Hofmeyer was gone. If you, yourself, had arrived at the appointed time for your envelope, we would have been too late to find you. But you were the one who was too late. By these little mistakes, even the best spy walks into the net, Miss Koch."

"I am *not* Koch. I am Sheila Matthews." Her Scots temper flared.

"Now we are back where we started," the man murmured. He looked over her shoulder, behind her. She suddenly remembered that someone had been standing there all this time.

"Do you want to continue the interrogation, Mr. Commissioner?" the man at the desk was asking the unknown. Sheila turned her head, her eyes widened. But only the small, thin man, who was now advancing towards the desk, could see them. He looked at her without any sign of recognition, but there was almost a warning in the blankness of his eyes. He held her stare so coldly that her "Mr. Olszak!" froze on her tongue and remained unspoken.

"No thank you, Colonel Bolt," Mr. Olszak said crisply. "I think you have handled it as fully as possible at this stage, and you have treated it with your usual thoroughness and brilliance. The case of Margareta Koch is on the files of my little department, and I think it would probably clarify matters if this young woman were to be put under our care, until a full check can be made of several interesting points which she has raised."

Colonel Bolt, obviously pleased with the beginning of that speech, seemed somewhat ruffled by the time it approached its end.

"We are handling Hofmeyer, and it would seem that this case is linked with his."

"Hofmeyer was never under suspicion until four o'clock this afternoon. The files on him have only been opened. Koch, on the other hand, has been one of our subjects for the last six months, and the files on her past activities have grown in that time. In any case, Colonel, you have more important business at the moment than the tedious verification or disproval of this young woman's statement. How's that Gottlieb case coming along? My dear fellow, I thought your analysis of his reasons was really brilliant, if I may say so." Mr. Olszak had seated himself casually on the corner of the desk. He picked up Sheila's handbag. "Examined these papers in here yet?" he asked as he opened the bag to show it stuffed with a woman's usual concentration of odds and ends. "Of course not," he added quickly, "it takes time to examine all these innocent-looking little scraps of paper and letters."

"There was no gun, no weapon," Sheila's first escort volunteered from the background.

"Good," Mr. Olszak said. "And now—"

"We've wasted considerable time on this Koch-Matthews possibility," Colonel Bolt said quickly. He was still inclined to be difficult.

"Not wasted, I assure you," Olszak said equally quickly. "And my department is in your debt, Colonel."

"For the matter of our records—" Colonel Bolt continued, but Mr. Olszak interrupted him with polite magnanimity.

"The records, of course. By all means, Colonel, have it placed on your files that a young woman calling herself Sheila Matthews, but possibly Koch, was apprehended by your department at Hofmeyer's shop in suspicious circumstances. That the said young woman, having failed to satisfy your department that she had no connection with Koch, was transferred to the care of my department because of our special interest in that case. Now, I think I'll take Miss Matthews or Koch along with me. I think I can find a quick method of verifying certain necessary points in her statement. I shall let you know at once, of course, so that your records on this case may be completed."

Sheila, her arm grasped by a thin, surprisingly strong hand, found herself being led determinedly from the room. In his other hand, Mr. Olszak had an equally determined grip of her handbag.

# CHAPTER VI

## Mr. Olszak

"WELL, young lady," Mr. Olszak said at last, when they had reached a small room of indescribable confusion, "you do make life very complicated for yourself." He pushed aside two wire trays filled with papers, and perched himself on the corner of his desk to face Sheila, seated in his only chair. Now her back was to the light and it was Mr. Olszak who faced it. Sheila felt as if he had reversed the positions deliberately. She suddenly relaxed for the first time in the last two hours. Her hands trembled slightly as she smoothed her linen skirt over her knees. But she managed to smile.

"That's better," Mr. Olszak said in his crisp way. "Much better." He removed his rimless glasses, and fingered the thin bridge of his nose where they had pinched it into a red groove. His graying hair had receded so deeply from the temples that what was left of it formed an exaggerated widow's peak, making the high brow still higher. His face had the white look of a man who worked too much, slept too little, and cared about neither regular meals nor exercise. His clothes and his manner of wearing them were quiet and neat, but nondescript. He was completely undistinguished to look at, except for his eyes and his hands. Both of these, Sheila thought, were unexpectedly powerful, once he let you look at them. It wasn't the color of the eyes so much—a strange mixture of gray and green—as the expression they held. Behind his glasses, they had been quick and intelligent. Now, as he looked past Sheila to the tree branches which brushed the window, there was a brooding quality which combined thoughtfulness with decision. This man, Sheila realized, did not know fear. He believed in something so far apart from himself that he had left no place in his mind for selfish emotions. Nothing that happened to him personally would seem important enough to be terrifying. She envied him at this moment.

"And what do you think of our policemen?" he asked, still watching the tree, still smiling in that sardonic way of his.

"I'd think you were wonderful," quoted Sheila with some bitterness, "if I weren't in my position. For a moment or two, they had me almost convinced that I didn't exist."

Mr. Olszak didn't bother to answer. He was looking through

the contents of her handbag now. "Where did you find this?" With a movement as sudden as his question he had extracted Hofmeyer's leaflet. He watched her closely as she explained it all, beginning with Hofmeyer's visit to Korytów yesterday evening.

"You believe me, don't you? You know I *am* Sheila Matthews," she ended desperately, as Mr. Olszak remained silent.

"Why else should I have rescued you from the efficient logic of Colonel Bolt?" He smiled without any sarcasm this time, and added, "But my belief didn't come from anything you contributed to the discussion in Bolt's office, Miss Matthews."

"What do you mean?"

"I met you through Professor Korytowski. He met you, like Barbara and her mother, through Andrew. Andrew met you in London through some letter or other from his aunt. But if he or she cannot be found to substantiate your story—if, for instance, a German bomb or bullet took care of them within the next few days—well, then! What's more, you had a strange reluctance to leave Poland. Edward Korytowski told me about the station incident last night. Of course, we could have checked with the British Embassy to find out why you were staying. I presume you informed them?"

Sheila's face was answer enough. She said, at last, to end his obvious amusement, "I went this afternoon. That was why I was late for Hofmeyer's. But everything, everyone was so busy ... Really, I didn't think I mattered so much just then."

"I see." It was an encouraging rather than a polite remark. Sheila felt that not one of her most hidden emotions could escape these sharp eyes.

"Why do you believe me, then?" she asked.

"Because," and he paused and his voice was very quiet, "I knew your father. You are very like him. The resemblance is extraordinary. Except that your eyebrows and eyelashes are darker, but perhaps that isn't nature's fault."

"You knew him?"

"Yes, I was at the last meeting he and Madalinski attended. I had just left. It was raided by the Germans. They were shot." He looked at the girl almost gently. "When you get angry, and push your hair back from your face, and lift that chin and your eyebrows, I can see enough of Charles Matthews to please me."

"Then why didn't you tell Colonel Bolt? Why didn't you? He would have believed you."

"Yes. I'll explain that later, once you have answered a

few questions. Now, quietly, Miss Matthews. Please be patient.
The questions are important to me. First, what did you
know about your father? What did your uncle tell you?"

"Only that my father was killed in the war."

"Did you never ask for more information than that?"

"Of course. But you don't know Uncle Matthews. He isn't
very communicative. There wasn't even a photograph of my
father. And it was only last winter, when Andrew Aleksander
came to London, that I found out that my father had died
in Poland. I had always thought it was France."

"Men like your father, Miss Matthews, don't go about being photographed, and don't have medals pinned on their
chests. When they are wounded, it must be explained by
the word 'accident.' When they are killed, there is no military funeral, no name on a Roll of Honor. Their families can't
talk about their deeds, for their families even don't know
about them."

"My father was a spy?" Sheila asked haltingly.

"A spy, to me, is someone who finds out information for
a certain amount of money. The money smothers his
conscience if he is a traitor. If he is a patriot, the money
softens the lack of public recognition. But there is another
word which I prefer to give to men who care neither for
the money nor for any recognition. Their lives are often
ruined; they may meet an unpleasant death; but they fight in
their own way—with their brains, secretly, courageously—
because all that matters to them is what they are fighting
for. I think it is only fair to give them full credit for that.
Shall we say that your father was a secret agent?"

Sheila didn't answer.

"Now tell me another thing. . . . Why did you come to
Poland this summer?"

Sheila said with some difficulty, "Partly because I wanted
to see the Aleksanders. Partly because I wanted to see where
my father had died."

"I want you to be frank, for I have been frank with you.
You came to see the Aleksanders?"

Sheila's color deepened. "Andrew wanted to marry me. I
wasn't quite sure. I . . ."

Olszak seemed pleased. "That's better," he said. "Now you
are being as frank as I am. Good. And when you came to
Poland, you intended to leave before any trouble started?"

Sheila's face was scarlet. "Yes. It sounds mean and callous
now. But I never thought of it that way then, somehow."

"Why didn't you keep your intentions?"

"I've been trying to find out the reasons for myself. Perhaps I stayed so long because Poland was so like, and yet

so unlike, anything I had expected. We, the people at home I mean, don't know so very much about Poland. And when I stayed here, I found a lot of answers which I hadn't found in books. You can't capture the spirit of a people by just studying facts. You've got to live with people, and talk and argue and laugh with them and see their worries, before you begin to understand why they believe certain things, do certain things. I felt I was beginning to understand a little. And it was important to me that I should at least begin to understand. For although I never knew much about my father, I've thought of him . . . a good deal. When I learned he had died in Poland, I wanted to know why. I mean, I wanted to find out what he believed in so strongly that he was willing to risk his life here. I felt if I learned about Poland, I might learn something about my father."

"That's one reason. Any other?"

Sheila hesitated. She was embarrassed that Mr. Olszak should be playing father confessor, embarrassed in case she bored him. But he didn't seem impatient or bored.

He was saying, "Yes?" very quietly.

That gave her courage. "Another reason, a lesser one but still another reason, was the fact that I have never known much about what we call 'family life.' I got plenty of it with the Aleksanders. I liked it. I wanted to hang onto it as long as I could. That was how the weeks vanished."

"Yes?"

"And then, I just lost my temper at the station last night, I think."

"Why?"

"Because . . . Oh, just because."

"Because?" Sheila had a feeling that Mr. Olszak was waiting eagerly for the answer, as if much depended on it.

"Well, I felt—perhaps I'm wrong—I felt that the people at the station weren't leaving Poland so that they could join the fight in their own countries, or because they wanted to go on fighting in other places. I felt all they wanted was to get away from the fight. And do you know what I wanted? I wanted just one bomb, only one, to be dropped right on top of them. That's how they made me feel."

Olszak's smile didn't appear. "I am glad you didn't tell that to Colonel Bolt. He would have thought you were an anarchist. What are your politics, if you have any?"

"A liberal," Sheila said firmly.

"I didn't know there were any left. What makes you so sure of being a liberal, Miss Matthews?" His voice was amused, now.

"My conservative friends say I am a radical. My communist friends say I am a reactionary. So obviously, I must be a liberal."

Olszak wasn't smiling at all, yet strangely enough she knew he was laughing. It seemed as if the sardonic smile was there only when he was not amused.

"Now, what do you know about your uncle?"

"Uncle Matthews?" Sheila was on guard although she still smiled. "Oh, he's a businessman. He's been very good to me, really. It must have been a frightful bore to have a month-old baby dumped on him. Especially when he is what you might call a total bachelor."

But Mr. Olszak wasn't to be sidetracked.

"Come, Miss Matthews, you promised to be frank. It saves so much time."

"I know nothing except the usual things any niece knows about her uncle. He has been very busy recently. Exporting and importing, you know."

"Shall I phrase it another way? What do you think about your uncle?"

"I'm very fond of him. He's rather a pet, although he looks formidable enough."

"Miss Matthews, you are fencing. Why? Did your uncle send you for any reason to this country?"

"Send me?" She felt relieved that she could once more give a direct answer. "Why, he wasn't even in England when I left! He travels a good deal. I sent him a letter explaining why I had decided to accept the Aleksanders' invitation. By the time the letter reached him, I was already on my way here."

"Didn't he ask you to come home?"

"Recently there have been telegrams from him," Sheila admitted.

There was a pause and a sharp look from Mr. Olszak. "In a way, I am pleased with the way in which you have fenced. It proves a certain loyalty, a certain control. And they are important. But I am not asking you to betray your uncle. I know about him. More than you'll ever know. *And*," Olszak tightened his voice to a command, silencing Sheila's lips as they opened, "don't give me that export-import stuff once more. I know your uncle would not tell you anything important, but I think you can add two and two together as well as anyone. You have the advantage of being pretty, so that most people will underrate you. I, however, have not fallen into the mistake of underrating you. I know you must have had suspicions about your uncle, but because he didn't want you or anyone else to have them, you very loyally avoided thinking about them. Isn't that so?"

Sheila's memory was already working. Things, little things she had noticed about her uncle's life, about his visitors, about his trips abroad, came crowding into her mind. Old unanswerable questions, old half-formed guesses now began to take the more solid shape of possibilities. Particularly after the news about her father . . . secret agent. She returned Mr. Olszak's stare.

"Remembering now, Miss Matthews?"

"Nothing very much," she said, and didn't let her eyes waver.

"Your uncle will be pleased with such obstinate discretion. But it adds to my difficulties. All I wanted to know was whether you came here with a particular mission entrusted to you, or not. All I wanted was any information or knowledge which you had gathered here in recent weeks. It might save me much time. More important, it might save lives. We are on the same side, aren't we?"

"Of course we are. But I can't help you in any way; I would like to, but I can't. For I know nothing. I am what is called the innocent bystander."

Olszak replaced his glasses carefully. "Well, that's as far as we get, I see," he said, and swung his legs off the desk.

Sheila rose with relief. "May I go?"

"Only next door, I'm afraid. You'll have to stay near me or be locked up as a suspected enemy agent. Colonel Bolt still has you on his little list."

"But you could tell him all about my father!"

"Yes."

"Then why don't you?"

Olszak took a long time to light a cigarette.

"Miss Matthews, just as Colonel Bolt found the evidence pointing to you as a German agent, I found the evidence pointing to you as a probable British agent. Don't look so incredulous. I admit I am beginning to think I was wrong, too. But that was why I let the drama in Colonel Bolt's room almost reach the third act. I can, as you very pointedly say, close it now. If you have no wish to help us, I will close it. I can go to Colonel Bolt, tell him I find you absolutely innocent, and your name will have that description written after it in his records. You will then be free to go. Will that please you?"

"It would be something of a relief."

"But if I told you that you could be more useful to us, to Poland and Britain and our friends, by allowing Colonel Bolt's records to have a grave question mark against your name, would you let that question mark still remain?"

Sheila looked puzzled. She was groping for a meaning.

"What do you mean by 'useful'?" she asked at last.

"That depends on the future. If we are faced with a catastrophe, then people like you who are willing to fight with only courage and brains for weapons will be very useful, indeed."

The only meaning that Sheila could discover in Mr. Olszak's words was so fantastic that she simply stared.

"I only hope the future for which I must plan now will not happen," the exact voice continued. "I hope this with all my heart. I see you look horrified, Miss Matthews. I am not a defeatist. I am being a realist. In the past, I've had grim experience in how to organize and fight hidden battles. I am talking, you see, of the possibility of a temporary German victory. For, if Germany's overwhelming preparations for war do win, then there will be some of us who are already prepared in our turn to carry on the fight until the day Germany is ultimately beaten. That is one possibility of the future. And this is the one time that I hope all my plans and preparations will never need to be used."

Sheila decided to risk her fantastic guess. "In such a future, the Germans would be interested in anyone who was marked down in your police records as a possible traitor to Poland?"

"I should think so."

"If you could have people on these records who were innocent of such charges and who would work with you, then you would find them useful against the Germans?"

"That could be possible."

"Was that interview with Colonel Bolt a complete farce? Did he know I was innocent, after all?"

"Good God, no. There's only one man in the Security Police who knows why I have been appointed as Special Commissioner. Bolt would have apoplexy at the idea we were using his records for our own purposes. Of course, many of those whose names appear on the records are guilty; they get their deserts. Those I know to be innocent either 'escape' or are released under 'strict surveillance.' But the question mark remains against their name in Colonel Bolt's files."

"And they become your men? For future use, if necessary?"

"You make me sound very autocratic," Olszak said gently. "I assure you that I and my friends have merely decided on a certain course of action as a precautionary measure. An insurance policy, shall we say, against evil days?"

Sheila studied a blot of ink on the surface of the desk. *They either "escape" . . .*

"Was Hofmeyer really a German?" she asked innocently.

Or was he an English agent, working under her uncle as her father had done?

Olszak arranged some of the papers on his desk very casually. "I hardly expected such a wild guess from you, Miss Matthews."

Sheila, feeling very young and very stupid, offered her justification. "There seems to be a strong connection between my uncle and Hofmeyer. You have hinted that my uncle is no mere businessman, that he is more interested in other things, that he is doing the kind of work my father did. Then you jumped to the conclusion that I was an agent as soon as you saw that Hofmeyer leaflet which I had in my handbag. And Mr. Hofmeyer *did* say Matthews correctly. And he seemed to recognize me when he first saw me, so perhaps he knew my father, too. And then, he *did* escape in time."

Olszak ignored all that. "Matthews ..." he was saying. "Anyone can say Matthews correctly, if they only read it correctly."

"You don't say it correctly, Mr. Olszak."

They looked at each other steadily, and then Mr. Olszak surprised her by throwing back his head and laughing loudly. "Well," he said at last, "I don't pronounce Matthews correctly. Imagine that!" But Sheila felt that he had turned her question about Hofmeyer very adequately.

Mr. Olszak looked at his watch. "The last train for refugees leaves at seven. In half an hour, to be exact. What is it to be? Do you take the train, with your name cleared of all charges against it? Or do you stay here, and help us as I have proposed?"

"I will not take the train."

"Then you have no alternative if you stay in Poland. You see Miss Matthews—rightly or wrongly pronounced—you have been caught up in a chain of events, which will make it dangerous for us to have you here unless we can trust you fully. I know you aren't against us. But that isn't enough. Knowing what you do, you must be with us, completely. For I must be sure of one thing. To put it quite brutally, your name, left in the doubtful category on our police files, will ensure your silence."

Sheila said slowly, "I see." She did, only too clearly. She brushed the hair back from her forehead. She looked suddenly so young and uncertain that Mr. Olszak came over to her and took both her hands in his.

"You mustn't think I enjoy talking to you like this. But either you go straight back to England, having taken a very solemn oath never to speak of these matters, never to think of them, again ... and I'll have to send someone with you to make sure you do arrive safely. I shall also have to write a report to your uncle, so that he will see that you remain thoroughly discreet. ... Or, you stay here and leave your name on the files of the Security Police. I won't have to worry about you then."

"But I would have plenty of worries if you got killed, or if my friends heard I had been arrested. I couldn't explain anything to them."

"No, you could not." Olszak looked pleased, as if she were showing the right responses.

"But why would you have to send someone to protect me on the journey home?"

"I am quite sure that your arrest will have become known to people who take an interest in these matters. Your name will also be on the German files."

"So soon?"

"You are so trusting, Miss Matthews. It must be very pleasant to be so trusting." He looked at her still more closely. "Perhaps you don't want to accept my proposal unless you know exactly what it entails. Yet, I'm afraid, that's what I can't tell you. You must take my word for it that I shall ask you to do nothing impossible or useless."

Sheila smiled, but she still didn't give him an answer.

"Why don't you rest next door? You can think about it, and if you decide to return to Britain, I shall see you get there, train or no train. You'll find some magazines and a radio and a comfortable chair. And be sure to black out the window before you switch on the light. I'll order a tray with some food, and I'll telephone Korytowski so he will stop worrying about your absence. I have other work to do, meanwhile. Orthodox work, approved by Colonel Bolt's investigation of diversionist activities."

"Diversionist?"

"Oh, Germans pretending to be Polish-Germans of great loyalty, who will inform against all Polish-Germans of great loyalty once the Germans get hold of them. Or Germans pretending to be Polish-Germans, to stir up trouble and spread untruths and panic among Polish-Germans. Or just Germans, doing their best to defeat us before the war even starts. What is wrong, Miss Matthews? You look amazed."

"It is all so mad, so difficult to believe. I mean, things all being planned under the surface, while ordinary people just eat and sleep and think about their own problems."

"Life is never simple, Miss Matthews, except for those who close their eyes and will not see. You thought I was being overdramatic at the beginning of our conversation. Perhaps you even thought I was at the stage of inventing secret and mysterious plans to satisfy my wild imagination.

I said I was a realist. I am. But I don't blame you for not quite believing my urgency. Anything outside of one's own experience always seems 'unreal,' 'fantastic,' 'unconvincing.' That's the way most human beings react. Do you still think that I and my friends are mad?"

"No." Sheila smiled as she added, "I begin to think that I and all my friends may be the mad ones. At least, we haven't been exactly realists, and I suppose it's madness not to be realistic. My only worry now is—well, I don't think I'd be any good to you at all, Mr. Olszak."

"Won't you let me be the judge of that? After all, I've been watching you more closely than you think, during this conversation. I must say, you've shown a certain alertness and mental agility." He was waiting for her answer, she knew.

Sheila took a deep breath, and walked to the door leading into the next room.

"You have work to do," she said in a low voice. And then, as she opened the door, she paused. "Mr. Olszak, what happens to a simpleminded person like myself who finds out too much, and can't cooperate with you?"

"I was hoping you wouldn't bring that up, Miss Matthews."

She closed the door behind her, leaving Olszak examining a sheet of paper.

"You may not have found out too much, yet," she told herself bitterly, "but you certainly guess too much."

She turned on the wireless set, in order to divert her worries. Her purpose was certainly achieved. She felt an increasing disgust with herself as she listened. The news was still worse, and here she was insisting on making her own choice of the way in which she wanted to help. At a moment like this, choice became a selfish privilege. And why didn't she want to accept Mr. Olszak's suggestion? Was she afraid? She might as well face it: she was afraid. Afraid of being called a traitor when she wasn't one. Afaid of living with fear and worry and lies. Afraid of being incapable and unsuccessful. Afraid of a possible death which would not earn her any kind memories. She was not only a coward, but a vain little coward.

The announcer's voice was saying "... certain amount of unrest on the Polish frontier, due to diversionist activities. The Government asks ... continue to keep calm ..."

She listened to the radio voice, to the traffic sounds dying away on the street outside. She watched evening come to the waiting city, to people heart-sore and mind-weary. She saw the cold wind rising, blowing the dry dust in little swirls off the pavement. Darkness came, and with it were no lights.

When Mr. Olszak entered the room, it was fully eleven o'clock. He stopped at the doorway in amazement, silhouetted against the brightness of the other room.

"Why in the darkness?" he began, crossed over to the window to close it and its screen of black cloth, and switched on the light. He shook his head as he noticed the half-eaten food on the tray, the untouched magazines. He switched off the radio, now talking of Danzig, and waited for her to speak. Sheila rubbed her cold hands together. Her foot doubled under her as she rose from the edge of the chair.

"Take off your shoes and stand with your foot flat on the floor," Mr. Olszak commanded.

Sheila began to laugh.

"What's so funny? Standing that way to cure cramp?"

"No. Just having cramp at this moment. I wanted to rise, erect and noble, and say, 'Mr. Olszak, I agree to do what you think is best.' Instead, I stand here listing to starboard, trying to straighten my leg."

"That's better," Mr. Olszak said, "that's much better." He wasn't referring to her cramped foot. Behind the solemn gray-green eyes he was thinking, she can laugh at herself again. For a moment, his thoughts touched on the girl's dead father. When Matthews had joked about a personal emotion, it had meant a depth of feeling that had better not be underestimated. And then, Olszak's mind switched back to the cold room and the girl whose loose, fair hair fell over her eyes as she bent to find her shoe. He knelt quickly and replaced the shoe on her foot, and smiled to himself as he noticed her confusion. They are so independent nowadays, and at the same time so young, he thought. She was twenty-three. At twenty-three, his mother was not only married, with three children, but had followed his father into political exile in Czarist Russia. At twenty-six, she was a widow with four children, and all her possessions in Poland had been confiscated when her husband was executed. At thirty-seven, she was a grandmother, and had seen two of her sons imprisoned like their father. At fifty-seven, she was a great-grandmother, with all her sons (except Olszak himself) killed in the last war. She too had taken part in that war, sheltering escaped prisoners from German camps, aiding her grandsons and their friends when they were wounded in guerrilla fighting. She still lived, in a neat little house in a small village, high in the Carpathian mountains. People had always thought how gentle and frail she was.

And then Olszak became aware that Sheila was watching him. "You aren't really so terrifying as I thought," she wanted to say. But the quick change in Mr. Olszak's eyes silenced her.

"What do you want me to do?" she said, equally business-like.

"At the moment, nothing. I want you to go back to Korytowski's flat. I'll have a story ready for Colonel Bolt in the morning, so don't worry about that. Shall we say that you are still under my department's observation? Forget everything we have been talking about. Be natural. But keep alert. That's all."

Sheila looked keenly at Mr. Olszak. Her initial disappointment over the first sentence of his speech now vanished. She thought she detected a rather satisfied look in Mr. Olszak's eyes.

"I shall take you to the flat, now."

"I can manage, really. You are probably too busy, Mr. Olszak."

Mr. Olszak said patiently, "I shall take you to the flat."

In the cold darkness of the street, an unobtrusive man silently joined them as they entered a cab. Nothing was spoken throughout the slow journey. They left the cab more than a block away from Korytowski's home. The unobtrusive man lagged behind them, so that he was out of sight when Sheila and Mr. Olszak were admitted through the wrought-iron gateway by a sleepy Henryk.

Henryk was curious in spite of his half-closed eyes. He gave Olszak a nod of recognition, but his chief interest was in Sheila. The lamp, now blue in color, above his house door gave a feeble light which sicklied their faces. Three ghosts stared at each other. Then Olszak had taken her arm in his special grip above the elbow, and they left Henryk's square white face with its two black shadows of close-set eyes.

"He looked like a clown, a clown with a whitewashed face," Sheila said.

"He's hardly a clown. He may be many things, but not that. I like clowns. I don't like Henryk. But then, I dislike inquisitive people."

After that very final remark, Sheila's next question remained unspoken. In any case, she wasn't supposed to know if Professor Korytowski had any further connection with Mr. Olszak than that of an old friend. She wasn't supposed to know anything.

In the flat, there was once more a roomful of tobacco smoke and men's voices. But this time Olszak led her into the living room. "It will be all right," he said aside to Professor Korytowski. "For one thing, she's perishing with cold—didn't have any coat with her. She needs a warm drink or we'll have a pneumonia case on our hands. For another, I think they should meet her. She's Matthews' daughter, after all."

Korytowski's look of worry and indecision disappeared. "Splendid!" he said with such enthusiasm and relief that Sheila knew he had been wondering how else to cope with a guest who stayed out so late and came back shivering. So Olszak was in command here, too.

She was plunged into a sea of unknown faces. The men stopped talking, but they must have known her father, for their eyes were friendly and welcoming. The warmth of the room, the sense of returning security reacted strangely on her. She couldn't say anything as she bowed shyly to each man who kissed her hand as he was introduced. Most of them had indeed known her father. She bit her lip, and her eyes were too bright, but none of the friendly faces laughed. There was only understanding and sympathy. That weakened her still more.

Russell Stevens appeared at this moment, carrying a glass of colorless liquid. "I was told you needed this," he began, and then with a quick glance at her face he added, "Thawing out, I see." That started her laughing. It wasn't a very good attempt, but still it was a relief.

"So you are still in Warsaw?" he said severely. "What do we have to do to get you home? Hit you over the head and shanghai you?"

"But you are still here too."

"I have a job to do."

Sheila looked at Mr. Olszak and returned his smile.

The inevitable telephone gave its harsh ring in the hall.

"For me, I expect," Stevens said quietly. There was a new tension in the room as he left. The faces were openly anxious now. The smiles and friendly talk of the last hours seemed very far away.

When the American came back, he was grim. "Got to leave now. Emergency."

Korytowski was hurrying with him towards the door. But Mr. Olszak had taken Russell Stevens by the arm—a strong, polite grasp it would be, Sheila thought—and that way, they entered the hall together. She heard their voices. Mr. Olszak was being firm. The American was being firm, too.

"I'll lay my bet on Mr. Olszak," Sheila said to herself wryly. What was the argument about, anyway? If she suffered from too many guesses, then Mr. Olszak certainly enjoyed too many ideas. He was serene when he returned to the room, but you couldn't tell anything from that. The outside door, banging abruptly, told Sheila much more.

"I think you would be wise to go to bed," Mr. Olszak was saying quietly. "The dawn is already here, you know. Soon it will be morning."

Sheila moved towards the hall. Her head was heavy, her eyes felt as if two pennies were laid on them. She began to notice each time she swallowed. Bed would be not only wise, but infinitely pleasant. I'm going to catch a cold, she thought miserably.

The man whose shoulders were bent over the radio suddenly stiffened. He held up one hand. His head was thrown back, his eyes were white circles. The announcer's voice cut through the sudden silence of the room.

It had come.

*"Less than an hour ago, German planes bombed Polish territory. Without any declaration of war . . ."*

It had come.

## CHAPTER VII

## *Surveillance*

IN THE dark street, the unobtrusive man paced slowly under the chestnut trees. Twice he halted at the gate and peered into the gloomy cavern of faint light. The third time he approached the iron gateway, Henryk came limping forward.

"Well?" he said, with a truculence that usually disposed of unnecessary visitors.

"Cold night," the man said, and buried his neck further into the shelter of his upturned collar. "Should have brought my coat."

"Get a move on there. Or I'll call the police."

The man shrugged his shoulders, lifted a hand out of his pocket to turn the palm towards the porter. A metal disk gleamed there for a moment in the blue light. "No need," he said, and slipped his hand deep into his pocket once more.

Henryk lost his truculence. He dropped his voice and added a smile. "You got business here?"

"Yes. This the only entrance? No others?"

"No. . . . Who is it?"

The man shivered slightly. "I wish to heaven this sudden wind would bring some rain. We could do with some rain. They tell me the roads are baked dry."

"It's warmer in here," Henryk suggested. "You can sit in the doorway. Less of a draught there, and you can see everyone going or coming. People are moving about tonight. Can't settle." He swung the gate, and the man entered.

From the porter's apartment came a rhythmic snoring. "The wife," Henryk explained. He lowered the volume of the small radio beside his chair. "I was having some tea. I'll get you a glass. Aye, there's been a lot of traffic in and out here, tonight. I've got to stay up until it stops. Why they can't stay in their beds at this hour is something I'll never figure out."

"Wish I could be in mine. You and I appreciate our beds, and that's why we've both got jobs that keep us out of them."

Henryk laughed and limped into the kitchen for more tea. "Someone been breaking the law?" he asked jokingly when he returned with an extra chair as well. The two men settled themselves comfortably in the little cubicle of a doorway, and stared out into the gloomy vault of the entranceway as they sipped the tea.

"Someone I've just got to keep an eye on," the visitor said.

Henryk's small, deep-set eyes studied the simple face beside him. "We are all highly respectable here. Can't imagine you've come to the right place."

"This is the house, all right."

"You followed someone here? Well, that's different." The deep-set eyes were inscrutable now. The man, concentrating on his glass of tea, seemed lost in his thoughts, too. But they would have surprised his amiable host. Hurry up and get to the point, the man was thinking: the boss told me you were a curious chap. What's happened to your curiosity all of a sudden?"

"Do you know the people here well?" the man asked at last.

"I'm getting to know them and their visitors now. Took a week or two to remember them by name." Henryk's voice was casual, almost diffident.

"Any strangers recently?"

"A girl. Came late last night, too. She's a guest of Korytowski's. Say, there's nothing wrong up there, is there?"

"Korytowski's all right. Just another dopey professor as far as I know."

"But the girl is a friend of the family. My wife was told that today."

"He thinks she is. What do *you* think of her?"

"Looked good to me." Henryk outlined a curve in the air with his two hands, and laughed with the other man.

"Would you say she was English? Have you heard her talk?"

"She's a foreigner for certain. Might be English."

"She didn't seem German?"

Henryk was impassive. Except for the slight pause there

was nothing to show that the question had startled him.

"No. Didn't get that impression. In fact, I was out with Madame Sarna's dog today—she's the singer, third floor over there to your right—" he pointed into the dark courtyard— "and this girl appeared. She didn't know much Polish, it seemed. Just stared at me when I wished her good day, and then said something which sounded like French to me. I wouldn't know. I remember thinking her legs looked kind of French. What made you think she was German?"

The unobstrusive man lowered his voice still more. "I don't get told much. Do this, do that. And no explanations before or after, see? But today the hunt is on for a German spy. Hofmeyer's the name. And she's a pal of his. That's all I know. It isn't much, but it's enough when you're dealing with Germans."

"And Korytowski doesn't know? Why, his house is always filled with good patriots!"

"And that's it. Who would suspect her if she were there? She's a clever one."

"Aye," Henryk said. He moved his stiff leg. "Wound from the last war," he explained. His guest had no objections to changing the conversation, now. They talked of the old days.

Henryk turned the radio louder. "Soon be morning," he said cheerfully.

"I'll take a turn on the pavement and let you have a nap."

"Don't feel like sleeping. I'll get some in the afternoon when the wife's on duty." His hand played nervously with the radio's station-finder.

Footsteps running through the courtyard caught their attention. It was the American. He gave them a nod as he clanged the gate after him.

"An American," Henryk explained. "Friend of Korytowski's. Always in a hurry, coming or going."

Silence filled the courtyard once more. Only the radio voice was speaking. There was a sudden pause, a sudden rush of words. *"Less than an hour ago, German planes bombed Polish territory. Without any declaration of war . . ."*

The two men stared at each other, and then Henryk rose quickly to his feet.

"Elzbieta, Elzbicta!" he was shouting into the bedroom. "Wake up, woman, wake up. It's started!"

The quiet man sat stiffly in his chair. "Dog's blood," he swore, "dog's blood and dog's bones." He didn't look at the staring-eyed woman, her straight hair stiff in thin pigtails, who clutched round her throat the shabby coat which she had thrown over the shoulders of her nightgown. Together

with her husband, she bent over the radio to catch the
uneven words. Henryk's hands trembled. He wiped his mouth
and the back of his neck with a rag of a handkerchief. The
Pole, still sitting on the chair beside him, cursed the Germans
for what they were in a steady, even flow.

Other footsteps were hurrying through the courtyard, now.
Olszak looked at the little group in the doorway as he opened
the gate.

"You've heard?" Henryk called after him. Olszak nodded.
His quick footsteps died away on the pavement outside.
"That's another friend of Korytowski's," Henryk explained.
"He's an editor of a paper that no one buys. He's probably
rushing to write an editorial that no one wants to read.
Say, what are you going to do, yourself?"

The man said dully, "Can't leave this job until they get
another man set."

Ten minutes later, Henryk's phone rang.

"Someone wants to know if the man waiting in the street
outside this building can be brought to the phone," Henryk
announced with a grin. "Better not tell them you've been
warming your back on my chair."

The man rose and went to the phone. He did the listening.
Elzbieta had to wait until he returned to the doorway before
her curiosity was satisfied.

"Got to go now," he said.

"What about——?" Henryk motioned with his head in
the direction of Korytowski's flat.

"That's taken care of. Another man is set across the road,
now that the daylight has come." He stopped at the gate. "I
wouldn't say anything about this," he advised. "These Germans are wary birds. She'll fly at the first sign."

Henryk nodded. "I'll say nothing. I'm too busy to notice
anything." He pulled out the hosepipe onto the pavement. He called back to his wife. "Get some clothes on.
We'll have breakfast when I've finished this job."

The unobtrusive man had already disappeared round the
corner of the street, as Henryk started playing the jet of water
round the roots of the chestnut trees.

Sheila, in her bedroom, heard the cheerful hiss of the water. Someone down there was whistling quietly to himself.

"What has *he* got to whistle about?" she said savagely to
her white face in the gray mirror. The mirror only answered
her with unhappy eyes and trembling lips.

The weight was pressing on the back of her neck, now.
Her hands were hot, her spine was cold. The bed linen was
as icy as a midwinter pond. She started to shiver.

# CHAPTER VIII
## Escape

WHEN she awoke, the room was dark and stifling. If this were night again, then she hadn't much to show for today. She could remember a man, one of those who had met her in the living room last night, sitting beside her bed. He had taken her temperature, felt her pulse. He had made her swallow some small, square-shaped pills. Uncle Edward had stood watching her silently. The apartment no longer had any voices. She had thought, dismally, everyone had gone home: everyone, except herself. And she had started to shed a sympathetic tear for herself, and then she must have fallen into a sleep so deep that she couldn't even gauge its length. Later, when the sun filtered through the leaves outside to cast moving shadows on the wall, someone had wrapped her in a blanket and propped her in a chair. It was a woman, she had noticed dimly, a woman with a straight wisp of hair over staring eyes. And the woman had talked, low quick words. Sheila remembered feeling alive enough only for a brief space to mumble, "*Ja, jawohl . . .*" in answer to a repeated repeated question. It must have been asked in German, although she hadn't realized that at the time. She had been too busy watching the shadows on the wall. One had turned into a fox's face. It chased the other shadows up and across the wall, and then it would suddenly drop back to its original position and the fox's mask would start its chase all over again. The woman hadn't believed her even when she pointed out the exact position of the cunning face, had helped her firmly into bed, had covered her with sheets that were all smooth and cool once more.

But now the sun had gone, the shadows and the fox's mask had gone, the doctor and the woman had gone. Only Uncle Edward was still there, still standing silently watching her from the doorway. He was so quiet that it seemed strange he should have wakened her. Her thoughts were slow like her movements. She wasn't shivering now. The bed was as hot as an oven. The pillow felt damp when she moved her neck. All air seemed to have gone from the room. There was a jangling in her ears as if she were listening to a distant, violent fire-alarm.

70

"I really don't think you can be moved," Uncle Edward said. He walked slowly into the room and switched on the small light beside her bed. "But I think you ought to know, now that you are awake, that we are again under attack."

"Again?" Sheila swallowed painfully. Even the voice didn't seem to come from her dry throat. It sounded as if a ventriloquist were using her for a dummy. She raised herself on one elbow, but there was no support in her arm, and she was glad to sink back into the pillow's furrow.

"Yes. The first came this morning, just after the doctor had given you some pills and put you to sleep. Then there was a second attack, fairly quickly. I'm beginning to lose count now. The air warden from upstairs has been trying to herd us over to the trenches in the Park, for the recent raids have been coming closer to this district. But I don't think you should go."

"And you?"

The blue eyes, tired, worried, suffering, smiled at her. "I helped to dig them during the last two days. I prefer to stay here, myself. Four walls give an illusion of protection."

An angry, staccato rattle sounded from the courtyard.

"Antiaircraft," Korytowski said gently. "It was set up in our garden this morning."

Sheila nodded. Her hands were clenching the sheets in the same way she used to clench her handkerchief while the dentist's drill ground out a deeply decayed tooth.

"Just rest, and you'll be all right. Two or three days, and we'll have this fever beaten. If we could only send you to a hospital, it would be better for you. But the hospital beds are being kept as empty as possible." He shrugged his shoulders. The kindly face looked so sad that Sheila tried a smile.

The sound of airplane engines seemed closer. Sheila shut her eyes. She couldn't bear that sound: it was worse than the explosions as the bombs landed. For the bombs had at least finished when they crashed on the ground, but that loud coughing from the sky went on and on, threatening those still alive, promising pain and destruction.

Korytowski sat on the edge of the bed. "Words are extraordinary things," he was saying. "They persist through the centuries as if they had a real life of their own. Stevens was telling me that the vulgar expression for legs in his country is—" There was a violent blast, the room seemed to rock, glass smashed on the pavement outside. Korytowski looked at the black square of window speculatively. "It really was fortunate that I boarded it up this afternoon. Never did believe in these strips of paper. Well, the vulgar expression is *gams,* I believe." Another blast tightened Sheila's body into a rigid stretch of bone and muscle. "Now the extraordinary thing is this: back in the days of Rome, the soldier who didn't speak proper Latin would insist on a rough slang all of his own. His word for a pretty leg was—" The room moved again, this time more insistently. Sheila's eardrums were bursting, but her hands couldn't leave hold of the sheets to shut out the overwhelming sound. Professor Korytowski waited patiently for silence, as if he were facing a crowd of coughing, shuffling students in a classroom. "His word," he continued when the first short lull occurred, "his word was *gamba.*"

The planes had gone. The antiaircraft guns had fallen silent in the courtyard. But the ringing in Sheila's ears was louder. He noticed her tenseness.

"Fire brigade," he said briefly. He poured a glass of water and held it to her lips. "This bed has got to be changed again. We are soaking the fever out of you, anyway. I'll go and get Henryk's wife. She said she would look after you until Teresa arrives."

"Madame Aleksander is coming?"

"She has already left Korytów with Barbara. They decided they ought to be here at the hospitals. Stefan and little Teresa have stayed with Aunt Marta. It will be safer in the country. The Germans will not waste bombs on anything so small as Korytów. Marta phoned me after Teresa and Barbara had left; couldn't reach me on the phone before then."

"Then only Aunt Marta knows I am still here?"

"So far. And do you know what she said about this chill of yours? 'Never did wear enough clothes.'"

Sheila wanted to laugh, and found she couldn't, somehow.

"I'll go down to the porter's lodge. I don't think there will be another raid for at least an hour."

"Uncle Edward . . ."

"Yes, Sheila?" The blue eyes smiled kindly, reassuringly.

There was a slight pause. And then, "Aren't you afraid?" The question came hesitatingly.

"Yes, I was. Very much so. But I'm getting accustomed to the idea that bombs can drop around me, and as soon as you get accustomed to that, you begin to feel so many other emotions—anger, chiefly—that fear loses some of its importance."

"Is there much damage?"

"What you'd expect." The blue eyes had hardened.

"Has London been bombed?"

"No. Nor Paris. Not yet. We are fighting alone so far."

Sheila closed her eyes.

"Don't worry," the quiet voice was saying. "We'll hold on

here until our allies can reach us. All you've to worry about is recovering as quickly as possible. I'll tell the porter's wife to come up here, now. When she has left and you are back in bed, I'll give you some medicine." He nodded towards a bottle standing on the table beside the bed.

The door closed.

Sheila stared at it, miserably. It was one of those moments in life when everything seems wrong.

The door opened again, cautiously this time. The pale-faced, pale-eyed porter's wife came into the room.

"It's only me—Elzbieta," she said. "I've brought you some herb tea. Sip it, while I straighten this bed."

She wrapped Sheila methodically into the blanket, and propped her once more on the chair. Sheila began sipping the tea. It was weak and bitter: it smelled of a wooden chest with scented clothes, long undisturbed. Sheila collected her thoughts in German. A lot of Poles knew German, used it with foreigners if Polish failed. Yet Sheila felt she should be surprised at this woman. At the moment, she was incapable of feeling anything except worry. Over the edge of the wide cup, she watched the woman methodically change the bed linen. She was dressed in an old skirt, a shapeless knitted jumper. Yet there was a neatness, a clean-scrubbed look to her in spite of the old clothes. Her straight hair was tightly pinned into a plaited coil at the nape of her neck. Only one short strand of hair was out of place, and she would blow at it out of the corner of her mouth as it fell over her eye. Then, quick-temperedly, she'd tuck it back into place, scarcely pausing in her work. Sheila took some time to notice that the woman was watching her as much as she was watching the woman. "You're slow in the uptake, today," she told herself, and at that very moment realized why she should have felt surprised at the woman's German. It was good German, accurate and hard, with the clear enunciation of Berlin.

On an impulse, Sheila said to the waiting woman, "Are you German?" Her voice was a ludicrous whisper: the effort of sitting up in this chair must have been more of a drain on her strength than she had imagined.

Elzbieta looked at her with a strange smile. "Oh no!" she whispered back. "Are you?"

"No."

Elzbieta laughed suddenly. She spoke in a normal voice again. "There's no one here. You can speak as loud as you want. Old Korytowski's down gaping at the bomb-holes."

Sheila tried to focus her mind sharply. The callous impertinence in the woman's voice had warned her.

"You work for Hofmeyer, direct?" the woman asked suddenly.

"Hofmeyer?" Sheila felt her mind dulling again. She was too tired to cope with all this, she thought in desperation.

"You don't know anyone called Hofmeyer?" The voice was sarcastic.

Sheila shook her tired head.

"Come off it," the woman said almost savagely. "Stop wasting time." She went over to the dressing table, opened Sheila's handbag, pulled out the airplane tickets and Hofmeyer's leaflet. Sheila, who had imagined that Olszak had destroyed that sheet of paper, could only stare at the fact that it was still in her bag. And there was a reason behind that fact. So much she could guess, even at the moment, when her head felt it had fallen off her neck and was rolling around on the floor.

The woman said bitterly, "I found that this morning. Fine credit you are to us! Letting them dope you until you can't even see what's happening to your own handbag. Heinrich got in touch with Hofmeyer about you this morning, after the policeman left us."

Heinrich. Not Henryk. Heinrich. And Johann Hofmeyer playing a double, yet single-purposed game. Hofmeyer, neither German nor Pole, living in Warsaw for twenty years as a German-Pole. Hofmeyer taking orders from Uncle Matthews, working now with Olszak, accepted by the Heinrichs. Surely that must be it. Surely Hofmeyer was in German pay in name only, for his own purposes. Surely—Policeman. . . . What was that about a policeman?

"Policeman?"

"Political police. Watching you. A fine mess you've made of it. What did you spill at headquarters, yesterday?"

"Nothing."

"Hofmeyer will be pleased for that small mercy. If it's true. Wish he could see you now, so doped that when the police pick you up again they'll get everything out of you."

"Where is he?"

"Hofmeyer? Safe. And still in touch with us. He said you would hear from him." The woman smoothed the top counterpane with quick decisive strokes of her hand. "What's your idea in staying here, anyway?"

Sheila felt that the woman hated her for being here. There was certainly resentment in her eyes.

"It was safe." Sheila was now praying for Korytowski's return. She was feeling too tired, she was losing the alertness which her fear had given her. She would make a mistake. Why didn't Korytowski come?"

"It was a good front, all right," the woman admitted. "Hofmeyer's a sharp fellow. But my guess is that he will tell you to clear out now, before the police arrest you again."

"But the police were satisfied yesterday."

"God, what innocents we are using nowadays! Don't you know that the police are never satisfied? Listen, you are fairly new to this game. Not like me or Margareta Koch. And the first thing you'll have to learn if you want to stay alive is that you've got to smell danger. I've just got to take one look at this set-up and I smell plenty of danger all round you."

"Margareta Koch? Where is she?"

"Haven't heard for nigh on six months. One of our men in the police building reported yesterday that Koch had been arrested disguised as an English girl. But it turned out to be you and not Koch. I won't say you weren't a surprise. But then, Papa Hofmeyer usually has one or two up his sleeve. I'll tell you one thing: he's pretty angry with you, right now. Called you a string of names to Heinrich for getting onto the police list. You won't be much good to us now, not until we take over here. Come on, back into bed with you. Clever of you to have chosen to be the English milady. No one expects them to speak Polish correctly." She picked up one of Sheila's shoes, and shook her head admiringly. "Trust Papa Hofmeyer. Everything correct down to the English shoe label. Nice piece of leather. I haven't been allowed to wear anything like that for a long time. Too damned long. Wait until you're made a caretaker's wife some day. You'll know, then!"

Sheila pressed her head further into the pillow, as if to shut out the woman's venom. She suddenly felt at the mercy of this woman's bitter heart. She almost cried out with joy when she heard the outside door being opened. The woman dropped the shoes and picked up the empty cup.

"No more medicine!" she said quickly. "Remember. You're not ill. They are doping you to keep you here. And you've got to leave. The plans are being made."

Elzbieta was opening the bedroom door, now. "Good evening, sir," she said very timidly, very politely to the man who came in. It wasn't Korytowski. It was Olszak.

"Well," he said to Sheila, "don't tell me you are a casualty. Where's your host? I brought him a copy of my war editorial." He uncorked the medicine bottle. "Want some now? One of my best accomplishments is holding a spoon of nasty medicine for someone else. Allow me."

"No," Sheila said as clearly as she could. "No, thanks. I don't need any more medicine."

"Too bad." Olszak corked the bottle again, regretfully.

They both listened to the closing of the outside door.

Olszak moved swiftly, in strange contrast to his diffident entry, back into the hall.

"Thoroughly locked," he said when he once more returned. "Now, what did she say?"

Sheila was so amazed that Olszak should expect the woman to have said anything interesting, that she could only stare at him.

"Quick, Miss Matthews, tell me everything that happened." His voice was strangely excited. "I know you are ill, but if you ever wanted to help in this war, by God I think you are going to do it now."

The wild enthusiasm in his voice lifted Sheila out of her lethargy. She told him about Elzbieta, haltingly, yet as accurately as she could force herself to speak. Sometimes she would forget something (why should she have to be ill at this time?) and then she'd pause, force herself to go back and straighten out what she had jumbled. Mr. Olszak listened patiently, intently, without interruption or prompting. He let her choose her own tempo, and his silence helped her. It wasn't so long, after all, before he could piece together the whole scene.

"Good," he said. "In fact, excellent. That's all I wanted. You know, it is a nice feeling when you have a suspicion that no one else will share, when you work out a little plan to deal with it, to find that everything does fit into place and that you've a neat success on your hands. It's a nicer feeling than many a bigger, more obvious victory."

He looked at Sheila critically. "You're tired. You should sleep. I'll wait for Korytowski in the other room. Anything I can get you?"

"Some medicine. I want to get out of this bed as soon as I can."

Olszak nodded approvingly. "I think I'd better warn you," he said as he poured a careful tablespoon of medicine, "that your real name is supposed to be Anna Braun. It was the first name that Hofmeyer could think of, when Henryk contacted him with the news that you were under suspicion. Henryk, of course, wanted to know all about you. There: that's the way. Swallow it quickly when your mouth is wide open. Now here's some water. That's the way."

He relented suddenly. "I suppose you have earned more of an explanation than that," he said. "I had a suspicion or two about Henryk. Only, my sources were not reliable, and although we have watched him and the woman we could find out nothing definite. Hofmeyer knew nothing about them. But last night, one of my men was instructed to inform them very carefully that you were under surveillance, that you had some connection with Hofmeyer. This morning, Henryk contacted another German who knew where Hofmeyer is hiding. He actually met Hofmeyer. Now we know Henryk and Elzbieta are Heinrich Dittmar and Lisa Koehler. We've more than enough proof."

"Elzbieta knew who Hofmeyer was. She called him Papa."

Olszak repressed a smile. "Only by reputation," he said. "Just as Hofmeyer had heard of Dittmar. But he never met him until this morning. We did a good job of work last night."

"I wish. . . ."

"What do you wish?"

Sheila stirred restlessly. "Somehow I wish Hofmeyer could just have come along here and found out for himself who Henryk really was."

"And let the Germans' suspicions be aroused against Hofmeyer when Henryk is arrested? No, I'm afraid that isn't the way we have to work. In fact, you will have to be arrested again, along with the porter and his wife, just to keep yourself safe from the Germans. I've already arranged for a nice place for you to hide after you 'escape' from our police. But meanwhile the problem is that Henryk will be planning how to smuggle you out of this apartment so as to hide you from the Poles."

Sheila said, "But I don't want to leave here. Madame Aleksander and Barbara are coming. I want to see them." Her voice was foolishly on edge.

"I'm afraid you'll have to leave. It's a matter of your own safety. Henryk and the woman are too interested in the unknown Anna Braun. And Hofmeyer has got to invent a life story for you that will fit, and you can't answer any German questions until you learn that story. You've got to get out of here and be well hidden." Mr. Olszak began to walk about the room. "The best way," he said at last, "will be to let Henryk do his planning, to let him smuggle you out. You will appear then to have escaped from this room with his connivance, whereas you really have escaped from him." Olszak was looking pleased, now. "Yes," he added, "that would be a neat way to use Henryk, and catch him."

"Madame Aleksander—" Sheila began miserably. "I want to see her."

"Yes, yes. Don't worry. I'll look after all that. Don't worry. Get some sleep." His voice was reassuring and strangely gentle.

Bombs wakened her again.

Olszak had come back into the bedroom. He was standing beside her.

"I'm afraid it would be ungallant to climb under your bed," he shouted, and won a weak smile.

"Uncle Edward?"

"Still not here." He glanced impatiently at his watch. "I can't wait much longer. Yet I can't leave you alone." Sheila thought, it isn't the bombs he is worrying about so much as the woman downstairs. As long as someone was with Sheila she would be safe from Elzbieta's curiosity.

At that moment, even as if their thoughts had attracted the woman, they heard a pounding at the entrance door. Olszak gave Sheila a warning glance and moved quickly into the hall.

"Everyone to the shelters!" Elzbieta was yelling. "Air warden's been hit. I'm following his instructions." She pushed past Olszak to enter the room.

"Get dressed before the next raid. This is going to be a bad night. Everyone's to get to shelter. Orders." She stared at Sheila and then turned on her heel.

"Miss Matthews is ill," Olszak's voice was saying.

"I'll help her to the shelter. Orders." She left them as a building shattered to the ground. That bomb had landed not so far away. She didn't even flinch. Her eyes, as she left the room, gave Sheila a final look and command. The entrance door slammed shut once more.

"She's without fear," Sheila said.

"She's enjoying it. If I were in Berlin and the bombs started dropping, I'd dance with joy."

"Have they dropped there, yet?"

"No."

"England, France? Are they fighting?"

"Not yet."

"America? The other countries?"

Olszak shook his head. In a quiet moment, he dropped his voice to normal and added, "This approximates my idea of hell." He sat on the edge of the bed, as the torrent of noise broke loose once more. He had taken hold of one of her hands as if to give her strength, and she clung to his wrist desperately. The antiaircraft guns had burst out again with renewed venom. The angry coughing of the planes was nearer. The living room window, which Korytowski hadn't had time to board up—his guest's room had seemed the only urgent one, to him—shattered suddenly. As the curtains blew wildly aside, and the doors were sucked open, Sheila could see a strange light sweeping through the blasted window to reach into the hall. Its rhythmical ebb and flow told her it was only a searchlight. Perhaps because her first fear had been so great, she felt almost calm in her relief. If only she could be out of this bed, if only she could identify these ripping, smashing, tearing crashes, she would feel better. She felt vulnerable because she felt so helpless. If she could see other people waiting for the bombs, too, she would lose this feeling of war waged against her personally. It was always easier to bear trouble if you felt you weren't the only one.

The noises slackened at last, and then ceased. She could smile to Mr. Olszak and say, with more determination than truth, "I think I'm getting accustomed to it, now." She let go his wrist and added frankly, "But I'm glad you were here."

He said urgently, "Can you get dressed? Can you travel for a short distance? I have a feeling that Henryk has planned your rescue from this room during the next big raid. Elzbieta gave you the warning. You saw that, didn't you?"

Sheila nodded.

"I may have to leave you, for I have our own plans to put into action." Olszak glanced at his watch. "It has stopped," he said fretfully. "Damn Edward... what's keeping him?"

And then the phone bell rang, a pathetic, plaintive little sound after all the noise of the last fifteen minutes.

"Edward!" Olszak said in relief and hurried to answer the phone. First, he listened, and than he insisted on something he proposed. He ended with the words, "Hurry, Teresa." So it wasn't Professor Korytowski. It must be Madame Aleksander, Sheila thought drowsily. It must be. She must ask. but when Oszak returned to the room, she was already deeply asleep.

She was still asleep when Madame Aleksander arrived.

"Michal, what's wrong?" were Teresa Aleksander's first words.

"Gently, Teresa." First I must calm her down, he thought. His voice was reassuring. "You are looking well, if a little tired. Come and sit down while I explain." He locked the front door carefully.

"Where's Edward? You were so strange over that phone. Why didn't you let Barbara come up here? Why did you insist that she should go to your flat? What's wrong?" She halted at the doorway of the living room. "Oh, look at this glass everywhere!" Her domestic instincts were outraged.

"Gently, Teresa," he said again as he watched her white face. The silly disorder in the room seemed as if it were the breaking point of Madame Aleksander's resistance. Small things like that were always the last straw. He tried to make the blackout curtains secure once more, so as to shield the room's one small light from the courtyard. "As if it mattered, anyway," he said irritably, thinking of the city so brightly illuminated now by flames. "Now tell me your story, Teresa. How did you get here?"

By the time she had finished her story of hopeless roads, of crowded fields, of children and women machine-gunned, she was again in control—as if by talking of these things she could bring herself to accept them for the harsh reality they were. Just as Barbara and she had reached Warsaw, walking the last ten miles on foot, the raid was taking place. "All we did was to stand and crane our necks," she said in surprise. "So did everyone else. I suppose it's because it is all so strange: it is like another world, somehow. I kept thinking, this can't be Warsaw. This can't be me or Barbara. . . . We just stood and looked. Then it was all over, and the trams started running again, and people got into them, or started walking down the streets. And then I phoned Edward and found you; and I've sent Barbara to your flat as you insisted But why?" She pulled off her hat wearily. "I hate hats. They make my head ache. But my feet feel worse. Fortunately, I made Barbara wear a pair of sensible shoes this morning. Otherwise we wouldn't have been here yet. Now, where is Edward?" She smoothed the heavy braid of silver hair which encircled her head. She looked more tired than she would admit: the shadows under the eyes were stronger, the high cheekbones seemed more pronounced.

"He is out. But the news is Sheila Matthews. She's still here. She didn't go to Britain."

"Sheila!" Madame Aleksander was first aghast, and then dismayed. "Oh, Michal!"

"And she's ill. Caught a severe chill. I want Barbara to nurse her at another address. I didn't want Barbara to be seen coming here at all. No, don't go to see Sheila now. She's asleep. And I have more to tell you, for I must leave here, now that you have arrived to take charge."

"What's wrong, Michal?" It was not for nothing that Madame Aleksander had known Olszak for twenty-five years.

"I am sending Sheila to another address. She is in danger here."

"But this house isn't any more dangerous than other buildings. Really, Michal, bombs don't respect place or person. We've all the same chance."

"It isn't the bombing that worries me. Let me finish, Teresa. Sheila was instrumental in uncovering certain German agents. They know she is here. She must leave and hide."

"Well, tell the police at once, Michal. Surely you've done that?"

"Teresa, things don't work so simply. The police are very busy right now doing a hundred jobs outside of their own duty. Besides, we have little time. We shall have to help Sheila. We can protect her. When the next raid warning comes through, get her dressed. When the concierge or his wife come upstairs, let her go with him or her. But you must stay behind. Say you want to wait for your brother; give any excuse that seems natural. But don't say one thing more than that to the person who comes for Sheila. If you do, you will kill Sheila."

Madame Aleksander looked at him unbelievingly. "Michal!" she said. Yet he was serious: he really meant what he said.

"You will hear the full story later," he was saying. "I will see that Sheila is safe. And Barbara. In two or three days, you will see both of them again. Please trust me in this."

"But of course," she said slowly. "Of course I trust your judgment." She followed him into the hall. He opened the bedroom door and they stood looking at the sleeping girl.

Madame Aleksander crossed quickly over to the bed. "Her brow is damp. She's flushed. Her breathing is heavy. Michal, I don't think she should leave this bed. Really, I don't."

Olszak said firmly, almost coldly, "She must go. Now do you see how desperate the situation is if I insist she must get up and go in her present condition?"

Madam Aleksander nodded. "She looks so young at the moment. There is always something so pathetic about the young when they are asleep: all their grown-up ways quite gone."

"She's twenty-three. What were you doing when you were twenty-three?"

Madam Aleksander smiled gently. "In Siberia, with my husband. Andrew was only a year old. Stanislaw had such dreadful bronchitis I never thought he would live."

"But he did. You all did. Hardship and danger destroys fewer people than indulgence."

"Sometimes I used to think that if we suffered, then we would save our children from suffering," she said sadly. "Now it seems as if no generation escapes suffering."

"Each generation suffers so that its children will be strong, for children whose fathers have escaped hardship come to think that life is easy. Soon they believe that easiness is life. There is no greater danger to a country than when its citizens assume that danger no longer exists."

"I wish I didn't believe you," Madame Aleksander said. "I wish I didn't." At the door, she gave him her hand to kiss.

In the kitchen cupboard she found a dustpan and broom. She turned the radio on, so that she might hear the next air raid warning. She took off her costume jacket, and rolled up the sleeves of her white silk blouse. How do you begin to clean up so much broken glass? she wondered.

She had almost finished the seemingly impossible task, when the radio suddenly interrupted its concert, and in place of violins came the impersonal voice of the announcer. "Look out! Look out!" So many enemy planes passing this zone, and then this zone, and then this zone. They were heading for the center of the city. She hurried into the bedroom. "Wake up, Sheila, wake up," she was saying frantically as the radio voice warned the last zone of all: "Warsaw! Warsaw!"

"Quick, Sheila, quick." Madame Aleksander was already drawing a thin stocking over Sheila's damp instep. "Wake up, Sheila. Air raid warning. Wake up." Madame Aleksander was in tears, tears shed in anger at her own weakness at ever having promised to get Sheila out of this flat. "Sheila, my dear Sheila," she was saying. "I'll never forgive myself." She hugged the girl tightly.

Sheila forgot to be surprised. The quinine was playing havoc with her head. She had begun to shiver again once she had left the warm bed. Only when Madame Aleksander had managed to close the zipper on her girdle, and had slipped her skirt over her head, did she say, "Madame Aleksander! I thought you'd never come." Madame Aleksander blinked back the tears, and gave Sheila a second hug, and then pushed her arms into the sleeves of her linen jacket.

"Where's your coat?"

Sheila nodded towards the curtain which disguised the pegs on the wall. But even with the coat's warmth belted tightly round her, its collar turned up round her ears and across her throat, she was trembling with cold.

The antiaircraft guns were going into action. As Sheila fumbled weakly after a shoe which her foot had kicked by accident under the bed, the door opened and Elzbieta entered. She had pretended to retire for the night. She had pinned a shawl round her head to hide the thin plaits of hair. A coat hung over a tentlike nightdress. Her bare feet had been thrust into an old pair of sand-shoes.

"Everyone downstairs," she said in Polish. "It's a big raid. Orders."

Madame Aleksander, kneeling beside the bed with one arm stretched under it, produced the missing shoe. It was probably her exertions which made her face so red and unnatural.

"Miss Matthews is ready," Madame Aleksander said. "I don't think she is well enough, but she insists a shelter would be safer."

"It certainly would. Hear that? Come on, I'll help her," Elzbieta said.

"I'll follow. I must get my own coat, and my bag, and my brother's manuscript. He would want me to take it with me."

Elzbieta nodded agreeably. She was pleased at this turn of events. Madame Aleksander saw a last, almost despairing, look from from Sheila, as Elzbieta urged her out of the door. The woman was holding the girl very firmly around the waist. A sudden chill struck Madame Aleksander's heart. She was afraid, not of the bombs beginning to fall so methodically, so callously. She was afraid for Sheila, for Barbara, for little Teresa and Stefan and Marta. She was afraid for Andrew on a crowded road leading to the front, for Stanislaw who was still in Warsaw. Even for Eugenia, his wife, much as it was hard to like her. For if anything happened to Eugenia, it would hurt Stanislaw; and anything that hurt one of her children hurt her. She had become part of them, just as they had once been part of her.

This war has scattered us, she thought sadly. Now none of us even knows what the other is doing, where he is, whether he needs us. We are all shut off from each other as if we were strangers. Each time a bomb falls, I shall wonder if it is worse for them wherever they are. . . .

The planes were almost overhead now.

Madame Aleksander switched off the meager light. She clasped her slender fingers and knelt beside the bed in the deafening darkness.

# CHAPTER IX

## The Arrest

"HURRY UP. No time to lose." The door had closed on Madame Aleksander's anxious face. Outside, the babel of sounds had increased. The woman's arm tightened around Sheila's waist, urging her through the dark courtyard, past the shouting men, round a pointing gun, into the entrance gate. Tonight no blue-painted bulb was needed to light the vault. A dim glow was reflected from red patches in the sky.

"In here, quick." The woman pulled her into the doorway of the porter's lodging.

"Here," a man's voice echoed sharply, and firm hands guided her through the dark narrow hall into a poorly lit room. The smell of stewed sausage and sour cabbage was everywhere. The hands freed her, and Sheila caught the edge of a table for support, its dishes rattling nervously as her weight shifted them. She wished she liked the smell of stewed sausage and sour cabbage. The nearest chair seemed so far away, and her legs had suddenly lost the power to move. Olszak was right: this was worse than bombs.

"As soon as the raid is over," Henryk was bellowing, "Martin will have the car here. And as soon as the car's here, we can all stop worrying." The outside noises slackened, and he could drop his voice to a shout. "So you're Anna Braun, Hofmeyer's little surprise packet. 'You're a fool,' I told him this morning, 'to think that you're important enough to pick and choose your own private agents. What do you think you are? A head of a department?'"

"You were the fool," Elzbieta said. She paused for a sudden burst of gunfire to finish before she went on. "Hofmeyer's got influence. He soon will be the head of a department."

"I'm superior to any Hofmeyer. Just remember that, my girl."

The background of noise lessened again. But the last crashes and slams and smashes had seemed to make Elzbieta angrier.

"Yes. You were. But his time is coming. He's chosen the right friends. He will probably be made the head of a district. It's a pity you didn't use a little more tact, my man. I'm tired of playing a porter's wife. It's time you got something better for us than this. Before I tied up with you, I lived in the Athene Palast, and the Dorchester, and the Waldorf-Astoria. *This* is what I get *now*." She flung her arms tensely apart.

Sheila was praying, let them go on using their bad temper on each other; let them bicker, and perhaps they'll forget to question me. But her legs were treacherous. She sank to the ground, kneeling beside the table, shifting it with her weight. Henryk took a step forward, peered down at the flushed face leaning against the table leg. Sheila's eyes were closed. Her breath came in short stabs.

"She's ill," he said, and felt her brow. "She's damned ill."

"Doped," the woman said. "Why all the sympathy? Last week I had a worse cold than that. I had a pain which bent my back double. But I kept on my feet and did my work. Much credit I got for it, too."

"Shut up. She's ill. She'll never stand the journey out of Warsaw. Martin will have a dead woman on his hands. What will Hofmeyer say then?"

"None of us is irreplaceable."

"Tell that to Hofmeyer."

"So you think he's important now, do you?" Elzbieta sneered.

"Shut up," Henryk said savagely. "Help me get her onto this chair."

The noises offstage had burst out again with uncontrolled fury.

"It won't matter whether she's ill or not if a bomb hits this dump," Elzbieta shouted. "Did you hear that one? It was the closest yet."

"Why didn't you tell me she was ill? We could have made other plans. Too late now."

"I still say she isn't ill. Just—"

"Oh, shut up!" The planes and guns obeyed him incongruously, leaving the angry voice to shake the room.

Footsteps hurried on the flagstones outside. Someone thumped a fist on the porter's door.

"Too early for Martin," Henryk said. "See who it is."

Elzbieta was gone for only a few moments. "The air warden," she said quickly. "He's all bandaged up. Thinks he's a hero. He wants the hosepipe."

The footsteps had entered the hall.

"Damnation," Henryk said quietly, and pushed his way past Elzbieta. "Keep them outside, you fool." He was speaking in his usual tone of voice when he reached the hall. "Here's the hosepipe, gentlemen. Right here."

"Good," a strange voice replied. "Any extra spades? There's digging to be done on the next street. We'll need you. Did your wife get everyone out of this building?"

"Everyone except the old cripple on the third floor. She wouldn't leave her dog."

"Better get her down to the first floor, anyway. Bring the dog too."

Sheila could almost hear Elzbieta's unspoken protest as she obeyed the warden. The men's footsteps died away too. She opened her eyes. She was feeling better now, except for this trembling: she was shuddering with cold. For a moment, she thought of going out into the street, to wait for Olszak there. He had indeed been right. She would rather face an air raid than this little room, smelling of sausage and sour cabbage. Henryk and Elzbieta, she named them, and giggled weakly. Sour cabbage fitted Elzbieta so exactly, and sausage wasn't too bad, either, for Henryk.

When Elzbieta returned, the raid was almost over. The larger explosions were less regular and more distant, almost far enough away to sound like grumbling thunder. The anti-aircraft guns had reached a last frenzy of protest and were silent again. There was only a strange patter of heavy hail, now. And after two or three minutes, that ceased too.

Elzbieta had been running. Apart from a slight breathlessness, she was as calm and hard as ever. She sat down on the chair opposite Sheila, and wrinkled the small square of tablecloth with her elbows as she cupped her chin in her hands. A sharp chin, a sharp nose, pale eyes, pale hair. That was Elzbieta. The two women sat staring at each other. She doesn't trust me, Sheila realized. Elzbieta was probably sensing that danger she had talked about today. *Smell danger*, she had said. All Sheila could smell was sour cabbage.

"Wipe that grin off your face," Elizbieta said. "You don't need to try to fool me. You didn't like the big bad bombs, did you? I never saw such a coward. You're trembling all over."

In the street, a car's brakes grated.

"There's Martin. Too bad Henryk wasn't back in time so that you could extract a little more sympathy. Come on, get on your legs. They've got to do more than look pretty. No time to lose."

But the man who came into the room was obviously not Martin, to judge from the woman's face. Two other men followed him.

"Martin stopped a piece of shrapnel," the first man said. And then to Sheila he added, "Come on!"

Elzbieta looked at him strangely. Her eyes narrowed, her thin nostrils were dilated and rimmed with white. She *could* sense danger, Sheila admitted in amazement.

"What are you talking about? Who are you?" Elzbieta flashed at the men. "This is a young lady from upstairs, too ill to go to the shelter. I'm the caretaker's wife. She is certainly not going out of this house with strange men." She had all the shocked dignity of an honest working woman.

"Come off it," the man said. Once more he turned to Sheila. "Hurry up. The car can't wait forever."

Sheila rose unsteadily. One of the men caught her arm.

"Don't go!" said Elzbieta suddenly. "Don't you go with them!"

"You'll get into trouble for this," the man said.

The woman outstared him. "Shall I?" she said with every inch of insolence. "War or no war, no young man is coming to my door and taking away a young girl. I'll call the police, that's what I'll do. I'll show you who will get into trouble. Now go on; clear out of my house."

The men exchanged glances.

"Take her too," one suggested. "There's nothing else to do now. Come to the same thing, anyway."

Elzbieta made a dash for the door. After her late conversation with her husband, it was strange that the one call for urgent help which came to her lips was "Henryk, Henryk!"

Either the woman was a star actress, or she really was in love with Henryk. Sheila watched her again in astonishment. She was still more astonished when the man nearest the door acted even more quickly than Elzbieta. One movement blocked her way, another had her in a firm hold, and as she struggled with a fury and skill which threatened to free her, a third movement had her limp and senseless. It was hardly a vulgar clip to the jaw, but it had the same results.

"Well," the man who had first entered was saying, "I don't see what else we could do. Who tipped her off, anyway?" The other two shrugged their shoulders. "And what about the man?"

"Out digging with the air warden," Sheila said slowly, and received a curious, unfriendly stare.

"Let's move," said the man who held her. "We'll help you to get these air raid victims into the car. And then two of us will come back here and wait for the man. Stop worrying, Tomasz; they were to be picked up later tonight, anyway. This saves us a double journey."

The first young man shook his head. "It still worries me. We've gone beyond our orders."

"What else could we do?"

Tomasz shrugged his shoulders in agreement, and the procession started for the entrance gate. Sheila went first, firmly supported by one man. The woman was carried by the other two.

An air raid warden looked at them with all the authority of his official position.

"Casualties. Shrapnel," Tomasz said, who seemed hypnotized by that explanation. "They *will* look at the airplanes. . . ."

The air raid warden, whose particular worry was people who would come out of shelter to look at airplanes, nodded sympathetically.

At the edge of the pavement, there was a large black car with its windows screened. Far back in the car's depth sat Mr. Olszak.

"Really!" he said in protest, as Elzbieta's inert body was bundled onto the seat beside him. "Well, explanations later. Hurry."

"Two of us must wait for the man. He was out," Tomasz said.

Olszak's polite voice was in contrast with the phrase he used. Then he leaned forward to say to the quiet man who sat beside the driver, "You wait with these two for Henryk. You can identify him." And as the unobtrusive little man, who had kept watch at the gate last night, got out of the car, Olszak said quickly to Tomasz, "You come with me and tell me how this happened."

The car moved off, and Tomasz explained.

"I see," said Mr. Olszak. "Once she refused to let the girl go without creating a scene, you hadn't much choice. Pity she didn't come quietly like the girl."

"Oh, *she's* scared stiff," Tomasz said with returning confidence, and turned to look at Sheila. "She's still trembling."

"Shock, no doubt," Mr. Olszak said. In the darkness his cool hand touched Sheila's gently to catch her wrist and feel her pulse. Then he patted the back of her hand. But he didn't speak to her, and Sheila had gathered enough from the young man's tone to know that for this journey, at least, she was classified with Elzbieta.

She would have liked to be able to speak. She wanted to say, "That woman felt danger in the room, and nearly escaped you. Perhaps I've been infected by her; but I too felt danger, there in the dark street. I felt someone standing back in the shadows, watching us. Not the air raid warden, either. There was someone else, I felt. I think it was Henryk." But silence was imposed on her now, and doubly imposed because of Elzbieta lying so limply in the car's other corner. Elzbieta might not be so limp as she pretended. Elzbieta might be listening, waiting for her moment when the car at last halted. Mr. Olszak had been waiting too, for the woman's sudden desperate movement as the car slowed down had no success. There was a brief struggle, and then the woman was being carried, cursing and fighting, up the broad steps which led to the hall outside Colonel Bolt's office.

Sheila felt as if the last remnants of her strength were ebbing quickly away. Now that Elzbieta had gone, there was no need to try to keep her mind working. And as her mind relaxed, her body sagged. Mr. Olszak had stayed with her, was guiding her into an empty room through a doorway into another empty room, through another doorway into a small dark hall. Then there was the cold touch of open air on her brow. There was hurry and silence, and Mr. Olszak guiding her firmly and quickly. There was a car, waiting so quietly in a side street that Sheila's overtensed nerves jumped as Mr. Olszak pulled her quickly into it. The engine came to life as Olszak closed the door, and the car was moving expertly through these smaller streets which had so far escaped bombs.

After the car, there was a flight of stairs, an open door, familiar voices and faces. She thought she heard a man speaking English. It sounded like Stevens' voice, which was a silly kind of idea. And there was a woman. It was only when she was touching Sheila that Sheila could be really sure the woman was there. At last the room stopped lurching, and swayed gently instead. Sheila, the sheets and blankets drawn up to her chin, which wouldn't stop its trembling no matter how she clenched her jaw, opened her eyes to see fair hair and very straight eyebrows focus for a moment before they swam into a white haze.

"Barbara," Sheila said softly, and smiled, and then stopped smiling. That too was a silly kind of idea.

"I've such a terribly bad cold," she complained to the room. A silly, irritating kind of room with faces and then no faces. So many faces. So many Olszaks and Barbaras and, yes it was after all, there he was, Stevens. Too many for her to look at without getting dizzy. Sheila closed her eyes and wondered who could be breathing in such a peculiar way.

## CHAPTER X

### Besieged

IN THE fields that summer, the peasants had first marveled and then complained at the long drought. Towards the end of August, even the townspeople and city dwellers, who normally paid little attention to the weather unless it was unpleasant, were shaking worried heads too. In September, this cruel trick of nature bore bitter fruit. Over the hard, dry earth came the tanks and the armored cars, running smoothly, rapidly, ruthlessly. The Polish cavalry, which could have efficiently attacked so many of these monsters if they had been wallowing through the usual universal mud of autumn, found that their quick brave sweeps ended in grim death traps. The dry fields were sown with blood and flesh. Horses and men were plowed under by the relentless caterpillar wheels.

Russell Stevens, in the short hours when he rested in his rooms, would rave against the very idea of cavalry. Barbara Aleksander, in the short hours she could spend there away from the emergency hospital now established at the University, would listen in silence. Both of them were suffering; each expressed it differently. Once Barbara said sadly, "But if eighty per cent of Poland lives on farms and not in factories, then we have got to depend on horses and men and not on machines. We haven't enough." And the American nodded glumly. You can't, he was thinking, go to a shop and buy so many tanks and planes. You can't hand brave men guns and then say you have an army. In his own mind, he was acutely unhappy. For months previously, newspapers in the anti-Nazi countries had had editorials and articles on Poland. All men in anti-Nazi countries had hoped that Poland would fight, had cheered when there was a sign of resistance to Nazi demands. He ought to know: he had broadcast in the belief that the Germans must be stopped in their continuous course of blackmail. And now Poland had opposed Germany, now Poland was fighting. And only two allies had come forward so far, and these two weren't able to help. You can't go to a shop and buy so many tanks and planes. And all the other countries were either silent, or saying what an evil thing war was. As if every sane person didn't know that. He had seen enough newspaper articles recently from the outside world to make his stomach turn over. The assumption that countries at peace were either especially sensible or virtuous, or both, at a time when the fight against Nazism had begun, seemed nauseatingly callous. And for the first time in his life, he found that he was entirely with Poland.

Once, he had argued angrily about Poland, had denounced the inequalities, and the conservatism which clung to the past. He had admitted that Poland had inherited a bitter legacy, when she won her independence: for nearly a hundred and fifty years she had been divided between three countries with different religions, different languages, different laws. He had even gone so far as to admit, when pressed, that the Jewish question in Poland had risen only under the tyranny of these three masters. Poland, before its partition, had been one of the first European countries to have religious toleration. Three foreign conquerors had found that a subject people's unrest and unhappiness could often be turned away from the conqueror if another outlet could be provided, and invariably that outlet was the Jew. Stevens could see the basic truth in that, but his crusading zeal —a zeal shared by all liberal young men who have had the good fortune to be born into any country without a conqueror's heel on its throat—made him want to see Poland as part of the modern scheme of progress. Like all young men, he was impatient of those who asked only for time. It is with age that men discover how necessary time is.

Today was the seventeenth day of the siege of Warsaw. Russell Stevens stood at the window of his living room and wondered if he would be able to stand there tomorrow and say with equal amazement, "This is the eighteenth day." He looked down into the quiet street bathed in sunlight, and thought how strange it was that the rain of bombs and shells had missed this part of the town almost entirely. The houses round him here looked indecently normal. Sev-

enteen days of pulling people out of ruins; of washing blood
off sidewalks; of digging trenches for bodies (trenches for
human protection had long been abandoned as an unnecessary waste of time); of helping in any way, like the other
foreigners who had stayed in Warsaw, as if by their wild
efforts they could atone for the inaction of their countrymen.
... There was a Swede who worked and cursed like a man
possessed. There was the wife of an American wounded
during one of the earliest raids who nursed him along with
sixty others in a school, where mattresses spread on the floors
formed emergency wards. There was an elderly Frenchman
who had turned surgeon's assistant, an Englishman who had
the self-appointed task of getting into ruined basements from
which came weak cries, a Swiss and a Belgian who helped to
pull the wounded into the courtyards when the hospital wards
were in flames. They were kept busy: the hospitals were under constant attack. There was an Italian, bitterly ashamed
of the ally his country had chosen, who drove a makeshift
ambulance through bomb-pocked streets. And there were others: some were bandaged, one had been killed, all had
stayed when there had been a chance to leave. There were
those, like Stevens himself, who argued with their head offices
and firms back in their own countries that their jobs still required them to stay on in Warsaw. And some of them, who
would lose their jobs if they refused to leave with the last
parcel of journalists and diplomats, refused to leave. Not
out of heroics, Stevens had decided, but simply (as he himself
felt) out of shame and a sudden disquietening humility.
You had only to watch the faces on the streets, watch the
women and the children, to feel chastened. For you knew
they could have avoided this if they hadn't resisted the Germans. And it seemed as if the German guns which now
had the city well within their range were being specially
vindictive to make the Polish people pay for their rejection
of Nazism. Even now, as the shells fell with savage accuracy
on warehouses filled with food, on hospitals crammed with already broken bodies, there was no sign of faltering in
these faces on the streets. There was no evidence of bribery
or treachery or cowardice. Differences neither in politics nor
religion nor wealth mattered. The people of Warsaw closed
their ranks. The soldiers who had survived the battles round
the city had now entrenched themselves in the ruined suburbs. Together, soldier and civilian, they faced the enemy
who was advancing on them from the northeast, from the
west, from the south. They neither asked for mercy nor
expected it.

"The seventeenth day," Stevens said. He stopped peering
through the strips of white paper, and turned back into the

room. "I bet I am one of the few possessors of window-panes left in Warsaw."

Barbara nodded, and went on with the dusting of the room.

"Wouldn't it be better to sit down and rest?" the American suggested. The girl's movement in the room made him irritable. He was tired and he wanted to rest. She was equally tired, and she wouldn't rest. "Let Madame Knast look after her precious two rooms if she feels like it." Madame Knast was the owner of the apartment. She had rented two rooms to the American, called him a "paying guest"; and in this way managed to keep on her apartment in this pleasant section of the town after her husband's death last year, without any loss of pride.

"Madame Knast is out looking for her son," Barbara said quietly, and arranged the couch so that he would sleep more comfortably. Stevens hadn't slept in a bed since the first day of the war; Olszak had brought the English girl here then, and she had been lying ill in the bedroom next door ever since. Stevens searched in the pocket of his stained and wrinkled jacket for a cigarette. He had lost his clothes as well as his bed: the suitcases which he had taken to the office, in his first obedience to instructions to leave, no longer existed. An incendiary bomb had landed on the office building, and his clothes and his notes for that book he was going to write some day had gone up in flames. Now all he possessed was the clothes he wore, a typewriter, and the pictures and ornaments he had bought to make his two rooms more homelike.

"What's wrong with the son?" Stevens thought of the thin, nervous boy who had just begun an engineering course at the University last year.

"He's been wounded. He was brought here from the East Prussian front, and he's in one of the hospitals. But as the wounded have been moved to different buildings each time a hospital is blasted, Madame Knast doesn't know where he is. So she goes each day to the new hospitals and wanders about in them, looking for him."

Stevens said something under his breath. "Nothing," he said aloud to Barbara's "Beg pardon?"

He made an effort to be polite, too. "How's the invalid?"

"Much better. She wants to get up. I had to take away her clothes and hide them. It's too soon, yet. Normally, she wouldn't be out of bed for another week at least."

"Normally, yes. But I wouldn't call these normal times. In another week, God knows where we will be."

Barbara ignored his pessimism. "I am going to take her

some soup, in a minute. I managed to get a cupful today from the canteen kitchen, and I brought it here in a bowl. How could we heat it? The gas doesn't work today."

"I had a spirit lamp." He rummaged in a cupboard set into one of the walls and produced a small chromium object. He unscrewed the wick on the little cup, but the contents had almost evaporated.

"We can try," he said doubtfully. "What about a candle?"

"We'll have to use them carefully. The electric power plant has been destroyed."

"So I heard. And the printing presses were shattered today, too. No more newspapers."

"So that is why you are depressed." She was smiling, and Stevens gave her a grin. Any joke is better than no joke, he was thinking.

"How are your children?" he said. "All two hundred of them?"

"A hundred and eighty-two, now," Barbara answered. She wasn't smiling any more. "They keep me so busy that I haven't time to worry about my own family. Not much, anyway."

"Have their relatives been found?"

"No."

Both were silent, thinking of the children who had been found wandering in the fields and ditches in the first week of the war. They had been among the refugees from the west, driven forward by the Germans. They had been machine-gunned and bombed on their long journey across Poland. By the time they neared Warsaw, many children were orphans, alone in the middle of a battlefield.

"If we don't find any relatives, I have a plan. After the war, I'm going to take them to Korytów. Aunt Marta will find room for them, somehow. She's wonderful at that. And mother will have a wonderful time playing teacher. She always loved doing that."

Stevens looked in silence at the girl. Hadn't she heard? She returned the look with eyes trying very hard to be calm. Then her self-possession ended. She sat down on the couch, and her face was suddenly old.

"Yes, I know," she sat at last. "The last pocket of resistance to the southwest of Warsaw was wiped out two days ago. I know. Korytów is in German hands. What are we to do? Mother is nearly demented. She's nursing at the hospital organized by the Knights of Malta, and there are so many wounded that she hasn't been outside of the building for five days. If only she weren't needed here, if I weren't needed, we could try to slip through the German lines and reach Korytów. That's the only way we can learn about little Teresa, and Stefan, and Aunt Marta. What shall we *do*, Russell?" It was almost a cry.

Stevens shook his head slowly. What could he say? What could anyone say?

"Don't worry. We may get news. Korytów is probably all right." It wasn't important enough to be bombed or shelled. "You leave it to Aunt Marta. She can rout most men, even a German. Have you heard from Andrew?"

"His division was shattered. What was left of it joined the Eleventh Infantry. We heard that from one of mother's patients who fought with Andrew at the beginning."

"How's the Professor?"

"Digging away. He looks very noble with a bandage round his head and a spade over his shoulder. He reminds me of some painting I once saw. The. . . ." She halted. "Oh, I can't remember anything these days."

"He was lucky. Just a fraction of an inch nearer the brain, and that piece of shrapnel would never have let him return to his apartment."

"That was so long ago now," Barbara said sadly. "That was the—first day of the war, when Sheila was brought here, and mother waited and waited for Uncle Edward at his apartment. When she went down to the porter's lodge she found three men who questioned and questioned her, and she was late in reporting for duty at the hospital. That's so long ago now."

"Today's the seventeenth." Tomorrow would be. . . . Perhaps it wouldn't.

"Sunday. The churches which are still standing are packed. As I came here I saw people kneeling on the pavement outside, joining in the Mass through the open windows." She brushed the white dust on her skirt. Stevens noted that the white smears were at knee level. Now he knew how they had got there.

"Did you see any of the leaflets the Germans have been dropping today? An ultimatum. Surrender, or else."

"Surrender!" Barbara said contemptuously. "I like that, I must say."

"Don't look so angrily at me, Barbara. I'm not a German." Barbara calmed down. "Sorry."

"How's the soup?"

"Lukewarm. Do you think that's the best we can do?"

"I think it's a pretty good best, considering everything. I'll come in and see her too. She's been asleep every time I've mustered a few jokes and knocked on the door. I never thought anyone could sleep through the bombing and shelling and machine-gunning as she has done."

"Mr. Olszak says that is why she is recovering. He was quite worried about her, as if it were his fault that she had pleurisy."

"How's friend Olszak?"

"Digging with Uncle Edward. Do you know, Russell, I went round unexpectedly to see Uncle Edward yesterday, and I could swear that they were digging where there was no bomb damage. Am I mad, or are they mad?"

"I'm quite sure Olszak isn't," Stevens said with much feeling. "He's the only man I know who would be a match for Aunt Marta." He knocked at the bedroom door.

Sheila was awake. Her eyes were larger than ever in the thin, white face; the color in her lips and cheeks was gone; the hand she gave Russell Stevens seemed frail and weak, as if the fever had burned up all its strength. He looked doubtfully at Barbara; perhaps Sheila should be kept in bed, after all.

As if she had understood that look, Sheila said firmly, "I must get up."

"Drink the soup, Sheila."

"Where are my clothes, Barbara?"

"Drink the soup. All of it. It tastes awful, doesn't it? It was the best I could find today."

"It's wonderful," Sheila said. "I could eat anything now, even a piece of horse." She didn't notice the look that Barbara and Stevens exchanged, fortunately, or she might not have finished the soup so enthusiastically. "First, I did nothing but sleep. Now I want to eat and eat."

Barbara said, "If Russell will stay here and look after you, I shall dash round to see mother. She may have some food. People are bringing all their food round to the hospitals so that those who are wounded and ill may get something nourishing."

"This is enough," Sheila said, handing back the empty bowl. But Barbara moved determinedly towards the door.

"No," she was saying. "If you want to get up you must have food, the right kind of food. Or else, you'll be too weak to move, and you won't be able to help."

"To help . . ." Sheila said, and laughed. It was a thin, weak laugh. Stevens was startled. As he pulled the high-backed chair over towards the bed, he was thinking: it must have been God-awful for her here, with all the rest of us so busy that we could only thrust medicines on a table beside her and tell her to help herself.

"What is it like—out there?" Sheila was asking. "What's happened? I daren't ask Barbara. You must tell me everything before she gets back. Sometimes I see the flames reflected into this room. Sometimes I can smell horrible burning smells. I lie and try to identify all the noises, as if I were suddenly blind and had to try to learn to live without eyes. That was a house, that was solid road, that was a hundred windows, that was an engine exploding, that was an enemy plane, that was one of ours."

"Ours?" Stevens smiled gently.

"That's how I feel now. Don't you?"

"Yes." His voice was so harsh that Sheila raised herself on her pillow.

"Go on," she said, "tell me. Then I won't get such a shock once I do go out into the streets."

Stevens told her. After he ended there was a long pause, broken only by the renewal of some antiaircraft guns from the western side of the city. There were fewer guns now than there had been yesterday. Each day saw the death of more.

"Another attack," Stevens said, stretching his legs and reaching for a cigarette.

The British girl didn't seem to hear him. "What's to be the end of all this?"

Stevens studied the flame of his lighter, and then killed it with a characteristically decisive flick of his thumb. He shook his head.

"You think it's hopeless?" Sheila was amazed and hurt. She would keep believing that people who fought so bravely and so unselfishly must be rewarded with victory.

"I'm not a Pole. That's why I seem gloomy, I guess."

"If this were happening to your own country? To New York?"

"I suppose then I wouldn't think it's hopeless. I'd keep fighting as long as I had a gun in my hand and something to go in it."

"I know. I've been lying here thinking about London."

"New York . . ." Stevens was saying. "All the bridges under heavy air attack. Brooklyn and Queens leveled to the ground. Last-ditch stands by the soldiers in all the outlying boroughs. Manhattan itself under heavy artillery fire. Airplanes swarming over. The Empire State Building gone, and all the blocks around it. The stations just a heap of twisted girders. Radio City a ragged shell, with burst water-mains pouring down Fifth Avenue. The museums in flames. The Metropolitan and Times Square a shambles. The Medical Center in ruins. All its equipment gone. Blood running down the trolleycar lines on Broadway. The dock area one line of blazing warehouses. No power, little food, less water. Gaping windows, crushed walls, buildings smashed to pieces. And no one complaining, everyone helping, all trying to tidy up after each night's new destruction. No one talking about peace, no one wanting to accept an ultimatum."

"And the Poles were so proud of their Warsaw. They've rebuilt it, and cleared the slums, and made gardens and parks and driveways..."

"Even if it's in ruins, it is still a city to be proud of," Stevens said shortly. "Hell and damnation." He began pacing the room.

"I really must get onto my feet again. Have you any idea where Barbara's hidden my clothes?"

"Don't ask me! You just stay where you are. If you have a relapse, you'll be less of a help than ever."

Sheila relaxed obediently. She saw the sense in that. She said, with a touch of bitterness, "It's rather a joke on me. I stayed because I wanted to help. And all I did was to lie in bed through the siege of Warsaw. My grandchildren will have a very poor opinion of me."

The American was looking at her in amusement. "I have a suspicion you will have at least one story to tell them."

Sheila pretended to be wide-eyed and innocent. How much did Stevens really know about her? Mr. Olszak had somehow persuaded him to give her this room, so that she might be well hidden from any friends of Henryk who still searched for her. How much did he really know? She had such an impulse to tell him everything, if only to release the worry which still pressed on her mind.

And then, his next words told her that he knew really very little, that he was puzzled, that he wanted the key to that puzzle. "I have one source of information on the fringes of the Second Bureau—Military Intelligence, to you. He gives me gossip. No state secrets, so you can look less shocked. He told me an interesting story a few nights after you were brought here."

Sheila still said nothing, but her heart had started that off-beat again.

"It seems a German agent, pretending to be an English girl, had smuggled herself into a reputable Polish family. She was arrested on the day before the war started. She was handed over to a Mr. Kordus, who was head of a special department. He released her and placed her under close observation in the hope of catching two other spies. She was arrested again along with one of the spies, who was the porter's wife at the apartment house where the girl was staying. The porter's wife was sentenced and shot. But the girl escaped, and she hasn't been traced so far. Interesting story."

Sheila said "Yes."

Stevens laughed.

"All right," she said with an answering smile. "Do you think that English girl was a German spy?"

"I might, if I hadn't found her diary in my car."

"Diary?" Sheila had forgotten all about it. It must have fallen from her lap in that drive from Korytów to Warsaw.

"There was no name on it, and half a dozen people had been in my car that day, so I had to read an entry or two to make sure whose diary it was." The American's voice was half-apologetic, half-teasing.

Across the river, the bombs were falling steadily now. Sheila caught her breath and counted them. At last she said, "Of course. It must read rather strangely now." She thought, all that life is dead, as easily abandoned as the diary was forgotten—and she felt a mixture of surprise and shock at the idea.

"I didn't read much, but it was enough to make me sure that the girl wasn't a German spy. Anyway, no spy would bother to fake a diary and then lose it carelessly. A spy would have produced it at a convenient moment along with her passport."

Sheila relaxed once more. How utterly satisfactory it was to be believed.

And then Stevens said, in that smooth voice which he kept for his most alarming statements, "But the most interesting thing of all is this: once, I had Kordus pointed out to me. He was a thin little man with receding hair and pince-nez. Friend Olszak would have been peeved."

Sheila was really aghast this time. The casual voice, the fact that the American didn't fully know the dynamite he was handling, were as upsetting as the actual statement. "Have you talked about this?" she asked.

"Not even to Olszak. I've just been trying to place his game. It gives me a laugh. Privately, of course. But then all those high-signs and name changes are a natural for a laugh. You can't enlighten me on anything, can you? Just between friends?"

"I know less than you, it seems," Sheila said. It was true in some ways. Kordus was a new angle to her. Kordus ... Well, Mr. Olszak had his own reasons and they would be good ones. So much she had learned about Mr. Olszak. "Russell," she added suddenly, and wondered why he repressed a smile, "Russell, don't please talk about these things. Don't think about them. Don't even guess. Please."

"Why?"

She wanted to say, "See what has happened to me." She said, "Because I like you, and you've been more than decent to me. This Kordus affair is of no value to you. It would only lead to complications for you. Mr. Olszak will tell you about it some day, when he can."

"Not Olszak. He's been a reporter himself. All I've been able to figure out so far is that he visits police headquarters as Olszak the editor, who writes on specially interesting criminal cases and miscarriages of justice. He's been doing that for years, I know. I've gone with him, on occasions. And then he becomes Kordus when he has any other work to do. It's the other work that interests me."

"Russell, please. I gave you my advice. Why get mixed up in such things?"

"Oh, the inquiring reporter." But the smile he gave her proved that he wasn't convinced that she was as ignorant as she pretended.

"What does Barbara know?" she asked.

"The Aleksanders think you're a heroine. You spotted a German spy and risked your life to catch her."

"What were you told?" It was interesting to find out the ways Mr. Olszak had disposed of her.

"Much the same. That I was saving you from German agents by having you here."

"And you don't believe much of that story?"

"I know that the Poles are looking for you."

"And it doesn't make sense?"

"No, it doesn't."

And you are going to try to make it into sense, Sheila thought as she looked at the man who was watching her so intently.

"Probably the whole story about Kordus was a fake. I don't believe that's his name at all," she protested. But looking at the American's clever face, she knew that he wasn't impressed by her amusement.

After that, they talked of the news and pretended not to listen to the falling bombs. At least, it was Stevens who did most of the talking, as if he guessed that Sheila had begun to tire. He was exhausted, himself. He thought wearily of the couch next door, but Sheila's eyes pleaded with him to stay here and go on talking. Once she said apologetically, "It is sort of monotonous to listen to all those loud noises by yourself." And once he thought she was summoning up courage to tell him something. But just at that moment, Barbara returned, flushed with her running through air-raided streets. She carried a small basket triumphantly.

"We shall soon get you well," she said happily, and plunged into long instructions from Madame Aleksander, as she moved busily about the room. Russell Stevens moved tactfully into the living room as Barbara started shaking pillows. He was too tired even to make a joke.

He did say, "When Sheila is up and about again, I'll take you both out to dinner. How's that?"

"It sounds wonderful," Sheila said, and laughed. Bombs might be falling, but people still went out to dinner. The idea cheered her, somehow.

Barbara said, "You know, you *are* looking better. I believe seeing people does you good. Perhaps you ought to get up soon, after all."

Sheila nodded happily. It was pleasant to share things, even air raids, with people.

## CHAPTER XI

### The Eighteenth Day

NEXT DAY, when the sun was at its warmest, Barbara came for her hour's visit to the apartment in Frascati Gardens and Sheila was allowed to have her clothes. Apart from a treacherous weakness in her legs, so that the first steps made her totter like a baby learning to walk, she managed to pretend she felt very well indeed. When she came into the strange living room, she was telling Barbara cheerfully that all she needed was to move about and make her legs strong again.

"Not too quickly, though," Barbara admonished in such an unconscious imitation of her mother's voice, that Stevens, trying to shave off a thick growth of beard with a half-cupful of cold water, turned to give Sheila a grin.

"What are you two laughing about?" Barbara asked tolerantly, and began transforming Stevens' bed back into a couch again. Sheila only smiled. She walked determinedly, if slowly, towards the window. It was funny to see how like Madame Aleksander Barbara really was. Sheila wondered what traits she had inherited from her own mother and father. Or didn't you inherit them if you had never lived with them? Uncle Matthews would tell her, some day, now that she knew enough to be able to question him intelligently. She felt suddenly so happy that she was ashamed. But all the worry and insecurity and pain of the last weeks were well worth while, after all: some day, she could question intelligently. If she lived, she added; and looked down on the trees in the street.

"It seems so untouched," she said in surprise. "The parks are still beautiful."

"This district is the luckiest, so far," Stevens said briefly. He thought of the long lines of trenches which she couldn't see from this window, trenches which yesterday had begun to be filled with dead bodies. The cemeteries could hold no more. He dried his face carefully, and turned on the radio.

A man's strong, encouraging voice filled the room. "The Mayor," Stevens said. "You'd never guess he's speaking from the ruins of his office, would you? Still works there." He switched the knob around for a foreign station, and found a German one. Always German, he thought angrily: either German or jammed by Germans.

"Oh, not that," Sheila said, "not so much drama. Don't they *love* to threaten? And if they don't threaten, they gloat."

Stevens silenced her with a hand. He held it there, suspended in the air, his head bent to one side, his eyes narrowing. He turned strangely, unbelievingly, to the two girls who weren't even bothering to listen. Barbara was telling Sheila that Mr. Olszak said it would be perfectly all right if Sheila were to come and help Barbara with the children, once Sheila was strong enough. Suddenly, they noticed the American's face. He was still listening.

"Another ultimatum?" Barbara said scornfully.

Stevens shook his head. He could hardly speak. Their curiosity turned chill.

"The God-damned liars," he was saying. "It can't be true. It isn't true. The——!" He seized his jacket as he moved quickly to the door. "Have to see if I can broadcast to America," he said. "That was a German report that the Russians entered Eastern Poland yesterday. Can't be true."

He was out of the room before either of them could speak.

"They've come to help," Sheila was saying. "Perhaps it's help."

They listened to the German announcer's triumphant voice. Barbara shook her head slowly, and sat down on the nearest chair. This news had managed to do what the bombs and shells had failed to accomplish. The first tears since she had said good-by to Jan Reska were streaming over her cheeks. She just sat there, crying quietly, gazing at the blue sky outside, as if all action and courage had been sapped from her veins.

Sheila stared down at the street. Well, that was another prayer that hadn't been answered: she had hoped so much, to the point of believing that it would come true, that help would come from the east. Perhaps this new invasion really meant only a defense of Russia before the Germans got too far to the east. And yet the German announcement was using the tone of victory. Even the element of surprise had made it more victorious. Yesterday, no one had known, no one had guessed what had taken place. Today, the Germans were the first to announce it. That doubled the weight of the blow. It made you feel twice as helpless. And helplessness could become hopelessness.

"What will Warsaw do?" she asked dully.

"Do?" echoed Barbara, still unseeing. And then a fury seized her. "We'll fight on. We'll never stop fighting until we have Poland again. Not even if it takes twenty, thirty, forty years. We'll fight on." Her voice rose. Her face had paled, her neck flushed red. Her blue eyes were as hard and brilliant as granite caught in sunlight. Sheila switched off the radio and let her talk: it was the best thing for Barbara. Her courage was back, all the stronger because of her anger. At last she paused, and the two girls stared at each other. Only the loud ticking of a cheap alarm clock broke the silence.

"You are so quiet, Sheila," Barbara said at last. "Don't you feel anything?"

"Feel?" Sheila walked slowly over to the couch. In the same low voice, she clipped out the words, "Damn and blast all politics to hell."

Barbara was gathering up her coat and basket. "I must go back to the children, to games of let's pretend, where the bad men gets shot, and the good man lives, and all are happy ever after. I'll come to see you tomorrow. Take care. You'll soon be able to come and help with the children." Her voice was normal, as if she had forgotten the last quarter of an hour. And then she began to laugh, a hysterical bitter laugh.

"Eugenia," she explained, "Brother Stanislaw's wife. . . . You never met her. But you've heard Aunt Marta on the subject. . . . In the first week of the war she was in Warsaw, and then she found enough petrol—that kind of person always does: she approves of rationing except for herself—and she set out for the Aleksander house in Polesie, with her maid and trunks and jewels and best furs. . . . She hadn't enough room in the car for little Teresa or Stefan, although Stanislaw made her offer to take them with her. She almost embraced mother in relief when we said we preferred to have the children nearer Warsaw. We heard last week that she had a 'perfectly frightful' journey; but she did arrive. In Polesie. And do you know where Polesie is? Right on the Russian frontier. It's the only funny piece of news in a long time, but I dare say that to no one but you."

"What about Stanislaw?"

"He's in Warsaw. He resigned his diplomatic job last week and put on an armband and took his best hunting rifle. He's over in Praga now, stalking Germans in suburban streets."

"Barbara, have you heard anything about Jan Reska?"

Barbara shook her head for an answer, and then walked slowly out of the door. Her footsteps were slow and heavy on the wooden stairs.

Sheila wished desperately that she had left that question unasked. She searched for something to read, but all Stevens' best books had been burned along with his clothes in the suitcases. She found a battered Polish grammar. As long as she had to sit in here, she might as well learn something. She had a feeling that she was going to need as much Polish as she could master. Besides, a grammar made you concentrate, made you forget other things. Like a good Scot, she began at the beginning and methodically revised the earlier lessons which she had already learned. Now that she was sure of the right pronunciations, the words were easier to memorize than they had seemed in London last spring. She found she could recommend studying a foreign grammar book to anyone who had to sit through air raids.

At six o'clock she was hungry, and picnicked on a strange assortment of food. Mr. Olszak had sent bread and butter today. Calf's-foot jelly and a peach came from Madame Aleksander, and the small bowl of milk had been brought by Barbara. Stevens had discovered some bouillon cubes for her. Uncle Edward had brought a thermos bottle of soup, a small bottle of red wine, and a bunch of flowers. None of them had forgotten her, however busy and worried they were. And each item of food was now a luxury which not money, but time and trouble had discovered.

As dusk came to the city, she didn't bother either to light the candle or to draw the blackout curtains. She was suddenly as exhausted as if she had worked all day in the fields. She watched the red glow, deepening and widening in the smoke-covered sky—unaware that it was the Royal Castle which tonight was ablaze—until she had gathered enough energy to take herself to bed.

Outside, the eighteenth day of bombing, the tenth day of artillery bombardment, came to its close. People were still toiling in the numerous parks which had once been Warsaw's pride. They were filling in the trenches which they had dug almost three weeks before, covering the corpses carefully and wearily with the soft, dry earth. The sisters in the burning hospitals pulled the wounded men into the courtyards, sheltered them with their bodies when a German plane swooped low to machine-gun the living mass.

Barbara quieted the children. The night attacks would wake them from uneasy dreams, and they would start remembering their mothers and fathers. Some of them would still think that they were wandering alone in machine-gunned fields.

Stevens had paused for a cigarette along with the Swede beside whom he worked nowadays. Their work tonight was useless. The precious flour in the largest bakery flared beyond all human effort. Neither man spoke any more as they worked, but they kept together.

Over in the Praga sector, once a workers' suburb across the Vistula River, Stanislaw Aleksander silenced the nagging worry about his wife with the machine gun to which he had been promoted.

Edward Korytowski and Michael Olszak were busy with the cunning concealed doorway which they had made between two adjoining cellars. The printing press in one cellar was now completed, and hidden by protecting sandbags.

Jan Reska lay in the shelter of an eastern forest beside men who were strangers to him. All his old comrades were lost. This was the fifth company he had fought with, and now it seemed as if they were to be surrounded, too. Here under the trees, they could rest from the bombers, perhaps think of some way to join with the survivors of still another division.

Captain Adam Wisniewski had gathered the remnants of his calvalry platoon from the slaughter fields of the Poznan bulge, had led them silently at nightfall away from the west. The south, too, was in German hands. Their nearest hope was Warsaw. A knock at the darkened window of an isolated house brought them any food there was, perhaps a moment's warmth by a stove, or in a barn where the exhausted men could rest. And then the alarm of a scout sent the half-sleeping men and the stumbling horses stealing away in the cold darkness once more.

Eugenia, her furs and jewels quite forgotten in her misery, watched the earnest, angry face of the young Commissar as he berated the peasants who had dismantled the Aleksander house, who had dressed in their best clothes to celebrate the day when every man was his own master and need not work. They were as bewildered as Eugenia was unhappy. The big house was not theirs to plunder; it belonged to the State. Their gay clothes were useless: the State wanted workers soberly dressed, soberly thinking. Her face was a proud mask as she set off on the nightmare journey into an unknown country. Furs and jewels were useless to staunch the blood which oozed through the cracks in her hand-sewn shoes.

In Kawka's kitchen at Korytów, Aunt Marta lay in bed with Teresa and Kawka's two little girls. The German officers in the Korytowski house grumbled at the lack of linen and silver, at the empty pantry shelves, at the kitchen's disorder. Aunt Marta smiled grimly to herself, and listened to Teresa's breathing. She would be all right, now, although her right hand would never play on a piano again. Stefan lay awake in Kawka's room. He couldn't sleep because he had so much thinking to do. What could he do to hurt *Them* most? He had seen what *They* had done to the village and to Wanda and Teresa. What could he do to *Them?*

Andrew Aleksander lay in a cattle truck, his right leg shattered at the thigh. He listened to the moaning of the wounded men jammed into this evil-smelling box as the train lumbered slowly into Germany. It was strange how he persisted in living when he wanted to die. He had seen so many men, who wanted to live, die. If this truck was left unattended in sidings for eight hours, as it had been yesterday, perhaps he would. The body, crushed against his, twitched in a violent spasm and then lay still. The dead man's arm was across Andrew's mouth. He hadn't the strength left to shake himself free.

Madame Aleksander was attempting to rescue the few scraps of equipment still recognizable from the ruins of the operating theater. She worked silently, trying not to think of the flames leaping greedily on the other side of the small courtyard where the western wing of the hospital had been set on fire. For one moment, the hot red light disappeared; the crackling and hissing and guns and roaring planes were silent. In the cool darkness, the family were around her. Teresa's nose was crinkled over its freckles as she laughed; Stefan, large-eyed and silent and smiling; Andrew waiting for her to speak, with one eyebrow slightly raised; Stanislaw, serious, worried, bitter, gentle; Barbara, her head thrown back, her eyes seeing some pleasant secret of her own. . . . The fainting spell could only have lasted a moment, for when the faces had gone with the cool velvety darkness, the flames had come only a little nearer. Madame Aleksander looked up at the young Sister who had taken three steps to reach her where she had fallen on her knees. The girl moved over the rubble and dust with the grace that her training had made natural for her. Did she ever think of ballet, now? Madame Aleksander wondered. But then, there was so little time for thinking these days. So little time for sleep, and escape into dreams.

The Sister's graceful arm helped her to her feet.

"Perhaps we should rest," she said, looking at Madame Aleksander's driven face.

"Perhaps."

They worked on.

## CHAPTER XII

# Barbara

SOMETIMES Sheila, when she had an interval free for thinking, would imagine that the last days of Warsaw were the very essence of Greek tragedy. You knew there could be no hope, no happy ending. Yet this knowledge did not end the suspense. The drama mounted steadily, intensely, until you felt that the human mind and body could bear no more; until the last scene reached the final anguish. For the very character of these people of Warsaw would not let them end their miseries. If they had been made of more selfish, worldly stuff, then they would have found an excuse long before the end to save themselves from the full course of the tragedy. Their pride, their nationalism, their courage, their fatalism made their actions inevitable. Even their individualism, which had served them so ill in the past, now strengthened their resistance. Their strong historical ties bound them to their decision. Above all, the vision of another captivity made life seem something not to be hoarded.

The American, gray-faced and taciturn, had looked at her curiously for a moment when, under the influences of a plate of hot food, she had told him these thoughts. They had met for that promised dinner in the restaurant of the Hotel Europejski. Barbara, at the last moment, had been unable to come. One of the other nurses had sprained an ankle, and Barbara insisted on doing extra night duty with her children. She had also insisted that Sheila should go to the restaurant. Sheila, she had said with much truth, was still not completely well, was working too hard, was in need of a warm meal and a two-hour rest; and Russell Stevens would just be the right person to cheer her up. So Barbara had insisted. So had Stevens. And here Sheila was, trying to concentrate on a kind of soup made with boiled meat and rice which was the regulated and only choice in all the restaurants, trying to think of something to say which wouldn't deal with the war. It was difficult.

Stevens must have felt that too. He looked at his plate speculatively. "Ever eaten here, before?"

"No. In June, Barbara and I ate at the smaller places." She smiled. "We didn't have any expense accounts, you know."

He laughed in spite of himself. "It's a pity you didn't see

some of their chief places. Good food and wine. Boy, I lie awake and dream of them, now."

"This food is better than I've tasted in a long time."

"Which proves one of my theories. Good cooking is only the daughter of invention. The more disguises you have for food, the bigger chef you are. Now this stuff—" He jabbed at his plate with his fork. "Well, we all know just what kind of meat is left in Warsaw. I believe even cardboard would taste good if it had the proper seasoning and sauces."

"I'm too hungry to be disillusioned," Sheila said. She tried not to think of the horse which had been machine-gunned today on the street near the children's hostel. Nor to think of its skeleton, stripped bare, only an hour later.

She tried very hard to look round the large room non-chalantly. "Not so many people here tonight," she began, but the American's amused smile stopped her.

"I guess that was what you might call a light conversational gambit."

"There's enough heavy conversation from those guns." Sheila now gave up all pretense of not appearing to listen to the constant, methodically timed shells. "Twenty hours, now," she said. "Twenty hours without pausing for five minutes."

"Don't tell me you're still counting them?"

"Why do I amuse you so much?" she demanded frankly and suddenly.

He looked as guilty as a small boy caught inside a jam cupboard. "Not *amuse*," he said. "There's the wrong sound to that word."

"But you laugh at me. Half the time, you are laughing inside yourself. What's so funny about me?"

Stevens was taken aback. "You've got me all wrong," he protested too vehemently. Amused? He wondered. Surprised would be nearer it. She surprised him into smiling. He was feeling cheerier than he had felt for almost a week now.

"What have you been doing since you left the apartment?" he asked.

"Reading simple Polish stories to the younger children. Drawing funny pictures. Making rabbits out of handkerchiefs. Barbara won't let me do much of the heavier work, yet. Sort of funny, isn't it, to spend the last six days since I've seen you doing nothing but thinking up things so that the children won't think of other things? And what have you been doing?"

"The usual."

"The last of the diplomats and the journalists left four days ago."

"Meaning, what am I still doing here? Much the same as you are. Probably less." He smiled and added, "How's friend Olszak?"

Sheila was smiling too, but her eyes were watchful. "Tell me, Russell, did you ask me to dinner tonight because you were being polite, or because you wanted to keep track of Sheila Matthews?"

He wasn't smiling now, although this was the biggest surprise she had yet given him. "I had a much more natural reason than either of those," he answered, and saw he had routed her. She was still watching him, but this time she wasn't quite sure whether to be pleased at the implied compliment or to be afraid that she had seen a compliment where none was intended. She shifted her ground and got back onto a safer level of conversation.

"What about your job?"

"That's over, meanwhile. I think that I'll get it back once I do get out of Poland. The New York office will come round to seeing it my way. If ever they wanted a big story, then this is the place to get it and not on the road to Rumania." He was being casual about it, but Sheila guessed he was more worried than he sounded. He had been enthusiastic about his job; now, perhaps, he had ended the career he had chosen by his decision to stay here. He went on talking as if to persuade himself that all was well. "There's one other American reporter left. He has the same idea as I have. And my Swedish friend and several others on the staff of the American Bank are still here. The bank is going to keep open even if the Germans do take over. Then there are skeletons staffs at all the neutral embassies. So we aren't the only foreigners left in Warsaw."

"But why doesn't your head office see it your way now? Why did you have to lose your job?"

"I'll get it back again, perhaps. That's more than you can say for the guys in this country. And anyway, the New York office was probably right. It's quite a chance that my big story will be cold news by the time I leave here."

Sheila's face was such a study in horror that a smile was forced out of him.

"But people have *got* to listen," she said. "If they don't, then all this sacrifice is useless."

"People react in ways you don't expect. Some will see the writing on the wall, and start taking action. Some will say its propaganda and warmongering. And some will say that it's all too tragic—give us something with a tune in it. Why should they listen anyway? I agree with you, personally. But why should they? Why shouldn't they just go on concentrating on pleasanter subjects?"

"Because it weakens them, because they are making themselves incomplete, because—" She floundered in her attempt to express what she felt: her emotions were racing far ahead of the words on her tongue. She took a deep breath. "Look. This evening I arrived here babbling about Greek tragedy. Now I know I really meant it. For why did the Greeks believe so much in tragedy? They must have, or they couldn't have written such good ones. Didn't they believe that men must have a periodical housecleaning in their minds and emotions? Wasn't that why they gave men drama which roused their pity and fear? Pity was for the characters in the tragedy; fear was for the audience's own chance of having the same kind of experience. Pity and fear together make a powerful purge for any mind. A public which won't look at or listen to tragedy develops a sluggish mind. That's what the ancient Greek knew. And the richness of their minds has never been equaled."

"Didn't I hear some place that Athens once fell? And for good?"

"Yes, it fell when its people didn't want to hear or believe unpleasant things." Sheila relaxed again. "You see," she said more quietly, "I really *feel* this. I really believe it. I am worried for those people outside: not the people here—I pity and I admire *them*. And I feel so angry when I see what is happening to them that I could go out and kill fifty Germans with my own bare hands. I could. . . . If I couldn't I would be a callous wretch. But I worry. . . . Poland is nailed to the cross. And the rest of humanity will not be warned in time. If what you say is true, that your news of the siege will be cold news in a month or two, then this whole sacrifice is in vain."

"You speak like a Pole."

"No," Sheila said slowly, "like a Scot. If I were a Pole, then sacrifice in itself would be so noble that I wouldn't worry about what it pays for. I can't bear to see sacrifice wasted."

The old waiter stood beside them. "Another alert has been sounded. The management offers the wine cellars as suitable shelter." He had said it so often in the last three weeks that he might have been announcing that veal was off the menu today. "This way," he added, and waited for them to rise.

Stevens looked at Sheila with an eyebrow raised.

"No one bothers, now," she said, and Stevens shook his head at the waiter. The old man nodded and went slowly as if he had expected that. His shoulders were bent, his feet hardly lifted off the ground. He was very old. He went to the other tables. Only three people rose, and these hurried out of doors with the businesslike look of some duty to be done. Air raid wardens, Sheila thought. They had probably come here to relax in an off-duty interval. But they had known there was no off-duty time for anyone when a big raid was announced.

"It must be a very big one," Sheila. "They don't bother to let us know about the average ones, now."

The American nodded, lit another cigarette, and kept looking at her.

"The Greeks . . ." he said. "I believe we were talking about the Greeks. So you don't believe in modern progress?"

"Bigger and better battles?" She flinched suddenly and caught the edge of the table. "Wish I wouldn't do that," she said shamefaced, after the explosion had died away.

"I was almost under the table, myself, at that moment." They both laughed at that, rather too loudly, rather too vehemently.

"Let's keep talking," the American urged. I didn't bring her here to have her talk, he thought and laughed again, this time at himself.

"I'm overtalking," Sheila said. "I don't know why. . . . I don't usually do this."

"It's the reaction to the bombs," Stevens said gently. "Some people think of food all the time. Others want to sleep. Others want to make love. Others talk their heads off."

Sheila smiled. "Unfortunate for you that I am the kind that . . . " She paused, as if she had said more than she should have.

"Talks," the American concluded. He was laughing again. This is mad, he thought. The bombs are falling, and I'm laughing and I haven't much to laugh about; this evening isn't going to end as I had planned at all. And I'm laughing. "You loved Andrew Aleksander like a brother, and you love me like a father confessor. What's wrong with you anyway? Or should I ask what's wrong with Andrew or with me? Sorry: I see I'm embarrassing you. But some day I'd like to know."

Sheila searched for one glove which was, as usual, under the table.

"I'd like to know, too," she said in a low voice and accepted the glove from Stevens. There was a loose thread in its thumb. If she pulled it, there would be a hole. It would be nice to outwit that rule, she thought. She pulled the thread. "Perhaps," she said, "I want to be quite sure. The way Barbara and Jan Reska were quite sure. I'd rather be alone all my life than not sure." Her thumb came through the opened seam.

"Stop doing that!" Stevens said. "You're ruining it."

She obeyed, much to her own surprise. And she suddenly knew what she had missed in Andrew: she wanted someone who could say "stop doing that" now and again. She stared at Russell Stevens and thought, if I could mix

you and Andrew together, I'd be sure for the rest of my
life.

"That was a big one," Stevens said, listening. "not far
from here either."

Sheila listened, too. The long, dull roar from the east
gathered intensity. She was suddenly afraid. Not for herself, not for the people round her. She rose, clutching her
opened powder box and lipstick. She jammed them into her
bag as they were. "I must go," she said.

"Hey, wait. The check," Stevens called to her, and then as
he saw her reaching the door, he threw down some notes
and coins on the table and started after her. He caught her
arm as she stood hesitating in the doorway. Together they
looked out into the street, dark under its black ceiling of
smoke, as if they were reconnoitering. It didn't take long to
develop little habits for self-preservation when you lived in
a beleaguered city.

"Must we?" Stevens shouted.

Sheila nodded. We must, she told herself as she shrank
from the noise and desolation of the street. She tried to
shake herself free from the terror she had suddenly felt inside the restaurant. Someone called my name, someone
called me, she was thinking. She tried to tell that to the serious face beside her, but she couldn't. Stevens thought she
was mad enough already. Perhaps she was. *Sheila, Sheila!*
... How could she have heard that, inside the restaurant?
How could anyone hear anything in this noise? The attack
was more to the east of the city, over towards the banks
of the Vistula. The black smoke above the buildings became lined with orange. Somewhere there was fire. The
American was looking down at her face. His grip tightened
on her hand.

"Keep to the doorways. One at a time. When I say dodge,
dodge," he shouted, his mouth close to her ear. And then
they were out into the street, into Marszalkowska Avenue
which had once been Warsaw's gayest. The smart clothes, and
the laughing voices, and the music and flowered window
boxes, were gone. Only the trees still stood untouched in their
neatly spaced circles of earth. A gaily striped awning flapped
pathetically over a boarded window. The solid buildings
stared across the avenue at each other's wounds. The names
over the shops and nightclubs and cafés were meaningless.
On the roadway were fragments of bodies instead of taxi-
cabs and red tramcars. On the pavements were broken slabs
of concrete, like the crushed remains of a huge ice floe
ruptured by its own force. The people who walked there,
now, were people with urgent heart-twisting business. They
walked quickly, dark figures moving through a nightmare of

sound. There was the constant thunder of the encircling guns, the scream of plunging shells, the angry bark of planes, the whistle of dropping bombs, the roar of explosions, the staccato crescendo of machine gun fire as a plane swept contemptuously low. Then suddenly there would be a terrifying blank of silence; a short lull to be counted only in moments, before the dentist's drill plunged once again into the naked gum.

"Where?" Stevens asked in one of these moments.

"The children's hostel," Sheila had time to answer, and only time. For Stevens pushed her violently into the slight alcove of a boarded doorway and stood behind her, pinning her flat against, almost into, the wall. Then she heard the planes' sudden roar as they swooped low, heard the sound of heavy hail on the pavement behind her. It was over before she had even grasped the coming of danger. In the street, others were now stepping away from the walls, or were rising from the ground where they had flung themselves. Two women remained on their knees to finish decently the prayer they had begun. Some bodies didn't rise.

Stevens was staring at the sky beyond the University buildings which they were now approaching. The children's hostel, Sheila had said. And the children's hostel lay over there. Sheila was staring too. The low-hanging smoke clouds and the coming of night made it difficult to see clearly. And then the flames broke loose, leaping higher than the black clouds. Stevens pointed suddenly to the north and center of the city. Flames all round were growing. The fires had begun. The clouds became scarlet. Sheila, remembering how Warsaw had been set on fire with incendiaries three nights ago after the water supply had been blasted into uselessness, gripped Stevens' arm in desperation. Five hundred fires three nights ago. Tonight, how many? They cast all caution aside, and broke into a run towards the once pleasant garden and the once quiet square of houses.

"It's the hostel," Sheila kept saying. Stevens couldn't hear her, but he knew, too. They were near enough to realize now that it could only be the hostel or one of the buildings beside it.

They reached the open square flanked by well-spaced, modern houses. One of the buildings was already being devoured by flames.

"It's the hostel," Sheila said again.

A warden shouted "No nearer: the walls are dangerous." He pulled them roughly to a halt. "Help with the sandbags," he yelled over his shoulder as he rushed towards a group of firemen who were entering the other buildings. The incendiaries were just beginning their work on these houses. Fire fighters already on the rooftops, were silhouetted against the knee-high fence of dancing flames. They were emptying the sandbags, which had once protected the buildings' foundations from blast, over the greedy tongues. No water, Sheila remembered—no water. Stevens was already lifting a bag of sand onto his shoulders.

"Stay back," he shouted to her. "You've been ill. You can't manage this." He pushed her towards a woman who had paused to wipe the streams of soot-stained perspiration out of her eyes. "She's been ill," he yelled in Polish, and plunged into the stream of people carrying the sandbags towards the doorways of the buildings. At the doorways, they were met by others who came down the stairways to seize the bags and carry them up to the roof. The procession of old men, women and boys never halted. Some of the younger men had found ladders and climbed, with their load of sand, like flies against the face of the buildings.

The woman pulled Sheila back roughly as she tried to lift a load of sand.

"It takes strength," she said not unkindly, and pointed towards the center of the square, towards the huddle of figures on the grass and flower beds. "Help there!" She herself lifted a bag of sand and joined the moving stream as Stevens had done. Sheila looked towards the women lying on mattresses and blankets in the middle of the broad gardens. They must have been evacuated from the maternity hospital across the square. Nurses were with the women; ambulances were already arriving to take them to new quarters. A young girl, too young to be able to lift a sandbag, was dragging it slowly over the grass. The desperation on her face decided Sheila. She caught the other end of the bag. Singly you and I aren't much good, she thought, but together we can help. And to help with the fire-fighting, now that the people inside the buildings had been evacuated, seemed the most important thing to her. Stevens passed them as he returned for another load. He saw Sheila and the girl. He shook his head, but his face relaxed for a moment.

On one of the roofs, the fires had been extinguished. There was a sigh of relief from the crowd, almost swelling to a shout of triumph. But the neighboring house had suddenly five little crowns of fire, and the people's work was all to begin over again. Other houses were less lucky: there the flames were higher, but they were still fought. It was then that Sheila heard the increased drone of planes, like a mosquito's hum mounting at her ear. The planes were so low that the flames, leaping above the pall of smoke, lighted their sharklike bellies. Some swooped even down between the flames. Machine guns added their noise to the crackle and roar of fire. And the firemen, fighting their desperate battle on the rooftops, suddenly ceased to be black silhouettes: there was nothing left but the orange flames. A woman cried out in helpless anger. Looking at the tense faces, blackened with smoke, wet with sweat, Shela saw the woman's impotent hate repeated in the bloodshot eyes as they stared at the sky.

Other fire-fighters had climbed to the roofs to replace those who had been murdered. And again, just as they seemed on the point of controlling the flames, the planes roared down. Again the machine guns leveled at them with the precision of scythe strokes in a cornfield. Only two of them were left standing. The flames roared higher in triumph. Sand was useless now.

Stevens came to Sheila, pulled her hands from her eyes, and led her away from the building across the grass. "It's no good," he kept repeating, "it's no good. Damn and blast them all to hell." They sat down on an upturned barrow which one woman had trundled until the flames had shown them all that it was useless. He kept his face turned away from Sheila, and Sheila, weeping openly, looked towards the big building which had been the first to flare up. The red walls were now crumbling, falling like a row of children's red and yellow blocks.

"That was where we were," she said at last. "I wonder where Barbara took the children. Perhaps to the shelter?" She looked at the dark hump in the middle of the grassy square. She rose unsteadily. Her back felt as if it would never straighten, her feet were heavy, her hand throbbed. She looked at it curiously. It had a raw, shiny look. It began to throb and burn.

Stevens rose too, and then he looked at her and said, "What's wrong?"

"I seem to have got my hand blistered. I can't think when ... We'd better find Barbara. She will be with the children."

He took her arm, and they walked towards the dark mound of earth. There was no one sheltering there. There were only two nurses who had come with some first-aid equipment. A line of injured women and men began to form. But the stock of medical supplies was low, and only the worst cases were being treated. The most desperate of these ("I told them the building was going to fall," an exhausted warden was repeating to everyone who would listen) were being taken to the emergency hospital cars which were now arriving.

"I'll take you to the apartment. I've got some vaseline there which will cover your hand. Hold it up. Don't let the blood run down into it." He turned away from the crowd of exhausted, worried, suffering people, and led her away from the shelter.

"Barbara," Sheila kept repeating. "We must find Barbara." Everyone kept repeating his words, as if by saying them over and over again other people might understand, as if he hadn't heard himself speak and thought other people hadn't heard him speak, as if . . . Sheila stopped thinking, for even her thoughts were repeating their words.

Stevens took her back across the plots of earth and grass towards the few people now left on the scene. There was no Barbara among them.

"She will have taken the children to some safe house," he said. "They will be far from here, by this time." But his eyes still searched among the small groups of people. He felt Sheila tug his arm suddenly, and she was looking at a slender fair-haired girl standing silently beside an air raid warden. Sheila's heart leapt with relief. Stevens was smiling, too. They hurried over. Just as they reached the fair-haired girl she turned round to face them. It wasn't Barbara. Sheila's relief turned to fear.

Stevens was saying to the silent man, "We are looking for a girl, blonde like this young lady with you here. She was one of the volunteer nurses with the refugee children. This evening, there were three nurses and the children in that building which is almost burned out now. Where did they go? Do you know? Or where could we find out?"

The warden didn't answer. His exhausted eyes were fixed on the American's. He seemed to be trying to speak his sympathy, but no words came.

"They . . .?" began Stevens, and stopped. Sheila was a statue beside him.

The man shook his head slowly, sadly. The girl beside him suddenly said in a frightening voice, "My sister was a nurse there. She was there." The hopelessness and anguish in her face were answer enough.

Sheila turned away, and began walking blindly towards the street.

"I'll see you home," Stevens said as he followed her, "and then I'll come back and look. I'll look until I find her. They don't know what they are talking about. I'll find her."

They walked towards the center of the town in silence. Stevens had slipped his arm around Sheila's waist and that helped to steady her. A first-aid car halted beside them on a ragged street.

"Any help needed?" the driver was saying. "I've room for one more."

"Going south? Anywhere near Frascati Gardens?"

"As far as the Bracka Emergency Hospital."

"That's fine. Thanks." Stevens jammed Sheila into the car on the front seat beside a sleeping man. "Stay at my apartment. I'll be back as soon as possible. Medicine cabinet is next to the radio shelf." He didn't wait for them to drive off. He was already running back to the ruins of the children's hostel.

The car plunged on, avoiding the holes in the road as if by a miracle. Sheila didn't look at the people crowded into the rear seats of the car; she could hear them. She rested her throbbing left hand up against her shoulder, and tried to avoid lurching into the sleeping man. Once, the car twisted suddenly round the edge of an unexpected crater, and the man's head fell sideways against her. She knew then that he wasn't sleeping. She stared into the orange-streaked darkness and listened to the middle-aged driver, his good-humored face puckered into fury, giving vent to his overcharged emotions with a constant stream of descriptive adjectives to fit the Germans.

At the hospital on Bracka Street—once a recreation hall—the car was emptied.

"I must return. I cannot take you further. I am sorry." The man's gentle voice was in quiet contrast to his recent rage. He was leaning heavily over the wheel.

Sheila nodded to let him see she understood. She gave him her good hand. He held it, and patted it gently.

"Go down that way," he said and pointed. "You will pass a large bank at the corner where Bracka meets Main Street. Keep on south, through the square, into Wiejska Street. Then you'll be home. It's quiet down there, tonight."

Sheila nodded again. She couldn't even say thank you. She just stood there, looking at him, and nodding, and looking at him. The car started northwards into the center of the burning city.

Sheila's body had become a machine. It was like a child's toy which is wound up and runs on, unable to stop its rhythm long after it had struck a wall and lies sideways on the floor. Without thinking, or seeing, or feeling, she walked the distance to Stevens' flat. At the same even, unfaltering pace she crossed torn streets, skirted shell holes, stepped over debris; at the same even, unfaltering pace she climbed the stairway to Stevens' rooms, and passed through the half-open doorway into the hall. Later, when she tried to recall that journey, all she could remember was that she saw the stranger drive away, and then she was standing in Madame Knast's entrance hall, listening to the voices which came from Stevens' living room, staring into the desolate kitchen.

Stevens' two rooms were at the front of the building; the

kitchen, across the hall from them, faced into an enclosed garden. Once it had been as cheerful and gay as the trees and flowers it overlooked. Now, lit theatrically through its empty window by the reflected glow from the sky, it was desolate. The table was cluttered; dishes had fallen off the shelves and had smashed on the floor beneath. The curtains, without any glass to restrain them, were waving dolefully out into the garden. No one had lived in this kitchen for many days. Madame Knast's rooms, farther along the hall, were silent too. Only from Stevens' room came voices. Voices talking in English.

Sheila stood in the hall. The forsaken kitchen had sapped her will power. The machine had run down: her legs wouldn't move any more. She stood and looked at the kitchen. Once, she thought, this was the life of the house. Then the son had been lost. Madame Knast must be lost, too. Lost, searching for her son. The curtains flapped back against the window sill, then blew out into the night again. Madame Knast was lost. And Barbara was lost. Lost, lost, lost, the curtains echoed gently.

Stevens' door creaked behind her. A man's voice said in English, "Hello, I thought I heard someone. Come on in, whoever you are." He was an American. When she didn't move, he repeated the invitation in Polish. Over his shoulder he called back in English into the room. "Tuck in your shirt, Jim. It's a woman."

The man came towards her curiously. "Come in," he said for a third time, and touched her gently on the shoulder.


CHAPTER XIII

*The Outlanders*


NO LONGER would Madame Knast have thought of calling her "paying guest's" rooms "nice." Here, the disorder had spread too. But it was of a different kind. There was a friendliness in the opened suitcases sprawling over the floor, in the bottles standing on the table, in the saucers filled with cigarette ends, in the sheaves of ill-arranged papers beside the typewriter on top of the bookcase, in the blankets hanging over the armchairs. Candle stubs burned cheerfully in the necks of three empty brandy bottles. Roughly hacked sardine tins and a piece of marbled sausage, a knife and a corkscrew and a can-opener completed the still life on the table. The window now was boarded-up. Russell Stevens had lost his bet.

The man who had been washing the cuts on his cheek in a bucket of much-used water paused in drying his face with a shirt to stare at the newcomer. Another man, with a decided wave to his hair, had one foot on a chair and his trouser leg rolled above the knee while he wound a puttee-like bandage round his calf. He had paused to look up at Sheila, and he kept looking at her while his fingers finished the knot on the ragged piece of muslin round his leg. Sheila recognized the remains of Madame Knast's best white curtains lying at the man's foot. A third man struggled with the waistband of his trousers. He must be Jim. He was staring, too.

"Well, it certainly can't be Madame Knast," said the man who was drying his face, and threw the shirt into a dark corner of the room. He had spoken with a decidedly French accent.

"No, thank God," the American said. Then he began slowly and carefully in Polish, "Did you come to see Madame Knast or Stevens? Madame Knast hasn't been here for almost two weeks, now. Stevens will be here any moment. We are expecting him."

Sheila made an incredible effort. "He sent me. Here." The words seemed to have been uttered by a stranger.

The man called Jim said, with a hint of cockney in his vowels, "You're English, aren't you?"

Sheila nodded.

The man with the wave in his hair tucked the last strand of bandage in place, unrolled the wrinkled trouser leg methodically, and walked stiffly over to her. He bowed with great politeness and said, "Gustav Schlott. You must be Miss Matthews. Steve has spoken of you."

The men lost their first curiosity. Another kind, more subtle and less staring, took its place.

"Have a chair," suggested the black-haired American. He tipped one forward to empty it effectively of its mixture of clothing and books, and carried it over to her.

Schlott had noticed her hand and was searching for the first-aid box. It had wandered considerably from its usual place, and no one seemed to remember who had put it where. With Swedish perseverance he found it at last, stuck inside a biscuit jar.

Jim was saying with humor made heavy in his embarrassment, "Don't tell me you've been out for a stroll in the moonlight."

Schlott smeared her hand generously with petroleum jelly. His middle-aged, heavy face creased in a smile as he patted her shoulder encouragingly. "That will cure it. Now, would you like vodka or wine or schnapps?"

"Wine," the Frenchman said decisively. "It's both nourishment and drink." He chose a bottle carefully from underneath the table, kissed it mockingly and uncorked it gently. "We can even offer you some food. Bill, our American friend here, has produced a suitcase of delicacies. There is pâté de foie or caviare or pâté de foie. Bill is a very wise man. He chose to save these tins of food rather than his clothes."

Bill said, "Nuts. That was the first suitcase I could grab. That and my manuscript. Just didn't get round to finding my clothes."

"All I'm dreaming about is a slice of soft white bread with lashings of butter, and a pot of tea," Jim said. "Never thought I'd sink to dreaming about them."

Bill handed her the wine in a kitchen measuring cup. "Try this," he urged.

Sheila wished she could smile. They were all so eager to help her, as if they had read in her face all she had seen and heard in these last hours. She raised the cup slowly, but when she tilted it the rim wasn't at her mouth after all. She only realized that the cup's rim was pressing below her underlip when the wine trickled coldly down her chin and splashed on her coat.

The men exchanged quick glances. Schlott unclenched her hand as gently as he had applied the vaseline, took the cup and held it to her lips. She swallowed the wine in quick hard gulps.

"What about resting on the couch?" Bill said. He was already arranging a blanket for her. "Sorry we can't offer you the bed next door. But there are a couple of fellows in there, dead to the world. You can go on sleeping here until Steve or one of us gets back again. Steve doesn't know it, but his boarders are increasing. We're the Bombed-out Brigade. This part of the city is the luckiest, so here we are. Steve's going to be the most popular guy in Warsaw before the siege ends."

"A doubtful honor," murmured the Frenchman, looking round the confusion in the room.

The Swede was tucking the blankets methodically around her legs, folding them envelope fashion. "Warmth is necessary," he was saying to himself.

Jim, watching him, nodded in agreement. "Lord, the things we've learned in the last weeks!" he said, as he helped Schlott arrange everything to his satisfaction.

"Try and sleep. Yes?" Schlott said, and then moved away with Jim to sit and talk quietly with the others. They kept their voices low, but everything they said now sounded twice as loud to Sheila, as if, by lying so still and not having to move or talk or make any effort, her power of hearing had been strengthened. She wasn't listening, and yet she heard every word in spite of the constant roll of noise from outside. She wasn't sleeping, and yet she felt she wasn't in this room. It was only the body of Sheila Matthews, and not Sheila Matthews, which lay so still.

The serious voices argued on. The problem was ammunition: for the last week it had been rationed sparingly. The problem was food: none was left in the shops, and the warehouses had been bombed to bits, and the city was surrounded. The problem was water: the waterworks had been destroyed, and the old wells were inadequate now. The problem was the hospitals with so many in ruins, so much equipment destroyed; thirty-six thousand wounded soldiers and more than that number of civilians lay on floors and in corridors. The problem was the burst water mains; the sewage pipes blasted; the increasing tempo of night raids which made burial more difficult. The problem was the guns which smashed day and night at the city: they were getting worse and worse, and soon people wouldn't be able to move about the streets to help where they could; no human being could stand this much longer.

The serious voices argued on. The only thing they agreed about was the fact that there were problems.

Schlott came over to her once more. "Not asleep?" he asked gently.

She could answer him now. "I'm much better, thank you. I'm all right, now."

He seemed pleased.

He turned back to the others. "Time to go now," he said to them. The men gathered up their odds and ends of equipment silently. And then they started to talk again as they left the room. They filed out slowly. Only by their slowness, not by their faces or by their voices, could you tell that they were loath to leave this room. Here at least you could rest. Here at least you were together. Here at least the walls shut out the sight of the streets.

When the storm of sudden tears had passed and she was calm again, Sheila listened to the bursts of snoring from the sleeping men next door. How strange, she thought, to be able to sleep like that through all this shellfire; and then she remembered that she had slept equally deeply through the worst raids in the early part of the siege. But this shelling was worse than the bombing. The center of the city must be crumbling. Bill, that new American, was right. Steve had chosen a lucky spot for his apartment. Steve ... Sheila found herself wanting to smile at the precise way in which she had called him "Russell." Of course, his friends would call him Steve. Russell was probably only used by his great-aunts. She sat up on the couch and moved her legs onto the floor. She was feeling better now. She had almost smiled for a moment. Are we really all heartless? she wondered in amazement and shame as she reached the boarded window. Two hours ago she couldn't have smiled. Two hours ago all she could do was to walk and walk and walk. She couldn't even think then. She hadn't been afraid of bombs or shells or things lying before her on the street. Now she could smile. She could think. She could be afraid.

The bedroom door was flung violently open, and a thin dark-haired man stood staring at the candle-lighted room. "They've gone, damn them. I told them to waken us." He spoke bad German. Behind him stumbled a young man, with rumpled hair and a blond beard. They looked at Sheila curiously for a moment.

"Where did they go?" the bearded man asked. He had the soft accent of Vienna.

"I don't know. They left about an hour ago."

"You are a German?"

"No. British."

The two men forgot about her. They were searching for their coats, cursing the others for having left them behind even out of thoughtfulness. The dark-haired man was probably Spanish, Sheila guessed, as he burst into a long stream of fluent phrases which neither she nor the bearded Viennese could understand.

"If we miss them," the Viennese was saying, "tell them we've gone to the Poniatowski Bridge. Tell them to come along there when they've had some sleep. They'll be needed there."

The Spaniard nodded, took a drink of wine and passed the bottle to his friend. Together they left the room. The Spaniard was limping. He had a rifle slung over his shoulder and an armband round the sleeve of his torn jacket. The Austrian had stuffed some empty bottles into his pockets, and caried two in his hands. They were discussing something about petrol for the bottles.

She was alone once more. She moved a board which had been fastened only at one end so that people could "open" the window. She stared towards the north, to the heart of the city. It was bright blood-red.

## CHAPTER XIV

# Battle without Glory

IN THE eastern suburbs across the river Vistula, the cloud of dust from crumbled bricks and shattered cement blotted out the night sky. To the men, crouching behind the ragged walls of houses, or lying in trenches slit through the rubble of gardens, there was left neither night nor day. Time was remembered only by the gnawing hunger under their belts, by the taste of sulphur and lime on their parched tongues. None of them turned to look at the flaming city behind them to the west. Their red-rimmed, sleep-heavy eyes stared towards the east, towards the shroud of dust, suspended like a cloud on a volcano's rim, which wrapped their enemy round.

That afternoon, on one of the smaller streets which ran parallel to the main road into the city, a group of nine men, two of them wounded, had settled themselves in the little Café Kosciusko. Formerly, it had been a basement room. Now, the upper part of its window, which reached above street level, served very adequately for a combined machine-gun slit and observation post. The machine gun was silent. Like the watchful man beside it, like the others resting wearily behind it, the gun waited. Above the men's heads, above the gaping ceiling and the empty space where two other stories had once formed a neat house, was the unseen arc of whining shells aimed at the city across the river. A dull glow warmed the dark shadows of the room, turned the white faces gleaming with sweat and streaked with black to bright copper.

"First the tanks, then the flame-throwers, then the mopping-up parties," one man said.

Another nodded wearily. "No more shelling now, anyway." He sounded almost hopeful.

A third soldier, sitting beside the two wounded men, examined his rifle carefully and adjusted the bayonet once more. He looked up to catch the eyes of a comrade watching him. "I *know*," he said savagely. "I know, for God's sake. But it's all I've got. How the hell do they think we can stop tanks with a bayonet? Why the devil don't they send us the reinforcements we asked for?"

The man's outburst was the sign for the officer to rise and walk towards the window. His movement silenced the oaths behind him into an indistinct mumble. Well, why don't they send something? Why in all hell don't they? He looked up at the gunner.

"Nothing out there, as yet, Captain," the gunner said.

The officer nodded. He climbed heavily onto the solid table which had been jammed with massive beams against the window to support the gun. Standing there, his head close against the wall, his neck twisted forward, his eyes above the pavement's level, he could see as far as the haphazard pile of concrete blocks which straddled the street. By this time, the Germans must have occupied the remains of the houses beyond that freak barricade. But the snipers he had posted near there this afternoon were still silent. The man lying on the half-ruined ledge above the café's entrance was still silent. There was nothing out there, as yet. He wiped away the sweat which blinded him, streaking his face with his grimy hands. His fingers scraped over the heavy stubble on his jaw and rested on his chin. Five days' beard, two days' hunger and sleeplessness, a handful of ammunition, a spoonful of water in the last twelve hours. So we've come to this, he thought; we are fighting like rats from a basement. His bitter eyes followed the broken line of buildings which fenced the street. They rested on the pitted surface of the road. If only we had some petrol, he thought once more. Even one bottle of petrol.

"Nothing there," he said abruptly. He knew that the man beside him and the men behind him were watching him. They were waiting for orders, for a last word of encouragement, and suddenly his bitterness turned to anger: anger with them for depending on him, anger with himself for his uselessness. They had relied on him for four weeks now, and he had brought them to this. Caught like rats, fighting like rats with bare teeth. Yet, what else should he have done? At what point in the last four weeks could he have made another decision which would not have led to this? It seemed laughable now that he should have been so proud of the way in which he had led his men to Warsaw. After the slaughter-fields of Poznan, after the scattering and encirclement of the remaining armies, Warsaw had seemed the one hope. There, men could make a stand and fight, men could hold the Germans until help came. Well, they had held the Germans. The Germans hadn't been able to cross the Vistula, not with all their planes and tanks and ammunition, not with all their ten divisions in a tight noose round the city's neck. Ten divisions... He stared at the house opposite the café. There, Cadet Kurylo waited with the other machine gun and five men. Four snipers. One outpost. Nine men here. Twenty altogether. A nice round figure. Twenty of them, and only four of his original command. He had brought them to this. His sense of failure was so complete that the whole catastrophe became his personal fault.

He turned quickly away from the window, and stumbled down from the table. He faced the waiting men. Now was the time for a neat little speech; now was the time to tell them that everything would be all right. All they had to do was to hold this basement for one more hour, and then the trenches guarding the approach to the Poniatowski Bridge would be reinforced, and they could fall back to join their comrades evacuating the other streets, and together they would fight along the Vistula.

He steadied his voice and said, "Well, we know what we've to do." A traditional beginning. Excellent. Wonderful. His voice grew more bitter as he gave the final instructions which were demanded of him: ". . . hold your fire until the tanks—" He halted. If he could see what was beyond all this for these men, he could face them more easily. What the devil was wrong with him, anyway? All he could see was the last round of ammunition and the eventual capitulation. Capitulation. The muscles in his throat knotted when he thought of the word, as if someone had stuck a knife into his side. Capitulation. He kept repeating the unbelievable word, twisting the knife cruelly in his wound.

He stared at the men, waiting so patiently in their exhaustion. Michal Olszak had been right, he thought. Two nights ago, he wouldn't let himself believe Olszak. Two nights ago, he had insisted a break-through could still be made, and to prove it he had tried it with some four hundred men. And of these four hundred . . . He said roughly, in sudden fury at himself and all the world, "Repeat tactics of this morning." But this morning, they had had grenades and petrol and phosphorus. This morning, their numbers had been three times as great. This morning, they had had a well-built shelter, and a field telephone, and another machine gun. And these men knew all that as well as he did.

The soldier who had been so preoccupied with fixing his bayonet gave a slow grin. "Kill what we can. We'll give as good as we get, Captain."

"Aye, Zygmunt," one of the wounded men said, "the more we kill, the less left for someone else to kill."

The captain's tight face relaxed. He reached into his pocket and fumbled for the last cigarettes. He looked at them, crumpled and flattened, in his blackened palm. "Three," he said, his voice even once more. "If we cut them up, they'll go round." What the devil had been wrong with him? he wondered again. His anger had given way to shame that he had doubted the men. They'd go with him all the way.

He found himself saying, very quietly, very slowly, "There

will have to be a capitulation, of course. There's no hope now of connecting with the outside world. This whole sector has just a few more hours' ammunition left. But before then—" He halted abruptly. He had said more than he should have. Two days ago he would have cursed an officer who had let himself speak so frankly. Before then, he had been about to say, before then we have a job to do. But he hadn't said it, and he wouldn't. In this desperate moment, men had a right to choose whether they lived or died. He waited tensely for their reply.

One of the men, the civilian with the armband to prove he was a soldier, said thickly, "There's no such thing as capitulation." The lines round the officer's mouth slackened.

Zygmunt, one of his four remaining cavalry men, was watching him fixedly.

"Yes, Captain," he was saying, "we'll take a few of those Szwaby along with us when we go." He looked as if he wanted to add, "What were you afraid of, Captain? That we'd go out to meet them with a white cloth waving above our heads?" Instead, he grinned. It was a slow, wide grin, showing strong teeth against his ugly, blackened face.

Captain Adam Wisniewski smiled as he dropped the last fraction of his piece of cigarette onto the broken floor. Looking at the faces circling him, he was happier than he had been all this day. His smile broadened. He felt less like a man who has condemned others to death along with himself.

From the window, the gunner's voice ended the feeling of suspended time.

"Movement from the German end of the street," he reported crisply. "And something's been moving at the other end, too.'"

Adam Wisniewski returned to the window. Once more, he stared into the red-lined shadows of the street. "Machine gun nests, probably." He listened carefully, trying to catch the sounds of this particular street against the dull roar of battle. But the snipers were obeying orders, however much their fingers itched on the trigger. The angry chatter of German machine guns swept the street, but there was no reply. The machine guns ceased.

"They'll think we all got killed in that shelling this afternoon," the gunner said.

Wisniewski nodded. All the worse for them, he thought, when they do make up their minds to attack. Each of our bullets will have double value.

Why don't they attack, and get it over?" the civilian with the armband said angrily.

But the captain was staring at the western end of the street. He could see nothing. "Sure you saw a movement there?"

"Yes, sir. Jozef up on the ledge saw them first. He gave me the signal. Two men at least. Perhaps they are ours. About time some more ammunition was coming up. Unless they've forgotten us."

"If they have ammunition, they'll send it," his captain answered. Perhaps they are ours, he was thinking. Or perhaps the Germans have forced their way along a neighboring street and are setting up machine guns in the rear. Encirclement—that was all he could think of nowadays.

"How far away?" he asked.

"Less than eighty yards. More like sixty. Just ahead of that church which is burning."

Adam Wisniewski jumped down from the table. The tiredness had lifted from his muscles. There's another hour's life in them yet, he thought. His eyes rested naturally on Zygmunt. And Zygmunt, just as naturally, had already risen to his feet and was moving towards the doorway.

"The usual, *rotmistrz?*"

Adam nodded, and watched the large, solid shoulders crouch to slide through the hole in the cafe's western wall. Good man, Zygmunt. He met you halfway. The use of the word *"rotmistrz"* twisted Wisniewski's tight lips into a bitter line. Fine captain of cavalry he made now, he thought, and turned to the civilian with the armband and two other soldiers.

"Time to get along behind our snipers. About fifty yards to the east. Each of you choose four possible places to work from, as you did this morning. Hold your fire until the attack comes. You know what to aim for."

"Yes, sir."

The civilian said, "Still don't see why they haven't attacked. Sort of funny when you think of them trying to clear the street for a column of tanks to sweep through, when one tank and a couple of flame-throwers would finish us completely."

Wisniewski looked wearily at the man. "Yes," he admitted, "it's sort of funny." The Germans were playing a clever game. Its shape was still vague, but it was clever. He added quickly, "And it's funny, too, to hear us talking, when we could be getting into position."

"Yes, sir." The man with the armband followed the others quickly through the jagged slit in the wall.

"And blacken your helmets and bayonets," the captain shouted after them. God, he thought, sometimes I feel like a nursemaid. He posted a soldier to watch for Zygmunt's return. The gunner was on the alert at the window. Josef on his ledge would be lying still, watching, waiting. The two wounded men were propped against the bar. One of them, only, would be of any use. When Zygmunt got back, that would make five men here. He looked at the less severely wounded man. Four and a half, he thought, as he picked up the other one's rifle and secured its bayonet. His eyes traveled round the room once more. "*Rotmistrz,*" he thought again; and he smiled grimly as he kept his eyes on his watch.

At the end of six minutes, the sentry at the western wall gave warning. "Zygmunt. Two men. Civilians. Carrying something."

Civilians, and only two of them. No reinforcements, then. Wisniewski cursed silently.

"Good," he said briskly. He climbed up beside the gunner, and watched the German end of the street.

Behind him Zygmunt's voice exclaimed, "We've a chance, now, *rotmistrz!* Eight grenades. A couple of bottles of petrol. Phosphorus. *Rotmistrz!*"

Adam turned away from the window. No reinforcements. He faced the two men who had come with Zygmunt. They were resting on the ground, their breath coming in heavy stabs. Then the younger of them walked unsteadily towards the box which they had dragged here with so much difficulty. "It isn't much, I'm afraid," he said in his precise voice. The pride on his thin face hesitated as he blinked nervously through his spectacles at the silent captain.

"It's what we needed," Adam said, and watched the smile return to the boy's white face. A student, Adam thought, probably rejected for military service. He smiled too, and said, "Excellent!" Eight grenades. Two bottles of petrol. Well, that was something. "Excellent," he said again, and this time he meant it.

The young man was talking on and on. "Left the car at the foot of the street when that machine gun started. Didn't know the Germans were so near."

But Adam was no longer paying attention either to him or to Zygmunt, who was ripping up the last piece of his shirt into shreds. Loosely plaited, soaked with phosphorus, jammed into the narrow necks of the petrol bottles, they would serve as a fuse. Wisniewski stared now at the other newcomer.

"Just what the devil are you doing here?"

Michal Olszak took his pince-nez out of his pocket, wiped them carefully on his sleeve, and the settled them on the thin bridge of his nose. "I wanted to see you. This was the only way to come, as combined ammunition-carrier and dispatch-rider. I bring you some orders from Sierakowski."

"You've come from Sectional Headquarters? What's new?

We've had no direct communication with them since that barrage smashed everything this afternoon."

"They are trying to establish a field telephone at the end of the street, now. Your orders are to gather your men together and withdraw to that point. The Germans have begun a serious attack on the main road leading to the Bridge. Sierakowski is of the opinion that if you don't get your men back to the junction of this street and the main road, then you are in danger of encirclement. Besides, you may be needed back there to help in the defense of the main road."

Adam didn't speak. He sat down on the ground beside Olszak. He passed his hands over his eyes as if to wipe the sleep out of them. It wasn't as simple as all that, he kept thinking. It wasn't so simple. If only the telephone wires hadn't been blasted away, he could have talked to Sierakowski, could have persuaded him.

He said, "Did the man I sent to Sierakowski this evening get through?"

"Yes. Wounded badly. But he got through."

"And Sierakowski isn't sending us reinforcements?"

"He's sending them to the main road. That's where the attack has come."

Wisniewski smothered an oath. It isn't as simple as this, he thought again.

Olszak was watching him keenly. "I wanted to see you," he repeated. "I thought you might have now changed your mind about that job. Have you?"

Wisniewski raised his head. He returned Olszak's look. "No," he said at last.

The blank look of amazement spread across Olszak's face. When he spoke, his voice was angry, sarcastic. "Still believe in no capitulation?" I've been mistaken, he thought, as his cold eyes rested on the younger man. His disappointment increased as his amazement ended. He tried to think of something to say which would cut through this young fool's stubborn pride, but his chargrin was too great to let him speak. May he rot in his own blindness, Olszak thought savagely. If he couldn't rid himself of that, then he was of no use. Not with all the qualities of courage and honesty and energy in the world would this young man be of any use. Olszak rose to his feet. It was particularly bitter that he should have always prided himself most on his ability to judge essential character.

"No," Adam Wisniewski said again. "There will be a capitulation." He paused and then said slowly, quietly, "You were right."

Olszak's anger gave way to further amazement. He sat down once more, and wiped his brow. "You shouldn't speak in such riddles. It's bad for my temper." He was looking at the younger man once more, and he knew how much such an admission must have cost Wisniewski. *You were right.* Two nights ago, when Olszak had spoken of capitulation, of continuing the fight by guerrilla warfare, Wisniewski by violently denying the possibility of one had refused the other. But now that he admitted the possibility of capitulation, why did he still refuse the task of forming a guerrilla force? And then, still watching Wisniewski's face, he guessed the reason.

Olszak said, "Two nights ago you refused because you thought I was wrong. Now you refuse because you found you were wrong. You don't trust yourself, any more. Why don't you leave that decision to me? Why blame yourself? There was no chance of success."

So Olszak had heard about the failure of the breakthrough. Well, that saved some explaining. "Thank you," Wisniewski said with overpoliteness. His voice hardened. "Ninety-five per cent of my men lost. That's a franker way to state the case." He rose and walked towards the window.

"It was a miracle that the five per cent did get back," Olszak said as he rose and followed him.

"All quiet, sir," the gunner was reporting. "Can't make head or tail of this. Can you, sir?"

"Don't worry. They are coming soon enough," Wisniewski said. "Keep your ears open for any signal from our snipers."

"Yes, sir!"

Olszak said too casually, "Surely five per cent could have slipped through. Why did you bring them back?"

"A few men wouldn't have formed a break-through." The younger man's voice was tired, as if he were weary of explaining that to himself. Yes, some of the five per cent could have slipped through, but that wouldn't have been a fighting wedge. That would have been merely escape, and escape didn't help those who were left behind.

"No," agreed Olszak. So you came back, he thought. To this hell. Admitting defeat. His thin, neat hand rested on Adam's arm.

"Time enough to escape when there is nothing left to fight with," Adam Wisniewski said roughly. But he didn't shake off the other's hand. He nodded to the red sky, smoke-streaked, above their heads. His eyes turned towards the direction of the Vistula. "And we needn't be sorry for ourselves. These are the people I'm sorry for, Olszak. You and I are trained for fighting. These civilians aren't. They are the ones who suffer most."

From the street, so strangely silent amid the uproar of destruction to the north and to the west, there came three sudden shots, evenly spaced. Adam Wisniewski's hand tightened on Olszak's arm, gripped it as if pleading for silence. The machine guns' angry chatter began once more.

"Damnation, it wasn't so simple," Wisniewski burst out. "It wasn't so simple, damnation." Over his shoulder he shouted, "These bottles ready, Zygmunt? Take a couple of grenades. Two for me. Leave the rest here. Quick." He motioned the less seriously wounded man to stand by the gunner. To the sentry at the gap in the wall, he gave last instructions about the grenades, about signaling Cadet Kurylo and his men on the opposite side of the street. In fifty seconds, the dejected room was an alert battle station.

Olszak said, "Anything I can . . . ?"

"Get back to Sierakowski or the nearest field telephone. The frontal assault on the main road is only half of the attack. The Germans are about to send a column of tanks through this street. If they carry it, they'll outflank the main road. Tell him to reinforce the junction of this street and the main road. We'll try to delay the tanks until his men are in position. Half an hour. That's the most we can promise."

"But how do you know?"

"I didn't. Not until the snipers gave us the warning. I could only guess. This afternoon, this street was blasted by artillery. Since then—nothing, except machine gun fire to try and draw us out. An hour ago, I went up towards the German end of the street. They were digging. Clearing away. The street at their end had been blocked by ruins which were practically tank-traps. Now, a sniper has given us warning that he has seen tanks being moved up to enter this street."

"Then retreat to the end of this street. Face them there, with reinforcements."

"No. Once they really start moving, they are hard to stop. The place to face them is up here. Just at that part of the street where it is narrowest, where it twists, just where they will think they have got free of these blocks of cement." He turned towards the gap in the wall where Zygmunt waited impatiently. "Better reach Sierakowski," he said to Olszak. "We can't stop them permanently. We can only delay them for a little."

"And what about that job I wanted you to do?"

Adam Wisniewski was placing the two grenades in his pockets. Like Zygmunt, he held a bottle of petrol with its phosphorus-soaked cork in his arm.

"Better wait and see how far I am wrong, this time."

Olszak's thin lips smiled. "The meeting is on the twenty-seventh. Usual place. At the same time. Remember?"

"I hadn't forgotten." There was an answering smile. There

was a touch of the old Adam Wisniewski as he pulled his helmet over one eye. The weariness had gone from his face, the stiffness from his body, as he bent to step through the gap in the wall.

Olszak watched the crouching figure, grenades in his pockets, petrol-bottle cradled in one arm, the borrowed rifle slung over his shoulder, reach the impatient Zygmunt. They knelt for a moment by a shellhole, smothering their helmets and covering their bayonets with a coating of mud. And then the two men, doubling low, were circling round like hunters towards the German end of the street.

"Come on," Olszak said to the very tall, very young man who had come with him here. He removed his pince-nez and placed them carefully in his breast pocket. "Quick."

"What about this wounded man? We ought to take him back."

"Later. Come on."

The other followed unwillingly. "But—" he began.

"Come on." Olszak was already through the informal door. He crouched as Wisniewski had done, choosing each available patch of cover with a quick eye and determined pace.

"I didn't mean to overhear you," the young man was saying as he caught up with Olszak, "but don't you think he is mad? An attack through this narrow street, where there is only machine gun fire? The Germans can't be taking this street seriously."

"Shut up, and come on," Olszak said angrily. "If we get separated, run for that outpost and field telephone, near where we left the car. You know what to tell them. Seemingly."

That silenced his companion. Even at the field telephone, he offered no addition to Olszak's quick sentences.

"Well, I only hope he is right. That's all," he ventured as they at last reached their abandoned car.

The first explosion answered him. The ground danced beneath their feet. Olszak looked at the other man, as they picked themselves up. This time, he didn't need to say anything.

Adam Wisniewski squirmed round the last block of cement which separated him from the road. Twenty yards away, Zygmunt would be crawling forward too, under cover of a broken wall. By this time, Cadet Kurylo should have received the final signal: two of his sharpshooters would now be stationed as far forward as the other snipers, and the nose of his machine gun would be pointing to crossfire with the gun in the Café Kosciusko. The snipers were picking their shots carefully, enough to distract the Germans' attention, yet not enough to destroy the Germans' belief that this abandoned street was theirs for the taking. Adam Wisniewski listened to the savage machine gun fire replying to the single shots. He thought of his seven men crouching in the ruins of the street, shooting, eluding, changing positions. He was listening now to see if their firing power had been diminished. Six now instead of seven? Five or four? The shots were fewer, farther spaced. His men were silent now. Were they obeying orders, or had they in fact been wiped out? The machine guns, seemingly satisfied, had fallen silent too. In this desert of jagged stone and powdered brick, Adam waited. Desperation was in his heart. And then, out of the background of harsh noise, came a definite sound. It grew louder, focusing itself on this street. The first tanks were approaching.

He kept his head low and waited. At least, he thought, it looked now as if the snipers hadn't been killed. It looked now as if they had been following instructions; some of them, anyway. Sweat, as intense as his relief, lay cold on his brow.

The noise of the tanks ground nearer. He tightened his grip on his box of matches, if only to steady the sudden treacherous trembling of his hand. His stomach was caught in nausea. He swallowed painfully, and drew his arm across his eyes to wipe away the sweat. The waiting moments always got him this way. The waiting moments were the worst. Once he started action, once he saw the tanks, he'd forget all these fears and worries. He'd only remember, then. He had a lot to remember. These damned murdering swine. He'd remember.

The first tank was edging its way cautiously past the ruined walls of the houses. Once it cleared that narrowed piece of street, it would be less skittish. It would increase speed. Let it. Kurylo and the gunner in the café would know how to deal with it when it was isolated. For it wouldn't be followed by the row of tanks which it now led so arrogantly. The second tank was his. The third was Zygmunt's. At this narrow part of the street, two flaming tanks would hold up the traffic. Long enough. Long enough for Olszak to give his warning. And then, the snipers would know what to do. They all knew what to do. God give them accuracy and timing.

Then he saw the first tank, nosing slowly into the street in front of him like a lumbering monster out of a hideous underworld. He raised his body slowly to free his shoulders. His fingers were on the pin of a grenade as the tank gathered speed. The second tank followed. He pulled out the pin, counting. His arm followed through in a careful arc. I've missed, too late, I've missed, he thought with growing desperation. And then the grenade exploded under the tank's tracks. The huge bulk swung round to face him as its direction was lost. It twisted uneasily and then lay helplessly across the narrow street. A sniper was shooting to distract attention. Another sniper joined in. The cupped match in Wisniewski's hands spluttered against the phosphorus cork. This time, he threw quickly, aiming for the tank's waist where body and turret met. He saw the bottle gleaming strangely in the phosphorous light as it landed safely. And accurately enough. He flattened himself tightly against the earth as the explosion's hot blast scorched his neck and hands. All his breath was smashed out of him as the air current lifted him a few inches off the ground and then dropped him. The massive block of concrete beside him trembled, and then against its other side he heard the sharp hail of machine gun bullets. He couldn't even allow himself the pleasure of looking at the flaming tank. Here was one that no more would grind horse and human flesh into pulp. He began to crawl backwards, away from its blistering heat and sickly smell, away from the fireworks of its ammunition. As he reached the cover of ruins farther back from the road, he was thrown on his face once more. Zygmunt had aimed his petrol bottle well.

Wisniewski found he was shouting. How long he had been shouting was something he didn't know, and what he was shouting didn't make sense. He stopped suddenly, and then laughed at his caution. No one could hear him. Not in this inferno of sound. All he had to worry about now was a German machine gunner, or a German sniper. Or a shell. They were using trench mortars again. There was an explosion behind him, and a wall to his right crumbled as a shell's fragment plowed into it. He picked himself up again, and, his rifle held ready, ran for new cover. That shell had been aimed at the large block of cement behind which he had sheltered as he waited for the tanks. The Germans didn't take long, he thought savagely. Well, even they weren't infallible. This was one time they hadn't been so clever. A handful of men had deluded them. A handful of men . . . He felt better when he discovered that thought. He felt so much better that, crouching under the rim of a shell hole, he was surprised to find that the spreading stain on the shoulder of his tunic was not oil but blood.

From where he lay, he could see two columns of flame from the street. He wondered where Zygmunt was now, where the others were. Probably crouching into holes in the ground like himself, waiting as he was for this sudden barrage to spend its temper before they could make their way back to the Polish lines. His fingers touched the wet stain on his tunic. Nothing serious, not serious enough to prevent him from reaching the Vistula. Nothing was going to prevent him now from doing that. Not now. The twenty-seventh was the meeting day. Tomorrow he could give Olszak his answer. He edged cautiously out of the shell hole and began his slow journey back to the Café Kosciusko. In front of him, the sky over Warsaw was bright blood-red.

## CHAPTER XV

### Recruitment

SHEILA HAD LOST all count of time.

When the door opened, it wasn't Steve or Schlott or any of the others. It was Olszak, a thinner, wearier, grimmer Olszak. "You'll catch another chill," he warned her. His calm voice brought her back into the room. "And somebody may think you are showing a light to attract enemy planes."

Sheila guiltily pushed the board back into its position across the window. "I forgot," she said inadequately. "I truly forgot about the candles."

Mr. Olszak was smiling. "Frankly, I don't think it matters so much now. But it's a waste of good candle. How's your hand?"

"It's all right." She looked at him quickly. "Who told you? Steve?"

"Yes. I found him at Korytowski's flat when I reached there tonight. He has now gone with Korytowski to find Madame Aleksander."

"Should they tell her, so soon?"

"They were discussing that when I left them. Their courage in that respect was very low. You may seen them here, instead."

"Why didn't you go with them and give them some support?"

"Well, Stevens was worried about you alone here. And I thought I'd like to see you."

Sheila was touched that this man should have made the frightful journey through the streets to see her. She smiled.

"So, you've forgiven me for nearly killing you?" Mr. Olszak asked. "I hardly expected such a warm smile of welcome. Thank you." He sat down at the table. He thought, it would be wise to talk about past things and to avoid tonight's happenings. Sheila's eyes were too hard, too bright. "Well, we got the woman, Elzbieta. Again, thank you. You did a very good job."

"What about the man?"

"Henryk, or rather Heinrich Dittmar? He never came back to the porter's lodge. He has disappeared."

Sheila suddenly remembered the feeling of being watched as she had entered the police car in the dark street, that night. Perhaps she had been right, after all. . . . Perhaps . . .

"Yes?" asked Mr. Olszak.

She told him what she had imagined that night and then had laughed away.

"If you were right, we shall soon know. He will make it unpleasant for any of us he can recognize again. You will be all right. In fact, your case will be stronger with the Germans. If I remember rightly, one of my men had you in a very decided grip, which rather distressed me at the time."

Mr. Olszak poured himself some vodka. "I am glad," he went on in his quiet, smooth voice, "that you recovered so well from your illness. You are still somewhat thin, and probably—if I could see your cheeks—too white. But I must say you worried me for quite a while. You never thought I had a conscience, did you?"

"I think you believe in what you do, and nothing will stop you."

"Same thing. Won't you have some wine?"

Sheila shook her head. She had promised herself the pleasure of giving Mr. Olszak a shock whenever she saw him again. And here he was, and she couldn't remember what she had been going to say to him.

"Why don't you wash your face?" Mr. Olszak, it seemed, was determined not to let her think.

She stared at him. He was drawing a handkerchief out of his pocket as he went over to the bucket of water. "Come here. I'll get rid of the worst streaks." He bathed her face carefully, and while she finished the cleaning process, he searched for a towel. Madame Knast's best curtain had to suffer some more tearing.

"Organize yourself. That's the thing. Organize," he was saying. He surveyed their joint efforts critically. "Much better. But as I thought, too pale. Did you eat all the butter I sent? And the eggs? And did you drink the wine?"

"I ate and drank everything. I couldn't stop eating. Barbara said—" Sheila's voice faltered.

"Comb your hair. It's terrible," Mr. Olszak said quickly. Then as she looked round in a puzzled way, "Isn't there a comb here?" He fumbled through his pockets.

"My handbag. I can't remember what happened to it. I had it—" Steve had taken a sack of sand over his shoulders and he had left her and she had helped the young girl, had used both her hands to grasp the slipping heavy corners of the sandbag. And then there had been nothing but hurry and effort and strain ...

Olszak, watching her eyes, said sharply, "What's that tearing your pocket's seams?"

She looked down slowly and began to laugh. "My handbag. I jammed it in. I must have." It was tightly wedged into the pocket. Her coat tore farther as she tugged and pulled.

"Easy now," Mr. Olszak was saying. "That's a nice coat." He didn't add, "And it may be a very long time before you have another one like it."

Sheila was still laughing as the bag came free.

"Stop that. Stop it, and comb your hair. Here, give that bag to me." He opened it and his thin fingers searched quickly for the comb. "I remember the first day I looked into this small contraption. I wondered how anyone could ever cram so much inside. Do you remember that day? In Colonel Bolt's office?"

Sheila took the comb and began tugging at the ends of her hair. They were harsh and singed. Her eyebrows had the same dry feeling. So had her eyelashes.

"Do you remember?" Mr. Olszak insisted.

She nodded. As she combed her hair, she was remembering. Mr. Olszak and Mr. Kordus and Steve. Steve who knew so much without understanding the full meaning of what he knew.

"How is Colonel Bolt?"

"Everywhere. The man's energy is boundless." There was a little smile in Olszak's eyes as if he believed in other ways of spending one's energy.

"And how is Mr. Kordus?"

The smile was still in place, but there was a hard edge to it. "When did you hear of Kordus?"

The frank question took away much of Sheila's assurance. She heard herself give the direct answer she hadn't meant to give so quickly.

"Steve heard that a Mr. Kordus was Special Commissioner to the Security Police."

"I believe he is. But who told Stevens?"

The story was neatly extracted with Mr. Olszak's usual skill. Sheila was left with no feeling of triumph at having jolted Mr. Olszak, who had consistently dominated her since their first meeting. She began to wish she had never given in to her impulse to watch Mr. Olszak jump. For he hadn't. On the contrary, he was in full cry after a probably innocent Stevens.

"But he has no ax to grind," she protested in the American's defense.

"My dear young lady," Mr. Olszak was at his silkiest, "have you ever known a journalist without an ax to grind?"

"I'm sure he would have told you himself whenever there was time. He's been busy." Somehow, her sarcasm was wasted. She said, suddenly uncomfortable and chastened, "Shouldn't I have told you then?"

"Of course. And before this. And found out the name of Stevens' informant, who points and talks too much."

"But the man didn't know you were Olszak. He pointed you out as Kordus. And Russell Stevens didn't tell him the truth."

"Stevens is really too inquisitive."

Sheila's temper flared as her worry over Stevens grew. "All right, then. I shouldn't have told you. I should have let you go on thinking that no one ever found out that Olszak was Kordus, or Kordus was Olszak."

"No one knew, except three men who made my appointment possible and who are working with me. No one knew. ... See, you've shaken my confidence, Miss Matthews: I should say, 'No one, I hope.' Does that please you?" There was a gentle little smile round the thin lips. She was not only worried, but ashamed.

"I'm sorry," she said miserably.

"No, don't be. I'm glad you had the very natural impulse to—shall we say, tease? You're a high-spirited creature, Miss Matthews, and you've resented the way I've used the curb and the snaffle. You don't like a tight rein, do you?"

Sheila smiled in spite of herself. Mr. Olszak's idea that women were like highly bred horses amused her. "And now you are giving me a lump of sugar," she said.

"It's surprising," Mr. Olszak said, "how well we understand each other." And then he was silent, his arms folded, his chin sunk, his eyes watching the flickering candles. "When a man knows too much," he said at last, "either you make him one of your party or you eliminate him. These are the only ways to silence him."

Sheila stared. "Not Steve!" she said. "He's on our side. He will promise to keep silent. I know he will."

"Promises are not so binding as dangers shared. Promises are merely good intentions. They are not enough. You see, Miss Matthews, every day and every hour make my plans more real. You've seen Warsaw. You know, as I know, that nothing more can be done. We have nothing left, neither light nor water nor food nor medicine nor ammunition. Not even clean air. But although we shall have to capitulate, the battle will go on. As long as we have one ally left in the world outside, we will fight. Even without that ally, we'll fight. We must. No nation is ever free which lets other nations fight for its freedom." He regained his calm voice and said, "You see, Miss Matthews?"

"I see."

"Did Stevens ask any questions about me?"

"Nothing very much."

Olszak looked almost comical in his sarcastic disbelief. Then he relented. "Don't worry so much about your American friend. I happen to like him. Why don't you sit on that couch? It's comfortable, at least." He rejected his own longing for sleep, and searched for something to say to this girl whose eyes were still too hard, too bright. She had taken his advice, but she was sitting bolt upright on the couch, resisting its comfort as she resisted consolation. She would keep staring at the boarded window, as if she could still see that sky smothering the city and its suburbs. He could feel its color in the heat of this room. He thought of the streets across the Vistula. By this time ... Well, he thought, what good will worrying do? Either he is alive, or he has been killed. Worrying will do no good.

The silence had become as intolerable as the heat. Olszak moved restlessly. He said, his thoughts still across the river, "You have met Adam Wisniewski, haven't you?"

At first he thought she hadn't heard him.

And then she was saying, "Is he dead, too?"

He looked at her curiously. "No," he said quickly. "He's alive. At least he was very much alive two hours ago."

Again there was a pause, and her face was quite expressionless. Then she suddenly bowed her head, and all he could see was the crown of smoothly combed hair.

What's wrong now? he wondered. He saw her body relax, and he knew that whatever he had said hadn't been wrong after all. For a moment, he sensed something which he couldn't explain, couldn't fit into a logical pattern, and it exasperated him. There were so many tangents to a woman's way of thinking. Men were simpler. Either they thought in the same or in a parallel direction as you did, or their way of thinking crossed yours at decided angle. But these women ... and the younger they were, the less understandable. Youth in itself was so involved. What was the process of becoming old but a choosing of the essential things, a discarding of too many impulses, a forgetting of too many dreams? How would it feel to be young again and have so many personal emotions cluttering up one's life? These young people would pity his age, his dry way of living. They would never guess the relief he felt because he had achieved a perspective of life. He was master of his own mind and of his emotions. He depended on no one. He was less vulnerable. He indeed traveled fastest who traveled alone.

Sheila had fallen asleep. Quite unexpectedly, her eyes had closed, her body had slumped forward, and she was unconscious as if an ether mask had been covering her face. She would have been surprised to see the care with which Mr. Olszak straightened her into a more comfortable position and covered her with a blanket. She would have been surprised to see him wait so patiently beside her until morning came, and with morning an exhausted Stevens and a grim-faced Korytowski.

She awakened to hear Steve's overhearty, "Nice domestic scene." Mr. Olszak only nodded benignly. He let the other men talk on. They had been unable to speak to Madame Aleksander. Her hospital had been bombed again, and she had been too busy with the remaining nurses moving the survivors from the courtyard, where they had been dragged to safety, into another building.

"I'll wait until tomorrow," Korytowski repeated. The lines on his face, thin and white under the soiled bandage round his head, were deeper. His eyes were dark caves; the blue light had gone from them.

The American threw himself on the floor beside the couch. He seemed relieved to have found Sheila so quiet and composed.

They talked spasmodically of the city.

No one mentioned Barbara.

Then Mr. Olszak said to Sheila: "I think you need more sleep. It will be easier next door."

She knew what that meant. As she left the room, she looked at Steve. Her tired eyes said, "Steve, be careful. Don't be smart. Be ignorant, and careful. And give the right answers."

He was looking at her too. He saw the expression in her eyes and thought, she's as unhappy as hell. To the two men he said, as the bedroom door closed quietly, "She must have been very fond of Barbara."

Edward Korytowski closed his tired eyes, nodded wearily. He was thinking of his sister Teresa. Barbara was the first of them to go. Or was she? What of little Teresa, or Stefan, or Andrew, or of Stanislaw? The longer he postponed breaking the news, the harder it was going to be for him to do it. He ought to have insisted that they search tonight until they had actually seen Teresa. But both he and Stevens had been loath to find her, to tell her. They had welcomed the excuse that the time was ill-chosen. And if there hadn't been that excuse, they would probably have found some other reason. The city was being bludgeoned into unconsciousness, its grip was weakening. Before the end was called, anything could happen. Why not wait until the death of the city? If

Teresa or he were still alive then, that would be enough for her to know. If she weren't alive, then he would have spared her one sorrow more. He looked at Olszak as if for help. Michal would know what ought to be done.

Korytowski rested his head wearily on his arms; his mind had begun to reel as if his emotions had made him drunk. Helpless anger and grief gave way to hate. He could do nothing but hate. Hate the men who had ruined his country, shattered his city, killed his people so ruthlessly. One month ago, they had all been living here in peace; sleeping, eating, working in peace. There had been light and warmth and flowers in the streets, there had been music, there had been people who laughed. There had been families and birthdays and visits to friends. There had been books to read in neat rooms, with only the voices of children playing in the gardens or the singing of the birds to break the quiet. The sky had been dark and cool at night, unclouded blue in daytime. And as he thought of these things, he could do nothing but hate. He had felt this since the first bomb had fallen, but Barbara's death released it from the secret places of his heart. It was now in command of him. All he could do was to hate. And he hated the Germans all the more for having taught him to hate like this.

Stevens, watching him, felt an upsurge of pity. The gentler you had been in your own life, the harder it was to bear all this violence.

Korytowski suddenly rose from the table. "I must find Teresa. I must tell her," he said thickly.

"Wait," advised Olszak, "wait until I can come through the streets with you. I shall go with you to Teresa."

"Then you would tell her?"

"Yes. Teresa never avoided bad news in all her life. She would prefer to know."

"Let us go now, then."

"Shortly, Edward." Olszak turned to Stevens. "Well, it will soon be over now. Listen to that new barrage since dawn broke. . . . What are you going to do, Stevens?"

"Can't seem to think about that."

"Surely you have plans?"

"Thought I had. But now that it's near the end, I don't know."

"Why don't you go back to America at once? Your Warsaw story will still be news for another week or two. You could tell the people outside how we fought in here. How Warsaw Fell. Exclusive."

"Shut up, Olszak." Stevens had risen to his feet and was standing over the Pole. "Shut up. I'm not so much under control these days. Perhaps I don't want to be under control. So shut up."

Mr. Olszak seemed far from offended by the American's savage tone. The sarcasm was gone from his voice when he said: "But perhaps you *could* tell them of our mistakes. For we have faced a new kind of warfare, and we didn't know how to meet it. No country does, unless it has been studying war and war only for the last seven years. Whatever our faults as a nation, we have at least been a willing guinea-pig in the cause of humanity. They could be warned in time through us."

"You mean I should go and give them advice? Me? I'd never stop talking if it would do any good. But you don't talk a democracy into anything. Each member wants to do his own thinking, his own talking. The people make up their own minds. If you try to rush them, they start yelling holy propaganda. It was the same with the British. They had to argue about Czechoslovakia before they decided Germany was dangerous. And it's the same with all forms of democratic government in Europe. They are still discussing the war, and voting on it at elections. How can you expect America to be any wiser than countries on Germany's doorstep?"

Korytowski said suddenly, bitterly, "Then the sacrifice is all in vain. Other countries may be attacked without warning and suffer cruel defeats, because they would not see what happened to us."

"Not in vain," Olszak said. "In the end, we'll win. Even if there are few Poles left, even if all Poland is entirely devastated, there will be other lands where there still are railways and factories and modern housing. By taking the first blow from the German fist when it was strongest, we may have helped to preserve buildings and lives in other countries. So in the end, we'll win, for Poland will live in the hearts of men. Or, do you think," he added with his peculiar smile, looking so innocently at Stevens, "that men will forget us as quickly as they forgot us after we saved Europe from Mohammedanism?"

Stevens didn't answer.

"You know, I like you. Just as I like that girl next door," Olszak said unexpectedly. "You both have that same angry, helpless look when you contemplate future injustices which you hope won't, but which you fear may happen. But let me ask another question. Why should you worry whether your return to your own country would be valuable? Why don't you just return, take up any new assignment, and go on building your life like millions of other fortunate young men?"

"Hell, no. What do you think I'm made of? Do you think

any of the foreigners here, who have been through this with you, are going to go away to their different countries and turn off these last few weeks like a water faucet? I guess we were all committed permanently when we first decided to stay. We didn't know it then, but we chose sides, all right."

"You are decided then? You are going to fight on?"

"We all are. There's another American here. We've talked of getting to England and learning to fly a bomber. There's a Swede I know. He's staying in Warsaw, at his job with the American Bank. But he thinks he has enough contacts to be able to smuggle people out of Poland. There's a Frenchman and an Englishman; they are going to reach their countries by Rumania and then enlist in their air forces. We all want to be on the giving end of a bomber, just for a change. But there isn't one of us who is going to start tending roses in his own back yard."

"What is your Swedish friend's name?"

"Schlott. Gustav Schlott."

"His idea has certain possibilities. But it needs silence. Tell him to keep absolutely quiet. Has he any Polish friends he can work with in his future enterprise?"

"I guess so."

"Find out their names. Bring them to me tomorrow. That will be the twenty-seventh of September. Come to Korytowski's flat at three o'clock in the afternoon. Now where can I get in touch with Schlott if I want to see him? Not at the bank. Preferably some place more private."

"He's living here now. If you wait long enough, you'll see him."

"God forbid." There was such an expression of alarm on Olszak's face that Stevens grinned.

"Some checking-up in order, first?" the American asked innocently.

"You talk too much. What is worse, you think about things which are dangerous. We need friends. But we don't want friends who are merely interested. If that is the most they can feel for us, then they are a danger to us the moment the Germans take over the city."

"What are you getting at? If you think I'd give information to a lousy Hun, I'll—"

"You'll what?" asked Olszak mildly.

"Skip it. Stop ribbing me. My temper is not what it was."

"Neither is mine," Olszak said with a touch of steel in his voice.

"What are you getting at?" Stevens said slowly. Incredulously he added, "Don't you trust me?"

"I can trust no one until he has proven himself. Do you trust me, for that matter?"

"No."

The two men looked at each other, and then Olszak laughed.

Korytowski, watching the American's face, said quickly, "Michal, I rarely interfere, but I feel that all our nerves are frayed to breaking point. We know Stevens. He's a good friend. He's been fighting with us. What more proof do you want?"

"Only a very little more. But first let me ask, what does Mr. Stevens intend to do with any information he has recently gathered? Not telling it to the Germans is only a negative plan. The Germans don't always wait for people to tell, or not to tell. Suppose you were in London or New York. Suppose you were at a party and there met a charming woman or a sympathetic old man who deplored Poland's situation. In your friendship for us, might you not rise to our defense? Might you not say that you knew there *were* certain men in Poland who were going to fight every attempt at domination? Later in the evening you would find yourself being asked about life in Warsaw before the war, about the people you had known there. Then months later you might learn that Korytowski, or I, or one of the men you used to meet at the flat, had been arrested. For the Germans are logical. If you knew about it, it was only through the people you had known in Warsaw. That's how it can happen. I know. I've seen how they have approached exiled Czechs here, in the last years. Always very innocently, always very sympathetically, and *never* as Nazi Germans. Even the cleverest man can be duped by these agents. For there are moments when it is hard to keep silent, to keep from denying a lie or from justifying your friends. Yet the only way with these Nazis is to be able to seem callously silent. Can you do it, Stevens?"

The American shook his head slowly. "I'll never be able to converse again. Damn you, you know I like a good argument." He laughed ruefully. "I may as well admit now that I said I didn't trust you because I was mad at you for not trusting me."

"That's better," Korytowski said in relief, and relaxed again. He began pouring drinks into the measuring glass and a shaving mug.

"Here, what's happened to my best crystal?" Stevens said in surprise, and looked round the room as if he were really seeing it for the first time. He cursed softly and steadily.

"Someone has been drinking a toast," Olszak said and pointed to the corner of the room where broken wine glasses were scattered. He handed the shaving mug to Stevens. "Do you feel like a toast?"

"Meaning?"

"Meaning that I have a job for you to do. It will put you on the Nazi black list. It makes you one of us, not just a sympathizer but an active member. If things go wrong for you, I must warn you that the American consular representative could do nothing for you. I am giving an invitation to danger."

Stevens raised the shaving mug. "Good-by to the bomber," he said. "I'll fight your way. On the receiving end." He began to drink.

"You know what you are giving up?" Olszak asked slowly, raising his drink to his lips.

Stevens looked towards the bedroom. "If she can do it, what's going to stop me? When did a Limey ever do what a Yank couldn't?"

The kitchen measuring glass and the shaving mug smashed against the wall and added their large coarse fragments to the delicate ruin of crystal on the floor.

The bedroom door opened, and a startled Sheila stood there.

"Come in," Olszak said almost genially, "come in, Sheila. We didn't need to shoot him."

Sheila relaxed. She smiled at Olszak. Until now it had always been a very careful "Miss Matthews." She knew that somehow he was pleased with her.

"What's that? Shoot who?" Stevens asked with more vehemence than grammar.

Men's voices and heavy footsteps sounded on the staircase. The tension in the room reappeared. Olszak was already at the door. Korytowski paused to kiss Sheila, and to shake Stevens' hand.

"Tomorrow afternoon. Three o'clock. Bring Sheila. Your jobs begin then," Olszak said softly and left the room.

"Hello," Bill said as he entered at the head of the tired group of straggling men. "Who were the two old geezers we passed on the stairs.?"

"Looking for Madame Knast," Stevens said briefly. Sheila's eyes met his and smiled approvingly. "You're back early."

"There's little to be done. It's going to be a day of heavy shelling. Most people are making for the cellars. We'll have to wait until this barrage slackens."

The others were filing slowly into the room.

"You've additional guests," Schlott said.

Stevens looked at them. "So I see. Well, we have still got a floor here," he said. "How's the world outside?"

"Pippa isn't passing," Jim said slowly. "God's not in his heaven." He opened his jacket and set down a small thin frightened dog on the floor. He fondled the shivering little animal, scratched the ears lying so flat against its head.

"Carried him all the way here," Schlott said. "He's crazy. Does he expect us to eat a dog that made friends with us?"

"I didn't adopt him. He adopted me. What could I do? He wouldn't be a bad-looking little tyke if he were clean and happy."

The shivering dog, its tail tucked well between its legs, moved uneasily round the room. It came to Sheila and cowered at her feet.

"He's filthy," she said softly, sadly. We all are, she thought. And we are all just as afraid. She rubbed the dog's head gently as the men talked. She felt her eyes close in spite of her attempt to hold them open and be polite. The dog had stopped shivering. He looked up at her. As one human being to another, he seemed to be saying, just *what* is wrong with the world these days?

"How's your hand?" Steve was standing beside her. She smiled for an answer; she was too tired to speak. He pushed her shoulders gently down onto the couch. The dog jumped up beside her, and none had the heart to put him down. Sheila listened to the men's voices growing more blurred. The candles became a haze. The dog stared at her solemnly. She scratched his ear, and his watchfulness relaxed. He settled comfortably, and gave a small sigh.


## CHAPTER XVI

## *Capitulation*


THE BOMBARDMENT CONTINUED unceasingly. In Stevens' rooms the men were restless. When the guns seemed about to level off, they would talk and argue. They would make brief sorties out into a grotesque world where volunteers were useless. The end was near. The men felt it, and each made his own plans, his own preparations for that moment. Only the Americans and the Swede would be free men once the Germans came, and even they had to plan how they could keep that freedom.

During the day, Bill's remaining tins of food were scraped clean. The last bottle was emptied, and the final candle was inserted in its neck. The boards over the window had been loosened to let some light into the room, so that the candle could be saved for the night. A cold wind swept into the room and huddled them together in their coats. Once, either because the guns seemed to be directed more against the north of the city, or because sitting in this room had become unbearable ("It's madness to go out," Jim said, "but it's misery to sit here and just wonder"), the men rose and left together. Sheila seized the chance to tidy the room. Now that she was alone, she *had* to do something. She couldn't sit still and let herself just think. Even the Polish grammar book was no longer a diversion. She moved the conglomeration of private possessions into neat piles. She tried to get rid of some of the thick dust which drifted in clouds through the open window. After she had swept the white powder into heaps three times in succession and found that the coating of dust still lay on everything, she was forced to close the window boards. Barbara, she thought as she looked round the room, Barbara would have made a neater job. Barbara . . . She lifted the pail and almost ran downstairs, and went searching for the nearest well.

It was farther away than she had thought, and it was an unpleasant journey. She almost wept with rage when a sudden blast, nearer than the others had been, made her duck so that almost half of the precious water was spilled onto the road. The little dog had followed her to the well, had waited patiently beside her in the long queue. He had kept very close to her, padding along beside her, looking up into her face now and again as much as to say, "See, I've got one of those humans, again. She's got some quite good points, too. Might be intelligent. At least, she tries very hard. Perhaps I'll get round to teaching her some tricks one of these days. She certainly learned very quickly how to walk on all fours this morning when she was retrieving the things on the floor." His tail was carried proudly, his ears were erect. It hadn't been the guns or the lack of food which had cowed him so much, last night. It had been the feeling of being lost, of being unwanted. He now lapped up the pool of water spreading at Sheila's feet, and cocked his head to one side as he looked up waiting for more. His cool assumption made her laugh, and her rage vanished. Strange, she was thinking, that things never seemed so bad if you had someone—even a dog—to share them with. The last stretch of the journey seemed the easier for having the dog trotting along so closely beside her.

The men had returned in her absence.

"I told you to stay here," Stevens said sharply. "You gave us a scare, walking out on us like that."

Schlott took the half-filled pail of water and said gently, "We can do this."

"You had other things to do. Besides, all the other women and children are standing in line for water. That's our job now. I'm sorry my hand would only let me carry one pail. Doesn't seem so much, does it?"

"The pioneer woman," Bill said and looked round the neat room in amusement.

"The woman's touch," Jim said with pretended scorn. "Now it will take us two hours to get things comfortable again. I see the dog didn't desert us, anyway. What shall we call him?" He reached down and shook the dog's paw solemnly. "What shall we call you, funny face?"

"Try some Polish on it," the Frenchman said.

Schlott obeyed, and they all laughed as the dog cocked his head to the side and his tail fluttered like a flag.

Sheila, watching the relaxed faces round the little animal, thought, it's a good thing that Jim did salvage this dog; it has given them all a new topic for conversation. For the arguments were now centered on breeds of dog, on dog-training and animal intelligence.

"What shall we call it?" Sheila asked when these subjects had been exhausted.

"Him, not it," Jim said, as he tried to straighten the tangled coat with his broken comb. "Wonder who owned him? If you washed this soot off him, and combed him correctly, you'd have a good West Highland terrier. What about Prince Charlie?"

The game started; each had his own idea of a name, and each idea led to another.

The Frenchman said incredulously, "If anyone had told me a week ago that I should spend my last hours in Warsaw naming a dog, I would have said he was completely mad."

"This may keep us from going mad," Schlott said.

"What about me?" Sheila asked. She held up the torn jacket which she was trying to sew in order to keep herself occupied. "I think I ought to warn you that I've never sewn a man's jacket or shirt before, in my life."

"No embroidered rosebuds on the collar, please," Bill said.

"What, none? I thought a spot of *broderie anglaise* would have been appropriate. Or perhaps you might prefer some Richelieu work round these holes? I can't disguise them, I'm afraid."

"Just stop the seams from bursting altogether," Jim said. "We only want these things to be able to hang onto us. It can't be helped about the wide open spaces."

The man from Vienna alone said nothing, and didn't laugh. He sat on the floor with his head resting against the wall, his eyes counting each unseen shellburst. But then, he had known what the Nazis were like: he had escaped from a concentration camp.

He spoke only once. He said, "Do you realize the Germans may be crossing the bridges? Do you realize—"

"Yes," Bill said. "Hope some of them stick in the wire entanglements I met last night. If a Pole hadn't shown me the way out, I'd have been hooked up there still. That is what made the holes, Sheila."

"We thought it was moths," Stevens said, but Sheila noted that he too was listening openly to the falling shells, now. They all were. Schlott blew out the candle and removed a window board. A red glow spread over the opposite wall. Schlott began to curse, solemnly, sincerely.

"Come on," he said suddenly, and left the room. The others followed. They didn't even pause, this time, to gather their equipment. Their footsteps clattered on the top stairs, and then were lost as the guns' thunder grew louder. The dog whined uneasily and then lay down, its nose pointing to the door which swung half-open. Sheila collected Madame Knast's sewing materials and replaced them neatly in their little wicker basket. She pretended to be busy, but the red glow on the wall was deepening, the house trembled with the distant blows like the engine room of a ship plowing its way through heavy seas, the air which came into the room was hot and dry and smelled of sulphur. The dog coughed uneasily and padded about the room with its ears flat against its head. This is the end, Sheila thought as she lay down on the couch. No one was going to live through this night. For a moment she had the impulse to go out and face this terror in the streets as the men had done. But then she remembered that if any of them did get back to find she was gone once more, then they'd come out searching again. She would have to stay where she was. Wait... wait... You waited for everything, for food and water, for the bombs to fall, for the night to come, for another day. Nothing but wait...

The dog came over to where she lay. He took her forefinger gently between his teeth and held it that way for some moments, as if to say, "I'm here, too, you know." She rubbed his cheek, and he jumped up beside her and crept to her side.

She had to think about something. Not about people. Just about something. So she thought of London. She would take a bus-ride: from Hampstead down Tottenham Court Road into Charing Cross and Coventry Street and Piccadilly Circus. Then she would go up Regent Street, and along Oxford Street and then down Park Lane and through Hyde Park Corner along to Knightsbridge and Kensington. She was on her way back to Piccadilly, heading for Trafalgar

Square and the Strand and Fleet Street, when she fell asleep.

The silence awakened her. It was morning. She sat up quickly on the couch and listened. Yes, the guns had stopped. The planes had gone. The silence was so immense, so overwhelming, that it terrified her.

Outside, in the street, there were people. They were looking at the sky unbelievingly. They moved as in a daze.

"Come on, dog," Sheila said, and was shocked at the loudness of her voice. Had they all been yelling at each other in these last two days? The dog's tail thumped on the floor. "Come on, dog," she repeated quietly, and went down into the street carrying the pail. She had learned never make any trip without doing something necessary. The dog padded heavily on the stairs behind her. Yesterday she had only seen the movements of his paws: now she could hear them. Yesterday she hadn't heard his tail thumping on the floor, she hadn't even known the handle of the pail creaked. The little noises could live again.

In the street, a gray-faced woman stopped her. "What is wrong?" the woman asked. Sheila heard others asking the same question. You talked to strangers, to anyone, to the windowless houses. The guns had stopped, and you asked "What is wrong?"

She saw the two Americans and the Swede walking slowly towards her. Their faces were old and lined with fatigue. Their clothes and skin and hair were covered with a fine dust. Bakers out of hell, she thought. "Where are the others?" she asked.

"The Englishman and the Frenchman have gone. It was time for them to go," Schlott said heavily.

"The Spaniard and the Austrian?"

"They went over the Kierbedz bridge. They haven't come back."

Sheila looked up at the gray haze of sky as the others had done. The men's eyes followed hers. Their little group stood closely together. Grim faces moved quietly along the ruined streets, searching for food, for shelter, for water, searching. Three children stood at the edge of a bomb crater, filled with water wasted in its muddy hole. Sheila saw one small arm raised to throw a stone, heard the high-pitched little laugh as the water splashed round the boy's feet. The others were playing that game, too. "I'm a bomber. See!" one child yelled suddenly as he threw a larger piece of stone. "I'm a machine gun," cried another, and scooped up a double handful of gravel to shower into the pool. "Hear it! I'm a machine gun!"

The shrill calls of the children were the only sound in the street.

Stevens turned away, and the little group followed him.

Upstairs in Stevens' room, the men dropped wearily onto the couch and the floor.

"What's to do, now?" Schlott asked. "What's to do, now that it's all over?"

"Some still want to fight on," Bill said. "Some are weeping in the streets because they aren't to be allowed to die any more. I saw men in tears." He picked himself up from the floor, and tramped blindly into the bedroom. They heard the springs creak as he threw himself heavily on the bed.

"What's to do now?" Schlott repeated.

"I'm damned if my side is going to lose," Steve burst out. "I'm God-damned if it is going to lose. It—"

Schlott pointed at Sheila, and Steve grew silent. He rose too and paced between the hall and the room.

"We must not sit here with our thoughts for company," Sheila said to Schlott. "I've these rooms to clean properly. There's water to fetch and food to be found. There are friends to see. Perhaps they still need our help. But first of all, you must sleep. You've been out all night."

"Stuck in a cellar. No damned good to anyone," Steve said bitterly.

Sheila unfolded a blanket. "Sleep, Steve," she suggested. "Here, or in Madame Knast's room? There's a comfortable bed there.

Stevens shook his head and slowly wound a small alarm clock. "This is my own place," he said. "I guess we are damned lucky to have it." He took the blanket from Sheila. "There's that meeting, this afternoon. Four hours, just give me four hours of sleep." Sheila glanced anxiously over at Schlott to see if he heard, but he was already asleep. Steve stretched himself on the floor and placed the clock beside his head.

Sheila went into the wreck of the kitchen, and the dog followed her.

"What is it to be, dog?" she said. "Shall we clean up, or shall we get some water and food?" The dog cocked its head to the side, thumped its tail, and waited with bright brown eyes.

"All right," Sheila said. "Water and food."

She lifted the pail once more, and they went downstairs and joined the searching people.

The strange thing about a bucket of water was the way its weight increased. She set down the pail at her feet for the third time on the homeward journey. The dog sat down, too. It waited, watching her face.

"Stop looking at me!" she said half angrily. The dog's tail circled, and she laughed at the sideways-held head. The boy who had been walking along the pavement towards her, his eyes fixed on the ground, looked up when he heard the laugh. He stood looking at her with angry, blue eyes.

"It's this dog," Sheila said. "He makes me laugh."

The boy said nothing. His eyes followed Sheila's pointed hand, and now he stood looking at the dog. The dog looked at him in turn, and cocked his head to the other side. The boy's fingers snapped halfheartedly, and the dog's front paws beat an excited little tattoo on the pavement's dust. The boy smiled involuntarily. The dog sat up and begged.

"It's a nice dog," the boy said slowly, and knelt to rumple its coat. He kept his head bent, his face well-hidden.

Sheila picked up the pail, once more. The boy straightened. He kept his head turned away. "I'll carry it," he said in a muffled voice.

"I haven't very far to go," Sheila said.

"I'll carry it." He lifted the pail out of her hand.

When they reached the hall of Madame Knast's apartment, the boy hesitated awkwardly.

"Do you need more water?" he asked.

"Yes."

"I'll get it. Have you another bucket? I can carry two."

Sheila searched for the second pail. "Thank you," she said when she had handed it to him, "this is really a great help to me."

The boy clattered down the staircase eagerly.

When he came back, he seemed happier. The tight lines had gone from his mouth. And when Sheila, cornering the last heap of broken glass and china and dust beside the cardboard box, said "Splendid!" he seemed happier still. He insisted he could fill the box with the rubbish and empty it downstairs. He made several journeys, carrying the box carefully so that no dust spilled over. When he came back he stood at the kitchen door.

"Anything else?" he asked shyly, but there was such a pathetic eagerness in his voice that Sheila halted her final thanks.

"I was going out to try to buy some food," she said instead. "Do you know where I could buy any?"

"Not buy." The boy stood thinking, and then added, "I may find some."

Again he clattered down the staircase. When he came back

he had a cabbage tucked under one arm and a small piece of raw, roughly-hacked meat in the other hand.

"We'll build a fire in the courtyard," the boy said. "We'll make soup in a covered pot. I'll go and get scraps of wood from the street."

"Perhaps the caretaker has a wood stove," Sheila suggested.

"The caretaker isn't there. I looked in his kitchen. The stove has gone too."

Sheila looked at him in amazement. "I don't know what I should do without you," she said truthfully. The boy flushed, and his face became more alive. He jumped down the staircase, three steps at one time.

Before he came back for the soup pot, Sheila had wiped the withered-looking cabbage—she couldn't waste water in washing it—and had cut it into strips. She did the same with the hunk of meat, averting her eyes at intervals. There was salt and some herbs in the little hand-painted jars on the kitchen dresser. She sprinkled them liberally into the water covering the meat and the cabbage, and handed the tightly lidded pot to the waiting boy. The dog, watching all these preparations with instinctive pleasure, looked apologetically over his shoulder as he trotted after the boy and the pot of food. "I'm not deserting you," he seemed to say, "I'm just guarding this pot, you understand."

From the courtyard, she heard voices. The fire was burning brightly in its three-sided nest of stones. The boy had found a piece of iron grille, a pretty thing with a twisting pattern of flowers and vine, and had placed it across the top of the stones. "There's room for other pots, too," she heard him say proudly, and saw some women in once smart clothes hurry away to carry out his suggestion. "Go and find more wood," the boy was saying to the children who hung round to watch the flames. They obeyed him with excited whoops.

But they all must live here, she thought in surprise. And then she smiled at herself. Of course they did. It was like the last night on a stormy sea voyage: people whose existence you never had suspected suddenly appeared out of their cabins, and the whole ship became amazingly inhabited.

The alarm clock rang. Sheila after cleaning the rooms had made a determined attempt to clean her dress and her shoes. She had discarded the shreds of silk which had once been stockings. She had wiped her face and combed her hair and even thought of powder and lipstick. She felt much better. Now she stopped admiring her handiwork and rushed through to the living room to silence the alarm.

Stevens and Schlott hadn't moved. Four hours. Did Stevens

really mean four hours? Yet Mr. Olszak's meeting was at three, and the time was almost one o'clock now.

Sheila shook Steve's shoulder. "Breakfast is ready," she said. It took some time and perseverance, but at last he opened his eyes and sat up stiffly on the floor.

"Breakfast?" he said. "That's no way to wake a man when he knows there isn't any." His temper was as bad as the taste in his mouth. He reached into his pocket for a cigarette. The pack was crumpled and empty. He threw it angrily at the opposite wall.

Sheila picked up the clock and pointed to the hour. "The meeting is at three," she said. The second time, he understood.

"All right, all right," he said irritably.

"Why don't you wash and shave? You'll feel better with that beard off."

He looked at the neat table in surprise. "What's happened to the bottles?"

Sheila pointed to their orderly row on top of the bookcase. "Drinking water," she explained. "And I found some clean towels and soap in Madame Knast's room. I think you'd better wash in here: something has gone wrong with the bathroom —it's a frightful mess."

He still looked surprised, but he didn't say anything. He began morosely to shave and wash.

"Who the hell is this?" he asked suddenly and stared at the doorway. Sheila, folding the blanket into a neat bulk, looked up to see the boy standing hesitatingly in the hall. The dog ran into the room, and jumped up and down excitedly with short sharp barks.

"Oh shut up!" Stevens said. Schlott sat up on the couch and frowned heavily.

The boy carried the pot into the kitchen, and then, watching Steve's lathered face uncertainly, backed slowly towards the front door.

He thinks we don't want him, he thinks I don't need him any longer, Sheila guessed. She ran through the hall and caught the boy by his sleeve and pulled him back into the room. He came slowly, willingly, and yet unwillingly.

"What's wrong with him?" Stevens asked. In Polish, he said, "Come in, come in. What's your name?"

"Casimir."

"Well, come in, Casimir."

"He's been our friend," Sheila said in Polish. Her arm kept a tight grip on the boy. "He got us this water, and food, and made a fire, and cooked the food. Please come in, Casimir. I am Sheila. That man is Steve. That man is Gustav, and our friend Bill is sleeping next door. Will you help me to put the soup in the bowls and we shall all eat together?"

The boy followed her silently into the kitchen. The dog begged for food, standing erect in its eagerness. From the living room came Schlott's voice chanting "Food! Food! Food!"

"This is Steve's house," Sheila explained carefully to the silent boy. "He has given us shelter. We had no place to go."

"You are refugees, too?" the boy asked with unexpected interest. Sheila felt suddenly happy as she watched the round face with its short nose and anxious blue eyes: she had said the right thing, thank God. She smothered a question about his home and people and said, simply, "Yes."

The boy's confidence returned. He was no longer an intruder. He was one of them.

"Here's some soup for the dog. You give it to him, and then he will be your dog."

"Whose dog is he?"

"He is a refugee, too, like all of us."

The meal wasn't large, but it was enough for them after the little they had eaten in the last few days. Everything was finished, down to the last shred of stringy and now colorless meat, to the last strand of tasteless cabbage. The dog came round to them, each in turn, to wag its tail and jab a cold nose against their ankles.

"He's saying thank you," the boy said delightedly. And then the delight faded, and he rose clumsily to his feet. "Thank you, too." He bowed jerkily, bent down to pat the dog's head, and started towards the door.

"Quick, Steve, ask him to stay here. Quick," Sheila said in English.

"What about his own home?" said Schlott. "If he has people, they will be worried."

"If he has people," Sheila said quietly.

"But we may have to leave here," Steve said. "What then?"

"We can cross that bridge when we come to it."

The boy had halted at the door. His movements were very slow. "Go back," he was saying to the dog which had followed him. "Go back." There was a sudden lost look on the boy's face.

"Why are you leaving us? We would like you to stay here," Steve said. "Would you like to stay here?"

The boy nodded and came slowly back into room. He watched them anxiously.

Schlott rose and thumped him on the back. "You're our food-scout, Casimir. We need you."

"And look how happy the dog is," Sheila said quietly.

The boy nodded, and sat cross-legged on the floor. He began to play with the dog.

Steve looked at his watch and then at Sheila. She rose obediently.

"Where are you two going?" Bill asked rashly.

"Out," Stevens said. Schlott and the dark-haired American exchanged amused glances.

"We'll make a tour of inspection of the bridge," Bill said to Schlott. He paused as if thinking of the two men who had crossed it yesterday. He went on with mock light-heartedness which deceived no one. "It will be good to walk along the streets without having to dodge into a doorway every two minutes."

"What about the boy and the dog?" Schlott asked. "A family is a serious matter. You have got to think about them."

Sheila said to the boy, "We must go out now. Would you look after the dog? I'll give you a small piece of soap and a comb. Wash him in the river, or in a shell hole. And if you can find some more food, we will have soup again tonight. Tell the children in the courtyard to keep that fire burning. Will you do that?"

"Your Polish is improving," Steve said, "but let the poor kid rest. He needs it."

"Yes, but not alone, by himself. He can rest tonight when we are all together. Now he has got to do things, to feel that he *is* needed here."

The men looked at her strangely, and then nodded their agreement.

In the street, Stevens took Sheila's arm. They walked northwards to the center of the city. They walked in silence. The ruin and destruction around them were too eloquent. Past them moved white faces, sad, sorrowful, sick. Warsaw was not only written but carved upon their hearts.


# CHAPTER XVII

## The Meeting


THE PORTER'S HOUSE was empty. It looked as if it had been unoccupied since the night that Elzbieta and Sheila had been taken from it. The garden was in ruins. The remains of the antiaircraft emplacement looked like a half-finished grave. Across from the porter's gate, there was now another entrance to the courtyard. A gaping hole had been driven in the middle of that side of the apartment house, leaving a moraine of stones and smashed household belongings spreading towards the garden. Through the neatly sliced gap, with its remnants of flowered wallpapers and tilted picture-frames still clinging to its exposed walls, could be seen the black, burned walls of a church. Fire had seared the top floor of Korytowski's side of the house, but his apartment was still there. Like the others which still gave shelter to their owners, its windows were neatly covered with bright-colored cardboard. Their brightness was like the smile on a dead man's face.

Sheila and Stevens climbed the stairs carefully. There was a tilt towards the well of the staircase, and the railings shook loosely when touched. The door's framework had a lopsided look. The door itself had separated from its hinges and was propped shut. As their footsteps stumbled over the fallen plaster, the door was lifted open. Two men looked at them, two men in stained and ragged uniforms with guns at their belts.

"Get the old man," said one of the guards. The other left him holding up the door and watching the newcomers carefully. Sheila stared back. Even Stevens looked as if he hadn't quite expected this. Mr. Olszak's invitation had scarcely prepared them for such a welcome. From the living room came the murmur of many voices. Sheila quickened with excitement. The deathlike acceptance of the ruined buildings had gone. Here was challenge and defiance. Here was hope.

Korytowski, with a red scar taking the place of the bandage across his brow, led them through the hall into the living room. He was excited, too, for he only smiled and didn't speak when he saw them. The large room was a warm mass of dark shapes. The only light came from a candlestick on Korytowski's desk, so that those who leaned against the walls of the bookcases stood in the shadows. Afterwards, Sheila wondered if the concealing darkness was intentional rather than economical. There were some women in the room. They sat on the few chairs. The men sat on the floor or stood beside the bookcases. All looked towards the desk, each with his own attitude of attention, as Olszak rose to speak. Above the candle's broad flame, the lines on his face were etched more deeply, the eyes were more sunken.

An officer, his torn coat draped round his shoulders, placed a chair beside Sheila. She looked up to thank him as she sat down. Even in the twilight of this room, she saw his face had grown gaunt and white. There was a loose lock of hair which fell over his brow. His mouth held no smile now, and the laughter had gone from his eyes. For a long moment they looked at each other. Then as silently as he could, he had left her, and once more was leaning against a bookcase. Adam

Wisniewski. She remembered the warm evening sun as she had leaned out of a bedroom window, the black horse rearing in front of four white pillars, the cavalry captain who had looked up towards her and saluted as he dismounted. She remembered a dinner table, and mocking brown eyes which had watched her as she had pretended to talk to Andrew. Adam Wisniewski. She forced herself free from her thoughts. Like Steve standing so silently behind her chair, like Wisniewski leaning with his tired shoulders against the bookcase, like the group of three workmen sitting at her feet, like the two young students beside her, like the priest, the soldiers, the women who might have been schoolteachers or secretaries or housewives, the men who looked like substantial burghers, the men who looked like skilled craftsmen, she set herself to listen.

". . . our last free day. Tomorrow the enemy may come. We have this day, by the grace of God. That is why I have called you together. Some of us have met before, some have only been recruited to our ranks in the last few weeks, some have been chosen to join us in the last few days to fill the gaps in our ranks caused by enemy action. Our purpose is one, whoever we are, whatever we have been. We fight on. Poland will not die, while we still live.

"We meet here together for the first and last time. We have renounced our names. We have no families, no loyalties except one alone—our country. I have asked you to come to this meeting, innocently in ones and twos, carefully, secretly, not so much as heads of the departments of our organization, but rather that you each may learn that you are not alone. That feeling will be important to you in the months ahead. However heartsick and despairing you may be, you will take comfort from the fact that we are all part of each other. And neither torture nor the threat of a painful death will allow us to betray what we know, for one word wrung out of our lips will mean not only the end of our own department but the end perhaps of all the other forms of our resistance. Each of us will remember we are dependent on each other. Without each other, organized resistance is lost.

"The time is shorter than even the most realistic of us had feared. Before the enemy installs his occupation forces, you must have your chief men and women in their places, ready to organize and function. For safety, I have urged you to choose two deputies unknown to each other, who in turn choose two deputies who do not know each other. And so on—until we have a small army of patriots with the arms and the grip of an octopus. First, organize. Second, gather your strength slowly. Third, test your strength before you use it fully. For there is no hurry: the more thoroughly

organized, the stronger and surer we are, and the greater
will be our ultimate success. The war will be long, unless our
allies betray us by making a peace with the Nazis. And I have
no fear of that. As long as we have one friend fighting outside, we can hope.

"In preparing for this new German tyranny, those of us
who experienced the last . . ."

Korytowski was beside Stevens, saying something in a low
voice. Stevens nodded. Korytowski bent down to repeat his
words in Sheila's ear. "Olszak wants you both to memorize
all the details. That's why you are here. Memorize the details,
forget the voice and faces." Sheila, wide-eyed, nodded in
turn.

Olszak's quiet, yet strangely moving, voice was saying
". . . planned this organization to be able to attack the methods
of occupation we knew then. For the Germans always repeat
themselves. We must also expect additional miseries due to
the Nazi refinements on Prussianism. I have studied their
methods in Czechoslovakia and I have planned accordingly.
But the organization is not static. We may have to add further departments to take care of any Nazi inventions which
we have failed to visualize, remembering that when you are
under the Nazis life is always worse than the worst you had
imagined. Your monthly reports go either to our chief in
Warsaw who is Number One, or to Number Three in Cracow,
Number Five in Lodz, Number Seven in Lublin. That depends in which district you work from. Reports from your
deputies are sent directly to you; their deputies furnish them
with reports. By this system of steps and stairs we shall safeguard our work.

"Now, we shall review our departments. Some of us may
work closely together, such as radio and press. But remember
that all information which you yourselves cannot use must be
forwarded either to me, or to Number Three, Five or Seven.
We shall send it to the departments that can use it. We are
together. However different our departments, we are one.
That I cannot emphasize too strongly."

Olszak paused. The men and women were motionless.
Stevens' arm was tense on the back of the chair. Korytowski
beside them whispered, "Now, forget nothing."

Olszak was speaking again. "Our first department has been
given the name of Number Ten. Number Ten, are you
here?"

"Here," a voice said quietly. One of the watchful men
straightened his back. The thin, anxious face waited ex-
pectantly.

"Department Ten: editing of news. You have your initial newspapers planned and located, your editors chosen and their staffs selected?"

"Yes."

"Department Eleven: printing of news."

"Here." A broad-shouldered artisan raised his hand.

"You have the nucleus of a printing press gathered together and hidden, as we arranged? You have contacted trustworthy presses for secret help?"

"All set."

"Department Twelve: distribution of newspapers."

A young woman's voice said, "All arranged as you advised. All we need are the papers."

"Good. Departments Ten, Eleven, Twelve will work as a unit. Make your final arrangements today."

"All made," said the quiet voice of Number Ten. The other two echoed him.

"Number Ten will also work closely with our next department, Number Thirteen: radio."

A tall, thin man with a bandaged shoulder said, "Here. Transmitters and receivers installed in key points. Hundreds of radio parts being hidden for future use. Reliable men are in charge. Subdepartments for sending and receiving have been formed. A special group for code messages is already at work. A network of six stations encircling our central station will be in contact not only with each other and the central station, but with our allies in the outside world. Smaller stations will form their networks round each of these six stations. Thus, we will maintain contact between the various districts of Poland, and between Poland and our allies. The plan should be working smoothly and fully by the end of a year."

"Excellent. Now we come to three departments working closely together. First, Number Fourteen: communication."

"Here," a businesslike voice answered. "Routes are being planned for the escape out of Poland of those in political danger. Contacts outside Poland are being established for two initial underground railways."

"Department Fifteen: papers and passports."

"Here," a dark-haired man said. Sheila stared at him. He reminded her of someone. "Our chosen men are ready, but we must wait for the German issue of permits and passports before we can copy them." The voice was familiar; an Aleksander voice. Stefan . . . this man was like Stefan. Sheila strained to see him better. Was this Stanislaw, the diplomat? His tweed suit, well-tailored, was now stained and torn. There was a bandage at his neck. He still wore the armband of the irregular soldier. Then Olszak's voice caught her attention again.

"Department Sixteen: transit in Poland from one district to another."

"Contacts established before outbreak of war. Main routes already planned. We found no lack of volunteers. The people are willing. But like Number Fifteen here, we must wait to see how the Szwaby orders us about. We're ready for them." This time, the speaker was one of the workmen in blue dungarees who sat near Sheila. He had the alert face of a man who has been accustomed to secret political planning. There was confidence in his voice and in his quick eyes.

"Good. All of us will need the help of Number Sixteen."

The man grinned and rubbed his nose self-consciously. "We'll take care of you," he said. The others stirred restlessly as if they had relaxed into a grim smile for a moment.

"Our next seven departments might be put under one head, that of sabotage. But they are each so important in themselves that we have subdivided them and made them autonomous. Department Number Seventeen: railways."

"Here," a man, with a greasy leather cap worn at an angle, spoke up. "I've got my first batch of men all chosen. But we'll have to wait until the Szwaby build the railways again before we can blow them up." The group of workmen round him grinned, and then waited tensely to give their answers in turn. Two soldiers straightened their backs and held themselves ready.

"Department Eighteen: power stations."

"Here." That man might be an engineer. White collar, roughened hands.

"Number Nineteen: fuel dumps."

"Here," said a workman with the armband of the irregular soldier.

"Number Twenty: ammunition dumps."

"Here," one of the soldiers answered.

"Number Twenty-one: bridges, tunnels, canals."

"Here." This time it was a neatly dressed man who had lifted his right arm. A construction engineer, a draughtsman, a builder? Sheila couldn't guess. In past life the man had been successful. You could tell that at least from his voice.

"Twenty-two: troop trains, shipment of arms and military supplies."

"Here," the second soldier said. He was a countryman. He seemed restless in this warm room.

"Number Twenty-three: factories."

"Here." The man carried the responsibility and pride of a workman who had risen to the position of foreman through his own efforts.

"These seven departments are waiting only to see what the Germans offer them." The sabotage group nodded, and a variety of phrases to signify agreement formed a sudden chorus. Even Olszak's face relaxed for one moment.

Then he said, very crisply, very evenly, "Number Twenty-four: assassination."

Sheila took a deep breath, but the serious-faced student who answered "Here!" was as calm as Mr. Olszak had been. "We, too, wait for what the Germans have to offer us. Weapons are being hidden, men are being chosen. At present, we intend to avoid indiscriminate assassination and reprisals. A few well-chosen key Nazis will be worth more than a thousand soldiers."

"Number Twenty-five: intimidation by anonymous messages, warnings, signs on walls and public places."

"Here." This time it was a woman, perhaps a schoolteacher, middle-aged, placid, resolute.

"Number Twenty-six: whispering campaign to affect the German soldiers' morale."

"Here!" another woman said. "We are ready for both the men and the officers." She was well-dressed, with just too much care spent on her clothes and face. Her eyes were hard, her red lips smiled as if she were already welcoming the unwelcome customers.

"Number Twenty-seven: direction of citizens who are faced with deportation to Germany for forced labor."

"Here," a professional man said. He might be a doctor or a lawyer. "Those we can contact before they are seized will have their orders."

"Hope you don't have to give them to me," one of the workmen said pointedly. The men around him again smiled grimly.

"Number Twenty-eight: maintaining the morale of the Polish population. Counteraction against the probable introduction of drugs; of cheap, crude liquor; of pornographic books and entertainment; of excessive gambling; with the purpose to demoralize our people."

"Here," the priest's deep voice answered.

"Good. These last departments, dealing with morale— either attack on that of the Germans or defense of our own —cannot be fully envisaged until we see how the Germans use their power. But your men and women are ready?"

There was a solemn chorus of assent.

"Now we come to counterespionage. Number Twenty-nine. That representative cannot be with us today. But I know him well. You can trust him, as I do, to achieve his purpose." Sheila wondered if Twenty-nine were Olszak himself. Or was it Hofmeyer?

"Closely allied to counterespionage is Number Thirty, who is responsible for contact with our allies in the world outside. Both will naturally work in close contact with Number Thirteen. Department Number Thirty?"

"Here. All initial contacts prepared." This time there was no doubt. The quiet voice was Hofmeyer's. Sheila looked in his direction, but he had chosen an especially dark shadow. No one, not even one of his comrades, was going to be able to identify Mr. Hofmeyer.

"Now we come to one department which cannot be organized by the same method of deputies and sub-deputies as the others. For in this department of guerrilla warfare, the leader works with a staff of specially chosen officers, and all must fight along with the men they recruit. The essence of successful warfare of this nature is participation and personal direction. Number Thirty-one."

"Here," Captain Wisniewski replied. All the voices had been eager. His was hard and angry as well.

"Yours will be a long task," Olszak continued. "Such warfare can only be carried on after bases have been established, after ammunition and supplies have been collected and hidden, after your men have gathered in sufficient strength and have been trained to know their terrain and to work together."

"We haven't had much time to prepare."

The listeners saw a smile on Olszak's thin lips.

"Naturally," he agreed.

The defensive tone left Wisniewski's voice. "But we have made a beginning. Under the terms of capitulation, all officers are to become prisoners. Tonight, those whom we have chosen will leave the city and make their way through the German lines. Our first base has been selected. We shall proceed there. Give us six months to collect and take what we need, to gather recruits and train them in this way of fighting, and we can start preparing our campaign. At the end of a year, we should be strong enough for co-ordinated attacks, both in the countryside and in city streets. It will be one of our jobs to find which men are suitable for those different types of resistance."

"Good," Olszak said. "You will need the co-operation of Numbers Fifteen, Sixteen, Twenty, and Twenty-two. See them before you leave Warsaw."

Adam Wisniewski nodded. The men of these departments were already making their way to where he stood.

"Our last department is that of education. Number Thirty-two: the organizing of secret Polish schools. We have no reason to hope that our children will be allowed to learn anything except German ideas. During the last German tyranny, our schools and our universities were abolished and our language was banned. Then, for one hundred and fifty years, we depended chiefly on the mothers to teach their children. And they did it nobly in spite of imprisonment and punishment, for otherwise we Poles would have become either pseudo-Germans or one mass of illiterates. Today, we are organizing secret schools to be taught by trained teachers. If that is impossible in some locations, then our schoolteachers will secretly help and advise the mothers. Number Thirty-two is still in hospital, I believe. He will be discharged tomorrow. He is sure of full support from his fellow teachers."

Mr. Olszak paused and looked round the silent faces. "That," he said, "is our programme. We may add to it, or alter its direction, as the need arises. Any questions, or suggestions?"

The red-faced soldier cleared his throat. "What about the farmers? The peasants should not be left out of this. They've got to be united secretly."

"The farmers have their Peasants' Party," Olszak reminded him. "And so far no political opposition has ever managed to crush it. And many of our departments will contact the country people. We need their help in guerrilla warfare, for instance. They can smuggle food and horses to us. They can give us shelter and clothing. We haven't forgotten the peasants. We depend on them, now."

The soldier nodded, as if satisfied. Others rose to ask their questions. Twice, Olszak noted down before him some new idea, but the question about religious persecution was referred to the Church. "Our priests have always defended us," he said. "The Church of Christ will know how to save."

The problem of safe hiding places for those in sudden danger, of houses where men wounded in this new struggle could be secretly nursed back to health, was answered by Department Number Sixteen. "We'll take care of you," Number Sixteen said once more.

"One question has not been asked," Olszak said finally. "And that is the question of reprisals taken by the Germans on civilians for acts which our agents will commit in line of duty. If the Germans follow their practices of 1914 to 1916 in Belgium, or of 1916 to 1918 in Poland, we can expect harsh treatment for the innocent. But we must remember that every man, woman or child who is murdered by the Germans in reprisal falls as a soldier on a battlefield. We ourselves face death. We have all accepted that constant threat. If we ask no quarter for ourselves in the secret battle which we fight, then no other Pole will hesitate to pay the price we ourselves are willing to pay. For unless each of us is willing to die, we can never win. The choice is this: either we let our purpose be conquered by the blackmail of reprisals, and then we are conquered too; or we harden our will and our hearts, knowing that without sacrifice, the Germans would have a comfortable victory, and Poland would be forever dead."

"Never, never!" the editor exclaimed with rising emotion. Others joined his cry: "No, never, never!" Olszak silenced the threatened shout with hands that commanded obedience. "Quietly, quietly. We must not be heard. Quietly." And then his voice strengthened. "Poland lives, for Poland fights on," he said. He sat down abruptly, shading his eyes with his hands.

The priest rose. The room's sudden silence was broken by the rustle of kneeling men and women. Their voices repeated a short oath of allegiance, and their heads were bent to the priest's brief prayer. It had the intensity, the finality of a prayer before battle. ". . . God, in whom we trust," the priest ended, and his arms fell slowly to his side, and the men and women rose to their feet.

Stevens stood up quickly and helped Sheila to rise. He avoided her eyes and pretended to be absorbed in the people around him. Korytowski was beside them again.

"You understood everything? You will remember?" he asked Stevens anxiously, and the American nodded. Korytowski noted the puzzled look on Stevens' face. "Olszak will explain," he said. "We are to wait for him next door. The others will take some time to leave. They cannot walk out of here in a body, you know." He turned towards the door, obviously intending that Sheila and Stevens should follow him. They did so unwillingly: they would have preferred to stay in the room and watch these people. But perhaps Olszak wanted them out of the room for that very reason. Sheila's last glance round the room ended with Adam Wisniewski. He was still leaning against the bookcase, his officer's long coat thrown cloakwise round his shoulders. His face was that of a man who had been savagely wounded, of a man who was so exhausted emotionally that all he could do was to stand unmoving, his face a determined mask, his eyes fixed in a brooding stare on the opposite wall. Number Sixteen was talking earnestly. Wisniewski answered. Number Sixteen nodded as if pleased. Wisniewski was talking again. Sheila suddenly realized that the mask was there to hide his wounds, that there was a depth to this man which she had never suspected. But then, she thought, she had never given him a chance to prove what he was or what he wasn't. And it was too late now. They would never meet again. The time was out of joint.

For one moment, his eyes looked directly at the doorway and rested on her. She felt the look rather than saw it. Russell Stevens pulled impatiently at her sleeve. He too was watching Wisniewski.

"Come on," Stevens said, "we are supposed to be in the next room." He looked at her in that quick, clever way of his. He stood aside to let her pass into the hall.

Adam Wisniewski had stopped talking, stopped listening. The men beside him saw him take a step towards the door. One of them repeated his question quickly. "You said you would need someone in the villages surrounding your camp to be responsible for guiding your recruits. In each village? Or in a key village, Captain?"

Wisniewski halted. She had gone, and the American was following her.

The men around him were waiting for his reply. He turned his back to the door. "In each village," he said. "We'll need help from every village in the district, not just from one or two." Grimly, he forced his whole attention on the man's answer. If there had been no time for personal feelings in the last four weeks, there was even less now.

In the hall, Korytowski waited impatiently for Sheila and Stevens. "This way," he was saying, "this way," as he led them to the guest room. Behind them was that low, busy murmur of voices. The two soldiers on guard leaned against the twisted door.


## CHAPTER XVIII

### Anna Braun


SHEILA SAT ON one of the narrow beds. Korytowski sat on the hard spindle-legged chair. Stevens paced the room.

"How long will it take the others to leave?" Sheila asked, if only to break the silence and interrupt her own thoughts. This was the second time they had met; this was the second time they hadn't spoken. Then it had been people, now it was events which had kept them apart. It wasn't likely that they would ever meet again. But somehow, she wished he had spoken.

"Long enough," Korytowski answered. "They must leave singly or in groups of two or three."

"Who are the guards at the door?"

"Two of Wisniewski's men."

Stevens stopped his pacing. "How long has he been with this outfit?" he asked.

"Who? Wisniewski? Since yesterday. Until then, he had thought it possible to break through the German lines. He led two attempts this week. But yesterday he saw that capitulation was inevitable, and so he agreed to Olszak's original proposal, and will fight on this way."

"Why do you look like that?" Sheila asked Stevens.

"Like what?" he countered, with pretended obtuseness.

"So—so contemptuous."

"All I wanted to know," the American said with emphasized patience, "was how long the brave captain has been associating with workmen and businessmen and schoolteachers and newspapermen. That surprised me, I admit. I thought he only knew beautiful women and handsome horses."

Sheila was angrier than Korytowski, who repressed a smile. "Really, Steve," she began indignantly. And then, rather weakly, "He's Andrew's friend."

"Yes. That attraction of opposites, I guess."

"Not so very much opposites," Korytowski said mildly. "And he has something in common with you too, Steve. Only, you've been educated under different systems, and the result seems different on the surface." He looked at Stevens' heavy frown. "It's strange," he went on, "I should have thought the violent energy which has characterized Adam Wisniewski's exceedingly colorful life would have appealed to an American. That is what made America, after all. He is so very much—alive. He's a good soldier, a magnificent horseman, a fine shot, an excellent hunter. The ladies admire his conversation." Stevens muttered something under his breath which Korytowski tactfully ignored, although he smiled. He continued, "I must confess that there have been moments in my own orderly existence when I have admired, and even envied, Captain Wisniewski's ability to enjoy life."

"He's a damn fascist," Stevens said. "He's not on your side, nor on mine. What about that students' riot two years ago? In the Jewish quarter? Wisniewski was passing with some friends. He didn't stop them, did he?"

"In all fairness to Wisniewski, you should remember he didn't begin the riot, and he didn't even join it. He had great contempt for the 'bourgeois fascists,' as he called the type of student who began that riot. His contribution to the evening began by snatching a policeman's helmet. True, he might have tried to stop the riot instead of taking the opportunity for some fun at the expense of the law. I agree with you there. And yet, I don't suppose either you or I could have stopped that riot, or even wanted to act as policemen, if we had been having an evening's celebration such as Wisniewski and his friends had had."

"What happened to the policeman's helmet?" Sheila asked.

"It was found floating down the Vistula with four others which Wisniewski managed to collect before his evening was over." Korytowski smiled. "As far as I can remember, they had paper sails rigged in them."

The tension slackened much to Sheila's relief, but Stevens still didn't speak.

"I've been teaching young men for almost twenty years," Korytowski continued, "and there is one thing I've learned. If a large number of them get together and start looking for what is called 'fun,' they invariably end in trouble. The sense of power which the mass feeling provides is intoxicating; and, as in the case of that riot, the direction which that power takes depends on the merest chance. One man of ill will can affect others, and high spirits can be turned into blind violence. Tomorrow these young men may be ashamed, but at the moment they are intoxicated and their individual judgment is lost. Surely you have seen that happen in your own country, too?"

"Of course." Stevens was too polite. "I don't believe in pogroms, or in the men who don't stop them, that's all."

Korytowski was silent for a long moment. Then he said quietly, "Every country has its minorities, whether they are racial or religious or political. And minorities are always resented, sometimes with cause, sometimes without. The only difference in countries is that some raise the mob emotion against minorities into an official policy, and become totalitarian; others seek to educate their citizens against resentment and mob emotion. Their success in that depends on how long a space of peace has been granted to their countries' natural development."

Olszak entered briskly. "A short lecture on the dangers of Nazism, I see," he said, and looked at the cracked ceiling, the boarded window, the plaster and dust on the floor.

Korytowski smiled. Stevens' frown disappeared. "My fault," he said, "and now I feel like a heel. I wasn't attacking Poland, Professor."

"No?" Korytowski said gently, and Sheila laughed.

"Was I?" Stevens demanded indignantly.

Sheila said, "Just the foreigner's usual holier-than-thou. I know, Steve: I have had attacks of it myself. I suppose we mostly believe 'my country, right or wrong,' whether it's cooking recipes or social systems we are discussing. What we have been brought up with always seems more sensible than what is different."

"The foreigner visiting any country is a rarity if he

doesn't criticize and think 'At home, we had ... or did ...' "
Korytowski said.

Stevens watched Olszak's strange smile. "I got into this
through a very simple statement. I said, and I still say, that
Adam Wisniewski's out of place."

Sheila thought, perhaps I shouldn't have defended Adam.
Then Steve might have stopped harping on this subject. . . .
But she couldn't resist saying, partly to find out Olszak's
verdict, "A damned fascist." Steve looked at her angrily. By
her tone and face he saw she didn't believe him. Wisniewski
had watched her plenty in the meeting, and that last look
she had given him hadn't been particularly short or cold,
either. Damn Wisniewski. What was he doing here anyway?

"All right, then," Stevens said. "He *is* a damn fascist.
I said it before, and I'll keep on saying it."

Olszak watched him keenly, and then looked at Sheila. "I
am going to shock you both," he said with mock seriousness.
"I never pay much attention to a young man's politics, as
long as he doesn't specialize in cruelty or violence. He makes,
if there is any good in him, at least one major change before
he reaches the dangerous age, before his convictions harden.
What is more, I am in revolt against the recent fashion of
attaching so much weight to political ideology. For the last
fifty years, we have paid too much attention to political
differences, just as we used to pay too much attention to
religious differences. Nowadays the word Communist or
Fascist rouses the same emotions as Protestant and Catholic
once caused. If these religious factions can learn to live together by giving up all persecution and forms of torture, it
is quite possible that a future world will see many forms of
political ideology living and working side by side. We will
have that as soon as politics and politicians become adult.
If the Church has found that the Inquisition and St. Bar-
tholomew's Day are not necessary for maintaining its authority, politics too can achieve that perspective by giving up
concentration camps and murder. If Adam Wisniewski believed that one nation alone should be master of the world,
even if he believed that nation should be our own Poland, I
would fight him to the death. But his love of Poland only
means freedom for the Poles, freedom for everyone, to live
in their own houses, to till their own fields, to ride over their
own roads with no foreigner to interfere or command. He is
a nationalist, but not a fascist. For a fascist is one who
uses a political ideology to grab more power for his country, his Party, and of course for himself. He is identified
completely with his Party, and it in turn is identified with

the State. He can tolerate no differences of opinion for that very reason."

Mr. Olszak's voice had become grimly serious while he talked. As the Britisher and American remained silent, he went on, "Adam Wisniewski and I have disagreed in politics in the past. Yet he trusts me in our common fight. I would be a lesser man if I could not trust him. Our differences were merely ones of having and not having. In the past, he and his friends wanted to keep what they had. I and my friends wanted more than we had. On their side it was fear, on ours it was envy. That is how mean politics can be. But today, with German bombs and soldiers to level rich and poor homes, to make us one in suffering, our differences seem petty. Nothing matters now but the freedom we have all lost."

Neither Stevens nor Sheila spoke yet.

"When a conqueror lives in your cities, destroys, mutilates, kills, you will know then what I mean," Olszak said, and fell silent too.

Stevens kicked aside a piece of plaster. "I don't need that experience. I guess you're right. At least, you always sound as if you were right."

Olszak smiled, a strangely gentle smile. "With age men lose their hair, their teeth, their eyesight, their strength. Their only compensation is their experience. If they have lived without achieving that, then their lives have been quite useless." He turned to Sheila. "You understood all that was said at the meeting?"

"Yes. I've learned a lot of Polish in the last few weeks. I had to."

"Good." To Stevens he said, "You remember the meeting quite clearly?"

"Yes. I won't forget it.".

"Good. I have a job for you to do. The Germans will round up all foreigners when they arrive. Unless the neutral foreigners have established business here, the Germans will certainly send them out of the country. And they will see that they get safely out of the country. They don't want any extra witnesses here of their treatment of the Poles. I want a full report of that meeting to reach our friends in the outside world. The only way in which there would be no possibility of the Germans intercepting such a message would be if it traveled out of the country safely locked up in a neutral brain."

"Then I am not to stay here?" Stevens' face was a study in disappointment.

Olszak was pleased. He gripped the American's shoulder.

"You are the only neutral, so far, who is in our organization. This would be a major service which you would render us. Coded messages sent by radio would be too dangerous in this case: that is how important it is. And although the German will give you safe-conduct, there will be plenty of danger. You'll need to use your wits all the time. They'll have spies well disguised. I'll give you full instructions later. Meanwhile, don't forget what you saw and heard today."

"And after that?" Stevens was still disappointed.

"There will be another job for you to do . . . and then, another, and another. We work our good men very hard."

"And where will I be?"

"Wherever it does the Germans most harm."

Stevens smiled grimly. "All right," he said, "that suits me. But what about Sheila? She can't stay here pretending to be a Pole. She has only got to speak and the Germans will know at once she is a foreigner."

"We've thought of that." And we've made our plans, the voice implied. Mr. Olszak turned to Sheila. "I've heard from your uncle. He was not very pleased to hear that you were still in Warsaw. He thinks you are a nuisance to us."

"What did you reply?" Sheila asked. She wondered why she should feel so upset at the idea that she might have to leave Poland after all. There had been hours in the last few weeks when she had been miserably homesick. Now she knew she still wanted to stay. Madame Aleksander needed her: Madame Aleksander who once had so many children round her, who now had none.

"I waited to hear your answer before I replied."

Sheila brushed back the hair from her forehead. There were little beads of perspiration under the curls. "Have I been a nuisance?" she asked.

Olszak shook his head slowly.

"Then I shall stay. Madame Aleksander. . . ."

Olszak and Korytowski exchanged glances. Uncle Edward was smiling happily.

"I'm on the side of her uncle," Stevens said quickly. "She has already done her job here. She should leave. Or else, she'll spend the rest of the war in a concentration camp—if she's lucky." His voice was harsh.

"But Steve, I've lived through the bombardment and siege. The war may last only another year. Once the Siegfried Line is cracked there will be nothing to stop us reaching Berlin."

Steve tightened his lips. "What you need is a firm hand, my lady," he said.

Olszak said quietly, "Yes, she already has done more than

enough—if that phrase is valid in time of war. But remember, she won't have the neutral's prerogative to leave on a train, as you will have. She must go by underground. Until a safe route has been established, I do not want to risk sending her. She would be better waiting here. As I said, we have thought of that. We will give her a name and story that the Germans won't think of questioning. And she can go on living in your flat, Stevens. Madame Aleksander will join her there. It will all fit into the story we have prepared for the Germans. She will be as safe as anyone can be under the Germans. Safer than many."

Sheila avoided Steve's angry eyes. "What's my new name?" she asked quickly. The meeting had given her hope and courage. It only needed Mr. Olszak's latest suggestion to end completely the sense of frustration and uselessness of the last few days. Perhaps there were other things she could do, as well as look after Madame Aleksander. She looked at Olszak and saw he had half guessed her thoughts.

"Perhaps I could be of some use?" she suggested hesitatingly, without waiting for Olszak's answer.

Mr. Olszak only smiled. But she knew him, by this time. If he needed her help, he would make use of her.

He said, "You'll find Mr. Hofmeyer next door. From now on, you are under his advice and orders. He has your papers and life story all ready. He has enlarged considerably on the name of Anna Braun, which he first found for you in an embarrassing moment with the man Henryk. Stevens was right when he said you couldn't be disguised as a Polish girl, so we have kept your old story of being a German girl who adopted the identity of Sheila Matthews. If the Germans question you, refer them to Mr. Hofmeyer whose secretary you have now become. That and the police records of August 31 will be enough to keep you safe. Now, I shall give Stevens his instructions if you will have a talk with Mr. Hofmeyer. I may not see you again for quite some time. Meanwhile, good luck."

Sheila smiled wholeheartedly. He would never have taken all this trouble about me if he hadn't hoped to give me some job to do, she thought happily. She felt as if a very high compliment indeed had been paid her. As she closed the door carefully behind her, Olszak was saying, "Now about your Swedish friend . . . We find nothing against him. I think his best plan would be to . . ." How miserable, she thought, Mr. Olszak would be if there were no plans left to be invented. She was still smiling as she entered the large living room.

Mr. Hofmeyer was reading peacefully at the desk. The candle stub gave a deep yellow light which rounded out the lines on his face, softened its furrows. He removed his horn-rimmed glasses, stuffed them into the breast pocket of his neat, dark suit and came to meet her with his quick, light step. She seemed to be standing again in the music room at Korytów, listening to these footsteps in the hall. In the dining room, the Aleksanders and their friends sat round a table rich with food and wine and silver. It was little Teresa's first grown-up party. The children outside had played round the American's car. The gaily dressed women from the village had brought their songs and laughter and friendly curiosity to the windows of the big house. The evening sky was slate blue. There was the lingering warmth of a summer's day to carry the sweetness of flowers and trees into the softly lighted rooms.

It couldn't be only a month ago. It couldn't, Sheila thought, as she took Hofmeyer's outstretched hand. It wasn't possible so much could have happened in one month. But the boarded window, the dust gritting under her heels, the torn plaster, the guttering candle were there to prove the nightmare was a reality. There was no awakening, no escape from this dream.

Mr. Hofmeyer was speaking in English. Sheila knew by this time that it wasn't a foreign language to him: his hesitancy was due to the fact that he had used English so little in many years. To serve his country, this man had been willing to renounce it. Living with foreigners, Hofmeyer had become one of them. Even the square-shaped head with its bristling white hair, or the way he bowed with his heels together and made a little speech of welcome, was now quite un-English. She wondered if he were ever really happy, or was his happiness a sense of having accomplished a difficult task well?

"I am under your orders, Herr Hofmeyer," she said, and sat on the nearest chair.

"Yes, Fräulein Braun." He smiled as if to himself, and turned back to the papers he had been reading at the desk. "Here are the necessary documents. First of all, birth certificate. That gave us the greatest difficulty of all your papers: it had to be a blend of fact and fiction. We had to find a real man called Braun who lived in Munich and was killed in the last war. We found one called Ludwig Braun." Mr. Hofmeyer repeated the name slowly as if to emphasize it in her memory. He was to do that with all the names and dates he mentioned, quietly, insistently. Sheila found herself repeating the name to herself quite naturally.

Mr. Hofmeyer's clear voice went on, "Ludwig Braun had a wife Frieda, who married a year after his death and went to live in Cologne. She died two years ago. The Brauns did not have any children, so I have given you a birth certificate showing you were born six months after their marriage. Its date is the 15th May, 1916. For good middle-class reasons, your birth was kept secret from Frieda Braun's ultra-respectable family. She boarded you out temporarily with a retired governess. Before Mrs. Braun had found courage to reveal your existence to her family, her husband had been killed and she herself was thinking of a second marriage. Naturally she had less courage, then, to own you. But Mrs. Braun found, even after she was successfully married for a second time, that confession grows more difficult with postponement. So when Mrs. Braun, now Mrs. Mühlmann, went to live in Cologne, you were still living with the governess. She was a Miss Thelma Leigh who had retired in the city where she had spent thirty years and had become a naturalized German. That is actual fact, by the way. She is a friend of mine and now lives in Switzerland. She already has received instructions about the little girl whom she looked after in Munich. Her address there was Theresienstrasse, 25. You lived very quietly with her until you were sixteen. Miss Leigh tutored you, for she didn't want to send you to a State school and yet the money which Mrs. Braun, now Mrs. Mühlmann, sent her each quarter was insufficient to pay for a private school. In this way, you did not have school friends and grew up almost unknown in Munich. Like many governesses, Miss Leigh was a snob and wouldn't let you mix with the neighborhood children. Miss Leigh was your constant companion. That was your simple life until you were sixteen, and you followed her through museums and art galleries obediently."

Mr. Hofmeyer brought a small red book across to her. "Baedeker. He has a fine chapter on Munich. I understand that is the city you know best in Germany?"

Sheila nodded. She knew it well.

"Good. Then all you have to do is to refresh your memory. Don't be worried about that part of the story. Any girl who has been away from her native town for almost ten years is not photographically clear about its details. All you need to do is to memorize the streets round your old home and the chief shopping centers. Remember what you can of the English Park and the old Pinakothek Museum."

Sheila nodded again.

"Anna Braun left Munich when she was sixteen. That was in 1932, the year before the Nazis came to power. Miss Leigh wanted her to finish her education abroad, to learn languages, so that some day, when Miss Leigh was dead, Anna Braun could earn money in a ladylike manner. By this time your mother had stopped paying the small allowance to Miss Leigh, and the governess had informally adopted you. So Miss Leigh arranged for you to go to England, where she had been born and still had some relatives. You traveled third class, and spent a quiet year with a dull English family. Their name was Carson and they stayed just outside of London. You can pick any district you know. You were teaching their daughter Margaret to speak German in exchange for room and board. At the end of that year, when you were about to return to Munich, Miss Leigh had lost her last savings in the depression; she had to become a governess once again with a family in Switzerland, this time. You were offered a temporary position, well paid, as a governess in a London household. Your employer was a Mrs. Bowman of Eaton Square. As things grew more difficult in Europe, you thought you must stay in a secure position. Mrs. Bowman helped you become a foreign correspondent in a business firm which exported to Germany. For the sake of being able to continue your position in this business firm and for the sake of future promotion, you wanted to become a naturalized British subject. Your mother's selfishness had given you no pleasure in the name Braun, so you even chose an English name, Sheila Matthews. Your security was assured. You were highly thought of in your firm, whose name was Matheson, Walters and Crieff."

Hofmeyer ignored Sheila's upraised eyebrows. He pointed to a thin dark blue book and some papers on the desk. "There are the citizenship documents, the legal papers for your change of name, and your subsequent passport. They are excellent copies. You need have no fear about any suspicion rising from them."

Hofmeyer didn't wait for any questions. He went on, "You had, of course, been little interested in politics during all this period. You were much too intent on trying to fight for yourself in a world where you had neither influence nor money nor a recognized name. Then the AO—the *Auslands-Organisation*—approached you. As the AO has some ten million Germans throughout the world organized in all grades of treachery towards their adopted countries, you are perfectly safe in maintaining that you agreed eventually to help your Fatherland. I can testify to that. For when you were visiting Miss Leigh in Switzerland, in 1938, I was in Switzerland too. I met you, and through my connections with the AO working in Poland, I decided the form of your service in that organization. You returned to London, and we corresponded. You sent me several pieces of requested information which verified my opinion of your ability. Then in the winter of 1938-1939, you met Andrew Aleksander and had many enjoyable evenings together. You wrote me that he wanted you to visit his family. He thought you were English, of course, on account of your name, of your business connections in an old established British firm, and of your accent. Thanks to Miss Leigh's early teaching, you had an excellent English voice. This summer when I was searching for a reliable secretary to replace Margareta Koch, I decided that you must be brought to Warsaw. I ordered you to resurrect the Aleksander invitation, and you arrived here welcomed as an English girl. Everything went according to plan, except that a careless member of our AO here betrayed me and drove me into hiding. You were arrested, released pending further investigation, rearrested along with Elizbieta Dittmar, and escaped during an air raid. Since then, you have been waiting until I can open my business house here again, and then you will begin working with me. And that is the story of Anna Braun who became Sheila Matthews."

There was a pause.

"Now, let's begin at the beginning," Hofmeyer said with a smile.

Sheila felt herself grow tense as she strained to repeat the names and dates which she had tried to memorize. She was too anxious: she made a mistake, fumbled, halted, and bit her lip in annoyance at her own stupidity.

"Easy, now," Hofmeyer said. He prompted her carefully, insisting that she repeat the names after him, spelling them out slowly.

"Again," the quiet voice said, when she had finished her account.

Again she told him. This time, the names were becoming familiar, the dates and events seemed more plausible.

"Good," he said, and her confidence increased.

"If you could give me a piece of paper and a pencil, I could write down the German names. I'd remember them much better, then."

Hofmeyer raised one of his eyebrows, but he followed her suggestion, watching the look of concentration on her face as she wrote. The resemblance was so strong, he thought. Charles Matthews was dead, and yet he still lived, still shared in life through this girl.

"There!" she said, and watched him anxiously as he examined the sheet of paper.

"Good," he said once more. And then, as if to keep her from being too confident, he added, "There are two *n*'s in Mühlmann." He held the piece of paper to the candle's flame. "Well, that's about everything, Miss Matthews."

"But what work shall I do?" Sheila asked quickly. "I mean, the Germans will expect me to do more than typing, to justify all the trouble you took to get me into Warsaw."

"I have already informed the proper authorities that you are invaluable to them for counter-espionage, which is my own field. You are to maintain the name and character and friendships of Sheila Matthews, by German permission. They believe that you will be able to give them necessary information from time to time because of the trust which your Polish friends have put in you."

"But when I don't report to the Germans, when I don't give them information, won't they guess something is wrong then?"

"I shall credit you with some information, Fräulein Braun. We have to throw a sop every now and again, you know, to justify the money the Germans pay us. Now, here are your papers. Your birth certificate, your naturalization papers, your deed of name, your passport with its visit to Switzerland correctly dated, and your identification card in the *Auslands-Organisation*. Keep these safe."

He watched her open her handbag, and transfer her powder box, cigarette case and comb into her pocket to make room for the papers.

"You may as well give me your real passport," he said. "It has too many summer holidays stamped on its pages which would not at all agree with our story.

Sheila removed the thin, dark blue book and held it in her hand thoughtfully. "I don't know why," she said, "but I don't like giving it up. Silly, isn't it?"

"I assure you it must be destroyed."

His quiet voice prompted her. She placed it in his outstretched hand.

"Now, Fräulein Braun, tell me the story of your life."

Sheila looked startled, but Mr. Hofmeyer was waiting. She began, "Born in Munich, May 1916. Fifteenth May, 1916. Parents Ludwig and Frieda Braun, later Mühlmann of Cologne..." When she ended, he nodded sympathetically.

"The only slips were with the English names, strangely enough. Repeat it all, once more."

This time he said, "Good. Don't worry about how you spent your London years. Now that the war is on, the Germans don't have the same facilities for inquiries there. But they have no doubt checked on Miss Leigh in Switzerland.

However, I have sent her full explanations. Even photographs which she can produce of Anna aged two, Anna aged six, and Anna aged twelve. Miss Leigh's brown hair is almost white now, by the way. And she stoops slightly when she walks. That's how you saw her last, in 1938. And you need not worry either about the house where you were brought up. We placed it especially in a row of houses which has since been torn down to make way for Party offices and barracks."

Sheila's eyes widened. She had better stop being surprised. She had better concentrate. There were questions she wanted to ask, questions which even now were slipping away from her just because she wanted to ask them so much.

"What if I am questioned?"

"Both the Gestapo and the AO have their lists of secret German agents. They will not question you. If you get into any difficulty with the military, all you do is show them that AO card, and refer them to me. You may never have to face questions on the story I have just given you. But to keep it alive in your memory I suggest that you send yourself to sleep each night by repeating your life story to yourself."

"I shall end by believing I *was* born in Munich."

"Good." Hofmeyer smiled encouragingly. "Frankly, I don't expect you to meet any complications. You are responsible only to me. You are a secretary on my staff. You were chosen for your assured loyalty to Germany and your special qualifications. But actually you will do no spying. I will give you only routine work to do. You see, I intend to keep you alive. Your uncle would never forgive me if I didn't."

Sheila's sense of elation faded. "You mean . . . ?" she began incredulously.

"I mean that you will leave Poland safely when the time is suitable."

She flushed with annoyance. "Mr. Olszak didn't lead me to expect this."

"Mr. Olszak docsn't know your uncle personally."

"But he knew my father."

Hofmeyer came over to her and took her hands in his. Sheila, looking at the kindly face with its worried eyes, felt her emotions smooth out. "So did I," Mr. Hofmeyer said.

There was a pause. "You wish I had left Warsaw before the war began," Sheila said with a very small smile.

"Well, I can imagine other things I might have been doing in the last week, instead of worrying about Anna Braun."

Sheila looked down at the guidebook which lay on her

lap. She slipped it into the remaining free pocket of her coat as she rose to her feet.

Mr. Hofmeyer said, "Read your Baedeker, remember your catechism, and if you can find a typewriter, practise some fingering. You are supposed to be a secretary, you know."

Sheila smiled wryly. *"Ja, Herr Hofmeyer,"* she said.

He was looking at her almost sadly. It is so easy to disappoint the young, he was thinking; they expect so much. He followed her with his light step to the doorway into the hall. "One last order," he said. "Positively no bright ideas, positively no heroic gestures."

Sheila tried to smile. But that was the unkindest cut of all.

In the guest room, there were only Professor Korytowski and Stevens. Olszak had gone, and Sheila felt cheated of a last court of appeal. And yet, on second thoughts, perhaps it was just as well that she had been cheated. Hofmeyer was her boss, now, and there was nothing else to do but accept his plan of strict nonintervention and say nothing. Mr. Hofmeyer was the serious professional and he wasn't going to trust any amateur performance. And that was that.

She sat on the bed. Korytowski sat on the hard, spindle-legged chair. Stevens paced the room. An hour ago she had sat here like this and watched the other two as they waited for Olszak. Then she had been confidently Sheila Matthews; now she was this strange Anna Braun, so strange and yet somehow so incredibly real. The blend of fact and fiction had been convincingly measured. Mr. Hofmeyer had taken an actual couple, who had been childless. He had given them a daughter, and reasons for her life with Miss Leigh. Miss Leigh had been an actual person, too, and she was a friend of Hofmeyer's obviously willing to back the Anna Braun legend. Miss Leigh was probably in Mr. Hofmeyer's own line of "business." And all the rest had been invented, except of course the firm of Matheson, Walters, and Crieff. No doubt, by this time, Uncle Matthews had been informed of Anna Braun and had given instructions to his firm that any innocent questions from strangers about a Sheila Matthews, a foreign correspondent, would be satisfactorily answered. She smiled suddenly, partly in admiration of Mr. Hofmeyer's powers of invention, partly because she now felt confident. It was a pleasant feeling, for a change.

"But what are you going to do?" Stevens was asking Korytowski.

"I'll stay here. Why shouldn't I? I have no fine paintings or *objets d'art* to attract German collectors. Even my books wouldn't be of any value to their libraries, and they wouldn't find my manuscript interesting. It is quite unpolitical. Besides, my students know they can find me here, and some of them may need my help. Those I know well, I can direct to Jan Rcska."

"Reska? Here in Warsaw?" Sheila asked in surprise.

"In hospital. He escaped from the Russians and came back through the German lines to Warsaw. He is in charge of Department Number Thirty-two, by the way. I recommended him; I know his worth. He will be able to leave the hospital tomorrow."

"I suppose he made his way back to Warsaw because he knew Barbara would be here," Sheila said slowly. "Does he know? About Barbara?"

"Yes."

"Does Madame Aleksander know?"

"Yes."

There was silence. Stevens stopped his nervous pacing.

"How is she?" Sheila asked at last.

"She is still working at the hospital, but she will be leaving in a day or two. She's— Well, I think it would be a very good thing if Sheila would look after her for some time. She needs someone like you, Sheila; someone who is young enough to make Teresa think *she* is needed. She always gathers strength if she thinks someone needs her." Korytowski smiled half sadly. "I offered her a room here, but as soon as she heard that you were living alone at Stevens' flat with a pack of men, she was horrified. She accepted Olszak's idea that she should go there, as soon as she heard that."

"I was very thankful to be allowed to stay there," Sheila said. "Steve and his friends took good care of me. Didn't you tell Madame Aleksander that?"

"I tried to," Korytowski said, so ruefully that both Sheila and Stevens wanted to smile.

"It is so like her," Sheila said, "to have time to worry about me, when she herself has suffered so many blows."

"And they are heavier than we thought," said Korytowski with deceptive quietness. Suddenly, his hand went over the scar on his brow, and tightened on it as if the agony of his soul required his body to suffer, too. "Korytów was in German hands when Wisniewski and his men passed near there in their effort to get to Warsaw. The house was standing. But a scout found that German officers were quartered there, that there had been some trouble in the village. We don't know where Marta or the children are. Wisniewski's own house had been burned to the ground along with the village houses. His father had defended the village along with the peasants. They were all executed as snipers. There was nothing left except some half-crazed women and children searching in the black ruins. And yesterday," he paused, speaking with increasing difficulty, "yesterday we learned that Andrew is missing. One of the men in his battalion met Teresa in the hospital. He said that Andrew had fallen, wounded; he said that the German tanks had advanced over the wounded men lying before them, but that Andrew probably escaped death because he had rolled into a ditch. After that, he didn't see Andrew any more, but the Germans had captured that district and those who were wounded and had escaped the tank treads must be prisoners."

"Andrew!" Sheila said. "Andrew, too."

Stevens smashed his fist at a piece of bulging plaster on the wall. His face was rigid.

Sheila rose and went over to Professor Korytowski. "I'll look after Madame Aleksander," she said with difficulty, and gave him her hand. His blue eyes looked up at her with real affection. She turned away swiftly and hurried out of the room. She heard Stevens' feet running to catch up with her.

They joined the city's silence, and made the slow, heartbreaking journey back to Frascati Gardens.


CHAPTER XIX

*Inspection*


FOR SOME strange reason, the Germans postponed an immediate entry into Warsaw. Perhaps they were afraid of a city where there was no water, no light, no food; where there were graves along the public streets and bodies still buried under piles of rubble; where buildings still collapsed with a sigh as if they were glad that the mockery of their hollow walls was at last ended.

Sheila argued the point: whether the Germans were afraid of looking at the chaos they had created, or whether they were afraid of being torn apart by angry hands in dark streets.

Russell Stevens supported the latter view. "These boys aren't squeamish over destruction," he pointed out. "If they were, they wouldn't have trained so enthusiastically for 'battles of annihilation.' The term is theirs: they invented both

it and 'total war.' God, I hope I see the day when they
learn the meaning of these phrases."

"Sometimes I wonder—" Sheila's voice faltered.

"Wonder what?"

"Whether any of us here will be alive . . . then."

Steve said quickly, "That's the first time you've said a
thing like that. And it's the last."

"Sorry. I think it's this waiting. Have you heard from Olszak?"

"No. After all, it's only two days since the meeting."

"Two days." Two months, two years. She forced herself
free from this paralyzing gloom. She said, with a pretense of
lightheartedness, "How is your new home with Schlott's
friends? I feel I'm as bad as a Nazi, the way I've taken
over your flat."

"Oh, that's all right. You and Madame Aleksander and
Casimir will just about fill it. There wasn't going to be
much room for Schlott and me. Or Bill."

"Have you seen Bill since . . . ?" She paused, tactfully.

"Since that dust-up two nights ago? No." Steve's face took
on his stubborn look.

"I'm sorry," Sheila said.

"Guess all our tempers were a bit frayed by the end of the
siege. Bill will come round to seeing it my way: when he
stops drinking he will know he shouldn't have brought that
girl round here."

"After all," Sheila said, "if I am here, I expect Bill saw
nothing wrong in bringing Lilli, too. I was sorry for the
girl."

They were both silent, remembering Bill's noisy entrance
with his arm round a large-eyed girl, his voice repeating in
English, "Come on in, Lilli, Liberty Hall. Come on in. Liberty Hall." The girl hadn't understood, but Bill's confident arm
had pulled her into the middle of the room. Even then, the
girl had sensed that something wasn't right. She had looked at
Sheila, and then at Casimir teaching the dog to walk on its
hind legs, and then at Schlott's brick-red face. Only Bill
was oblivious to the sensation he was causing. "Liberty
Hall," he kept repeating rather thickly and determinedly.
When the girl had tried to leave Sheila had risen and said,
"Do come in." The smile she gave the girl only caused
Lilli's embarrassment to deepen.

"No room," Schlott had said with an angry glare at the
impercipient Bill.

"Nuts to that," Bill said.

Steve had spoken, awkwardly, worriedly, "Sorry, Bill. No
room."

And then Bill's temper had flared. There was the beginning of a first-class fight, for Schlott was equally aroused. Steve got between them in time, and the girl had seized the chance to back out of the room. Bill decided to abandon the fight and follow the retreating girl. His good-natured face was puckered with anger as he gave his last opinion of them. And then they had heard him calling, "Lilli. Hey! Wait! Lilli!" as his feet slipped and stumbled on the stairs.

Stevens now broke their silence. "Pity it ever had to happen," he said. "Bill should have had more sense."

"I was sorry for the girl. Perhaps she *had* no place to go."

"Perhaps." Steve half-smiled. "I wonder what's keeping Madame Aleksander. She should be here by this time." He glanced at his watch with a frown. He was regaining the old habit along with his new clothes. During the siege, time had meant nothing.

"Smart suiting, Mr. Stevens," Sheila said gravely. "Are the big shops open?"

"Not yet. Those that weren't destroyed are being kept closed by German orders. I got this from a friend of Schlott's who knew someone who knew someone. There's a lot of sidewalk trading starting."

"I wonder why they aren't open. The large stores, I mean."

"Loot for the master race. First pickings for them," Steve said bitterly. Sheila looked down at her dress which no amount of sewing or brushing would make decent. She sighed.

"You always look fine. Don't worry," Steve said, paying her the most maddening compliment that man can pay a woman. *You always look fine,* as if that were going to make her stop feeling like a scarecrow.

"Before Madame Aleksander and the Professor arrive, I'd like to get one point cleared up," Steve said. He was nervous in spite of his quiet voice.

Sheila braced herself. She hoped it wasn't going to be what she thought it might be. I hope he keeps off that subject, she thought miserably. Like Bill's visit the other night, it would be better if the point were never brought up. She was very fond of Steve, and then she groaned inwardly at the damning phrase. He was what he himself would call a swell guy. But she wasn't in love with him. He probably only thought he was in love with her. The strain of the siege had made most people more urgent in their emotions, had quickened the tempo of all human relationships. Acquaintances became friends overnight. Marriages had increased in terrific numbers. People felt they had to get the best out of life before they died so soon. She looked at Steve, and her eyes said, "Please, Steve, don't. You'll be hurt and I'll be miserable. Please don't."

"I want you to leave here. Not to go back to England. I want you to come to Switzerland with me. That's where Olszak is sending me to meet one of your countrymen who's waiting for me in Geneva. Then the people out there will have an idea of what is being done in here, and they can plan to help us fully." His eyes hadn't left hers. He was walking slowly towards her.

"Will you come too?"

She was silent, searching for something to say which wouldn't hurt him, wouldn't sound banal, wouldn't embarrass her still more.

He had sensed something of the conflict inside her, and judged it part of her wide-eyed innocence. "Will you?" he repeated.

"I must stay here," she said in desperation. "Madame Aleksander . . ."

"Look," he said. "I'm trying to get past the little glacier wall of yours and tell you that I'm in love with you."

Still she couldn't bear to say to him, "But, Steve, I don't love you. Not enough. Not the way I want to feel. I wouldn't be able to reason with you like this if I were in love with you." Instead, she clung to the excuse of Madame Aleksander. "I must stay here," she repeated. "I can't leave yet."

"Why?" His clever eyes narrowed. "And don't say Madame Aleksander again." His mouth had an angry line to it. "Has Wisniewski something to do with this?"

"Steve!" She was suddenly angry, too, and startled that she could be roused like this. "Steve, don't be stupid, don't be a complete—"

And then the door opened. Korytowski's voice was saying gently, "Here we are, Teresa. See, they are waiting for us." He urged his sister into the room as if she were a child.

Stevens relaxed his grip on Sheila's arm. Together they stared at Madame Aleksander. Her white face was so thin, so quiet. The curve of high cheekbones was accentuated, the wide-set blue eyes were ringed with deep shadows. There was a straight line to the pale lips, a droop in the thin shoulders, a feeling of complete exhaustion in the slow movements. Her face, so taut, so smoothly molded and expressionless, was a death mask of human emotions.

Sheila went towards her. The words, which she had worried over, just wouldn't come out. Silently, she took Madame Aleksander's hand. It was cold and thin and lifeless. As she led Madame Aleksander towards the bedroom, she looked at Stevens. He turned quickly away. Now, he was thinking, I'll never be able to persuade Sheila to leave. He had seen her choice in that last look. Yet, as he accepted the decision, he resented it. If a girl loved a man, nothing would stop her from being with him if she got the chance. Sheila wouldn't say "yes" unless she was positively sure. That was the reason just as much as Madame Aleksander. But why the hell wasn't she sure? He stared at Professor Korytowski, who was finishing an interminable sentence.

"Yes," Russell Stevens said in complete agreement, and hardly noticed the surprised look which passed over Korytowski's face.

When Sheila returned from the other room, where she had left Madame Aleksander lying motionless on the bed pretending to sleep so that there might be no need to talk, Stevens was gone. Professor Korytowski found her responses to his efforts at conversation as peculiar as Stevens' had been. She pulled herself guiltily away from her thoughts to listen to his news.

". . . several attempts to break through the German circle and fight their way out," he was finishing.

"Any good?"

"Only as a diversion. Two nights ago, Wisniewski and five men made their escape through the German lines to coincide with such an attempt. Last night, half a dozen other officers left. So Wisniewski's group is the first in our movement to start action." There was quiet satisfaction in his voice.

Sheila's interest quickened. There was the beginning of a smile, of a light in her eyes. "So, we've made a start," she said. Wisniewski and his men had got through the German lines. She smiled happily. "We've made a start," she repeated. The depression of the last two days unwreathed its cold mists. She began to feel and see clearly again.

But the sight of Korytowski's sad face and stooping shoulders as he turned towards the door brought her back to the reality of Warsaw, of waiting in a slaughterhouse for the butchers to enter.

"I'm sorry, I . . ." she began.

"Sorry about what?" Korytowski paused at the door, and looked affectionately at the girl's worried face.

"Uncle Edward . . ."

"Yes?"

"Uncle Edward, is it wrong to worry about one's own emotions, or even to let oneself think of them, when there are so many more important things to worry about?"

He closed the door and came back into the room. He stood facing Sheila and placed his scarred hands on her

shoulders so that she had to look at him. "As long as people
are human they will always have personal emotions. We
each inhabit two worlds: the public world of events, and
the private world of the mind. If we couldn't smile now,
then the Germans would have a total victory. If we can still
keep some private emotions which they can't invade, then
it is a defeat to their purpose. There must be some moments of private happiness to help us live through so much
misery."

He moved once more towards the door, and as she still
said nothing, he halted and added with one of his warmest
smiles, "Because you see so much to make you sad, that
doesn't mean it is your duty to be unhappy. It isn't heartless
to say that, for none of us is ever going to forget those who
have been killed or who have suffered. It is only those who
forget who are heartless. But I don't think anyone who has
lived through these four weeks is going to forget. Ever."

Sheila nodded. No one is going to forget, ever, she thought.
Every life had been changed by these last four weeks, and
these changes would remain throughout each life. For the
major changes were not in the loss of possessions or in health;
the major changes were in the mind. When men have suffered, they see more clearly and less arrogantly what they
want from life.

"Does that answer your question, Sheila?"

"Yes."

The worried look left Korytowski's face. "I didn't choose
my words for your benefit, Sheila. I believe them, myself. I
am glad if they helped. For I can never thank you enough
for what you have done." He glanced towards the bedroom
and then the door shut quietly behind him. His slow steps
diminished.

Now she was glad she had persisted in staying. His last
words filled her with a strange happiness. And then she
wondered why Uncle Edward had never married. What a
fool some woman was, not to have fallen in love with him.
And then she thought of Andrew. And she thought of herself,
and knew she was just such a fool.

She moved quietly to the bedroom door. Madame Aleksander's pretense had become a reality. In sleep, the lines of her
face had softened, and its peace had returned.

Sheila turned back to the living room. The typewriter
would be too noisy. Anyway, she had practised enough on it.
She picked up Baedeker's *Southern Germany,* and found section 46: *Munich and Environs.*

Sheila listened to the footsteps. Not Steve. Not Schlott. Not

Bill. Not Casimir. Not even Uncle Edward coming back to tell her something he might have forgotten. She rose, remembering to stuff the Baedeker into the depths of Madame Knast's knitting wools in her workbasket, and hurried to the door. The man was already in the hall. In its darkness, she made a guess that this was some kind of workman. Something in his voice touched her memory, but the question he asked about the owner of the apartment was matter-of-fact and harmless.

"Madame Knast?" she answered. "No, I'm afraid I don't know where she is. We think something must have happened to her."

"Who's responsible, then?"

"Mr. Stevens, I suppose. But he isn't here at the moment. He rented the two front rooms."

"Have to see what repairs are needed."

"Oh." How very prompt, Sheila thought. Did that mean some Germans were going to be billeted here? "You'd better make your inspection, then," she said worriedly.

"You live here?"

"At present. I am a—refugee. There are others, too. One is sleeping in the front bedroom. Please go very quietly, there. She is ill."

Sheila re-entered the living room, still worried. If Germans took this apartment block, what was going to happen to the people that lived here? (Later, she would have smiled at her naïveté. What happened to the dispossessed was no concern of the Germans.) And then she was aware that the workman had followed her. He was behind her, closing the door. She turned in surprise. The surprise became fear. God, she was saying to herself, dear God. Her legs couldn't move. All she could do was to stand there, her heart thumping so heavily that the man surely must have heard it, her lips dry, her throat unable to swallow. God, she said again in her heart, dear God help me. For the test had come. The man moved forward, smiling and now unlimping. For all his workman's clothes and his younger appearance, the man was Henryk.

"Surprised?" he asked mockingly in German.

She put a finger to her lips and pointed to the bedroom door. With a quick easy stride, he crossed over to the door, looked inside briefly, and nodded. "Asleep," he said.

"She has been restless. Quiet. She may wake." Sheila answered him in German.

"Who is she?"

"Madame Aleksander."

"Ah, your late hostess." He looked round the room.

"You've been luckier than some of us. This isn't too bad. How do you feel, now? Better?"

"I—I don't like this waiting."

"It will soon be over. The first of October will see the occupation begin. The sixth is the date set for the parade before the Führer. The Poles have to clear away the litter from the main avenues before then. Doesn't that make you feel better?"

Sheila nodded. Gradually, she was becoming more calm. The first panic had passed without disaster. She could even look at the man with interest. It was incredible how he was still Henryk, and yet not Henryk.

"What are you staring at?" he asked, and sat on the edge of the table.

"You," Sheila said frankly. "You are so much younger than I thought."

That didn't displease him. "You look better yourself. You were almost a corpse that last night on Czacki Street."

"But they didn't get us," Sheila said slowly. Danger zone, she thought.

"They got Lisa."

"Lisa?" She widened her eyes. She remembered in time that Lisa was Elzbieta's true name.

"Yes. Shot. She wasn't so lucky as you. We'll get the men who did it, though. I have them listed."

Sheila said nothing. She hoped he would think she was being sad about Elzb—Lisa.

"How did you manage it?" the quick voice asked.

"Lisa had been unconscious." Danger, danger zone, she thought.

The man nodded.

"But of course you knew that, for I saw you in the shadows," Sheila said. She watched Henryk's expression with some satisfaction. "I was afraid that the policemen would see you too. It was a bad moment for me."

Henryk only smiled approvingly. He was waiting for the rest of her story.

"Inside the police building, Lisa recovered. She suddenly broke away and tried to escape. She ran down the hall, and just then a bomb fell near by. The man who held me tried to stop Lisa as she passed us. The lights were dimmed. I tugged myself free just as he grabbed Lisa, and sidestepped into a doorway. It was an empty room. I saw another doorway. It took me into a small passage. Another doorway. And then the street. It was unlighted, but I rushed on. I heard yells from the passageway I had just left. And round the corner was a fire which the bomb had started, and

I lost myself among the firefighters and air wardens and people who had come to help. In the Main Street, I found a droshki. I took it to the French Embassy. Then I walked here. I wanted to make sure I wouldn't be traced to the American's flat. And I thought the police wouldn't look for me in an American's rooms."

"What story did you tell him?"

"That I was in danger, from some German spies. That no one must know I was here."

"And he believed that?"

"I decided him by fainting. And I was ill. He noticed that. I was in bed for nearly three weeks, and only the Aleksanders knew I was here. Barbara Aleksander came to nurse me. I think the Aleksanders persuaded him my story could be true. They were always talking of German spies."

"Why didn't you go to Nalewki instead of here? Why didn't you let us know where you were?"

Nalewki. Nalewki. The Jewish quarter. Was that where Henryk and his friends had been in hiding? She looked squarely at the man. He was asking too many questions. He had no right to do this, she suddenly realized: she was under Hofmeyer's orders, not under Henryk's. She said coldly, "I didn't go to Nalewki for fear I had been allowed to escape so that I could be followed. And I didn't let you know, because I was ill. I didn't even know if you had been arrested or not. When I was well enough, I got a message through to Hofmeyer. That was all I needed to do."

The man nodded slowly, as if he accepted that explanation.

Sheila drew a deep breath. Oslzak had been right. He had said that once you start defending your life and your friends, you learned how to use your wits. He had said ideas came quickly, surprisingly. He had been right. Her confidence grew. She was actually smiling at the man. It wasn't one of her friendliest smiles, but it was sufficiently assured.

"When did you see Hofmeyer?" he asked very casually.

What was this man trying to do, anyway? Had he been given one story by Hofmeyer, and now wanted to compare her version?

"He will tell you," she said, with a show of temper. "I'm under *his* orders. And just what are you doing here today, anyway? Does Hofmeyer know?"

"What's Hofmeyer to you?" he asked, his eyes veiled.

"What's that to you?"

"Temper, temper." He shook his head mockingly, but he was now on the defensive. He stopped his questions. He said, "Hofmeyer may not always be so powerful as you think, Anna."

Sheila thought over that. She didn't like it, just as she didn't like the man's way of watching her. She drew her ankles out of sight, and covered her legs carelessly with her skirt.

"Hofmeyer won't like to hear that," she said, and almost shuddered at her temerity.

"But you won't tell him." Henryk's voice was soft as silk. His assurance was unbounded. "What I can't believe is that you should have lived in London so long without Bracht discovering you. It had to be Hofmeyer!"

"Switzerland suited my complexion better than London. Bracht should have met me there."

Henryk laughed. He had a fine set of teeth. Like a bear-trap, Sheila thought.

"Why did you come here?" she asked again. "Did Hofmeyer tell you my address?"

"I followed you two days ago. You were walking back from the center of the town with the American. You've got him neatly under control. There's nothing like a pair of pretty eyes, unless it is a pair of pretty legs. I wager Hofmeyer doesn't know your value."

"He has given me his orders. I am quite satisfied."

"And loyal, too. Brains, beauty, and loyalty. You'll go far. With the right boss." There was a coarse huskiness in his voice which irritated her.

Sheila suddenly thought, I can't bear much more of this. I can't bear it. I could take off my shoe to smash in these mocking, knowing eyes. She pretended to listen. "Thought I heard Madame Aleksander," she said, and lowered her voice. "Quiet!"

"The old girl's dead-beat," Henryk said.

"Why did you come here? Have you news for me? Or is this just a social call?" She rose wearily, and walked to the window. People were out there: people who were her friends and this man's enemies.

"Purely social." He was laughing again. Then with his voice very smooth again, and the hoarseness quite gone, he added quietly, "Used to know Munich. Was stationed there in 1932. Were you there then? I wager you used to walk past the Brown House in pigtails, and look at the men standing guard outside. I used to be one of them."

"Yes, I saw them. But probably not you. I left Munich in 1932. Fräulein Leigh must have heard you were coming to town." She turned once more to the window. There were two policemen now in sight. If she leaned out of the window and called down for help, she could have Henryk arrested. The Germans weren't in full control here yet. Not until the first of October.

"Who was Fräulein Leigh?" His voice was too gentle.

"She brought me up." If I could dash out of this door and lock it, Sheila thought, if I could tell the policemen that this man was a spy, they would know what to do with him quite unofficially but effectively. One spy less. One spy with his account rendered and paid.

"An orphan?" he murmured sympathetically.

"My father was killed on the west front. My mother was —I'm sorry. I must be boring you."

"Not at all. Your mother, Lotte Braun, was . . . ?"

"My mother, *Frieda* Braun, was in Cologne."

"What's so interesting in the street? Come and sit down over here. Did you ever meet Bracht in London?"

Sheila said, "I was keeping watch for the boy Casimir. He is entering the house now. He's another refugee that Herr Stevens is sheltering."

Casimir's clatter ended abruptly in the doorway. Henryk was standing before a cracked wall, prodding the loose plaster most expertly. Sheila had picked up a magazine.

"Quietly, Casimir," Sheila said. "Madame Aleksander is sleeping next door. What have you brought for supper? Wonderful! Would you fill the pot from the water-bucket in the kitchen, Casimir? I'll be with you in a minute as soon as this man leaves."

"Who's he?" Casimir asked curiously. The dog was pawing Sheila's knee to attract attention. Me too, it seemed to say. She rubbed its head and replied, "Some workman or other. He's just finished inspecting the damage."

Casimir went towards the kitchen with a last curious look at the man. The dog followed him, his nose surely pointed towards the food.

"Time to be going," Sheila said in a low voice to Henryk. She was surprised when he obeyed.

"Just routine check-up, ma'am," he said in Polish loud enough for Casimir to hear. And then he added out of the side of his mouth, "Quite the friend of the Poles, aren't you?"

"Those were my instructions."

"What are your plans?"

"Waiting further instructions."

He looked down at her, his eyes so impenetrable that Sheila wondered in alarm if she had betrayed herself. She was left with the unsatisfactory question unanswered, for Henryk was already moving into the hall. He was whistling. She remembered that early morning in Uncle Edward's flat and the sound of water as the hot dust was hosed off the pavement under her window. Again she echoed her thoughts of that morning; what has he to be happy about? But this time she knew the answer.

She stood at the window until she saw Henryk enter the street. Another workman, loitering in a near-by doorway, joined him. Together, they strode away, their feet keeping perfect rhythm. If she had called the policemen, she might have caught Henryk, but she would have endangered Hofmeyer. She took a deep breath. Now that she was safely alone, without a phrase or expression to betray her and threaten her friends, she suddenly felt terribly afraid.

From the kitchen, Casimir's voice called cheerily.

She roused herself. "Coming, Casimir," she said, and placed the magazine slowly back in place. She wished this man Henryk weren't so ambitious. She wished he weren't jealous of Hofmeyer. She knew she had good reason to be afraid.

## CHAPTER XX

## Mr. Hofmeyer's Apprentice

THE FIRST Germans entered Warsaw. The human-length mounds along the streets and gardens welcomed them. Rough wooden crosses were the banners which the city raised. The withering flowers on the unknown graves were the petals strewn in the conqueror's path.

The people, too busy with their search for food and water and jobs, for scattered families and rooms where they could live now that the Germans occupied so many houses, hardly seemed to notice the green-gray uniforms crowding their streets. *Ignore them* was the unconscious reaction. The Germans offered chocolate bars to children and took photographs. They offered bread and soup to the less proud and took more photographs. (Later, the bill for soup and bread was charged to the city; no photographs were taken of that event!) But the people seemed coldly oblivious. They were like men who have been sharply awakened from an evil dream, who moved and talked with the dream still haunting them. If there was bitterness in their hearts for their failure, bitterness on their tongues for those they blamed, still more bitter were their eyes as they ignored the Germans doling out little benefits with so much fanfare. The Nazis gave so little compared to what they had destroyed. The chocolate offered to a starving Polish child, even without the newsreel cameras cranking in the background, was merely added insult to his mother's sufferings. The smiling, confident Germans would have been amazed, even indignant, if that had been pointed out to them. Sometimes, Sheila wished she could enjoy that luxury.

But it was luxury to be alive at all. Even after a week of silent guns, she was still amazed that any people should still be left. She was still more amazed that she should be counted among them. As she walked along the partly cleared streets towards Central Station she could only think, "In spite of all of this, some of us still live. Some of us still have homes. And some," as she noted a man and woman hawking a tray of stockings outside a boarded-up shop, "some are beginning to plan their lives again." The extraordinary thing about human beings was their resilience.

She attempted a short cut to the station, and entered a quiet thoroughfare to reach Marszalkowska Avenue. But its end which joined the larger street was still blocked by an immense barricade. Men were even working now to tear it down. They worked grimly. No doubt they were thinking of how they had planned to retreat and fight behind these barricades. They had built them strong. But the failing supply of ammunition, the lack of water, had beaten them. And now the order had been given that Polish hands must tear the barricades down, so that the Nazis could stroll through the street.

One of the men straightened his back, pulled on his well-cut jacket with grimy hands. Another man had stepped forward to take his place: each citizen gave so much of his time as he passed by the barricades which ringed the center of the city; each stepped forward, worked for the same period of time, and then relinquished his place to another. The man in the well-cut suit was trying to wipe off the dust on his hands. He noticed Sheila's hesitation as she calculated what would now be the quickest way of reaching Central Station. She must not be late, not for her very first meeting with Mr. Hofmeyer.

"Trying to get to Marszalkowska?" he asked. "You'll have to make a detour. I'm going there. I'll show you the quickest way."

"Thank you," Sheila said in relief.

"Stranger?" the man said. He finished rubbing his hands. He wore the neat black jacket and striped trousers of a once prosperous businessman.

"Yes. British."

*"Hm."* The man looked sourly at her. After that he didn't speak until they had reached Marszalkowska Avenue. "There you are," he said abruptly.

"Thank you again." Her smile hesitated: this man didn't want any smiles from foreigners. But he had noticed the expression in her eyes and halted unexpectedly.

"What are you doing here?"

"I stayed. I thought I could help."

*"Hm.* You're one of the few foreigners who did, then."

"I'm sorry," Sheila said miserably.

The man stared at her. He noticed the bloodstains still smudging her coat, its singed cuff, the red skinless flesh on her left hand, her bare legs, her worn shoes.

"I'm sorry, too," he said gruffly. "Good day." But his voice had lost its hard edge, and the bitterness in his face eased for a moment. "Please forgive me," he said wearily, and then he left her.

It was a subdued Sheila who crossed the street and reached Central Station. Its twisted, blackened ruins increased her depression.

Hofmeyer was already there. He was walking with his light step quickly towards her.

"Good day, Anna," he said in German, "I was beginning to think that you didn't get my message this morning." He caught her arm to turn her round so that she faced the way she had come. "This way. I am taking you to my new office. I realized you might not be able to find it easily, but you would certainly know the way to the station, at least. Besides I wanted to have a little talk."

"I'm sorry I'm late. I took a short cut, which was like most short cuts."

Hofmeyer's grip tightened on her arm warningly. "Look happier," he said in a low voice, his face still looking straight ahead of him. "Our friends are everywhere now."

He spoke the truth. Apart from the uniforms, the Germans who had hidden themselves in Warsaw had come forth to enjoy their triumph. They were dressed like Poles. They were trying to look like Poles, for now their job would be to mix with Poles and spy on them. But today there was that certain exultation in their faces, which men find difficult to hide.

"They've won," Hofmeyer said in that very low voice, his lips scarcely moving. "Take a good look, Anna. That's how you feel when you win."

"It must be a pleasant feeling," Sheila said bitterly, speaking as secretly as her companion had done.

"And that's why you must look happier. You're one of them now."

"You depress me still more."

"Fortunately this walk to my new office isn't so very long. You can let your face relax there. Only you must guard your tongue once you are inside. Speak German at all times. If we have any private talking to do, then we shall take a little walk through the streets. And whenever we are taking such a walk, you are to talk about the weather as soon as you feel my hand knock against yours."

Sheila looked surprised.

"Just as the walls have ears in a German office, so the streets have ears in a German-controlled town. Now is there anything to report before we reach the office?"

"The man Henryk has been to see me."

"Henryk? You mean Heinrich Dittmar? The devil he did." He was silent for some paces. "Well, I won't deny that was a surprise. What did he want?"

"He called it a 'social call.' But I got the feeling that he disliked you, and—please don't think I'm exaggerating—I thought he would like to do you some harm."

Hofmeyer didn't laugh. He nodded grimly, and said, "You are not far wrong, there. Any further—feelings?"

"He was more interested in me than was necessary. I've worried ever since. What could have given him a suspicion?"

"Not a suspicion. At least, we must hope not. Heinrich Dittmar is well known. If he must work with women, he likes them young and pretty. Elzbieta was very pretty once, you know."

"But I am under your orders."

"What's that to Dittmar? My dear Anna, if you could see the energy and tempers that are wasted on little jealousies in the Party, you'd never criticize the democracies again. I have just been through a particularly tiresome session. About offices. Yes, you may laugh, but it's true. We squabble over offices—which are the most comfortable and the most impressive. It is a point of honor with small minds to put such emphasis on material display of importance. We are now fighting over the housing of our staffs and even about the staffs themselves. We all want the best, to show how much authority we have. We are jockeying for our future positions and power."

"It sounds fantastic. Then their supposedly united front is . . .?"

"No. It's united in the main things. They know that if they aren't united, then the little butcher or grocer of a Saxon village would cease being the Gaulieter of hundreds of square miles. The debt-haunted Berlin clerk would stop traveling first-class, staying at the best hotels, wouldn't have all the women and expensive dinners he likes to enjoy. The dull schoolteacher from Bavaria would no longer be able to have a mansion and motor car and servants. The—" His hand brushed heavily against her arm.

Sheila hesitated and then the words rushed out on top of each other. "It is getting so cold, and the rain is miserable now that it has come."

"Good," said Hofmeyer after a pause, and the man who had walked so closely beside them had passed by. "But there's no need for such zest. A bored remark will do."

Sheila said nothing.

"Oh, it was quite good for a first try," Hofmeyer added encouragingly. "Now, where were we? Ah, yes—the little jealousies behind the scenes. No, don't hope that a miracle will come of them. Remember that this is the end of one campaign and that many of them believe it is all they need to fight. Many think that England and France will ask for peace, and that they will then have plenty of time to plan for the next phase. They want to immobilize the biggest countries, make them disgusted with their leaders, play on their peoples' natural tendencies to reproach and criticize each other. Then they'll take over the small countries one by one, and the bigger countries will be in such a state of uncertainty that they will be unable to fight any war. So, thinking these things, the Nazis can relax and be their own nasty little selves. Before the campaign, everything was forgotten except the need to win. Or else, as I said, the butcher and grocer and clerk and schoolteacher would all be back where they started."

"But all Nazis can't have power."

"No. But they all think they share in the loot. They all see personal prosperity ahead of them at other nations' expense. Meanwhile, during this lull in action, they are flown with insolence and wine. They are confident enough to indulge in petty quarreling. Recently, I've felt that I have missed my true vocation. I should have been a tightrope walker."

"Have you never felt like that before?"

"Not quite so constantly." Hofmeyer smiled suddenly and said, "If this weather continues we must have glass on our windows."

Sheila looked at the gaping holes around them and said, in what she hoped was a bored enough voice, "Yes, indeed."

There was a pause for safety. And then Hofmeyer said,

half-amusedly, "Dittmar's interest in you is most annoying. It changes my plans for you entirely. I can't ship you back to England now."

"No. I suppose either I would have to go on pretending to be a German agent in London, or you would all be in danger here. I'm your discovery; if I behave suspiciously, then you'll be suspected too."

"Don't worry. Now that you've given us warning about Dittmar, Olszak and I can make our plans." He looked at her and smiled. "You might have the makings of an agent, after all. Perhaps Olszak was right about hereditary traits."

Sheila smiled happily at the oblique mention of her father. Hofmeyer had paid her a high compliment.

"Of course, if you did go back to England," Hofmeyer went on, "you could always disappear as effectively as Margareta Koch. In your case, it would mean complete change of identity for the duration of the war."

"In her case it was . . . ?"

Herr Hofmeyer's square white face looked blandly at a group of German soldiers. "Exactly," he said. Then, "She found out too much about us. Dear me, what a lot of cameras the German Army has!"

They had now left Marszalkowska for a quieter side street of balconies and three-storied houses. The architecture had been noble. No expense had been spared in workmanship. Hofmeyer halted before one of the large double-doors.

"Nothing private to be discussed," he said so quietly that Sheila wondered if she had heard all his words. She hadn't expected the journey to end so quickly; she still had questions to ask.

"Madame Aleksander and Korytów?" she asked hurriedly.

"Yes. But don't be too sympathetic."

The hall was of marble, with a floor of great beauty. This house had suffered less than the others on the street, and that was why it had been chosen by the Germans. One of the reasons, at least. Another might be its wealth. The ground-floor rooms seemed empty except for workmen. On the broad curve of stairs, she noted the elaborate pattern of marble underfoot, the pieces of sculpture still standing in the wall-niches. Even in spite of traces of dust and water, the beauty of the house survived.

"Who owned this house?" she asked as naturally as she could, as they reached the thick carpets of the first floor. Hofmeyer must have thought her question harmless, for he smiled and nodded approvingly.

"A lawyer. He is an officer in the army, but if he comes back here to see his wife and daughter he will find that his

property has been confiscated. He has been known to have
expressed opinions against us in the past. The wife and
daughter were told to leave two days ago. So the house is
empty except for some workmen doing repairs, and some
cleaners mopping up after them. In the next few weeks,
the other rooms will all be occupied as office suites. Surplus
furniture is being removed to Germany along with some of
these paintings. They are too valuable for a private house.
They belong in our museums or public buildings."

Sheila thought of the lawyer's wife and daughter. Like
the dispossessed in Western Poland, they had probably been
allowed to take one small bag with them.

Hofmeyer understood her silence. Perhaps he himself had
also thought of the wife and daughter. "Plenty of pretty
dresses and hats and furs still in the wardrobes," he said.
His smile was bitter. "Do you need some clothes? They'll be
removed soon." His smile deepened as he saw the look of
disgust on her face. He opened the door of his suite of
rooms.

They were in what must have been the library. Next
to it was a large, extremely comfortable study, and the room
beyond that was a bedroom. There was a feeling of great
comfort and charm in the rooms' arrangement. The lawyer
had been proud of his home, and the happiness of the family
still lingered inside the house.

"You see, I shall live here. It makes my business more
efficient," Hofmeyer said as they finished the tour of inspection, and returned to the library. "Now sit down, Fräulein
Braun. We can talk at last. This room will be the outside
office. You will work here with two typists who I am now
choosing. *Volksdeutsche*, of course. But even so, they will
be kept to deal with the problems of table delicacies only. My
own office will be that study next door. Fortunately, I had
copies of my files which were all destroyed by fire at
the Old Square, so once they are installed here you can start
work. These bookshelves will be cleared, of course, to make
room for our records. The books will be shipped home with
the contents of the Warsaw libraries and private collections.
A defeated nation does not need valuable books."

Home . . . Home, in this office, now meant Germany. But
something in Hofmeyer's direct stare at the wall of books
in front of him interrupted Sheila's thoughts. "The walls
have ears," he had warned in the street. She followed his
stare. *The walls have ears.* And he had drawn her attention
particularly to the books. Yes, a dictaphone might very well
be hidden somewhere behind these books. She wondered what
a dictaphone looked like. It was slightly comic to be domi-

nated by a little mechanical device which you had never seen. Comic? On second thoughts, the joke turned sour. It must be quite a strain to live with it constantly.

"Do you expect many Polish customers?" she asked. I hope to God none of them speak their minds in this room, she thought.

"Why not? The Poles have known this firm for many years, and if they can't pay me in money then they can pay in jewelry or valuables. Besides, I have my clients in Sweden and Switzerland to consider. We need their foreign money. As for my political position, the Polish police hadn't time to publicize their search for me. Colonel Bolt was killed in the siege. No more than six others at his headquarters knew about me. Five of these have already been arrested by us. Kordus, alone, is unaccounted for. It won't be long before we have him too. So, to the Poles, I am still a friend."

"I see."

"Now, here are two telephone numbers. One is for the phone in this office: 4-3210. One for the private phone in my own room: 4-6636."

As he repeated these numbers slowly, he extracted a small piece of paper from an inside pocket and handed it over to her with a gesture of silence. On it was a third number: 6-2136. Underneath was written "Emergency only. Leave message if unable to reach me." Sheila concentrated on the figures. So Hofmeyer had another refuge. The two telephones at this address belonged to district number 4. But the special telephone, coming under district 6, was in another part of the city. She handed the sheet of paper back to him.

"Cigarette?" he asked and opened his case. She took one, still memorizing the numbers, and watched him strike a match.

"What were the numbers?" he asked.

"Business number: 4-3210. Special number: 4-6636." Very special number: 6-2136; 6-2136....

They both watched the piece of paper curl into a gray tissue, watched Hofmeyer's pencil chop it up until all that remained in the ash tray was a fine powder.

"Talking of the Poles," Hofmeyer said suddenly, "how are your specially chosen friends?"

"I wanted to ask you about them. Frankly, I am worried. I understood that you wanted me to live with Madame Aleksander meanwhile?"

"That was the plan. Stay close beside her and meet her friends."

"She is recovering from her illness. And she wants to leave

Warsaw. She talks continually of going back to Korytów and looking for the children."

"But she can't, for then you will have no excuse for staying where you are. Your patient work all this summer will be quite undone. Are you convinced that you can't persuade her to stay?"

"I have already tried. Tactfully. For invalids are always suspicious. They lie in bed and brood. If I persuade her too much, she may even turn against me. If she insists on going to Korytów, shall I accompany her?"

"Out of the question. Absolutely not." Hofmeyer rose with one of his surprisingly quick movements, and searched for an atlas among the reference books. He opened it at Central Poland. "Out of the question, Fräulein Braun. See here. Korytów is too insignificant to be marked in this map, but roughly that is its position. Here. Just south of Lowicz. Isn't that so?"

"Yes."

"The line between German Poland and Occupied Poland, or the Government General, will run through that district. The proclamation of the partition of Poland will be published tomorrow. It will be put into effect by the twenty-eighth of October. If the Aleksander woman is allowed to return to Korytów, she may be in the incorporated part of Poland. And that means that she would have no contact with her important friends left in Warsaw. She would be quite useless to you for our purposes. You see, the western part of Poland, from the Carpathians just west of Zakopane in the south to the East Prussian border in the north, will become part of Germany. All property is ours. The Poles will be killed or kept for serf labor. That part of the country will be made completely German, this time. And there will be no communication allowed between German Poland and Occupied Poland. If Madame Aleksander were cut off from us here in Warsaw by going to Korytów you would lose your one asset. She will be entirely eliminated if Korytów lies west of the boundary line between German Poland and Occupied Poland. Her lands will be needed for German settlers from the Baltic States. She may be executed for treason. She may be shipped in a cattle truck to Germany, or to the northeastern plains of Poland where the weather will take care of those not strong enough to labor for us. So, until we know the definite boundary line of the partition of Poland, she must be kept in Warsaw. Do you understand?"

"Yes, Herr Hofmeyer."

"Let me see the assets you have in Madame Aleksander," Hofmeyer was saying as if he were counting the good points in a horse at a fair. "She has one son in diplomatic circles, another who had many friends in government service, a brother who has the trust of the Warsaw University faculty, a cousin who is a general, another who is a bishop, another was a member of that band of parliamentary fools they called a *Sejm*. Yes, it was a powerful family, and its name still carries respect among the Poles."

Sheila stared, fascinated. She hadn't known all that. "Her daughter-in-law comes of a great commercial clan, I believe," she said, remembering the ill-fated Eugenia. "It owned many big businesses and shops throughout Poland."

"Yes, a powerful family. That was why I wanted you to win their trust. For our office has two functions. One is to be in contact with people who might hear important news and unwittingly supply us with it. The other is to try and persuade some Poles to work with our Government General. That would always help us initially. Later when their usefulness to us was over, they could be disposed of like the other Poles."

Hofmeyer was pacing the room, now. His whole performance was convincing. It was cold, callous and calculating. Whoever was interested in the concealed dictaphone would only find two worried Germans shaping their plans to bring honor to themselves and power to their Reich.

Hofmeyer stopped his pacing, abruptly. "I have an idea, but I must discuss it with another department first. If they approve it, then you will make a quick journey to Korytów and bring back the children to Madame Aleksander and Warsaw. That will make you a heroine in Polish eyes, and your position will be assured. You can invent the difficulties you had to face. Actually, from this other department I hope to get facilities to make your journey there very simple. I shall phone you tomorrow, and give you instructions."

"The phone wasn't working this morning. I think it's probably going to be out of order for some days."

"Nonsense, Fräulein Braun. Do you think that we shall leave that excellent district, which has been less destroyed than any other, unrequisitioned? And naturally if our officers and officials are going to take over those apartments, we shall certainly see all repairs are done there before other districts. You are now living under your country's rule, Fräulein Braun, and not under slipshod English methods. I shouldn't be surprised to hear that our workmen have already started on their job in that quarter, while you were absent."

Sheila said meekly, "Yes, Herr Hofmeyer," and watched Hofmeyer's grave wink. That last sentence had seemed pe-

culiar in many ways. Why had he chosen to add the unnecessary "while you were absent" phrase? And why nod as
emphasis to the "you"? He was staring so fixedly now at
the bookcases that she realized he was trying to warn her of
something by the association of ideas. She looked at the
bookshelves, too, and she thought of a dictaphone. That was
it: the workmen might install a dictaphone. The walls had
ears. In her simple-minded way she had thought that only
meant the walls here. Now Hofmeyer, who had sensed her
mistake, was trying to warn her. He was watching her face,
and he now showed the relief of a man who had remembered in time to give an added caution, and who saw that
it had been accepted.

"You had better return to the Aleksander woman now,
and stay with her until you hear from me. Tell her about
your new position here: say that I am a friend of the Poles.
Arouse no suspicion. Find out, meanwhile, what you can
about the members of her family."

Sheila rose. Hofmeyer was already on his way to the
study to answer an insistent telephone bell. "Heilitler!"
he snapped, his hands deep in his pockets.

" 'tler," echoed Sheila obediently, and closed the library
door.

She clutched her handbag firmly as she walked down
Marszalkowska, turned left along Jerozolimskie Street. For inside the bag was her only security now: her identification
and membership card for the *Auslands-Organisation* with
the faint stamp across its surface reading SPECIAL SERVICE.
After that conversation for the benefit of a dictaphone, Anna
Braun was no longer a mere name on a piece of paper.


CHAPTER XXI

*Casimir*


INSIDE the living room of Stevens' flat, Madame Aleksander
and Casimir were waiting. The kerosene which Casimir had
"found" now burned in a lamp which he had "discovered."
Madame Aleksander sat with her legs wrapped in a blanket.
Casimir sat at her feet, directing the terrier as it tried to walk
backwards on its hind legs. Madame Aleksander was smiling at the dog's anxious eyes.

"I feel better each hour, Sheila," she said as the girl entered. "Casimir has been telling me long stories. And he has

been teaching the dog a new trick and it's trying *so* hard to please. Just look at it!"

Sheila felt happier as she heard the new note in Madame Aleksander's voice. The dull, dead tone had gone. She was indeed better, much better.

"I'll soon be able to leave for Korytów," she was saying happily. "Casimir is determined to come with me to protect me."

Sheila bent down to pat the dog as it scratched impatiently for notice at her legs.

"We've found a name for him," Casimir said proudly. "He's a Scottish dog, so Madame Aleksander said we must give him a Scots name. He's Volterscot."

"Walter Scott," Madame said with a smile. "I had to read his novels when I was learning English."

"Volterscot!" Casimir called and snapped his fingers. The dog cocked his ears and twisted his head to the side. He panted his smile. "See," Casimir said with delight, "he knows his name!" Volterscot wagged his tail happily, took Casimir's forefinger gently between his teeth and paraded before the boy, proudly leading his hand back and forward.

"Volterscot is showing that he owns you, Casimir," Sheila said. "If I had a nice bone, he would have it." Volterscot deserved more than that, she thought, as she looked at Casimir's face, young once more, and then at Madame Aleksander watching the boy and dog together.

"I'll get him one. Somehow," Casimir said, and leaped to his feet with all the unnecessary violence of a boy of twelve. "And there's our supper to find, too. Have you three zlotys? Prices are *awful* high, now."

Sheila counted out five zlotys. Almost seven shillings, she calculated quickly. She always seemed to translate money into English values. "Take good care," she called after him, but he was already out of the door with a last wave of his hand. Volterscot looked at the two women as if to excuse himself, and darted after Casimir.

"Volterscot, the almost human," Sheila said, and tried to look as if she felt like making a joke.

Madame Aleksander was watching her keenly. "Did you have a nice walk?"

"Yes. No."

"That sounds very mixed." Madame Aleksander looked as if she would like to hear more about Sheila's afternoon.

Sheila said quickly, "And what have you been doing, besides getting up against my orders? I must be a very bad nurse, if my patient will not obey me."

"Casimir helped me into this room. It was he who tucked

this blanket round my legs. He's a nice boy, Sheila. I've got very fond of him. And then we just sat and talked, and three hours disappeared."

"I am sorry I was so long."

"Nonsense. You need more fresh air. You've lost the color in your cheeks. But I'm glad you've stopped putting that horrid red stuff on your lips."

Sheila looked at herself critically in the small mirror over the bookcase. She wondered where she had lost that lipstick. Nowadays, everything got lost, and one never seemed to be able to remember where things had been put. It didn't matter. Nothing mattered but finding something to eat and disguising it as food.

"Pale. But interesting, I hope," she admitted.

"And we had three visitors. There was a man about the electric lights. And there was a man to see if the phone could be put into order."

Sheila's fingers stopped twisting the curls into a pattern over her brow. She turned away from the mirror. "Really? That's good." She looked nervously at the walls. Where did they hide those damned things?

"They told me that we should have running water soon. Men are working at the pipes day and night."

"Good. And who was the third visitor?"

"Mr. Stevens. He came to collect the typewriter. He is going away."

"So soon?"

"Tonight."

"Tonight?" Well, the Germans hadn't lost much time in getting rid of the neutrals. She felt twice as depressed. Parting from friends always made her feel as if she had lost something of herself: as each one went, a gap was left.

"Yes. He and another American and a Swedish gentleman called Schlott. It seems Mr. Schlott had his business here, but the Germans have taken a dislike to him and he must leave, too. Mr. Stevens is going to be a correspondent in Switzerland for an American newspaper. It is a better job than his old one. Isn't that splendid?"

"Yes."

"Sheila, couldn't you go with him? Can't you pretend you are an American?"

Sheila looked shrewdly at the blue eyes, too bright in the white face. So Steve had enlisted Madame Aleksander's help. "And what about a passport?"

"You could have lost it in the siege. Russell Stevens said he and his American friend would vouch for you. The Germans seem eager to get rid of neutrals. Perhaps they don't want them to see how they are going to treat us."

"I'm staying here." Sheila touched Madame Aleksander's shoulder lightly.

"You must not think only of me. You must think of yourself, Sheila," Madame Aleksander said gently. She took Sheila's hand and held it. "I can always go to Edward's flat. I feel I should have taken you and Casimir there, anyhow. I wonder why Edward and Michal were so insistent that I shouldn't go there?"

"Wasn't it bombed?" Sheila asked, her eyes on the wall in front of her.

"He didn't tell me! What about his manuscript?" Madame Aleksander was nervous again. Her voice was raised, her eyes were troubled. Sheila was sorry she had mentioned anything about the flat, and yet she had had to stop any speculation about Michal Olszak.

"Oh, I don't think the whole place was destroyed. And you know Uncle Edward. He would save his book first of all."

"Yes," Madame Aleksander agreed. She relaxed again, but she was still worried. Her thin hands plucked at the fold of blanket on her lap.

"Why don't you go back to bed? When Casimir brings back our supper, I'll cook it and bring it to you on a tray. And I'll read to you." She looked at the pile of American magazines which Steve had left behind, and wondered what story she might find suitable tonight. Madame Aleksander's taste ran to stories about New England villages, or about ranches in the West, or about plantations in the South. These were her escape from the ruins of Warsaw, perhaps because her life at peaceful Korytów had been a composite of all three.

"Casimir . . ." Madame Aleksander mused. "Sheila, do you know anything at all about him?"

"Only what I've guessed. I *think* his family were refugees from the west."

"Tonight he told me a little, a very little and yet so much. His mother had long black hair. When she was brushing it, it fell beneath her waist."

"How *did* you find that out?"

"I was brushing my hair. He was watching me in silence, standing over there at the bedroom door with this blanket over his arm. Then he said that."

There was a silence. At last Madame Aleksander said, "I am going to take him to live with us at Korytów. I think I'll try to leave tomorrow, or the day after. The sooner, the better. I'll never feel really well again until I get there."

"You must first get official permission."

"Permission? Korytów is only about forty miles away!"

"It is impossible to travel even five miles without the proper identification papers and a letter of permission. I saw the queue today outside the German Kommandantur: people waiting for permission. Sometimes it takes days."

"Nothing but waiting," Madame Aleksander said with rising anger. "First, we waited for the war, then for news, then for bombs, then for help, then for food and water. We waited to be killed, we waited for word from our families, we waited for the Germans to take over the city. We do nothing but wait. And there's still more waiting to be done: waiting for the Nazis to be driven back into their own country. But a lot of us here won't sit around and wait for that day. We didn't in 1916. After the first shock of this defeat is over, I know there will be men who will—"

"Madame Aleksander, if you want to be strong enough to travel, you must rest." Sheila glanced nervously at the walls. "I thought I heard Casimir," she said more quietly.

"Oh, he couldn't be back so quickly. It takes him at least two hours to reach the end of a queue on a lucky day. I've timed him. I used to worry about him when the Germans first appeared on the streets. He said he would—"

Sheila spilled the pile of magazines which she had been examining.

"Sheila, I think *you* need to rest. How selfish I am, always speaking of my own worries. You are missing England, aren't you? If you really won't go with the American, I am going to speak to Michal about you, and he will be able to plan something. I have great confidence in him. He's very clever, and he knows so many—"

"I am all right," Sheila said quickly. "I think I'm hungry, that's all. It seems a long time since supper yesterday. Now do go to bed. Let me help you."

"If anyone comes asking at this house who you are, do you know what I'm going to say?"

Sheila shook her head. She could only hope it would be nothing that would incriminate Madame Aleksander.

"I shall say you are Barbara."

"Barbara." It was the first time they had mentioned her name.

"Who is to know but our family and friends? And no Pole will tell." Her face looked happier, now. "It's a very good idea of mine," she said firmly. "I can't imagine why I didn't think of it before." She unfolded the blanket and rose slowly. She looked round the room and forced herself to talk of everyday things. "Tomorrow we shall clean this place thoroughly. I do wish we had Maria here. She is so good at making things shine."

Sheila's amazed look turned to one of amusement. Madame Aleksander didn't believe anything was well done unless she had at least superintended it, herself. Wars may change ways of thinking, but they don't change instincts. Sheila looked at her hands, roughened by so much cleaning and scrubbing. She began to laugh.

"Are you all right, Sheila?"

"Yes. I almost forgot to tell you one piece of good news. I have a job. That will earn enough to buy us food and clothes. You see, someone must make money. Uncle Edward has been robbing himself to provide for us, but he will get no more salary from the University. All the teachers are looking for jobs. Wasn't I lucky to find this one?"

Madame Aleksander looked doubtful. "What is it?" she asked slowly.

She looked relieved when Sheila explained, although she still frowned.

"But this man's a German."

"Of German descent. He is Polish now."

"And he knows who you really are?"

"Yes, he knows." That was one truth which the dictaphone could repeat without condemning her.

"Then either he's a fool or a very brave man."

"He considers himself a Pole," Sheila said, and Madame Aleksander gave a strange little smile.

The bedroom door closed gently.

Sheila picked up the magazines which she had dropped, pretended to hum a song, folded the blanket, rearranged the table mat, moved a chair, and then sat down and stared at the walls. I just can't bear the idea, she thought: I just can't go on living here with this continual trap around me. She could guard herself; but Madame Aleksander? She still broke into a cold sweat at the innocent remarks this evening which, if they had been completed, might have disclosed enough to the Germans. As it was, Madame Aleksander was convinced that Sheila was heading for a nervous breakdown. She would be worrying now in that room, as if she hadn't enough to worry about.

Sheila jumped as the telephone bell rang. Was it tapped, too? Probably all telephones were.

"Telephone, Sheila," Madame Aleksander's voice called.

"Yes." She went into the hall and lifted the receiver from the hook as if it exuded vitriol.

It was Steve. She almost wept at the sound of his voice. She couldn't speak.

"Sheila, what's wrong with you? It is you, isn't it?"

"Yes."

"Say, is anything wrong?"

"No."

"I wondered if you might have changed your mind. About coming. We are all gathered together in the Europejski, like sheep in a pen. We leave in an hour. There's just time for you to join us."

"But I've got to stay here, Steve."

"Perhaps you feel you ought to, but there is no 'got' about it."

The operator's voice said, "That is all the time allowed for a telephone conversation. Are you finished?"

"No, damnation," Steve said, "Sheila, listen—"

The telephone went dead.

Sheila had just re-entered the room when the bell rang again.

This time it was Bill.

"Steve wasn't allowed to make any more calls. There's a mob of us here. We are allowed one each. How are you Sheila? Sorry about that night. Remember?"

"I hope Lilli's well. I liked her."

"She's a good kid. But say, Steve's at my elbow. Why the hell don't you come with us, and stop us all worrying? Schlott is here too. The Germans didn't like his face. Just a minute, Sheila, Steve's jabbering at my elbow."

There was a slight pause.

"Sheila, he says, and this goes for all of us—"

The operator's voice said, "That is all the time allowed for a telephone conversation. Are you finished?"

"Hell, no," Bill said, "and you know that damned well."

"I'll be all right. Don't worry," Sheila said quickly, as the telephone became blank sound.

There was the same blankness in the living room. First the Spaniard and the man from Vienna; then the Englishman and the Frenchman; now Bill and Schlott and Steve. She picked up the guide to Munich and started work on it once more. Work. Something to do. Something else to think about than a room which had become too neat and clean and quiet.

It was dark now. The curfew would be on: anyone on the street was to be shot at sight. It was with relief that she heard the door open and Casimir's voice calling triumphantly, "Got something."

There was a look of delight on his face. Not even the small piece of salt pork, which he laid on the table along with the two potatoes, could account for such exaltation. Sheila remembered the unexpected quietness of his entry. Usually his clatter on the staircase told everyone in this block of apartments that Casimir was returning. His face was flushed with running. His eyes were excited. He made a joke about Volterscot and laughed too heartily.

"What is it, Casimir? What have you been up to?"

The bedroom door opened, and Madame Aleksander appeared fully dressed.

"I thought you had gone to bed," Sheila began in amazement.

"I decided I was tired of bed. We've no time left to be ill now, anyway. I feel better when I am up. Now what have we got to cook this time, Casimir?"

"Casimir's been having some fun," Sheila said. She tried to look severe, but the boy's unabashed smile spoiled the effect.

"What is it, Casimir?" Madame Aleksander asked, with the authority of a woman who has brought up a family and instinctively knows what kind of voice to use.

"Nothing," Casimir began, "at least, nothing much. Nothing as much as I'd like." But his grin widened.

And then Sheila remembered the dictaphone. She sat down heavily on the nearest chair and moistened her dry lips.

"I just," said Casimir, his pride beginning to need an audience after all, "I just—"

"Sheila, what's wrong with you?" Madame Aleksander hurried over to the girl.

"I think I'm just weak with hunger. I would love some food. Wouldn't you?"

"Yes, I believe I would. Even this." Madame Aleksander looked at the piece of pork curiously. "Once I wouldn't even have offered it to a dog."

But Casimir, having once decided to tell, was not to be cheated.

"I tore down a poster," he said. "One of those anti-British posters the Germans have been putting up everywhere. It showed a picture of the ruins, and Chamberlain's face, and one of us pointing at him and saying 'This is your fault.' So I just ripped it right off the wall, and then we ran. Didn't we, Volterscot?"

"You shouldn't have done it. I'm glad you did. But you shouldn't have done it," Madame Aleksander said slowly. "Did any German see you do it?"

The boy shook his head, and Madame Aleksander's look of anxiety disappeared. "Then that's all right," she added. "I'm glad you did it."

"Casimir, do you know what happens if you tear down posters?" Sheila asked.

"Yes, I know. I saw the bodies today."

"What's that?" said Madame Aleksander quickly.

"Two boys tore some down last night. This morning six were shot in front of the wall. No one was allowed to remove their bodies all day."

"Where was this?"

"In the center of the town."

Madame Aleksander's nostrils dilated. "Think they can terrorize us, do they? Think they can—"

"Please, Madame Aleksander."

"I'll go out and tear down these posters, myself."

"You'll never reach Korytów if you do."

Casimir looked at Sheila anxiously. "You wouldn't want these lies on the walls about England, would you?" he asked.

Sheila hugged him suddenly. "I don't want to see you shot, Casimir."

"Someone's got to be," the boy answered gravely. "If we don't do these things, we will be slaves. You are glad I did it, Sheila? Are you glad?"

Sheila tightened her grip on his shoulders, with an intensity that surprised them both. She nodded her yes. Casimir's anxious little face cleared. He opened his mouth, but Sheila laid a finger across his. She pretended to laugh. "You've got to look after Madame Aleksander and me, you know. So don't go and get killed, Casimir. You won't?" She kept the smile on her lips as she stared at the treacherous walls. She couldn't bear this, she thought for the second time that evening. How many honest remarks might not condemn good friends? As she returned Madame Aleksander's curious gaze frankly, she made up her mind what she was going to do. Hofmeyer would call it a sign of the amateur. A professional like Hofmeyer himself would either solve it in a more clever way, or be able to harden his heart. If her decision was an admission of defeat then here was one time when she would choose defeat.

"Shall I cook supper?" Casimir asked eagerly. He was so like Volterscot, so anxious to please.

"Yes, do," Madame Aleksander said quickly, and Casimir lifted the small piece of pork and the two potatoes as if they were precious crystal. Volterscot trotted happily after him into the kitchen.

Sheila didn't look at Madame Aleksander. She hunted for a piece of paper and a pencil. Where was that stub which Schlott had used to draw diagrams of the city, so that she would not get lost? Had he taken it? She searched frantically, feeling Madame Aleksander's eyes on her every movement. She was thankful that Madame Aleksander kept her silence. Silence was safety. She found the pencil at last, lying in a pot of dry earth which held a wilting aspidistra. She couldn't find any paper, so she took one of the magazines. Above its title, she wrote in English, "I think this room is tapped for conversation, just as all telephone wires are now tapped. Do you understand what this means? I am *not* exaggerating."

Madame Aleksander's brows knitted as she read the message. She looked sharply at Sheila and saw the girl's desperation. She kept silent and, taking the pencil which was held out to her, wrote her reply among the list of contributors. "Yes. Do not worry. Now I understand. But is this possible?"

On the bottom margin, Sheila wrote, "Yes. Believe me, yes. Trust me. Michael Olszak does, but never mention this to *anyone* unless you want to see me shot."

Madame Aleksander's eyes widened. "Sheila!" they seemed to say. "Sheila!" But she still kept silent as the girl searched for the precious box of matches. Together they watched the title page curl into black tissue. And it was Madame Aleksander who crumbled its ashes into powder on the floor, all her housewifely instincts silenced.

"We are just coming," Madame Aleksander called to Casimir. Her voice was even. Her arm was round Sheila's shoulder. She has the strength, now, Sheila thought: I now depend on her. And she didn't care if Olszak or Hofmeyer were angry. She couldn't go to Korytów, leaving Casimir and Madame Aleksander unwarned. After all, Herr Hofmeyer only pretended to serve the Nazis so that he could help their enemies. And that, Sheila decided, was exactly what she was doing now.

Through the unboarded kitchen window, the chill wind of a wet night struck shrewdly. The lights were on once more in Warsaw, small flickering lights of candles and kerosene lamps. In the other kitchens which still stood, other women and children were gathered round pots of thin brew cooking slowly on the coal or wood stoves which had been resurrected. Casimir had "found" a small stove, had rigged a somewhat leaky pipe-chimney out of the window. Now he was blowing gently, carefully, on the small heap of glowing coals.

"It's 1916, all over again," Madame Aleksander murmured. Sheila knew she wasn't referring only to the cold, the scanty food, the feeble lights of the city. "But we'll come through it."

And suddenly to Sheila, the sparse pinpricks of light in the darkness were no longer pathetic. In their tragedy was promise. Through the mist which covered her eyes, the lights seemed to grow and spread until they touched each other, and there was no darkness left. For a moment, there was only one blurred glow. She brushed her eyes with the back of her hand. The darkness and its meager lights had returned. But the glow and the brightness remained in her heart.

## CHAPTER XXII

## *New Clothes for Old*

CASIMIR may have wondered why his bedtime followed supper so quickly that night, why Madame Aleksander and Sheila sat up late writing on magazine margins and burning discarded pages in the rusty stove in the kitchen, why they rose so early next morning and worked so silently about the flat, why he was given so many little tasks to do that he, too, had no time to talk. But, with the unexpected patience of the very young who will trust infinitely if only their affection is answered, he obeyed all Madame Aleksander's suggestions because he saw that it pleased her so much. He felt happy too, because she seemed to be quite better today. Her voice and all her movements weren't ill any more. He whistled as he cut out muslin "windowpanes" and tacked them into place; the plywood boards, he had decided, were to be used as shutters for bitter weather and night-time.

Sheila, as usual, wanted the dog to be washed. Madame Aleksander had said she was going to see her brother and then to visit the Kommandantur. Sheila said she would have to go out too, but she thought Volterscot needed one more bath before the weather got too cold.

"But isn't that his natural color?" Casimir asked.

"Not yet. He should be white. He will feel much better if he is really what he should be."

Casimir rose, still reluctant to leave the hinge he was trying to invent to make a neat shutter. "All right Sheila. If that makes him feel really better. But you are awful fussy about baths. Come on, Volterscot!"

"We'll all meet here again this afternoon," Madame Aleksander called after the boy and his dog. "Take care, Casimir."

To Sheila she said, "I am going out, now. Are you coming?"

"Not at the moment. I have some sewing to do."

The two women exchanged smiles as if each knew what

the other was thinking: how stilted and self-conscious the simplest phrases became if one was not sure of privacy. And then Madame Aleksander had also gone, and Sheila was left alone to put her plans into action. First, she must get in touch with Hofmeyer. Casimir had to be hidden, before the Germans arrested him. If she phoned that very private number, she could leave a message to be given to Hofmeyer when he visited that address.

Yet, somehow, she wanted to reach Hofmeyer without delay. The problem about Casimir was urgent. Perhaps it was too late even now. Suddenly she thought of a way to telephone Hofmeyer at his office without arousing suspicion. She arranged her thoughts into a line of conversation, and the more she examined what she would say, the surer she was that this would be not only the quickest but the safest method. It was only natural that she should want some respectable clothes and a decent meal. Anna Braun would demand those things. And Sheila Matthews would be a more efficient person if she fell less like something the cat had dragged in. She looked like a beggar; she was beginning to feel like one. She urged her courage with these thoughts, and called the number 4-6636 before she could change her mind. She listened to the phone's distant summons, and looked at her disreputable coat and her cracked shoes. Never again would she wonder why soldiers and sailors should keep their uniforms smart. Never again would she smile at button-polishing or deck-scrubbing.

Hofmeyer sounded abrupt and busy. Her initial confidence ebbed slightly. He was probably going to be furious with her. Her first question about any further instructions sounded painfully weak. But perhaps it was that hesitancy which caught his attention. "What else?" he demanded.

How pleasant and easy it would be if this were a normal world and she could say "Casimir's in trouble. Please help him." Instead, she said as Anna Braun might have said, "I thought I'd like a decent meal. I'm cold and depressed. What restaurants would you like me to use?"

"So that's it. How much money have you?"

"Little, and it belongs to the housekeeping. I wondered if I might have an advance on salary? I need some clothes too. I lost all my luggage in one of the September fires."

"Call at this office and collect some money, then. You can eat at the Europejski Restaurant."

"You mean I can go there alone?" Sheila hoped that her inflection on that sentence would be enough to make Hofmeyer realize she wanted to have one of those little walks with him.

But he ignored the question. "You can choose some clothes from the bedroom wardrobes when you call here. You should have taken some yesterday, as I suggested: the best of them are gone now." He turned away from the phone to talk quickly to someone else in the room.

"Those clothes may not fit me," Sheila said. She would rather wear her present rags than loot some unfortunate girl's . . . .

"I see," Hofmeyer said abruptly. She hoped desperately that his tone and manner were for the benefit of that someone else in the room. He was talking to the unknown man once more.

"Are you there, Fräulein Braun? I am sending round one of our young men who will take you to one of the larger shops, together with entry pass and credit check. This is a great nuisance, Fräulein Braun."

"I am sorry, Herr Hofmeyer," Sheila said meekly. She was beginning to wilt like a child under its parent's disapproval.

"My man will collect you in half an hour. His name is Hefner. He may seem Polish, but you can rely on him. He is a true German. Are you alone at the flat? All the better."

Well, Sheila thought as she replaced the receiver on its hook, she had tried to arrange a meeting, and all she got was a shopping tour. She began to analyze the conversation once more. No, she had made no slips. She couldn't have risked anything more obvious. Surely Mr. Hofmeyer didn't really think that she had troubled him only because of a meal and some clothes?

After that, she worried about Mr. Hefner until he arrived punctually. Mr. Hofmeyer had warned her, at least. *He may seem Polish. . . .* Don't, Anna Braun, forget your catechism.

Anna Braun answered the polite knocking on the outside door. The man was in civilian clothes. He was thin, blond and blue-eyed. With his broad brow, high cheekbones, wide mouth, straight nose, he might very well have been a Pole. His bow and greeting were also Polish. He had an excellent accent. He had obviously been given a description of her, for his identification card was already showing in the palm of his hand. Sheila slid hers quickly out of her bag. I would laugh, she thought, I would laugh if the price of a smile wasn't a bullet against a stone wall. A sense of humor was costly, nowadays.

"Miss Sheila Matthews?" he asked, and listened intently for any sound of life in the flat. His excuse for this visit was on the tip of his quick tongue.

"There is no one here."

He looked relieved, bowed again, said "Hefner!" as he bowed. "Are you ready, Fräulein Braun?"

"Yes." Preparations to go out certainly became very simple when you had to wear your coat indoors.

In the bright light of the street, he frowned at her coat and her shoes. He didn't seem to enjoy walking beside her. He hurried her into the car which he had left innocently around the corner. Sheila's smile disconcerted him. He was probably ashamed of being ashamed at accompanying a poorly clad German. He certainly had his own ideas of the comforts a German should have, even when imitating a bombed-out Pole. Anyway, he didn't speak during the short ride in the car, and Sheila had decided to ask no questions and to offer no conversation. She wondered what shop could be open to sell clothes. All the buying she had seen recently had taken place from hawkers' trays. She marveled that the route into town which she knew so well, and had always considered rather long, should in reality be so short.

She concealed her surprise when the car stopped in an alley, at the delivery entrance to one of the large shops which yesterday she had noticed was among those boarded-up. It still appeared to be in that category, for the noise of workmen's hammers clattered spasmodically into the street. But at this side entrance, there was a guard. As soon as Hefner had produced a ticket with the proper shape and color, the guard swung the heavy door open, they entered quickly, the door closed firmly behind them. Aladdin in his precious cave could not have been more blinded than Sheila.

The strangeness of the bright electric lights at first dazzled her, and then as her eyes became accustomed to the glare she saw that her first unbelievable impressions were really true. Behind the boarded windows, the long counters were heaped with merchandise. Perplexed shop assistants were helping an array of uniforms to make their purchases. Wehrmacht, Luftwaffe, Gestapo uniforms jostled each other and the few Germans in civilian clothes; all madly buying; all talking at once; all using elbows and stretching hands freely. Yards of cloth, underwear, perfume, blouses, hats, dresses—it didn't matter what they bought, as long as they found something. The only impulse was to buy and buy; the urge to spend, to acquire, was on. There was plenty of occupation money. With this arrangement, even the most expensive articles were practically given away free. Why bother with the farce of worthless notes at all? Sheila thought bitterly. She noticed with some embarrassment that there were only nine women in sight (apart from the *Volksdeutsche* behind the counters) and these were definitely camp followers: streamlined, chromium-plated camp followers with elegant hair and shoes and voluptuous fur jackets, but still camp followers, who would share in the loot in return for favors rendered. Sheila remembered a phrase of Steve's. *On the receiving end: . . . we've been on the receiving end.* And now, here she was on the opposite side. She had seen what it was like to be defeated by the Germans; now, she was seeing the other side of the picture. Herr Hefner didn't seem to notice what little zest she had for choosing new clothes.

Perhaps that was because he himself seemed to enjoy arranging what she should buy. "Something which would be smart enough for a secretary, and yet not too outstanding for your Polish friends to live with," was his judgment.

"Yes," Sheila said, looking at his extremely expensive suit and delicate tie. Herr Hefner had his own rules for himself, it would seem. The only thing that surprised him was her moderation. He looked at the heavy brown coat, the gray wool suit, the brown wool sweater, the simple gray felt, the brown shoes and warm gloves.

"Are you sure that's all?" he asked with a puzzled frown.

"On my first month's salary, yes. Secretaries don't earn so much, you know. Besides, I have some other things to buy."

"Oh, yes, of course," Herr Hefner agreed with a smile, looking in the direction of the underwear department. "Over here, I think."

Sheila didn't move. "Later," she said sweetly. "But first I must buy something for the people with whom I am living."

He frowned again. "Is that necessary, Fräulein Braun?"

"They would accept my new prosperity more naturally, if I did buy them something." She saw by his face that she had won her point.

"Not in this department, then," he said. "These clothes are wool. We'll find cheaper things."

Sheila concealed her disappointment with an effort. When you are hungry, you always felt twice as thwarted, it seemed. She followed him to the other side of the shop where fewer officers and more private soldiers were selecting clothes for those at home. She chose the warmest black dress she could find for Madame Aleksander, and a thick sweater for Casimir. She tried to buy a heavy scarf for each of them too, but Herr Hefner would have none of that. "You've bought more than enough for them," he said. "This is unusual, Fräulein Braun." He still looked undecided, as if he were calculating what Hofmeyer would have to say to such unnecessary expense.

"They are so cheap," Sheila said, and left the department before he thought better of his acquiescence. She led the way through a crowd of soldiers buying silk and lace underwear. Hefner was beside her, much to her surprise. "You'll need some of this, I suppose," he said, watching a tall, lean soldier holding up a peach satin nightdress in front of him with a critical eye.

Sheila said, "I shall have a cold winter if I live with the Poles. I'll need warmer things than that."

As she chose the heavier, plainer silks (she was not Spartan enough to choose the dull and depressing cottons), Herr Hefner was saying, "I admire your restraint. I suppose it is necessary."

"I must live my job, after all, Herr Hefner," she replied, and that satisfied him completely. "Now, I'm going to wear some of these things, and the rest can be parceled." She headed determinedly for a possible fitting room, evading two Luftwaffe men who were measuring silk stockings along their own legs. Herr Hefner hovered outside the cubicle. It was an extraordinary thing, Sheila thought as she changed her old clothes for new, that no one in the building had looked around him and burst out laughing. She had never seen so many little groups of people all so intent on their own little purposes, and yet all coming under one large theme: loot. Breughel, she decided, could have filled one of his enormous canvases with them. He would have enjoyed their petty preoccupations and painted them into one sweeping satire. Here in this corner, would be the two airmen measuring stockings. Here the soldier with the nightdress in front of him. Here the three Gestapo men stretching girdles to see if the rubber was good. (They ought to know a lot about rubber with their experience in clubs.) Here the two officers each with an armful of perfume bottles and bath salts. Here the lacquered blonde with her hand held under the lace and ninon bed-jacket. And behind the hundred little groups would be the ragged outline of a murdered city, a pyramid of bones, and a mad woman wandering.

Herr Hefner looked at her critically when she at last left the fitting room. His impatience vanished. He looked surprised, pleased. "Good," he said.

"I think you chose the right things." That pleased him still more. And she added one more drop to his cup of self-esteem by saying, "I must tell Herr Hofmeyer how very efficient you have been."

He lost all the stiffness he had shown in the car. He was now far from ashamed at being seen with her. In his relief, he became effusive.

"Now, what about a cocktail? And you needed a good meal, too. I remember that. Why don't you have an early lunch with me now at the Europejski? The best people go there. And it has a corner left for Poles, so we will be safe if any of our Polish friends see us enter the restaurant."

"Splendid," Sheila said, and hoped she was enthusiastic. "What about letting Mr. Hofmeyer know where we are going, in case something urgent turns up for us to do?"

"Good. I'll phone, while you collect the packages."

Sheila bought two woolen scarves in the more expensive department. They were much superior, softer, warmer, than those she had first tried to buy. They were neatly included in her parcel by the time Hefner had returned from the telephone booth. He arrived in time to watch the last knot of string being securely tied, and remarked pleasantly, "They take a long time to get packages together these days. But I expect many of these girls are new to this job."

Sheila agreed with a bright smile. The two hidden scarves were her own small triumph. She would have smiled at anything Herr Hefner said at this moment.

They lunched well, except that Sheila found she couldn't eat so much after all. She spent the latter half of the meal in sipping a glass of weak tea, avoiding the sight of Herr Hefner's excellent appetite as tactfully as she could. She found herself longing for the cold draughts of Steve's rooms. The warmth and noise of the restaurant, instead of being as exciting as she had imagined, only made her feel still more sick. Remember in future, she told herself, whenever you think you are missing bright lights and laughing voices and interesting food, that these things aren't the fun they used to be. It was all relative: if you weren't free, a palace for a house would be less bearable than a poor cottage where friends could be together. Better a dinner of herbs where love is than a stalled ox and hatred therewith.

Mr. Hefner did most of the talking, which consisted mainly of questions. Sheila had to pretend to be quite unguarded, while her mind quickly analyzed each harmless remark to find how deep the bog was before she could venture one foot in it. The only way to cross safely was to scatter some conversational bracken leaves over the treacherous surface, and in this way she gave the appearance of having evaded not one question, without having given any particular answer. Hefner wanted the details of the Warsaw siege (he had just arrived from Danzig) and the only difficulty there was that she had to remember she was supposed to have enjoyed every minute of it. Hefner talked about Munich, where he had once spent a year at the Geopolitical School. That was answered by lots of chatter about Aunt Thelma, about pleasant days at Nymphenburg, with its charming Dutch kitchen in the hunting lodge where Amalie and her ladies had liked to cook for the King and his court, about the Dachau Museum with its walled garden and thin brown pears and its view of the Bavarian Alps and the Zugspitze.

"Dachau..." mused Hefner. "That's become a very interesting place in the last few years. But of course it's been some time since you were there, hasn't it? Why didn't you ever go back?"

"Money," she explained with a sad smile. "And when I had saved enough for a trip to the Continent, my aunt was in Switzerland and Mr. Hofmeyer met me. He persuaded me to go back to London, to continue, to wait. He had plans for me."

She watched Hefner, but she must have said approximately the right things, for the clever look in his eyes was gone and he was genuinely sympathetic. He became quite sentimental. "The lives of our German brothers and sisters who must work in foreign countries are indeed sad," he said.

"But necessary."

"Of course, very necessary. We have a second army in them. Their rewards will be high. Don't worry, Fräulein Braun. You will enjoy the benefits fully, some day. Only have patience for a little longer."

"It won't be long, now?"

"Absolutely not. Another six months at the most, if peace isn't negotiated before then. Our Führer has promised that. He is never wrong."

What, never? Well, hardly ever, Sheila thought: and watched, with relief and rising hope, the white head and lined face which had just entered the restaurant. Mr. Hofmeyer had not misinterpreted her telephone message, after all. He walked towards them as if by accident, as if he were merely looking for a table.

Quietly he motioned Hefner to sit again, and pulled over a vacant chair from the next table.

He looked at Sheila and said, "Well, you didn't waste your time, I see."

"That was due to Herr Hefner. He was very helpful, and very kind."

Hefner beamed. "It was a pleasure, Fräulein Braun."

Hofmeyer ordered an elaborate meal and said casually to Hefner: "Don't wait for me. Dittmar said he wanted to see you at his office."

Hefner rose abruptly, his face already obedient at the name of Dittmar. He said to Sheila, "I hope we meet again, soon. You like dancing?"

"Yes, when I have time."

"Good. I'll phone you, if I may?" He bowed to each of them in turn, and hurried away.

In a low voice, Sheila said, "I thought he was your young man, not Dittmar's."

Hofmeyer was very absorbed in measuring salt and pepper. "He serves us both. Dittmar was in conference with me this morning when you phoned. It was he who suggested Hefner should accompany you this morning." His voice dropped. "I've been worried ever since. Hefner is a very percipient young man. But I see you did well. I could tell that from his manner."

He ate with remarkable speed. "I see that I've been left with the bill to pay, however," he said dryly as he called for the waiter. "Hefner will be a rich man, some day." Then he looked at the large package which Sheila was pulling out from underneath the table. "We can't walk far with that," he said.

"But I'd like a short walk. I need fresh air. It is too hot in here."

Hofmeyer paused in counting his change. "So?" he said slowly. He lifted the package and carried it towards the street without any more delay.

"Why are you smiling?" he asked as he turned in the direction of his office.

"Herr Hefner was too dignified to carry that parcel. He's quite the most graceful snob I have ever met."

"In the restaurant you were very serious for a moment. I knew you must want to see me when you phoned. But is it as bad as the way you looked when you said you needed a walk?"

She told him quickly about Casimir. "And I am sure there's a dictaphone. There were too many workmen pottering about the flat yesterday with no obvious results to show for their labors. Where would that dictaphone be?"

"Anywhere. It's a small thing. Probably linked up with the telephone."

"Then our words would be heard as soon as they are spoken?"

"Yes. All telephones are operated by Germans, now."

"Then Casimir could be arrested at any moment?"

"When we think it's worth our while to arrest him. We've plenty of more important people to arrest. He will be on the black list for treatment as soon as we have the time.

That may be tomorrow or next week. Today we are busy."
He paused and then said still more gravely, "Edward Korytowski was arrested at dawn this morning."

Sheila turned white. She was going to be sick. She halted
and leaned for a moment against a bullet-scarred doorway.
The attack of nausea passed.

"For what reason?" For the meeting in his apartment?
her eyes asked anxiously.

"Professors are being arrested. That's the only reason."

"What will happen to him? To the others? Most of them
were too old for military service."

"He is being sent to Dachau." *A very interesting place,*
Hefner had said. In spite of the midday sun striking through
her new wool clothes, Sheila shivered. The pavement under
her feet lost its even surface for the next few steps. Uncle
Edward. Dachau.

"Polish culture must be destroyed," Hofmeyer said in a
hard voice. "The orders were issued yesterday. No Polish
universities, or colleges, or high schools. No Polish libraries,
newspapers, priests, law courts or radio. The great silence
has begun."

Sheila couldn't speak. She stared unseeing at the buildings
in front of her.

"As for Casimir, either Department Fourteen will help him
to leave Warsaw at once, or perhaps we could find some use
for him with Number Thirty-one."

Sheila forced herself to pay attention. Those who still
could be saved must be thought of, first "Thirty-one," she
said. Casimir would rather be with those who helped the
guerrillas than be sent out of Poland. "He's so alone,"
she added.

"As soon as you get back to the flat, send him away at
once. To Warecka Street, Number 15. They will hide him
until we can make arrangements for him. He seems a brave
boy, this Casimir."

Sheila nodded. "Worth helping," she said. When Poland
was free again she would need all her Casimirs. "Shall we ever
see him again?" she asked.

"No. And better keep the dog with you. Don't let it follow
him. It could give him away. You understand?"

She nodded wearily.

"We shall soon be at the office. It was better not to take a
long walk today. I am bringing you back here to discuss the
problem of Korytów, so that this journey here together will
seem natural."

Something in his tone aroused her. "Is Dittmar suspicious?"
she asked quickly.

"He trusts nobody. There are too many gambling for power to let us be generous and trustful with each other. Don't worry. The dictaphones and tapped phones are merely part of the Nazi methods. They like blackmail. They don't expect state secrets: they are content with an ill-chosen friendship or a hidden love affair or an unadvised opinion to give them a hold over their fellow spies. Dittmar thinks he is clever: he watches me because I'm a serious rival; he watches you because some day he may want to use you against me. That's all. Besides, I watch Herr Dittmar just as carefully." Herr Hofmeyer smiled, as he transferred the weight of the parcel from one arm to another. I, too, have enough influence to have dictaphones installed, he seemed to say.

"I still think he doesn't accept me," Sheila said. "He cannot forgive me the fact that I escaped and Elzbieta didn't. He's possessive. Her death was an injury directed at him."

"He accepts you slightly more since Captain Streit approved of you yesterday morning."

Sheila looked sharply at Hofmeyer. What riddle was this?

"Streit is Gestapo chief for our district. He commended your information on Gustav Schlott as a future helper of the Poles. Don't look so distressed. I assure you Schlott was too warmhearted and simple; he had already talked too much. He would have been caught red-handed helping the Poles. Then he would not have been evicted. In fact, we saved his life. I forwarded your report on him two days ago. Yesterday, action was taken."

"What a miserable kind of person you've made me out to be," Sheila said resentfully.

"But what an excellent Nazi, Fräulein Braun. And after all, I have got to justify your existence here, from time to time."

Neither of them spoke as they approached the large house where Hofmeyer had his suite. They kept their silence until they were inside Hofmeyer's own private office.

"I brought you here," he said crisply as he rubbed circulation back into his fingers, "because a decision about Korytów has been reached. It seems that the village has been giving us trouble. A punitive expedition is to be sent against it. An example will be made of the village, and certainly the Aleksander woman will not receive permission to travel there. I, at the moment, am too busy to be able to find a solution for you. So are the other departments. For the victory parade into the city takes place on the sixth of this October; that is the day after tomorrow. The Avenue Ujazdowskie has at last been made fit for the parade, and our Führer will himself be present. Naturally, we are busy finding prominent hos-

tages and arresting potential troublemakers. You can see how
the problem of Korytów is now one for you alone."

He watched the amazement on her face and continued:
"I have done all I can at the moment. Here are the necessary permits which will allow you to make the journey. If
you do so, it will of course be on your own judgment and
risk. Herr Ditt—the other department which I hoped would
facilitate your journey refuses to help at this moment. They
consider the Aleksander woman and her children are of no
importance."

Sheila's horror over the fate of Korytów gave way to dismay as she realized that if Herr Dittmar's policy (for that
slip of Hofmeyer's tongue as he referred to the department
which had been so uncoöperative was no accident) meant
no Aleksanders, then that meant, in turn, no Sheila Matthews. As Anna Braun she would be given some real German
work to do. Dittmar might even try to have her transferred
to his department.

A telephone call interrupted Hofmeyer's account of how
she might attempt the journey to Korytów if she decided
to make it. Sheila sat tensely while he answered it. Surely
Hofmeyer realized that this was Dittmar's thin end of the
wedge to ease her out of the Aleksander-Matthews relation-
ship? Surely—and then, looking at the number of permits,
clipped together, which Hofmeyer had pushed across the
desk to her as he reached for the telephone, she knew that
he fully realized that. He wanted her to go to Korytów and
keep the Aleksanders together, together with her own excuse
of being Sheila Matthews. He knew, too, that any other solution would lead her into grave complications, perhaps himself and Olszak into danger. He knew. Otherwise he wouldn't
have taken the trouble to get these permits for her. If his
permission now seemed grudging, it was only because he
was maneuvering against a department or combination of departments which were powerful. She examined the permits:
they allowed her considerable freedom of movement. She
couldn't help thinking what an involved way of wasting time
and energy all these pieces of paper represented: this was
carrying German method to a ludicrous extreme. She thought
of Uncle Matthews for the first time in days: how he used
to grumble over the inanities of income tax returns. He
ought to see the complexities of German rule. And then she
realized that Uncle Matthews, attached to some branch of
British Intelligence as he must be, would probably see sam-
ples of all these permits. And Department Fifteen of Olzak's
organization was no doubt making excellent copies of them,
at this very minute. Department Fifteen. Stanislaw Aleksan-

der. There was her plan. Her main problem was solved. Once she could get the Aleksander children and their mother reunited, Stanislaw could attend to their papers and credentials. She would get them safely out of Poland, yet. The feeling that she must go to Korytów was strengthened. And she must go at once. If only Dittmar's department had been helpful, she could have made the journey so quickly, so easily. With an official car, she would have been there in less than an hour. She would have been in time to warn Korytów. She stuffed the papers into her handbag, wondered how quickly she could make the journey on her own initiative, worrying if she would reach the village in time, wishing Hofmeyer would stop phoning and let her leave.

He ended his series of abrupt *"Ja!"* and *"Jawohl!"* He replaced the receiver, looking at her with eyes suddenly worried, with lips tightly closed. "Herr Dittmar would like to see you. He has sent Hefner round here to collect you. He wants you to identify Kordus."

"Kordus?"

"Yes, they have a body over at the Gestapo headquarters which they believe to be Kordus. The man would not admit anything before he died."

"I am to go to Gestapo headquarters?" The look on her face awakened Hofmeyer's pity.

He stopped looking worried, and said lightly as if to cure her of this sudden stage-fright, "Yes. They are in the former Ministry of Education building on Aleja Szucha. That isn't so far from Frascati where you are living. Consider it just a break on your journey home with your new autumn clothes."

Sheila smiled weakly. "That parcel is becoming a nuisance," she said. "I think I'll ask Herr Hefner to take me to Frascati Gardens first. That's on the way, anyway." And then I can at least tell Casimir to leave, she thought. Perhaps she herself would never come out of the Gestapo building once it swallowed her up.

Hofmeyer was obviously relieved at the casualness of her voice, but he noticed the tense neck, the hands held too stiffly. "So we've got Kordus," he said. But he shook his head warningly. Don't believe it, his eyes said, don't believe it.

"Now I have some work to do, Fräulein Braun. While you wait for Hefner, here are some copies of the newest decrees and regulations. They will show you how we intend to treat the Poles." He handed her a pile of printed sheets with impressive headings. On a slip of paper attached to the top page, he had scribbled: "Careful. Fake."

She left him, with a newly lighted cigarette in his mouth

and a piece of flaming paper in his hand. His eyes were on her as she closed the door. He gave an encouraging smile. That was the last time she ever saw Herr Hofmeyer.

Herr Hefner set himself out to be fascinating. He talked gaily all the way to Frascati Gardens. Sheila had an uncomfortable doubt as to whether all this charm was the result of a genuine liking for her, or he was only following special orders. He was extremely obliging about halting the car round the corner from Steve's flat and letting her carry the heavy parcel towards the doorway.

"Only a few minutes!" Sheila called over her shoulder to the waiting car. As her neat new heels sounded smartly on the pavement, she was already planning how to use every available second.

She called out halfway up the staircase so that they would know she was coming. Madame Aleksander was blowing out a match. In a soup bowl, the pieces of paper on which she and Casimir had been writing, remained unburned. She was smiling, partly in welcome, partly in relief.

"We have been playing that funny game you taught the children this summer," Madame Aleksander said. "What *is* its name?"

"Consequences," Sheila answered in a very normal voice, but her fingers had become all thumbs and she could hardly open the parcel. She looked sideways at the pieces of paper which Casimir and Madame Aleksander were now smoothing out to show her. So Madame Aleksander had been forced to tell him something about the dictaphone to silence his otherwise irrepressible remarks. Now he was excited. Like all children he loved a secret, especially one so strange and mysterious. His blue eyes were shining, and there was a flush on his pale cheeks. This was a game which he enjoyed, and perhaps even understood better than the two women.

Madame Aleksander had noticed Sheila's clothes. "But how nice you look," she said delightedly.

"I asked Herr Hofmeyer for an advance in my salary." Sheila pulled out the dress for Madame Aleksander, the sweater for Casimir and the two scarves. "For you," she said, and watched Madame Aleksander's surprise give way to pleasure.

"I was feeling cold," Casimir admitted, grinning happily because he had not been forgotten. Sheila had lifted his pencil and piece of paper. To Casimir, his head emerging with ruffled fair hair from the neck of the new sweater, she made a sign of silence. She began to write:—

*"Casimir! The Gestapo already know of the torn posters.*

*You must leave at once. Friends wait for you at Warecka 15. Keep silent.*"

The boy looked wonderingly at the piece of paper, at Sheila, at Madame Aleksander. The new game was no longer funny. He knew what the message meant. He was to leave this house, and his new friends, and all the happiness he had begun to find again. Madame Aleksander was clasping his hand with a pleading intensity. She was nodding and biting her lips and laying a finger on his to keep him silent, all at once.

Sheila said, "Casimir, we need some more wood for the stove. It is quite dead now. There's supper to be cooked for tonight, you know." She pointed the pencil to the written "Warecka 15" and kept it there.

"Shall I take Volterscot?" he asked slowly.

"No, I think he should keep Madame Aleksander company, for I have to go out once more."

Madame Aleksander gathered Volterscot, protesting with a strange half-smothered whine, in her arms. She held him there, struggling frenziedly, as Sheila pushed the reluctant boy out of the door.

"Please," Sheila said as they reached the hall.

"As you wish, Pani Sheila," he said. He looked slowly back at the room, at Madame Aleksander and the violently straining Volterscot, at Sheila. "As you wish," he said again. He suddenly took the paper and pencil and underscored "Warecka 15" to show that he had indeed understood.

And then his footsteps, no longer lighthearted or clattering, faded into the distance.

Madame Aleksander's face was drawn with sadness once more. She laid her cheek with its silent tears against the excited head of Volterscot.

"I must go to," Sheila said. She struck a match and burned all the pieces of paper, being particularly careful that nothing but fine dust was left of "Warecka 15." "I'll be back quite soon," she promised. She watched the last curling ashes and through of the lonely boy walking blindly towards the strange address. What kind of people would welcome him? Her heart swelled with pity and affection. It choked her. At last, "I must go," she repeated in a voice which seemed hardly her own. "I'll be back soon."

On sudden impulse she kissed Madame Aleksander's wet cheek, touched Volterscot under his chin.

Madame Aleksander didn't speak. She was biting her lip cruelly, her cheek still against Volterscot's alert ears.

Hefner greeted her affably. "More than a few minutes,"

he observed, "but better than I expected. How did they like their new rags? Did you have a touching scene?"

"Yes," Sheila said. She let him talk of the victory parade as the car turned south in to Aleje Ujazdowskie, and then southwest into Aleja Szucha. Sheila, seemingly intent on his phrases with a concentration in her brown eyes which obviously pleased him, was thinking of Warecka 15. She was thinking of a boy of twelve, with a new wool scarf round his neck, plodding obediently towards that street; of a boy concealing his unhappiness behind an unconvincing frown. If only she could have told him that he wasn't just going to hide in a strange house, if only she could have said, "You may eventually join a guerrilla army," how much more quickly he would have walked. But she hadn't dared tell him that. He might not reach Warecka 15.

So she listened to the affable young man beside her, fixed her eyes politely on his face, and kept saying to herself, "Please let him reach Warecka 15. Please, God, let him reach it."

## CHAPTER XXIII

### At the Ministry of Education

HEINRICH DITTMAR, in a smart gray suit, waited with three uniformed men in a pleasant room. On a large desk were flowers, a huge ash tray of heavy crystal, a silver framed photograph. The chairs were comfortable and decorative. The men seemed in excellent humor. They rose to their feet and saluted her in the Nazi manner. Hefner remained tactfully in the background.

The black-uniformed man with the exaggerated armband brought his heels sharply together, bowed and echoed "Streit!" as Dittmar said "Captain Wolfgang Streit." He resumed his commanding position at the desk, his elbows on the polished rosewood, his fingertips joining his outspread hands as he waited for the other introductions to be completed.

The man in the green uniform of the Waffen SS brought his heels together as Dittmar said "Captain Hans Greiser." He bowed and echoed "Greiser!"

The man in gray uniform with a black square and silver embroidered letters on his sleeve brought his heels together. Dittmar said "Herr Josef Engelmann." Again there was the sharp bow from the waist, again the echo. "Engelmann!"

Sheila inclined her head. She restrained herself in time from a full bow, heel-click and "Braun!" She took the offered chair, feeling as if she were on a stage and each small movement had become magnified into a gesture. She waited, her throat closing treacherously. The short silence probed like a knife at her heart. Fortunately, Dittmar was in a hurry.

"We asked you to come here, Fräulein Braun," he said quickly, "because you are the only person in Warsaw at the moment who can identify the man we have downstairs. All of us here, in our own way, are interested in that man. We believe he is Kordus. You can help us; for you were examined by Kordus, after Colonel Bolt had questioned you, and then escaped."

"Discharged," Sheila said. "The first time, I was discharged. The second time, I didn't wait to meet Kordus."

"Oh, yes! Discharged." Dittmar's watchful eyes smiled benevolently. "Anyway, you can help us. This way, Fräulein Braun."

The three uniforms exchanged glances. Their faces were expressionless as they could do nothing but follow the too quick Dittmar, who was already guiding Sheila out of the door. The short procession went down into the large, well-built cellars. Every inch of space in the enormous, modern building had been turned to use. Partitions had been erected to create more offices out of the cellar rooms. Men in and out of uniform hurried through the long basement corridor, stood respectfully aside to let pass Dittmar's personally conducted tour. Sheila was glad of the length of the journey: it gave her time to prepare herself. *Fake*, Hofmeyer had warned her. And now Dittmar had warned her too. "Escaped," he had said. He had said it purposely, as if trying to trip her up. Perhaps it was only what he thought passed for a sense of humor. But possibly it was a test. What if Dittmar knew that the body in this building was not that of Kordus? What if she said it was Kordus, hoping that would end the search for him? She had been tempted to identify whatever she might see as Kordus. Now she knew that such a clever piece of work was not clever enough. It was all that Dittmar needed to hear in order to condemn her. He still had doubts about her, then. She was glad she knew that, however unpleasant it was. It's war between you and me, Herr Dittmar, she thought, smiling at him sweetly when he halted at one of the end doors in the cellar. As he swung it open, and led the way into the room so that he could turn and face her as she saw the body, she was already guarding herself against the chance that Hofmeyer had been wrong, that she would really see the body of the man whom the Germans knew as Kordus.

A brilliant, cruel light came from the large naked bulb overhead. The smell was heavy and loathsome. Even after the smell of death in Warsaw streets to which Sheila had become accustomed, the thick, threatening air in this room was too much for her. She turned her head away, and fumbled for a handkerchief.

One of the men behind her said, "Whew! They don't take long, do they?"

"This will be cleared as soon as Fräulein Braun identifies them," Captain Streit's slow quiet voice said. "Quickly, Fräulein Braun. This way." His highly polished boots struck the cement floor with self-possessed rhythm. He was taking charge, now. Dittmar was too busy watching her face to worry about that.

She held the handkerchief over her mouth and nose, and followed Streit. Dittmar kept beside her. The others stayed near the door, sacrificing curiosity to comfort.

"Come in and close the door. Don't want it all down the corridor," Streit ordered. They obeyed reluctantly.

The first stiff figure, bent into a grotesque angle like a piece of hammered tin, had been thrown on a narrow table. Two other bodies were stretched on the floor.

"Is that Kordus?"

Sheila's glance flickered over the gashed face, the gouged eye, the earless head. It wasn't Olszak. In her thankfulness, she almost forgot her mounting sickness.

She shook her head.

"Definitely?"

She nodded.

"Know this?" Streit turned one of the bodies on the ground with the toe of his long black boot.

She nodded. The battered face had a ghastly smile, as if the man had welcomed death when it came.

"And that?" Streit pointed to the third body.

She shook her head.

The heavy door closed behind them.

In the corridor, there was only the smell of Turkish tobacco and talcum powder, of men who were well-dressed and careful of their well-being. In Captain Streit's office, there was the smell of roses from the vase on the desk. But she still felt ill, still crushed the damp ball of handkerchief in the palm of her hand.

Dittmar began, "Well, that's that. Now—"

And then Captain Streit asserted his authority for the second time. He interrupted Dittmar unfeelingly, said quietly but firmly, "You were sure, Fräulein Braun, that the first body was not that of Kordus?"

"I never saw that man before."

"The Chief Commissioner did question you when you were first arrested by the Poles?"

"First, Colonel Bolt questioned me. Then someone who was called Special Commissioner questioned me. I did not hear his name."

"That second man was Kordus. What was he like?"

"Medium-height, thin, undistinguished." By the way Streit had glanced down at a pad on his desk, she guessed that Kordus' description was already known. But even so, that put Olszak in little danger. There were so many men of medium height who were thin and undistinguished.

"Age?" Streit asked.

Sheila shook her head slowly, helplessly. "Middle-aged," she said. Streit nodded as much as to say, "That's what anyone who has seen him tells us." He pursed his thin lips in annoyance at the undistinguished Kordus.

Dittmar wanted his innings, too. "Who was the man you identified?"

Truthfully she answered him, "He was with the police when Lisa and I were arrested."

Dittmar's eyes flickered. He concealed his disappointment well.

"And the third body?"

"No one could recognize that," Sheila said briefly. The men laughed, shortly, quietly. Sheila was conscious of a slight change in their attitude. The tension eased. The faces were not merely polite now. They smiled, too.

"Well, that's all, Fräulein Braun," Streit said. "You were right, Dittmar, the markings inside the man's clothing saying he was Kordus were either coincidence or purpose."

Sheila rose, bowed and moved towards the door. She had been dismissed. It was over. She had told the truth throughout. It was over.

"One moment, Fräulein Braun," Dittmar called and roused a sharp stare from Captain Streit. "After your release from questioning by Kordus, where did you meet Herr Olszak? Remember, you arrived that night at Korytowski's flat with him."

"I met him in the street outside. He was going there for a visit."

"You met him in the street?"

"Yes." Mild surprise at such a question was in Sheila's voice.

"Was there another man with him? Someone who looked like that second exhibit downstairs?"

"No. He was alone. He almost knocked me down in the blackout. But there was no one else there at the time."

Dittmar frowned. This time he could not conceal his disappointment. Her mention of the blackout had reminded him that in such conditions she could not be expected to see anyone. He had had his theory nicely developing; now, a blackout made any other questions about that night quite pointless.

"What's this you've got up your sleeve, Dittmar? What's this about an Olszak?" Streit asked with a pleasant smile. But he and Greiser and Engelmann exchanged an almost imperceptible glance. "You're a fine fellow, I must say, after we all agreed to pool our knowledge on the Kordus affair."

Sheila saw the others watching Dittmar's sudden, bland smile.

"Oh, this had nothing to do with Kordus," the man answered coolly. "This is a little question just between me and Fräulein Braun. I never get the chance of seeing her. She's in Hofmeyer's department."

Sheila smiled. She could only hope the smile betrayed none of her nervousness. For now she was convinced that Dittmar had found some cause for suspicion. He was on the right road. He was trying to connect Olszak with Kordus, and Kordus with Hofmeyer. He considered her the hand which would tie the loose ends round Olszak's neck into a tight, satisfying knot. Why didn't he make his charges against Hofmeyer? she wondered, and then realized that Hofmeyer's position with other departments was too assured at the moment for unprovable statements to be made about him. All Dittmar needed was one small piece of proof. One small stone could start an avalanche.

"When did you last see Olszak?" he asked suddenly.

Sheila was conscious that the others' manners were strained. But they didn't watch her, strangely enough. They were watching Dittmar.

Sheila stared at him, too. "Frankly," she said with a puzzled frown, "I cannot remember the exact date. Some time during the siege. He came to ask about the Aleksanders."

"Why?"

"He had just heard that Barbara Aleksander was dead." Sheila looked at the three men in uniform. "She was burned to death with nearly two hundred children in one of our big raids."

They ignored her remark. Hefner, alone, seemed shocked by the idea. "You must be mistaken," he said sharply, and received a look of disapproval from the others, not for his naïveté but for the fact that he should have spoken at all.

Sheila looked pointedly at her scarred left hand. "I was nearly burned alive, too," she said. "A dinner engagement saved me."

"We all run risks, Fräulein Braun," Streit said coldly, but he looked at her with sudden interest. Something in her emotional outburst was connected with Dittmar. Sheila took a deep breath. The first phase of her attack had been launched. To strike back at Dittmar had been instinctive: this was the only way to defend herself and her friends. At the very least it would serve as a diversion. Subconsciously, Hofmeyer's remarks about departmental jealousies had linked up with the look on these men's faces as they had watched Dittmar take the center of the stage. If she had had time to think it all out, she would never have had the courage to attempt her next move. If she had been a man, she would never have tried it.

She returned Streit's look with wide brown eyes. "Yes, Captain Streit. I have been running risks willingly for three months now." She was almost weeping with indignation. "And today I find that all my work during these three months may be sabotaged. Not by the enemy. By someone among us, someone who may want to usurp Herr Hofmeyer's power.

"What's this?" interrupted Engelmann sharply. "What's this? Hofmeyer is one of my men. He has been of outstanding service to our new branch of the *Sicherheitsdienst*. Who has been interfering with his work?"

"I don't know. Herr Hofmeyer didn't say. He is loyal," Sheila said, but her eyes flickered towards Dittmar's bent head. He was pretending to examine the arrangement of roses on Captain Streit's desk. Streit had at least caught Sheila's implication. His thin, clever lips became thinner. Sheila's guess that he didn't like Dittmar was confirmed. Her fingers stopped their hidden trembling. She unclasped her hands and smoothed her skirt.

"Sit down, Fräulein Braun," Streit said pleasantly. "How sabotaged? That is a strong statement."

"By some unexplained refusal to let me make a short journey to Korytów."

"Why must you go?"

"I don't *want* to go. The journey will be unpleasant. But there are three people there—two children, one elderly female—whom I must contact. I can only do that by going to Korytów."

Streit looked puzzled, disappointed; but he was still watching Dittmar, who was now looking unconcernedly out of the window. "If they are necessary to your work, Fräulein Braun, then we can telephone and have them sent here."

"Then they would know we are behind this move. The Poles are very suspicious. I must accomplish this as Sheila Matthews, not as Anna Braun."

"What is this Korytów?"

"A very small village near enough to Warsaw."

"Is Hofmeyer against your going?" Captain Streit was beginning to get bored, but he was thorough.

"No. Yesterday it was his solution to my biggest problem. Today, he finds that another department which he had to consult is against the idea."

"Why so much fuss about a mere trip to an unimportant pigsty? There should be no difficulty for any agent to reach there. The question should not even have arisen. So much time wasted on these petty misunderstandings!"

"I believe the trouble arises because Korytów is to be destroyed. That was the reason given Herr Hofmeyer."

"Then that is a military matter," Streit said, and marked the conclusion of a disappointing conversation by slapping the gleaming rosewood with his open hand. "For the moment, the military is in control."

The case was closed. She had lost, Sheila thought. And in more ways than one, she realized, as Dittmar turned round to face the room and looked at her.

But Englemann said, "There's a department for liaison with the military in matters of reprisals. I was to have headed it, but owing to pressure of my own duties, Arndt was appointed instead. Where is Arndt? He will explain. He advises the military which areas we want cleaned up."

Dittmar broke his silence. "He had to visit Cracow. I have been acting as deputy here for him."

"Then you advised the military committee that a village should be selected as an example?" Engelmann said. "Such a decision should have been suggested first of all to Streit, or Greiser, or to me. On what authority do you make your decisions, Herr Dittmar?"

Sheila's eyes counted the roses. She had offered a diversion from questions about Olszak. She had stirred up something far more than she had intended. She was now too nervous even to enjoy Dittmar's sudden uncertainty.

"As Herr Arndt's chosen deputy—"

"Arndt is responsible in such matters to me. He would have had me ratify such a decision. As for this Korytów . . . where is it? I haven't heard of any trouble recently, there. I never even heard of it until these last minutes."

Streit picked up the telephone, and gave brisk instructions. He then settled himself comfortably in his chair. All his interest had returned. He was no longer annoyed over his time being wasted. "We shall wait until the right department is found, to explain to us why Korytów should have been the selected village," he said amiably to the room.

Sheila stirred uncomfortably. "I am sorry—" she began apologetically.

Streit silenced her with a careless wave of his hand. "Not at all, Fräulein Braun. Several little difficulties have kept arising during the few days we have been in Warsaw. We are always interested to see who is causing unnecessary complications for purely personal motives. Warsaw is difficult enough to organize, in any case. The place is a mess of ruins and intrigue. We have got to establish a firm order and discipline, not only among the sniveling Poles but among ourselves. There is no time for personal ambitions."

It was easy for Captain Streit to talk, Sheila reflected as she listened gravely. His position was already attained: now he didn't have to worry about personal ambitions of his own. All he had to do was to worry about the personal ambitions of others who might reach for his job.

Dittmar said, his face white with anger, his voice compressed and hard, "There is no need to find any department. I am responsible for the definite choice of Korytów. We had to make an example of one village to bring that district round Lowicz to its senses."

Sheila's horror couldn't be restrained. For a moment she stared at the man's set face. The others saw that stare. They remembered the term she had first used: sabotage. Now it seemed to them as if she had found proof that the village of Korytów had been picked maliciously to embarrass Hofmeyer's plan. It was obvious that she was outraged by Dittmar's statement.

"We all know the record of that part of the country," Streit said brusquely. "I agree that one example, perhaps two, possibly three must be made. It doesn't matter which villages are chosen, whether they are actually guilty or not. But it does matter that you recognize the correct procedure in such matters. In that way, no department will have its plans—complicated." In the slight but careful hesitation there had been the suggestion of a stronger word. Streit continued in the same even tone, "The AO has done good work in preparing the ground first for the military occupation and then for the Gestapo. But now that we are here, we do not need the AO to help us make decisions. We decide, Herr Dittmar. The AO merely suggests."

There was an uneasy movement from the embarrassed Hefner. He was worried, Sheila saw. Loss of prestige for an overambitious Dittmar meant loss of security for Hefner.

Captain Greiser stretched his long legs and then rose. "A most illuminating afternoon," he said, "and now I must beg your leave, Captain Streit. I have a committee meeting in ten minutes. I regret I must go. I am sure we shall all benefit from this most interesting discussion." He saluted negligently, and left the room.

Dittmar, his broad face impassive, saluted quickly and said, "I must beg your leave, too, Herr Hauptmann." He hurried after the Wehrmacht captain, as the Gestapo arm raised its cold consent, and Hefner hurried after him.

"Was it possible that he chose Korytów purposely, and not accidentally?" Engelmann was asking. This last half-hour had upset him more than anyone except Sheila.

"Most possible," Streit said. "Isn't that so, Fräulein Braun? I think Fräulein Braun could tell us a lot, if she weren't so afraid. Isn't that so, Fräulein Braun?"

Sheila, who had hoped that Dittmar's exit would also be the cue for her dismissal, sank back again into her chair. She felt the cold sweat break down her spine.

"Don't be afraid, Fräulein Braun. You can say what you think. We should like to know what you think."

"Captain Streit, Herr Engelmann." She stopped. Tears of desperation were not far away. "I may need your protection." She tried to stop twisting her innocent handkerchief.

The two Nazis looked at each other in amazement and then in mild amusement. Herr Engelmann was even a little touched by such a pleasant idea. The colder Streit merely waited for this frightened girl to explain her hysteria. His eyes had scarcely left her face since Dittmar had gone.

"Dittmar told you he never sees me," she said in desperation. "Yet he forced his way into my apartment a few days ago. He told me that Hofmeyer would not last. He told me a clever girl would look for another boss. He meant himself. I refused. I told him I had my job to do. He knew it concerned Korytów. That was why I challenged him today, as you saw, Captain Streit. He will not forget that. And yet I do not see why a man like Dittmar should be allowed to elbow his way into power. For power is the reward of service and bravery, not of scheming. Isn't that true of our country, gentlemen?"

Captain Streit smiled approval of such a pretty speech. The

more excitable Engelmann cursed softly and paced the room. "Hofmeyer is one of my men," he said at last. "I'll see he is left to work without any threats." The attack on Hofmeyer had now reached the dimensions of an attack on Engelmann himself. He bit his thumb savagely.

"Get hold of a car and send her in it to Korytów," Streit said curtly. "Surely we can spare one car, when so many are being used by our gallant young officers on leave?"

Engelmann nodded in agreement with Streit's passing jibe at the army, and reached for the telephone.

"You look pale and tired, Fräulein Braun," Captain Streit said. "Perhaps you have been overworking?"

Sheila, praying that the hard gray eyes would give her just two minutes' respite from their watchfulness, smiled shakily and said, "You know, I still can smell that room downstairs."

Streit reached a long-fingered hand towards the vase and broke off a rose. "Try this," he said. "I often do. You come from Munich, Fräulein Braun?"

She took the rose. Its perfume was soft and sweet and clean. "Yes. But I lived many years in London."

"So I noticed. When you are excited, there is quite a hint of English inflection in your accent. It is extremely interesting."

Sheila was holding the rose to her face as if it were a bottle of smelling salts. Engelmann, replacing the receiver, said jovially, "Now I know why you've been reminding me all this time of Chicago."

Sheila looked blankly at him.

"One of my best men, when I was working in the AO, was sent out to Chicago to organize the loyal Germans there. He was there for five years. When he came back in '38, he spoke German with a Chicago accent. I heard him with my own ears. Incredible!"

Streit was amused in that cold way of his, but he looked at the telephone suggestively.

Engelmann said hurriedly, "A car is coming round here for Fräulein Braun. She had better leave at once, in order to reach Korytów in time. She will make her own plans to deal with her contacts there."

"Any escort?"

"Can't be spared today. She could have one tomorrow if she waited."

"What does Fräulein Braun say?" Streit asked mockingly. "It may be dangerous."

"I'll go today," Sheila said quietly. Engelmann was

pleased, obviously. Captain Streit had a tantalizing way of hiding his emotions.

The telephone bell rang as Sheila rose. For a moment she was paralyzed with dread at its possible message. But Streit's voice was normal when he answered, "Too late now." He replaced the receiver unconcernedly. "Only about the Dittmar-Korytów-military-liaison-office affair," he said to Engelmann. He rose to his feet and said to Sheila, "Perhaps we may have dinner together some night, and discuss what you saw and heard at Korytów, Fräulein Braun. And come to me with any other information."

Engelmann had saluted and was already marching into the corridor.

Captain Streit's voice was so gentle that Sheila had to strain to catch all his words. "Information not only about Dittmar. About anyone. *Auf Wiedersehen,* Fräulein Braun!"

Sheila smiled and acknowledged his salute, as Engelmann's worried voice called, "Fräulein Braun, we have little time."

As she closed the door, Streit was arranging the photograph on the desk to his taste. As serious-faced woman and wide-eyed little boy stared out from their silver frame at the red roses.

Sheila found she didn't walk quite steadily. She lurched against Engelmann as they descended the broad stone staircase. She pretended her high heels were treacherous on the stairs. But Engelmann was too preoccupied to notice anything. She looked at him curiously. He was still the same tall thin man with an unhappy face. But now she also saw the worried eyes, the intent mouth. He had ordered the car, not because he was sympathetic to her or to Hofmeyer as he had pretended, but rather because he had wanted to assert his authority over Dittmar. If he hadn't done so, his authority would have been permanently weakened. All these people, these self-appointed lords of creation, were vulnerable. They lived with the perpetual fear that their power was threatened, because the foundation of that power was opportunity. That could explain the broken bodies in the evil-smelling room. The *nouveau riche* displayed his yachts and pictures to silence his doubts. The *arriviste* in politics displayed his brute force for the same purpose. Cruelty, like all forms of display, was the compensation for the hidden, nagging fear of inferiority. Yes, that could explain the mutilated bodies. And yet Sheila, having known men and women who could live happily without the display of either force or wealth, felt that such people were the reason why she condemned the Nazi even as she explained them. If some of the human race could be gentle and decent in face of poverty and worry and ill health, then there was no excuse for those who denied gentleness and decency. Explanation was no excuse at all, not even in the recently fashionable terms of Freud or Dali.

Engelmann had thought she was wondering about the removal van which had drawn up within the courtyard. "The school teachers," he said. "That's the first of them." He might have been talking of the swallows over Lisbon. Sheila averted her eyes as the human load was dragged out of the truck.

"I can see the car's outside in the street," Engelmann was saying with evident relief. His caution had advised him to see this young woman safely on her way, and yet he hadn't wanted to waste much more time on her. The prompt arrival of the car had granted both his wishes. He became almost jovial. If Sheila had been a man, he would have slapped her heartily on the back as he gave her last instructions. As it was, his hand grip was as encouraging as it was prolonged.

"I'll follow your results with interest," he said. "Your report on your success at Korytów will of course be forwarded to me by Hofmeyer." About Dittmar he said nothing, but Sheila felt that Dittmar was the real reason why her hand was being shaken so enthusiastically. Dittmar was no longer so dangerous as a rival, because Engelmann knew his danger and, knowing that, could guard against it.

Sheila nodded and tried to smile, tried not to look at the file of men encouraged with harsh words and gratuitous blows to enter this ministry of new education. It seemed incredible that one removal van could hold so many human beings. She turned her head away sharply, and walked quickly through the gate. Engelmann strode along beside her. "You can leave everything to the man who is driving. He knows your destination," were his final words to her.

To the dark-haired, dark-eyed man in corporal's uniform who was standing very erect beside an open army car. Engelmann said, "Fräulein Braun will give you any further instrutions, Treltsch." He had changed back to his official manner. The confiding air was gone. His salute was brisk. He walked quickly towards a row of parked cars.

The first thing Sheila did was to take one long, deep breath. And then she glanced at her wrist watch. It was scarcely three o'clock. She had been less than an hour in that place. In one hour she had felt ten years of her life surely slip away.

# CHAPTER XXIV

## *Ambush*

THE JOURNEY to Korytów had begun. So quickly, so strangely, that for the first five minutes Sheila's thoughts and hopes and fears had become one huge jumble inside her brain. The rigid control with which she had defended herself in Streit's office could relax in this car; but she seemed to have lost all power of arranging her thoughts in a logical order. She had had to think too tensely; now she couldn't think at all. Then a panic seized her; the journey in this high-powered, smooth-running car with the efficient driver at its wheel would be short; but all she could do now was to keep repeating to herself, "I've so much to do, I've so much to do." The more she tried to think how she should try to plan, the more she thought how much there was to plan.

Strangely enough it was the Germans, the cause of this panic, who now helped her out of it. The car was halted after it left the city. As the driver gave his brief answers, Sheila suddenly saw her face reflected by some oblique ray of sunshine in the windshield before her. She didn't look afraid. She didn't look worried. Her face was quite expressionless. It was like a portrait done by an artist more interested in line and texture than in emotions. Where did I learn all this? she wondered. She stared coldly at the image of quiet assurance. Her mind became as calm as the face she saw in the windscreen. The car moved on. The image in the glass disappeared. The wide road and wider fields were all she saw ahead now, but this feeling of calm stayed with her.

There was no sense of triumph when she thought of the last hour. She had been partly lucky, partly careful, and partly trying very hard. She had never been so hard-tried in her life. But this journey, this car, the snub to Dittmar, gave her no sense of triumph. All she had done was to let herself be entangled more deeply in the Nazi web. When she returned from Korytów, Hofmeyer would have to start disentangling her. One Gestapo interview, even a friendly one, was quite enough for one lifetime. She could never manage another. There was a limit to the length of time an amateur juggler could keep his eyes fixed on three balls at once. If Streit had detained her just five minutes more, she would have been lost. She might as well admit that, now. Heroics only gave you a false idea of yourself. Heroics would only land her firmly trussed in the center of the web.

But one thing she had accomplished as well as Korytów. Now she could warn Hofmeyer that Dittmar *was* suspicious, and she could have Olszak warned that Dittmar had a theory about the little-known Kordus. That was at least something. Having allowed herself that crumb of comfort, she began to plan the method of approaching Korytów and the manner of leaving the village. The chief problem was to warn the peasants to leave Korytów without their escape being linked up with her visit. She watched the wide road and fields and thought of a story with which to safeguard herself. She frowned as she concentrated.

"Terrible country, isn't it?" the corporal said suddenly as if in agreement with the frown. "Give me the mountains, every time." His tone was polite, deferential.

"Where do you come from? Bavaria?" she asked. She regretted her question instantly. It always had been one of her weaknesses to respond to pleasantness. Now it was obvious that she was in for a spate of conversation.

"Franconia is my part of the world."

"Oh."

"I know it's flat, too, miss. But the towns and villages are all neat. Look at *that!*" He waved to a line of houses stretching along the road to form a village. Sheila looked and saw the trampled gardens, the blue-painted walls of the cottages cracked and blackened by smoke, the burned thatch roofs, the pitted fields.

"Of course," Treltsch added generously, "there's been heavy fighting around here."

"Yes."

"But just take a place where there hasn't been fighting, and what do you get?"

"What?"

"Nothing that can equal our towns or villages. We Germans are neat and we work hard. We are thorough."

"Yes," Sheila said. She thought of the people of Korytów who had seemed never to stop working. She thought of the village, rebuilt after the last war. She thought of the German towns and villages which had never known destruction and pillage as Poland had known them for almost two centuries. She looked at the fields. Hardly one of them was empty. Each had its heaps of what seemed rags or old clothing, lying where they had fallen scattered under the machine-gun bullets. Wrecks of carts and skeletons of horses still edged the ditches.

"Glad I don't live here, anyway. It's a desolate pigsty."

Sheila didn't answer. All she wanted to say was, "It was pleasant enough before you came here. Those who lived here didn't ask for any change. If you hadn't come, it wouldn't look either desolate or a pigsty."

"It just proves everything," Treltsch said with great conviction. "The Poles are a shiftless lot. It just shows you some people have no right to govern. They just spoil everything."

"They've had a long history of war," Sheila couldn't help saying and then bit her lip. Fortunately for her, her voice was too tired to sound either indignant or sympathetic. Fortunately for her, the man obviously thought she was critizing the Poles as troublesome neighbors.

The man nodded and then, as if he thought that one word had been too generous to the Poles, he said, " 'History'!" He laughed. "What history? What real history have *they* ever had?"

Sheila didn't answer. Treltsch's schoolbooks would never have mentioned Poland as a nation. The Germans hadn't even bothered to publish a Baedeker Guide to Poland.

"What history?" the man insisted. The word was staying with him: his laugh hadn't chased it away after all. Sheila looked at the youthful face, at the frank brown eyes so intent on the road before them. This man was not setting a trap for her. He was honestly ignorant. He just did not know, he really didn't believe that anything good existed outside of his own country. He was willing, alert, obedient; he was smug, stupid, short-sighted.

Sheila was very casual, almost bored.

"I have heard that the University of Cracow is nearly six hundred years old," she suggested, keeping purposely silent about the defeat of the Teutonic Knights by the Poles. One of the oldest in Western civilization, she wanted to add: older than Heidelberg. Treltsch's amazement was obvious. So was his disbelief. What would he have looked like if she had told him that the French Huguenots had appealed to their king for freedom from persecution in the sixteenth century and had cited Poland as an example of religious tolerance? Or if she had told him that the Poles had saved Vienna from the Mohammedan invasion; if they hadn't, there would be mosques and veiled women in Austria, perhaps even in Germany, just as these reminders of Islam remained in Serbia to this day?

"Six hundred years old," Treltsch said with a laugh. "That's what the *Poles* say, I bet. You can't trust a Pole. You should have seen the way they fought us! They were like demons. They aren't human. The Führer was right. If we had let them get strong, they would have overrun our country. We were wise to attack them first. It was the only way to win."

"But Germany would never be beaten. No country can beat us. We are invincible."

"You're right there, miss." Treltsch looked happy again: she was speaking of the things he knew.

Then why on earth are you afraid of being attacked? Sheila thought bitterly. If you are invincible, then you need fear no attack. But Treltsch, unaware of the inconsistencies in his logic, was whistling cheerily as the car speeded on.

"Hope you didn't mind me talking, miss," he said. "It's real good to talk to a German woman, again." And then he was whistling, softly, tunefully once more.

They slowed up as they passed a cluster of houses. In the lifeless stubble of a long-harvested field, a line of men were digging a trench. A group of women and children, closely huddled, were standing near them. The women's bright kerchiefs matched the autumn leaves at the edge of the field. Facing them were green-uniformed soldiers setting up their machine guns. Two officers in massive field-coats were smoking cigarettes as they watched the shallow trench grow deeper. At the sign of the village inn, a man was hanging. He had been hanging there for some time. Treltsch halted the car beside the wooden table and bench in the inn's side-garden which bordered the road. Two soldiers patrolling this end of the empty village came forward. Treltsch answered their questions rapidly with the same formula which had brought them through the last patrol. Sheila stared at the calm image of her face in the windshield, tried to forget the creaking of the inn's sign just behind her.

"More sniping?" Treltsch asked as the soldiers relaxed, and nodded over his shoulder in the direction of the field.

"No, they cut *him* down last night." The soldier who answered jerked his thumb towards the hanging body. "He got his for food-hoarding. Told us lies about what he had, and then gave food to a couple of refugees. He's been up there for four days. Orders. But last night they cut him down. Buried him in a grave, too. But we found him. And he's back where he belongs."

"They'll all soon be where they belong," the other soldier said with a laugh.

Sheila glanced at her watch. "The light fades quickly, now," she said to Treltsch. "We ought to hurry."

The soldiers pulled themselves erect, returned the corporal's salute. The laughing one, serious now, called after the car, "Go carefully. There's been trouble round here when it gets dark."

Treltsch was silent for so long that Sheila, looking curiously at the man's pleasant face, wondered if he felt some pity for the condemned village. She smiled sadly, thinking that perhaps he was beginning to understand why this countryside should be so depressing.

He smiled too. Sympathetically, it seemed to her. And then he said, "You know, miss, I was just thinking: wouldn't it be funny if one of them was sent to my house?"

He noticed her bewilderment.

"One of these women," he explained, his eyes on a more difficult part of the road. The trees were thickening now; no longer sparse or isolated, their gay autumn colors formed small masses of shaded reds and yellows. "You see, miss, I've got my name down for a Polish worker. My wife always wanted help. Half the day she used to complain about having so much to do. She's young, you know. So I put my name down on the list. That ought to keep her happy. She can take it easy for a bit and let the Pole do the hard work. It will cost us nothing, not even in food or bedding."

"But the Pole will eat and sleep, won't she?"

"Table scraps and a heap of straw out in the shed. That's almost nothing. It's what the Poles are used to, miss. Treat swine as swine, that's what we say in my part of the country." The man's voice was casual, friendly. He was simply repeating his creed.

"What happens if—the woman dies?" she heard her voice ask.

"Oh, they're strong. They aren't human. They are like animals. Besides, there's plenty more. Thirty-five million of them. Yes, when I looked at that bunch of women I thought, 'You'll be setting out for Germany, I bet, as soon as the shooting's over.' And then I thought, 'What if I were to see that big, strong yellow-haired girl scrubbing my doorstep the next time I go home?' Sounds a bit fanciful, now that I put it in words. But there's the way things happen. It's a small world, that's what I always say."

"Wouldn't it be dangerous?" Sheila said in a low voice. "I mean, if a Polish woman, like the—the yellow-haired girl you mentioned, were separated from her children and sent to work for you, might not that be dangerous? For your wife and children?"

Treltsch was serious now. All the amiability left his pleasant face. "Just let any Pole try it. Just let them!" he said with unexpected depths of anger.

Then his face cleared as he remembered the solution, and the voice was easy once more. "They won't try it. Not with

relations left in Poland, not with their children in our camps.
No, miss, don't you worry about the wife and baby. We'll
look after them. The first thing the Pole will be told will
be just what will happen to her family if she tries any
tricks. No, don't you worry, miss."

Sheila nodded and pretended to study the woods, now
spreading widely over the flat fields.

When Corporal Treltsch spoke again, it was to say, "Nearly
there, miss. Four miles to go. We've made it in good time."

"Excellent," Sheila agreed and looked at her watch. "Now,
I don't want you to bring this car into the village. Drop
me there, so that I can enter the village on foot."

"Shall I wait for you there, to take you back?"

"I wish you could. But my problem is difficult. I have to
bring three Poles back to Warsaw, without their knowing
that we are responsible for taking them. They think I am
pro-Polish."

"I see, miss. But it's a long walk back to Warsaw. Perhaps I could pretend to give you a lift? I'll wait for you on
the main road just where it joins the village road. It will
all look natural."

"We can try it, anyway," Sheila said. After all, perhaps
Aunt Marta was ill. Perhaps she would be unable to walk
very far. "I think that's a brilliant idea."

Her words pleased him. "Got to use your wits nowadays,"
he said with a knowing air.

"Do you do much of this kind of work?"

"Driving's my job. Confidential kind of work. People like
you, miss, on special missions. I never know what they are
doing, but you can't help wondering."

"You must never let yourself wonder too much," Sheila
said coldly. She had begun to feel some brake must be
put on this man's quick wits.

"Oh no, miss," Treltsch said hastily. "I never say a thing.
I'm the silent type." He looked at her respectfully with a
touch of uneasiness, and didn't speak again. Thunder and
damnation, he was thinking, who in God's world would
have thought she was one of those stuck-up martinets? He
ought to have guessed, though, by the way she talked: all
very exact and proper as if she were reading a damned
grammar-book. That was the way they talked in the big
cities, in the best houses. Well, some day his children would
be talking like that. And he'd have that piece of land he had
already chosen in Southwestern Poland, with a view of a
mountain too. And he'd have his Polish workers. And he'd
give his children the best education. They'd be talking
like that. They'd be driving round the countryside in their

own cars. He began to whistle again, softly. She didn't seem to object to his whistling, anyway. She was looking as if she were worrying about getting these three Poles to Warsaw. Well, that was her picnic. That's why they paid her and gave her such fine clothes. Old Papa Engelmann would look after her well. Funny that a young girl could go for an old man. Plenty of the younger officers would give her a better time. A nice little piece like her . . .

"What's that?" Sheila asked. Unnecessarily. She had learned to know what that sound was. But the quietness of this empty stretch of road, the sleepy curve shielded by trees which they were now approaching, the low mass of gray clouds above their heads, had made the shots all the more unexpected.

"One of our patrols. I can hear a car," Treltsch said evenly. He swung the wheel to guide the car carefully round the curve of dense pine trees. They could see the short strip of road ahead of them, now, before it twisted again to resume its usual straight line. They could see the German patrol. Six gray-coated men lying on the road, their arms outstretched, their legs twisted, their bodies sprawled as they had been thrown from their motorcycles. The noise of the "car" which Treltsch had heard was the running engines of two of these motorcycles as they lay on their sides near the men, their wheels turning helplessly. The other four had traveled aimlessly into the muddy ditches and lay as grotesquely silent as their riders.

Men in ragged uniforms, in civilian jackets and cloth caps, were kneeling beside the dead soldiers. They looked up as the gray car swept quietly round the corner. Treltsch's careful driving and the noise of the motorcycles had no doubt deadened the sound of the car's approach. For the fraction of a second, Sheila saw the white faces staring up at the car, saw the men kneeling as if they would never rise. Treltsch, his face grim and hard, pressed the accelerator so that the car seemed to leap at the men. The car jumped as it struck the German corpses in its path, but the Poles had scattered to the side of the road.

Sheila was knocked forward on her knees. She had thrown up her arm to protect her face as she fell. There was a sharp blow on her elbow, a wrench in the back of her neck as her forehead struck against her own arm and the arm struck the dashboard of the car.

Treltsch cursed and swung the car with one hand towards the last of the men as they reached the ditch. In the other hand, he held his revolver. Before he could aim it at the faces so near them, the windshield had a sudden sunburst of fine cracks, the car plunged crazily down into the broad ditch, and the brakes screamed frenziedly. The car rocked, remained upright. But the deep soft mud held the churning wheels fast. Treltsch's last curse was unfinished. He screamed as the brakes had screamed. He tried to rise, stiffly; his knuckles round the steering wheel showed white as his weight was held by that arm for a moment. Then the arm bent slowly, and he fell forward.

Sheila stared sideways at the unmoving man beside her. She tried to raise her head away from her arm, tried to rise from her knees. She closed her eyes as she heard the Polish voice giving commands. "Hurry. Weapons, coats, papers off these sons of bitches. Silence the cycles and car, or we won't hear anything else coming. *Do stu djablów!* Hurry."

Someone was standing beside the car on Sheila's side. She could hear his heavy breathing, as if in that last desperate leap for the ditch the wind had been knocked out of the man.

"Two dead here, *rotmistrz*," his voice said slowly. "Two dead here, Captain."

Sheila opened her eyes, saw the man's mud-smeared face within a foot of hers.

She tried to smile. "Not dead," she said. "I'm not dead."

The man had whipped his revolver into sight as she spoke. And then, instead of shooting, he stared. He smiled, too, and the smile broadened into a laugh.

"*Do jasnej cholery!* What's there to laugh at?" the captain's voice asked savagely.

"She's only saying her prayers. She's not dead. She says she's not dead. She says, cool as you like, 'I'm not dead.'"

"She soon will be," a third voice said grimly. "We've finished over here, *rotmiztrz*. We're waiting."

"Scatter. Get into cover. Don't drop anything."

"Yes, *rotmistrz*."

The mud-stained man said, "What are we going to do with her? I shouldn't have listened to her. 'Not dead,' she says, and spoils my aim."

Sheila tried to rise to her feet. She looked up at the man who now stood beside the mud-stained man. A captain. A cavalry captain, if he were called "*rotmistrz*."

"Wisniewski," she said desperately. "Adam Wisniewski."

The captain's hard blue eyes narrowed. He reached into the car and pulled her roughly to her feet.

"Korytów," Sheila said, "Korytów is in danger."

The captain's hard look, compressed lips, lowered brows were unchanged, but he had opened the door of the car. He was still pulling her. The pain circled from the nape of her neck up round her head.

"I should have shot her when my blood was hot. But, God help me, I've never shot a woman," the first man was protesting.

Sheila said "Adam Wisniewski" and stumbled forward. Her hat was somewhere in the car. And her gloves. And her fine new coat with Treltsch's blood over it had caught in the doorway and had fallen off her shoulders as she had been dragged out. It trailed over the car step, and a large mud-colored footstep was blotted on its lapel. She still held her handbag. She would die, it seemed, still clutching it. But the mud-stained man had noticed it too. He snatched it out of her hand, and opened it.

He said in amazement, "No gun, *rotmistrz!* Only papers."

"Don't lose them," Sheila said, "don't lose them." She looked anxiously at the man. She put her hands up to hold her head, and closed her eyes.

"Keep a grip of her arm, Jan," the captain was saying. "No time to lose, now. Keep going." He took the bag from Jan, and stuffed it inside his jacket. "I'll have a look at these later. Keep going, Jan."

They hurried her between them to a place in the ditch where branches had been thrown over the deep mud. They crossed it at a run, dragging the girl. Jan stopped to pull the branches away and scatter them under the trees. Then they were hurrying and twisting through the pines. The captain held Sheila's arm in a vice-like grip. Jan, when he caught up with them, followed with his revolver held pointed at the small of her back.

Sheila kept saying, "Korytów. Korytów. We are going away from Korytów."

"Keep quiet!" The captain shook her impatiently. His grip twisted, and the pain in her arm silenced her. He pulled her up from her knees. They entered the wood. On the road behind them was the heavy peace of autumn dusk.

CHAPTER XXV

## Hostage

THREE of the men were waiting in the thickness of the trees. Their faces were alert, their guns held ready.

"The others have gone ahead with the coats and rifles. A

good haul," a short, muscular man said. He looked at Sheila. So did his companions. Their eyes were hard.

"Korytów," Sheila repeated weakly.

"She's crying," Jan said, his good-natured face trying to look as hostile as the others. "She's scared."

Sheila shook her head desperately. "Korytów," she said, her voice breaking on the word.

"Keep moving," the captain said. "Get away from the road. We'll question her when it's safe."

*"Psia krew! psia kosc!"* It was the short, broad-shouldered man. "Why didn't you shoot her with the others?"

"It wasn't so easy," said Jan. "Not when she's on her knees looking up at you and telling you she's not dead."

"The bigger men come, the softer they are," the other said angrily.

"Quiet. We'll get some information out of her before we shoot," the captain said. "Keep moving."

The men scattered once more through the trees. The captain wasn't holding her arm any more, but he watched her out of the side of his eyes. Sheila stumbled on, trying to keep up with the quick lope of the men. The light was fading now, and the army of pines closing in around her increased the darkness. Her heels twisted under her on the surface roots of the trees. Once she fell forward on her face. The captain waited for her, watched her pick herself up so slowly and then try to run after him. She was too tired to notice that his revolver was held ready to use. He slipped it back into its holster as she came even with him again. He held her arm once more, but this time the grip helped, instead of forcing her, along beside him. At last, the journey was over. Or at least, temporarily over. The men who had gone on ahead with the German coats and rifles had heaped them outside a woodsman's hut in a small clearing. There they had waited for the captain and the others. Nine men altogether, Sheila counted. Three of them, at a signal from the captain, walked separately into the woods. They carried rifles. The rest of the party dropped wearily onto the ground.

Now that she could see the sky clearly once more, Sheila knew that evening had come. Night would not be far away. Again she thought of Korytów, and a picture of torches lighting its darkness, of shallow trenches and weeping children, flared up before her.

"Korytów," she said again.

"She's always saying Korytów," Jan remarked. "Perhaps it is all the Polish she knows."

"Is this as far as we take her?" the short man who believed in shooting her demanded.

"We shall soon know," the captain answered. He sat down on the soft earth covered with faded pine-needles. "Sit!" he said to Sheila. She obeyed him.

The captain asked quietly, "Where were you going in that car? Where did you come from? Better tell us before we get it out of you."

"I was going to Korytów," she began in Polish, and then stopped. She held her aching head in her hands. "Oh God," she said in English, "If only I could get my thoughts straight!"

The men around her stopped their quiet talking, and looked at her. In her own language, the captain said, "Why did you speak English?"

She said wearily, "But I come from England. My family is Scottish. And I can't think of the right Polish words at this moment. They've all gone."

"Well, we shall talk in English then. Two of us understand it fairly. Now go on. You were going to Korytów. Why?"

"To warn it. The Germans are going to make an example of it. Perhaps tomorrow, perhaps even tonight. I couldn't find that out."

"So you traveled in a German car to save a Polish village? Did you intend to bring the inhabitants to safety in that car?" The captain's quiet irony quickened her reply.

"I'll answer all your questions. But first, send someone to Korytów. We must not waste any more time. Please!"

"We aren't wasting time. We are going to find out a few things," the captain said coldly. The broad-shouldered man knew English too, for he was translating freely to the others.

"Why were you riding in a German car?"

The short man laughed. "Why do pretty blondes in pretty clothes ride in German cars?" he said in Polish. All the men laughed. It wasn't a pleasant laugh.

The captain shook his head slowly. "That doesn't explain this case. She wasn't with an officer. Corporals don't have large staff cars to take blondes for pleasure-rides." The men were silent again, and the captain said in English, "Go on. Tell this story of yours."

"But first, send two men to Korytów."

"First, we shall hear your story."

Sheila stared at the man. And then she knew he was right. Too many traps had been set by Germans.

She told the story quickly. The captain and the man, who disbelieved everything she said quite openly, were listening attentively. Jan had drawn near to listen to the foreign voice. The others stretched themselves more comfortably on the pine needles and talked together in a low murmur about the ambush.

The story was given, simply and as directly as Sheila could manage. She told of her visit to Korytów this summer, of everything that had followed. She didn't mention Olszak's name: he was described as "a friend of the Aleksander's uncle," just as Hofmeyer became "one of his assistants." She didn't speak of her father, of Uncle Matthews or of Olszak's underground movement. These particulars were too dangerous even to be told to the enemies of Germany. But the essential part of the story, the part that would win these men's trust and help Korytów, was clear enough. When she had finished her hurrying sentences, she looked at the men. In the growing darkness she couldn't see their expressions. Jan, not having understood one word of her story, moved uneasily as if asking her not to expect anything from him. The other two were motionless. Their silence worried her.

"If you examine the papers in my handbag," she said, "you'll find my British passport as Sheila Matthews, and the forged birth certificate of Anna Braun, and the AO identification paper, and the forged change of name from Anna Braun to Sheila Matthews, and the permits which were given me to let me accomplish this journey under false pretenses." Her head still throbbed with a deep steady pulse, but the feeling of grave danger had cleared her mind. She was seeing things now with a terrifying clearness. What a futile way to die, she thought. How abjectly silly....

There was a rustle of paper. The thickset man held a torch carefully pointed downward. The tall Jan cupped his large peasant's hands round its weak light. The captain turned over the various pages, studied the text and the photographs and the seals. Sheila watched in an agony of impatience. They were so slow, so thorough, so slow.

At last the torch was switched off.

"Well?" Sheila said. *"Will* you send someone to Korytów?"

The men ignored her. They talked quickly together. The short man argued.

And then the captain said, "There are some points in your favor. You didn't use the corporal's gun on Jan, although it had fallen beside your hand in the car. You didn't struggle away from us at any time. You made no attempt to escape among the trees when I released your arm. These points are in your favor."

"Well," Sheila said, "well—" Her relief choked her.

"On the other hand, how do we know that your story is really true, that you were not instructed to use it if ever you were questioned by some Poles?"

"Well—" Sheila halted again. In desperation, she said to the watchful men, "Doesn't *any* of you come from this district? Does no one here know Korytów? He could question me about it."

"We all belong to this district," the captain said quietly. "I used to visit the Aleksanders. I know them. What was their house like?"

Sheila plunged into a brief description of the house and garden.

"All very well," the short man said, interrupting her flatly. "The Germans occupied that house on their push to the east. The Germans could have told you what that house is like."

The captain nodded, but he called softly to one of his men who was stretched on the ground. The man came forward.

"Your girl lived in Korytów. When did you last see her?" the captain asked him.

"August."

"Do you recognize this woman here?"

"Can't say I do."

"Did you hear of any foreigner staying at the big house in Korytów this summer?"

The man thought over that. "Believe I did. My girl did mention some funny kind of clothes she had seen in the village. Yes, now I think of it, there was a visitor at the big house."

"Did you hear the visitor's name?"

"It was one of these foreign ones, twisting your tongue."

In Polish, Sheila said, "Did you know Kawka? How is his mother who was so ill? Did you know Benicki—Wanda, the little goosegirl—Jan Reska the schoolmaster? Felix, Maria?"

"Aye, all these I knew. Jan Reska ... There was a lot of talk about him and—" The man looked at his captain. He had remembered in time that he was a friend of the Aleksander family.

"Pani Barbara is dead," Sheila said quietly.

"God rest her soul."

"And Pan Professor Korytowski has been arrested. Pan Andrew is missing."

The man said, "He is?" And then slowly, as if the name had struck some thin note in his memory, he added, "I remember now. There was talk he was going to marry the foreigner, that was it. That was why she was there."

Sheila could feel the captain's eyes staring at her. Thank God, in one way, for the peasant's chief interest—gossip. In one way, thank God. In another way—she felt her cheeks flush hotly under the captain's unseen scrutiny.

"You have said you met Andrew Aleksander in London," he said softly, "and that Madame Aleksander invited you to Korytów. This last piece of information adds a little more sense to your story, even if it does embarrass you."

"What about Korytów?"

"I think we'll let you handle that. We must push on to our camp fifteen miles south of here. We could set you back on the road near the scene of your accident. You could make up a story of lying unconscious in the wood to which you fled. You will find the Germans all right. They will be there by this time. And then you can go on to Korytów and complete your mission there." He held out her handbag to her.

She didn't take it. She said dully, "And then I'll be back with *them* again."

"But they trust you. So you told us."

"Yes. But my luck can't hold forever. I managed to scrape through this afternoon at the Gestapo headquarters, only because one of the men was despised and distrusted by the others. And because four Nazis were all in different branches of the service. But if I were to meet four Gestapo men, all solidly together—"

"Then why were you chosen for this kind of work?"

"I wasn't especially chosen or trained. I've *told* you. It just sort of happened. Things have a habit of becoming more complicated than the way they were planned. If I go back, I'll be in deeper than ever . . . Streit, the Gestapo man, invited me to dinner. . . . He meant it. . . ."

"Couldn't you handle that?" The Pole's voice was mocking.

The wind, rustling the pointed pines, had risen to blow away the clouds. Above her head now was a clear sky. The darkness gave way to the half-light of stars. The shadows round her were now faces. She could see the smiles on the two men's lips.

She rose abruptly. "Yes, I'm a coward. I know that. I want the easy way of disappearing." It would have been a good way, too. No suspicion on Hofmeyer. Only a minor fanfare for Anna Braun, kidnaped and missing in the line of duty.

"All right," she said slowly. She passed one hand wearily over her brow, held out the other for her bag. She turned towards the path which had brought her here. Her steps were as slow as her words; her feet dragged. The broad-shouldered man moved quietly round to block her way.

"One moment!" the captain called after her. "Three things I want to know. Who is the man you called your chief—the friend of Korytowski?"

"I can't tell you that."

"Who is the man you called his assistant, the man who employed you?"

"I can't tell you that, either."

"Why did you say 'Wisniewski' down on the road?"

Sheila caught her breath. She answered slowly as if trying to find for herself the reason why that name had come so spontaneously to her lips, "Your men called you *rotmistrz*. That meant you belonged to the cavalry. So did he."

"There are several cavalry officers of that name. Surely you didn't expect me to know your Wisniewski."

"He was a horseman I thought you would know. Adam Wisniewski. He represented Poland at the international riding competitions. Surely you must know him if you are in the cavalry? I thought that if you knew him and saw that I knew him, then you wouldn't shoot me at once. You'd give me a chance to explain. All I wanted was not to have a Polish bullet in me. It seemed a pity to die so—so unnecessarily. And then . . ." She hesitated, and looked sharply at the listening faces. Did the rest of these men really not understand English?

"And then?" the captain repeated patiently.

"Well, he is doing something of the same kind of fighting as you are. I suppose when I saw a cavalry officer leading a guerrilla attack I thought—at least I suppose I thought subconsciously of Adam Wisniewski."

"I think," the captain said very slowly, "I think we have still more information to find out. Your story was not so complete as it seemed. Sit down. Just how do you know what Wisniewski is doing? When did you last see him?"

Sheila looked at the man who still blocked the path. Jan had moved up obediently beside him.

She said angrily, "I don't believe you ever meant I was to leave. You still don't believe me. Why did you tell me to go when you didn't mean it?"

"To see if you would go readily, eager to reach your German friends with the news that our camp was fifteen miles south of this point. I believe you more than I did ten minutes ago."

"But what about Korytów?" To the man whose girl lived at Korytów she said in Polish, "Korytów is to be destroyed by the Germans. Someone must warn the people to scatter to the woods, to other villages."

"I can handle my own men, thank you," the Polish captain said in a hard voice. Then wearily, "Korytów will be your final test. I'll send two men. If they don't return or if they find no Germans arrive within forty-eight hours then we shall know you are too clever to live."

To the man whose girl lived at Korytów, he said, "Go with Jan. Warn the people. Then watch for two nights and two days to see if the Szwaby arrive. You know where to join us. We'll wait for you there until the night after your watch is ended. Take great care. I may be sending you into a trap."

From the irritation in his voice, Sheila suddenly realized the risk the captain was taking. He was half-angry with himself that he should have listened to her. He was torn with doubts between a possible danger to Korytów, probable danger to his men, suspicion of such a story, belief in certain extraordinary details. To hold her as a hostage was the most generous thing he could afford to do. The broad-shouldered man obviously shared none of the part-belief which had been awakened in the captain. Sheila, listening to the captain's worried voice, knew she should be thankful for even this small mercy. Her own irritation over the slowness of his decision vanished.

Jan was looking at her. He said with a broad grin, "You wouldn't make *me* dead, would you, miss?"

Sheila shook her head. She was smiling, now. She said to the man who knew Korytów: "Find Pani Marta and the two children, Teresa and Stefan. Tell them they must go to Warsaw and Madame Aleksander. She is ill and alone at Frascati Gardens, 37. She needs them." She opened her bag quickly and searched for her re-entry permit into Warsaw. "No good. Oh damn and blast and damn," she said in English to herself. The permit was in the decided name of Anna Braun. "Tell Pani Marta she must swear she lived in Warsaw and was a refugee who is now returning. She must do that. Otherwise she won't get in. Remember: Frascati 37."

The men nodded, looked to their captain for a sign of dismissal, and then moved silently towards the path back towards the road.

"I'd almost believe she meant what she was saying if I hadn't seen the results of so many German lies." It was the broad-shouldered man who was speaking. He stood, compact and solid and watchful.

"Enough, Thaddeus," the captain said. He stared at the ground before his feet, and then looked suddenly at Sheila. His eyes were bitter. If you've lost me two good men, by God I'll shoot you, myself, he seemed to say. For one moment, Sheila thought he was going to recall the men and let

Thaddeus have his way. He rose suddenly, and moving towards the other men gave them quick orders. They lifted the spoils they had won, wearing part of them, carrying the rest.

An owl gave its sharp cry behind Sheila. She started. But it was the broad-shouldered man called Thaddeus. He repeated the mournful cry as she watched him, and then smiled in spite of himself at her amazement. From three places in the wood came the hoots of other owls, irregular, so natural, that Sheila thought of the three sentries stationed there only after she saw that the rest of the men were leaving the clearing. They scattered, walking singly or in pairs.

The captain said, "I'm afraid I must burden you with my presence. Only keep silent. We have forty-eight hours for talking in the safety of our camp. That will be a pleasant way to pass the time."

"And if your men don't return?" Sheila asked wryly.

The officer smiled stiffly, too formally, as if she had made a remark in doubtful taste. "It will still have been a pleasant way," he said calmly.

The sharply pointing pines rustled in the wind. It was a sad wind, sighing and lamenting. The stars were remote and cold. The other men had vanished into the deep shadows of the wood. Sheila kept the steady pace of the man beside her, and his silence. Beyond the wood were long stretches of solitary fields. Beyond the fields were other woods. Beyond the woods were further fields. The distance was much longer than fifteen miles. Fifteen miles, he had said. Fifteen miles to the south. Yes, fifteen miles to the south for the Germans' benefit. Fifteen miles to the south for her information if she were in German pay. Now she knew that they weren't traveling due south, either.

When dawn came, mist shrouded the endless plain behind them and the wide forest which lay ahead. Within the shelter of the first band of trees, the captain let her rest for ten minutes. And then her heavy feet were following his, deeper into the thickness of the forest. Once he caught her as she stumbled drunkenly against his side. After that, he kept a grip on her arm and helped her through the wet, thick underbrush.

"One more mile," he promised her, looking at her white face. "A short one," he added encouragingly. Sheila was too tired to answer. She was too tired to smile. She could only try to keep erect, to wade through the heavy white mist which swirled round her legs and hid her feet like the cold hungry surf of a surging sea.

# CHAPTER XXVI

## *The Spy*

AS THEY left the masses of russet-colored honeysuckle, which, covering the ground, had dragged at their feet and twisted round their legs with the pull of a quicksand, Sheila heard the clear whistle of a bird. It came from behind the trees, near the path which the captain at last allowed himself to use. Once this path had been a cart-track, perhaps even a forest road. Now, fine green grass grew over the ruts at the edge, and led them with leisurely twists through the crowding roots of trees. The captain was hurrying once more, urging her on with concealed excitement, as somewhere ahead of them in this gray morning mist another bird answered. Then there were, suddenly, no trees. Just a stretch of frosted dew gleaming coldly. She heard men's voices welcoming them. The captain was saying, "Well, we've made it. We're the last, I see, but we made it," and Sheila raised her eyes for the first time from the path. The silver mist was rising. It unveiled the forest circling round this clearing, and the trees were scarlet and bronze and yellow. Sheila stood there, looking at the trees and the soft mist. It was like watching a curtain going up in the theater, when you hold your breath at the unexpected beauty of the stage.

The captain spoke.

"Yes," she answered. "Yes." But she hadn't known what he had said.

He took her arm and led her to the small wooden house which stood close up against one side of the forest clearing. A long-handled ax with its edge buried in a broad stump stood at the door. A two-handed saw with rusted teeth rested on wooden pegs driven into the house wall under the broad overhang of roof. The captain pointed to the back of the house. "There's a stream behind these trees. You can wash there. Then you can rest."

Sheila nodded. She passed Thaddeus, who didn't even bother to look at her. Two other men were standing beside a wooden bench outside a small shed. They had been examining the pockets of the jackets and coats which they had taken from the Germans. The papers and documents and maps which they found were in neat groups on the wooden bench. Large pebbles were used as paperweights. These men, too, didn't look at her.

She followed the narrow path past them. Three men still unaccounted for. They might be on guard in the forest. Well, two of them might. The third was at the stream, stripped to the waist, washing his shirt and socks. A healing wound ran its red tongue down his side. A violent bruise, brown with purple shadows, spread over his shoulder. As he turned round, she saw the small cross hanging from a silver chain round his strong neck. He rose quickly from the edge of the pool, gathered the wet clothes in his hand, and passed her without a glance. Like the others, he had an even mixture of contempt and hate in his face. Sheila felt as a leper must feel when he approaches a village, hungry for a human word, and finds some scraps of food placed where he may reach them without contaminating others. She must learn to forget her old peacetime belief that people were innocent until you proved them guilty. In a war such as these men were fighting, everyone was guilty until she proved innocent.

She concentrated on the problem of washing. She was too sleepy. She was exhausted. She hadn't any soap, any towel. The water was too cold. Any old excuse came tumbling into her mind, anything to pretend she didn't have to get her clothes off and scrape herself clean. She could imagine the effect if she went back to the forester's house and asked for a towel.

"What, no towel, no bath salts, no powder for her ladyship?"

As she knelt at the edge of the bank, where the stream, flowing slowly, had been dammed to form a round pool, and tested the water halfheartedly with a finger, she remembered how in the stifling air of burning Warsaw she used to dream of a clean cool stream and water which didn't need to be carried in a pail. Now she had the stream: it was clean, so clean that she could see the gravel in the bottom, and it was certainly cool. The pool was almost waist-deep, the bushes and trees were thick enough to give at least the feeling of privacy. Perhaps the guards, no doubt posted to make sure she wouldn't try to escape, couldn't see her. Then she laughed at herself, and she felt better. It was a long time since she had laughed at herself. She undressed quickly, shaking her clothes and hanging them on the scarlet and yellow leaves around her. She slipped hurriedly into the water before she could change her mind. It was very very cold. The morning's frost still pierced it.

When she hurried back to the forester's house, carrying

her wet underslip which had served as an inefficient towel, she found the captain, Thaddeus and two men examining the papers and weapons which they had won. The German coats and tunics and caps were piled on the corner bed.

The captain looked up as she entered. "Why were you running?" he asked sharply.

"Cold. Trying to get warm." It was true. Her teeth were chattering. The men lost interest in her once more.

It was, much to her surprise, Thaddeus who picked up a bayonet from the table, skewered a thick slice of sausage which lay there along with a bottle and some empty tins, and held it out towards her.

She thanked him. He looked at her with little liking in his light gray eyes, and turned once more to the table. Then he looked up again at the girl now sitting on the edge of the wooden bench in front of the unlit stove, poured some vodka out of the bottle into a tin mug and came over with it to where she sat.

"Drink this quickly."

In her nervousness, she gulped it so that she choked and coughed. He took the mug away from her, ignored her thanks, and went back to the table.

The icy bath had chased sleep away. She was still exhausted, but her eyelids were no longer weighted down. She finished eating the hard sausage, and then spread out the wet petticoat over the bench beside her, so that it might have a chance to dry.

"Better hang it outside," the captain said unexpectedly. He spoke in Polish to one of the men—the man she had seen at the stream this morning—who rose and followed her to the door.

"Where are your stockings?" the captain added quickly.

"They were in shreds."

"You left them at the brook?"

Now what have I done wrong this time? Sheila wondered. "Yes," she said.

The captain spoke rapidly in Polish once more. The man took Sheila silently to the stream, picked up the stockings from where she had thrown them under a bush, and then led her back to the large linden tree at the side of the house. There, round a rope strung under its thick cover, she knotted the shoulder-straps of the underslip beside the row of toeless socks. A drying shirt filled with the breeze, and swung like a fat, headless, legless man.

In the cottage, the men were now on their feet. The papers had been sorted and were being replaced in the tunic pockets.

"Did she leave anything else lying about?" the captain asked.

"No."

"Good." To Sheila he said, "Rest on the bed."

"I—"

"Get over to the bed. You'll be out of our way, there."

Sheila went to the corner of the room where the high wooden bed stood. There was a very old, very faded striped mattress, and three equally ancient striped pillows in a hard neat pile at the head of the bed. She watched the men, sorting the clothes on the floor as if this were some kind of card game. A coat, a tunic, a cap, sidearms, here. A coat, a tunic, trousers, a cap, sidearms, there.

"We need extra ammunition, and four more trousers. That's all. Then we'll be complete," Thaddeus said with satisfaction. "We can get the trousers from the laundry-line at Brzeziny. There's a garrison there."

The captain nodded. He had taken her torn stockings and thrown them on a pile of rubbish. "Bury them as usual," he said to the man beside him.

The insecurity of these men struck Sheila with renewed force. In this hidden house, with a depth of trees to give a margin of safety, there was still no security. Litter had to be buried. No fire was lit to give the warmth they needed. Everything had to be arranged so that, at the first alarm from an outpost, each man could seize his load and escape into the forest. Even the shirts washed free of bloodstains had to dry, not in the sunshine of the clearing, but carefully hidden from any passing plane under a broad tree. And none of these men sat in the sunshine: they couldn't enjoy even that. They crossed the clearing by circling round it, keeping close to the cover of forest. Sheila looked round the ominously neat room. These men couldn't relax, not even here at their headquarters. Their margin of safety was too narrow. She looked at the thin, tight faces, and she saw them clearly for the first time.

The hours passed slowly. The men ignored her; to them, she was either a treacherous danger or a necessary nuisance. The only words spoken to her were those telling her to eat or giving her permission to walk down to the stream. She knew she was as much guarded then—though tactfully, secretly—as when she lay on the coarse linen-covered mattress. She stared at the beam across the ceiling with its framed pictures and painted flowers. She stared at the straight row of sacred pictures on the wall in their heavy wooden frames. She stared at the roughly carved figure of the Madonna with her blue painted gown, at the candles and crucifix on the broad ledge at the Madonna's feet. She stared at the top of the tall whitewashed stove, followed with her eyes its simple design down from the ceiling to the bulge of cooking oven and the wooden benches fixed round it for a friendly hour on a cold winter's night. On top of the oven, someone had spread a neat piece of newspaper: weeks ago, someone had spread it, intimating that the oven was no longer going to be used until he got back from the war. And on the newspaper, its edges neatly matching the square of the oven top, was a prayer-book. She stared at those things. She knew them all by heart, just as she knew the shape of the table with its square solid legs suddenly twisting into a soft curve as they reached the hard earth floor; or the shape of the wooden bench, built into the wall opposite the stove, with its curved end-arms and its attached footrest. She knew this house as if she had always lived here; as if she had been the one who had painted the flowers on the beam so proudly; as if she had let the stove die, and had raked it clean for a fresh start, and had covered it with a newspaper headlining war, and had laid the Book on it with a prayer for a safe return.

Then, to stop thinking about the forester who had not returned, she would sit up and stare at the open door and the patch of grass, no longer whitened with dew, but warm and fading in the autumn sunlight. Sometimes, when the men were not in the room, she would rise and walk to the window, and lean on its broad sill of dark wood, and look out over the empty flowerbox at the trees, and forget everything that worried and nagged her by watching their leaves. Their rich colors, so sharply divided and yet merging into each other, would stare back at her until she could only think of red and yellow and orange and purple and bronze and henna. It was strange that anything so violent should be so peaceful. And then the crisp air would end its deception and strike at her shoulders, bring a shiver to her spine, and she would go back once more to the high, boxlike bed. She would begin staring at the ceiling beam with its framed pictures and painted flowers.

She would think of the Aleksanders and of Uncle Edward and of Casimir. She would wonder if Steve had reached safety, if Bill and Schlott were with him. And she would think a lot about Uncle Matthews. That always brought on a bad attack of conscience. He had been more fond of her than either he or she ever admitted. He would be worried. He might sit in his anonymous office, pretending that a lost niece was just another of life's unnecessary complications, but he would be worried. As for herself, she could now admit that she had never appreciated Uncle Matthews. She knew that now, when it was too late. Often she had used to think of Uncle Matthews as someone who was being unnecessarily dogmatic, or interfering, or boring, or embarrassing. Now she realized that she must have often seemed equally dogmatic, interfering, boring and embarrassing. But the chief difference between the old and the young was that the old knew what the young thought about them.

She thought about her father and her mother and then her father, again. When she was a child, her questions about her mother had been answered. But the discouragement given her when she asked about her father had only stimulated a greater secret interest in him. For that reason, she generally thought more about her father when she thought of these vague nebulous characters whose only reality to her was the fact that she did exist.

Night had come, and had gone. Still there was no sign of Jan and his comrade.

This was the last day. She had until tonight. Perhaps, if the Poles followed polite convention in such matters, until dawn. She couldn't sleep and she couldn't think. The guard outside the door spoiled both of those attempts. It was his silence that worried her. He made no sound, and then, just as she was beginning to think that he wasn't there, the slight shuffle of his feet, a smothered cough, a bored sigh would bring her right back to the growing idea that Jan had met with some accident. His accident would be her tragedy. Silly kind of tragedy, too. There was something ludicrous in being shot by your own side. Her father had died more efficiently than that.

She rose and went to the window once more. The soaring wall of leaves gave her courage. She looked at their brave colors and thought, nothing is inevitable, not while you have two legs and a sound body and wits still working. She had at least until tonight.

She stayed at the window, watching the fading light and the darkening leaves, until the captain came back to the house. He looked tired, as if he hadn't been able to sleep either. He entered the room without looking at her, now obediently back in her appointed corner, threw some papers on the table, pretended to study a much-folded map.

He looked up suddenly and said, in a burst of irritation, "Why don't you sleep?"

"If your two men don't hurry I don't think I'm going to need any more sleep."

He stared at her for a moment, and then bent over the map once more.

"You said we would have plenty of time to talk here." Sheila's voice was calmer than she had expected. "The forty-eight hours are nearly up, and we haven't talked more than twenty words."

"There's nothing you can say which interests us at the moment."

"I had hoped to tell you about Captain Wisniewski. Now that the others aren't here, I could tell you about what he and his men hope to do. Why don't you join him?"

The Pole's thin face tightened. His eyes looked at her coldly.

Sheila was silent. She wanted to say, "But this camp of yours is so impermanent. Nine men striking aimlessly, here and there. Nine men being picked off, one by one. It is merely pinpricking compared to becoming members of a larger force with real striking power. Wisniewski's chosen a winter camp. You may be sure it will be remote enough, well-buried enough to be safe. At least, safer than this forest. This is an open part of Poland. You daren't even light a fire. The frost is on the morning grass now. Soon you will need warm food and heat to thaw frozen clothes and bones. You are brave, and your men are brave. But that is not enough."

But, looking at the thin, proud face she merely said, when at last she did speak, "He needs men like you."

The door opened and Thaddeus came in. When he sat down at the table, the breadth of his shoulders and the large head and body made him seem a tall man. He was discussing her now. His eyes were watching her. The captain argued wearily.

"You are a fool," Thaddeus said, and rose in anger. He was no longer a tall man. He was only a little more than Sheila's height, certainly not more than five feet six inches. The captain had risen too. His fist crashed on the table.

"I say we give her until morning. Jan may have been waiting all day for the light to fade. He may need darkness to travel in."

The two men tried to outstare each other. Sheila rose quickly from the bed. She said to Thaddeus, "I'm not worth a quarrel. If you must lose your temper, then lose it with the Germans and not on your friends. You'll never win, that way."

Thaddeus turned his stare on Sheila. She found herself wondering what his face would really be like if he could shave and wash properly. She wouldn't be able to recognize any of these men if they had a shave, a haircut, a warm bath and decent clothes. But then, they wouldn't recognize her either if they had first seen her two months ago. And then Thaddeus turned on his heel and walked out of the room.

The captain's voice changed. He said gently, "If you knew his story, you would not think he was so hard. His wife, his father, his two children were killed because of a German spy. They gave shelter to our soldiers cut off in the retreat. A Polish soldier was their guest one night, but next day he came back in a German uniform with German friends. A servant girl out searching for a stray cow was the only survivor in that household. She told Thaddeus the story when he reached his home and found it burned to the ground."

Sheila looked at the captain's drawn brows. You've got a story, too, she was thinking: you've got a frightening story locked in behind those cold eyes. For a moment, his head bowed wearily, and then he was in control again, fingering the papers, examining the map, working with the intensity of a man who is driven by some inward compulsion.

A bird's whistle trilled; fell silent; and then, as if in love with its own liquid note, trilled again.

"They've come," Sheila almost shouted, "Jan's here!"

The captain, folding up his papers with quick fingers, shook his head. "Not Jan," he said, watching the girl's face change from joy to despair. "We've a visitor. But not Jan. Not Germans, either." He placed the papers in his torn, stained tunic. He took out his revolver, examined it, slipped it back into its holster.

Thaddeus was at the door again. The captain joined him. The two men, together, watched the darkening forest and the path from the outside world.

"It's Dutka from the village. Dutka and two strangers," the captain said at last. His voice was reassured.

"Hope he's brought that razor and piece of soap he promised. We'll never be able to use the uniforms until he does," Thaddeus said.

"One man's a soldier. The other looks old—a peasant—but he walks briskly enough."

Sheila, sitting on the bed, didn't even look up as the men entered. She listened bitterly to the sudden flow of words, to Dutka's loud jovial laugh. She buried her head in the pillow. She had been so sure it was Jan and his friend. She turned her face wearily to the wall.

Not only had Dutka brought the razor and soap, but he had also cigarettes and a bottle of vodka. Triumphantly, he set them all out on the table. "They've been hidden for a week until I could get to you," he explained in his deep hoarse voice. "Today was the first time I could manage to slip away from the village." And then he started to account for his companions. "This here is Galinski," he said, "a soldier in the Eleventh Infantry Division who fought round Lwów. He's been sheltering in the village for the last four days. He seemed a likely recruit. Go on, Galinski, tell them what happened to you." The soldier obeyed eagerly, quickly. He was alone in the world now. He wanted to go on fighting. After Lwów, he had been captured by the Russians east of Dublany. He escaped and walked back through Central Poland only to find his family had gone and his house occupied by the damned Szwaby. He had fled again, wandered for a week, and then found a hiding place in Dutka's village. The Germans were there, too, now. A patrol had been stationed there. But he had just kept quiet in Dutka's loft, and this evening, when the patrol was out on duty, he had slipped out with Dutka.

"It's good to be here," he kept saying. "It's good to be here." Something in his voice, perhaps its joy and relief, made Sheila turn round curiously to look at the man. He was young, tired, strained, but happy. She envied him his happiness.

The men who weren't on sentry duty had crowded into the room and had listened to the story silently. The shutters were closed, the candle in the empty vodka was lit, and the captain sat at the table with paper and pencil before him. He asked the soldier many questions. The answers were immediate. They seemed to be satisfactory. Then the other men were questioning Galinski eagerly, asking news of the outside world from which they had separated themselves. One of them knew Galinski's home town. It was the captain who listened now. Finally he seem satisfied. He turned to the other stranger, who had remained silently leaning against the oven, his cloth cap still pulled over his eyes.

Dutka said quickly, "He's no recruit. He came asking for you at the village. Zabka from the next village brought him to me, so he was sent by the right people. I brought him along, for if you know him, as he says, then good and well. If you don't—then you know what to do."

The captain nodded. "Take off that cap," he said sharply.

The man leaning against the stove didn't move. "I'm glad to find you," he said. "I heard two days ago that you were somewhere in this district."

The captain stared unbelievingly, rose to his feet as if to a superior officer. As he was about to speak, the stranger made a sign with his hand and silenced him. "Later," he said quietly. "Later."

The captain smiled, and then sat down again. He opened the cigarettes and passed them round. The new bottle was uncorked, and each man had a mouthful of vodka. Sheila, sitting motionless in her dark corner, listened to the rising voices, the laughter, the short questions, the long answers. She was watching a scene from a play in which tension and gloom had suddenly and dramatically changed to lighthearted gaiety. Dutka was giving them news; they had cigarettes between their lips, the taste of vodka on their tongues. When a man is hungry for these things, it doesn't take much of them to please him. Each man's high spirits increased the others'. Only the captain and the stranger with the cloth cap pulled over his eyes didn't join in the sudden uproar of voices. The captain had a smile on his lips. His face looked happier than Sheila had ever seen it. His eyes were watching the stranger. He in turn watched the men. And it seemed to Sheila, as the hidden audience to all this, that Galinski watched everyone, but especially the unidentified stranger. Quietly he watched him, secretly, as if he didn't quite trust him.

The stranger, despite his clothes, was not a peasant. His voice as he now spoke was that of a commanding officer. "Who is this?" he asked, and nodded towards the corner of the room. Sheila suddenly realized that he had noticed her from the first. The men stopped talking. All had turned their heads to look at her. Galinski laughed and said a few phrases which brought a sudden guffaw from the others. Sheila's cheeks flushed and she drew nearer the wall. Dutka came forward to see her more clearly.

The captain said crisply, "Enough of that. She's our prisoner."

"A German spy," added Thaddeus bitterly.

"Why don't you shoot her?" Dutka asked curiously. "That's what to do with a spy."

"She will be shot at dawn, and no later," Thaddeus said, and looked pointedly at the captain. No more reprieves, either, his tone implied.

The man with the cap stopped leaning against the stove. He moved quietly towards the door, motioned with his head to the captain, who followed him out into the night. He wants to find out more about me, Sheila thought; or he may have something to say which he doesn't want a spy to hear, not even one who is to be shot. And no reprieve. She closed her eyes.

"Let's have a look at this spy," Galinski said and caught

up the bottle with the candle. Sheila opened her eyes to see the flame flicker, nearly vanish, and then burn more wildly as the man stood holding it above his shoulder. He was a young man, with a fair-haired, fair-skinned look in spite of a deep tan and streaks of dust. Like the others, he needed a shave. His uniform was stained and ragged. His eyes above the gaunt cheekbones were a clear blue in the candle's golden light. He stood with his back to the room and stared down at her.

"A spy, eh? A damned German spy." His voice was harsh and savage. But his lips were smiling; a strange, meaning smile which only she could see. The blue eyes were serious: they were trying to tell her something. The bitter voice went on, "And where in God's name did you pick her up?"

"On the Lowicz road. First we got a patrol. Then she arrived in a staff car with a German corporal," one of the men said eagerly. "He got his all right. But she was still alive, so we brought her here. Information, you know."

Dutka drew closer, too. "Did you get information?" he asked.

"A pack of lies." The Pole who was talking was enjoying himself. By his voice, you would have thought that he was responsible for everything. "She pretends she isn't German, says she's English, says she's got friends at Korytów who will swear she's all right." He laughed at the idea. "Just look at her. She's a German. A German telling lies to save her skin."

Sheila said nothing. Her eyes were fixed on the man in front of her. Dutka shook his head and turned away. "You should shoot her at once. Mark my words. A German's a German. And a pretty woman never did no good. You'll have trouble on your hands."

Galinski's eyes swept over her as if he were memorizing every detail about her. "German," he echoed Dutka with even more hate in his voice. He spat. Sheila flinched. But her anger was stifled by amazement. The man had grinned, a friendly encouraging grin, and his left eye winked deliberately. "I wouldn't mind helping with the examination," he said as he turned to face the room again, "or is that the captain's privilege?"

"Here," Thaddeus said suddenly. "That's enough of that." One of the men who had begun a laugh didn't finish it.

Galinski placed the candle back onto the table and said, "Any food to spare?"

"You'll have to wait till tomorrow," Thaddeus said gruffly. "We've been too busy in the last few days to bother about food. Some of us will forage tomorrow."

Dutka said, "If I had known, I could have tried to smuggle something up to you. Not that the Germans in the village leave us much. But I could have tried." He looked worriedly at the bottle of vodka and cigarettes, as if wishing they would transform themselves into a piece of ham and some bread. "You've never been needing food like this, before."

"We've been busy," Thaddeus said.

The talkative man—it was he who had cut short his recent laugh—once more found his tongue. "We are all set now. All we need are some breeches and some bullets."

"Ammunition?" Galinski asked. He walked over to the bench where the uniforms and weapons were neatly piled. "German ammunition you're needing? Hey, Dutka, you tell them."

Dutka looked at him stupidly. "Tell what?"

"About the patrol in the village. Haven't they plenty of ammunition?"

"Plenty." Then he was explaining in his deep voice about the patrol which had come to the village so unexpectedly only three days ago. They were quartered in the old Posting House. They used the outbuildings at the back for supplies. Two guards looked after that.

Galinski interrupted to say, "I know every step they take. I lay and watched them for these last three days from Dutka's hayloft."

"Didn't they search the village first, to make sure it was safe for them?" Thaddeus asked suddenly.

"Oh, yes," Dutka said, "they searched. But they didn't find him. Galinski used his wits. He will tell you what happened."

"Let us talk of this ammunition, first," Galinski said. "That's the important thing. Give me a knife and I'll take care of those two guards in the darkness."

Sheila wanted to scream, "This is a trap. Don't you see, all of you, Dutka, Thaddeus, it's a trap?" She wanted to scream, "Thaddeus, remember your family. Remember the 'Polish' soldier!" But she forced herself to sit rigid and silent. Thaddeus had never believed her. None of them believed her.

She watched Galinski as he let the others develop the idea he had so cleverly proposed. The talkative man was elaborating on the plan. His voice quickened, his eyes gleamed as if he already saw two Germans waiting in the dark for a tight Polish arm round their neck, a quick Polish knife to silence their first cry. And as he talked, and the others nodded their approval, the whole idea seemed to become his. His comrades added their ideas. Between them all, the plan became easy—a mere matter of lifting what they needed from the German supply hut and vanishing into the night.

Dutka alone was silent. He was thinking of the village, of the consequences it would have to face. Thaddeus noticed his silence. "We'll wait for the captain. He never let us do any raiding so near the camp. We'll wait for him."

"We could all go. Make it a full attack," the talkative man said. "Only two dozen Germans. We know how to work in the dark. We could take care of them. Two dozen Szwaby less."

"And then one village less," Thaddeus said, and turned, with relief no greater than Sheila's, to the door as the captain and his strange friend entered. They had the look of men who had talked and decided much. The stranger was satisfied. But Sheila had the feeling that the captain had been persuaded against his will: he had the preoccupied air of a man who still argued with himself.

Thaddeus gave the new information quickly, outlined the idea, which had grown from bullet-snatching to wholesale slaughter.

The captain listened gravely, watching the excited happy faces of his men.

"You see," he said to his visitor, "all they want is action."

"And dead Germans," the talkative man said.

"The village is too near the camp," Dutka suggested. "They will search every inch of this forest, afterwards."

"We are leaving this camp," the captain said slowly, and looked at the stranger beside him. "Tomorrow, we leave." The stranger nodded. "But for the sake of the village, Dutka, we won't kill any Germans. We'll be satisfied with the ammunition. We shall send two men back to the village with you, dressed as Germans. That way, the guards may not need to be killed. Tie them up, and gag them well. But you keep out of it, Dutka. Let my two men do everything. You will get to the village inn, and have an alibi. We shall take what we need and then clear out. Quietly. No noise of fuss. Fifteen minutes will do the job."

He noticed the men's disappointed faces. "This is more dangerous than killing the guards. Killing is the quick, easy way." He smiled as he saw their faces clear. Suggest danger to a Pole, and he prefers it that way. The more danger, the greater honor.

"Now, outside with you. Thaddeus, you detail the men. Supplement my instructions. Come back here when you've finished; we have new plans to discuss."

Thaddeus, already picking up two German greatcoats, nodded.

The men filed out. Their humor was high. Galinski was the last of them to leave. He shot a quick glance at Sheila. "Courage," he seemed to say, "courage." And all Sheila's remaining courage melted into panic. She had only enough sense to keep silent. Not now, she told herself: wait, until he is out of this room.

And then he was gone too, and there were left only the captain, the stranger, and herself.

They were looking at her. "Come over to the table. We want to talk a little," the captain said.

"Don't let him go. Choose two men, but don't let him be one of them."

They stared at her.

"That soldier who came here tonight. Don't let him go. He's a German. He's a spy."

The captain turned to his friend. He raised his hands helplessly and let them fall on the table. "You see?" he said. "She has the most fertile imagination."

"Believe me now. Please believe me!" She plunged into a description of all that happened.

The two men listened gravely, and that encouraged her.

"But we have only your word for it," the captain said when she had finished, "and we have no proof that your word is honest."

Sheila's frustration ended her calm. Her Scots temper flared. She didn't know what she was saying, but there was a rhythm and intoxication in the intense stream of words which gave them more meaning than any dictionary. When she ended, she was no longer angry. She was amazed at herself, even ashamed. She was quiet and cold and miserable.

"Let me ask some questions," the stranger said unexpectedly. He removed his cap, placing it carefully on the table beside him as if it held his rank and insignia. Sheila saw his high forehead, redstreaked where the cap had pressed too tightly, turn towards her. The eyes were keen, the eyebrows strong. It was a young face with old lines and whitened hair. His crisp, cool voice began a probing examination of her story.

"You are concealing something," he said at last. "Who is the man who arranged everything for you? Was he Wisniewski?"

Sheila shook her head.

"You will not tell?"

She shook her head again.

"But how else can we believe you? You mean you are willing to be shot as a spy rather than give his name?"

"Would his name prove my story?" she asked with a flare

of her past temper. "Once you had learned it, you might say I had been taught his name to use when necessary."

"But the Germans do not know his right name."

"Then you know him!" Her relief choked her. And then she was on guard again. Once she used to think that friends were friends, that questions and answers could be frankly given between them. But now she knew better: now she was learning. A mask went over her face and she stared coldly at the man.

"Look," he said, "you and I are both afraid to make the first move. We have reached an impasse. Yet we must break it. Much may depend on that."

"Much," agreed Sheila bitterly, thinking of the dawn that was marching so steadily towards her. But she said nothing more.

"Does Wisniewski know this man?"

"Yes. Adam—Captain Wisniewski belongs to his organization."

"What department? Come. I know it. What department?"

"Thirty-one." She was weakening. She felt this man was genuinely trying to help her, respecting her for what she would not tell about Olszak; and she was weakening.

"How do you know that?"

"I was at the meeting, the first and last meeting of the organization, just before the Germans entered Warsaw. Another foreigner was permitted to attend with me. He was to take a report of the meeting to friends in Switzerland. I was there to meet the man who was going to employ me as secretary. It was then I became Anna Braun, attached to Department Thirty."

"This foreigner, a Swede I believe—"

"An American."

The white-haired man leaned back against the wall. His eyes had never left her face, but now they had relaxed just enough to let her know that she had indeed given the right answer.

Then Thaddeus entered. "They've gone," he reported.

"Not Galinski? Not the man calling himself Galinski?" Sheila cried involuntarily.

"I'm tired of her play-acting. It's getting on my nerves," Thaddeus said irritably, and lit his cigarette at the candle's flame.

"It isn't play-acting," the stranger said. "She knows too much. If the Germans employed her, she could have put the noose round a certain editor's neck weeks ago."

Sheila stared at him. She began to smile. "You *do* know him," she said.

"I once had the doubtful honor of holding him under protective arrest. That was after he had made a very savage attack in print on the colonels. An interesting man, even if I disagreed with his politics at that time. But now the colonels are gone." He smiled sadly as if laughing at himself. "And politics have gone, and Poland depends now on her captains. Wisniewski . . . you—" he looked at the man sitting beside him—"and hundreds like you." He interrupted his thoughts abruptly. "Send a man to trail the others to the village. One who can take a short cut, who can bring us back word of the success of this expedition, or of its disaster. It is too late now to stop it. All we can do is to find out what happened to it, and be prepared for what it may bring."

"I've sent a scout after them," Thaddeus said. "After they left, I sent one in case of an accident. I should have sent one after Jan: we'd have known now what happened at Korytów to our men." He looked quickly at the captain's worried face. "Is there something more than routine behind this sending of another man?" he asked sharply.

"Remember your wife," Sheila said in a low voice. "Remember the 'Polish' soldier, Thaddeus."

Thaddeus turned to stare at her. His face seemed larger, whiter; his bloodshot eyes were closed into slits. "Dutka was right," he said slowly, "she's a troublemaker. We'll have no peace until she's gone."

The stranger shook his head. "Perhaps," he said, "or perhaps she has given us a real warning. In any case, I want to talk to her."

The questioning began once more. The stranger watched every line of her face, every fleeting expression, every uncontrolled muscle. Nothing escaped the granite eyes. The captain waited eagerly. He was obviously relieved that he hadn't shot this girl: he would have had to live with a nagging conscience at the thought of having murdered a friend of his friends. Thaddeus, without the personal link with Andrew Aleksander, would feel regret and sadness if her death had been unjustified, but he wouldn't have the same bitter memory of a tragic mistake. At this moment, however, Thaddeus sat with his eyes averted, a look of distaste on his face. Every answer this foreigner gave only seemed to make him believe still more that she was a spy.

An owl shrieked. Again its startled cry rang through the forest. The three men were on their feet. They were out of the cottage. Sheila was left staring at the flickering candle with its rough coating of congealed drips. "Expect the worst," Uncle Matthews would say, "and you won't be disappointed."

From now on, she was going to believe Uncle Matthews. . . .
Someone was approaching; a friend, possibly, for the three
officers had taken no weapons. But the friend was Dutka or
someone else from the village. It wasn't going to be Jan
and his comrade. Expect the worst . . . Sheila prepared herself for it. The candle flame was burning steadily once more.

She heard voices, many voices. Not triumphant voices.
Bitter, hard, sad voices. It couldn't be Jan. Uncle Matthews
was right. The door opened at last. White smudges of human
face, like a painter's daubs on a black canvas, stared into
the room. Six men entered with Thaddeus. Behind them came
the captain and his friend. And a boy. The white faces took
shape. Jan there was. But not his companion. The others
were men from Korytów. She gave them a weak, unbeliev-
ing smile. And then the boy came forward, and she didn't
give Jan a second glance. She stretched her hand out to the
boy with the strained dark eyes and the haunted face.

"Stefan!" she cried. And Stefan Aleksander forgot the watching men. His self-imposed restraint broke down. His thin
arms were round her, and nothing seemed so wonderful to
Sheila as the tight grip and the intense hug. It was her
reprieve from distrust and veiled hatred. She forgot she was
cold and hungry, forgot she was tired and sleepless. Nothing
mattered, she thought, nothing mattered in this whole damned
world except this warmth, this feeling of being welcomed and
loved. She tightened her own grip and laughed through her
tears.

She remembered Jan. "Then you were in time?" she could
say at last. But where was little Teresa, where was Aunt
Marta? Had they gone to Warsaw to Madame Aleksander,
while Stefan had chosen to serve with these other new recruits?

The men's silence gave her answer. It didn't need Stefan's
hysterical grip on her hand, or the slow unhappy shaking of
Jan's head to warn her of the words he would speak.

"These five men and the boy are what's left of Korytów,"
was all he said.

## CHAPTER XXVII

## Death of Anna Braun

AT THE END of an hour they were ready. No explanation
of Korytów's fate had been asked or given. They all knew

what Jan's words implied. But with Sheila's story proved, the threat of danger from Dutka's village became more real. Silently, obediently, the men prepared to leave. The captain was taking no chances this time.

All traces of the occupation of the forester's house were removed. The uniforms and weapons were distributed among the men. The table was cleared of everything except a map of Poland and the burning candle. The guards outside were replaced with men who had already been given their last instructions, and the remainder, some of them with strange, freshly shaven faces above green-gray uniforms, gathered round the table. Stefan, quite suddenly and unexpectedly, had fallen asleep, and had been carried to bed. Sheila sat beside him. He would be angry that she had let him sleep while all these orders were being given, but it was better that he should sleep. However determined a boy of fourteen was to prove himself equal to a man, the shock of the last two days would not be fought against in the way that a man would master it. It was good for Stefan to fall asleep, and sleep well.

The captain stood at the table in front of the map. The white-haired man was at his elbow. Together, they gave the final instructions. Immediately the house was abandoned, the men were to separate. They were to travel either singly or in pairs to the south. There, some sixty miles away, they would reach the forest land to the southeast of the Province of Lodz. In the part of the forest which they all in turn examined from the map, they would find one of Wisniewski's camps. It was hidden in that forest, a forest of great depth and safety, where fires could be lit, and game was still to be found in plenty. Meanwhile, they were to travel carefully, at night. They were to avoid the Germans' attention by neither fighting nor giving any cause for suspicion. They would find shelter through the day, and food, in the villages through which they would pass. The peasants had already proved themselves willing to accept that risk. So had the big houses. So had the priests. The one danger was a German pretending to be a Pole. Therefore, they were to steer clear of other wandering men. The people they could trust lived in the villages and were known to one another. When they reached the forest district, they were to ask at any of the villages which encircled it for a woman called Jadwiga. It was all arranged: each village had its chosen Jadwiga, and each Jadwiga would either show or supply them with a guide to reach the first outpost of the camp. The password was "The Reapers." That was the name the men of the camp had chosen. It was wise to have a guide to reach the forest camp of the Reapers, for a man from the open plains or towns would find the forest a grim place to penetrate. In its depths were stag and lynx and wild boar. There were parts of it where no human beings had ever been. The thick trees and bushes formed a matted wall. Also, wandering strangers with no guide to vouch for them were apt to be killed first and questioned afterwards.

The captain had finished. The white-haired officer repeated the commands, carefully and slowly. In the same words, all the men once more repeated what he had said, telling it to themselves unforgettably. After that, not even the slowest-thinking man in the group could have mistaken any of the orders. Not, thought Sheila, that there was a stupid look on any of the faces. Danger sharpens wits; hunger increases alertness. There wasn't a placid face among them. Each jaw had an edge, each eye had a quickness, each mouth was set. The excitement and laughter of the earlier evening had given way to grim purpose. The men waiting so silently had seen death, had felt danger's cold breath, had known tragedy and sorrow. There was nothing left to fear. Everything had been taken from them. The Germans had made a mistake in leaving them nothing, in conceding no hostage to fortune.

The captain and his friend came over to her, while the men sat on the floor, smoked the last of the cigarettes, and waited with eyes which saw beyond the room into their own personal tragedies. It was as if they strengthened themselves by remembering the evil that had been done to them and their land.

The captain said, "Miss Matthews, you are our worst problem. What are we to do with you?"

"I can go back to Warsaw and make up an elaborate story of an escape from you, as you once suggested," Sheila said unhappily. Back to Warsaw and Dittmar, and Captain Streit, and the weaving of a further net in which she herself would at last be caught. There was no escaping from Captain Streit: she wasn't clever enough.

The two men exchanged glances. It's strange how every nation thinks that foreigners are mad, Sheila thought. She said "I must reach Madame Aleksander and the head of my department. The last he heard of me was that I was summoned to Gestapo headquarters to identify a body. He will be rather worried." And then she ought to warn Olszak too to tell him that Dittmar had been doing too much thinking.

The white-haired man smiled, with his lips, at her choice of phrase. His eyes never smiled, it seemed.

"I will let him know. And Madame Aleksander will be

taken from the flat in Warsaw, and she can meet you and the boy. It will be arranged. But I, for one, would not advise you to go near Warsaw."

Sheila was watching the gray eyes, flecked with brown: that was one of the reasons why they looked like granite. "If it can't be arranged . . . ?" she asked slowly.

"We can try. We have a better chance than you have. You and the boy will travel with one of the men to the camp, and wait there. Captain Wisniewski will take good care of you until we hear from Warsaw what you are to do."

"Is he there?" Sheila asked quickly, and then was angry with herself. But the white-haired man didn't seem to notice her embarrassment.

Suddenly the captain said to Sheila, breaking his worried silence, "Were you quite sure that the man was a spy? You didn't misinterpret his expression?"

"I am sure. He was in sympathy with me, because he thought I was a German. He left as quickly as he could so that the Germans would be here before dawn. I was to be shot then. He knew that."

"Yes, he was in great haste. At the time, haste seemed natural if the village were to be raided before the dawn came. But now, with your interpretation, this haste seems to point to the man's guilt. I was wrong about Korytów; you were right. You may be right about the man Galinski. We shall not know, until he returns either with ammunition or with German soldiers."

The white-haired man said, "You have decided to leave here, anyway. It is better to leave now than to wait for confirmation of Pani Matthews' suspicions. If he isn't a spy, then the others can be directed to Wisniewski's camp when they return here. If he is a spy, you cannot save Dutka, or your man who went with Galinski. Perhaps you cannot even save the scout whom Thaddeus sent to watch their progress. Not unless Thaddeus reaches them before Galinski leads Dutka and your man into a German trap." At the mention of Thaddeus' name, Sheila looked round the crowded room. Now she realized she hadn't seen him since Jan and Stefan and the other survivors from Korytów had arrived. She felt that Thaddeus' action was a gesture of atonement: he would blame himself for Korytów. The captain might have believed her, if Thaddeus hadn't been so much against her.

The captain was saying, "The scout should already be in position. His short cut takes little more than half the time to reach the road."

"Are you sure Dutka won't take his party by a short cut, too?"

"He always sticks to the path at night. He isn't a woods-man."

"Galinski might persuade him to risk a short cut. If he is a German, he will search for the quickest way."

"Yes, there's that to worry about too. In that case, our scout would be useless and Thaddeus has gone in vain."

"I advise leaving at once, Captain Reymont. Your men are ready."

The captain nodded, looked at his watch again, gave his last orders. The outposts stationed in the woods were given their warning to move. Their answering bird call proved that they had heard it and were obeying. As the men in the forester's house started to move out of the door, Sheila wakened Stefan. And then she remembered that she, too, had preparations for leaving to complete. She found her hand-bag, which had been placed on top of the oven, near the worn prayer-book. All the permits and identification papers would have to be destroyed. Anna Braun was dying. There was unbelievable pleasure in feeling the thick sheets of paper tear between her fingers. The British passport was the most difficult.

"If I may . . ." the white-haired man said gently, and held out his hand. He must have been watching her all this time. He ripped the resisting cover of the passport in two. "Would you like me to dispose of these where the Germans might think they were very clever in finding them? That would make them so proud of themselves."

"Of course. I am supposed to be dead." She laughed happily.

"Or worse than dead. Naturally, the barbaric Poles would either have murdered and buried you, or carried you away for further torture. Naturally, the same barbaric Poles would try to hide the evidence of your capture. But the Germans, being a superior race, cannot be misled by such petty tricks."

"May I keep my bag, at least? Empty except for the comb and things like that?"

"Bettter throw everything away. If they think you left with a handbag safely under your arm, they won't think so much of the destroyed papers which they will find."

She gave him the bag slowly. Now I'm neither Anna Braun nor Sheila Matthews, she thought, as she watched the strong fingers rip the bag's lining and break its clasp.

"Take off your jacket, too," the quiet voice was saying. "The material is much too like Warsaw for a trip through the fields. The boy will give you his. Later, at a village, you can get appropriate clothes, and burn your blouse and skirt."

He watched her transformation with approval. He picked up the jacket and the underslip which she had stuffed into its pocket. "When these are discovered, you will be in the headlines of all the Nazi papers."

Sheila smiled grimly. "Yes. She died for her Führer." The stranger laughed suddenly, so unexpectedly that the captain looked up in surprise and the few men remaining in the room smiled in sympathy. Sheila looked at the stranger's transformed face. For a moment, she thought of the change in all these men: this was how this man should look, this was how all men should look. Not aged and sad and grim, but laughing honestly. His teeth were white and even. She thought of Russell Stevens. He had wanted her to go, to leave for a world where men could laugh every day. She had chosen to stay, and in choosing had chosen strain and sadness. Yet if she were now asked whether she regretted her choice, she would say, "No. Not now. This afternoon, lying on that bed, waiting to be shot—yes. But now—no." For now, watching the strength as well as the sadness in these men's faces, she felt herself a part of something bigger than ever an individual could be by himself.

Jan had brought Stefan over to them. "We travel together," Jan said to Sheila, and then grinned good-naturedly. "Did you hear I'm to get a medal because I didn't shoot you? I'm the hero who saved the camp."

"How does that work out?" one of the men called over from the door. He was waiting for his time to leave.

"Well, if I had shot her then she wouldn't have been here to see that fine recruit that Dutka brought in for you, would she?"

The man at the door said, "If they give you a medal, it will be a nursemaid's one." He grinned at Sheila and Stefan. "I'll get them to the Reapers quicker than any of you grown men can travel."

"What do you bet on it? My knife to your daggger, eh?" The man's time had come. He slipped through the opened door, and gave a last wave of his hand to the room.

"Jan, *are* you to get a medal?" Stefan asked, his excitement wakening him fully.

Jan smiled. "When we drive the Germans out of our land, we'll all get medals. I'll carve my own out of Himmler's jawbone, and wear it on my hat."

The room was empty. Only the captain and Jan and Stefan and Sheila remained. The white-haired stranger had gone, as silently as he had come. She hadn't even seen him leave.

The captain smothered the candle with his hand. "Better go now," he said. "The other men have gone ahead to clear any danger out of your path." He was looking at her, but she couldn't see his face in the room's darkness. Through the opened door came a short path of faint moonlight. The shrewd night wind cut into the room's thick warmth.

"And you?" she asked.

"I shall wait for Thaddeus and any other who gets back here. They must be told where to go."

If there is any other, Sheila thought. If there is any Thaddeus.

"*Dowidzenia!*" Captain Reymont said quietly. Jan had already moved over the path of moonlight into the silvered grass.

"Good-by," she echoed, and gave the dark silhouette her hand. "Good luck!" He would need it.

"Good luck!" Stefan repeated.

Sheila followed Jan and Stefan round the edge of the clearing. The trees, now a wall of black bronze and white silver, shut out the forester's house, and the man waiting in its darkness. If Thaddeus or the scout returned first, he would have a chance. If the Germans got here before them, there was none.

The sky with its fitful clouds and veiled moon was blotted out. Overhead were only the rustling, whispering leaves. The forest seemed alive. Sheila's alertness increased. Inside four walls it had been possible to relax a little, to feel a supposed security. But here, in the nakedness of the night, every shadow and every whisper might suddenly become an enemy.

Jan had said, "Follow me. Do as I do. The boy walks last."

In this way, like the men who had gone ahead of them, they crept through the woods. Through Polish land they crept, hunted through its forests and fields as if they, and not those who hunted them, had been its thieves.

When the woods ended, open land as flat and broad as a sea stretched in front of them. Its islands were solitary trees, a line of hazel bushes, a group of houses clustered together in solid blackness. Above them was limitless night: in this countryside the horizon was not where the earth rose in rugged folds to touch the sky, but where the sky reached down to join the straight line of farthest fields.

"We'll follow the edge of the wood for a while, and then cut south," Jan said. He was smiling. He was glad to see the plains again. The open fields and the wide sky were his country. He felt safer there.

They must have been more than a mile from the wood on

the journey south, when the first distant shots echoed across the fields.

Jan stopped. He cursed softly. He stood, looking back at the wood, as if he were about to run towards there again. Sheila found she had taken hold of his sleeve. It was as if she were saying, "Don't leave us. We are lost without you."

He looked down at the girl's anxious face. He cursed softly again, and turned away from the direction of the shots. They were closer together now, dull, distant, but unmistakable. Thaddeus and the captain, instead of escaping, must be shooting it out with the Nazis. The Germans must have come quickly: perhaps they had been waiting on the outskirts of the wood near Dutka's village for "Galinski's" return. For now the meaning of the stationing of the German patrol in the village just after "Galinski" had arrived there became clear. The Germans were moving against guerrilla bands. This was the method they had devised: first a spy was sent to a village near any suspicious locality; then some troops, ostensibly as a road patrol. No wonder "Galinski" had not been discovered by the Germans when they searched the village. No wonder he and Dutka had been allowed to reach the wood without any trouble. And now Thaddeus and the captain were shooting it out, perhaps to give the rest of them time to scatter to safety.

Jan urged them on madly. They raced towards a group of darkened houses. Sheila, breathless, had no time to ask why this sudden speed should be so necessary. The Germans hadn't followed them. Thanks to the captain and Thaddeus, the Germans were well occupied round the wood. But as they waited in the shadow of a long, low cottage and Jan rapped gently at a shuttered window, she began to guess the reason of Jan's urgency.

"We are still too near the forest," she whispered. "Should we stop here?"

Jan said, "You need proper clothes." And that was all. But even before the sleep-dulled faces welcomed them into the long dark corridor which formed the hall, even before she and Stefan were being given peasant clothes and a bowl of thin soup, even before Jan disappeared as they swallowed the warm liquid and sat round the wooden kitchen table, she knew that her guess was right. Jan had done what he had wanted to do as soon as he had heard the shots. Jan had gone back to the wood.

"He will be here before dawn. He promised," the peasant's wife assured her and offered her some more soup. Sheila refused politely. Heaven only knew if she and Stefan were gobbling up the family's ration for a week. She kicked Stefan adroitly on the shin as he seemed about to accept a second helping. He refused suddenly, and would not be persuaded again. The two little girls, flaxen-haired and wide-eyed with excitement, stood with their bare feet showing under their long white shifts, and stared. An older girl helped her mother serve the food. There was no sign of the woman's husband. Sheila watched the broad-faced, broad-hipped woman moving so silently about the kitchen in her shapeless plaid nightgown. How often, in the last few weeks, had she taken strangers into her house and shared its warmth and food with them? Her placid face gave no answer.

At last the soup bowls were emptied to the last shred of cabbage.

"You and the boy can share a mattress in front of the stove," the woman said. "It's warmer here than in the bedroom next door. He is your brother?"

Sheila nodded. She was too tired for explanations.

"Poor souls," the woman said to the wooden beam across the ceiling, "they're dropping with sleep." She lifted a candle from the table and said to Stefan, "Help your sister get the mattress. It's next door. I'll show you."

In the next room, leading off the long corridor which ran the whole front length of the cottage, there was a striped mattress and a gay bedmat and high-piled pillows. But the room was cold, and Sheila changed her mind about suggesting she would sleep here after all. As she and Stefan pulled the bedding along the corridor to the kitchen, they heard the roar of motorcycles.

The woman blew out the candle, and they finished their task in darkness. The light in the kitchen had been extinguished too. The children were back in bed. The older girl sounded as if she were clearing the table of all signs of their meal. They felt their way to the stove by its warmth.

"Quietly," the woman's voice came through the darkness, as Sheila stumbled against a bench. "Open a shutter, Weronika." The girl's footsteps crossed the floor unerringly. A shutter was gently pushed aside, just enough to let the intense blackness give way to dim shadows.

"Remember," the hushed voice from the corner bed was saying, "you are my niece and nephew from Lowicz. Your parents are dead. Your names?"

"Sheila and Stefan." The words were out before Sheila could stop the boy from speaking.

"Sheila? What a strange name!" Weronika said. "It doesn't sound Polish." She was helping Stefan to straighten the mattress in front of the whitewashed stove. Then her bare feet ran towards the crowded bed. The children exclaimed and were hushed by their mother as Weronika climbed in and pushed them over to the wall. Then there was silence.

The motorcycles had swept through the village. Now they were followed by two cars. And then there was silence once more. Sheila shivered in spite of the warmth of the kitchen. She couldn't stop worrying. Korytów ... she would need to know what had happened there. She had failed, and she wanted to know just how far she had failed.

"Stefan," she said softly. But the boy was already asleep. Steady breathing came from the corner bed. There was a nice placid sound in the unbroken rhythm. It was warm on the floor, and more comfortable than Sheila had imagined. Her last thought was one of amazement at the discovery, and then yawning loudly, without benefit of a restraining hand, she hugged her shoulders and closed her eyes.

When she awoke, the others were all moving about the kitchen. From her mattress she could see nothing but strong legs and bare feet.

"Well, she's back with us," a man's voice said. It was Jan. She raised herself on her elbow. He and Stefan sat at the long table with their backs to the wall. They were eating again.

"It's all right," Stefan called. "Jan brought us some food."

Sheila rose slowly. Cold sunlight filled the kitchen. The corner bed was stiffly neat. The woman and her children were dressed now as Sheila was, with wide black skirts and white blouses and sleeveless jackets and aprons. Like those which had been given to Sheila, their clothes were neatly patched and darned. Weronika was examining Sheila's discarded skirt, holding it up in front of her.

"That and the jumper and the boy's jacket should be burned," Jan said between generous mouthfuls of food.

"Such a waste. Such good material," the woman said. She looked at the stained and torn pieces of clothing. "If they were washed ... I could alter them and the Germans would never know them."

"Then alter them quick," Jan said.

"They ought to be destroyed," Sheila suggested. She looked worriedly at the others, but no one wanted to hear her.

Weronika ran happily for her mother's carved wood sewing box. "We'll alter them first before we wash them," the woman decided, "and then no one can recognize them when they are on the drying line." She looked up at Sheila, who was watching her busy scissors doubtfully. "You must eat, for you will be leaving shortly. The cart will soon be ready for the journey. Hurry."

As Sheila ate the simple meal which one of the flaxen-haired little girls put shyly down before her, Jan was talking to Stefan about his farm and a cow that had given him a lot of trouble. The woman added her advice on that subject as she stitched. There was only a feeling of peace in the neat room. In many ways it reminded Sheila of the forester's hut. Only, its decorations were cleaner, its white-washed walls and ceiling were fresher. Its similar array of pictures and imitation flowers tacked along the overhead beam was brighter. And the same love of brightness and color was in the cheap prints along the wall, in the striped bed cover and gay pillows piled high on the wooden bed. From her high place of honor, the Virgin Mary smiled down on them, in her robe as blue as the children's wide eyes. A prayer-book had been laid neatly, reverently, so that its edges exactly paralleled the corner of the little table under the Madonna's outstretched arms.

Jan rose suddenly. "Time to leave," he said.

The woman gathered the new shapes of cloth together, spoke quickly to the children. They ran obediently out into the street. The girl, Weronika, stood with her fair head leaning against the door. Her blue eyes under their thick eyelashes and strongly beautiful brows were watching the children at play.

"It's safe," she called back over her shoulder.

The woman watched Sheila tie the yellow handkerchief round her head.

"Not that way. This way," she said with a smile. Her tanned cheeks creased into fine wrinkles. She took the two long pointed ends of the kerchief in her thick, square-shaped hands. She knotted the scarf firmly. "Like that," she added, and pushed Sheila gently towards the door. "Go," she said, and then as Sheila tried to thank her, "You would do the same for me and mine."

She was already bending to pick up the bedding from the floor as Sheila followed Jan and Stefan into the street. Weronika turned back from the door, and gave them a shy side-wise smile. From the kitchen, her mother's voice was telling her to clear the table and hurry up about it. The children in the street stared at them for a moment in the way that children do, and then remembered suddenly to go on with their game. Their high laughter was the last memory of that staunch house.

In front of the blacksmith's open shed, an ancient horse was harnessed to a long boat-shaped cart. The blacksmith, standing well back in the black shadows of his shop, watched Sheila and Stefan climb into the low cart. Jan stooped for a moment, as if examining something beneath it, jammed his revolver quickly behind one of the slats, and lifted the reins. He gave a reassuring nod to the old man standing so silently within the shed, said quietly, "We'll leave the horse and cart with the blacksmith at Rogów as your daughter arranged." The old man, still silent, watched them drive away.

"He didn't want us to take the horse," Jan explained cheerily, "but his daughter persuaded him."

"That was the woman who took us in, last night?"

"Yes. I knew her husband. We were in the army together."

"Where is he now?"

"Killed. All the best men get killed." And then with a sudden laugh, Jan added, "So I'll live for many a day, yet." He tilted his cloth cap forward to shield his eyes from the strengthening sunlight, and whistled quietly as the horse plodded forward.

The road they followed was broad and badly constructed. Its surface had churned into mud. It wound crazily southwards over a flat plain of harvested fields, with thin trees marking its way. Without the trees, the road might have lost its name as well as its direction.

They passed other peasants, mostly walking. The lumbering carts were few. When German motorcyclists or a Nazi car approached, Jan would slip from the driver's seat and stand holding the horse's uncertain head, as if all he had to worry about was the frightened animal. Sheila, clinging to the edge of the shallow cart, still unsure if it really was going to remain upright, felt that the rearing horse couldn't be any more terrified than she was. But the Germans passed with mud hising out from under their tires, and Jan took his perch once more on the rough board across the front of the cart; and the hammock-like wicker basket, its sides supported by wooden slats, rolled along on its four shaky wheels.

Once Sheila said, "This takes a long time, Jan."

And Jan, turning round to look down at her and Stefan jolting about with the remains of cabbage leaves, wisps of hay, goose feathers, cucumber rinds, poppy seeds, had grinned and said, "Those they are looking for won't travel slow."

And once on a lonely stretch of straight road, which went on and on until it hit the blue autumn sky, she said, "What happened last night, Jan? At the wood?"

This time, Jan didn't turn around. He said, his eyes fixed on the long road in front of him, "The wood was surrounded. The Germans had called up reinforcements. The shooting

was over before I got there. I saw Dutka. Dead on the road.
So was our man who went back with that spy. At the edge
of the wood, there was another body. The cars' headlights
were on it. It was our scout. And then I met one of our men
just outside Dutka's village. He had been there to warn Dutka's wife and boy. It was an idea of his own, but it
worked. They got away."

"The captain? Thaddeus?"

"The Germans were still searching when I left. The search-
lights had been brought up."

"There's a chance, isn't there, Jan?"

"There's always a chance." But his voice was heavy, and
his shoulders drooped.

Sheila's next question about Korytów was stifled by Jan's
expressive back, by Stefan's dark face. They would tell her
when they wanted to. Stefan, now that the excitement of
being in a guerrilla camp was over, now that they were
faced with a tedious and ignominious journey, had relapsed
into heavy gloom. Nothing Sheila could say would pull
him out of it. He sat with his arms round his hunched knees,
swaying to the rough rhythm of the cart, staring ahead of
him with unseeing eyes.

He altered that position only once, and that was when
they were stopped by a patrol on the outskirts of one of the
larger villages. And then he turned his eyes on the Germans
with such burning hate in their black depths that Sheila was
afraid. Surely the Germans would notice it, and Jan's explanations would be useless. But the Germans, after a quick search
for weapons on the three stiffly held bodies, after a look
into the dirty cart, seemed satisfied. Possibly they had come
to think that the look which Stefan gave them was a natural
one for a hard-faced, glowering Pole. The main thing, anyway, was kept secret: Jan's gun, jammed between the wicker
cradle of the cart and one of the supporting slats of wood,
had not been discovered.

Sheila, in her nervousness as the examination ended and
they were still free, missed her foothold on the cartwheel and
slipped. The soldiers laughed. Perhaps it was funny. She
picked herself up from the ground and shook down her
wide skirts. She bent her head to hide her scarlet cheeks. The
Germans thought that still funnier. Jan waited patiently,
stupidly, until the soldier who had been holding the horse's
head let it go at a signal from the sergeant. The soldier gave
the horse's nose one last pat.

"I'm fond of horses. Even an old nag like this," he said.

The soldiers, now that they had found these three peasants
harmless, stood in an amiable group in the middle of the

road. Well clothed, well fed, they looked at the poorly dressed Poles and their ramshackle cart and their ancient horse. There was nothing here to be commandeered. They could indulge themselves in the very pleasant feeling of being so vastly superior. Their mockery was generous. Their humor was broad.

Jan urged the horse forward. As soon as the Germans had started to discuss the girl in particular terms, he had felt it was indeed time to be moving. Many a joke had ended in earnest, before now.

A car, traveling quickly towards them out of the village, was the deciding factor. The half-dozen soldiers formed up neatly, the sergeant saluted, and by that time Jan's efforts had driven the horse into the beginning of the village.

From the branches of the trees in front of the Posting House were suspended four bodies, hands tied behind their backs, toes pointed, heads drooping forward.

Sheila turned her head away quickly. She said in a hard, strange voice, "I'm fond of horses. Even an old nag . . ."

Jan's back was as rigid as Stefan's eyes.

## CHAPTER XXVIII

### *To the Forest*

AT ROGÓW, they left the horse and cart. They also left Jan's revolver—after a short, bitter argument.

"It's a good gun," Jan said, "It's fought bravely."

"You'll get as good a gun where you're going," Sheila replied obstinately. (She still broke into a cold sweat when she thought of the casual way Jan had hidden it in the cart.) And Stefan, rather unexpectedly, supported her mutiny, perhaps because Jan had made him discard his penknife before they started the journey.

"All right, my lady," Jan said at last, and pointed out the revolver's hiding place to the man who had taken charge of the horse and cart. "Five good bullets," he added slowly. And these were the last words he spoke for the next three hours. Even after they were stopped and searched to the south of the village, he still conveyed by his gloomy silence that he would have hidden the gun, that he could have fooled a German any day.

But, apart from this obstinacy, he was as cunning and careful as Sheila could have wished. They avoided any village where, as the peasants warned them, a German garrison was quartered. Jan had no desire to test his story, of traveling to the nearest town to register for work, before a group of officers. And he also avoided any repetition of the cart incident, when the soldiers had shown signs of interest in Sheila. For as soon as they left the village of Rogów, he shouldered her into a ditch. When she struggled out of it, not only were her legs and hands covered with its filth, but her clothes were liberally clotted. Even her face was streaked, and her hair at the temples was splashed with its nauseating mud. She tried to brush it off. That only made matters worse: it would have to dry first. She looked at Jan angrily. "You *would* choose the ripest part of that ditch," she said bitterly, but he merely stared stolidly back at her. "I gave up my gun," his eyes were saying. "You can give up looking pretty." Stefan was no consolation. But at least, Sheila thought, we've made him laugh: that's something. He's a boy again. Her anger changed to self-pity, and the journey continued in silence.

But Jan had been clever enough in his own peculiar way. Certainly, the German soldiers who stopped them after that seemed to take little pleasure in searching a disreputable peasant girl.

"Careful of lice, there," one of them even warned his comrade, watching her from a safe distance, in disgust. "God in heaven, what a race of filthy pigs!"

For a day, a night, and a day they traveled. Traveled like three restless ghosts, without proper food or sleep or warmth. Jan was determined. He refused low-voiced invitations to rest overnight in the little villages they passed; and the food which was offered them—a piece of hard black bread, a slab of cold sausage—he would thrust in his pocket. Later, when he allowed them one of their brief ten-minute rests in some small cluster of trees, they would swallow the cold hard lumps of food, and wash them down with water from a stream. Sheila's mouth seemed to taste permanently of the leaves which floated on the water: an earthy taste, bitter, sharp, neither sweet nor sour.

Jan wouldn't let her try to wash off the mud. It had dried, but it still stained her clothes and skin. Its smell still clung to her. She seemed to be living in a state of permanent nausea. "No," he said sharply, towards the end of the first day, when she tried to scrub her face and hair. "That is why we don't stop with the villagers. They'll be cleaning us up, making us look respectable. They'll start talking. They'll be wanting news. They'll keep us late."

Sheila looked at Stefan, propped wearily against a tree. He never complained. If a boy could do it, so could she. She had to content herself with a mild "*Must* we hurry quite like this?"

Jan nodded.

She looked at him accusingly. "You are trying to win that bet, Jan. That's the reason." Later, when and if they reached safety, she would perhaps be able to smile at the expression on Jan's face at that moment.

"I'll win it all right," he said. "I'll get you there before the others arrive. . . ."

"It's safer anyway," he went on after a pause, as if to excuse his determination. "If we stay in one place, the Germans will start asking questions about us. If we are going to town to look for work, as we say, we wouldn't be sitting beside someone's fire. We'd be going to the town."

Jan was already on his feet. "Come. The time for resting is over," he said. "We've twenty miles to cover before day breaks." And they covered the twenty miles or more before dawn. As a reward, in the bitter hours before sunrise, when a rising wind cut through their thin clothes, Jan let them have an hour's sleep under a neatly thatched haystack in a field of harsh stubble. They slept huddled together for warmth, Jan sheltering the two smaller bodies from the wind with his broad back. But before dawn came with its cock-crow from the near-by village, Sheila and Stefan were shaken awake. Looking at Jan's haggard face, Sheila knew he hadn't slept. He had been their guard as well as their shelter. Her annoyance faded; she forced herself wide awake, and they walked on.

That was the last sleep they were allowed. The occasional ten minutes of rest were granted more sparingly, and only whenever they reached a fringe of thin wood. But in the open country, they kept their steady pace. Except, of course, when they came to a wayside cross or a little shrine. Then Jan would take off his cap and kneel. So did Stefan. Sheila forgot her Presbyterian conscience. Religious differences didn't matter, now. At first she had welcomed the kneeling in the soft mud of the road as a chance to rest. And then she found she was praying, and she felt better. She felt stronger and better. There is no evil in man's mind when he prays; and it seemed as if the shrine before which they knelt had kept something of the good will and hope which had flowed into it from the hearts of the simple peasants who had prayed there. It seemed as if the shrine's symbol had been given, by their honest faith, the power to encourage all those who knelt there.

As they managed to pass two more German patrols, Sheila's confidence revived. But she still had one fear. She mentioned it, at last, as they rested (ten minutes by Jan's idea of time; he owned no watch, but he seemed to have been born with a clock in his brain) towards the evening of the second day.

"Jan, what if we were ever to meet the same patrol twice? What if they heard we were going to look for work in a town which had changed its name since they last questioned us?"

"What's to be, will be. If we meet the same Germans twice, moving at the rate we move, then God never meant us to reach the Reapers' camp."

Sheila couldn't be quite as philosophical as that. But she comforted herself with the thought that it would be a rare chance if a patrol left its appointed district. Patrols were like sentries, with their own beats to watch. The Germans were methodical, thank Heaven. Looking at Jan and Stefan and what she could see of herself, she could believe the story which the German road-patrols accepted. They really looked as though they were a family who had lost everything in the war, and now, hearing that people were being registered for work, were trying to reach the nearest town.

"What papers do you keep showing them, Jan?" she asked curiously. They couldn't be German documents and permits, for the countryside hadn't been fully registered yet. It was only in the larger cities that the Germans had been able to satisfy their bureaucratic instincts, so far. In a few weeks, no doubt, the villages would be under card-index control. Then Jan, if ever he made another journey like this one, would have to change his story.

Jan took his papers out of an inside pocket of his ragged jacket. That was where he kept his blunt stub of pencil, a piece of string, two small coins. Sheila could see them all spread out on a broad German palm, could see them thrown on the road, could hear the soldiers laugh as the Polish pig rooted in the mud for his possessions.

She took the papers silently. They were much folded, stained, and thin at the edges. They almost tore as she opened them.

"Have a care," Jan said, anxiously.

The writing was faint, sharply angled, brown. The seals and flamboyant signatures still looked imposing.

"What are they?" she had to ask.

Jan said, very seriously, "Communion certificates. Certificate of merit for the cow I showed at the autumn county fair. Birth certificate." He folded them carefully, and replaced them in the inner pocket. Sheila was reminded of the reverent

way in which he offered his papers for the Germans to see.
The Germans were never interested: as often as not the
papers followed the pencil stub and string and coins into the
mud of the road. But the papers had an effect all the same.
Together with Jan's emphasis on the word "work," they
stamped him as a harmless serf willing to accept authority.
When the inevitable search, thorough and methodical, revealed neither weapons nor possible loot, then Jan was classed
as a negligible, indeed. Let him go to the town and be shipped into Germany for work. If he went without having to
be driven, so much the easier for the Germans. They had
plenty to do rounding up the ones who wouldn't go even with
a bayonet behind them.

"We'll be moving," Jan said. "There's a storm coming."

"What town are we supposed to be going to now? We've
left Lodz to the north of us," Sheila said.

"What town, now?" Jan asked Stefan. "Where's that geog-
raphy of yours?"

Stefan's brow wrinkled. "Let's say Radom. It's in the next
province, but that's the direction we're traveling in now. Or
if you want a town farther west, there's Piotrków. That's
almost due south of Lodz, as far as I can remember."

"Better keep to the one province. Piotrków it is," said Jan.

"I feel like one of the Three Sisters," Sheila said, and
Stefan laughed.

"What's that?" asked Jan.

"They kept saying they were going to Moscow, but they
never did get there."

"Keep moving," Jan said. "God preserve us from reaching
any of the towns we've been traveling to. But if we don't
keep moving, we'll never reach that forest."

As Sheila stumbled after him, she thought: the first twenty
miles were painful, the second twenty miles were hell, but
the third twenty miles are such agony that I've stopped even
feeling them.

"We'll be there before dawn," Jan said cheerily. "If we
keep moving with no more asking for rests," he added,
looking pointedly over his shoulder at Sheila.

Jan was right. Well before dawn, they came to a small
village, and in the distance, stretching along the whole
horizon, as far as they could see, was a heavy blot of darkness.
Under the clouded moonlight, it was like a ribbon of black
velvet joining flat gray fields to a threatening night sky.
"Yon's the forest," Jan said.

Sheila, too tired to be able to say "I hope so," just looked.

Trees, many of them, stretching for miles, so dense that they formed one wall, one unit, almost a world.

Jan left her and Stefan under a hazel tree. He was going to the cluster of houses by himself. "That storm's been threatening all night. It's following us," he said. "You'll be safe here, if it breaks. Lightning never struck a hazel tree."

Then he was gone. Sheila, crouching close to Stefan, tried to follow him with her eyes. But after the first few minutes, she couldn't see him.

He was gone far longer than she liked. Even Stefan had become impatient. The storm had something to do with their nervousness. It struck cruelly at the cowering houses and the moaning trees. Sheila glanced uncertainly at the branches overhead.

She said, "Let's get into the open."

Stefan whispered, "But this is a hazel tree. Jan chose it specially. All you have to do is to pray to Jesus, Mary, and Joseph. The hazel tree sheltered them on their flight to Egypt. It will never be struck by lightning."

"Do you believe that, Stefan?"

"All the country people do"

Sheila hesitated, and then started to edge her way into the open. But a white flash lit the earth in front of them as clearly as any searchlight, and she stopped, lowering herself onto her elbows, and then flat onto the ground. On the road beyond the field she saw two cars. The angry voice of the storm had hidden the roar of their engines. They were rushing towards the village. Then the flash was gone, and the cars vanished into the stormy dark.

She pulled herself back under the shelter of the long grasses round the hazel tree's roots. She would have to trust the peasants. In any case, she'd rather face a bolt of lightning than a car full of Nazis.

Jan came when the sheets of white light no longer played over the fields. The thunder rolled away farther to the south. The rain alone remained. Cold and heavy, it lashed their shoulders and whipped their legs as they followed Jan along the windbreak of trees.

"Germans in the village," Sheila whispered, as Jan paused to steady her over the treacherous roots.

"Aye. The storm brought them. They've stopped for shelter. I had just found our Jadwiga. She keeps the inn. She's serving them with drinks now. She had to send her son to guide us, instead."

"Were you in the inn when they came?"

"I got out the back window. It was a near thing. I could do with one of those warm drinks they are swilling."

"So could I," Sheila said feelingly, and brushed the rain from her eyes.

Jadwiga's son was waiting for them at the last tree. They joined him silently, without pausing, and silently they followed the thin small figure, slowly crawled with him across the open field, crouched as he did while they hurried through thin fringes of bush or tree. And the rain slashed at their brows and blinded their eyes, cut their hands and legs, flailed their hunched shoulders. There is a time in the state of human discomfort when additional miseries suddenly cease to be counted. At first Sheila had kept saying to herself, "This is not me. This can't be me." Now, her body moved and stopped in obedience to the shadow ahead of her, but she had passed the stage of amazement, of useless anger, of self-pity. She didn't even try to protect herself any more. When her feet sank into deeper mud, she let them sink. When a branch whipped towards her face, she didn't even turn her head aside.

Suddenly it was darker: so dark that they had to walk, each holding the jacket of the man in front, like a file of blind men. The air was still and smelled sweet; the wind had ceased with the rain. High above them, there was a drumming noise, a hollow ryhthmical music. Cold drops fell in unexpected showers. Sheila began to realize they had entered the forest. The ground was firmer. Leaves rustled underfoot. A twig cracked. There was a feeling of deep silence, of brooding peace, broken only by the sudden scurry of a startled animal. Dawn must have come, for the forest was no longer a series of black depths stabbing at her eyes; it was a misted gray with unending ranks of ghostlike trees.

The boy leading them paused, and gave a bird's shrill cry. When the answering cry came, he moved on. Suddenly he halted again. Sheila, still clutching Jan's torn jacket, leaned her head on his broad arm. Her neck seemed to be loose. Her head wouldn't stay up. She needed Jan's arm to prop it into position. I'm a doll with the sawdust running out, she thought, and stared dully at the boy's raised arm. "He want silence," she told herself. "He is whispering. What can be wrong now? Dear God, what can be wrong now?" But the boy didn't seem frightened—he was excited, but not frightened.

"Old Single, himself," he whispered. His eyes were shining. "Keep still and he won't attack us."

Sheila's eyes followed the pointing arm. At the roots of an oak tree there was a black bulk, all shoulder, bulging brow, and mean snout. The two powerful tusks pointed towards them. The boar's eyes glowered at the trees behind which they sheltered. Its enormous head and shoulders turned away and it was staring in another direction. Then, without warning, and moving with a quickness which made Sheila flinch, it was lost in a maze of bushes.

"He heard the others. They must be coming near," the boy explained. But his eyes, still shining with excitement, stared in the direction which the boar had taken. "Isn't he a beauty?" he kept saying. "We saw him, didn't we? That's Old Single, and we saw him."

Altogether too much of him, Sheila thought. She found she was clutching Stefan's hand in a paralyzing grip.

Old Single had been right after all. Sheila hadn't heard them approach, but they were there. Two men carrying rifles, with pheasant feathers in their caps, stepped out of cover. They looked well fed, and clean; and their clothes weren't in rags. But it wasn't this so much that made Sheila stare. It was they way they walked and held their heads. Free men live in this forest, she thought, as she watched them advancing towards the boy.

She looked at Jan and Stefan, and smiled.

The boy had left them. He had gone, imitating the soldiers, with a careless wave of his hand and a proud smile. His shoulders had broadened as one of the men slapped him on the back. That was the reward he wanted. He was one of them, even if he was not yet ten years old. Back in the village, his mother would be waiting anxiously, would make him change his sodden clothes, would force him to drink that cabbage soup, would bother him with low-voiced questions. He would tell her of Old Single, but the soldier's greeting he would keep for himself.

Five miles ago, Sheila had determined she was going to walk into the camp on her own feet. No one was going to carry her. If she had come as far as this without needing help, she would finish the journey by herself. Perhaps, subconsciously, she knew there was no chance of staying at the camp unless she seemed strong enough. And she wanted to stay. She was tired of being hunted, of pretense, of uncertainty. She would cook, she would carry water and wash clothes, she would nurse, she would do all the jobs she had once hated and shunned, if only they would let her stay. When she saw the two soldiers, their heads held high, their movements bold and free, she knew she was right. Here she would find men who believed in attack. *That* was what she wanted now. As the men led them through the trees, her excitement grew. She drew strength from it. She forgot how miserable she had been only half an hour before. Stefan was looking happier. So was Jan. A weight had slipped from all their hearts. It didn't matter if their bodies were stiff and slow-moving.

One of the men went ahead, setting the pace. The other brought up the rear. The men talked naturally as they strode with their steady confident step along the bewildering path. No longer was there need of whispers or silent gestures. Deer started before them. Gray hare cocked long ears, vanished on longer legs. Pheasants walked jauntily across the path. From dense bushes and undergrowth a flurried wood-grouse would rise.

They came to a small hut, almost hidden by undergrowth. Four men came out to watch them pass.

"Much farther?" Sheila asked in desperation, when they didn't stop.

"Not so far now," the man following Stefan said. He looked at her face. "Need help? Hey, Tomasz, we'll give her a carry."

"No," Sheila said and walked on.

There was a second hut, a third hut, each with its watching men. "Wood-grouse," the leader explained as they passed the huts. "This is where they used to shoot them: the wood-grouse sing here at dawn."

"No shooting now," Jan said.

"Bigger game now," the man agreed, and laughed. "But we can shoot here. The center of the forest is ten miles from anywhere. A shot doesn't carry so far. We have to be careful near the forest's edge, that's all."

"We could use bows and arrows," Stefan said excitedly. "On the birds, I mean."

The man said, "We've got a lot of things planned out." His smiling confidence was infectious. Jan nodded, with interest. Stefan's questions multiplied, in spite of his tiredness. And Sheila, seeing the trees thin out ahead of them, seeing the bright color of their leaves blotted out by the weathered logs of a long, low house, knew she had managed it. She had won not only against the German patrols; she had won against herself. She was walking into the camp on her own two feet.

The room was long and dim. The small windows, far-spaced, didn't allow much of the early morning light to enter. At one end of the room was a large open fireplace; at the other, under three small windows, a table. High on the brown pine walls, heads of animals looked glassily down on the three strangers. Open rafters stretched across the room's breadth, showing a dark triangle of roof above them. There was a smell of tobacco, of coffee, of roasted food. Sheila didn't know whether it was staring up through the rafters at the pointed shadow of the roof, or the feeling of sudden warmth and civilized life, which made her feel so dizzy. She had walked in unhelped; it looked as if she would never get out that way. She swayed, and Jan's strong arm helped her to steady herself. Stefan, his eyes fixed excitedly on the large wall-map, on the uniformed men, noticed nothing else.

The officers grouped round the table had raised their heads as the two soldiers shepherded the newcomers through the doorway. They looked with an annoyance at this interruption, which gave way to silent pity. Adam Wisniewski was there, two other officers, and the white-haired man. One of them said brusquely to the soldiers, "Three more of them? Well, give them something to eat. We'll question them later. And, for God's sake, scrub them." Adam Wisniewski didn't even look at them any more. He was too busy explaining something. The white-haired man was the only one who still stared.

Sheila's sustaining excitement ebbed. She looked at Jan, holding her up so determinedly. He had more sense than to expect anyone to be excited over what they had done. Nowadays, a journey such as their was mere routine. Most of the men here would have wilder, grimmer tales to tell. The roof's pointed height, the soaring antlers on the stags' heads, made Sheila feel still smaller. She made as if to turn around to the doorway, but it was as if she were standing on ice: her feet were afraid to turn.

The white-haired man's voice was coming nearer. " . . . recognize that man," he was saying, "and the boy."

Jan let Sheila go, straightened his shoulders, and saluted. "Jan Pietka from Captain Reymont's camp, sir," he said with natural pride.

"You've traveled quickly. I arrived here only two hours ago, and I was alone. You've done well." He looked as if he needed sleep, too, but he had bathed and shaved and discarded his peasant dress for his cavalry uniform. Everyone looked so clean, Sheila thought. Clean, clean. She suddenly realized how filthy she was. Even the white-haired man hadn't recognized her this way.

"Any of the others here yet?" Jan asked quickly.

"No, you are the first. Better get washed, find some dry clothes, something to eat, and rest. We'll question you after that." And then, as if he had just remembered, "You were in charge of the English girl, weren't you?" He stared at Sheila, then suddenly reached forward to pull the handkerchief back off her hair.

"We'll question them later, Colonel Sierkowski," Wisniewski said impatiently, and moved some papers aside to make room for a map. "Now if you come here, I'll explain what we..."

Sheila saw in Sierakowski's eyes unexpected sympathy. She turned shakily to take a step out of the room. She wanted to get away. She had perhaps wanted praise, but she couldn't bear pity.

Sierakowski was speaking quickly. Chairs scraped at the table. Footsteps hurrried across the room. Adam Wisniewski was beside her. He was saying something. He had caught her arm. She kept her face turned away from him. And then, suddenly, her feet were lifted off the treacherous ground, her body relaxed in a firm grip, and Adam was carrying her into the sunlight streaming sideways through the trees.

## CHAPTER XXIX

### *The Reapers*

THERE WAS warmth, the soft rise and fall of light voices, the lazy feeling of security. Sheila stretched her body under the coarse linen sheet. The straw mattress rustled. The voices halted. Sheila, too contented with this new world of comfort, kept her eyes closed. She didn't want to talk, she didn't want to move; she just wanted to lie here forever and ever.

The voices began again.

"... until the potatoes stick to the meat, and the marrow juice comes out of the bones..."

"Water only drowns it..."

"... headache fit to split..."

"At least forty threads to the inch..."

"Rat's teeth... never saw such stitches. And she..."

Two women gossiping gently. Cooking, dresses, the weather, illness, other women. Women gathered round a village well, round a bridge table, round a factory bench, round a silver coffee tray. Women talking together.

Sheila kept quite still, and listened drowsily. It was wonderful to feel so warm and safe and clean. It was a spell she didn't want to break.

At last, one of the women rose and came over to the bed. Sheila had kept her eyes closed too long. Now, as the woman stood beside her touching her brow with a businesslike hand, Sheila found she really couldn't open her eyes and show she had been awake—awake, listening to the women, without telling them.

"Much better," the crisp voice said and the cool hand left Sheila's brow. "She's been quite normal for two days now. I feel rather proud of her, as if she were my first case all over again."

"You'll soon have plenty more," the softer of the two voices said. "I wonder when the raiding party will be back? Did you hear what they were out for, this time?"

"Supplies, as usual. But mostly clothes, this time. We'll need warmer things as soon as the real winter sets in. The Chief went himself on this raid. It's a big one."

"I wonder where?"

"Far from here you may be sure. There's no raiding done near here. Don't want the Nazis to chase us out of this camp just as we are getting it nice and cozy. You can see a difference every week. When I came here at first, there was only the hunting lodge, unused for years. The forest damp had got into it. Moldy: that's what it was, perfectly moldy. And all the huts unusable, practically falling to pieces. When they brought me to this one and said, 'Here's your hospital, nurse!' I burst out laughing."

"I hope they bring in some more supplies for our new shelves."

"Antoni got the Chief to send some men after drugs and dressings. They are going to lift the contents of a field ambulance. Not a bad idea. That would set us up nicely."

"It would. Where's Antoni? He hasn't been to see her this morning."

"He will be over here soon. He's been busy with that case you brought in. The amputation, you know."

The gentle voice sighed. "I *never* thought he'd live. The other cases were straightforward wounds, but this one—"

"I know, dearie."

"Sorry." There was a forced laugh. "Always keep wanting to talk about it. Sorry, Marian."

"That's all right. I talk plenty, too. Sort of gets it out of your system. But the Chief's against talking about the past. I remember the first night we came here. Just a handful of us then, more and more coming every day, some of them straight off the battlefields, some from the woods where they had been hiding, some from the villages, some from the towns. A funny bunch of scarecrows we were. The Chief said, 'No talking here about what we've lost or suffered. That belongs to the past. What we will suffer together is shared by us all. So no talking. And no arguments. I don't care what politics or religion you have. We are here to fight together, not to fight against each other.' "

"He sort of frightens me."

"What, him?"

"He's—well, he seems hardly human."

"As the Germans will learn. Yes, he's driven us all pretty hard, but he drives himself hardest. And if we hadn't a man like him, where would we all be? We wouldn't have turned this abandoned forest into a well-prepared camp, ready to face a hard winter. Once he's satisfied with this place, he's going into the mountains to start preparing a bigger base for the spring. And that's a dangerous job he's planning. The weather is fierce in the Carpathians in the winter, and there's not only Germans but storms and wolves. That mountain camp will be our main training base, and then this forest one will be one of our advance bases for special raids. Antoni thinks all of us here will be moved up to the mountain base in the spring. He's hoping that, anyway. He always liked a mountain."

"I'd like to see them, too. Just once. In the spring? Wonder if we'll be alive in the—"

"Franziska! Where would you rather be than here with us? With Germans to cart you off to the brothel in their barracks? Or watching your brother being trucked off to Germany as a serf?"

"No, Marian, no. Please. I just get so sad. I sometimes wonder—why should anyone try to live at all? Sometimes, those who have died seem the lucky ones."

"I'll send the priest to you, Franziska, if you start that again. You'll be crawling on your knees all over the forest as penance for such talk, all four hundred square miles of it!" Marian began to laugh.

Franziska's gentle voice was shocked. "Marian, you shouldn't say such things. You don't take religion seriously."

"Oh, I do my share of praying. But if you want to die, then at least wait until you've killed a German or two. Don't worry, Franziska. If we in this camp are going to die, it will be so exciting we won't even notice our last moment has come. Or would you prefer cancer? As a nurse, Franziska, what illness of old age would you prefer to a bullet? My Antoni says that the most depressing thing about being a doctor is just to see what people get for hanging onto life."

"Marian!"

"All right, all right. Keep your voice down. Don't waken *her.* But how she does sleep! You would think she was paid for it."

"She won't recognize herself when she wakens. When she

came she was just a mass of rags and mud. And the Chief carried her here, too. That gave me as big a shock as seeing her. Wonder what she went through?"

"Oh, you'll soon find out, Franziska. Several of our worst-smelling ditches, I thought, myself. Antoni says that kind is always tougher than she looks."

"I suppose she must have been a friend of his?"

"Of the Chief's? Looked like it, I must say. But I don't remember ever seeing her in Warsaw with him."

"Did you know him then?"

"By sight. Who didn't? I remember the last time I was at the Opera with Antoni. The Chief was there. I always did like those cavalry uniforms. And the girl with him! White velvet cut down to here. Off her shoulders, like this. Black, black hair, and rubies in her ears. And a sable cape. It touched the floor, all round. Antoni knew her husband, at least he knew the uncle. Nice old thing. I met him once at a University reception. He was a professor. And, do you know, Antoni says he's among the arrested. He's on the latest Dachau list. The name's on the tip of my tongue. Kory-something. Anyway, you should have seen that cape. Funny thing was, when the Chief came in here carrying that bundle of rags so carefully, I kept thinking of that last time at the Opera, and the sable cape over his arm."

Sheila moved restlessly. She had heard more than she wanted to. This was the just reward for pretending. She was angry with herself, with these curious women, with sable capes. A sable cape was unfair. Any idiot could catch an eye with a sable cape.

"She's awakening," Franziska said with sudden interest.

"Now you can find out all about her to your heart's content," Marian said with her good-natured laugh. "I'll get Antoni." From the doorway, she called "Antoni! Antoni!"

Sheila opened her eyes. Unwillingly. That moment could no longer be postponed. A sad-faced girl was watching her curiously.

"Well!" she said. She turned to Marian at the door. "We were both wrong," she said. "They're brown."

Marian, older, broader, plainer than Franziska, came bustling over to the bed. "Well," she said in amazement, "so we were. Unusual, aren't they? She wouldn't look bad in a sable cape, either."

"None of us would."

"You'd be surprised. It takes a good neck and shoulders."

A small fat man, quite bald and red-faced, entered the hut.

"Well, well," he began in his best bedside manner, and reached for Sheila's wrist. He sat down beside her.

"Looks surprised," he announced. "Didn't she know she had reached the camp, poor thing?"

Sheila smiled. Somehow, from Marian's way of saying "Antoni" with such adoration attached to the word, she hadn't quite expected this middle-aged, ugly little man. Sheila's smile broadened.

"She's better," Antoni said delightedly. "I told you sleep would do it." Marian, towering over him, clapped him on the shoulder as if he were entirely reponsible. Franziska looked strangely at Sheila, and then slowly, almost unwillingly, smiled too.

"Tell the boy," Antoni said. "He's been moping round this door as if she were going to die. Better tell big Jan, too, if you can find him. He was over helping the men at the new huts."

Franziska obeyed him promptly. The doctor and his wife, watching her running steps, exchanged amused glances.

"What she needs is a husband," the doctor said cryptically.

"Yes, that would give her plenty to worry about," Marian added affectionately, her hand still on the little man's shoulder.

To Sheila, Antoni said, "Your Jan thought he had killed you. He got a lecture and a half for the pace he set. Forgot you were a city girl, the big ox."

Stefan came first. He didn't say very much, but he looked so pleased that Sheila could have hugged him. Then Jan came in. He was equally speechless, and more than nervous.

Sheila looked at him solemnly. "Not dead," she said, "I'm not dead."

Jan stared and then broke into a shout of laughter. The more he tried to explain the story to the startled doctor and his wife, the less understandable it became. But his laughter was infectious. Even Stefan, with his solemn dark eyes, was half-smiling.

Marian became suddenly businesslike. "Well, there's work to be done. If you men take yourselves back to your jobs, I'll get her dressed. She'll sit outside on a bench at the door: some sunshine and a look at the camp would be the best tonic she could have. Antoni, tell Franziska to start changing the dressings in the men's hut. I'll get over to help her as soon as I've finished here."

Marian's actions were as quick as her words. In little time she had Sheila dressed and seated outside in the sunshine, with an army blanket over her shoulders and a doeskin rug tucked round her knees. Marian had asked so many questions that there had been little pause for any full answers, and between the questions had come such a jumble of friendly advice and information that Sheila's head whirled. She was glad when the kindly but overenergetic woman left her at last, left her to watch the long, low loghouse under the tall thick branches. From this bench she could see only one other hut, quite a large, newly built one. That was where Marian had gone, so the rest of Antoni's "hospital" must be there.

Except for the distant sound of men's voices, and occasional laugh, a sudden burst of hammering, the forest seemed deserted. A leaf, its rich color faded into brown, would be torn from its branch by some unfelt breeze. A patchwork of cold blue, where the leaves had already fallen away from the tree's black arms, formed the sky. A column of wood pigeons wheeled above, with silver underwings flashing brightly as it twisted and maneuvered in the sunshine. This was the forest. Its vastness gave strength; its peace gave hope.

Antoni came out of the hospital hut, lighted a cigarette, and then, with his hands in the pockets of his faded army trousers, strolled over to the watching girl. His good-natured eyes, wrinkled at the corners, looked at her over his spectacles. His nose was so short that the spectacles had slipped almost to its snub tip, and clung there precariously.

"Envying the birds?" he said gently, pushing his spectacles back into place as he sat down beside her.

Sheila stopped watching the flashing wings. "No. Admiring. Not envying. They have hawks to prey on them, too." She hesitated. "Actually, I was thinking about airplanes."

"Haven't you left them behind you?" The kind eyes were studying her face.

"Difficult. . . . Don't they ever fly over here?"

"Yes. But the thickness of these trees keeps us safe. Even in winter, their branches will camouflage us, and there are plenty of evergreens scattered about. You notice, we haven't tried to make any clearing. We've dispersed the huts over nine or ten square miles. The lodge, as you see, is the center of the camp. The men come there for orders, or for an evening in its warmth. For we are very careful about fires. Smoke in daytime would give us away, or any glow at night. Yet, we must have heat. So we light a fire in the lodge when darkness comes, and we've built a canopy over the chimney so that no red glow of sparks can be seen from the sky. We kill the fire before dawn, so that there's no smoke left to give us away. Then we take the hot ashes and—do you see that kind of mound over there by the lodge?—well, we spread the ashes there, in a kind of hole in the ground, with earth over the top. It bakes things for us slowly. The main cooking is done either over the lodge fire, or at three covered kitchen fires. All at night, of course. We have had to change our mealtimes to suit the fires, but at least we do have one hot meal a day. It looks as if we'll have to build more kitchen fires, if our numbers keep increasing as they do."

"How many are there in the forest?"

"Well over three hundred, now. At the end of a year, we'll be counting in thousands."

"But there won't be room."

"There's room in other forests. There's room in the mountains."

"It all seems so quiet, as if no one really lived here at all."

"We keep apart. We take turns working and relaxing. Even at the lodge in the evenings, there's never more than fifty together at once. We share and share alike. Some look after the food, some look after the patrolling, some build and help with the improvements. There's always some raiding party out. The men take their turns. It's all a matter of planning and organization."

"Food. Where does it come from?"

Antoni laughed and smacked his knee. "You ask us that in this forest? Four hundred square miles or more, with everything from hare and rabbit to boar and deer? The peasants in the villages around do what they can to help us, too. There's a lot of smuggling going on in these parts, nowadays. And then, now and again we lift something we especially need from a Nazi's larder. We don't starve. We eat carefully, but we don't starve."

"But if you hunt in this forest, surely the shots may be heard?"

"Not if we do our hunting in the central part of the forest. We've marked out a boundary line a certain distance from the camp. Beyond that, no more hunting."

"What if the Germans come hunting?"

Antoni shook his head. "There's a woman for you—always thinking of trouble."

Sheila smiled at the wrinkled brow which meant the invisible eyebrows were raised in mock disgust.

Then seriously he added, "You don't miss a trick, do you? It was a good point you made. But when the Germans take time off for some ordinary hunting, and not just the mere hunting of human beings, then they are going to spend their shooting holidays in the forests where the game is known to be so plentiful that they'll bag big results. There has been a rumor for many years among the peasants—and we keep it alive, you may be sure—that this forest is poor in big game. Years ago it was too much hunted over, and it never was restocked. There's a forest to the east of us with bigger and richer game. Marshal Goering won't waste time here if he has better tracts of forest to explore. As for a less ambitious hunter . . . well, if any of them comes here, we'll lie quiet that day and let him shoot around the forest's edge to his heart's content. Our patrols will follow him and his friends, and they'll probably have some ripe criticism to make on the German's way of hunting when next they spend an evening at the lodge. I hear the Germans are pretty busy right now emptying our libraries and hospitals and factories of their equipment. What would they want with a forest where there wasn't even a decent hunting lodge to spend a night in? No, the danger would only come when they formed a suspicion that this forest isn't so desolate as it seems."

He looked at Sheila laughingly. "You don't believe me?" The spectacles were slipping again.

"And if they formed a suspicion?"

"We shall have our warning. We have our patrols round the forest night and day. And we've good leaders. They've their plans made. Yes, even the optimistic Pole has his plans against a possible attack!" He watched her face with amusement. "Remember, no motorized division can surprise a large forest. The Germans will have to use men and not their machines for that. And we will have time to retreat."

He pushed hs spectacles back into their rightful position with a broad forefinger. "Just wait until you've rested here for a week or two. Just wait until you see the men and the Chief. I know how you feel. I came here the same way, not quite believing. Guerrilla army? A storybook adventure . . . something out of the Middle Ages . . . fantastic. Perhaps we are all these things; but we are also the only army left to a conquered country. Some of us at any rate will be here to help those who start pushing the Hun back where he belongs. Then we won't be just a storybook chapter; we'll be in the history books as well." He touched her arm gently. "We all came here with our courage shaken, our pride badly wounded, our hopes quite gone. All we had left was cold rage. But now we have somethig more; we have learned to believe in ourselves again. We expect danger, we live with death; but we've got our courage and we have action. Plenty of it. Look to the faces of the newcomers when they first arrive. You'll be filled with pity. Look at these same faces just a few days later. Then you'll see what I mean."

"I've already seen. Jan. Even Stefan."

"The boy was in a bad way. He will take some time to mend. Jan told me about it."

"About Korytów?"

"You know about it?"

"No. And yet I must. I tried to get there in time. I failed."

"You don't want to know about it."

"I must. I have to meet Madame Aleksander. I can meet her better if I know. Jan wouldn't tell me. Stefan—I am afraid to talk to him about it; can't.... You are a stranger. You can tell me better than anyone. If you know, then tell me."

"I know only the outline. But it is enough. It's a common enough story in the last six weeks, yet it is one which you always seem to be hearing for the first time. That's the kind of cold, unbelievable shock it gives you." The kind, simple face was worried. He jabbed at the unruly spectacles crossly. Her request worried him. He looked miserably towards the hospital as if wishing Marian would appear and help him out of this.

Sheila's voice was tense. "If you don't tell me, I shall never know. And I shall go on worrying about it and thinking about it. The name of Korytów is haunting me. I feel as if someone had told me that a friend had died, and then refused to tell me what illness had killed him. That's how I feel. I am not being sordid. It is just that Korytów was the one place in Poland which I knew as if it were my own village. Don't give me details. But just tell me: are Stefan's sister and aunt dead?"

"They were taken away with the others." Antoni watched her face. Suddenly he was the doctor, again. "I think you are right in wanting to know, or else you will always torture yourself about it. If you know the worst, then you know. It's healthier that way. Now what did you learn about Korytów's end?"

"Only that Jan and another man went to warn the village. Only that Jan and five other men and Stefan came back. That's all I know."

The early sunset now bathed the forest in its rich rays. The evergreens seemed darker. The breeze had gone. There was a strange hush through the trees, as if they waited breathlessly for night.

Antoni cleared his throat and stared at the copper beech opposite them. Its leaves were like molten metal.

"Jan and his friends came to Korytów in the late evening. Jan went to warn the people at the big house. His friend went to the village: his girl lived there. There was absolute peace in the village. There had been no Germans since the officers billeted in the manor house had gone, taking the soldiers with them. The Germans had requisitioned most of the food supplies. In fact, there was so little left that the people of the village thought the Germans wouldn't bother about them again. So both Jan and his friend had some difficulty in persuading the people that there might be some danger intended for them. They didn't get very excited about it. They had heard too many false rumors from refugees, they hadn't anything left for the Germans to plunder. They didn't believe the story very much that Korytów had been giving trouble and was to be punished. For one thing, all their weapons had been taken from them. And they knew that the Germans knew that.

"Well, at last, some families did move into the woods. They lay there all night, and watched the peaceful village. Rain came on, and a cold wind. By dawn the Germans hadn't come. By dawn, those who had listened to Jan and his friend thought they were alarmists. They found reasons for wandering back to the village where those who had refused to leave had spent a pleasant comfortable night in their warm beds. The day passed, and still there was no sign of any approaching Germans. In the woods beside the village there were only left Jan and his friend and five men who wanted to join Captain Reymont's band, and Stefan. Stefan wanted to fight, too, and he had been so insistent that his aunt finally agreed he should go back to Reymont's camp with Jan. I think she knew that if he stayed in the village he would do something desperate and get them all into trouble. Stefan's aunt promised she would set out for Warsaw with the little girl as soon as the child was well enough to travel, for she had been wounded at the time of the fighting round Korytów and her hand wasn't healing properly. From what Jan told me I think the whole arm had become infected." Antoni passed a hand wearily over his brow. "So many of our doctors have been killed or imprisoned," he said heavily. "So many wounds have gone unattended." He stared at the copper beech, each leaf outlined in gold.

"Well, that was the situation. And then, on that evening after that day of waiting, Jan and his small band set out from the woods towards Reymont's camp. They didn't go very far. They were only about a mile away when they heard shooting. They knew that was the Germans. They started back to the village. Not that they could stop the Germans. Only Jan and his comrade had guns. But they thought that the people might have fled to the wood, that they could help them. When they got to a place where they could see the village—it was lighted by floodlights from the German trucks and cars—there were some bodies scattered on the road to the wood. So some of the people had tried to escape. But the Germans had come too quickly, too efficiently.

"Jan and his men saw the villagers being herded out of their cottages, being dragged back from the trees in their fields where they had tried to hide. The lights were still burning on the cottage tables. Some people carried a small bundle in a handkerchief. Others hadn't even time to collect that. They just carried a picture or an ornament or a Bible, just something they had caught up when they were told to leave. You could see everything clearly, because as well as the floodlights, there were now torches being lit, and one house was already in flames. Jan said you could see the villagers kneeling in prayer outside their cottage doors; that was the way they were saying good-by to everything they owned. Then they were made to pick up their bundles, and they were divided into groups like so many animals. The younger women and girls were forced into one truck, the older women into another. The children were pulled from their mothers and pushed into a third. They were open trucks, and you could see the people jammed so close in them that they could neither sit nor turn around. The boys and men were grouped together and shot in the back. The parish priest was shot too, standing beside the truck with children as he tried to quiet them. Then the houses were set on fire. One old man had hidden in the stables beside the manor house. The Germans set fire to the stables, too, and they shot at the window when the old man tried to climb out. He got stuck, there, wounded."

"Felix!" Sheila said involuntarily. He had stood shaking his head under her window, that last evening at Korytów. "Sad," he had said so calmly, "all the young people going away again." Somehow she had always thought that Felix, no matter how the young people went and came back or didn't come back, would always be there.

"Then the trucks drove away," Antoni was saying. "Jan's friend broke loose from Jan's grip. He ran towards the road and the truck with his girl. He shot two soldiers before he was killed. The Germans stopped the trucks, a machine gun was turned on the older women for a minute. Ten Poles must die for every German killed, you know. Then the trucks rolled on again. The women's truck must have had many killed, certainly many wounded, but it left with the others. The Germans must have thought that Jan's friend was by himself, perhaps one of the refugees whom they had overlooked. For they left the village. The last truck with soldiers comfortably seated was gone. The manor house was on fire too. The whole village was one mass of flame and smoke."

Sheila hid her face with her hands. She had asked to be told. She had been told.

The doctor's professional voice continued, "The old women will be dumped out on the frozen plains northeast of Warsaw and left to wander. The middle-aged are sent as serfs to Germany or are given the dirtiest duties about the barracks. The younger women and girls will be sent to the soldier's brothels. The children are being sent to Nazi camps. They will be taught to be slaves."

She had asked to be told. She had been told.

Antoni was saying, "If I told you more than you asked to know, it is only because we all should remember." His voice was no longer the doctor's voice. "If we don't know, if we won't listen or see, then we shall not remember. We shall forgive too soon, too easily, as we did before. And in the next war, we, the people who forget, will be destroyed even as Korytów."

In a gentler voice, he said to the still silent girl, "Go in and rest a while. You are cold. You must not get cold."

She didn't move.

"I'm sorry," Antoni said miserably. "I shouldn't have told you, after all."

"No. You should have. I had to know. We all have to know." She was thinking of Dittmar, now. "I should have killed him," she said.

Antoni stared at her. She looked up suddenly and caught his expression.

"A man who does evil because he is evil. I should have killed him."

"Come in now. We'll rest for a space. Come in."

She shook her head. The beech tree was now one purple shadow. "I'm warm," she said. "I'm all right. Let me stay here." She reached out her hand and touched his shoulder. "I thought they loved children," she said sadly.

"Who? The Germans? Yes, they love children: German children. They glorify youth: German youth. They talk sentimentally of motherhood: German motherhood. In the last war, the worst famines were in Belgium and Poland. Our starvation was caused not only by the blockade but by the Germans who ate all our cattle and grain and left us nothing. But did you ever hear of German Relief for starving people? Unless for German peoples?"

Sheila's halting voice said, "They suffered, too. Perhaps that is what twisted them."

"Yes, of course." Antoni's voice was bitterly sarcastic. "Think how they suffered and starved. That's why they have so many rickety cripples in their armies today! And such

small armies! And all because they suffered more than anyone else in the last war. Think of their countryside with its
cattle and grain all stolen by invading troops. Think of their
towns ruined in the battles fought on German soil. Think of
all the rebuilding they had to do, with half of their population shot, and the other half working with bloated bellies.
Don't you see how their bodies have suffered through the
the terrible hardships and cruelties which the Allies forced
on them when they invaded the Rhineland in 1914 without
warning? What wrecks, what invalids they are! Why, the
poor dear Germans have never done anything at all! Their
land has been the cockpit of Europe where other more powerful nations came to fight and rape and steal. That's why
they have so few people in their country, today, compared
to other countries of the same area! Don't you see it all?
Surely it must be clear to you. That's why they have no in-
dustries, no factories, no well-equipped laboratories. That's
why they've no trade, why they can't reach South American markets or the Danube. And all these German firms
and salesmen you find throughout the world, even in India
and other far places? Why they aren't Germans at all! It's only
a capitalist lie, a stab in the back by Jews and Communists.
They are merely—"

Marian's voice said cheerfully, "I got thirty eggs today.
Isn't that wonderful? If the hens don't stop laying when the
cold weather comes, we'll be able to have one egg each every
two weeks. Isn't that wonderful?" She was watching Antoni's
sad face. There is something pathetic in a face which is sad
when it seems made only for laughter. Marian said quickly,
"You just can't trust a man, can you? Turn your back fifteen minutes, and he's talking to the prettiest girl in the district. That's what I get for not taking my mother's advice.
'Marian,' she said, 'never marry a good-looking man. He'll
roast your soul.' " She placed a hand gently on her husband's shoulder, and Antoni looked up at her as he patted it.

He was smiling once more; a round faced little man, with
kind eyes and spectacles that kept on sliding down his nose.

"I hear that our outposts have just seen the first of our
men coming back from the raid. There's been a relay of signals from the edge of the forest. Better get things ready,
Antoni. I've set Franziska to boiling water and sterilizing the
knives."

Antoni rose. Now he was the capable doctor, moving
quickly, neatly. He touched Sheila's head as he passed her.
"Keep your illusions about human nature," he said. "Life is
stark without them. It is wonderful to keep being broad-
minded."

Sheila smiled sadly. "Now you make me feel still more smug," she said. "People like me who have never suffered —I mean in the way the people of Korytów and all the other millions of Poles are suffering—can afford to be broad-minded. You and the people who have really suffered must think people like me are not only smug, but callous."

"Only if you tell us that it is wrong to hate," Antoni said. "That is callousness to the men who have been tortured to death, to the women who have been raped and the children who have been brutalized. That is callous and blind selfishness disguised as nobility. Let everyone think of himself as a villager in Korytów, and then if he does not hate the men who do these things, then he is truly broad-minded. If he can see his mother dragged off to destitution, his wife being forced to work German latrines, his daughter sent to German brothels, his son shot in the back or left dangling from a tree, his young children kidnaped and their minds distorted, his house burned, his lifework destroyed in a few short minutes, and can still honestly say, 'I do not hate the men who do these things,' then he has my respect. But I have none for those who only hear of those things, and still say so very nobly, 'Of course, *you* should not hate.'"

"Antoni, the men will start arriving," Marian warned. "I'll come over and help as soon as I get our patient in bed again."

Marian looked after him with a mixture of pride and sadness.

"He was the kindest, happiest, best-natured fellow you ever met," she said slowly. "He still is, to those who are human beings. Come on, here's my arm. That's the way. Stiff? You'll soon be running about this place. Can you nurse?"

"I could try to learn," Sheila said.

"Good. We need help."

"Are you and Franziska the only women here?"

"In the camp. Yes. And that's because we have work to do—plenty of it. When the men get leave, they go to the villages round the forest. No weapons or uniforms, then: they are just relatives from another village. When they first came here, all they did was to sit about the camp in their free hours, sit and stare at the forest. It worried me. But now they go to the villages. They've got girl friends there, some even have wives now. That's better. That's more natural. Can't sit about moping. That drives a man mad."

Marian had helped remove the wide black skirt and the bright petticoat.

"Pretty, isn't it?" she said. "We sent down to one of the villages for it when you arrived. You know, I wish they'd let me go on a raiding party sometime. I've got a list of things I need: just a few needles and some threads and an extra pair of scissors—I'm always losing mine—and some buttons and a few books and some real handkerchiefs. I always like a neat handkerchief; I hate these little scraps of cloth I've got to use nowadays. But you can't ask the men to risk their lives for these small things. They've got to get rifles and ammunition and uniforms and food, and they've got to find good hiding places to cache them in. We don't use much of the stuff we are collecting now. It's for later, when we've enough trained men and our Allies start attacking from the west. Then we can help. Then we'll show the world that Poland was not beaten in four weeks."

"Yes," Sheila said. "Yes." And she smiled. To think of the word victory, even a remote and faraway victory, cheered her. She stretched her body comfortably; bed, she decided, was a good place after all.

"It's just patience we shall need," Marian said. "We won't always have to live secretly in a forest."

Franziska's running feet almost blotted out her words. "Three back," she gasped delightedly. "No wounds."

Three, only three? Sheila watched the two women clasp each other in their joy. Marian's keen eyes had noticed the expression on her face.

"The men slip back as they slipped out, in twos and threes," she explained. "You didn't think we marched out in a column with flags flying, did you?"

The two women laughed good-naturedly. They were so happy that they could laugh at the smallest thing.

"Takes a raiding party two days to get out, and often a week to come back in," Marian continued. "Now, I must dash over and hear the latest news. Franziska, fetch her some milk. And then she can get up for a warm supper this evening when the cooking starts. You've never told us your name, you know. It's an English one, isn't it? You talked English in your sleep."

"Sheila. Sheila Matthews."

Marian and Franziska repeated it solemnly, and then giggled at their efforts.

"Such queer names foreigners have! Can't think for the life of me how they can ever pronounce them," Marian said, and gave Sheila a warm smile, and was gone to hear the news from the world outside.

Sheila sipped the strong-tasting yellow milk from a square-shaped cup of bark.

"Birchbark," Franziska explained as she moved around the room, tidying its simple belongings. "It gives a strange taste at first, but you get used to it. We can even boil water in buckets made from it. The milk came from our goats. We have three of them, kept specially for our invalids. We've got hens. And last week, Zygmunt brought back two young pigs. We are fattening them up for Christmas. The only trouble is keeping the fox and the badger away."

"I've so much to learn," Sheila said. "This life is all so strange."

"Oh, you get used to that too." Franziska had almost finished her tidying: not that there was much to straighten. Life was decidedly utilitarian in this hut. There was another straw mattress on the ground with half of an army blanket neatly folded across its rough cover. The earth floor was hard-packed, swept clean. A natural wooden table, new-looking and stoutly made, was against one log wall. An equally new bench stood along the front of the table. There was no glass in the small window, only inside shutters. Franziska was now hanging Sheila's strange clothes on one of the large wooden pegs driven into the wall at one side of the narrow door. On the wall beyond the door was a wooden crucifix.

"It won't be long before it is dark," Franziska said, "and then we can go across to the lodge to warm ourselves round the fire and have something to eat. Or don't you feel strong enough, yet?"

"Oh yes," Sheila said quickly, "I'm all right. I wasn't ill. Only exhausted. And now I've exhausted my exhaustion. All I want to do is to move about, and see, and do." She smiled and said once more, "Everything is so strange." It was a new world, she thought.

"When I first came here, I missed everything I had been accustomed to think was a necessity. You will be surprised how very little is necessary in life, and how simply one can improvise. It becomes a kind of game—like keeping house or playing shops when we were children. Then you find yourself beginning to despise your old way of living, you begin to like this way. If I live to see the day when we return to our towns, I expect I shall miss this forest. Funny, isn't it?"

"A thousand years ago, most people lived in forests," Sheila said, "for the forests were deep and thick all over Central Europe, then. Forests like this one."

"The Dark Ages," Franziska said slowly. "I used to think that name meant people couldn't read or write. But if they lived in forests, then there was darkness all around them."

"When I saw the churches of the Middle Ages, I used to think the people who had built them were still remembering the forests of the Dark Ages. The tall windows are like the winter trees, and the light strikes through them as if it were piercing a forest. Even the way the stone pillars branch into the curve of roof . . ."

The two girls smiled together at their fancies. Then Franziska suddenly came over to her, saying eagerly, "Can you nurse?"

Sheila stared at the anxious, affectionate face. "No," she said in mild surprise. "But I can learn. It's really a matter of *not* being lazy, isn't it? Like being a good cook—just taking every trouble you can and not finding easy ways for anything?"

"I'll teach you. I'll help you. Say you can nurse when they ask you. I'll show you."

Sheila's surprise deepened. Now that the sadness had gone from this girl's face, Sheila thought of Barbara. Here was Barbara, a little older, a little less pretty, a little less decided. But here was Barbara.

"Why?" Sheila asked gently.

"Because I want you to stay here. I don't want you to be sent to live in one of the villages. I want you to live here. You see—" Franziska's quiet eyes were half-smiling now—"you see, it isn't a husband I need. Antoni is wrong. In fact all the men would be insulted if they knew how little I wanted them—as men. Men wouldn't understand that. But you do, don't you? I just want someone who will talk with me, will laugh with me. Marian has her Antoni. I've felt so alone. But now we can work and talk together. Isn't it strange how two women can spend an hour together talking about nothing really very important, and yet there is such a nice satisfactory feeling at the end of it? With men—well, either you are everything or you are nothing. Either they make you feel that you are being hunted like an animal, or that you are as unattractive as a stone wall. It's—it's disturbing. Either way."

"Yes," Sheila could agree. "It's disturbing. Either way." Then they both laughed.

Marian's voice, talking, explaining, was outside the hut. She entered, her head turned to answer the man who followed her. It was the white-haired man who had come to Reymont's camp, the man who was a colonel and served under a captain.

"Well, you certainly sound much better," he said.

Marian said, "Franziska, Antoni needs you. Two more men

have reached the camp. One has smashed his shoulder in falling off a roof."

Franziska picked up the empty cup obediently, and gave Sheila a parting smile.

"Perhaps you will be needed, too," the colonel suggested smoothly.

"Yes, Colonel Sierakowski," Marian said regretfully. The conversation between these two had promised to be so interesting. . . . And then, as if to assert at least a little of her authority, "Now don't you go tiring my patient. She's doing very nicely."

"Yes," the colonel said, and waited until the doctor's wife had left the room. Then he pulled the bench across to Sheila's bed. He obviously was not going to speak his information across the length of the room.

He spoke in English. His voice was quiet, exceedingly businesslike.

"We sent a man to Warsaw. He got through. We've just had a brief, coded message. So your warning has been given into the right hands."

Sheila looked both relieved and puzzled.

"We have a radio, of course," he said quickly. "We can receive messages. Soon we shall be able to send them; we have an electrician here who is putting smuggled parts of a transmitter together. Anyway, we do know that our man got through and that he gave the message about you."

"I keep wondering what they'll do with it."

"That will have been decided by this time. We will not know until Olszak arrives."

"Here?"

"For a brief visit. A meeting of sorts, in other words. Some changes must be made in the organization, changes to suit what we have learned from the Nazis. Their technique has changed in several ways from that of the German occupation in the last war. The Nazis have been even more cruel and ruthless than we had expected."

"Yes," Sheila said, and thought of Korytów. "Yes." It seemed as if anyone who had come under the power of modern Germany always found that the Nazis were worse than anyone had ever imagined. They were a perpetual shock. And the worst shock was to know that they were human beings. She met the man's sad eyes and said, "If they were some kind of monsters like robots or men from Mars, we could expect this ruthlessness. But I've come to hate them just because they are human beings like ourselves. That gives them no excuse at all for behaving the way they do."

"Quietly, quietly. Or we shall have Nurse Marian back

here, saying I am upsetting her patient. Now, when Olszak arrives we shall hear, among other things, about your friend Madame Aleksander. He will also have discussed your future with the man whose secretary you were supposed to be. All you can do, now, is to get quite strong again, and then you'll be able to do whatever Olszak has decided."

"I'd like to stay here." It was out, quite unthinking.

Colonel Sierakowski restrained a smile at her impulsive frankness.

"I can't go back to England," she said in embarrassment. "Not now. If the Germans were to find out that a Sheila Matthews was living there, then the whole Anna Braun story would come crashing down. Wouldn't it?"

"Unless your recent employer can arrange a suitable ending to it."

She thought desperately for some reasonable explanation why she should stay here. There were obviously no passengers in the camp. Everyone had his job. Her face lighted up. With a woman's instinctive leap in reasoning, she had found the solution.

"Colonel Sierakowski, there's no good pretending I'm a nurse. I can learn. But I've had no training. But there's one thing I really could do. I could be your listener-in for foreign broadcasts. I could listen to American, British, French and German news. I could be here all the time to listen and make notes. You do need to know what's happening abroad as well as in Poland, don't you?"

His rare smile appeared. "Of course," he said. "We have had a man listening, but you would release him for active duty. Captain Wisniewski will be interested I'm sure, when he returns from the raid." His smile deepened. "And then Olszak wouldn't have to think up any more plans for you."

Sheila flushed. "Well, he certainly has arranged it to his own taste in these last weeks." Her embarrassment grew as Sierakowski's smile deepened further. "Of course, he knows best—I suppose."

Sierakowski laughed at the tone of her voice, at her raised eyebrow. Then he sat and looked at her so gravely that she wondered what had brought that thoughtful look into his eyes. It was as if he were forming a decision about her.

"I'm afraid I'm dealing with a rebel," he said at last. But she knew that wasn't what he had really been thinking about in that long pause. "Perhaps if you start your job before Olszak gets here, you will have more chance of persuading him. There's a lot of weight carried by a successful *fait accompli*."

"And Captain Wisniewski?" Her words had been quite

evenly spoken. And why not? Captain Wisniewski was in command of the camp: his permission was necessary. Her question had been merely a routine one. That was all, she thought, as she studied the coarse weave of the blanket over her knees. That was all she was going to allow it to be.

"He will have no objections, I'm sure." He still watched her thoughtfully as she looked up at the slight inflection in his voice. He was puzzled by the sudden unhappiness in her eyes.

"Why do you want to stay?" he asked suddenly.

Sheila felt as if she were under examination again. She answered directly and simply, "Because I've done enough escaping and running away. I'm going to stay—and—and—" She halted. This sounded so much like mere heroics.

"Fight it out?" he suggested gently.

"In any way I can—yes."

He thought, this girl was honest: she wasn't a sensation-seeker, a wide-eyed romantic. She knew the dangers, she didn't minimize them. And she could be of use.

"Good," he said with unexpected brevity, and rose to his feet. His salute as he left the hut was equally unexpected.

Sheila stared at the rough ceiling's shadows thankfully. Sierakowski had believed her. She had won an ally. Whatever decisions were made about her, he would be on her side.

There were voices outside now. Darkness had come. Work was over for the day. We are gathering at the lodge, she thought: how many of the raiding party have reached home? We . . . home . . . the words had come naturally: this new world was no longer strange. She watched the black square of night in the window's frame, listened to the rustle of closely laced branches in the stirring wind. She thought of those others who were now moving back to the forest under cover of this darkness. When you hoped the way she hoped now, it was as if you prayed.


CHAPTER XXX

*Adam*


A CALENDAR became a curiosity. Time was measured by sun and moon, by patrols and sentry duty and raids, by increasing frosts and colder winds. Winter was coming, and as nature prepared for her long sleep, the men in the camp prepared for winter. The raids, in the last few days left of au-

tumn, were never-ceasing. Supplies, clothing, and food were
snatched from under the sharp greedy German nose, were
hidden nearer the forest for future needs. ("Nearer" meant
within ten miles of the forest's edge. The raids themselves,
as far as Sheila could discover, pushed as far north as
Lowicz, as far south as Cracow. It seemed as if man had regained the power of travel which nature had meant him to possess. These soldiers could cover ten miles as easily as if
they were walking down the street to buy an evening paper.)

Men who were resting between raids helped with the preparations in camp. Huts were enlarged and weatherproofed
with bark and thatch. Fuel, dried, and as smokeless as could
be found, was stored as carefully as gold. So were the sacks
of rye and potatoes, the barrels (fashioned out of birchbark
like the cooking pots and cups) full of salt meat. Animals,
hunted or trapped, also gave them skins for winter clothes.
The melted fat was used for cooking, for soap, for candles,
and for greasing rifles. Nothing was wasted. Everything, like
everyone, had its function. Life was primitive and simple
work was hard, the sense of danger was constant. But perhaps
because there was no time to sit and brood, perhaps because
each man had learned savagely and cruelly why they were
fighting, for what end they were fighting, there was unity of
a broad and deep kind.

It was the best kind of unity, Sheila thought as she studied
the men's faces in the lodge each night. Work—except for
the constant forest patrol—and the one meal of the day
were over. The camp relaxed in the warmth of the large
room, gathered together with tolerant, unforced friendship. Perhaps it was the cold wind rising outside, symbolic
of loneliness and anger, that made officers and men appreciate these hours together. Perhaps men always enjoyed
themselves when they got together after a good job well
done. There was talk—plenty of it, for no one could accuse
the Poles of lack of conversation. There were boasts and
arguments and discussions and stories. There was singing,
with verses invented to fit every man in the camp. Music
and poetry seemed to be rooted and growing in every Polish
heart. Even Jan, that prosaic silent man, could turn a rhyme
to set the others laughing. It was the best kind of unity, for
each of those men was still an individualist. You could see
that in their reactions and unexplained prides. The engineer
was still the engineer; the lawyer remained the lawyer; the
farmer and landworker still belonged to the villages. But these
differences were like salt and pepper in the flavor of a broth.

The communal dish was all the better for their varied seasoning.

Strangers still arrived in camp. Some stayed, and filled the gaps in its ranks after each raid. Others left: either they were better suited for another branch of the underground movement than for guerrilla fighting, or they had come for training in the camp's methods before returning to their distant villages. There they in their turn would organize and adapt what they had learned, for the use of their own districts.

The rest of Reymont's band arrived. But Captain Reymont didn't. Nor did Thaddeus. Jan had awaited their coming. Then suddenly he said one day, "They won't come." And he turned away in disappointment from the two ragged strangers who had come out of the forest. After that, he stopped looking for newcomers. So did Sheila, but she kept thinking about Reymont. She owed him her life.

"I don't think he ever wanted to leave his own camp," she said to Jan that night. Jan was silent. They were sitting in the lodge. The shutters and doors were secure. The voices round them rose and fell with the rhythm of men who enjoyed themselves while they could. There had been food, there was vodka, there was story-telling, there was warmth, there was laughter. Hard faces softened in the candlelight, and coarse voices mellowed into music. Jan didn't look up at her. He was fashioning a long stick, strong and pointed, into a spearlike weapon. "No?" was all he would say. But he believed her. Reymont had enjoyed his own command too much: he had been proud of it. Sierakowski had persuaded him that only in co-operation with a larger group was there any chance of permanent survival. So he had sent his men where opportunities were bigger. For this camp, here, with the work and united effort of so many men, seemed fantastically efficient and luxurious compared with Reymont's camp. He had been a good leader, probably as good in some ways as Wisniewski, but he had worked on too small a scale. He had lacked Wisniewski's vision.

When she reached that conclusion, Sheila was startled at her own choice of words. Vision . . . She looked over at Adam Wisniewski sitting with his soldiers.

This was the first evening he had spent at the Lodge since his return to the camp four days ago. He had been absent for over three weeks. This was the first time she had seen him since that morning she had arrived in camp. Or rather, she told herself as she averted her eyes and pretended to be watching Franziska, this was the first time she had allowed herself to see him. At the moment, she wished she were back in the loneliness of her hut, away from the warmth and life of the Lodge. Her will power was weakening: she was still telling herself that she must rise and leave, when Franziska came over to her.

"Anything wrong, Sheila?"

"No," Sheila answered sharply. And then she saw she had hurt Franziska, and she added more gently, "Of course not."

Franziska shrugged her shoulders and sat down beside Stefan. She, too, pretended. She listened to Stefan's enthusiastic description of his work at the radio-hut with Sheila, of the new transmitter which was being perfected. But she wondered about these last few days and the change in her friend; she wondered what she had done to cause this feeling of separation. She listened to Stefan, but she watched Sheila, and Sheila seemed to be staring at the middle distance.

Now Adam Wisniewski was listening to a story, his intelligent eyes on the teller's face, his lips ready to laugh. Sheila had her second surprise then. He likes men, she thought; and men like him. She watched him, almost incredulously. And then she smiled at her naïveté. Hadn't this camp been proof to her that Adam Wisniewski got on well with men? Hadn't this been the reason why Olszak had chosen Wisniewski? Horses and women: proto-fascist ...

Russell Stevens had been quite certain about all that. Would he be as certain if he lived in this camp for a week? Wouldn't he be sitting there now, laughing along with Wisniewski? Probably, Sheila thought, he would be laughing at himself: for Steve was honest. Perhaps too quick to pin identification tags on people's shoulders, perhaps too prone to simplify; but fundamentally honest. If Wisniewski had lived up to the label Steve had pinned on him, he would now be sitting in Warsaw or Cracow, collaborating with the Nazis. There he would have had women and horses and a comfortable house; there he would have seen the people who opposed him either killed or imprisoned. If this man were a fascist by inclination, he would have welcomed the chance to "cleanse" his country of the people he disagreed with. He wouldn't be working with them, living with them, all political differences buried under the common battlefield. Fascists never buried politics. They kept them sharpened, like a dagger to plunge in your back. The Nazis were looking for a political stooge in Poland. They had searched among politicians, among generals, ambassadors, princes, landowners, professional men. Not one Pole had accepted the chance to gain the whole New Order and lose his own soul by working with the enemy. The reward for their refusal was always torture and death for themselves, imprisonment and persecution for their families. Yet, each week, the execution list of these men was growing. Nothing the Nazis could do would convince or persuade or force the Poles to become Nazis, or the allies of Nazis.

If ever she were to see Steve again, she would argue this out with him. "Labels, Steve, are just misleading," she would say. "They are meant for laboratory specimens, not for human beings. All the so-called 'enlightened' would have had Poland quite taped and labeled. Poland was 'feudal,' Poland was 'undemocratic,' Poland was 'fascist.' And now the Poles are giving a demonstration to the world of what honor and freedom really mean. If a country doesn't love freedom, why should it die so willingly against oppression? Why doesn't it jump on the German bandwagon and say, 'Of course, we'll co-operate'? The Germans gave it the chance to do that. They churned out propaganda on the radio—you heard it as well as me—about the stupid cowardly government which led the poor Poles into this war. They've slandered, they've even fabricated proof of the guilt of Polish leaders. They offered the Poles every opportunity to say, 'We've been betrayed. We lost the battle because we've been betrayed.' But the Poles won't take that soothing excuse. Their honor is real, not just national vanity. And the more they refuse to co-operate, the more they suffer. Korytów, and the hundred other Korytóws, would be still standing to-day if the Poles would only co-operate. How many other countries, even the most democratic ones, would pay this price for their honor, Steve?"

The voices swept in warm gusts around her. Above was the black shadow of the pointed roof, and the static animal heads peering down through the haze of smoke. Those beasts must have seen many a hunting party here. Now they were watching the strangest hunting party of all. She looked across to the priest, tall, thin-faced. He was listening to the man who had lost an eye. How unreal and yet real; how mad and yet sane! •

A voice, strong and confident, was speaking. She looked up, startled. There was no escape this time. "You look very serious." It was Adam Wisniewski. He didn't wait for a reply, but sat down cross-legged on the floor at her feet. Something in the ease of the gesture reminded her of the first time she had seen him. There were four or five answers she could give him: each sounded sillier than the other. She kept silent, and smiled.

"That's much better," he said approvingly. He was watching her as he drew a package of cigarettes out of his pocket. He offered her one. He lit it carefully. Jan placed his cigarette behind his ear: he was concentrating on smoothing his spear-point into sharp perfection.

"I've almost lost the taste of a cigarette," she said. She was annoyed with herself for her nervousness. She couldn't seem to think of anything else to say.

"So you *do* talk?" Wisniewski said slowly.

She returned the long look which he gave her. (How unreal it is, she was thinking. We have at last spoken, and I find I have nothing to say.)

"Occasionally," he said gravely, answering for her. That made her laugh.

"Actually," he went on with a smile, "I think you've been avoiding me."

There was enough truth behind the light words to make Sheila lose the composure she had gathered so determinedly.

"You've been busy," she said with little originality. What a lack of wit and intelligence she was displaying! The cat had not only got her tongue: it had got her brain.

He wasn't smiling. Strangely enough, he wasn't looking bored. He was watching her face very intently. He had watched her that way at Korytów when she talked to Steve at that last dinner in the Aleksander house. That look had been disconcerting then. Now it also made her happy.

"You've been busy," she repeated. That was true. And sometimes she had felt that he had been avoiding her too. Each avoiding the other, as though they were afraid of something they couldn't avoid.

"You yourself haven't been exactly idle," he was saying. "In fact, you've been too busy. Where's the smile you used to have in your eyes?"

"Had I?"

"I remember when I first saw you. You were leaning out of a window, talking to old Felix. I recollect thinking, 'That's the way a woman should look, with a smile in her eyes and a soft word on her lips.'"

"Felix," Sheila said slowly. "'My friend Felix,' as Teresa used to say."

He was quick to notice the strained look on her face. "Come," he said, with unexpected gentleness. "Come now." He took her hand and gave it a reassuring grip. He turned to Jan and said, "What's the spear for?"

"Old Single," Jan said without looking up. He was wetting his thick forefinger and running it along the wood.

One of the men near them laughed. "He's heard those brave stories about bears."

"A spear and a saber," Wisniewski said. "They are brave weapons against a bear, Zygmunt."

"If a man can fight a bear that way," Zygmunt said disbelievingly.

"It's been done. It gives bear and man an even chance. When you face a bear that way, then you know it's either him or you. That's the most satisfactory way to kill."

"You might fight a bear that way. But not a boar. Old Single's too clever," Zygmunt said. "Why, he even knows just the limits where we are allowed to shoot. He's been keeping down to the forest edge since we came here. He knows we dare not shoot him near there."

Jan said, "I'll catch him." He tapped the spear. "I haven't met the pig yet that I couldn't stick, Goering included."

Wisniewski was examining the spear. "It will need a crossbar just about there, as a grip." He felt the spear, and then shook his head. "It's strong, but not strong enough. Not for Old Single. He's carried bullets about in his fat for several years now. You need steel for that job."

Jan grinned and patted the sheath of the long thin knife he now carried—as all the men did—at his waist. "Little sister will make sure. First big brother." He pointed the spear like a javelin. "Then little sister." He drew his finger across his throat with a quick slashing gesture.

"How much would you bet on it?" said Zygmunt, with real interest.

Jan's fingers rubbed the side of his nose.

"Careful," Sheila said to Zygmunt warningly. "If you make a bet with Jan, that's enough to make him win."

Wisniewski released her hand. She was all right again. She had stopped thinking about Korytów. He thought, it seems impossible that anyone as lovely as she is should be so unconscious of her power. He looked at her. And, for once, she accepted his challenge.

"Yes?" she asked.

Rather surprisingly, he didn't accept hers. "Why do you stay here when you could go back to your own country?" he countered.

"Why does Jan, who knows little about forests, want to brave Old Single?" she answered.

Jan looked up at her quickly. "I'm learning," he said resentfully. "I'm doing the best I can."

"Some would say it's because he's mad." Wisniewski's hand on Jan's shoulder turned the words into a compliment. "Or some would say he is proud, and never refused a challenge." Adam Wisniewski was smiling now, watching her eyes with that very straight disconcerting look of his. "Or some would say he has courage."

"I've hardly that." She was trying to laugh. "I scream at

a rat, I'm afraid of snakes. I turn sick when I see blood.
I've tried hard. But I still scream, I still turn sick."

"And the rat Captain Streit? And the snake called Dittmar?"

Sheila looked at him in surprise. The brown eyes were
amused, and yet, somehow, serious. She felt the blood rise
in her cheeks, and she smiled uncertainly, and she felt a
warm gentle surge in her heart.

"I know so much about you, you see," he was saying
quietly. "First it was Andrew who talked. Then Madame
Aleksander and Barbara. Then Korytowski, Olszak, Sierakowski. Even Jan. It seems as if the only person who won't
talk to me about you is yourself."

"Oh!"

"Yes, oh!"

The laugh in his eyes had died away. The smile on her
lips had gone. We've always known each other, Sheila thought.
We've always talked and laughed and been silent together.
We've always been together."

Jan was looking at them curiously. Franziska, beside Stefan,
was watching too: she seemed to be saying reproachfully, "But
you never told me!"

Sheila rose quickly. "I must go now." She was running away.
She knew it. She didn't look at him now. "Good night," she
said. She wished her voice hadn't been so uncertain.

Adam Wisniewski had risen too. He was even taller than
she had thought. He cleared a path for her to the door. For a
moment, the room was silent.

"Good night, Captain Wisniewski," she said again. But he
didn't seem to hear her low voice. He closed the door behind them, shutting in the sudden burst of voices. For a
moment they stood together. He took her arm, and they
walked slowly away from the lodge.

The black sky with its misted moon and stars spread like
a blanket over the forest. The naked trees moved and sighed
in the soft night wind.

## CHAPTER XXXI

### Old Single

AS USUAL, Franziska had risen before the dawn. She had
bathed at the pool. Her cheeks were pink and her fingers
chilled and white. She was kneeling before the crucifix on

the wooden wall. Sheila kept still until the girl had finished her morning prayers, and then jumped out of bed too. She dressed quickly, shivering slightly.

Franziska said, "It's getting colder every morning now. I almost froze going down to the pool this morning." And then, too casually, she added, "I met the Chief on his way to the lodge. He starts work early."

Sheila was smoothing her short hair with the rough wooden comb which Jan had made for her. She ignored Franziska's lead.

"Where's Marian?" she asked.

"Still on night duty at the hospital hut. That amputation is taking an awful time to heal. I'm just going over there. Have you time to relieve me at midday?"

Sheila nodded.

"And we've those dressings to wash," Franziska said. "And the patients need more milk. If you've a spare hour this morning, you might try and explain that to the goats."

Sheila said "Yes." Franziska, she thought, always seemed to think of the most unpleasant tasks early in the morning. It was as if she lay worrying about them all night in order to produce them in a neat row when she rose from her bed.

"This place needs a good scrubbing," Franziska said, taking the twig-broom and brushing vigorously at invisible dust.

"All right," Sheila said, and smiled. She was accustomed to the idea, by this time, that short-wave monitoring wasn't considered real work either by Franziska or by Marian. "I'll do that. I'll bring back a pail of water when I go down for my bath."

"I'll help you," said Franziska, suddenly relenting. "Two of us make the job easier." She looked at Sheila. "But how long are the two of us going on working, now? Why didn't you tell me? You can't really think I'm your friend after all." The girl's voice was hurt, reproachful.

"Franziska, what's wrong with you this morning?"

"You made me think you didn't like him. Why, you never spoke to him. You kept out of his way. Purposely, too. I could see that. And then last night: both of you looking at each other as if the rest of us didn't exist."

"You're imagining things," Sheila said stiffly. She wished Franziska would go to the hospital hut. She wished Franziska would stop probing. This was her own affair, she thought, and stared at Franziska. "Yes, I'm in love," she could say, "and I've been in love with him since the first moment I saw him." But she wouldn't say it. She would tell neither about that nor about anything else connected with Adam. And then Sheila's anger disappeared: poor Franziska, she thought, Franziska whose fear of men frightened men away.

"Better relieve Marian," she suggested gently. "I don't have any important broadcasts until eight o'clock. I'll have this place scrubbed and the goats milked before then. I'll see you at midday." She put her arm round the thin shoulders. How soft and fragile women's shoulders felt. She turned quickly away and started straightening her bed.

That was Franziska.

Then there was Marian, as brisk as ever even if she needed sleep and rest. At least, she was direct: startlingly direct.

"So you've made up your mind at last," she said approvingly as she unbraided her hair. The heavy plaits fell over her shoulders almost to the waist. It gave the thick middle-aged figure a strangely girlish look. She was rubbing some grease into her face. "When the spring comes, we'll search for some herbs and make this stuff pleasanter. I feel as though I were an axle every time I put it on. Antoni's done his best to purify it, but grease is grease. Still, it protects our skins from those red sores that the frost brought on. Last week my face cracked every time I smiled."

Marian unbuttoned her skirt, and stepped out of it neatly. "Of course," she said, folding it with excessive care, "I knew all along. I said to Antoni—"

"I've got to get down to the pool for water. Franziska wants this floor scrubbed."

"Nonsense. I washed it two days ago. There's a war on. We've given up polished parquetry for the duration. Now, as I said to Antoni, there's a well-matched pair, and if she doesn't know it, then he does, and she'll soon learn. What this camp needs is something to give us a bit of real happiness. What this camp needs is a wedding. That's what I said, and I was right."

"Marian!"

"Don't look so shocked, Sheila. If I were you I'd be shouting the news from the treetops."

"You go too fast."

"Not me! I'm not so green as I'm cabbage-looking." Marian slumped into bed. "When people fall in love they usually marry, unless something prevents them. What's to prevent you two? Nothing, absolutely nothing. I knew it all along, anyway. Ever since the morning you came here. He carried you in as though you were an armful of precious glass, instead of a bundle of rags. And the row he kicked up when I cut off your hair! Had to.... Couldn't get a comb through it. But you should have seen his face when he came to see you before he left on that raid. And you still sleeping away...."

She pulled the deerskin rug over her shoulders. Sheila breathed in relief. But Marian's head bobbed up again, and she was saying, "People in love are always the same. They think no one knows about it except themselves. It's the most open secret in all the world. As for trying to keep any kind of secret in a camp like this . . . ! Why, you might as well try to do it in a large family. Don't you worry: no amount of talk will scare the Chief, if that's what's worrying you. He's a man, not a milksop. He knows where he is with himself. He is what he is, and no false pretenses. We could do with more of his kind in the world. Ask Antoni. He used to doctor—oh, what's the use? If you don't believe what I'm saying, then you're not worth the Chief's little finger."

Sheila was so silent that Marian relented. "I'll talk no more about it. Antoni would say I'd talked too much. It's just that I like you, Sheila, and I don't want to see you cheat yourself. You could. You startle as easily as a deer." She laughed, and added, "In some things, anyway. Did you hear Jan's latest story about you? You shot two Germans, strangled another, and caught three spies. He's getting it almost perfect, isn't he?"

Sheila began to laugh in spite of herself.

Marian's eyes were closed firmly. Case dismissed.

Stefan helped her with the goats. It was impossible to try to milk a goat and not think the world had humor in it. They made progress, despite the advice shouted to them from two men weaving a wattle fence round the hen run. Sheila, her face scarlet with exertion, was laughing at one of the men, more helpful than the other, now retreating back to the protection of the fence with speed rather than grace; Stefan was looking with great seriousness at the amount of milk they had rescued. "It really isn't very *much*, is it?" he was saying.

And then three men walked towards her. Sheila, laughing, saw the two soldiers salute her, the little thin man in peasant's dress bow gravely. They had been talking earnestly, their heads slightly bent, their hands clasped behind their backs. Neither Sierakowski nor Olszak faltered in the deliberate pace. Adam's step slowed, imperceptibly. And she saw, too, the serious eyes suddenly lighten as he watched her as he passed. The line of his lips, grim and hard, softened for a moment. No one else had noticed, no one else could; only she could notice, and know what he meant.

Olszak asked something quickly, and Wisniewski's stride caught up with the rhythm of the others, as he replied. Then the trees hid him.

Sheila could have shouted with joy. It came in a wave, filling her heart and her whole body. "Shout it from the tree-tops," Marian had said, and she had been right. "Stefan thinks that I'm looking at him, that I'm smiling because of him," she said to herself. "He's wrong. I'm on the tip of the highest tree, shouting and shouting. And no one can hear me except Adam. Just as I can hear him, and no one else can." It was only after that strange, disturbing exuberance had spent itself, and she felt sane and ordinary again, that she remembered to be surprised that Olszak was here. Olszak had arrived at last. Olszak in peasant clothes, Olszak unshaven and so different, Olszak still so much Olszak in spite of the mud and the grime. And he must be leaving soon: probably tonight. For he hadn't bothered to wash off a week's accumulation of dirt. Yes, Olszak was still Mr. Olszak, the realist who didn't lose any time.

Stefan was saying, "Is that another recruit? We soon won't have room for any more. We've got *dozens* sleeping in our hut."

"Stefan!" Sheila wasn't laughing as she should have been. She was too busy wondering whether she should say, "Stefan, that 'new recruit' will have news of your mother," or not. Probably not. No use raising the boy's hopes, in case . . .

"Well, we've nine, anyway. Jan calls it the hen-roost. He says we'll soon be sleeping standing up, like horses. That's why there are no more huts being built just now."

Sheila tried to leave Madame Aleksander, and come back to the forest. "What was that, Stefan?" she asked.

"Didn't you know? We are going to get more horses. The stable's being built for them over there. When the spring comes they'll sweep down on the plains. They'll—Sheila, you aren't listening."

"Yes, Stefan," she said meaninglessly, and then saw her blunder in the boy's disappointment.

"What's wrong with you, Sheila? You never listen now."

"Come on," she replied gently. "We'll take this milk over to the hospital. They probably need it over there."

"I'm free until this afternoon. I've got leave." His voice emphasized the word proudly. He was a soldier: he got leave. "That's because I worked all week without stopping. At least, hardly stopping. Jan has his leave too, but he's not going down into the village like Zygmunt. Zygmunt's *always* going to Dwór. But Jan's going hunting. He's taking me with him. I made him promise. I'm not allowed to go down to one of the villages."

"I should say not," Sheila began emphatically.

"Why not?" There was a small smile at the back of Stefan's eyes.

"Well, hunting's better fun than a dull village, isn't it? What could you do down at the village except talk and look at people? You couldn't even fight if a German patrol came visiting." That was the rule of the camp: the men on their visits to the villages were not to provoke suspicion. They went unarmed and behaved as the villagers would behave.

"Yes. Specially—" He stopped too quickly.

Sheila said, "Specially what, Stefan?"

His cheeks flushed. "Oh, nothing. Not really, Sheila. Besides, it's a secret. Jan's secret."

They were reaching the center of the camp, now. And then she saw Jan. He was waiting for Stefan not far from the lodge. He carried a long wooden spear. There was a crossbar fixed near the butt. His knife was sheathed at his waist.

"Stefan!" Sheila said sharply. But the boy had already relinquished his grasp on the leather thong-handle of the bark bucket, and was running towards Jan. "Sorry I'm late, Jan," she heard him say. "I had to help Sheila. She's not very good at . . ." and then the man and boy were gone into the forest, and Sheila was left alone at the hospital door. There was no one else in the half-clearing in front of the lodge, no one else to whom she could call to stop these two fools. She almost ran into the hut. Franziska looked up from the wound she was dressing. Her patient was Zygmunt, gloomily watching the girl's fingers handling the nasty gash on his leg. He would take a long time to reach the village for his night's leave with that leg. Three other men were stretched in rough cots on the floor.

"Careful!" Franziska said in a low voice. "You'll spill the milk. Put it over there Sheila." She nodded to the table.

"Jan. Stefan. They've gone hunting Old Single."

"*Ssh!*" Franziska nodded this time towards the sleeping men on the floor.

Sheila lowered her voice. "I'll have to try and stop Stefan at least. His mother may be here any day now. I can't let him get killed just before she arrives."

"I wonder if he's got a chance, that Jan," Zygmunt was saying. "He's got an eye on my rifle. He bet—"

Sheila said quickly, "then he's determined to win. I told you *not* to bet. You heard what Ad— Captain Wisniewski said last night. The spear won't be strong enough. He knows. He's hunted boar. He knows."

"So that's why Jan was questioning the patrol that came back from the north edge of the forest this morning. Old Single was moving farther in, they said." Zygmunt added, "Damn to hell the misbegotten ax that argued with my leg. I'm going to lose the best gun a man ever picked out of a dead German's hands."

"Where's the patrol?"

"Sleeping, of course. What do you think they would be doing after twelve hours on duty?"

Sheila started towards the door. Franziska thrust the long strip of bleached linen into Zygmunt's hands. "Hold that. Just there," she ordered, and followed Sheila outside the hut. "What are you going to do?" Her face was unexpectedly sympathetic.

"I'll have to go after them. There's no one else to send. I'd only waste more time running round the huts trying to find someone who hadn't a job to do."

Franziska said, "Don't worry if you aren't back by midday. I am staying on duty anyway. That boy with the amputated arm is worse again. Marian says— Oh well, I'm not going to lose him now, after all the trouble I've had. When I think of—"

Sheila knew the story well. She gave Franziska an unexpected hug. "I'll be back before midday," she said. She was looking round the clearing. No one in sight. Hammering from the distance. A voice giving commands over at the training school. Here, there was no one. She would have to go by herself.

She set off at a run. Franziska understood. She wasn't going to lose her patient after all the difficulties they had overcome together. Sheila wasn't going to lose Stefan. Not needlessly like this. Madame Aleksander— Oh, damn that big lump of a man. Why couldn't he wait till Old Single moved still farther in, moved into the shooting zone? Why was he so set on getting Old Single this way? And when she caught up with Jan and Stefan, they would probably laugh at her: fuss about nothing, they'd say. Women are always like that, always worrying and interfering with men's business, they'd say. They might be right; but she wasn't going to take the chance. Not with Madame Aleksander . . . Madame Aleksander had lost enough already.

Sheila was hidden by the forest.

She was right, Franziska thought as she re-entered the hut. This idea of Jan's was too dangerous. Someone had to stop Stefan. Only—well, it wasn't any of her business. She picked up the bandage slowly. Then she looked at Zygmunt.

"Where's the Chief?" she asked suddenly.

"With that stranger. The little fellow."

"In the Lodge?"

"Yes."

Frankiska thrust the strip of yellowed linen back into Zygmunt's hand. She ran out of the hut.

"Hey!" Zygmunt called after her, and then he grinned as he began winding the bandage, himself. A woman, he was thinking, never knew how funny she looked from behind when she ran. Or none of them would run. Must be the way they kicked up their heels, like a scampering cow.

Inside the Lodge, the three men sat at the table. Olszak was studying the map, Adam Wisniewski was studying Olszak, and Sierakowski was lighting a cigarette.

"Good," Olszak said and straightened his back. He looked at Sierakowski. "You'll be in charge of the camp this winter, then." To Adam he said, "I am glad you found everything working smoothly in these last three weeks. You turned a raid into quite a tour of inspection, I hear."

"I thought it was wise to see, before I left here, just how our arrangements with the villages were working out."

Olszak nodded his approval. It had been wise. "And you are leaving this week?" It was a very polite form of suggestion.

Adam Wisniewski smiled. "I shall leave before the first heavy snows come to the mountains."

"That will be soon, then?"

Adam didn't answer. Sierakowski found his cigarette hadn't been lit properly, after all. Damn, he thought, and then wondered if he were angry with the cigarette or with Olszak's insistence. "Damn this," he said sharply.

Olszak was speaking again, very casually, very gently. "Actually, Adam, I had expected you to leave as soon as you got back from that raid."

Sierakowski said quickly: "Oh, there's time enough. Adam will reach the Carpathians before winter sets in." He glanced at his friend as if prompting him to reassure Olszak. The little man was fussing like a hen with its chickens. He wasn't satisfied, as though he had guessed something. And I'm responsible, Sierakowski thought worriedly. It was I who brought Sheila Matthews here. And yet, back at Reymont's camp, this place had seemed the most obvious: especially with Reymont's men all coming to the forest. Pity about Reymont. The Germans must have killed him. Pity. Clever, sensitive kind of chap.

Adam Wisniewski said as quietly as Olszak, "I'm thinking of getting married."

Even Sierakowski flinched. Adam, he thought, what in heaven's name made you speak so bluntly? Why didn't you at least prepare him for the shock?

Olszak's face was a mask. At last, "That's a bad joke," he said coldly.

"It's far from a joke," Adam said in the same even voice.

Olszak took a deep breath. Only his thin hands, suddenly rigid on the map in front of him, showed his temper. Just as evenly he replied, "Then it's the greatest piece of foolishness I've ever heard of."

Adam's jaw tightened. But he said nothing.

"You are in earnest?" Olszak went on. "Where is she going to live? What about security? Hers? Yours? Who is she, anyway?"

It was then that they heard the running footsteps.

"Coming here," Sierakowski said for all of them. "What's wrong now?"

Franziska's face, flushed and worried, answered him. The girl hesitated in the doorway of the lodge, suddenly afraid of her own temerity.

She heard the little, thin man ask in his cold voice, "Is *this* she?"

The Chief didn't answer. He was watching her. "What is it?" he asked. His voice sounded angry. She took a step backwards. All her courage had gone.

"What it it?" he asked more gently.

"The English girl. I shouldn't have let her go. Alone. I shouldn't have let her—"

Adam Wisniewski had risen abruptly. He was coming towards her. "Where? When?" His hand reached out and gripped her shoulder. She winced, but the intensity of his grip forced the story out of her. The stranger had come over to the doorway with Colonel Sierakowski. "Madness," he kept saying. "Incomprehensible. Mountain out of a molehill."

Adam Wisniewski turned on him savagely. "Keep quiet, Olszak. Let me hear this!" Then he said more gently to the nervous girl, "What path did she follow? Come, show me." His grip moved from her shoulder to her wrist. He pulled her out of the hut into the forest glade.

Olszak's voice was cold and quiet no longer. "Wisniewski, damn you, stay here!"

But Wisniewski was pointing to the paths into the forest. "This one? Or that one? This?"

Franziska nodded.

Without any further pause, he started to run.

Olszak turned back into the cold shadows of the Lodge. Sierakowski stood at the doorway until at last he heard the far-off whistle and its answering call.

"He's made contact with one of the sentries," he said

as he came back to the table. "The sentry will have a rifle, anyway."

Olszak looked up from the pretense of studying the map. "Is that so necessary?"

Sierakowski looked at Olszak's set face. For a moment, he felt a certain pleasure. You know so much, Mr. Olszak, but not everything, he thought.

"Have you ever hunted boar?" he asked politely.

"I've been much too busy with other things," Olszak said with a touch of sarcasm.

"Then you don't know in what danger Miss Matthews is, or the boy Stefan, or even Jan."

Olszak's voice lost its grating edge. "Then it is Miss Matthews?"

"Yes."

"Since when, may I ask?"

"Since they met, I believe."

For the second time, watching Olszak's expression, Colonel Sierakowski had a mild feeling of amusement. Mr. Olszak indeed did not know everything.

"I know nothing about Miss Matthews' feelings," Sierakowski went on, "but Adam is my friend, and I do know him. I'm afraid this affair is neither a joke nor a piece of foolishness, Mr. Olszak."

Mr. Olszak traced the course of a river on the map with his finger. "So I see," he answered at last. And this time, there was sadness in his voice.

Sheila was breathing unevenly, in heavy tearing gasps. She halted and tried to master the short stabs in her breast. She swallowed the hot saliva, rested her hot hand against the cold rough trunk of a tree. She was following the right path for the north. That was the one Jan and Stefan had taken. She must catch up with them soon. They hadn't so very much of a start. Surely their pace couldn't be as quick as hers: hunters don't hurry. And then she remembered that Stefan was due back on duty by the afternoon: they would be hurrying after all, to cover the six, seven, eight miles that would bring them towards the last stretch of forest. She kissed her knee quickly, and the stitch of pain at her side softened. She ought to have remembered that child's trick before now. She had come about a mile already: she had scarcely begun the journey. Too bad if she still gasped like a fish out of water. She started northwards once more.

At the end of the third mile, her lungs had seemingly decided she wasn't going to rest, so they stopped rebelling. She was traveling more quickly now. Her feet, too, had resigned themselves to this inevitable pace, and were picking their way more cleverly. It was as if all parts of her body realized they'd better look out for themselves because the mind controlling them was certainly thinking about other things. She passed some huts standing modestly back among the trees. Nobody was there. By this time, the men would be at work. She reached the tree on the path with the blazed markings. Beyond this, shooting was absolutely forbidden. Beyond this, she hadn't walked since she arrived. And because this new part of the forest was strange to her, it seemed more threatening. "Perfect nonsense," she told herself, but her words didn't convince her. She was nervous now, as well as worried. Jan and Stefan were still invisible. She stopped to listen. But she heard nothing except the constant whisper of branches. She couldn't get lost if she stuck to this path, and surely Jan wouldn't leave it. No one left the paths except the outposts, and they were chosen because they knew forests, because they could move as confidently through trees as the others would walk down a city street. She must have passed an outpost now, although she couldn't see him when she stopped and looked round her as the bird's call came suddenly out of the forest. A round-breasted pheasant, his long tail straight as a rudder, rose in a straight stiff angle with a hoarse cry of protest. He had the same heavy look as the bombers she used to watch over Warsaw when they had lifted away from antiaircraft shells.

Sheila stopped in sudden annoyance. This is futile, she thought; absolutely futile. And all the thanks she would get, if she did find Jan and Stefan, would be scorn. Men never liked advice from a woman. They didn't even call it advice; "nagging" was the word they would use. Knowing that only made her annoyance deepen. She used the scrap of linen which she had cut for a handkerchief to dry her brow. Her face must be a fine vintage purple by this time. Moistening the corner of the handkerchief, she tried to stop the irritating trickle of blood from a cut on her lip. Her hands and arms were scratched too. There were red scores on her legs. She sat down on an overturned tree and stared at its surrendered roots in disgust. A rabbit scampered towards her. Two wood-grouse flapped out of cover. Two more rabbits. A squirrel abandoned a beechnut, and fled to the nearest tree. Yet she was sitting quite still. It couldn't have been her movements which had startled them

And then it seemed as if she saw them all at once. Coming back towards her on the path were Stefan and Jan. She rose, relief on her face, her lips open to greet them. They were returning, was her first thankful thought, they were returning: they had failed. But Jan wasn't looking at her. His eyes were fixed on a thick copse of thin trees to her right. Stefan only glanced towards her for a moment. He laid a finger on his lips, and then he too was half crouching, moving slowly forwards like Jan. He too held his knife ready. She looked quickly towards the thin trees. She could see nothing. But the feeling of nervousness which had so discouraged her for the last few minutes turned into fear. She was all the more afraid because she didn't know what she was to fear. She looked quickly over her shoulder. On the path, some distance behind her, was Adam. Adam and one of the sentries. Adam had taken the man's rifle. The man held his bayonet like a knife. Both men were stiff, unmoving, as if they were turned into rock. They weren't watching her. They were staring at the thicket as Jan had done. Her first thought was: Adam—how did Adam get here? And then he thought: there *is* danger; I was right, there is danger. She looked back again to the wall of bushes on her right. Moving slowly round the roots of a trunk which had blocked her view came Old Single.

The boar moved so slowly, so nonchalantly, that for a minute Sheila believed all would be well. If you didn't attack, he wouldn't attack. That was what the boy who had guided them into the forest had said. Sheila stood as still as Adam and the sentry behind her. Adam can't use the gun, she was thinking: the Germans might hear a shot. All we can do is to stand still and let Old Single wander off. She had been keeping her eyes so fixed on the huge beast that she hadn't seen Jan. He couldn't have noticed the Chief. Jan noticed nothing except the giant boar. Jan was moving forward.

Old Single, in spite of his pretense of rooting round the tree, had known they were there. The men had come again to trap him. The nearest man was rising now, standing there to give him challenge. Old Single accepted it. The shapeless mass suddenly swerved. The hulking shoulders, the long snout, the savage tusks pointed towards the man. He was at Jan with a speed which terrified Sheila. She saw the raised spear pointing forwards, plunging into the boar's shoulder with all the strength of Jan's right arm. Both the man and the beast seemed to stagger under the shock. And then, before the sharp edge of the spear had reached the boar's heart, the wood cracked, and the spear's shaft snapped cleanly in two. Jan stumbled. His knife was ready, but the tusks slashed mercilessly at him. Sheila was gripped by a nausea: she saw Stefan, his knife in his hand, start towards Jan and the boar. Then Sheila's sickness passed, and the weight which had anchored her feet to the ground was slipped, and she was moving towards Stefan. "No!" she was saying. "Stefan, no! Too late! No!" She had wrenched her apron from her waist with an impulse completely instinctive and unreasoned.

The boy stopped as he heard her voice. Perhaps he knew it was too late. Perhaps he realized the danger into which he was pulling her. He stopped, and he lost the one moment when he could have attacked and been attacked. The moment was gone, and Old Single had charged, and Stefan was safe. It was towards the running Sheila, not towards the motionless Stefan, that the bloodstained tusks pointed. The beast was almost on her. She dropped the apron and stepped aside instinctively to try to reach a tree. The tusks slashed the fallen apron and then swerved towards the girl. She heard a racketing crash through the silent forest. Old Single checked for a moment, as if in surprise. She had reached the tree. He was following her, but he was moving slowly, blindly, as if he were tired, as if all his strength and pride had gone. He traveled almost fifteen feet to the tree before his knees bent forward as though the heavy shoulders were too much to bear any longer. He grunted, and tried to rise. For a moment he stood, his small eyes staring stupidly, pathetically at Sheila. He made one last quick movement, no longer stupid, pathetic. For one moment he was Old Single again, with all the meanness and savagery that gave his huge bulk so much evil. And then he fell forward once more and lay motionless. He was only a shapeless mass of flesh and fat, a monstrous joke by nature to balance the beauty she could also create.

"I'll make sure," the man with Adam was saying, and used his bayonet. "They've the cunning of the devil." He wiped the bayonet on the bristling hair. "That's one that isn't cunning any more," he said. He walked over to where Jan lay. Stefan, white-faced, knelt with him. The man was shaking his head slowly.

Adam still held the rifle. With his free hand he grasped both of Sheila's, and then his arm was round her waist holding her fiercely. His strength gave strength to her. Their kiss was in defiance of death.

Then, still gripping Sheila's wrist, he was speaking, quickly, urgently, to the sentry and Stefan. The command brought them to their feet and over to their Chief. Stefan, the tears on his face unnoticed, received his instructions in silence.

"Stop thinking of Jan," Adam said sharply. "Think of the camp. Can I trust you to take this message to the village of Zorawno on the north side of the forest? You know it?"

Stefan was stung into answering. "Yes, sir. We went to

the edge of the forest before we started back—before we saw him." For a second, he looked down at the boar. "I saw Zorawno. It isn't so far away."

Wisniewski repeated his instructions. "Go to that village, carefully. Find Jadwiga. Find out if any Germans are in Zorawno, or near it. If any are there and heard the shot, then Jadwiga remembers that one of the villagers went out hunting last night. She heard the shot too. She thinks an accident has happened. If the Germans insist on searching, they will find a dead man, a dead boar, and a gun."

Stefan repeated Wisniewski's words.

"Now, quickly," said the captain. "And carefully. We are depending on you."

The boy saluted. He left at a run.

"Carefully!"

Stefan's movements became noiseless.

Wisniewski turned to the sentry. "Get back to camp, giving the alert signal as you go. Colonel Sierakowski is in command there meanwhile. Tell him to start Plan C at once. I'll be behind you." The man repeated the instructions, saluted, and set off at a half-crouching, silent lope. Wisniewski let go Sheila's wrist.

"I've bruised it," he said gently, and lifted it to his lips. "Wait here," he added. He walked quickly over to Jan, placed the gun carefully beside the bloodstained figure, paused for a moment as he picked the long feather out of Jan's cap, and came back to Sheila. He stood for a little, looking down at the feather, his face grim, his eyes thoughtful. Then he took Sheila's arm and together they followed the sentry. A strange birdcall echoed in front of them, one that Sheila had never heard used before. It was the warning. She heard it again, far and faint, strident and harsh. She shivered slightly: it meant, perhaps, the end of the camp.

They covered the long journey in silence. The pace was too quick for any talking. The time was too late for explanations. Each hut, as they passed it, was empty. Ahead of them, they heard the faint birdcall once more. Only Adam's firm grasp gave Sheila comfort. The long journey seemed short and easy. With him, anything would be easy.

They were near the lodge now. Already they could hear men's voices, words of command, directions.

Wisniewski halted suddenly, and pulled Sheila round to face him. The grim look on his face softened. He was looking at her with the old smile, half-mocking, half-serious.

"This may be a false alarm," he said quietly. He was holding her shoulders so that she was forced to look up at him.

"But we can take no chances. If it isn't, then you stay with the people in the camp, leave as they leave."

"And you?"

"I'll follow you later. Some of us must stay round the forest's edge. If the Germans come, we'll retreat into its depths. If they follow us beyond Old Single, then Jadwiga's story hasn't worked, and we'll have to do some shooting. By that time the camp will have dispersed. Each man knows where to go. You travel with Sierakowski." He touched her hair. "Sheila, you will obey me?"

She nodded. Their arms were round each other. With her last, almost despairing kiss, she told him what he had left unasked. He kissed her again, suddenly, this time gently. Then they were walking quickly towards the camp.

Sheila saw the men, in numbers which she hadn't even guessed, standing silently among the trees. They were armed and waiting. A look of relief came to the watchful eyes as they saw the Chief. "He's here," someone called. There was the beginning of a shout which Wisniewski silenced. Sheila, standing against a tree, watched him move towards the lodge. He had jumped up on a table pulled out at its door. She heard his voice, crisp, cool. She watched the faces around her, straining eagerly for his words. They knew the plan which had been prepared for this day, he told them. Each group of men had its orders, each man knew what he was to do. To Sheila, standing so watchfully, came the revelation of still another Adam. Sierakowski and the other officers beside him seemed pale cold figures. Wisniewski had control of these men. He spoke well because he spoke briefly, simply, honestly. He had their respect and their loyalty, not because of the form of his words, but because of the sincerity which lay behind them. Even at the end of his short speech, when his voice said clearly and slowly, "As for the event, which may force us to leave this camp—I take full responsibility. But now, my first duty is to see that we all get out of this mess. After that, when you are either in your new quarters or safely back here, you can appoint a new commander."

Sheila missed a breath; and then relaxed as the men broke their silence with a derisive shout. "Pox to that," a man beside her yelled. She could have hugged him in her relief.

Wisniewski said no more. He stood looking at the men for a moment, gave them a quick salute, and then leapt down from the table. The priest was speaking now. The men knelt. Under the arches of bared boughs, under the cold blue

sky, they knelt; their voices were like the voice of the wind
through the trees, surging, unfathomable, free.

Now the men formed neatly, soldierwise, into prearranged
groups, and the officers took their places with the men. And
then the groups took their various directions into the forest.
Adam had gone. Only the men who had been left to clear
the camp remained. Sierakowski gave them their orders, standing beside the table outside the lodge. There was a feeling
of life and bustle, of great haste and urgency. Faces and
voices were excited; movements were quick. But to Sheila
the camp was already deserted.

She went towards the hospital hut. She heard Antoni's
voice saying, "Of all the damned nuisances . . ." as he packed
a wooden case with his medical supplies in front of the door.
There was Marian, giving instructions to a man fashioning a
rough stretcher.

"Two will have to be carried all the way. Your men know
what to do?"

"That's why we're here," the man said abruptly, and silenced even Marian. Inside the hut, Franziska was packing the
last things. "Don't worry," she was saying to her patients.
"We'll get you out of the forest at night. You'll stay hidden in one of the villages till you are well enough to join
us again." She glanced at Sheila and said, "Well, here's a
fine how d'you do! We've all to begin over again." She was
almost weeping with anger.

"What can I do?" Sheila asked.

"Help get the stuff over to the pits. We are hiding it there
in case we have to move."

Sheila seised a bark-covered bundle. "Where are the pits?"

"Follow the crowd," Franziska said.

Antoni pointed out the way to her. "Over there through
the trees. That's our cache. Dog's blood, isn't this a damned
nuisance? How the hell did it happen anyway? Is it true
Jan Pietka is dead?"

Sheila nodded. Marian quieted her husband's language by
saying, "Well, the Germans may not come. We may not have
to leave this camp."

"Then we'll have everything to take out of those holes in
the ground again. I say it's a damned nuisance, and that's
what it damned well is."

Marian had no reply. It wasn't often that Antoni left her
with none. She looked suddenly at Sheila. "Here, I'll give
you a hand with that," she said, and lifted one end of the
bundle. But she had the sense and the kindness to keep silent
as they carried the heavy load to the pit.

It was more of an underground cave than a pit. It had props

to keep the roof from sagging, and the floor had been covered with boards to try to give it some dryness. Sheila and Marian watched their bundle stowed away with the few straw mattresses and furs and blankets.

"The hens are what I'm worried about," Marian said. "I won't have them killed until we get the signal to move out."

"What about the goats and the horses?"

"The last of the rearguard will use the horses. It may give them a chance." She stopped as she saw Sheila's face. "Don't worry. He's got nine lives. He's only used up five of them so far." She took the girl's arm. "Did you hear the men when he said he would resign the command? That's why they are for him. He's always first in and last out. He never asks one of us to do what he can't do himself. Come on, now. We'll give Franziska a hand with parceling up the wounded. They'll have to be taken down near the edge of the forest right away. Can't leave them to the last moment. Franziska's going with them. Sort of funny, she's leaving the way she came in. Didn't she ever tell you?" And when Sheila didn't answer, Marian plunged into the epic of Franziska: how she, as a nurse, had driven a horse and cart filled with wounded just one step ahead of the Germans for over a hundred miles. At the end of the war she had reached this district. By that time, only five men out of eleven were alive. "Machine-gunning, chiefly. Only those who could walk managed to get out of the cart in time to dodge. The villagers hid them, but after the war the enemy began searching the villages. So the villagers carried the five men here. Franziska came with them. Four of them are out in the forest now. The fifth one is that boy whose arm we had to amputate. That's why Franziska's worried about him. He's been her special property, somehow."

As they reached the hospital door, Marian was congratulating herself on her ingenuity. She had talked without letting her tongue trip her up again. *It may give them a chance.* How could she ever have said such a thing? Good job Antoni hadn't heard her.

Antoni's temper had recovered. His round face creased in a wide grin. "Well, this will be a good dress rehearsal, anyway," he said to them as he finished packing the box. He added, "Sheila, they've been asking for you. Over at the lodge."

He stood with Marian and watched the fair-haired girl turn silently and retrace her steps towards the lodge.

"Now what did you say to her? Only ten minutes ago her eyes were shining and she carried her head bravely. Look at her now: she's back to her worrying again." Antoni's voice was so sharp that Marian stared at him.

"Why, nothing at all," she answered indignantly. She looked at the men carrying the camp equipment into the forest. "It's going to be miserable sitting round here waiting, without warm food or bedding, until we get the signal to move. *If* we get it."

Antoni let her change the subject. "You're getting soft again," he said teasingly. "All the luxuries we've been having have softened you."

She looked down at her bare legs and broken shoes, at her darned skirt and her reddened hands. She drew the coarse shawl more closely round her shoulders. She smiled, and said, "Do you ever think back to our flat in Warsaw, Antoni? I wonder how the new lace curtains are—and that new tiled stove we got last spring—and that pretty rug you bought me for the bedroom in July? Funny: we took ten years before we got all the things we wanted for our house. I had just got all the colors right, and the little extra tables, and you'd got the pictures you wanted and that new bookcase. And then the Germans came. And there's a German doctor working in your office, with all the equipment we bought before we could buy my rose-covered chairs. And his family is sitting on the chairs now, and eating off our good mahogany table, and walking over my polished floors. His wife has my linen cupboard, and all the rows of sheets and pillowcases that I embroidered myself, every stitch of them. He's got your X-ray apparatus and your instruments and all your notes on those special treatments you were giving your diabetics." She paused. "Well, that's the way it goes."

Antoni took her roughened hand. "Do you ever wish you hadn't come here with me when Wisniewski asked me?"

"Antoni! The idea!" And then she laughed. "Do you think I'd let you out of my sight with all these pretty girls around?"

Antoni curved his arm round the thickening waist and gave it a light squeeze. "That's my Marian," he said. "You're the best and the prettiest girl in Poland. And that means in the world."

"Antoni!" She gave him a rough quick embrace and pushed him away. The woman of forty laughed like a girl. "Just hope they remember to water the window plants," she added.

Antoni stared at her. She was in Warsaw again.

"You know what I wish, Antoni? I wish our home had been utterly destroyed by the bombs. There I was, patting myself on the back because we didn't even have as much dust and splintered glass as our friends. Probably that's the punishment I get for being so selfish—knowing that a German family owns it now."

Antoni said, "Better see that each man knows what food to take with him. Look after the kitchen. I'll finish this job here. Franziska has been wrapping up the wounded. They're practically ready to go."

"All right, my dear." Marian moved off towards the kitchen. She halted and looked back for a moment. "Antoni, I'm going to get a haircut like Sheila's."

"No!" said Antoni. "You'll do nothing of the kind."

"It's handier. And Sheila looks so pretty now, like a boy with long curls."

"No," Antoni repeated firmly. He started rolling up a mattress, covering it with a rug of rabbitskins.

Marian shrugged her shoulders, but there was a smile on her lips. She was humming to herself, a gay little polka tune, as she passed round the back of the lodge to the place where the kitchen fires had been grouped. She looked through a window as she passed the lodge. She had a glimpse of a thin-faced little man sitting on the edge of the table. She heard Sheila's voice. There was something despairing in its tone.

Marian's song stopped. Her step slowed.

At the "kitchen"—three small, scattered pits, with large flat roofs, a thick fallen trunk smoothed off as a table—she found Zygmunt and another man in charge. Near them, a strange man and boy—their clothes still showing the signs of much travel—were eating some of the remains of last night's supper and talking to Sierakowski between mouthfuls. They must be the newcomers who had arrived just before dawn along with that thin-faced little man. They looked half-dead. Probably they had been pulled out of their sleep to come and eat while there was still time. A small, disheveled gray dog was busily gnawing meat off a bone. He paused when Marian came up to the group, and held the bone firmly between his paws, his head cocked to the side, his ears and eyes alert.

Marian laughed. "What's this?" she asked half contemptuously.

The boy said defensively, "He needs a bath. He looks fine when he's white. Only, he's been traveling. As soon as I give him a bath, he'll look fine."

"What next?" Marian said. "Children and dogs. What next?"

The stranger smiled, and the hard line of his jaw and gaunt cheeks softened. He had the strong body, the quiet large-boned face of a countryman. But his voice was not the voice of a peasant. He was saying, "We've more traveling to do, I hear. I shouldn't bathe him just yet, Casimir."

"I want him clean before Sheila sees him," said the boy. "She liked to see him clean. She was *always* telling me to go out and wash him."

Marian said, "You aren't *that* Casimir, are you? . . . Why, I know all about you! And this is *that* dog? Where's Madame Aleksander, then?"

The man answered. "In a village called Dwór just northeast of here. She had to rest. She'll be brought along here in a day or two." He paused. "At least, she was to have been brought here in a day or two. She's a nurse."

"Good. We shall need extra help, I expect." Marian still couldn't place the man. He wasn't an Aleksander, and yet he seemed to know them all right. There was that touch in his voice. "Who are you?" she asked.

"Jan Reska. I used to live at Korytów." There was a blankness about the words which said "And don't ask any more questions."

Sierakowski said, "After you've eaten, you can help to get this kitchen eliminated. The thing to remember is not to destroy. Just remove things and hide them for future use."

"I'll show them," said Marian. "I'm going to see no food gets wasted."

"Good." Colonel Sierakowski moved away.

Marian said quickly, "If you could, Colonel Sierakowski, would you look in at the lodge?"

He halted and looked sharply at her serious face. "Very well, Pani Roszak."

"Now," Marian said, "we'll finish this job. And when everything's done, we'll clean the dog. And you can tell me how you got here."

"That's a secret," said Casimir. "We tried out a new way, and it worked," he added, proudly.

"Did it, now?" Marian said. She lifted the wicker lids off the food-baskets, while the three men and the boy started to take the fire to pieces. Marian pulled out the food carefully. "Wonder what's the best way to divide this up?" she called to them. "How much food do you think a Pole would be allowed to travel with nowadays? I'm not up in the new regulations. How much could each of us carry, without arousing suspicion if we were caught and searched?"

"Nothing," Reska answered, "or next to nothing."

"What, don't they even let us eat nowadays?"

"Just enough to keep us from starving, not enough to let us live."

Casimir yelled over, "The best way to carry it is in here."
He pointed to his stomach.

Marian stared at him. "I believe it is. We'll have a big
meal first, and pack what food is left after that. Here, Zygmunt, hobble around and tell everyone to come here as
soon as they've finished their jobs."

Zygmunt said, "*Hm*. What about these bottles of vodka?"

"They will keep. We can hide them." She relented. "You
can each have a drink, if Colonel Sierakowski allows it.
That'll keep you warm tonight. But the rest will be buried
until we get back here."

"That's a woman for you, always thinking of the future,"
said Zygmunt in disgust. "Today we're here, tomorrow we're
dead. Why worry?"

Because, Marian thought, even if we are dead, there will
be others who will come after us; even if we die, we've
shown them the way, and they'll follow it. The fight won't stop
just because we got killed. There are others who'll take it
up where we left off. There will be others who will come some
day to use these supplies.

"Really now, you don't say!" she mocked. Well, if you
laughed loudly enough, you didn't weep. She started counting
the food supplies once more. If one man got a leg of a
pheasant, would he get as much as another, who got a quarter of a rabbit? She began to hum the polka which had
been running through her head all day. Somehow, she couldn't
stop thinking about Sheila.

## CHAPTER XXXII

### *The Decision*

THE LODGE was dark and cold and empty. Sheila paused at
the door, and looked for a moment at the stone fireplace. Its
warm ashes were now scattered. Last night, there had been
songs and laughter. Last night, she had sat over there with
Adam and watched Jan and his spear-making with amusement. Accidents fell so sharply, brought tragedy quite beyond
their proportion.

And now the maps on the walls had gone, the papers on
the table had gone, Adam had gone. "I'll follow you," he
had said. The worry that had chilled her eyes was leaving
her. Adam would follow her. He would find her. She could

even manage to smile for Mr. Olszak. He was thinner and smaller, but he had lost none of his alertness.

"You look well," he said as he took her hands. He looked keenly at her face. "Very well indeed. The forest agrees with you, I see."

"I am glad to see you," she said simply. "I've wondered how everything has been in Warsaw."

"Not very good." He let go her hands and walked back to the table. Sheila sat down on the bench. She rested her arms on the table: here it was where he used to work, the maps spread out in front of him just where her hand now touched the solid wood.

"Some of our departments were almost blotted out before they could get started. Jan Reska's, for instance. We'll have to organize the teaching of the children in another way. The schoolteachers have been slaughtered. There's no other word for it." Olszak's face was bitterly dark. Then he went on, forcing his voice to a cheerfulness he obviously didn't feel, "However, other departments have been more fortunate. We've two secret newspapers, with good circulation. The hidden radio system is having excellent results. We have established several efficient routes for secret travel, and we are managing to keep our contact with friends abroad. On the whole, I should say we have a lot to be thankful for."

"What about Jan Reska?"

"He's come here. He feels he will do better as a fighter than as an organizer."

Sheila stared at Olszak blankly. "But Reska's got brains. And he's got courage. He's liberal and sincere. He would be a good organizer."

"These qualities you mention are also needed in a good fighter. He himself doesn't think he's a good organizer. He wants action. I agree with him."

Then Reska had failed in his job. Olszak was letting him down as lightly as possible.

It seemed as if Mr. Olszak was back in his old habit of reading her thoughts, for he said, "When this war is over I shall retire to the mountains. And I intend to write a study on what makes, or doesn't make, a man capable of efficient leadership. It is nothing you can see on the surface. It may even be nothing you can explain. But I should like to try."

"When did Jan Reska come? I haven't seen him."

"Early this morning. He traveled with Casimir and Madame Aleksander and a dog. Madame Aleksander insisted on the dog. It was madness. But both Casimir and Reska supported her view." He shook his head with extreme disapproval.

"Madame Aleksander?"

"They had to leave her at one of the small villages north-east of the forest. Dwór, it is called. She is resting there. She was supposed to continue the last part of the journey with a village guide, tomorrow." He shrugged his shoulders as if to say, but that plan will have to be changed too. "She isn't so very well at the moment. And the journey from Warsaw tried her strength sorely."

He paused. Then he said in the same even, purposely cold voice, "Edward Korytowski was imprisoned in Dachau. Then the Germans gave him the chance to head a Co-operative Council. He refused. He's dead."

He paused again. "Andrew Aleksander is a prisoner of war in Westphalia. The camp is already notorious. We have proof that the prisoners are subjected to every kind of insult and beating. There have even been some cases of torture. There is little hope for prisoners of war in Germany if their country has no German prisoners of war. When the Germans hold the whiphand, they use it."

He paused again. And then, as if to try and dispel the horror in the girl's eyes, he said, "But all my news is not bad. Hofmeyer is still safe and working well. Russell Stevens reached Switzerland, and accomplished his mission, and had an interesting conversation with your uncle."

"Uncle Matthews? Steve's in London, then?"

"They met in France, actually. Stevens, by the way, has accepted a job in Geneva. On your uncle's advice. He is still fighting with us."

"I knew he would," Sheila said. "Schlott and Bill?"

"Fighting on, too. Each in their own way."

"I knew they would—at least, I hoped they would."

"What made you fear that they might not?"

"Well, it would be only human to—well, relax or ease up or something. Once you felt out of danger, that is. Once you were away from the bombings and the massacres. It takes a lot of self-control for a hungry man to look at a roasted turkey and then choose dry bread instead." She hesitated for a moment, and then added, "Uncle Matthews . . . Is he angry with me?"

Olszak smiled openly. "Annoyed in some ways, perhaps. In other ways, he seems to be quite proud."

Olszak watched the girl's startled eyes. His amusement increased. "So, you've nothing to be proud of!" he said.

Sheila reddened, shrugged her shoulders, traced the pattern of the wood with her fingers. Olszak was probably trying to cheer her up, after having depressed her so violently with the first part of his news. One thing was certain: she had no tears left. They were all used up. Andrew ... Uncle Edward ... They were now woven into the same grim pattern of sadness which covered her memory of Barbara, of Aunt Marta, of little Teresa, of Jan, of Korytów. And the pattern would keep increasing, it would become more complex still. Perhaps only one's own death ever ended it.

"You are fond of your uncle?" Olszak asked suddenly.

She looked up in surprise. "Yes."

"You would obey him if he gave a really sincere order? You trust his judgment, now?"

Sheila was suddenly wary. "I trust his judgment," she said evenly.

Olszak leaned against the table's corner. "He would like you to leave Poland. He has asked me to act in his place, and see that you do."

Sheila was silent. And then she spoke quickly as if to make up the time she had lost by that silence. "But when he decided that, he didn't know how much I want to stay. There's no question of going away. Not now. He was only thinking of my safety. He doesn't know that I am safe, that—" The sudden change in Olszak's eyes halted her.

"Yes," he said quietly, "the hungry man wants the roasted turkey...."

"But that's not fair, Mr. Olszak." Her voice was rising. Olszak looked quickly towards the window at the back of the lodge. But it was only the doctor's wife passing by.

"There's no choice about what is my duty this time, thank God!" Sheila was ending.

"No?"

She stared at Olszak. A sudden fear warned her. She searched desperately for reasons against her going. "You know I can't leave Poland. What about Anna Braun? She cannot come to life in another country. Mr. Hofmeyer couldn't go on working, then."

"Our Mr. Hofmeyer saw that possibility coming. The story of your abduction and possible death on the Lowicz road was generally accepted. Actually, we ourselves were extremely upset about it until we got your message from one of Wisniewski's men. You were in all the German-controlled newspapers. Not the headlines, I'm sorry to say. Just a small box headed POLISH TERRORISM. As far as my men can discover, Streit and Engelmann had no reason to doubt the official report on your disappearance. But there's a man called Heinrich Dittmar."

Sheila's face went rigid.

"Dittmar, it seems, didn't altogether accept the story of your probable death. He questioned Madame Aleksander with unnecessary violence. Oh yes, he vented some of his temper on her. But he learned nothing. Madame Aleksander was released; no doubt he hoped she would lead him to you if you were still alive. However, we have seen to it that her journey here was most secret. Except for that damned dog." Olszak shook his head slowly, incredulously: his love of perfection had been affronted by such an idea.

"Well, to return to Dittmar . . . He visited the Lowicz road. Then he questioned the spy who had reported your presence in Reymont's camp. Then he visited the camp itself. He collected the remains of your papers and clothes. Then he visited the two villages which lie to the southeast of Reymont's wood. For the spy was wounded severely, by the way, after the German attack on the camp. He was shot as he stood on the road beside a staff car. He was shot by someone who escaped over the fields to the southeast. That someone evaded the German soldiers who tried to follow him. Dittmar, two days later on the scene, guessed that the man who had tried to kill the spy must have been hidden in a near-by village while the Germans had searched the fields. Usually a man tries to get far away from the scene of his shooting; but when no widespread search found a wandering Polish soldier, Dittmar guessed that the man had stayed so close to the woods that he had outwitted the Germans who were searching. So Dittmar visited the two nearest villages beside the wood on its southeast side. He visited them very thoroughly."

He stopped and looked at Sheila's face. "Did you know about that shooting?"

"No. Not at the time. Now it—it seems as if I should have known." She remembered how the talkative Jan had been so abrupt about that return visit to the wood. She remembered his words to the blacksmith near Rogów: *Five good bullets*. At the time she had thought, why only five? The men had all loaded their revolvers fully before they left Reymont's camp. Now she knew. "Yes, it could have been Jan," she said. Dear Jan, she thought, you always did things which infuriated less impulsive people and yet they always liked you all the more in spite of their irritation.

"But how do you know all this about Dittmar?" she asked with veiled admiration.

"I've shared your distrust of the man," Olszak said with a narrow smile. "He's only made one mistake so far. He has a weakness for a young man. You know him. His name is Hefner."

"But Hefner isn't one of us."

"No. Decidedly no. He is merely a young man with a lot

of ambition attached to his snobbery. He isn't quite sure yet whether Hofmeyer or Dittmar is the man whose coat-tails are going to pull him into power. He accompanied Dittmar on his search for information, and Hofmeyer found out as much as he dared when Hefner returned to Warsaw. Hofmeyer can handle Hefner very neatly: he knows that young man's price. In return, he can always depend on stray pieces of information. They are enough for our friend Hofmeyer."

Mr. Olszak's smile was really very peculiar. "What would you have done, Sheila, if you had been Hofmeyer and had seen Dittmar's suspicions growing about your late secretary? Especially if that secretary, Anna Braun, was out of danger from Dittmar?"

Sheila's smile was nervous. "If I were Hofmeyer . . ." she began slowly. She halted. "No, I wouldn't. At least, I don't think so. . . ."

"Yes, you would. If you knew your whole organization was at stake, you would. You'd have to pretend to play the game your opponent's way. That's what Hofmeyer had to do. Anna Braun, the pawn, was sacrificed. While Dittmar was searching every corner of these two villages to try to find someone who had belonged to the camp, so that he could learn more about you: while Dittmar saw some pieces of gray wool hanging out to dry behind one of the cottages, and thought it looked expensive cloth for a peasant to own; while Dittmar found that the weave of the gray material matched your jacket which had been found at Reymont's camp, our Mr. Hofmeyer was having a most serious talk with Herr Engelmann and Captain Streit. It seems he had become suspicious about Anna Braun. He had been making complicated investigations. He still hadn't exact proof, but he was beginning to believe she had been 'planted' on the innocent Germans by the perfidious British. He disproved your life story as skillfully as only the man could who had invented it. He was careful not to disprove too much, just as he was careful to show you had not learned anything of value if you were a British spy. He agreed with Streit that you were dead. His opinion was that you suffered poetic justice at the hands of your own allies. All he did was to put his suspicions on record before Dittmar could drag him down with you."

"I *asked* them to burn that skirt and jumper," Sheila said unhappily. Olszak's brows frowned. She hadn't been listening to anything since he had mentioned that gray material.

He said sharply, "You should have done the burning,

yourself. You cannot expect anyone who has so little to throw away anything that costs good money."

She closed her eyes wearily. She was afraid to ask the next question.

"The woman and the children?"

"The woman was questioned—unpleasantly—in front of the children. They screamed out the truth. That last phrase is Hefner's, as recounted to Hofmeyer." Olszak paused. "The children were deported. The woman died from the questioning. But not before Dittmar had proof that you weren't dead, that you were traveling south with a man and a boy."

"And now?" An impulse to shoot a spy in the dark, a stained gray skirt whose weave and color matched a torn, discarded jacket—small things to end one's feeling of success, small things to bring such complete failure and tragedy...

"Dittmar is continuing his search for you. He didn't return to Warsaw with Hefner. He has disappeared meanwhile."

"It's you he is really after," Sheila said slowly. "I alone am not worth all this trouble."

"That he is searching for Kordus is nothing new," Olszak said coolly. "I think a psychiatrist would perhaps give us the real answer to Dittmar's persecution of you."

"He's searching for Olszak now. If he finds that Olszak isn't so harmless as he pretends, then he will have all Olszak's friends and contacts arrested, too. He has already killed most of Kordus' friends, and found that wasn't enough." Now she knew why this man had doubled his name. Not to keep his Kordus activities secret, as anyone would naturally suppose; but to keep Olszak's interests and friends quite safe. It was the use of the pseudonym in reverse.

And as Olszak still kept silent, his thoughts hidden behind his clever eyes, she said quickly, "Don't men ever suffer from intuition? Or, as Steve would say, haven't you heard of anyone having a hunch?"

Olszak was looking at her, at least.

"For I think Dittmar has one. And he doesn't want to chase away all the others he could catch with Olszak, if he hunted him slowly and carefully." The last time she had seen Dittmar, he had brought Olszak's name into the conversation. Subtly, cleverly. She tried hard to remember Dittmar's exact words, and failed. She had had so many things to think about recently... she was forgetting. She had believed that her life in Warsaw as Anna Braun was over, and she had tried to forget it. She had succeeded.

Olszak had risen from the table and paced in front of it, his hands clasped behind his back. "I don't disbelieve in intuition," he said. "I've had attacks of it myself." Then he stopped his pacing and faced her squarely. "Well, we won't discuss that any more. I've one thing to ask you." And it seemed as if the imperturbable Mr. Olszak didn't enjoy asking it. There was a pause, a sharp look from his quick eyes, some more pacing round the table. He wasn't looking at her any more.

"I want you to take Madame Aleksander and Stefan out of the country. You will have papers in order, you will travel by train to Vienna and then to Switzerland. You will be given suitable clothes and money and a story to fit your papers. Stanislaw Aleksander will do an excellent job for you. In Vienna you will be met and sheltered by an Austrian. In Switzerland, Stevens will see that you are sent safely on to France and then England. Others have already traveled this way. You need not worry. Just keep your head and stick to your story. That's all."

Sheila said in a low voice, "But now, more than ever, I want to stay here."

Olszak said with remarkable gentleness, "I know."

"I can't go," she said in sudden desperation.

This time, he said nothing.

"Surely, if the journey is to be so prearranged, surely Stefan is old enough to take care of Madame Aleksander?" Her voice became pleading. "Isn't he?"

"Yes," he said gently. "They could go alone."

"But you want *me* to go. Is that it?"

Watching the controlled face in front of her, she half-guessed the reason.

"Why don't you say it?" she demanded angrily. "You've never been afraid to hurt, before." And then she wished she hadn't said that. She had placed the barb too well.

Firm footsteps sounded on the hard earth threshold. It was Sierakowski. Sheila's face lightened as she turned hopefully to him. He was her friend. He was Adam's friend. He could answer Olszak. And then, as she noticed the relief with which Olszak greeted him, she realized that there would be little help here. Sierakowski had known of Olszak's plan to send her away. He had come, not to help her, but to join in persuading her.

She looked at both men in turn. "I won't go," she said. She was fighting for all her happiness now, the only real happiness she had ever known. Even in war, Uncle Edward had told her, even in war happiness need not be refused.

"If I were to say that sacrifice of individual happiness is sometimes necessary for the good of the whole?" Olszak asked.

"But that doesn't apply to us. I won't keep Adam from being a good leader."

*"White hands cling to the bridle rein, slipping the spur from the booted heel."* Olszak quoted the lines slowly.

"No!" Sheila protested. "No."

"Would Wisniewski have risked that shot this morning, risked the camp, if it hadn't been you who were about to be savaged by that boar?"

As Sheila's eyes widened and her lips, half-opened, couldn't speak, Sierakowski said quietly, "As his wife, you would follow the camp rules and live in one of the villages. You would always be in danger of being taken by the Germans and held as a hostage. If Adam weren't our leader, I should say that it would be your own choice to face that. As our leader, he needs a free mind."

"Antoni and Marian—"began Sheila, and then stopped. It was a weakening of her defense.

"Antoni is hardly Wisniewski, either in his duties or in his—emotions," Olszak said. When I chose Wisniewski for this job, I knew he had enough energy and training and brilliance for it. I had to wait and see if the responsibility would make him into a true leader. It has. He has learned to think of the good of the whole, rather than the happiness of the individual. His job is only beginning. This winter is only the planning stage. He has proven himself. We need him. He's more important to us as a fighter for freedom with eventually thousands of men depending on his leadership, than he is as the husband or lover of a pretty girl. All we are thinking of now is the freedom we have to regain."

Sheila felt the mild rebuke sting at her eyes, flail her cheeks until they were scarlet.

"I didn't think that—that one thing canceled out the other . . ." Her voice trailed even as her eyes said, "You are being too harsh."

"That is why, I suppose, that generals bring their wives or mistresses into battlefields? Why captains of warships have their women living on board?"

Sheila rose. She didn't look at either of them any more. Her heart rebelled but her mind agreed with them. That was why she had fought so badly: her mind agreed. The choice was not hers to make. It was only in peace and freedom that you could make your own decisions.

The tears, which she had thought were dried up forever, soaked her face. She turned her head away. She fought for control over her voice, and, having failed, kept silent. She walked suddenly towards the door. This large room was suddenly crushing her, stifling her. Sierakowski was at her elbow, holding her arm gently. She shook herself free and ran into the open.

She saw a man staring at her as he hobbled towards her. "We are going to eat," he was calling. "We ..." He stopped as he saw her face.

She turned and ran away from him, away from the lodge, from Olszak, from Sierakowski standing so silently in the doorway. As if to torture herself still more, she had chosen blindly the short path where Adam had led her last night.

In the lodge, Olszak said abruptly, "All plans made for me to leave tonight? Guide ready? Patrols warned?"

Sierakowski turned slowly back into the room.

"Yes, everything's ready," he said slowly.

"I'll take Miss Matthews with me as far as Dwór, where she will find Madame Aleksander. Is the boy Stefan here yet?"

"He hasn't come back yet. There is scarcely time for his return. It will be difficult to persuade him to leave us."

"He will do as he's told. He needs some discipline. He has lived too long with too many women. If he hadn't gone with that fool Jan, this morning, Sheila wouldn't have gone after them, Wisniewski wouldn't have left us when that young nurse told him where Sheila had gone, the shot would never have been fired, and all this emergency would never have arisen. If that Jan had gone alone, then the score would have been still the same—one dead man. ... But the results would have been very different."

"It *was* the shot, then, which decided you that Miss Matthews must leave? This morning, you accepted her here. You had plans for Madame Aleksander to join us here and help in the hospital." Sierakowski's quiet voice softened still more. "And yet I, myself, would have fired that shot. So would the rest of the men in the camp. So would you."

Olszak looked at him keenly. The smile which wasn't a smile appeared once more on his lips. "Are you trying to plead for them, Sierakowski? No, it wasn't the shot that decided me. I made the decision when that worried nurse came interrupting me, when Wisniewski leapt to his feet, left us—like that!" He cracked his thin fingers. "Until then I thought it was one of those mad attractions, infatuations, blood-fevers—call it what you will. But then I knew it wasn't. I saw his face. And now after this last hour, I know I am right. This isn't an infatuation that will spend itself in six weeks. It isn't a pleasant decision for me to make. The right one seldom is."

He walked over quickly to the silent Sierakowski. "When this fight is over, I'll be the first to find Sheila Matthews and bring her back. She will have earned her happiness."

"If either of them is still alive," Sierakowski said heavily.

"If any of us is still alive. It is everyone's risk." With his short brisk step Olszak crossed the patch of fading sunlight at the doorway. Evening was coming. Night would follow, and with the darkness, Olszak would leave the camp.

Olszak's arranged everything, Sierakowski thought bitterly, everything except Adam Wisniewski. Olszak won't be here to face him when he returns. I'll have to do that. And there will be hell to pay.

The colonel swore softly to himself. The shadows in the room were cold. He moved to the doorway and watched the reddening sky and the trees' dark skeletons. If the Germans hadn't heard the shot, if there were no attack, if this alarm were false, then the camp would settle back here. Adam had planned to leave this week at latest for the Carpathians. Sierakowski was to have been given command of this camp, while Wisniewski made the long preparations for a summer base in the mountains. It would have been pleasant to be in command, here. . . . Sierakowski shook himself free from his thoughts. There was no time now for regrets. Captain Mlicki would make as good a commander as he would: Mlicki had wanted the command as much as he had.

Under the tree, he paused again to listen. No shooting, as yet. No warning signals. Well the camp would know in another twenty-four hours. It would be able to judge better when the boy Stefan got back with any information from the village. Perhaps there had been no Germans near the forest at the time of the shot. Anyway, the camp would know in another twenty-four hours. If the Germans were going to attack, they would strike before then.

Sierakowski looked round him with approval. The men had worked well. The camp had been thoroughly prepared for evacuation. There was a certain sense of pleasure in seeing what had been prepared on paper, against such an emergency as this, suddenly working so smoothly, becoming a fact instead of a series of sentences. His soldier's training approved, even as he silently cursed this blasted dislocation of camp life. He heard the voices coming from the direction of the kitchen. Better find the English girl and persuade her to eat something, too. She would need it.

This was the path he had seen her choose. He entered it quickly as if to make up for these last minutes of hesitation. He was as nervous about meeting her as he was before a skirmish with the Germans.

When he found her, she was lying on the thick bed of leaves round the broad roots of a beech tree, her eyes fixed on the patchwork of sky overhead. She had heard a twig crack under his foot. She rose and came towards him. His nervousness began to disappear when he saw she was quite calm again.

"I think we'd bett—" he began hesitatingly.

"Yes," she said, and walked beside him back to the camp. Olszak's wrong, he thought suddenly. And so was I. She would take any amount of punishment without a whimper or complaint. She's as good a soldier as any man.

He said, "If the Huns don't attack and the camp settles down again, Adam will go to the mountains. All his plans are made. He's been ready to leave for the Carpathians ever since he got back from the raid." And now I know why he postponed it to the last minute, he thought, looking down at her guarded face. "That is where he is going to be this winter," he said.

"I know." She suddenly looked up at him. The brown eyes with their long sweep of lashes veiling them seemed to be saying, "Did you think I was afraid of mountains or cold or hunger or danger? Did you think I'd be afraid of anything, even ultimate capture by the Germans, if I were with him?"

"I am going with him."

"I thought you were to be in command here." The brown eyes were puzzled now, as if searching for the reason behind his decision.

"I am going with him," Sierakowski said, and he saw she had understood why.

The brown eyes softened, and her hand touched his arm for a moment, and she said, "I am glad."

## CHAPTER XXXIII

## The Village of Dwór

IN WARSAW, Volterscot had helped her. Now he helped again. He helped all of them.

The camp had finished its preparations: the surplus food had been eaten, the wounded men and Franziska had gone to wait at the forest's edge, the lodge was once more alive. For tonight, those who had been left in the camp were going to sleep here. Outside, the air had the edge of fine steel. Inside the lodge, the waiting men, closely grouped as if from habit before the unlit fire, were at least sheltered from the wind. Their coats—roughly mended now, but still carrying the dark stains of battle—or blankets neatly folded and belted, were round their shoulders. Their rifles were stacked at the door. Rations were in their pockets. Ammunition. They were ready to move. The feeling of tension slackened as their tired bodies rested, as the food they had eaten and their close grouping warmed them. There was the beginning of talk and laughter, of tall stories, of long discussions over the best routes to reach the mountains, over the best methods of dealing with German patrols. But on the subject of the unnecessary dangers which would face them, if they were forced to move to the mountains before spring, everyone was silent; and by their silence the admission of danger was complete. Volterscot helped all of them. Whenever the voices lagged, whenever an unguarded face became moody or morose, there was always Volterscot. Obligingly and with his delighted good humor, the little dog went through his tricks. And a dark face would lighten, an unexpected laugh would be forced onto grim mouths. Even the tricks that failed brought applause. And Sheila, watching Casimir's pleasure and Volterscot's antics, could sit as quietly as if she were alone in this room.

Jan Reska, equally silent, sat beside her. He had chosen the seat purposely, so purposely that Marian had nudged Antoni and raised her eyebrows with deliberately comic emphasis. But Reska, after the first halting, undecided phrases, had said nothing more. Either he wouldn't, or he couldn't, mention Barbara. And if they talked, they would talk about Barbara. It seemed as though Reska and Sheila each took comfort from the other, just sitting side by side, just saying nothing.

Stefan was asleep on the floor. He had brought back an encouraging report from the village. There were no Germans at the north edge of the forest at the time of the shot: a platoon had passed through there on the day before, but today there had been no Germans. Two of the villagers, out gathering wood, had heard the shot. So had a man who had taken refuge in the village. Jadwiga hadn't sent him on to the camp, because he hadn't known about it, didn't ask for it, didn't give any signs of knowing names or password. ("We are a very exclusive club, you see," Sierakowski had said to Sheila with a smile. "No one becomes a member unless he is proposed and seconded.") The man was still hiding in the village. He was looking for his wife and her young brother, who had gone to the southeast when they

fled from Warsaw. He had traced them to this district. He had
heard the shot and at first had been curious. But when Jadwiga gave him Stefan's explanation, he had accepted it. He
seemed a dull, stupid kind of person. He was too worried,
looking for his wife, to pay much attention to anything
else. That was what Stefan thought after watching him in
the inn kitchen. Anyway, even if the man were still curious
about the shot, he would keep silent. He was a Pole.

Sierakowski had been pleased with Stefan, and his grip on
the boy's shoulder had made Stefan happier. At any rate, the
strained look on Stefan's face had gone. He had eaten the
food Sheila saved for him, had sat on the floor at her feet,
and then the weight of his head had fallen against her
knees, and he was deeply asleep. It was just as well
for him to rest like that until Sierakowski, sitting near the
shadows of the door beyond the small circle of candlelight,
along with the little thin man in rough peasant clothes, gave
the signal for them to leave.

Volterscot abandoned his audience and came over to
Sheila. He still had the same little habit of holding her fingers
gently in his teeth, while he paraded up and down before her
at arm's length. "See," Casimir was saying, "he remembers
you." He watched Sheila's face anxiously; and his wide grin
was fading. "You've never noticed," he challenged. He
couldn't conceal his disappointment.

"We washed him!" Marian called across to Sheila. With
more heartiness than was necessary, she added, "Alone we
did it. Looks a real dog now, doesn't he?" She pretended
she hadn't been watching Sheila's face. She was joking now
with Casimir, drawing the boy back to her and to Antoni,
diverting his embarrassing attention. She had obviously tak-
en a liking to Casimir, and Casimir, with the disarming
confidence of a child, considered Marian already his friend.
Sheila felt a gladness in her heart as she watched his face,
old no longer. He was excited by everyone, by everything.
He was so happy he could scarcely sit still. Here, Sheila
thought, he could begin to live again. Danger or discomfort
didn't matter to him now. Even they seemed fairly wonderful.

Zygmunt rose from the tight circle of men. His limp was
controlled now, as though he were determined to prove his
leg was fit once more. He was coming over to her. Specially. She saw that in his eyes, in the stiff way he held his
usually fluent hands. She saw the group of men behind
him watching him intently as though they were coming over
to speak to her, too. They were a background of shadowy
faces, strong, sad, violent faces. And then Zygmunt, stand-

ing before her, blotted out the watching heads. His voice was very quiet for such a large man.

"Wish I had lost that bet," he began awkwardly. His gaunt face, looking more like a death's-head than ever in the feeble candlelight, lost its hardness. "Don't worry," he said. "The priest went down to be with the body. We'll give him a Christian burial as soon as this alarm's over."

She watched him rejoin his group of friends before she realized he was thinking of the dead Jan. After that, she had a feeling of guilt whenever one of the men looked at her. They were giving her more credit than she deserved; they were thinking she was sitting quietly like this because of Jan. Even Marian thought that. Antoni's friendly, comforting smile proved it.

She glanced at Olszak and Sierakowski, still talking as they waited. They had kept the secret of her leaving. Sheila thought bitterly, tomorrow some will guess why I went away, but none will know the right answer. I will be the English girl who deserted, just as Stefan will be the boy who put his family before his country. She looked at the sleeping boy, at the tired white face and the wild black hair and the large brown eyes hidden by the still eyelids. Sierakowski couldn't have had the heart to tell him. Stefan wouldn't be sleeping so deeply, so peacefully, if he had known he was to leave the camp. We shall be called the deserters, she thought. It wasn't a pleasant idea. Reska had noticed her expression, for suddenly and unexpectedly he began to talk of his journey with Casimir. They had left Warsaw secretly and traveled some fifty miles southeast to Nowe Miasto. There they had met Madame Aleksander, who had made a less direct journey. After the Nazis had questioned her in Warsaw, she had been released. Surprisingly, there was no more interference. The Germans even gave her the necessary permission to leave the city for Cracow, where she wanted to see some relatives. She had traveled quite openly, third class of course, as all Poles had to do now, by a local train as far south as Radom, with the dog in her arms. She wasn't going to abandon him in Warsaw. Then she had left the train quietly at Radom, where a "friend" waited for her. She had then traveled back the thirty-odd miles northwest to meet Casimir and Reska, walking, riding in farmcarts, guided by a succession of "friends." She and the dog had arrived at Nowe Miasto just before Olszak appeared. Olszak had been as angry about the dog as Casimir had been delighted.

Then they had made their way towards the forest. It had been a journey much like Sheila's—the same pattern of effort and pretense and exhaustion. Near the small village of

Dwór, Madame Aleksander's strength had suddenly given out. They had left her there, at the little village inn, with Dwór's Jadwiga keeping a close watch over her. "Madame Aleksander's an extraordinary woman," Reska finished. "Yet I used to be pretty scornful about her. Lady Bountiful, I used to call her. Then I saw her as a nurse when I was in hospital. Either people were different in times of peace, or we were all blind to one another's possibilities." He was silent for a moment. "Take Wisniewski, for instance—" He broke off suddenly. Perhaps he had remembered some camp gossip. Perhaps Sheila's face was too polite.

She said, "In times of peace.... What was peace anyway but a state of being left alone to use our own energies in our own way? Probably that was its weakness as well as its charm. We didn't all choose to use our energies in unselfish, impersonal ways. People weren't really different in peacetime. Now, it is only the different ways in which they use their energies that make them seem changed."

Reska nodded. He leaned his square-shaped chin on the strong hand with its red mouth of a wound scarring up into the frayed cuff of his army tunic. "The problem is to keep people using their natural energy in the right direction in times of peace, when there is no compulsion to use it in any direction except in their own way. The compulsion in war is one's country. In peace it should be the State."

"A confession of failure," a man beside Reska said unexpectedly. "When one's country, or the State, arranges what the individual citizen can't or won't do for himself, then it's a confession of moral bankruptcy. Totalitarianism is an admission that the individual must be regulated and conditioned to be a good citizen. And that's a confession of failure on the part of the citizens. They should be able to do it for themselves, without the State stepping in."

"But there isn't a country in the world that has such citizens."

"No, but when a country has such citizens, we shall at last see the perfect state. How to produce them? Education. Have teachers who are truly wise as well as clever, teachers who know all politics, possess no party beliefs, know and respect all great religions...."

The man's voice continued, but Sheila's eyes were on Sierakowski. He had been looking constantly at his watch. She felt his tension. Now he was rising to his feet. Now he was coming over towards Sheila and Stefan. Well, this was it, at last.

Sheila bent down and wakened Stefan gently. The boy was still yawning when Sierakowski stood before them. Looking up at the thin worried face, Sheila suddenly felt sorry for him. He wasn't enjoying this, either. He was saying "Stefan, you are to go down and meet your mother at Dwór. That's where she is now. Miss Matthews will go too."

Stefan looked startled. "Dwór?" he asked. "Why, I was only seven miles from there this afternoon." And then he was following the colonel out of the lodge with his questions. His mother, was she all right, when did she come, why hadn't she finished the journey to the camp . . . ? Olszak had already disappeared. Zygmunt was walking to the door. Surely Zygmunt wasn't going to be their guide down through the forest? Sheila, remembering his attempt to walk naturally, remembering his determination to visit Dwór, almost smiled. Suddenly she wanted to laugh. Hysterical, that's what you are, she told herself angrily. She touched Reska's arm—Reska still enlarging on education and a teacher's qualifications—and said, "I have to go too. Madame Aleksander." Reska interrupted himself to look at her with surprise. Perhaps her explanations didn't ring so very true, perhaps he was wondering why her lips were smiling while her eyes were all blurred with tears. She couldn't see the others very clearly either, now. She walked quickly away. Here it was, at last.

Sierakowski waited for her at the door. "Zygmunt takes you as far as Dwór," he said quietly. "Olszak will then travel on to Warsaw while you and Stefan and Madame Aleksander will be taken towards Cracow by easy stages. Outside Cracow you will be given your papers and suitable clothes. You will then find the journey easier. In three weeks' time you will be in Switzerland."

He followed her outside. The door was closed on Reska, on Marian, on Volterscot and Casimir, on all the friendly faces whose names she hadn't learned to pronounce, yet.

"Zygmunt's leg—" she began, to end the awkward silence.

"He can walk. If the Germans attack, he might not manage a running fight. He's safer in the village for a couple of nights. Anyway, he's the one man here who knows every blade of grass on the way to Dwór."

Sierakowski pushed a small revolver into her hand. "There are two schools of thought about this. Personally, I never go unarmed. You can always get rid of this in an emergency. It's reliable for twenty yards, anyway. Six bullets."

Sheila slipped the gun inside her blouse, tightened the skirt band over it to hold it firm. Its cold weight at her waist reassured her. It was extraordinary how one small weapon gave you so much comfort. It was extraordinary how at this

moment six bullets sounded so much more reassuring than
Switzerland.

"Take no risks," Sierakowski said. "We shall hear when you
reach safety. I'll depend on you for that news."

Sheila pulled the heavy coarse black shawl more tightly
round her shoulders. The night wind cut through the kerchief
over her head. They were two pale ghosts walking under the
moon's blue light towards the forest path. She was still unable to give that last message. The wind, or something, had
frozen her tongue.

*"Dowidzenia!"* Sierakowski lifted her cold hand and kissed
it.

"Good-by." She hesitated.

She said, with painful inadequacy, "Take care of him.
Please."

"Yes," Sierakowski said. She saw him smile. "Any other
message?" he asked gently.

His eyes were on her face, as though they were photo-
graphing not its clearly molded lines, not its smooth softness,
but its intensity and honesty. Her face gave the message
which her voice couldn't.

"I'll tell him," he said slowly. He let her hand drop, and
she was walking quickly towards the beginning of the forest
path. She turned around once, just as she reached it. Sierakowski saluted her. He had forgotten the others until he heard
Zygmunt say in amazement *"Psia krew!* Is she coming too?"
and Olszak say, not unkindly, "We must hurry now," and
Stefan say in a hurt bewildered voice "Sheila, we aren't
coming back. Did you know?" And then there was only the
vast silence of the forest and the repeated coughing of the
sentry outside the lodge.

Sierakowski walked towards the empty hospital hut. No
alarm yet. The Germans couldn't have heard the shot. The
boy Stefan's report was probably true. He would know
definitely when the two scouts he had sent down to the other
near-by village returned to confirm it. Tomorrow night the
rest of the men would be back here. Wisniewski would be
the last to come in.

*"Do stu djablów,"* he said with sudden vehemence, and
ground out his half-finished cigarette.

Olszak and Zygmunt were in front. Sheila followed with
Stefan. The dark forest closed round them. Bright stars
pierced the bared branches above them. Last night they had
laughed with her like the warm flames of Christmas candles.
Now they were cold and impersonal. Last night the forest

had been a magic place of warmth and life. Now its black-ness was a pit of despair.

Zygmunt's injured leg kept the pace steady and even, seem-ingly slow. But his knowledge of the path and its short cuts brought them to the forest's edge without loss of time. In three hours they reached the plains. The last trees were be-hind them, the last outpost, the last bird-cries which signaled their going. The wind was stronger, the air colder, the moon-light clearer. Now they walked Indian file, some distance apart, obeying their guide. Zygmunt's knowledge of the most sheltered path to the village made the journey simple. He used every haystack, each tree, each windbreak, cunningly, skillfully. He brought them eastwards round the village, to-wards its north side.

There, in the deep shadows of a wooden barn, with the sharp, frosted stubble cutting at their feet, he left them and entered the village from the north. He seemed to be part of the night, so difficult it was to follow his progress. Olszak, Stefan, and Sheila waited in silence. They waited unmoving, as though they were carved out of the rough wood against which they leaned. Only their eyes were alive, watching the sleeping village.

"No Germans," Zygmunt whispered. He had come back from another direction, so that Sheila, startled, bit her lip and stifled a cry. Olszak looked pleased, as much at Zgy-munt's skill as at the good news.

"This is where we leave our weapons, in case we are surprised and searched in the village. Rule of the camp," Zygmunt whispered. He was watching Sheila's hand, which had traveled so quickly to her waist when she had bitten off that beginning of a scream. She relaxed her grip, but kept her hand at her waist, and hoped it looked like a natural gesture.

"No weapons," Olszak said. Two schools of thought: here was the other of them, Sheila reflected. She made no move.

"All right." Zygmunt's tone was brusque. Either he had no idea of Olszak's importance, or he didn't care. Probably both facts were equally true: Zygmunt wouldn't care even if he did know. "The girl goes with me. You two will follow. You know the inn."

Olszak nodded.

"Give us a hundred yards' start," Zygmunt said. He was still watching Sheila's hand resting at her waist. But he said nothing more as he led her towards the village.

There weren't more than twenty houses, squat and lumpish, although it was difficult to count the number, so haphazardly were they grouped together. Large, age-twisted trees, isolated remnants of the primitive forest that had once covered all this land, sheltered the sides of the cottages, or spread over the scattered barns and straw covered root-houses. In daylight, Dwór might have the charm of disarray ("a pig's breakfast" Uncle Matthews would have said), but by night it was bewildering. Bewildering, but safe. Sheila felt more confident as she followed Zygmunt's tortuous course. It was almost midnight now. The villagers were probably abed: certainly no lights showed.

Zygmunt saved her in time from the cold water of a communal duck-pond, guided her across the narrow stone causeway of a lurking stream. They had reached the center of Dwór, a little open space too small to be called a village square. At one side was the tiny wooden church sheltering its cupola and cross under the protecting branches of its trees. At the other, was the squat gable-end of a house and the beginning of a narrow road, its ruts of mud now crusted by frost. The road wandered westward. It was Dwór's one link with the world outside.

They paused under the church's covered gateway. Then, following the trees round the open space, they reached the gable-end house. The inn. A very glorified title, thought Sheila. Or did people once stay here on hunting trips in the forests? Now it seemed as dead as the other village houses.

But she was mistaken. Someone had been waiting for them. The door at the left of the gable opened slowly and quietly. Quietly and slowly it closed behind them. "Careful," a woman's voice whispered.

They were standing in a dark, narrow hall, running the whole length of the house, like a corridor in a train with the rooms as its compartments. The blackness at first numbed Sheila's eyes, and then, as the woman began to move silently towards a panel of light near the end of the corridor, Sheila could distinguish the deep shadows which were the recesses of other doors. Five, she counted; four solidly closed. Through the nearest one, the one almost opposite the entrance to the house, she could now hear a murmur of voices. A laugh added itself to the murmur, so suddenly that her grasp tightened on Zygmunt's arm and her body stiffened. He patted her shoulder gently. She followed the woman. The floor was either stone or hard-packed earth, for there were no creaking wooden boards to betray them. Zygmunt had a wonderful bedside manner, she was thinking as they stepped into the panel of light: the right mixture of domination and reassurance. The woman—she was young, Sheila now saw, with a round pleasant face and a strong body—closed the door behind them, and they were in a small room.

How warm it was, Sheila thought, although the small wood stove now gave little heat from its low night fire. And how bright! It seemed a long time since she had seen a room as small as this one lit by a lamp.

Madame Aleksander had risen from the bench beside the stove. She looked smaller, somehow, and thinner. Her hair was completely white. But there was still that strange blue light in her eyes.

"Sheila!" she said in surprise and then in delight. "I didn't know you were coming to meet me." She was watching Sheila's face closely. "Something's wrong," she added quietly. "Something's happened to Stefan."

"No," Sheila said quickly. "No. Not Stefan. He's all right. He will be here any moment." She looked towards the girl who had waited for them at the door. Zygmunt had her firmly round the waist, and her feet were dangling. She was scolding him for being late, and he was interrupting each phrase with a well-placed kiss. He set her down on her feet again.

"Two more, milady," he said to her. "That old fellow who was here last night, and a boy. Quick." He helped her out of the room with a neatly timed smack with the palm of his hand. As he came over to the stove, there was a wide happy grin all over his ugly face. The three of them sat down on the bench and looked at the half-open door. They hadn't to wait long. Out of the corridor's shadows the girl's smiling face appeared, still flushed and happy, then the more somber countenance of Olszak, and last of all, Stefan.

The door was safely closed. Mr. Olszak and Sheila had drifted together naturally, as if driven by the emotion they felt all round them. He watched Madame Aleksander and Stefan with a strange sadness, and then looked at Zygmunt and the girl with almost a smile. "Yes?" he asked Sheila, so suddenly that she said what she had been thinking.

"I'll never know what you really feel, Mr. Olszak."

He took her hand, gently. "That's just as well," he said. "Do you still hate me as much as you did this afternoon?"

"I believe I don't," she said with some surprise at her own calm voice; "I think you meant well."

Mr. Olszak grimaced and dropped her hand. "That's the most damning praise of all," he replied. "But, like most clichés, it is true." He watched her again. "After all," he went on, "you've been a big personal responsibility, you know. Your father would have expected me to do as I've done. And he would have expected you to do as you have done, too. It is strange how much you resemble him, in every way. He had a great capacity for self-sacrifice."

And that, thought Sheila miserably, makes me seem willfully selfish if I ask Mr. Olszak to change his decision. The request had been on the tip of her tongue. She looked at him and began to laugh.

"No, no. Not that. Please." Mr. Olszak really looked unhappy. He turned to the astonished Zygmunt and his girl.

"Now, before I leave," Mr. Olszak was saying, "where's your mother? Any Germans appear?"

"No Germans," the girl replied. "My mother's in the front room. She's with Zak and Peter and a stranger."

"Another recruit?" said Zygmunt. "Fine, bring them all along." But the girl didn't share his lightheartedness.

"He doesn't know anything about the camp. He wasn't sent here by any of our friends. But he was asking about the forest. My mother got Zak and Peter to give him some drinks in the front room. She's just making sure of his story."

"How does that stand up?"

"It's true, I think. I feel sorry for him. He's had a pretty hard time of it."

"What about me, Kati? Haven't I had a hard time of it?" Zygmunt clipped her broad waist expertly.

Kati laughed and pushed him away.

"That's right, Kati," said Olszak with an unexpected smile. "Business before pleasure. Have you someone here to take these people to Nowe Miasto?"

"Peter," said the girl; "but he's in the bar, too."

Olszak consulted a cheap battered-looking watch tucked into a disreputable waistcoat pocket. "I don't want to leave until I see them begin their journey," he said, as if to himself. "But I may have to." He bit his lip. "Damn the man for coming at this time. Tomorrow night he could have drunk Peter under the table for all I care."

Madame Aleksander said slowly, "Michal ... What is all this? What journey? The forest isn't far away."

"We aren't going there," said Stefan. His mouth was a straight line. His large dark eyes were angry, mutinous.

Madame Aleksander sat down once more. "Just what are we doing, Michal?"

Olszak walked over to her. He was sitting beside her, talking quickly in his low precise voice. Yet, to Sheila watching them, there was a softening of the hard lines of his face, an earnestness mixed with gentleness that revealed more about the man than she had ever guessed. There was only one person to whom Olszak was vulnerable. That was Madame Aleksander. "I've known him for years," she had once said.

She had concealed a lot in that simple understatement: she wasn't the kind of woman to flaunt her past conquests. Watching them, Sheila realized the incredible: Olszak had once been in love. He had lost. Madame Aleksander had chosen to forget about it. But he was always aware that she had never reminded him of his defeat, and her power had increased instead of diminishing. Even now, she was unaware of it, and Olszak had to fight twice as hard because of that. Sheila, watching them, was suddenly hopeful.

"No, Michal. Really no. I will not leave Poland. If I die, I die here." Madame Aleksander turned to Stefan. "And would you have me take him away to safety, to a country where he could be separated from all the other boys of his age? Where he would grow apart, and come back to find himself out of touch with them, even an intruder? He cannot share honorably in the peace if he hasn't suffered equally in the war. Can he?"

Stefan's reply was to give his mother a wild embrace. Madame Aleksander tried to free herself from his arms. She still had something to say, and it was difficult. It wasn't only Stefan's bearlike hug that made her words halting, breathless.

"And I must be here, so that little Teresa or Marta or Andrew will find me here if they escape. They would need me. So I shall stay. And Stefan stays. As for Sheila—" Madame Aleksander was in control of her voice again—"as for Sheila, perhaps she ought to go. There's her uncle, for one thing. For another, this isn't her country, and she's done more for us already than we had any right to expect."

Sheila's hope was gone once more. "There are no countries any more," she said slowly. "Just people. People who are on your side, or people who are against you."

"But, Sheila, why don't you take this chance of going away? You have friends who are waiting for you, who want to see you. Your uncle." And then, hesitatingly, shyly, "And there's Mr. Stevens."

"Yes," Sheila said. So Olszak hadn't told Madame Aleksander about Adam Wisniewski. She looked at him bitterly. He pretended to be examining his watch.

"Every time you women change your minds," he said irritably, "I lose an hour."

"But I haven't changed my mind, Michal," Madame Aleksander protested. "I always meant to stay here."

"Then you intend . . . ?"

"To go to the camp, help with the nursing and cooking and sewing and mending and weaving and cleaning." She turned to Zygmunt. "You can take us back when you return, can't you?"

Zygmunt looked at Sheila. "Her too?" he said, with a wide approving grin spreading over his face.

"No," Mr. Olszak said firmly. "Peter will take her to Nowe Miasto. From there she will go to Radom by the way Madame Aleksander came. At Radom she will be hidden until her papers and clothes and story are all ready."

Madame Aleksander was still watching Zygmunt's face. Then she looked quickly at Sheila.

"I seem to have misunderstood something," she said. Then very quietly, "Michal, did you tell me everything?"

Olszak said rapidly, "There's hardly time now. When I visit the camp again, I can tell you all the details. The important thing now is to find that Peter."

Kati said, "I'll get him out somehow. Come on, Zygmunt, you can take his place in the front room. Better knock at the door as if you'd just come in. I'll be there to welcome you. You're my young man over here on a visit from Opoczno."

"That's right. I'm your young man," said Zygmunt.

She looked at his laughing eyes and evaded his arm. "None of that in the corridor," she warned. "Not until you've knocked at the front door, and I've let you in." They left the door half open. Kati waited there until Zygmunt had reached the front entrance and given a cautious knock. Then they heard her footsteps walking along the corridor.

"Clever girl" said Olszak approvingly. "How did Zygmunt let her know that we had arrived?"

"By the window. He knocked there gently. I didn't even hear it. But she did. She had been expecting him all evening. She put out the light and opened the shutters. They talked in whispers. Then he went away. And she waited in the corridor. It sounds simple now, but it really was quite a strain. For me, anyway. Kati doesn't seem to worry. She has no nerves at all. And no fears."

Mr. Olszak put a finger to his lips, went over to the door to close it gently. He paused. For the front door had been opened by Kati. Her voice was welcoming. There was a smothered laugh, a stifled squeal. Zygmunt was going into action. A man who must have come out into the corridor from the front room said boisterously, "Well, who's this? All safe? No Germans? Thought I'd better make sure."

Kati was explaining now.

The voice said, "Come in, come in and have a drink. Come on, fellow. You'll need it if you've been doing any traveling. What's the news?"

Other voices, more distant, more blurred, said, "Come on, Zygmunt."

Zygmunt was saying, "Never refuse a drink or a pretty girl." There was laughter. Then the voices, the laughter, the sound of footsteps were shut inside the front room. In the corridor, there was silence, darkness. All that remained was the mixed smell of pinewood and boiled cabbage.

Mr. Olszak finished closing the door. "That wasn't Peter who spoke," he said. "Was it Zak?"

Madame Aleksander said, "No; it must be the stranger. He sounded cheery. I'm glad. His story is so sad."

"You've met him?"

"Oh no. I've been kept in here. He only came this evening. But Kati heard it and she told me. He's lost his wife and her young brother. They were refugees. He can't find either of them."

"That's the man I met this morning," said Stefan. "He was in Zorawno then."

Olszak was watching Sheila. "Yes?" he asked.

She shook her head. The rough voice from the corridor had been familiar: a note, an inflection . . . Something so vague, so distant . . . yet faintly disturbing. She shook her head again. "Nothing definite," she said. "Just . . ."

She sat down on a bench and imagined the voice once more. *Come in and have a drink. Come on . . . What's the news?* The harder she tried to catch it, the further it slipped away. She looked up at the observant Olszak. "Nothing," she said. "Just a very faint imagination."

"Which was he?" Olszak said. "Anxious or curious?"

The two women and the boy looked at him in perplexity. Madame Aleksander said, "You don't trust this man?"

Olszak sat down on a bench. "Until I find out more about him, I shall have to stay here." He looked sharply at Madame Aleksander. "You were followed as far as Radom after you left Warsaw." She looked so amazed that he smiled. "Why else do you think the Germans gave you such quick permission to leave Warsaw, after questioning you? But we took great care you wouldn't be followed from Radom to this district. The only thing is the dog. He could easily have given you away. That was why I was angry about the dog, Teresa."

Madame Aleksander looked crushed. "Casimir was so happy to see him. Besides, I couldn't abandon him in Warsaw again. I couldn't do that, not even to a dog." Then her voice brightened. "But he was hidden for most of the journey from Radom to here. Inside bundles, inside jackets, covered with rags on the bottom of carts. He wasn't allowed to run along after us. Your men saw to that."

"You are positive no one saw him?"

"Only the people with whom I stayed. And you trust *them*."

"Yes. Then the Pole who is looking for his wife and brother-in-law may be looking for his wife and brother-in-law after all. Perhaps—" he silenced them with his hand. The front room door had opened, then the entrance door.

"Someone's going out," Olszak said. Other footsteps were running lightly along the hall. Kati entered, and held the door open for a man.

"Here's Peter," she said. "Zygmunt is taking the man out for—" she glanced at Madame Aleksander—"for a walk. He's showing him the barn where he can sleep tonight. They'll be back soon."

She was gone, leaving Peter, tall, red-faced, blue-eyed, waiting for Olszak to speak. He shuffled his feet in their clumsy high boots, rubbed his square chin with a very large, very red hand, and then scratched his wrinkled brow uncertainly. The straight straw-colored hair bristled like a haystack. On the broad face was a fluctuating smile. Peter swayed a little, the smile vanished, and then reappeared. He walked towards the bench with a slight list and rather too much determination. His audience looked at each other in dismay. Olszak said coldly, as the bench grunted beneath Peter's sudden weight, "Peter, I'm afraid you're drunk."

Peter shook his head. "Not drunk," he said. "Other fellow's drunk. Not Peter. Not drunk. Just tired."

"Then I hope he's drunker than you are."

Peter looked so shamefaced that Sheila wanted to laugh.

"Then what did you find out about him?" Olszak went on. "Or can't you tell us?"

Peter wiped his face with his hand as though to drive away sleep from his eyes. "Nothing. He's looking for his wife and her kid brother. That's all."

"Didn't he talk?"

"Plague on it, didn't he talk? He talked us all under the table."

Olszak continued his questioning. Peter, making an effort, concentrated. And he achieved something. The answers were slow, but conclusive. The man was looking for his wife. Once he had asked about the forest: was there good hunting there? Mostly they had talked about the war, about what the future held for them. Zak had asked him what he was going to do: was he going to fight on? The man—Ryng was his name, yes, that was it, Ryng—had said he was going to find his wife first. After that, he'd know what to do.

Even Olszak was satisfied. "He didn't ask about a white dog, did he?"

Peter looked surprised. "No," he said very decidedly. "No, No dog."

Olszak was pacing the small patch of floor. "Well," he said at last, to Madame Aleksander, "this man Ryng isn't interested in either you or the camp. That's one good thing." He turned to Sheila. "But I'm afraid I chose an unlucky night for your guide. You will have to wait until tomorrow night before you leave. When Zygmunt takes Madame Aleksander and Stefan back to the forest, then you will go with Peter. He should be fit, by that time." Olszak gave Peter a bitter look and received an apologetic grin in return.

"I'll be all right. Just tired. Sleep," said Peter. He curled himself comfortably if somewhat precariously onto the bench, pillowing his cheek on his arm.

"Not in here," said Olszak, and with unexpected strength he pulled the half-sleeping man towards the door. "Sleep it off in the front room," he said with a final push on the man's shoulder which sent him lumbering down the hall. "Fool," he added.

"You forget men aren't trains. They can't be made to run on time, Michal," said Madame Aleksander. He didn't answer. He stood at the door, listening.

Kati was helping Peter into the front room. And Zygmunt and Ryng were re-entering the house. Olszak waited until the babel of sound in the corridor had ended before he left the door. He was looking at his watch again.

"This is really most regrettable," he said. He went over to Sheila unexpectedly. "I would take you to Nowe Miasto myself. But by tomorrow night I have to be near Warsaw. There's a meeting which I must attend. I simply cannot come with you."

"I'll go with Peter tomorrow. It will be safe enough then. We'll take care." Mr. Olszak was watching her, measuring her lifeless face and the quiet voice. She would do as she had said.

"Good. Remember, after Radom the journey will be pleasanter."

"Where do I go from there?" Again that quiet acceptance. He felt angry with himself. His voice was all the colder.

"To Cracow. Then to Vienna. By train. Your story and papers will reach you at Radom, where you will be hidden until they arrive. In three weeks' time you should be—" He paused. He took her hand. "You must take care. You have suddenly become twice the responsibility you once were. I will be held doubly answerable for you now." His eyes were half-laughing, half-serious. For the first time since she had known him, Mr. Olszak seemed completely human.

Sheila smiled back. I don't know why I like you at all, she was thinking. I should hate you; and yet I cannot. I don't know why I should smile for you, except that I know you want me to. She said, "Yes."

He kissed her hand, and quickly turned away. "Trust is the most powerful flattery," he was saying in a low voice to Madame Aleksander. "She weakens my resolution, that girl."

"Michal, what have you been doing?" Madame Aleksander challenged him.

"Playing the thankless role of father," he answered.

Together they looked at Sheila. But the girl wasn't listening to them. She had walked over to the high bed which stood in the corner of the room. She was standing before the little shelf beside it, with its two small candles under the carved figure on its cross. She was watching the hollow cheeks, the deep eyes, with a strangely curious detachment.

"What is it, Sheila?" Madame Aleksander asked at last. Sheila turned to face her slowly. Then she became alive, as she noticed the room again. Olszak had left.

"He's gone?" she said quickly. And no reprieve. No last-minute reprieve. The last faint hope flickered and died.

"Come here, Sheila." Madame Aleksander took her hand and led her to the bench. "Now the simplest thing is to begin at the beginning."

But Kati had come back to the room. Her round pink face looked as if she were going to cry.

"Peter's dead asleep," she announced vehemently. "And Zygmunt's getting louder and louder. Everything's going wrong."

"Provided Zygmunt doesn't talk about the camp . . ." Sheila began.

"He's not doing that. He and Ryng was just telling stories."

And Kati is temporarily forgotten, Sheila thought. She said, "Peter passed out very suddenly. Does he always do that?"

"Usually he's careful, when he knows there's a job to do. It must have been that last drink Ryng dared him to take. He said it was dynamite. Peter didn't believe him."

"But it was?" Sheila felt suddenly very wide awake. "Ryng gave him a drink? How? I thought you were serving Ryng drinks."

"Ryng had a flask of his own."

"Oh." Sheila exchanged glances with Madame Aleksander. "Kati, you'd better get back to that room and watch that flask."

Kati looked at them. "Why can't I have just one quiet evening nowadays, with my sewing?" she asked plaintively. "Just one?" Only Stefan didn't understand.

Madame Aleksander watched the closing door. "The Germans have taken our food, but they let us have plenty of cheap drink. They've taken away our guns, but they let us carry flasks," she said bitterly. Then she noticed Stefan's heavy head and sagging shoulders. From the bed she lifted one of the solid pillows, straightened his body on the hard floor, cushioned his cheek. She pushed back the thick black hair from his brow, and kissed him gently. He was already asleep.

She rose to her feet, her hands straightening the mended skirt, the darned shawl, smoothing the white softness of her hair. She looked round the strange room.

"How lucky I am," Madame Aleksander said. "I still have Stefan and Stanislaw." She paused before the crucifix. "The Lord giveth and the Lord hath taken away. Blessed be His Holy name," she said quietly. She crossed herself slowly.

She came towards Sheila, tears for the first time in her blue eyes. She clasped the girl suddenly, and Sheila felt all her self-imposed barriers dissolving like the gray-edged ice of a glacier.

"Now," said Madame Aleksander, putting aside her own worries and troubles, "we'll begin at the beginning."

## CHAPTER XXXIV

### The Stranger

MADAME ALEKSANDER was asleep. Sheila raised herself slowly, carefully. She lifted Madame Aleksander's hand gently away from her arm, and slipped her feet over the edge of the high bed. The warmth of the room was stifling her. After the forest, the small room seemed overfurnished, overheated. Its small comforts irritated her. She opened the shutters more widely. Outside, there was silence, the gray shapes of trees, and houses, air which was crisp and cold and clean. She thought of the forest and the men who waited there.

Her feet began to freeze. She turned back to the bed and

searched for her shoes. She watched Madame Aleksander for a moment. The calm, gentle voice still haunted her. "Don't leave him without seeing him first, Sheila." Sheila's mouth was in a tight, unpleasant line as she buttoned the instep strap of one shoe. "He isn't a regular soldier any more. His fighting isn't governed by rules." Sheila forced the other hard round button through its tight hole. "Michal doesn't know him as I do. He lived beside us, often with us. I knew him as a child and a boy so I know him better as a man than all the Michals in the world." Sheila lifted the gun from under the pillow and secured it once more under her blouse. She reached for the shawl lying on the bench. "If he believes Michal is right, he will accept this. If he doesn't, he will become morose, bitter, sullen. He will take wild chances." Sheila walked over to the stove. Stefan's head had slipped off the pillow onto the floor. She eased the boy's strained neck back onto the pillow, tried to straighten the wrinkled blanket with which his mother had covered him last night when he had fallen asleep on the floor. "Adam's greatest asset was his directness. He was always honest with himself. He never pretended, never compromised. Michal has been too quick to decide." The ashes inside the stove's little door seemed dead, and yet when the fresh wood was added, their heat would kindle flame. She wanted to laugh at her weak symbolism. It was the result of five o'cock in the morning, no sleep, and a gentle voice telling her the things which made her still more unhappy.

She walked to the door. The restlessness which hadn't let her sleep, which had made it impossible to lie on that bed, now urged her on. Behind her, the still figures didn't move. She stepped quickly into the corridor, closed the door carefully so that the latch slipping into position would not awaken them. In the long hall's darkness, she felt her way with her hands pressed against the rough wall. There was heavy snoring from one of the closed doors which she passed. The smell of sour cabbage seemed stronger. Still the haunting voice said sadly, "Sheila, you were too honest to please me by marrying Andrew. You were too honest to go away with Steve on false pretense. Keep that honesty. It's the only thing that matters. Don't do what you think is noble or clever. Do what you know is right." In the front room, the half-opened door showed Peter and another man asleep over the large wooden table. The light was too dim—the shutter had been opened, but the sun had not yet risen—to let her see the other man clearly. Perhaps it was the man Ryng. No, he was going to sleep in the barn. It was probably the villager Zak, who had never got home to his own bed after last night's celebrations. It didn't matter, anyway. Everyone was alseep.

She opened the door of the house carefully, after fumbling for some time to find how its catch worked. The dim light from the front room helped her solve that problem. The quiet village greeted her, as she closed the door equally carefully behind her. She might have one half hour of peace before the smoke from the chimneys thickened, the window shutters were opened, and the people started another day of work and worry. She moved towards the back of the house. It seemed more sheltered. There, in this mixture of garden and field, she could walk and think. The hedge of bushes, now stripped of fruit and leaves, would protect her not only from the early morning wind which froze the dewdrops on the the thin brown branches, but from other houses. She wanted no eyes to invade her loneliness.

She halted beside one of the larger trees. Over the inn and its side building, over the rest of the village, over the forest two miles to the south, was nothing but silence. In spite of the dreary light, half night, half dawn, she felt suddenly happy. The forest was still safe. Surely if the Germans had heard that shot, there would have been at least a patrol out by this time. Surely the forest and its secret were safe. Perhaps it was the need for this reassurance which had brought her out of door. Certainly, she felt calm again.

She pulled the shawl more closely round her shoulders. She was thinking more clearly, now. By the end of ten minutes, she had given herself an answer. Both Mr. Olszak and Madame Aleksander were wrong. One had made the decision for her; the other wanted her to make the decision for Adam Wisniewski. And both were wrong. Adam alone could decide. He knew what he had to do, how best he could do it. The decision was his. And the tragedy was that she would be gone from this village before he knew there was a decision to make. It wasn't even real tragedy—death would have been that—it was merely frustration. And then she thought, what if Adam knew there was a decision to make, what if he had decided even before Olszak had come to the camp? What if he had been deciding all these last days, while he had watched her and she had avoided him? Then the frustration would be twice as bitter.

A movement from the door of the barn as it opened caught her attention. Weeks of caution make her shrink naturally back against the tree. It was probably the man Ryng, but it was just as well that he shouldn't see her. The less anyone knew about Jadwiga's guests, the better. She had drawn too far back against the tree to be able to see the barn doorway clearly: all she had seen for a moment was a man, his head turned away from her as he looked at the silent houses. Perhaps he had decided to leave. Perhaps he was restless as she had been. Those who traveled secretly would always be restless, always worrying about what was happening outside the house that sheltered them. She waited for a minute, and then looked again. The barn door was was closed. No one was in sight. She felt a sudden pity for the lonely figure she had seen. Had he begun to realize his search was hopeless, and yet he didn't want to admit it?

She shivered, and realized she was chilled. She left the tree and went back quickly to the house. The village would soon be stirring. Perhaps Madame Aleksander had awakened and was anxious.

Quickly she entered the inn and shut the door carefully behind her. She was left in complete darkness. That warned her. Someone had closed the door of the front room and its shaft of weak light into the hall was gone. That, and a sudden feeling of fear, warned her. She drew back against the wall and waited, staring along the blackness of the corridor. The house seemed still asleep. She moved one foot forward cautiously, stretched out a hand to guide her along the wall. She heard a movement, as careful as her own, and she froze. Someone was beside her, touching. A man's hand blundered along her outstretched arm and then gripped it. For a moment they stood facing each other in the darkness.

"Who is it?" the man asked quietly. "Who is it?" he repeated. It wasn't Zygmunt or Peter. It was the voice of the man Ryng. Last night, she had thought the voice was familiar. Now she knew that it was. But whose voice, whose voice? She said nothing. The grip on her arm, the hand reaching towards her head warned her. Here was danger, she told herself. Here was danger. He was forcing her towards the door. He was going to open it, he was going to see her clearly. He was trying to feel the shape of her head, of her face. The large hand touched her straining cheek, brushed against her mouth. She bit savagely, heard him curse, wrenched the other arm free as she struck sharply with the heel of her fist against his wrist. She ran along the corridor. His footsteps hesitated. One of the room doors was thrown open, and Kati was there, half-dressed, her fingers weaving the plait of hair which fell over her shoulder.

"What's going on here?" she demanded loudly. She looked at the desperation in Sheila's face, and then stepped into the hall, placing her body between Sheila and Ryng, who still hesitated near the main entrance.

"Came to see if it was time for breakfast," Ryng said.

"Found someone sneaking about. Thought it was a spy."

"It isn't time for breakfast. And that's my cousin Magda who comes to help clean the bar every morning. What did you do to her?"

"Nothing. She bit my hand."

"She doesn't like men, scared of them. You shouldn't have put a finger on her." Then Kati called over her shoulder gently. "It's all right, Magda. Don't worry. He won't hurt you."

Sheila stood quite still. She wished she could turn round and see the man's face, but she daren't risk that. Perhaps he might be able to see her more clearly than she thought. So she stood still, and leaned against the wall with her head bowed, and was a terrified Magda. Actually, she wasn't unterrified.

Kati's voice was abrupt. "Get back to the barn. I'll bring you something to eat when it's ready—what there is of it. Lucky for you that Magda wasn't a spy."

To Sheila, she said crossly, "Don't be a fool, Magda. Men don't eat you."

The front door closed behind Ryng's slow footsteps. Sheila turned to face Kati at last. The girl finished plaiting her hair and said softly, as she coiled the braids round her head, "Hope he believed me."

Sheila nodded. Her heart was still beating too insistently. There was sweat on her brow.

"Better get back to your room. You are shivering with cold. I'll come and show you how to feed the fire." Kati, still in her striped petticoat and white linen chemise with its pink ribbon slotted through the embroidered lace round its wide neckline, took Sheila's arm and led her towards the end of the corridor.

"Orders are that no stranger is to learn about visitors from the camp. That's why I had to make up that story. But what did he do to you?"

"Just tried to see who I was." Sheila shivered. "I hate people pawing me," she said fiercely.

"What? Everyone?" Kati asked with mock belief.

Sheila smiled, too. "Now I begin to feel I behaved like a fool. I should have answered him when he asked who I was. I should have made up a story like yours. Then there would have been no fuss. And yet, somehow I couldn't answer him. I really was quite dumb with fear. Kati, I've met that man . . . Part of me recognized him in the darkness, but the rest of me isn't clever enough . . ."

Kati was looking at her with mild tolerance. Zygmunt had told her about this girl. She was the Chief's girl. She was leaving him for no reason Zygmunt or Kati could guess. Sometimes that turned a girl's brain, sometimes that ...

"What's wrong now?" she asked patiently.

"The door of our room. I shut it firmly this morning."

"Well, it isn't shut properly now." It certainly wasn't. The slight draught from the window had been sufficient to draw the door, improperly closed, a long inch away from its frame. "The old lady has been up looking for you," Kati suggested, and then watched Sheila closing the door once more, testing the hasp. She shut it the way she had closed it this morning, cautiously, slowly. The door stayed firm.

"Ryng had looked into his room. He probably looked through every room in this corridor," Sheila said. She had got rid of that mad fit, Kati thought: her face was cold and hard now.

"They'd have heard him," Kati said, nodding towards the sleeping Aleksanders.

"They haven't heard us."

Kati shrugged her fine shoulders, but before she could answer, Sheila had crossed quickly over to the open window and pushed the shutters closer. Someone was outside, loitering. Ryng, no doubt. Loitering to see the dawn break, perhaps, just as he had loitered round this house looking for the food pantry. He made no pretense of silence now: he must have heard her footsteps. He was walking carelessly, kicking a stone along his path as he went. He was whistling softly to himself. Sheila tried to see out through the shutter's hinge, but there was nothing to be recognized from that angle. All she could do was listen to the careless kicking at the stone, to the soft whistling as it faded.

The practical Kati was attending to the stove. Madame Aleksander stirred restlessly, and woke. "Thought I heard something," she said sleepily, and Kati laughed. But Sheila didn't laugh. If I can just let my mind lie fallow, just for two minutes, just think of nothing, perhaps I'll remember, she was saying to herself. For there was something to remember. The coarse voice in the hall with its touch of dialect ... it held something of a voice she had heard once before.

Kati pointed a poker at Sheila and said to Madame Aleksander, "She thinks something is wrong. She's been hearing things, too."

Madame Aleksander had the good sense to keep quiet. She looked at Sheila, and then she sat up in bed. She began to fasten her corsets, button her dress, smooth her hair into its usual neat pattern.

Sheila walked over to the stove She stood watching the new flames, leaping greedily inside their litle cave. The stove door had been left open to increase the draught. She warmed her hands, and looked at the charcoal's orange glow.

Kati was worried about the continued silence. "What's wrong, anyway?" she said. "He was a man searching for food. What's wrong about that?"

"A man searching for something," Sheila said slowly.

"Aye. For his wife and her young brother, Zygmunt got bored to sleep with his story, last night!"

Sheila bit her lip. "Zygmunt. Get Zygmunt. And Peter," she said suddenly.

"Zygmunt? He's still asleep. When he's asleep, he stays asleep."

"Get him, Kati."

The girl shrugged her shoulders. "Well, don't blame me for his language," she said.

Madame Aleksander was wakening Stefan gently. "Please, Stefan. We may have to leave." Her eyes watched Sheila's face anxiously.

There were other signs of life in the house, now. A woman's voice, strong and confident, was giving orders. That would be Jadwiga—Kati's mother. Doors opened noisily. Shutters creaked. There was a sound of dishes, of a stiff broom sweeping a hard floor. Peter and the man Zak stumbled out of the front room, and Jadwiga's voice followed them. Sheila heard the hiss of water, as the two men wakened their heavy heads under the cold stream from the pump. The hiss of water . . . water hissing against a hot dusty pavement. A man whistling softly . . . whistling the same little tune she had heard that morning. . . . *What has he to be happy about?*

"God . . ." Sheila said. "Oh, God."

"What is it, Sheila?" Madame Aleksander came over quickly. Kati and Zygmunt, with wild hair and his half-opened shirt wet with water, stood at the door.

"Kati," Sheila said very quietly. "Ryng is not a Pole. He is a German. His real name is Dittmar."

Her denunciation ended in anticlimax. They all stared at her unbelievingly. Zygmunt's face was still half drugged by sleep.

"What's that?" he said slowly.

"He's a spy. I first met him as Henryk, a Polish concierge at Professor Korytowski's flat. When war came, he changed to an official in the German *Auslands-Organisation*, working closely with the Gestapo. He arrested and questioned you after my disappearance, Madame Aleksander."

Everyone turned to the older woman. She shook her head nervously, blankly.

"The name means nothing. . . . I didn't catch any of their

names when they questioned me. They were just . . . faces."

Sheila said, "A tall man of about forty, powerful shoulders, round white face, small gray eyes, straight mouth with thin lips, short nose, long upper lips, short bristling fair hair growing over a once-shaved head?"

Madame Aleksander looked amazed. "Yes, there was one with very short hair, almost a shaven head. And gray eyes, small and hard. . . ."

Kati was staring too. "That's Ryng, all right. You've got him pat."

Stefan suddenly broke his attentive silence. "That was the man who was at Zorawno, yesterday morning, when I went there to warn its Jadwiga about the shot."

Kati looked at Zygmunt in alarm. "It's the camp, Zygmunt. That's what he's after."

Stefan said, "Mother, perhaps he followed you after all. Perhaps that dog. . . ."

"No," Sheila said, "he came for none of those things, but he may have found out about them. Zygmunt, did he describe his wife to you? How she might be traveling?"

Zygmunt was very much awake now. His face still looked tired, but his eyes were alert. "She was a blonde, quite young, with pretty fair hair to her shoulders. She had delicate hands but the left one had been scarred by a pot of boiling soup. The brother was young, just a kid. They were traveling south, trying to hide from patrols. There was an older man with them at one time. A big fellow. Ryng seemed jealous about that man. Didn't know whether he was the reason his wife had disappeared, or whether it was the Germans. I felt kind of sorry for him: he was sort of worried."

Sheila looked at her left hand, and so did Stefan.

"You and Jan and me," he tried to say. Sheila nodded.

"Devil take his pock-marked soul! Bloody fool that I've been," Zygmunt said.

"You were out on a raid when we arrived in camp, Zygmunt. You didn't know that Jan and Stefan and I arrived together, or that my hair was longer, then. But at least we know that Dittmar came here looking for me. Not for the camp. But he traced us to this district, and then we vanished into thin air. Now, he has seen Madame Aleksander here, knows she evaded the men who followed her from Warsaw, knows she must have friends here to help her. Yesterday he heard a shot from the forest, although the villagers had told him the forest was a dead place with all its paths blocked by undergrowth. When he adds up all these things, the answer will be that refugees are hidden in the forest."

"But how did he know we came south towards the forest?" Stefan asked.

"He found out that we were traveling south. After that it was only a matter of searching. He probably examined all reports from patrols, and what he didn't learn from the Germans, he learned from the Poles who believed his story."

"But why should he follow you? What are you to him?" Zygmunt asked bluntly.

"Because I could tell him about so many things."

"You wouldn't, Sheila," Stefan said.

"I'd try not to. But they might take a long time to kill me."

"Sheila!"

Sheila shrugged her shoulders. "There's no use pretending to be heroic in the face of torture. No one knows how he will behave until he is actually being taken apart, bit by bit."

"Sheila!" Again it was Madame Aleksander. The others were silent.

Then, "What about the camp?" Kati asked.

"If he really knew about it, he would now be traveling to the nearest German garrison to give the alarm. His guess about the forest will only be that it's a refuge for hunted people."

"But even that is dangerous," Madame Aleksander said. "That could lead him to the camp."

Again there was that silence.

"We had better take care of him," Zygmunt said. "You are sure about him?"

"Yes," Sheila said, and then thought how strange it was to condemn a man like this. "I didn't see him this morning. But I'm sure."

Zygmunt limped towards the window and pushed back the shutters. "Dawn's here," he announced. "Stefan, take your mother eastwards to the line of trees there. Wait. When it's evening, move towards the forest. You can guide her that way?"

"Of course."

"First you go east, to the line of trees. Then when light fades, you travel south to the forest, then west until you reach the path by which you came last night. The patrol will see you coming. Got that?"

"Yes."

"Good." A grin spread strangely over Zygmunt's dark face. "No telephone from here—the line's been down since that last big thunderstorm. And the line's down too in Zorawno where he heard the shot. He knows a lot, but he can't get any information out. He will have to leave before he can let the Germans know. And he can't leave. He's got to watch us!" Zygmunt began to laugh, a deep low laugh which brought a smile to all the anxious faces.

"Must we go now?" Madame Aleksander asked, and the smiles faded.

Zygmunt nodded and Kati moved towards the door. "I'll warn my mother and Peter and Zak," she said as she left the room.

Madame Aleksander crossed over to a corner of the room, and picked up a small bundle. "My worldly possessions," she said, half sadly, half defiantly.

"Couldn't we go straight to the forest, now?" Stefan asked impatiently.

"If they knew they weren't seen?" Sheila asked in support. She didn't like the idea of Madame Aleksander waiting out in the open country all day. It seemed so dangerous, so vulnerable.

"*If* they knew. But it's a big *if*," Zygmunt answered slowly. He didn't favor the idea, obviously.

Stefan shrugged his shoulders. "And you?" he asked.

"I'll come on later." Zygmunt looked at his hands. "I've business to do," he said.

Kati returned with the news that her mother was taking the German some food to keep him quiet, that Zak was with her mother and was going to stay in the barn with the man. Peter was already outside, waiting for the boy and his mother to leave. He was to guard their going.

Madame Aleksander gave Sheila a long embrace. They had still much to say, and yet could say nothing. Stefan's grasp on Sheila's hand tightened.

"We'll meet again," Madame Aleksander said at last. "Sometime. We will."

Sheila kissed the wet cheeks.

"Dear Sheila," Madame Aleksander said softly.

Zygmunt was leading them out of the room. Kati pretended to fasten the blouse and skirt which she had added to her costume. Then she threw more wood on the fire, and closed the oven door. She picked up Stefan's pillow, began pounding the bed's mattress, and arranging the quilted cover. She avoided looking at Sheila, and Sheila was grateful.

"I liked her," Kati said suddenly. "Before the war, all of us here used to talk about people like her. We used to say 'Those others with the big houses and fine clothes, they are really soft and weak. We may be poor, but we are strong.' In the last month, I've seen all kinds of people coming through this village. There were cowards among them, and brave men among them. But never did the cowards all belong to one class, nor did all the brave men."

"Yes," Sheila said. It was a relief to talk about something impersonal. "Yes, we are a mixed lot. All classes have their brave men, and all have their shirkers. That's what my uncle used to say. He used to say the only true classes in a country were the first-rate men and the second-raters, and it didn't matter how much or how little they possessed."

"Was he a communist, this uncle?"

Sheila smiled, remembering Uncle Matthews and his contempt for revolution. ("Too many first-rate men get killed off because they aren't workers; too many second-raters among the workers are honored just because they have the right password," was what he had once said. "Revolution's wasteful.")

"No," Sheila said, "I wouldn't call him that. He believes that there are good men in all classes of society and that they should be preserved and encouraged. If anyone has to be liquidated or strung up to a lamp-post, then it should be those who just won't do *any* job well, whoever or whatever they are. Only, I don't think he would believe in having them liquidated. Just openly scorned and despised would be enough for his sense of justice."

Kati looked puzzled. "But he doesn't believe in classes, then. That's communism."

"He doesn't believe in one class dominating. He believes in the best men of all classes being the leaders. He doesn't divide people into horizontal levels. He divides them vertically: good citizens, bad citizens. He believes there's a natural aristocracy among people: an aristocracy of courage and brains and human decency."

"But those who have much, they think they are the best."

"In some countries, yes. In others, those who have little think they are the best. Both are snobs. Quote, unquote."

"What?"

"That's my expurgated version of my uncle's beliefs."

"I would like to meet this uncle," Kati said with a smile.

"I think he would like to meet you and Zygmunt and Madame Aleksander and—"

"What does he call this political party?"

Sheila was smiling again. "The Weed-killers," she said. Kati looked at her disbelievingly, and then she was laughing, too.

"Zak must talk with you," she said. "He's always discussing such things. He loves to argue." She paused and listened. "Zygmunt's a long time away." And then with an effort, as if she were trying to keep from worrying, "We Poles talk a lot. It was the only thing we could do in the Captivity. Our fathers could only meet in secret, and talk and talk and talk. We got the habit then, I suppose."

"Who is Zak?" Sheila asked. This waiting seemed interminable. Had something gone wrong after all? What was happening outside?

"The Elder of our village. We elect him. . . . A sort of mayor. We've elected him for many years. He is wise."

"Don't you ever want a change?"

"We couldn't get a better man. We might get a worse one."

The bed was neat, the room tidied. There was nothing else to do, except wait. Talk was no longer an escape from worry.

And then Zygmunt came, quite oblivious of the anxiety which he had caused.

"Well away," he said, his ugly and yet somehow not unpleasing face relaxed in a broad grin. "I stood and watched them go. No German patrol in sight. Peter went with them to the end of the village."

A small thin woman followed Zygmunt. She carried a plate of food. "I've brought you something to eat," she said in her deep, strong voice, and handed Sheila a slab of dry bread and sausage. "Don't wolf it," she said sharply to Zygmunt. "It's all you can get. The Szwaby have marked down every pig we own, every blade of rye. It's been a job, I can tell you, getting these supplies for the camp smuggled out of sight."

"We know, mother," Zygmunt said with his mouth shamelessly full. He patted the woman's wrinkled cheek, and finished his portion of bread and sausage in three bites. "But I prefer to have a good taste of my food." He pointed to Sheila. "See! She's wasting it. She doesn't even get one real mouthful."

They were laughing, partly at Zygmunt's good humor, partly in relief that all was going so well, when Peter entered the room.

"All well?" Zygmunt asked quickly.

"Aye." Everyone relaxed again, and smiles were easy. "They reached the line of trees. No German patrol in sight."

"Good. Now while the mice are nibbling at their food, we'll discuss our plans." Zygmunt settled himself comfortably on the bench along the wall, his arm round Kati. Her mother, whom Sheila only knew as "Jadwiga," sat beside Sheila near the stove. Peter leaned his tall body against a heavily carved table.

Zygmunt spoke again. "Zak is with the German. In the

barn. Talking. I'm going there now to take the German for a walk. Out of the village. I'll come back alone. What do you say to that, mother?"

Jadwiga nodded. "Out of the village," she said. "Keep the village safe, and that keeps the forest safe." She nodded again. Her blue eyes were strangely young against the fine network of wrinkles over her brown cheeks. She fingered the empty plate on her lap with her broad, large-knuckled fingers. "And then?"

"The girl leaves tonight with Peter. Keep her hidden in here. The less known about her, the better."

"Aye. Now, if you can let go my daughter's waist, get on with your dead German."

Zygmunt rose, grinning. "It isn't your daughter's waist which keeps me here. It's your beautiful bright blue eyes, my darling."

Jadwiga's hard, anxious face relaxed for a moment. "Get on with you," she said.

Zygmunt limped towards the door. He turned to say something to Sheila, "You're *sure* about—"

And then the door opened. An unpleasantly businesslike Luger pointed at them. Behind it was Dittmar, tight-eyed, tight-mouthed.

"Back against the wall, all of you. Hands high!" he commanded. "And drop that plate. Quick!"

The plate crashed on the floor.

His eyes traveled round them slowly, rested on Sheila.

"So all the birds haven't flown," he said. And a smile, which contained much satisfaction and little charm, spread slowly across his face.

CHAPTER XXXV

## Death at the Inn

DITTMAR had won that round, and he had won it entirely by the force of surprise. The first moment, when someone might have had a chance to snatch the initiative away from him, was gone. Now they were standing, controlled by the large efficient pistol, along one wall of the room. Amazement gave way to a feeling of foolishness as they stared at the man opposite them. Dittmar leaned against the little table near the door. His eyes and mouth were as determined, and ruthless, and impersonal as the Luger. He was in complete control.

He consolidated his gain effectively. The emotionless voice said, "Any move by any one of you, or a shout for help, and I aim for Kati. Any move from Kati, and I shall blow a hole in her Zygmunt. At this range, a Luger doesn't leave much of a face."

He looked at them in turn, made himself comfortable on the table, and his mouth loosened into a pleased grin; but the hand and the eyes never relaxed. "You won't have very long to wait."

"You're lying," Sheila challenged him. "You haven't got any word out of this village. There's no phone working from here or from Zorawno."

"What a clever girl you are," he answered mockingly. "Three days ago, before I reached Zorawno, I was in touch with my assistant—but of course you've met him. You remember Hefner?—Well, Mr. Hefner had found traces of an old woman and a little ragged dog as far as Nowe Miasto. Three days ago it seemed that we had both come to an impasse; now Hefner will have quite a lot of surprises. He's reporting to me here, today. For before I left Zorawno to come to this God-forsaken hole, I gave a message to a helpful farmer to take to Nowe Miasto on market day. That message would reach Hefner last night." His tone changed. The words were like flint, now. "Incidentally, if you have any stupid ideas about attacking me, please abandon them. Herr Hefner will want to know the reason why I am not here waiting for him. And he comes officially, not in this kind of fancy dress." Dittmar pointed to his stained and torn suit of cheap poor cloth. "And there will be others with him. This village will be another example of what the disobedient can expect—if you try any little tricks."

"You are boring us," Kati said. "Your voice is as bad as your breath."

"You keep quiet. You'll answer when I get round to asking you questions."

"Will I indeed?" said Kati. "Just you wait until Zak warns the village. They'll deal with you, *and* have answers ready for your uniformed friend."

"Zak will not warn the village." His smile was as confident as his voice was decisive.

Even Kati was silent now.

"Interesting district this," Dittmar went on. "Where were the old woman and the boy going, I wonder?" He paused; and then added, "To the forest where you came from, my little cousin Magda?"

Sheila didn't answer him.

"For you came from there, didn't you?"

Sheila looked at the others, pretended to smile, tried to look as if she were secretly pleased by the question. Let him waste time on the forest, was the implication: that's all right with us. We all know there's nothing there.

"I told you once before, Cousin Magda, that you would go far with the right boss. I didn't know then that you were on the wrong side, that the only end for you would be either your back against an execution wall or a soldier's brothel. If you don't talk, you'll get both."

She was silent.

"Come on, now. You could give me just a few facts. You could tell me about Kordus. You could tell me about Herr Hofmeyer, for he's in this too, isn't he? You could tell me who has been hiding you in this district, and where you could hide when you weren't to be found in any of its villages. If you told me just those few facts, you could spend the rest of the war in a prison camp. That's quite pleasant, compared with other places."

No one answered him. There was a restless look in Zygmunt's eye. He was planning something.

"Come on, now, Magda. Or do you prefer to be called Anna; or is it Sheila?"

Sheila thought, if I keep him talking, perhaps Zygmunt can work out whatever he's planning. She said, "You take a great deal for granted. How do you know that Madame Aleksander and her son have left here? Perhaps you are being too clever."

"People carrying a bundle are not out for morning strolls. Or is it usual that a man accompanies them to the end of the village, or waits there until he sees them safely out of sight behind a stretch of trees leading south—where there are no more villages, no more houses, merely forest? Is it usual that the man runs back to tell the others in the inn? Not, that is, if the woman and the boy have been only taking a morning stroll."

He watched Peter's openly crestfallen face with increasing amusement. Like all winners, Dittmar couldn't help pointing out the loser's weakness. "The mistake you made was to think that I would be content to sit in a barn with Zak blocking the door so innocently." Now he was laughing at Zygmunt. "Or to think that I would never imagine you might suspect me. That incident in the hall was unfortunate for me, in one way. If it hadn't happened, I should now be sitting peacefully in a cabbage patch, and the woman Aleksander and her son would no doubt have been still here, waiting with you all in this house—until my friends arrived. We'd have got you with no effort at all. But, in another way, the hall incident was fortunate." He shook his head slowly at Kati. "Your cousin had very slender bones for a country girl. Her hands were very smooth for cleaning out a bar. Except for one hand." He looked at Sheila now. "The left one. The skin was still healing."

Sheila took a deep breath.

"Did you think your boy's hair would cheat me?" Dittmar asked her derisively. Then his voice sharpened. "Keep still there!" He rested the Luger on his left forearm. His eyes narrowed.

Zygmunt's body stiffened and obeyed.

"I am going to drop my arms. Otherwise I shall faint," Sheila announced. Twenty paces, Sierakowski had said when he had given her the gun. If she could only lower her arms, pretend to rest one hand casually at her waist, near her heart.

"Keep them up. Higher. Quite the English little miss, aren't you? Men at Fort VII have stood in ice-cold rain with their hands above their heads all through the night. Don't tell me that you patriots here are less patriotic than they were."

Through the half-open shutter came the sound of a village stirring into life. A woman singing as she worked; children's voices laughing, quarreling, calling to each other; the noise of a wooden-wheeled cart lumbering slowly away.

Sheila looked at the rafters above her head, at the bright paper flowers and stenciled patterns along the whitewashed wood. Zygmunt, she felt, was going to do something desperate. She looked at the others. Did they know that when Zygmunt moved they must all move, or else be mowed down like ripe corn in a harvest field? If they all moved, all attacked at once, two would perhaps be killed. Dittmar wouldn't have time to shoot more than that in a room of this size. *If* they all acted together . . . Looking at their faces —Jadwiga, thin, wrinkled, impassive, her bright eyes steady; Kati, an angry scowl drawing her straight thick brows into an ugly fold; Peter, stolid, expressionless almost to the point of stupidity; Zygmunt, his weight balanced on his uninjured leg, his dark face brooding, his eyes restless—Sheila knew they were waiting, waiting for the right moment. Zygmunt would give it to them: Zygmunt, who was no doubt cursing his wounded leg at this moment.

The tension increased in the silent room. Dittmar felt it too. His eyes narrowed once more, his watchfulness tautened. Sheila's eyes closed. Perhaps that way, the hard face opposite her wouldn't be able to read her thoughts. For she had the beginning of a plan. If only Zygmunt wouldn't make his move until she managed it. If she could give a good imitation of a faint, just the moment before Zygmunt moved, then Dittmar's eyes might for one moment be off guard. And from the floor she could use her revolver: and that was something Dittmar would not expect. Dwór, like every village and town in Poland, had been looted of its guns; even the possession of a child's toy revolver had been enough to condemn a man to the firing squad. Last night, Dittmar had obviously discovered that neither Peter nor Zygmunt was armed.

Sheila looked sideways at Zygmunt. Yes, he had noticed her expression. She hoped he understood it. And now her arms sagged, she swayed on her feet, one hand went to her brow.

"Keep your hands up!"

Dittmar's voice was worried and angry.

A slow faint—that would have to be the way. Dittmar didn't want to shoot her yet. He wanted to question her. Knees bending, head bending, and then a relaxing of her body until it could sprawl forward and lie inert. Not too violently—no point in knocking herself out cold on that hard floor, still less in falling on the gun—just like this . . . on her left side . . . leaving the right arm free. . . . She let her body sag forward. . . . Her left shoulder struck the ground with a sharp shock.

The Luger's crash seemed to split her ears. Peter's leap finished in a stumble, and then his body huddled almost at Dittmar's feet. It had been Peter and not Zygmunt—Peter standing so quietly, so stupidly — who had fully understood Sheila's pretense. Zygmunt, a fraction of a minute too late, dropped, as a second bullet was fired. Sheila fumbled for her gun. Her waistband held it too securely. She tugged at it secretly, desperately, as Jadwiga and Kati rushed Dittmar. A third crash, and Jadwiga's hand let the uplifted candlestick fall. Kati alone had reached Dittmar, Kati unarmed, Kati hitting and kicking and clawing. Dittmar wasn't shooting any more. He could handle two women. They must be kept alive, or he wouldn't get his information. He smashed his fist into Kati's face, and, as she reeled, kicked her heavily in the stomach. The girl lay half gasping, half moaning, her body in a rigid angle of pain. Dittmar looked down at her, kicked twice again. The small strangled cries were silenced.

"That takes care of her meanwhile," Dittmar said. He looked towards the other girl. She was raising her head and shoulders now, supporting her body with one hand flat on the floor. The other hand was covered by the wide-spreading shawl. She looked white, and weak, and terrified. Dittmar's calm voice said, "A little of the same will keep you quiet, too, my friend." He walked over to her slowly. He was quite confident.

Sheila fired two bullets. The floor splintered beside her as the Luger cracked once more. At least she had spoiled Herr Dittmar's aim. His astonished face suddenly became quite expressionless. A shoulder tilted, an elbow dug into his left side. His rigid body listed sideways, and then pitched forward.

Sheila moved away from the sprawling arm that pointed towards her. He must be dead. One in the stomach, one at his heart. Two bullets. A third, to make sure? This time she found herself turning her head away and half-closing her eyes as she pressed the gun to his ear and pulled the trigger. She noticed her hand was beginning to tremble. Dropping the gun, she walked unevenly over to the bench by the door. Her whole body was trembling now, as though racked by some fever. It wouldn't, couldn't stop.

Outside, the sounds of the village had given way to a startled silence. There was a long pause. Then a shout broke the silence, unleashed the alarmed voices and the running footsteps. She could hear the movement of people round the window, the movement of people along the corridor. Behind it all was the rustle of questions. *What is it? What's wrong? What's happened?*

The door opened, and a white-haired man in shirt-sleeves, with his cap on the back of his head and a scythe held as a weapon in his hand, stood looking at her. And then at the room. And then at her again. A black-robed priest entered. His quick glance passed over Jadwiga and Peter and rested on Zygmunt. He knelt beside him, holding Zygmunt's shattered leg tightly above the knee.

"Call Tomasz," he said to those who tried to press curiously through the doorway.

"Tomasz—Where's Tomasz?—Tomasz, you're needed!"— the voices echoed.

Sheila rose, and the man with the scythe tightened his grip. She went over to Kati, knelt beside her. She was afraid to lift her or to try to straighten the unconscious body.

"What can we do for her? She wasn't shot. He kicked her insensible," she heard herself say.

The man with the scythe laid its sharp blade carefully against the wall. He took off his hat, and crossed himself, as he passed Peter and Jadwiga. He stood beside Sheila, equally worried and useless.

"What's wrong here?" a woman's voice said sharply from

the door. She pushed her way past the two old men guarding the entrance, and then stood aghast. A tall thin-faced man followed her, hurried over to the kneeling priest. By the way he handled Zygmunt's leg Sheila judged he must know something about doctoring. This must be Tomasz.

She called over to him unhappily. "Kati has been kicked in the body. She's unconscious. What can we do?"

"Leave her there till I can look at her," Tomasz said sharply. He was tearing his shirt into strips, winding them tightly round Zygmunt's leg above the knee.

The woman's stupefied horror broke. She gave a scream, rushed to the window. "They're dead, they're all dead! They've been killed!" The villagers outside were shocked into silence, and then the chorus of voices began.

"How? How? What happened?"

There was restlessness in the corridor outside. The people wanted to see for themselves The priest rose and took the woman's arm, quietening her. "Zofia," he said, "unless you want to stay and help, you must leave." To the people pressing against the window, he said, "There has been violence and death in this house. Some of its people have been killed, some injured. We do not yet know how. Be patient, my children. We will find out."

Once more there was silence.

Zofia crossed her arms and rocked herself slowly. She was weeping now. She looked down at Kati's mother, whom Sheila had known only as "Jadwiga." "Aunt Katarzyna," she moaned. And then, "Peter, too. And the stranger who came last evening, God rest his poor soul." There was an echo of sympathy from the doorway. And then Zofia stared at Sheila as if she were seeing her for the first time.

"Who's that? Who's that?" Her voice changed from grief to fear, and then to anger. She pointed at Sheila. "What's she doing here?"

Sheila looked up at the woman in sudden alarm. She had been assuming that they would all understand at once. Now she saw a long series of questions and answers, of explanations disbelieved. She saw Hefner and the other Gestapo men arriving in the village while the explanations still dragged on. She saw Korytów repeated.

She rose and went over to the priest, quickly marshaling her thoughts. "The village is in danger," she said urgently. "That man was a German spy. He killed Zak in the barn, then came here and held us up with his revolver. He knew we had become suspicious of him. He was going to keep us until his Gestapo friends arrived. He had arranged to meet them here. But Peter rushed him, then Zygmunt, and Kati's mother was shot too. He struck Kati, and then kicked her. He wanted to keep her and me alive for questioning. I shot him."

The priest's large-boned, hollow-eyed face watched her curiously. Even Tomasz had paused in his work to stare at her. The woman's nostrils dilated. "What does she say?" she cried incredulously.

"I said that man was a German; other Germans are coming!"

The woman looked scornfully at her, her mouth twisted. "He was a Pole. He was looking for his wife." Her anger increased at Sheila's slander of the dead. "If there's any German here, it's her. She can't even speak Polish properly. She shot them. She's waiting for her German friends." The woman's grief had become hysteria. Her face flushed. Her arm kept pointing.

"She did it. She's the one." Voices again rose from the corridor and the window.

Sheila sat down again on the bench. She looked at the priest and shook her head slowly. "There's the revolver I used," she said, and pointed. "There's the one he used. Anyone who knows about guns can see the difference in the wounds." *What's the use,* she was asking herself, *what's the use?* She looked at the grimly silent faces, suspicious, watchful. Damn them all, she thought savagely; let them take what's coming to them. I'm tired. I can do no more.

The priest was still studying her.

"Who are you?" he asked. His voice was kindly. He, at least, was willing to believe her.

*Sheila Matthews, the daughter of Charles Matthews, shot in Poland, 1916; niece of John Matthews of London...* How would that sound?

"The voice of one crying in the wilderness," she said bitterly.

"Hush, my child." The priest crossed himself.

"Sorry, Father. I'm just tired of explaining while the Germans are acting."

"But we must know who you are. Why did you come here?" It was as if the priest were trying to prompt her to give the right answer

"Ask Kati. Ask Zygmunt. I came here last night, looking for Jadwiga."

The faces around her became guarded.

"Who sent you?" There was relief, almost gladness, in the priest's voice.

"The Reapers. Peter was to guide me towards Radom

tonight." Sheila felt as if she had won that point. There was interest now, as well as watchfulness, around her.

"She knows too much," said Zofia. "She will betray us to the Germans when they come."

"I must be away from here before they come. They are searching for me."

"Are they now?" Zofia was quite unconvinced. "You leave us with guns and dead people. The Germans find the guns. The village will be lost."

Sheila's anger vanished as quickly as it had arisen. Looking at the worried faces around her, she felt ashamed of herself.

"It will be lost unless you hide the guns and can explain the bodies," she said quietly. "We must plan now, while Tomasz is doing what he can for Zygmunt and Kati. When they can talk, they will tell you the story. First of all, see what has happened to Zak. Zak was guarding the German in the barn. He must have been struck down. For in here, the rest of us heard nothing until the German stood at the door with his gun."

The priest silenced Zofia's reply with his upraised arm. He moved to the window and instructed two men to go round to the barn. Then he spoke to the white-haired man, still standing speechless, motionless. "Take the guns. Hide them with the others." To Tomasz he said, "What about Zygmunt?"

"The leg's no good to him. We'll cut it off."

"Kati?"

"She'll come round." And then Tomasz called on the two men standing at the door: "Come on there, give me a hand. We'll lift her over to the bed. Careful. Watch out for the blood on the floor."

The priest sat down on the bench beside Sheila. "We have accepted your warning," he said gently. The deeply shadowed eyes looked at her not unkindly. "But you must stay here until Kati or Zygmunt can talk. You understand? After all, we don't know yet who you are. We cannot let you leave until we do. We must think of the village."

"Yes," Sheila said. "I understand." She tried to smile. "Anyway, I don't know where to go. Not now." She looked at Peter. And then, "What time is it?"

"After eight o'clock."

"Then we have perhaps an hour's grace. Perhaps less. I don't know, really." It might indeed be only a matter of minutes. She stared at Heinrich Dittmar's limp body. Powerless now, and yet not powerless enough. He could still harm them if he were found by Hefner. He must be the first one to be hidden. But the two others and Zak must be hidden safely too. Not that the Germans objected to the Poles quarreling and killing each other; that saved the Germans a lot of trouble. But the bodies carried bullet wounds, and bullets meant hidden guns, and that the Germans would not tolerate. Sheila remembered their ingenious theory of "collective responsibility." Evidence of one gun in a village made the entire village responsible. Hostages were taken and shot. The number depended on the Germans' whim.

"What can we do?" she asked suddenly. "We must act at once."

The faces at the door nodded. They kept their grim silence. They were too stunned by the blow that had struck the village, to be able to plan. They liked time to shape their ideas: there was something wild and indecent about such haste. They were peasants, and they moved slowly, like the earth.

"Dig a grave?" Sheila asked, and then realized the hard frost would show the newly turned ground. And digging took time. Tomasz was shaking his head.

"Take them out of the village in a cart?"

"Where? And if Germans are coming they will meet the cart and search it," Zofia said scornfully.

Sheila, looking at the woman's face, kept silent over a third suggestion. A fire might solve the problem. Yet if this house burned, it might take an hour or two before the blaze was really strong enough to destroy all evidence of bullet wounds. In any case, Zofia and the others would be shocked. They would not let their dead be burned: their dead must have decent Christian burials.

"Well?" Sheila said. Her insistence must seem callous. And then she realized that, as the stranger here, she alone saw the tragic incident as part of one large pattern, involving not only this village, but the camp and Hofmeyer, and Olszak, and God knew how many others. To the villagers, the tragedy consisted only of the murder of their friends and of the threat of "collective responsibility." They could not realize that the tale of death would not stop in Dwór. Nor could she tell them. The explanation she had already given them had baffled them enough.

"Father," she said quickly to the priest, "in many Polish villages, there is a house with coffins displayed for sale in racks before its door. Is there such a house here?"

The priest nodded, gazed at her gravely. He wasn't going to approve of her idea, she knew. She explained with increasing desperation. When she had finished, his serious eyes confirmed her guess. But he hadn't refused to listen.

There was still hope. She waited impatiently for his reply. She saw that Tomasz agreed with her: so did another man. Zofia was looking uneasy, uncertain. They all waited for their priest. He would decide.

"God grant us strength for what we do," he said at last, and rose to his feet.

It was the signal for all of them. The spell of silence and inaction was broken: commands, quick movements, willing hands gave life to the room and were echoed outside. Tomasz was in charge. "Give us half an hour," he said.

Zofia, now that she had become accustomed to the idea that the Germans might come, that Sheila had not lied, worked eagerly, unquestioningly. She was even beginning to take pride in the plan, inventing little details of her own. Perhaps some day, if this story were told in the long evenings before her kitchen fire, the plan would become hers entirely.

Sheila relaxed. The village was together. It was working with an energy as intense as its gloom had been. Even the children did their share: some went to the main road, where the short track to Dwór branched from it; others carried water, brought sheets of linen from their mothers' store cupboards.

Half an hour, Tomasz had said. In half an hour, they were ready.


CHAPTER XXXVI

## Funeral


AT NINE o'clock, punctually, a large black car jolted over the rough road and halted in front of the inn. The children had taken a short cut over the fields and had shouted as children do when they race each other. Now their game was over. They stood in a breathless, wide-eyed group and stared at the enormous car. Behind the shuttered windows of the cottages, older eyes watched the four men who stepped out of the car. One wore a gray tweed suit and a fitted, dark blue coat. There was a touch of the dandy in him, with his casually worn Homburg hat, and the yellow gloves gripping the cane. The businesslike brief case seemed out of place but authoritative. The three men who accompanied him were in the black uniform of death.

At the first warning from the children's raised voices, the small procession had formed outside the inn, and the cortège of white wood coffins moved slowly over to the church. When the car arrived at the village, the first coffin had already been carried carefully into the church, the second one was disappearing inside the door, the third was being edged through the gateway, and the fourth was still being slowly borne across the small village square. For one moment, the file of mourners turned their faces to stare with village curiosity at the newcomers. Then they bowed their heads once more. The four men paused to look at the procession. Then they turned abruptly, swinging neatly on their heels. The women who had been watching through the half-closed shutters of the houses crossed themselves thankfully, and turned back to the younger children whom they were guarding. The older children outside in the square were completely silenced as they transferred their attention from the Nazi car to the funeral, and watched the last coffin pass through the church's narrow gate. The two slow-swinging bells commanded silence and respect for the dead. Everywhere, there was the brooding peace of mourning.

The four men halted at the inn door. Hefner and the Gestapo officer were in front; behind them, in neat order, were the two other black uniforms.

"This is it," Hefner said crisply. He was more businesslike than Sheila had ever seen him. "This is it."

The officer glanced over his shoulder. "All looks dead to me. How do they know, these people, when it's time to enter their coffins?" He laughed at his own joke, and Hefner joined in politely.

"Wait here," the officer was saying to his two men. He rapped briskly against the door. Sheila moved back from the half-shuttered hall window into the bedroom where Zygmunt was lying, as the Nazi pushed the door open and entered. Tomasz was comng out of the front room to meet him.

"They've come?" Zygmunt whispered hoarsely.

Sheila nodded and sat down beside the bed. It was strange how the panic which had first seized her, as she had heard the car approach, had now quite vanished. She felt calm, even sure of herself. We are so desperate, she thought, that we just don't care. She made sure that Kati's red handkerchief was knotted round her head so that not one strand of hair was shown. She placed Kati's thick black shawl over her shoulders, crossing it over her breasts and tying it behind her waist to give her a bulky look. Kati's long wrinkled boots hid her legs. The gray ashes from the stove with which she had touched her eyebrows had made them dingy and colorless; her cheeks and lips were pale, and she had added a streak of charcoal from her smeared hands. If the hands looked dirty enough, perhaps the scar on the left one might never be noticed. She tried to look like a patient, huddled woman watching beside a sickbed.

"You've left the door open," Zygmunt said.

"We've nothing to hide," she whispered. "Don't worry ... You remember your story?"

Zygmunt nodded. His lips were dangerously white. His head moved weakly against the narrow pillow.

"I'm all right." His words were halting. She touched the large, powerful arms, now so motionless.

"Of course you are. It's just loss of blood. Keep still, don't talk and try to sleep."

"Kati?"

"All right. She's been sick. That's all. Don't worry."

"You should have gone away."

"Not enough time," Sheila whispered back. She placed a finger lightly over his lips. She was listening attentively to the German voices, to Tomasz and his slow steady replies. The Nazis had pushed past him into the living room, hardly listening to his answers.

"There *is* no one here," the Nazi officer's voice was saying with a mixture of annoyance and surprise.

"Have your men start searching the houses and barns, Captain Winkler," Hefner answered. Then he must have turned to speak to Tomasz, for his voice had a sharp aggressive note which Sheila had never heard before. In Warsaw, his voice had been gentle, lingering over his words with an accent almost feminine.

"You said you were the doctor?"

"I'm a bit of a doctor. I'm a bit of a blacksmith, too. I'm a bit of everything."

"You said you had your patient here. Anyone else in the house?"

"The nurse. And Katarzyna Hulka's daughter, who has been ill."

"Hulka is the owner of this place?"

"She was. She died two days ago. Her daughter is recovering."

"Send her here."

"She isn't well."

"Send her here!"

"One moment." It was Captain Winkler's voice. "What's wrong, here, anyway? An epidemic which you haven't reported?"

Tomasz said slowly, "No, I don't think it is typhus."

"*Typhus?*" Hefner's voice rose sharply. Without seeing him, Sheila had guessed that he had backed away from Tomasz as he spoke. Charming Herr Hefner with his elegant taste in shirts and fine shoes. . . .

Winkler said angrily, "Hefner! You don't catch typhus from people. You get it from what they carry on them. We aren't going to sleep here, you know."

His heavy, assured step moved into the hall, and he was giving orders to his two men. "Touch nothing and no one," he ended, and came back into the room.

"Well," Winkler demanded. "Where's this woman's daughter?"

Tomasz' slow footsteps came down the hall. Sheila strained her ears, but the flood of German from the front room was too quick, too confused. All she could gather was that the captain was annoyed that they had to wait, perhaps annoyed with Hefner, too. Hefner was definitely subdued, anxious to find Dittmar and leave the village. Sheila heard Kati's light step added to Tomasz' shuffling.

"Stand there!" Hefner said. Tomasz and Kati must now be standing at the doorway of the front room. He began a series of sharp questions, scarcely giving the girl time to reply. Sheila felt her admiration for Kati growing. She had learned the story they had prepared, between attacks of vertigo and violent sickness, and yet, even with one shoulder hideously discolored, a broken rib at her side, and a green-shaded swelling across her stomach, she was standing there giving the right answers in an even, quiet voice.

Zygmunt was listening, too. He saw the sudden emotion in Sheila's face.

"What's wrong?" he whispered, staring at her anxiously.

Sheila bent over the pillow so that her lips almost touched his ear. "I was just wondering: what makes some people so brave, and other people such—" She searched for a word he would use. "Such——?"

Zygmunt gave a slow smile, with something of his old humor in it. He nodded his agreement and closed his eyes.

The voices still came unceasingly from the front room. To Sheila, straining to catch each point and counterpoint, the talk was like an unpleasant fugue, harsh, scraping, dissonant. It was obvious that Hefner and his friends had not come armed with questions: they had hoped to find Dittmar waiting. If they had expected any talking, it was to have been done by Dittmar.

No, Tomasz repeated, the village of Dwór harbored no criminals. Only the people of the village were here. As the elder of the village, he could swear to that.

Winkler must have consulted one of the documents in

Hefner's brief case. "You lie. It says here that the head man of the village is called Zak. Where's this Zak?"

"He's dead. He was cutting down a tree with another fellow, two days ago. We found them yesterday afternoon. Zak had died, and the other fellow's leg was pinned down and crushed into jelly."

"You mean the tree fell on them?"

"Looked like it."

"And your patient is the other fellow?"

"Aye. Just cut his leg off. It was turning green."

Hefner said, "You are wasting our time. We aren't interested in amputated legs. We came here searching for a man. A Pole called Ryng. You say he hasn't been here. I warn you that if our men find him in a barn, your village will regret that your memory was so short."

"I said he isn't here. And he isn't."

Winkler's voice cut in quickly. "One moment. He isn't here. I see. But was he here?"

Tomasz didn't answer.

"Was he? Out with it. Was he?" Winkler's voice rose threateningly.

Tomasz said slowly, as if fear were making him betray his news in spite of his desire to be loyal, "A stranger came yesterday to the village. I don't know his name. He didn't stay long."

"Now that's a lie," Hefner said triumphantly. His voice was mocking. "He didn't stay, did he?"

"Not when he heard of the sickness here. Wouldn't sleep in the straw of the barn. Queer man. Kind of mad."

"Did he say why he had come here?"

"Looking for his wife. Kind of mad."

"You were willing to shelter a stranger? You know it is against the law to shelter a stranger?"

"This is an inn. Any man can stay here if his papers are in order, and he's willing to pay for a bed."

"But you didn't rent him a room. You offered him straw in a barn." Hefner's voice was pleased. He liked the way in which he had handled the examination of this peasant.

"There were no more rooms for him. Katarzyna Hulka was lying dead in one. The fellow with the smashed leg was groaning in another. And in the last room was Katarzyna Hulka's daughter, very sick. She's recovering now, as you see."

"So you were going to rent a stranger some straw in the barn, if he could pay for it. Is that it?"

"Aye. But, when he heard of the sickness, he wouldn't stay."

"Another lie," Hefner said.

"I'm not so sure," Winkler broke in once more, but this time his voice had overemphasized politeness. He had probably given Hefner a look to match his tone. For there was a short silence. And when it was broken, it was Winkler who spoke.

"Where did this man Ryng go, when he left here?"

Tomasz didn't reply.

"Where was he going? What directions did he ask you? Where was he going?" Each sentence became louder. "We shall take six hostages, unless you tell us *where he was going.*"

Tomasz hesitated. "Nowe Miasto," he mumbled.

"Louder!"

"Nowe Miasto."

Two pairs of marching feet entered the inn. A new voice said, "Nothing to report, Herr Hauptmann."

"Nothing?"

"Nothing, Herr Hauptmann."

The pause which followed was more terrifying to Sheila than Winkler's anger had been. This is the crisis, she thought. This is the point where they either accept or disbelieve our story.

"One moment." It was Winkler again. "You have a patient here. Let me see this patient."

Sheila pressed her hands together, covering the left one with the palm of the right. She kept her back to the door, her eyes on Zygmunt. What did Winkler expect to find here? A man with his face bandaged, an unwilling captive? Herr Hauptmann Winkler must have a very low opinion of the Poles. Did he really believe they were stupid? Or did he believe that the Poles kept their prisoners, to torture more information out of them, like the Nazis? That was the extraordinary thing about cruelty; first, you might practise it for the ends it achieved; then you practised it because you had developed a taste for it; then you began to believe everyone practised it, that it was the normal way to deal with people; then eventually, when your power started slipping, you would begin to be afraid that people might do as you had done unto them, because you believed that was the way all people behaved. Captain Winkler was at the third stage, expecting cruelty as the normal state of man. She wondered when all the Captain Winklers would reach the fourth stage. That would be a very pleasant stage to observe.

Behind her, Winkler's voice said, "Take off that covering. Let me see this leg."

She realized just in time that he was talking to her. She pulled the mat obediently aside. The Nazi advanced a pace to stand beside her. He looked down at the blood-soaked bandages round the stump of leg.

Over his shoulder he called to Hefner, "Come in. Come in. It's amputation all right." His half-derisive tone implied, "And not typhus!"

Hefner entered the room only far enough to identify the man in the bed.

"No," he said, "that isn't Ryng."

Sheila heard his quick footsteps suddenly leave. Winkler still remained. He was staring round the room.

"Lot of blood on the floor."

"He bled a lot," Sheila said thickly. She sat down again. Her knees were treacherous now as well as her stomach. I'm going to be sick again, she thought. She turned her eyes away from the blood as she pulled the mat gently back over Zygmunt's ghastly leg. She stared at Kati's framed communion certificate which now hung over the bullet which had lodged in the wall. The one which had been aimed for her had been dug carefully out of the floor. Perhaps there was another which they had overlooked in their hurry. It certainly wouldn't escape Winkler's sharp eye.

She moistened her lips, and remembered to stop looking at the communion certificate. The moment of waiting seemed interminable. She was clutching her hands together, pressing her knees together, biting her teeth together. Her jaw felt rigid, her neck corded.

And then with a last glance at the bed and the white-faced man lying so inert and helpless, Captain Winkler turned on his heel. His footsteps rang on the bare floor. For once they were not ominous. For once they announced a reprieve. Sheila took Zygmunt's hand. He knew how she was feeling at this unbelievable moment, for the corners of his mouth were trying to smile. Not yet ... wait ... don't rejoice too quickly, she thought. But it was impossible to repress the feeling of relief, of triumph which suddenly intoxicated her.

From the front room, came Winkler's voice. "A waste of time."

A subdued Hefner said, "Let's get back to Nowe Miasto."

"A drink first," Winkler said. "Questioning is dry work."

"Let's get back to Nowe Miasto. You'll have a better drink there."

"What—Herr Hefner refusing a drink on the house?" Winkler was laughing. "This is indeed a surprise."

"Let us get back." Hefner didn't wait for further argument. He was already outside the house.

Winkler followed him, amused and superior, but conceding that drinks in this dump might not be worth swallowing.

Their footsteps became silence. The car's engine roared into life. Soon it, too, was gone. The quiet village square heard only the sound of uneven voices praying in the church.

Kati came into the room.

Sheila rose quickly and gave her the chair beside Zygmunt. "How's your rib?" she asked softly. "Better go back to bed."

Kati shook her head. Her face had lost all its strong, natural color. She was still weak. But she was looking at Zygmunt, and Zygmunt was looking at her.

Sheila moved to the door. Tomasz was standing at the front entrance of the inn, talking seriously to some of the older children who had grouped round him.

"That's your orders," he said to them and dismissed them with a thump on the nearest shoulder, as Sheila approached. He beckoned her to follow him into the front room.

It was large, low-ceilinged, oak-beamed. Bands of painted flowers had been stenciled along its white walls. One of the gable-walls of the house formed the end wall of this room. Along it there was an open fireplace with an enormous log resting over a heap of accumulated ashes. Opposite the fireplace was the bar—a large, solid sideboard with open shelves and doorless cupboards. On either side of the door was a long narrow table with side benches. Across from the door was a shallow stretch of window with potted plants along its broad sill, and under the trailing green leaves was a third table and the usual benches.

Sheila crossed to the fireplace and rested her head against its rough gray stone.

She drew a deep breath. "We managed it," she said quietly. "We managed it, but they'll come back."

"Aye, they'll come back when they can't find their man at Nowe Miasto. And the second visit won't be so easy for us. But first, they've to reach Nowe Miasto, and then they've to search for him." His grim, heavily lined face relaxed. "Think I'll lower that drink the captain's friend wouldn't let him have." He wiped his brow with the back of his hand. "Dog's blood," he said, "I never thought to God and all the Holy Saints that I'd live through that one." He moved over to the sideboard. There was the sound of heavy glass being set down on solid wood. His voice altered. "Now, what's this?" he asked.

"What?" Sheila replied dully. The sense of excitement and relief had gone. Now there was more planning to do, more efforts to make, before the Germans came back. She crossed over to the window, and kneeling on the bench, looked out into the rough road which led to the main highway. This was the way they would come back, bringing more men to search and question efficiently. Perhaps they would send a medical officer first, to find out if there was an epidemic brewing; and that meant the bodies in the coffins would be thoroughly examined.

"They'll *have* to be burned," she said.

"Eh?" Tomasz was standing at the table beside her now, holding something out to her.

She took the flask. "The bodies," she said heavily. "Either they must be burned or we must bury them secretly out of the village and say that we burned them in case of typhus." She looked wearily down at the flask in her hand. "What's this?"

"That's what I've been asking. Never saw it before in my life. It was stuck over on that shelf beside the best brandy we have."

Sheila looked at the curiously carved top of the flask. "What a peculiar cap," she said involuntarily. She studied its simple, bold and yet unusual design. And then she looked up at Tomasz.

"Never saw it before," he repeated stubbornly.

She said quickly, "Peter got drunk last night after he had some liquor out of Dittmar's flask."

Tomasz still looked at her without understanding.

"Dittmar called himself Ryng," she explained.

He was staring now. He took the flask out of her hand and strode into the hall with that strange, loping walk of his. "Kati! Kati!"

When he came back, he said. "This is Ryng's flask. He must have put it there without anyone knowing."

"Yes. . . ." To give a message. He had put it there secretly, beside the best brandy which friend Hefner would choose to drink, just in case any accident should happen to him. She examined the top of the flask again: its very distinction made her believe that this guess was right. The flask might be one that German agents carried with them, to identify themselves when necessary. If Hefner had found it. . . .

She said very slowly, "Yes, to give a message. To tell them that he had stayed here."

Neither spoke for a moment. The feeling of danger once more flooded into the room.

Then at last, "I'll have that drink later," Tomasz said. "I've lost the taste for it. And I'm just remembering we have much still to do. I'm thinking that the angels have been on our side this time."

"Yes." She remembered Winkler's heavy joke: *What—Herr Hefner refusing a drink on the house?* "Yes. I've never felt so much like going down on my knees and praying, in all my life."

"We'll do our praying standing up until we finish this job." Tomasz was grim, gray-faced once more. "I've sent one of the boys over to the church to tell the people, when the service is ended, that they're to gather here. The other boys are back standing guard on the main road. They'll give us warning if any Germans appear. When everyone comes over here, we'll plan what to do. The priest will help us. He will know. Then, let all the Germans come. Dwór's ready for them!"

Then he added, not unkindly, "But we don't know what to do with you. You cannot stay. The Germans would hear from your voice that you are a foreigner. You must leave. But how? Peter was your guide, and he is dead. Zak could have shown you the way, but he too is gone. I know the way, but I must stay here. The village . . ."

"Yes, you must stay here. Winkler and Hefner will expect to see you when they return." Sheila looked up at the man's brooding face. "Don't worry, Tomasz. I shall leave. But I couldn't travel by the Nowe Miasto route anyway. Hefner knows about it; that is why he was there. He traced the old lady with her dog. So neither you nor Peter nor Zak would be any use to me now. I shall have to take another route."

"You can go back to the forest and wait for instructions."

"No, I won't go back to the forest."

The man stared at her in surprise. The vehemence which she had suddenly shown startled him. Well, everyone had their likes and dislikes, everyone had their own idea about things. If she wouldn't go back to the forest, she wouldn't go back to the forest. And that was that.

"What's wrong with the forest?" he asked defensively. No one was going to talk against the forest to him. She's got nice soft eyes, he thought; they smile and cry all at once. So she liked the forest. She had nothing against it, after all. "All right," he said gruffly, and left the room, closing the door firmly behind him.

Outside there was the sound of distant feet. There were voices, too. The church service must be over. The people were coming to the inn.

Sheila sat down on the bench, put her elbows on the table, covered her face with her hands. How soon must she leave? And for where? She suddenly felt so alone that her thoughts were stifled. Uncle Matthews would say, "No good giving up hope, while you've still one breath to draw." But somehow this was one time when Uncle Matthews' advice didn't sound so very true. The villagers' voices were raised now.

They at least were happy. They at least could rejoice over their victory. She wished she could be like them, letting whatever the next day would bring take care of itself. She shook her head angrily, trying to force logic back into her thoughts.

The Germans would spend some hours at Nowe Miasto, searching or waiting for Dittmar. Then they would make inquiries at the villages on the way to Nowe Miasto from here. Then they would gather enough me to strike fear into the heart of Dwór. And then they'd come back. This evening? No, more likely tomorrow morning would be the time of their coming. Tonight, in the darkness, she would have to set off. Perhaps one of the children could guide her for the first few miles to the east, and then, after that, she would just keep going east. Eventually she might reach the Russian part of occupied Poland. The Russians weren't at war with Britain. Perhaps they'd help her. All she could do was to try. The Russians weren't the Germans. They hadn't been treating the people of Eastern Poland in the way the Nazis had dealt with their half of the country. Yes, all she could do was to try. She sighed. Mr. Olszak would be more alarmed than amused if he knew how much she missed him at this moment.

She heard the priest's voice now. For a moment she wondered why the villagers hadn't come into the inn as Tomasz had suggested. They had gathered outside, instead. There had been a babel of voices; there had been a feeling of relief, even of joy. Now they were listening out there to the priest's even tones, instructing them, advising them. The priest finished, and Tomasz was speaking once more. And then there was a third voice, strong and confident. Sheila lifted her face from her hands. It couldn't be. It couldn't. . . . People were moving now; there was a blur of voices and footsteps. The door of the front room opened.

It was Adam.

# CHAPTER XXXVII

## *Wedding*

HE CLOSED the door firmly behind him, shutting out the curious faces of Zofia and Tomasz and Kati.

He looked at her gravely. "Men have been shot for less," he said. His voice was serious, his face set. And then, as he watched her eyes widen, there was the beginning of a smile. He crossed over to her swiftly. His hands were leading her round the table. He pulled the red handkerchief off her hair, and rumpled its curls back into life.

"Sheila," he said. "Sheila...."

She smiled with all her heart. She laughed. Life was simple and easy and wonderful once more. Now she could walk not only to the Russian border, she could find her way alone to Vladivostok.

Between kisses he was saying, "I told her to wait.... She said she would.... And then she left in the darkness.... Rebel."

She struggled free to protest, "Adam, you *know* I didn't want to go."

He was serious again, and this time his face and voice were gentle. "Yes, I know." He kissed her once more.

She suddenly noticed her hand as it touched his shoulder. She remembered her appearance.

"Oh Adam!" And then as he looked at her in surprise, "I should have known you would come. You always see me when I'm..."

"When you are what, darling?" But he knew what she meant, for he was smiling now.

She had to smile, too. "Why can't you see me *just once* in my prettiest dress?" she asked ruefully, and unfastened the shawl from her waist.

He was laughing. He pointed to the stained peasant clothes which he now wore and said, "I don't look much of a bargain in these things, do I?"

"Wading through ditches ... milking goats—" she went on, but he silenced her with his arms, holding her so tightly that there was no more breath left in her lungs, and the rest of her words became a gasp.

He searched for a scrap of handkerchief in his pocket. He cleaned her face gently. "Why did you leave the forest?"

"You know why, Adam." Her eyes met his steadily.

He spoke very quietly now. "That was the only reason?"

"It was the only reason."

He was wiping her hands. He kissed them each in turn. "That was what I wanted to hear," he said.

She tried to speak. I love you, I adore you, I love you, Adam. I never want to leave you, but if I must I shall wait forever and ever. But all she did was to put her arms round his neck and kiss him.

"After I stopped cursing Olszak, all I could think was that perhaps you...." His voice hesitated. He wasn't sure of himself, any more. He looked at her uncertainly, pleadingly.

There was a sadness, a sincerity in his face which twisted her heart.

"You *do* love me, Adam," she said gently.

"I more than love you, Sheila. You know that, too."

"Yes. I know that."

"As I know that you love me?"

"Yes. I love you, Adam."

"Forever?"

"Forever."

"That is all that matters."

She nodded. It was all that mattered.

\*     \*     \*

Kati entered, preceded by a timid knock, and then by a second, more urgent rap on the door. She looked apologetically towards Wisniewski. He and the fair-haired girl were standing so close together, talking so earnestly and sadly that she was afraid to speak.

"Yes?" the Chief asked impatiently without looking at her.

"Father Brys and the first of the men have got back from the burial," Kati replied.

Zofia, her neck straining to see past Kati, had tried to edge into the room too. But Kati's broad shoulders and outstretched arm blocked the way.

"Father Brys wants to know where the meeting is to be," Kati added.

"I see." Adam turned to come slowly to the door, his arm still round Sheila. "In here, I suppose." Zofia was looking very impressed as she stood aside to let Sheila enter the hall.

"Tell the other men, as they arrive, to come here," Adam said to the round-eyed village woman. "And we shall all need a hot meal before we leave again." Zofia nodded her head and bustled away, well-pleased at having been given some commands to dole out. To Kati he said, "Tell Zygmunt I'll come and see him before the meeting starts. If he isn't asleep."

"No, he's been waiting for you to come. Captain—" Kati was unexpectedly slow, hesitating. "Do you think you could have him back in camp, please?"

"He is badly injured."

"That's what he keeps saying: a one-legged man is no use for the camp. And he is lying there, just miserable, not caring whether he gets well or not."

"I see." There was a pause in which Kati's unhappy, strained eyes watched Wisniewski's face constantly. "We'll find some job for him to do, out of camp. Perhaps as our key man, here. You would like that, wouldn't you, Kati?"

"Yes. That's what we used to talk about all the time—
about having this war over and the Germans away and all
of us living the way we want to live, and Zygmunt and me
here at the inn. And now he's got the chance to be at the
inn. And he doesn't want it. He wants to go back to the camp.
To finish his job, he says."

"He could do an excellent job here, Kati, now that Zak
and your mother and Peter have gone."

Kati looked unhappily at Wisniewski. "Could you make that
job seem important? Sort of dangerous?"

"Yes." He repressed a smile. "If that will help, it will
be very important and very dangerous."

"Thank you, Captain." Kati hurried along the hall with her
news. Sheila watched her go.

"What's wrong, Sheila?"

"I was just wishing."

"What were you wishing?"

"That you'd have a leg amputated."

He kissed her quickly. "That's the only way to silence
you, my girl," he said. "You don't often say things like that,
darling." She felt more ashamed of her words than any re-
proof could have made her.

"No, don't look like that, Sheila. God knows I've thought
of enough mad things since I got back to the camp this
dawn and Sierakowski told me you had left. Even before
then, when we waited in the forest for the Germans to
show up, I had thought of them."

"Perhaps it would have been easier if we had never met
here. I was becoming resigned to everything. Now I am
all mixed up, again," she said sadly.

"No, Sheila, this way is best. This way, we make our own
decisions. We aren't children to have them made for us. If
we aren't strong enough to make the right one, then we
are dishonest—pretending what we want to do is what
we ought to do."

She nodded.

"You believe me, Sheila?" he asked anxiously.

"Yes." She kissed him to silence his doubts. She tried to
smile, to make her voice light. "I'm bad for you, Adam. I
make you break too many rules." She patted the gun in his
pocket.

He smiled and said, "We came here for business, not for
pleasure. If you hadn't broken that rule, yourself, this visit
would have been purely a business one." In spite of his
smile, she saw that the journey he had made from the forest
to this village must have been a nightmare.

As she looked at him, she remembered the first time she

had met him. Now his face was thinner, older; his eyes were more thoughtful, his lips tighter. It was a stronger face, the face of a man who had come to know himself. Everything had been taken from him. All he had left was his body, his brains and his courage. These were the real man: not what he had owned in land, or in money, or in the prestige of a name. And he knew that, and he accepted it.

Adam Wisniewski watched the girl's face looking at him so intently. What was she thinking? From the first time he had met her, he had wondered about that. His memory of her as he had first see her—leaning out of the window at the Korytów house, her eyes and lips laughing, fair hair falling to her shoulders, warmth and life in her face—had haunted him. Then later, when she came downstairs for that last dinner and his impatience had increased as he waited for her to appear, she had seemed another being. Still with the same fair hair, the same large brown eyes, the same smiling mouth. But she had become suddenly cold and remote; there was a challenge in the way she ignored him. He had watched her all through that dinner, and he had discovered two things. One was that she didn't love Andrew Aleksander and never would. Somehow he had been relieved to know that. The other was that she was shy, and her coldness was a guard put up against a frightening world. He had been amazed that any girl with her beauty and charm should be shy, and his interest had quickened. Before he could talk to her, tease her, try to make her lose that self-control so that she would become as alive and warm as in the first moment of seeing her, events had crowded in. Personal thoughts and desires had to be forgotten. At the meeting in Korytowski's flat he had been angry that she should have been there: she was being drawn into danger; he wanted her away. Safe. It was then he had realized the incongruous fact that he was in love with this girl: incongruous because he had at last found what he most wanted at a time when he, who had always got what he wanted, couldn't even try to possess it. There was no forgetting her, either. There never would be. But there were other things to be done, and if he kept her near him she would always be in danger. The journey from the forest to this village, without knowing what had happened except that shots from the village had been heard, had been undiluted hell. But it had proved to him that she would have to leave. Not for Olszak's reasons, not for all that damned talk about leadership. He was a captain with a job of fighting to do. He would fight as well with her as he had fought without her. But what would happen to her if he were killed? Or if she were taken hostage by the Germans? They'd soon know that she wasn't Polish; they'd learn about Anna Braun. Did she know what danger she was in? Probably she did. But she wouldn't go away if that were the only reason for not staying. He tightened his grasp round her waist. Not for Olszak's reasons, then; but Olszak's reason would have to be used if he sent her away. These would be the only ones she would listen to.

They heard Kati clearing her throat more loudly than necessary. They were once more back in the inn at Dwór. Behind Kati was the white, furrowed face of Father Brys. He was watching them with his calm gray eyes. Sheila felt he understood everything. Without being told, he knew, and knowing, understood. Quickly she followed Kati out into the open.

In front of the inn there was a group of waiting men. Sheila knew the younger men, some seven or eight in number. They were from the camp. Adam had picked the toughest fighters, too, she thought, as she recognized them. They greeted her smilingly, with a sort of informal, vague salute.

"You cheated us out of a job, we've been hearing," one called over to her as she passed, and the others grinned widely. Then they started moving into the inn with the older men from the village.

"What you need is a good scrub," Kati said critically. "Tearstains and all. You're a beauty at this moment I can tell you." She led Sheila round to the side of the house where there was an open pump. "Go on, stick your head under that. I'll have to get you fresh clothes, anyway."

"How's your side, Kati?"

"All right. Zofia bandaged me up. It doesn't hurt. Not much."

"Where are the women?"

"Cooking. The older children are pretending to work in the fields near the main road. They are keeping watch."

"How did the men from the camp arrive?"

"When the old woman and her son got to the forest, they found the Chief setting out for the village. He had just heard you came here last night. They told him about the German spy, and about the shots they had heard (that's what made the old woman and her son go straight to the forest instead of waiting for night to come), and the chief then chooses some men to come with him, and they come straight to the village. Not all together, you know. Not marching. Just the way they slip into places. But they all got here about the same time, just as the service was ending in the church. I was looking out of the hall window to see if everything was all right. And what did I see? First the Chief and Ladislas, then little Jan, then Kasmierz and Julian, then Edmund, and then three men I didn't know. What excitement there was in the square! The Chief was talking to Father Brys and Tomasz. They were telling him everything. And then I knew we were all safe." Kati was happy: the village had been in danger, and the camp hadn't forgotten it. The camp was taking charge. All was well.

"What happened to the—to the coffins?"

Kati stared at her. "You know nothing, do you? What in the wide world have you been talking about in there?" She nodded over shoulder in the direction of the inn. "Nearly an hour, you were. And you know nothing."

"What happened?"

"The Chief's a quick one. As soon as he knew what had been happening here, he gave his orders. The—" Only the slight hesitation, the drop in the girl's voice as it spoke the next word, was there to remind them of Jadwiga—"the bodies must disappear so that the Germans wouldn't find them. We are to tell the Szwaby that we burned them in case of typhus." The sadness in her voice disappeared. She added, vindictively, "But we haven't buried Ryng."

Sheila, drying her face and scrubbing her arms with her apron, looked up in surprise.

"No," Kati went on. "See that cart with logs in it? He's under there. The cart is going to Nowe Miasto. Zofia's husband had orders from the Germans to bring in a load of his best wood before the end of this week. So he is going today. The chief and his men will meet the cart at dusk just before it enters the little town. They will take the body, and when they raid Nowe Miasto tonight, they'll leave the body with a lot of bullets in it on the road behind them. It will be found after they've finished the raid."

"Captain Wis—the captain is going on a raid?" Sheila tried to keep her voice calm.

"Of course. He told Tomasz that if the Germans get enough to occupy them at Nowe Miasto, they wouldn't come here for a day or two. And if they found the spy's body, then they wouldn't start searching for him here. If we had buried him the Szwaby would have kept on looking and looking."

"Dittmar met a raiding party and got killed. . . ." Yes, that was the easiest solution. Strange how easy, how simple things seemed; once someone had thought of them, that was.

Kati said, "He got killed, all right." She suddenly put out

her strong, broad hand and gripped Sheila's shoulder. "And you don't look as if you could kill a mouse."

Sheila laughed shortly. "I never have," she said grimly.

Kati looked at her strangely. She slipped her arm round Sheila's shoulders. "Come on," she said with surprising gentleness. "You'll need other clothes. You must brush your hair, and then we must prepare the food we have. We are giving the men a meal after the meeting is over. They are now making plans for the raid and for what the village is to do in the next few days. They'll deserve the best meal we can cook for them. Come on."

The little square was empty now. Four of the older men of the village were grouped outside the inn door. They stood motionless, in the timeless way that peasants have; their pipes were in their mouths, their thumbs were tucked into their waistcoats' high pockets. Farseeing blue eyes, with the same distant look that you see in sailors' eyes, were turned towards the main road. The brown, wrinkled faces were impassive. They were waiting for the first sign of warning from any of the boys down in the fields. From the open cottage windows, came the sound of pots and dishes; of women's voices, sharpened by haste, telling children to keep out of their way. There was the smell of cooking food to remind Sheila that she was hungry. The white smoke of wood fires curled under the cold winter sky.

Kati looked at the blue-gray clouds overhead. "It will rain, but not before tonight, I hope," she said. "Soon the snows will come." She half-sighed, as if she asked how many winters of snow would there be before this war was over, before women could look after peaceful kitchens and men could come home to their families in the evenings.

The old men's high boots shuffled aside to let the two women enter the inn. Through the closed door of the front room came the murmur of voices. And then Adam's voice was speaking.

"Come on," Kati said with a smile, and pulled at Sheila's arm. "You'll be hearing him plenty yet, if you ask me."

The kitchen lay next door to the front room. It was square in shape like the bedroom. The difference in furniture was a larger table, a taller cupboard, an extra dresser with heavy dishes along its shelves, a bigger stove with an oven at the side of its wood fire.

Kati looked for a moment at the bed in the corner, at the bright-checked apron hanging on its hook, at the spinning wheel near the oven bench. Her emotions, which she had been able to hide under the stress of danger and worry and action, were now released. She looked at the baking bowl on the table with its measure of rye flour. Jadwiga, Sheila guessed, must have been preparing to bake some bread this morning when Dittmar had interrupted it. Kati's face twisted like a child's and she burst into tears. She turned her back on Sheila.

"Next door," she said at last. Her words were muffled by the apron which she held up to her face. "Next door, you will see a carved chest. The clothes are there."

When Sheila came back to the kitchen, Kati was standing at the table. She was wearing the red-checked apron, and she was shaping the rough lumps of dough into smooth round loaves. Her face was white, blotched violently with red spots. But her voice was calm and practical once more. She nodded in approval as she looked at Sheila.

"It's too pretty," Sheila said awkwardly, smoothing the silk apron over the wide black skirt banded with velvet. She fingered the lace edge of the thin white blouse and looked at the roses on the gaily embroidered jacket. She knew that Kati had only two dresses: the one she wore, and this special one. This very special one, kept for feast days, for funerals and weddings. It would be Kati's own wedding dress. "Let's wash my clothes. We can scrub the blood and mud out of them. They'll dry before I leave tonight."

"No," Kati said determinedly.

"But—"

"No!" Kati placed the loaves in the oven, lifted the lid off the large soup-pot. She seemed pleased with the result. "In that cupboard over there, you'll find shoes. Lowest shelf."

Sheila searched unwillingly among old newspapers, stubs of candles, carefully rolled pieces of string. The shoes, wrapped in paper, lay beside a sewing basket. Kati's best shoes. Perhaps her only pair besides these long boots.

"I don't need them, Kati."

"You'll walk barefoot?"

"Why not? You do."

"And what would the Chief say to that?"

"Nothing," Sheila lied.

"Well, I'd say plenty. The idea! You feet are too soft. They're not like mine." She held up a proud bare foot to prove it. "If I have my boots for the bad weather, I don't need shoes. Put them on. Do they fit?"

"They are beautiful," Sheila said, and a look of pleasure came into Kati's eyes. "But really, Kati, I can wear the shoes I arrived in."

"No. They'd spoil the look of the dress."

"But, Kati—"

"No! Now put on that working apron and cover your dress

well, and you can help me. This is all the meat we have. Slice it thin, and it will go further." She handed Sheila a knife. "You are leaving tonight? Back to the forest?"

This time it was Sheila who said "No."

"That's what Tomasz said you said," Kati answered. She pretended to be examining the contents of the cupboard. "Why?"

"Because," Sheila began and then stopped. "Well, why did you try to get Zygmunt back to the camp, when you wanted him to stay here?"

Kati looked at her. "But the Chief's the boss. What he says, goes."

"Yes. And because he's the boss, Kati, he has got to obey the rules of the camp even more closely than the men. Don't you see, Kati?"

"No, I don't. Stuff and nonsense. If I were boss, I'd be boss."

"Yes, but being in command means you must also be in command of yourself. There's no one to give you orders, so you have to give them to yourself."

Kati pulled down the few jars of pickled mushrooms and cucumbers from the cupboard shelf. "Open these," she said. "If we don't eat them, the Germans will. We'll have one good last meal together." She counted the jars with her fingers, nodded her head. "Enough," she said in relief, before she suddenly remembered to rush over to the oven. She opened the square iron door carefully with an apron-covered hand. "All right, so far," she said. The smell of warm bread filled the kitchen and added to Sheila's hunger. "He's got queer ideas about it, too. You know, he doesn't like being called Chief. We've got to say just 'Captain' to his face. And yet he *is* the Chief, all right. Who else?" Kati took one of the loaves and broke it slightly to see if it were baked. "I don't understand these things very well. I've never been a boss, so I don't know. But if you speak the truth, then I don't want to be one. Ever."

"You are the boss of this inn, Kati. You and I are so hungry that we could sit down at this table and eat all this meat, right now. Why don't you? You're the boss. It is your meat. It is your kitchen. But you don't even touch one slice of meat; you want to prepare as good a dinner as you can, and you think of those others next door, who are just as hungry as we are. Do you see what I mean?"

Kati stared at her. Then she gave one of her old smiles. "I wouldn't make a very good boss," she said. "I tasted a piece of cucumber when you weren't looking."

They were both laughing when the door opened and Tomasz appeared.

"We're finished. Are you ready?"

"Almost. Tell the other women they can start bringing their food over here."

Tomasz nodded, and turned to go. "Pretty," he said, looking at Sheila.

"Yes," Kati said proudly. "Isn't it?" And Sheila laughed again. Kati was pulling off the working apron, preening the lace collar, pushing up the wide sleeves of the blouse so that it billowed out in all its starched whiteness. She stood back and surveyed her handi-work critically once more. "You'll do," she predicted.

"Agreed." It was Adam, leaning against the door, smiling as he watched Sheila's startled face. He stretched out a hand as he came forward to her. The meeting had been successful: the plan was well made. She knew that by his face. She took his hand with a smile.

"Too decorative," she said. "The Russians won't believe I can work for a living, I'm sure."

Adam was laughing now. "Russians? What have they to do with this?" He was studying the dress approvingly.

"I thought the shortest way for me would be to try and reach the Russian occupation zone. They won't arrest anyone British."

He said slowly, "You mean that you were going to walk out in that dress and reach Russia?"

"Well, I've been trying to tell Kati that my old clothes would be better, bloodstains and all. They'd be a more successful entry permit, I think."

"Sheila . . ." He seemed to forget about Kati, and Sheila forgot too.

"Sheila." He was smiling again. He caught her suddenly round the waist. "Mad, quite mad. As crazy as they come," he said, and kissed her unexpectedly on the nose. He began to laugh. "To Russia," he said, "to Russia, by God. Just like that." He laughed again and rumpled her hair. "Without papers, without a map, without anything except a pretty dress and a lovely face. Darling, at this moment I swear I shall love you forever and ever."

"What's so funny, Adam?" Sheila asked with stilted dignity. When he laughed, his head was thrown back and his teeth were white against the deeply tanned skin. The worried lines had vanished from his face. It was infectious. She stopped trying to draw herself away and look dignified. She began to laugh, too. Kati, the forgotten one, was smiling broadly in sympathy as she pulled the golden loaves out of the oven.

"Darling Sheila," he said, "when a woman marries she is supposed to relax and let her man do the worrying."

He pushed the hair back from her forehead and draped a curl over the edge of her brow. "Madame Recamier. Blonde, but still Madame Recamier," he said. Then he was serious. "Let me do the worrying, darling. I'll manage it, I think. It won't be Olszak's way, but even he will admit it is inevitable."

A hot loaf dropped from Kati's fingers. There was a half-stifled oath.

"Father Brys agrees. He's waiting for us now," Adam was saying. Then he turned to Kati. "You didn't know the meal you were preparing was to be a wedding breakfast, did you, Kati?"

To Sheila he said, "You'll obey me, my girl, when you're married. No more bright ideas. You'll be safe, from now on."

"You're equally mad, Adam," Sheila said. And then, with a catch in her voice, "I love you."

Kati was staring openly now. There was no more pretense of ignoring them. The sad look had gone from her face, and for a moment it was blank of expression. Then excitement came to her eyes and approval softened her lips.

"Well, someone has got sense," she said, and looked very pointedly at Sheila. "You and your slices of meat!" she added beneath her breath.

Tomasz looked round the half-open door. "We are all ready. We are waiting," he said impatiently.

Kati said happily, "Tomasz, didn't you know? Didn't the Chief—the captain tell you? It's a wedding."

Tomasz said solemnly, "A wedding followed by a funeral is bad, but a funeral followed by a wedding is a good omen. We shall all be the happier of it."

"And to hell with the long-nosed German swine," Kati added emphatically. "This is one thing they don't take away from us." She was pulling off her working apron. "I must tell Zygmunt."

"The food, woman, the food!" Tomasz called after her.

"There's no hurry," she answered from the other end of the corridor. "They've got to go to church first, haven't they?"

"You see," Adam teased, "they won't let you eat until you've been to church with me. Either you marry or you starve, my girl."

In the small village square, a sea of quiet friendly faces waited for them. Sheila halted at the inn door for a moment. She looked up at Adam, standing beside her. "This," she said, "is the loveliest of weddings."

Adam's eyes held hers, as they had done when they had first met. He loves me, she thought, he loves me so very very much. And it almost frightened her that she should have roused so much feeling and emotion in any man. Then he smiled, and she smiled too. She was so happy that she wanted to weep.

## CHAPTER XXXVIII

## *To the Mountains*

KATI had been right: the night wind had brought a threat of rain in its cold touch. Sheila pulled Zofia's coat more closely round her neck, moved her feet inside their wide shoes to keep them from freezing, hugged her body with her arms. The man, sitting beside her under the bare branches of the small wood, was motionless. He hadn't spoken since they had reached this place and he had pointed northwards into the darkness, and had said "Nowe Miasto."

Sheila strained her eyes. In front of her she could, with some effort, make out the black stretch of slow-moving water. Through the wind's sad song in the branches overhead came its steady, gentle rhythm. That was the river which flowed east towards the Vistula. Adam had insisted that she should wait for him on its south bank. On the north bank, towards the west, pinpricks of light showed that Nowe Miasto was still awake. Even as she waited, the lights were slowly dying out. Soon the town would be asleep.

She whispered to the man, "Soon, now."

He nodded. She felt he was angry with her because he had to sit and look after her, instead of taking part in the attack.

Sheila stared once more at the masses of dark shadows, at the patches and the blots of darkness which meant trees and houses and buildings. She was too far away to be able to see anything clearly. She could only guess. She wondered where Adam and his men were. Probably lying like this under some tree, waiting as tensely as she was. She thought of Dittmar's dead body, now lying in a ditch to the north of the town, with that identification flask in its pocket and its Luger beside it, as if the attacking guerrillas had only had time to shoot but not to search the man who had tried to stop them. And, thinking of the Luger, she said suddenly:—

"They've only got revolvers. They won't have much chance."

The man stirred and put out a hand to quieten her. "We've a cache near here. They wouldn't attack without visiting it first. Don't worry. They are well-armed." His bad temper seemed to have been drawn off by worry in her voice. "Don't worry," he whispered again. And then, to the silent village, he said softly, "Go out, little lights, go out. We are ready."

At last, there remained only two visible lights. The man was sitting erect now, leaning forward, alert. His excitement was obvious. "Time to deal with the sentries," he was saying. He put out his hand once more and gripped Sheila's arm. As the first explosion shattered the black curtain of night, his grip tightened. A second, a third explosion, a rattle of quick shots, blinding flashes of light. Men's cries of warning seemed little things in the violence of sound and jagged flame.

Sheila and the man had risen to their feet. He was cursing steadily, fluently, in an ecstasy of joy. He stopped for one moment to look down at her. "Well-armed, eh?" he asked, and then, as a large orange column of flame wrapped in thick black smoke rose straight into the sky, he added, "Holy Mother, that's the railway. Petrol-cars must have been standing on the lines." He hugged her in his joy. And then the explosions ceased. There was only the wild chatter of machine guns.

"We've left," he was saying now. "That's the Germans taking their turn now." He watched the orange pillar of flame. "Such damage, such beautiful damage." His voice calmed. "Well-planned. That's the way. First the sentries. Quietly, no fuss. Some dynamite well placed. And then the grenades: well placed too. And then some shooting from scattered places, so that they may think there's a big attack with a lot of men. And then a quick retreat just as the Huns are getting together. That's the way, meanwhile: hit hard, then run like blazes."

Sheila's excitement left her more quickly. She suddenly felt cold as ice. She watched the thick heavy curls of smoke, blacker than the black night sky, and wondered: How many killed, how many wounded? Adam?

The man pulled her down once again into the shelter of the bushes.

"That's what we have to watch," he whispered, and pointed to the river.

"Where's the bridge?"

"Too well-guarded." The man had guessed her worry, for he added confidently, "He will swim it, all right."

Sheila felt suddenly weak. He will swim ... She stared at the black cold water of the river. The man must have felt her dismay. "Don't worry. We are used to this. It's all in a night's work. It's nothing."

Nothing? Sheila looked at him angrily.

"Another five minutes. Give him five minutes," the man said calmly. His eyes never left the river. Then suddenly he gave the low call of a night bird. Just then a flare lit up the river-banks and turned the orange flames to green. The man thrust Sheila's face down and held it pressed to the earth. They didn't move, but Sheila's heart had quickened. She had seen Adam, a black shape now as immovable and indistinguish-able as they were, as he had thrown himself down beside a patch of bushes. Again the man beside her gave the low birdcall. As the flare's blue light died down, they heard Adam's running footsteps. The man's arm was raised; this time the bird's whistle was scarcely audible. A second flare ripped into the sky, but the three of them were behind a wall of trees and Adam's hand was round her shoulders as they lay side by side, face down, on the ground.

"Neat," the man said approvingly. "Neat job, sir."

Adam's heavy breathing quietened. He nodded. "If they are sending up flares, they aren't sure where we've gone," he said. From across the river came the roar of motors. "Now they think they know," he added. He listened. "They've followed those who went northeast to the Vistula."

The flares had ceased. Adam sat up. To the man he said, "Reach the forest by the south. Tell Colonel Sierakowski that three have gone towards the Vistula—Ladislas, Kasimierz, and Edmund— and that two others have gone to the north. They'll be in camp in a week's time. Julian is dead. Little Jan is wounded. He's gone to the Halicz farm. Send two men to pick him up there and get him back to the camp. Tell the captain I am proceeding to the south, as we arranged at our last meeting. I expect to see him there next month. He must ask Warsaw to tell Number Sixteen that the Radom-Nowe-Miasto route is now under suspicion and should be used no longer. Is that clear?"

The man repeated the message for Sierakowski quickly.

"Good," Adam said. "I'll see you in the spring, Ryszard. In the mountains."

Ryszard saluted. "In the spring, *rotmistrz*," he said cheerily. And then he was gone, a dark shadow slipping into darker shadows. Adam took Sheila's hand, and together they moved through the wood. Only the distant shouts from the little town, as the Germans fought the flames spreading with the wind, broke the silence of the night. Once the sound of distant shooting halted them. "German bullets only," he said. And then, "Our men are still safe. If they had been cornered, they would have shot back."

As they came out of the wood on its south side, Adam paused once more. "Our men got away," he said at last. The relief in his voice told Sheila how much he had been worrying. He caught her violently in his arms, held her for a moment against his wet body. He kissed her slowly, and then suddenly let her go.

"Nearly twenty miles to go before daylight," he said. "Or is that too much for the first part of our journey?" He took her hand once more.

"To the mountains?"

"Yes. I'll keep you there until Olszak and all his experts have a safe plan arranged for you—papers, clothes, and all that. If Olszak can't think up a safe enough one to please me, you stay until he does." His voice was determined.

They were moving into the open field now.

"What will Olszak say?" Sheila murmured.

"I've more to say about you than he has," was Adam's quiet answer.

The night became a number of hours, each with its accomplished miles. There was speed and tension and care, but none of the agony of her night journeys with Jan and Stefan. Adam didn't force the pace, and yet they appeared to cover more ground. He insisted on a ten-minute rest every hour, and whenever her pace lagged, his arm would be there to help her. Even that contact with him seemed to give her strength. Before dawn, they had reached the end of the first stage of their journey. A quiet-faced peasant woman welcomed them into her small quiet house.

The second night, they covered thirty miles. This time they were given shelter in a country house, whose owner had been a friend of Adam's father. Now, his wife dead, his sons killed, he lived alone in the almost empty rooms of his looted home.

When they set off on the third night's journey, which was through wide stretches of forest land and uninhabited country, they were given two horses. "Poor specimens, I'm afraid, compared with what you used to ride, Adam," their host had said, "but it was all I could hide from the damned Germans. These crocks will at least take you a little more quickly than your feet. Leave them at the monastery. They will be brought back here to lend to other travelers." He had watched them leave, half proudly, half sadly. Sheila felt that the deepest regret of this old man, who lived with perpetual reminders of regret and sorrow, was that he was too old, too ill to be of any use, except as the host of those who traveled secretly. The horses carried them a long distance that night. The flat plains had given way to rich forests and rolling grassland. They traveled far enough away from even the smallest road, so that they were unseen and unheard. Dawn brought them to the monastery. The white-robed priests gave them shelter in the small guesthouse outside the grounds.

The fourth night they traveled through a country of foot-hills, each with its small castle or little church on its crest. It was now much colder. The ground was hard with frost. The rain was turning to grains of snow. At dawn, they thawed out in a forester's warm hut. When they left, they had food with them, and the forester's wife had given Sheila a fur cap and long boots.

The fifth night took them to the mountains. At first, the mountains were simply steeper hills, tree-covered, snow-sprinkled. And then the hills heightened, sharpened. The peaks became ice-covered crags, the pine forests climbed only half-way up the steep sides. Adam led her along the fingerlike valleys, deep and narrow; along the paths beside the shallow icy streams that clattered down to meet them. Snow was underfoot now, yet either the mountains or the pine forests sheltered them, for Sheila felt warmer than she had felt on the open plains.

They rested for only an hour on the fifth day. Looking at the dark gray sky above them, Adam shook his head. "We are nearly there," he said. And then, anxiously, "Sheila, can you keep on walking? We can trust this place even in daylight. There's nothing to be afraid of here." He looked up at the sky once more.

"Except the snow?" Sheila suggested.

He nodded. "There's going to be a heavy fall soon. We must keep moving until it comes. Once it starts, we will have to wait until the storm is over. And it might last a week."

Sheila looked at the black rocks showing through the snow on the mountainside. The pine trees, green no longer, seemed black too. There wasn't a house in sight. She shivered, and said, "You lead, Adam. That makes it easier for me."

Their pace had slowed, perhaps because of the snow on the ground which made each step an effort of sinking and lifting wherever the flakes had drifted, perhaps because Adam watched Sheila's progress as anxiously as he watched the sky.

"Adam, you don't have to stop for so many rests," she said once. "I'm all right."

He kissed her and then straightened the fur cap on her head, again.

"What a bad mountain-climber you'd make, darling," he answered, his smile broadening as he watched her indignation, and then her answering amusement.

"Frozen?" he asked.

"Not as long as we keep moving." She pulled Zofia's coat tighter round her neck. She kept doing that nowadays, it seemed.

"I'll get you a fur jacket," Adam said.

She laughed at that. "The Germans seem miles and miles away, somehow," she said.

"Five miles, to be exact. Just over that wall of mountains on your right," he answered. "Over there is the railway from Cracow to Zakopane. They've taken over Zakopane completely. It's their mountain resort, where tired army officers and Gestapo experts take their little blondes for ten days' leave."

Sheila stared blankly. "And our village?"

"Quite near Zakopane. Sometimes there's safety in the lion's den."

At the end of the afternoon, the narrow valley broadened and they saw the village: red roofs on blue-painted houses scattered over the white snow.

Wisniewski was smiling now. The worry had gone from his face. "Our house is higher up the mountain. It stands above the village," he said. "We'll cut up through this pine forest. Just half an hour more. All right, Sheila?"

She nodded, and he kissed her. "It's extraordinary—" he said, shaking his head.

"What's extraordinary?"

He looked at her with a smile in his eyes. "Later," he said. "We'll talk later, Pani Wisniewska."

They climbed slowly through the pine wood. She needed his arm now. He felt her weight sag, and slowed his step still more. She didn't even notice it. At the edge of the fir trees, Adam halted. There was nothing but silence, and the gathering darkness. In a clearing was a loghouse. A long slope of mountain shoulder was the background. There was smoke from its chimney, a thin column pointing like a gray finger from the wide roof to the grayer sky. A small candle burned on a table at the window. Adam smiled, and gave a long, low whistle. They waited. The candle moved—as if someone had lifted it and put it back.

In the summer, Sheila was thinking, the meadow around the house would be green. There would be little yellow and red and blue flowers, white butterflies, birds, and the dark sweet smell of pine trees. There would be a high blue sky, pierced by the jagged mountains gleaming white in the sunshine. There would be red and purple petunias in the carved window-boxes, the sound of a woodman's ax in the forest, the clear voices of children bringing home the cows from pasture in the evening. The bells round the cows' neck would strike their slow note at each slow step. In the summer. . . . Well, that wasn't for her to see.

She tried to smile. "We managed it," she said.

In the valley below, she could see the steady pillars of smoke from the village chimneys. The houses themselves were hidden in the downward curve of pine woods. Beyond the valley was the range of mountains which divided the village from Zakopane. And the Germans. She gazed at the mountains and said once more, as if to them this time: "We managed it." She smiled happily. "I managed the journey better than the one with Jan, didn't I? It was longer, and yet I'm not so tired, Adam." She stumbled as she spoke. "Or am I, and I just don't notice it?" Adam's arm tightened around her waist. He lifted her across the stretch of snow-covered grass towards the house.

The door opened as they reached it. An old woman, her black knitted shawl drawn tightly by one hand across her throat, against the cold air, waited for them.

"You're late," she said to Adam in her faded voice. "I-was beginning to worry." She gave him her hand, and he bent and kissed it.

Closing the door behind them, she looked at Sheila. If Adam takes his arm away, Sheila thought, I'm going to fall down . . . how warm the room is . . . how safe and warm and safe. . . .

"My wife," Adam was saying. "Sheila, this is Pani Olszak."

Sheila's tired eyes opened. "Michal Olszak's mother," she heard Adam say softly to her. He led her to a low chair by the open fire. Pulling off her long boots, he began rubbing her feet and legs.

"Soup," Madame Olszak said. "That's what she needs. Hot soup. And a footbath. If your feet are warm, you're all warm. Veronika! Where's that girl? Veronika!"

Veronika came hurrying out of the kitchen, white-haired, plainfaced. She was a good twelve inches taller than her mistress; as broad-shouldered as a man. She wiped her large hands on her apron, and a real welcome came into her expressionless eyes as she saw Adam.

"My nephew, Adam Gunter, and his wife have come to see me," Madame Olszak was saying. "From Cracow. They are tired and hungry. Give them some soup, Veronika, and bring that washbasin and some hot water in here. Yes, in front of the fire. The bedroom's too cold to bathe in. Don't you see how frozen she is? Make them comfortable. They came all this way to see me because they heard I was ill. Imagine that, Veronika! We must take good care of them."

Veronika smiled at Adam, and nodded. "All the way from Cracow! Imagine that!" she echoed in her harsh voice. As she turned to look deliberately at Sheila, the welcoming smile gave way to a frank stare. Then, as if suddenly remembering all the things to be done, she whisked round and disappeared into the kitchen.

Madame Olszak's young blue eyes smiled out of her old, wrinkled face. A thin narrow face, in contrast to Veronika's broad bones.

"Does she really believe that?" asked Sheila. She was still shaken by Veronika's cold appraisal.

Madame Olszak laughed and looked at Adam. "You've chosen a smart one, Adam. Even if she is a foreigner." And then, watching his face, "*You* a married man! Well, well ... But it suits you. You're looking better than you did when you came to see us six weeks ago." She turned to to Sheila, as if she had just remembered the answer she had almost forgotten in her amusement over Adam's expression. "No, she doesn't believe it. It's a game we play. All the men who pass this way are Gunter, my nephew. Veronika thinks it funny. I find it useful." As she talked, her eyes never left Sheila. She watched the girl's face, her movements, her expressions. If Sheila hadn't felt so exhausted, she would have been embarrassed at such open scrutiny. But now all she could feel was a soft glow of warmth and safety and happiness and fatigue. She leaned her head against the high chairback, and smiled. Madame Olszak's soft voice went on: "I had two nephews here last week. An English branch of the family. Two British airmen who came all the way from a prison camp in East Prussia. Couldn't speak a word of Polish. They stayed here for five days and got some skin back on their feet. Wenceslas, from the the village, took them to their next stop. They were going east, to Rumania. And then to Constantinople." She shook her head admiringly. "Imagine! Such courage!"

"And such good Polish friends," said Sheila quietly.

"The only good thing about war is the friends we discover." Madame Olszak sat down on a bench at the side of the fire, and lifted the sewing which must have been interrupted when Adam whistled from the pine woods. It looked as if it might be a patchwork quilt, some day. "Soon need to light the lamp," she said, frowning at the growing darkness, pursing her lips as she concentrated on the squares of bright color. "Put out that candle, Adam! There's no need for it now. And your wife's all right. She'll live. And she needs two hands to hold her bowl of soup anyway."

Adam grinned, and obeyed. Sheila watched him as he went over to the window table and blew out the candle. Madame Olszak was watching Sheila.

"Did he ever tell you what happened to the candle on his last visit here?" She tried to thread a needle and said irritably, "Better light the lamp, Adam, and close the shutters. How short the days are now! No time at all for work. Now come and take your soup while it's warm. That's better." She shifted her sewing to let the yellow light fall across it. Veronika brought a wooden tub to the hearth-side and half-filled it carefully with hot water. As she passed between the kitchen and the room, with the alternately full and empty kettle, she would look sideways at Sheila. It was a strange look, half-reluctant, half-curious, wholly guarded.

Wearily, Sheila closed her eyes, let the warmth of the room soak into her tired body. Such luxury: warm soup, a fire, a bath, a comfortable bed, no Germans to worry about. Such luxury.

"Are you all right, Sheila?"

She opened her eyes. "Yes, Adam. I'm thawing out. It's wonderful." The round globe of light brought out the colors, deepened the shadows in the room. The oxblood walls were as comforting as a glass of burgundy. Veronika closed the kitchen door disapprovingly. Such a fuss about nothing, was the clear implication. Poor Veronika, Sheila thought: obviously no one had ever made a fuss about her.

" . . . On his last visit here?" Madame Olszak insisted.

"No," said Sheila. Madame certainly didn't give you time to think of your own aches or the pains of others.

"Well, I had the candle lit. My guests always arrive after sunset, and I always hear from Wenceslas—you know, Adam, that radio works perfectly. I never would have believed it. Wenceslas' son is learning to send out messages too, now. . . . Well, where was I? Oh, yes, the candle. It was lit. I had heard, you see, that my nephew Adam Gunter was to arrive. The soup was ready. The water was being boiled, the bed was being warmed. Everything was waiting. And then a party of Germans arrived at the door. Four of them. They had been mountain-climbing. 'You light your candle early, old woman,' they said to me. 'I need it for my sewing,' said I. 'When you are eighty years old, you will need a candle too.' They wanted food. What loud voices they had! You would have thought there were fourteen and not just four men in this room. It was then I heard a bird whistling in the wood. 'Why do you put out the candle, grandmother?" one asked. 'Because I save it when I don't do my sewing. You don't need it to find the way to your mouths.' And they began to eat the soup. But they didn't eat much. Two mouthfuls were enough. You should have heard what they said about Polish cooking. . . . Then they went down to the village where they had left their car, and went back to their Zakopane. Later, I lit the candle again. When the bird whistled this time, I moved the candle. Who should come in but my nephew Gunter! But he got no hot soup. We had to throw away the whole potful. Veronika had been too generous with the salt. Such a waste!"

Adam and Madame Olszak laughed. Sheila's smile wasn't successful: she couldn't manage to be as objective as that about such incidents.

Madame Olszak noticed Sheila's worried eyes, and quickly added, "I haven't seen a German from that day to this. They don't climb the mountains so much: they stick close to their Zakopane now. Such a lot of mountaineering accidents, we had."

She rose, carefully folding the quilt. "You'll find it warmer to get your clothes off and bathe in here. In this weather the bedroom is as cold as Siberia. We who live in the mountains have to take our comforts seriously." She moved towards the kitchen. "I'll give you my news in the morning, Adam."

"Good news?" he asked quickly.

"Yes. All the instructions you left here have been carried out. Wenceslas has a list of willing men. And there's other news. But not tonight. Tomorrow is time enough for the telling. Anyway, the snow is coming; you will be unable to move out of the house till the first heavy storm is over. You'll have four or five days to rest and hear my news."

Adam's voice became expressionless. "Have you had any message from your son?" His eyes met Sheila's and held them.

"No." Madame Olszak was watching them. "What's all this, anyway?" she asked with a smile. "An elopement? I *wondered* what she was doing here with you, Adam Wisniewski!" She came back into the room. "I must admit I am curious," she said. "It is one of the prerogatives of old age." She turned to Sheila. "Who are you, child? I've seen you before. I can't remember where. But I've seen you before."

Sheila roused herself from the warm feeling of sleep which

was beginning, so comfortably, to paralyze her thoughts. "I'm
Sheila Matthews." She caught a smile from Adam. "I mean,
I *was* Sheila Matthews."

Madame Olszak's blue eyes searched for a meaning to the
name; almost—not quite—finding it.

"Your son was a friend of my father, Charles Matthews,"
said Sheila.

"Charles Matthews," the faded voice repeated slowly. And
then, suddenly, more quickly. "Charles Matthews!" Madame
Olszak was really smiling now. The veil had dropped. Politeness vanished. Real emotion surged over the finely wrinkled
face. "Charles Matthews . . . of course . . . that's where I've
seen you." She crossed over to Sheila with her slow, even
step. "I've been staring at you all evening, my dear. I kept
saying to myself 'I've seen that girl before. But where?' It
worried me." She touched Sheila's cheek gently with her thin
brown hand. "Your father—" she glanced at Adam. "Yes, I
know. That will keep for tomorrow, too. Besides, Veronika
will be angry if I let my bowl of soup stand any longer."
Adam half-smiled. No one, not even Veronika, could bully
Madame. But the excuse was graceful: it made a tactful
exit. He opened the kitchen door, and waited.

"If she is as like her father as she looks, you couldn't
have chosen a better wife, Adam. Even if she is a foreigner."

"I know," he said. "Without knowing about her father, I
know." He raised Madame Olszak's thin hand to his lips,
and then closed the kitchen door firmly behind her.

Sheila had risen uncertainly from the chair, and having
made that effort, seemed incapable of more. She didn't speak.
There was a strange brooding look on her face. For a moment, he was jealous, and then cursed himself for a selfish
fool. Jealous of a ghost, of a dead father . . . jealous of the
moments when her thoughts were not his. He lowered the
lamp, saw its flame flicker and die. By the light of the fire,
he watched her hands slowly fumble at the waistband of her
skirt. Then she looked at him, and now she was thinking
only of him. Even before she spoke, he came over to her.

"Adam."

He held her shoulders. His hands slid to her waist. She
touched his cheek.

Suddenly there was fear in her voice. "Olszak has sent no
message. Could he? Has there been time enough?"

He nodded. How strange women were. To be so practical,
so worrying, when there were other things to think of. "Time
enough by wireless to the village," he said. He unfastened

the last hook. Her skirt fell to her feet. ". . . Even Olszak is human, it seems."

She smiled at that. "Yes. Even Olszak had a mother. Extraordinary."

"But logical." He tugged at the tape of her petticoat. "How in heaven's name do you unfasten this? It's knotted like iron." He knelt beside her, pretending to concentrate on that problem. His fingers were strangely numb and slow. Her soft voice was saying, "I've never quite found out yet. You sort of pull, and hope for the best."

Now he was smiling. His eyes looked up at her quickly. She laughed, and pushed back the lock of hair which had fallen over his brow.

"And I didn't mean *that*."

"No? And why not, Pani Wisniewska?"

They were both laughing now.

"Such luxury," she said, "to sleep without one's clothes, to wash in hot water, to stand before a fire, to have a warm bed, to forget about Germans." She stepped out of the wide circle of skirts spreading round her feet, and let the blouse and Kati's best pink-ribboned chemise fall from her shoulders. She looked down at him. "Such luxury to be in love, Adam. Such luxury to be truly loved."

He wasn't laughing any more. The light from the leaping flames of the fire flickered over her body, white in the room's dark shadows.

Outside, a crumbling cloud of snow descended on the mountainsides and valleys. In the villages, it blotted out the house across the street, the tree only ten yards away, the winding roads. On the lower mountain slopes, the scattered houses became still more alone. The large falling flakes hid the forests and the paths. There was no longer sky, or mountain, or valley. The white curtain smoothly, quietly, obliterated everything. Height and distance, shape and color no longer existed.

In the kitchen, Madame Olszak finished the last spoonful of soup, and refused a second helping. "It's begun," she said to Veronika, and nodded to the unshuttered window. Veronika replaced the cover on the soup-pot.

"Time was when we always had plenty of food to last us for months of bad weather."

"Times change. Close the shutters, Veronika. It seems warmer with them closed." She pulled the shawl more snugly round her shoulders.

Veronika peered out at the falling snow. "It's just coming

down," she announced. "My, it was lucky they got here before this started."

"I imagine," Madame said dryly, "that my nephew Gunter realized that fact. He knows the mountains."

Veronika cleared away the soup-bowls and crumbs of bread from the table. "It was only a year ago he was staying in the village with that shooting party. They still talk about that shoot."

"Veronika," said Madame Olszak, "sometimes a good memory is a dangerous thing, particularly if there's a loose tongue attached."

"I'm only saying it to you and me," Veronika protested indignantly. As if, she thought crossly, I didn't know how to hold my tongue when a German's about.

"And that's two people too many, my girl. Best not to get into the habit of remembering. You wouldn't want to be the one who gave him away?"

"But there have been no Szwaby here for weeks. They took all our extra food when they put our names on their list. They won't come, not until this bad weather is over anyway. And then there will be just some skiers, out for a good time. Those others with their lists and grabbing fingers won't be back until we have something else for them to lift." Her indignation changed to vindictive pleasure. "But they won't get the new calf or our chickens. Our own men will be eating them, this summer."

Madame relented, and nodded her head approvingly. The two women smiled. We are old, they seemed to be saying, but we are needed now as much as the young men: even we can help.

"You've put the Adam Gunter papers in his room? Good. They are getting worn. We'll soon have to ask for a new set. And the skis?"

"Wenceslas saw to them the last time he was here. They're in the attic, ready." Veronika finished wiping the bowls and stacked them neatly on the painted shelves fixed to one wall. "Time for some painting to be done round here again," she said, scrutinizing the fading colors of the flower decorations on the wooden beam above her head.

"That can wait till after the war," said Madame Olszak decidedly, and glanced at the hand-loom beside the window, at the spinning wheel inside the oven, at the small table with its growing pile of rough homespun.

"Aye," Veronika agreed. "They'll be needing a lot of cloth this spring when they come up to the mountains. There won't be much painting or woodcarving done in this or any other village from now on." She paused, and listened to the footsteps in the corridor. A door closed.

"I wonder what she's doing here with him," said Veronika. Her lips closed tightly and she shook her head.

Madame Olszak smiled slightly, but didn't answer.

"Married! She hasn't a wedding ring, even. I wouldn't feel married unless I had a ring on my right hand."

"Wouldn't you?" Madame Olszak smiled gently. She sat quite still, letting her thoughts wander back sixty years. Sixty years ago ... Veronika's voice kept insisting, kept pulling her back into the present. Madame Olszak frowned in annoyance.

"Is she going to stay here? That's what I want to know. When this storm ends, he's got work to do. He's leaving here, isn't he? He's got other villages to visit, hasn't he? And if she stays here alone, what will happen if German skiers come to the door at any time? They always notice the pretty ones. And even if she had papers, she's still a foreigner, by her accent."

"It is none of our business," said Madame Olszak sharply. She too had been worrying about that all evening, but somehow she felt irritated when these worries were put into words. Then, more gently, she said, "What's wrong with you tonight, Veronika? Come, we'll have a last half hour at the fire before we go to bed." She rose wearily from the hard bench. "Perhaps I am getting old, Veronika. The beginning of winter now makes me sad."

Veronika followed her into the other room. "It's the snow," she said slowly. "It makes you feel old. It makes you feel alone."

They sat close to the fire, and watched the dying log.


## CHAPTER XXXIX

### *The Last Days*

A FIRM, CRISP surface formed on the deep snow. You could walk on it as you could on icy ground, carefully and slowly, with each step judged and balanced. The white-gray skies changed to a clear pale blue. The sun set this clean, unmarked world glittering. The very air seemed to dance with light. Only the leeward trunks of the trees with their long winter shadows, and the walls of the houses which had sheltered under broad roofs kept their dark color in defiance of so much change. But even in the expanse of white loneliness, the feeling of being lost in space had ended with the falling snow. Sound and sight had come back to the world.

You could see once more the wisps of whitish smoke from the village chimneys; you could hear the light sound of sleigh-bells. And along the lower slopes of the mountain's side were scattered small brown patches, each with their column of smoke above them, which meant other houses. In the morning there were blue shadows on the snow, the sound of men's voices as they cleared paths to their doors, the echo of children's high laughter as they played, the occasional long-drawn call shouted from one neighbor to another. In the evening, the snow was streaked with gold and orange furrows from the large round sun sinking so swiftly behind the jagged edge of mountains. The shadows deepened to violet, the columns of smoke thickened and darkened, and the day's sounds (so small and simple, yet so magnified by the intensity of the silence) died gradually away. The people in the houses down in the village, or in the houses sparsely scattered along the hillsides or in the valleys, rested from their day's work. The cows and goats, brought down for the winter months from the high pastures, were fed; the baking and weaving and sewing and cobbling and carving and making and mending were over. There was time for talk in the kitchens and lamplit rooms. There were tales from the past, and stories, bloodier still, of the present. There were songs which brought tears and laughter, and whispered plans which brought hope for the spring. Night walked over the mountains, sweeping its train of stars, their brightness sharpened by the keen air. The carpet of snow became a cloth of silver. The shadows were as black as the windows where the lights died, one by one.

Wenceslas came on the first day after the storm had ended. But his mixture of news and gossip and information lost all importance to him when he saw Wisniewski. The warmth of his welcome was so infectious that Sheila, her face taut and fearful when she saw this man arrive, found herself smiling along with Madame Olszak as they watched his delight and relief. It was almost as if he were greeting his son.

"Used to hunt with Adam. Best guide in these parts. Best hunter too," Madame Olszak explained to Sheila in a low voice. "Come, we'll sit over at the window and let them talk. We'll keep an eye on the path to the village."

Sheila followed the old woman obediently. She looked back at the two men now facing each other across the table—Wenceslas red-haired, round-faced, broad-shouldered, slow-speaking; Adam silently listening, his large dark eyes narrowing as his mind played with an idea, a smile glancing over the determined mouth as the idea developed possibilities. He had pulled a sheet of paper in front of him, spread out a map. Wenceslas leaned over the table on his powerful forearms, marking his points with an upraised forefinger.

Madame Olszak watched Sheila's face. She touched her arm gently. "I know," she said half sadly. "A man has two things: his work and his wife. A woman when she's in love has only one. I know."

Sheila looked at her in alarm.

"It's all right: they'll never hear us," Madame Olszak smiled as she looked across at the two men. "They are in another world. I know." She nodded philosophically over the patchwork quilt.

At the end of the hour, Wenceslas rose to leave. He seemed to notice Sheila for the first time. "There was a message two days ago about her," he said to Adam. Sheila's heart missed a beat.

Wenceslas' tantalizingly slow voice went on: "Person accompanying Captain X to await further instructions. Full plan to follow."

Adam's arm rested round Sheila's shoulders. "Bring the message when it comes. As it stands. I'll decode it, Wenceslas." His voice was harsh.

Wenceslas looked at them in surprise. "Right," he said.

"You've never told me your news, Wenceslas," Madame Olszak said quickly, and led the red-haired man towards the door, listening gravely to the strange mixture of information: old Stefan was ill, badly this time; Maria's cow had stopped giving milk; more shooting of hostages in Warsaw; Ladislaw's younger daughter had a son, a ten-pound boy; Cracow professors had all been arrested and sent to concentration camps; five Germans at Zakopane had been caught in the snowstorm and frozen to death; the wolves were already prowling round the villages to the east—it was going to be a bad winter, more snow and bitter cold.

Wenceslas halted in the doorway. "The captain may have a chance to hunt wolves when he goes east," he said. "Think I'll have to come with you as your guide, Captain. Ladislaw can look after the radio for a while. He's always sticking his nose into it, anyway."

Adam smiled. "Wolf-shooting is out for the present, Wenceslas. German-shooting now."

"There's no law against doing both," Wenceslas suggested hopefully, but without success. "Well, I suppose when I took on this radio job I gave up hunting," he added sadly, and concentrated on fixing his skis.

"Plenty of hunting next summer when the camp has got to be fed, Wenceslas."

The grin came slowly back to Wenceslas' red, round face. "I'll be back in a day or two, no doubt," he said and looked at Sheila.

"Yes. I'll have further instructions ready for the district, then," Adam replied. His voice was businesslike, but his grip on Sheila's shoulders had tightened.

The door closed. Sheila felt that it had shut out all her hopes.

Madame Olszak picked up her needle once more.

Neither Sheila nor Adam had moved.

"She could stay with me," Madame Olszak said softly. "Must she go?"

Sheila felt her shoulder crushed. She knew the answer before he had spoken.

"Yes."

Madame Olszak's keen blue eyes looked at them sadly, but she nodded slowly as if in agreement. She rose and went slowly into the kitchen. "Must tell Veronika about the news from the village," she said.

Adam pulled Sheila round to face him.

"It would have been easier to say 'No.' That's what I wanted to say . . ." He watched her eyes anxiously. The lines on his face had deepened.

"I know," she said. "It seems strange . . . but I love you all the more," and the truth of her words was in her eyes.

She ended the long silence with "When will the instructions come?"

A shadow crossed Adam's face. His voice was quiet, expressionless, almost as if he were talking to himself, getting his own thoughts into order. "A few days, perhaps. Perhaps a week. There's a clever man at Zakopane who has helped us before. He would be the safest way. It depends if they can contact him and he is available. They must wait until he is. He's safe."

Sheila's body stiffened. She looked up at him. "That isn't why you are sending me away? Because of safety?" There was a rebellious line to her mouth.

Adam pretended to smile. He lied most innocently. "Of course not." He silenced her with a long kiss. "Darling . . ."

She said softly when she had enough breath to speak with, "I wish sometimes I were a man."

"Thank God you aren't," he replied with such fervor that she was forced to smile.

"That's better," he said. "That's how I like to see you.

With a laugh on your lips . . . That's how I first saw you. Remember?"

"So long ago it seems. Before the war . . ."

"Scarcely three months ago."

"How many more months before it all ends?"

He was silent.

"How long, Adam? Next year?"

His arms tightened round her waist. He kissed her throat.

"That's my favorite corner, just there," he said with a pretense of a smile. He kissed the soft curve where her neck and shoulder met. "One of my favorites," he added.

"How long, Adam? Surely next year."

"God knows." He shook his head as if he were trying to free himself from his bitter thoughts. "But never too long, Sheila. Never too long for us to wait."

Never too long . . . It might be years, then. Years, her heart echoed despairingly. But her eyes met his, as he wanted them to do, and accepted that fact.

Four days later, Wenceslas returned.

"Things are shaping up," he announced. He handed the message which he had brought to Wisniewski with evident relief. "The priest made sure I got it down all correct," he went on. "He's been waiting with me each night at eight o'clock for it to come. I told him it was important. And last night it came. But I thought I'd wait until this morning before I brought it along. Time enough, I said to myself, to bring it in the morning."

Veronika finished her pretense of dusting the room. In the last four days she had dropped her hostility to Sheila. The foreign girl was going away. She wasn't going to stay here and keep good men off their job. Much work any man would get done with her about the place.

"Come into the kitchen," she said with a sudden burst of tact, "I've got a nice bowl of hot soup ready to warm you, Wenceslas."

Madame Olszak had risen from her chair near the window. "I'll come and hear all the news, Wenceslas," she said.

Sheila crossed over to the table where Adam, his forehead resting on his hands and his elbows on the table, was reading the coded message. She sat down quietly beside him. Without looking up, he reached for one of her hands and held it.

"When?" she asked at last, certain he had finished reading the passage.

He still didn't look up. "Soon," he answered. "Very soon." She looked at the scrap of paper. It was a very innocent letter to a niece. Weather ... family health ... affectionate greetings ... *Your loving Aunt, Valeria.*

"And what does Aunt Valeria say?"

"Your clothes are already waiting for you. Your papers and story will be given to you any day after tomorrow, when Aunt Valeria arrives with them."

"Here?"

"No. At a small inn outside Zakopane."

She said slowly, "I should be there, ready to welcome Aunt Valeria when she does arrive." She was trying desperately to keep her voice calm.

"Yes.... I'll take you to the inn. We'll have to go carefully." He gave her a twisted smile. "Strangely enough, that may be the most difficult part of the journey. After that, with the right clothes and papers, it will be safe—easier."

"I feel safer with you than with any papers, Adam, no matter how clever your Aunt Valeria is."

"He hasn't made a mistake yet." Adam's voice was grim. He was convincing himself that this way would be safe.

*"He?"*

"Yes. Aunt Valeria is one of Number Fourteen's best men. Thank God he's on this job."

Her voice faltered. "Tonight we leave, then?"

"Tonight." Adam rose abruptly. He didn't look at her again. He opened the door, slowly climbed the path they had cut in the deep snow. If I had wept, she thought, as she stared at the pool of pale gold at the threshold where the sun's weak rays spread over the floor, if I had wept we never would have left for Zakopane. It was a relief that she could allow herself to weep now.

Madame Olszak came back into the room.

"I knew someone had left a door open," she grumbled. "Such a draught. This place is like ice." She moved about, closing the door, jabbing at the fire with a poker, talking incessantly as she moved. Sheila was in control of herself by the time that Veronika and Wenceslas entered.

"When?" Madame Olszak demanded suddenly.

"Tonight."

"That's what I expected." Her voice was almost bad-tempered. She was angry with everyone, herself most of all.

"Where are you going?" Veronika asked pityingly. Her hard face had softened.

Sheila saw Wenceslas, behind Veronika, shake his head warningly.

Madame Olszak had seen his advice, too.

"None of our business, Veronika," she said sharply. "Now you and I will start some cooking. We want a special supper this evening." She followed the slow-moving Veronika towards the kitchen. "Wars, wars," she was saying savagely. "People who should be together, bringing up the children God meant them to have, kept apart . . . . separated . . . I've always cursed the men who started wars. I must die cursing them . . . never an end . . . never . . ." It was strange to hear Veronika suddenly burst into wailing tears. And then the kitchen door closed.

"She's all right, that Veronika," Wenceslas said, "except she always wants to know everything. Well—" his round, good-natured face watched hers anxiously—"well . . . Think I'll just wait here." He sat down on the edge of a chair. "To see if the captain needs my help for tonight," he explained unnecessarily. And then he looked upset: oughtn't to have mentioned tonight, he thought. Pity she had to go. Yet no place for her here. The captain was traveling east. She would have to wait here. She couldn't go with him there. That was certain. And the Germans might come to the village, might come to this house. As they had done before, and would do again. The captain wouldn't have his mind on the job. He'd be worrying about her. Pity she had to go. No one's fault but the bloody Germans. Always the bloody Germans.

Wenceslas blew his nose violently. Then he was listening. "That's the captain," he said, and hurried to the window. "Walked his temper off, too, thank God. We'll get down to business, now." He looked anxiously at the girl. Funny how he kept saying the wrong things today. She was smiling, sadly, and he blew his nose again because he couldn't think of anything else to do.

They didn't notice him much, anyway. Not even when he suggested the arrangements for tonight: a sleigh, a sure-footed horse, and the third-rate little road which ran almost parallel to the main road to Zakopane. The German patrols kept to the main road in this weather, but even so, the time to make the journey was between patrols. On Tuesdays and Thursdays, the night patrols were out on the roads leading to Zakopane between ten and twelve, two and four. Methodical race, the Germans.

They didn't notice him much, but they had listened.

"Today is Thursday," the foreign girl said.

And the captain said, his face the same cold mask that his wife's was, "We set out at midnight, then."

"I'll have the sleigh waiting down by the last trees behind the post office," Wenceslas said.

He left them, then. They didn't even seem to notice his going.

## CHAPTER XL

## *Journey from Adam*

THE NARROW, open platform of the small railway station was crowded. Uniforms, holiday clothes and farewells jostled each other. Military boots, smartly polished and ready for duty once more, trampled on the hardened snow beside the ski-boots of those whose furlough was not yet over. There were women, too. Women with confident eyes and voices, furs, lipsticks, and perfume strangely heavy in the crisp pine-scented air. The voices became louder, gayer. Back-slapping, handshaking, good humor. Commands were kept for the thinly clad, overworked porters. These were Poles. Even the smartly dressed stationmaster and the man sitting in the warm ticket-office were Germans.

Sheila buried her chin more deeply into the fur collar of her coat, as if to shield her neck from the cold wind. If fear caused seasickness, then she was liable to be violently seasick at any moment on the solid platform of Zako-pane. The feeling of nausea, which had attacked her so suddenly this morning when she rose and thought of this journey had returned once again. German voices everywhere. German faces. She looked away from the crowd of well-fed, well-clothed bodies, stared at the village of Zakopane with its restaurants and hotels, its balconies and terraces, it summer villas and winter chalets strung across the lower mountain slopes. The Poles had been proud of their Zako-pane. Perhaps that was why the oversized black swastika in its round white circle was displayed so prominently over the ice-stadium.

"... another two weeks' leave in early spring," a captain was saying to a tall blonde girl in well-cut skiing clothes. "We'll have that in Berlin."

White teeth showed evenly against golden skin. "Let me know when, Franz. I'll be back in Danzig next week. Usual address ..."

An immaculate major, thin-jawed, hawk-nosed, said to the pink-cheeked captain who kept slow pace with him: "Pity you must leave before you got any real skiing. Perhaps in a month or two ... excellent in February."

"Yes. I was here last winter for the World Ski-championship. Some of the jumps reached eighty-five meters. I remember ... " Their steady pace drew them out of Sheila's hearing.

A dark-haired anxious woman passed with a lieutenant. " ... better, Walther. But are you sure you're fit to rejoin your unit?"

"Perfectly. Stop worrying, Lisa. Here's Johann."

"Walther! Seeing your wife off? When do you leave? Monday? So do I. Good. We'll travel together. Here are Martin and Sigurd and Frieda to say good-by to your Lisa. ... " There was a torrent of phrases and laughter.

Sheila waited patiently. The attack of sickness had passed. She watched the platform carefully. Soon, now. Surely soon. The train would be leaving in seven minutes. She walked a few paces across the platform, a few steps back. The clock was behind her now. She was standing in the right place. She tightened her hold on the book under her arm. Left arm ... that was right. It was a novel in a dramatic jacket of Party colors—black, white, red. That was correct too. She pretended to ignore any glances in her direction from the unattached men near her. She was one of the wives, whose husband were still too ill to be able to come down to the station for a last parting. She was wearing the right clothes. "Quietly, but nicely dressed," the man who had signed himself Aunt Valeria had said approvingly. "That and a purseful of money will ease the way. The German officials are always quick to differentiate between a woman and a lady. They admire the authority of good clothes. With your papers and escort, you probably will have a pleasant journey."

Pleasant ... Sheila tried to swallow the nervous lump in her throat. She was holding the new handbag so tightly in her neatly gloved hand that she felt it was growing onto her, had indeed become a part of her arm. In the handbag was what she valued more than the smart clothes or the money in her purse. In the handbag were the little pieces of paper which explained who she was, why she was here, where she was going—all so efficient with their flourish of signatures and authentic-looking stamps. Aunt Valeria had been pleased with them. "Beauties!" he had said and kissed them mockingly as he presented them to her with an imitation-official bow. Stop thinking of Aunt Valeria, she warned herself. Stop thinking of the ghostlike journey from Madame Olszak's house to the inn outside Zakopane. Stop thinking of Adam ... of the parting that had come so swiftly that it was over before she knew it had come. ... It was better that way.

Neither of them could have endured a long drawn-out farewell. . . .

Five minutes. She walked a few paces once more. And then she saw him. A short, thick-set man with a heavy white face. Hair graying at the temples; black well-marked eyebrows; gray eyes, serious and thoughtful. His German uniform was carelessly worn, only to be excused by the insignia of the Medical Corps on his coat collar. A busy man, a hurried man, a man too preoccupied with the problems of medicine to be worried about the correct way to dress as a soldier. And an important man, to judge by the respectful salutes given him and acknowledged in his own way. He walked past her very slowly, buried deep in thought. The title of the book he carried was clearly shown against its white cover: *System of Neuropathology*. Newspapers were under his other arm, a bulging yellow cowhide brief case in his hand. This was the man. And he had seen her, dressed in the fur-collared black coat, and the neat little green felt hat pulled down over one eye. But he didn't seem to notice her.

That was what she had expected. Aunt Valeria had gone over this routine so often with her, that she thought she would scream if he asked her to repeat it once again; but now she was glad of the care that had been taken. Now all she had to do was to follow the man in uniform, let him do the talking as he saw fit. The irritating lump in her throat was gone. Contact had been made. The first stage of the journey was already completed.

She pretended to watch the train backing slowly into the station. A chorus of good-bys, advice, laughter surrounded her as she followed the army doctor casually on board. She ignored the too loud remark of an officer walking beside her, avoided the bright smile he had given which meant to include her along with his friend in his joke. She had a last glimpse of the blond ski-girl with her strong teeth now in a firm smile, of the dark-haired Lisa with tears on her cheeks, of the pink-faced captain making a formal, heels-together good-by. And then she was out of the cold wind and into the suffocating warmth of the long corridor.

She searched for a pleasant compartment, and found the one in which the army doctor had already installed himself and his brief case. She sat opposite him and pretended to be interested in the emptying platform. An expansive colonel had followed her into the compartment. He disposed of himself amply, and greeted the doctor leisurely.

"Well, Dr. Lilienkron, chasing back and forward to your

Vienna, as usual? He spoke with benevolent condescension, and straightened his jacket with its row of decorations.

The doctor nodded and opened his newspaper. "Neurologists' conference begins tomorrow," he answered. "I shall be a day late, but I've been busy. Didn't know if I could manage to be there at all. I've had some interesting cases, recently."

"Seems to me to be a waste of time to have those meetings during a war," the colonel said bluntly. "What d'you do?"

Dr. Lilienkron raised a black eyebrow. His voice had the Austrian thick softness. "Save lives," he said, and tried unsuccessfully to study a newspaper column. The colonel talked on. Each phrase breathed success and satisfaction. He was quite conscious of the possible audience he had; the confident voice, the constant note of self-assertion showed he was aware of Sheila even if he did pretend to ignore her.

She, for her part, concentrated on Zakopane, wheeling out of sight as the train curved away from the sloping valley. On the dwindling platform, one of the Polish porters still stood, watching the train. At the last moment he had halted outside this compartment, and the apparently blank eyes had rested on her. Sheila had returned the look, and into the man's eyes had come relief and happiness. For that one short moment, Sheila knew that she had had a friend as she had stood on that platform. These eyes had watched her carefully, ready to report if the slightest thing had gone wrong. Nothing had. And now he stood watching the train, ready to report, "All well at Zakopane."

She didn't listen to the conversation which the colonel was relentlessly pursuing. She didn't even worry now whether he would be a handicap or an asset to their plans. Dr. Lilienkron would know how to decide: this was his problem. She glanced over at the tired white face, with its dark-circled eyes. Dr. Lilienkron was watching her with puzzled politeness.

He leaned over slightly and said, "I believe we have met. . . . . Please excuse me. I forget names so easily. Your husband is one of my patients, isn't he? Didn't I see you when you visited him?"

"Yes," Sheila heard herself saying. "Captain Hellmuth Kraus." She managed a smile as she said the last name not too distinctly.

"But of course. How stupid of me. You must forgive my rudeness. I have a habit of forgetting names but remembering faces." Introductions followed to the waiting colonel, but Sheila was too nervous to catch his name. It didn't matter anyway. He did most of the talking. The ticket collector was quickly chased out of their compartment with his what-the-devil-are-you-bothering-us-about-now stare. And no other traveler had either the courage to resist the colonel, or the inclination to be bored by him, for no one else entered the compartment although the small train was well crowded.

"I forget where your home is," Dr. Lilienkron was saying to her with grave politeness.

"It's near Vienna."

"And that's where I am going," He smiled kindly. "So we are traveling companions."

"I'm traveling as far as Bohemia, myself," the colonel informed them.

After that, the doctor seemed willing to forget about both his newspaper and his patient's wife. He listened constantly and politely to the colonel. It is possible that the colonel had never had such an attentive audience. His constant repetition of "out of the question," "in my opinion," never had more patient hearing. Dr. Lilienkron of the sad eyes and tired face was turning the colonel into an asset.

Their journey led them back into Poland as far as Cracow. There they changed trains to travel towards the southwest. The colonel stayed with the doctor, and the doctor stayed with Sheila. She seemed worried, and nervous, and sad. That was sufficient excuse for him to see that his patient's wife was escorted out of this strange, wild land. The colonel approved, too. He had been impressed by Sheila's restraint and by her clothes. Aunt Valeria had chosen well.

Sheila solved the problem of conversation by pretending to be tired. She spent the journey out of Poland either listening to the steady flow of opinions which passed for conversation in the colonel's mind, or resting with her eyes closed and her head leaning wearily against the white mat which decorated the back of the compartment seat. She feigned sleep. It was all the more difficult that she should be really fighting against it. She mustn't fall asleep, or let her mind slip into Polish or English phrases. She mustn't think of Adam, of the stark loneliness of these last two days when he was no longer with her. That was the price you had to pay; the more you loved, the greater this sense of loneliness.

"Are you all right?" Dr. Lilienkron was asking gently. His observant eyes were studying hers with a doctor's perception.

She nodded.

"You must not worry so much about your husband. He will be quite well very soon."

She nodded again.

The colonel cleared his throat impatiently, and brought the

doctor back to the problems of keeping troops healthy under desert conditions. He kept talking of some Afrika Korps.

The rolling foothills of the countryside south of Cracow gave way to pine trees and rocky crags. The white mountains and the huddling villages swept by. The train was once more in the Carpathians. They were approaching the southwesternmost corner of Poland, of the Poland that was—for all the names and signs in the villages were now in German. Soon they would be at the old border. The train would travel across the southeast tip of Germany into Czechoslovakia, into the country the Germans now called Bohemia to satisfy themselves that it was German too.

The rhythm of the train wheels changed. There were movements in the corridor as some passengers prepared to descend at the old frontier town of Bogumin to catch the Breslau express.

A young lieutenant glanced into their compartment as he passed leisurely along the corridor. His face was familiar, and he had recognized her. She could feel he knew her. Sheila looked abruptly away, fear and worry once more churning inside her, and pretended to watch the station into which the train was now sliding slowly. Slowly it stopped. Impatiently she watched the passengers who dismounted, made their good-bys, joined other groups. She searched desperately for the known face. And then, as she saw the man's slight figure walking confidently across the rails towards the waiting Breslau train, she remembered, and remembering, she could have cried out in relief. The man dressed as a German lieutenant had been at that Zakopane inn to meet Aunt Valeria. He had been nameless and uncommunicative. She had met him only once. He had been there for instructions, Aunt Valeria had said. Now she could guess what these had been: the young man was to proceed into Germany itself. She watched the slim shoulders with amazement and admiration. They moved so confidently, so calmly into the German express; somehow his assurance comforted her and gave her added courage.

She could smile now at her alarm. Frontiers, even in peacetime, had always worried her. If she hadn't been so nervous she might have recognized him sooner, and saved herself an unpleasant three minutes. And yet the man seemed so altered, so different, that she probably wouldn't have recognized him easily, in any case. She leaned more comfortably against the arm-rest in her corner of the compartment. It was comforting to know that people could merge so successfully into a new background. And it was comforting to think that another friend had been so near her on this journey.

First, the porter at Zakopane. Now this young "German,"
whose journey had been arranged to coincide with hers. She
began to wonder if this kind of supervision was going to follow her all the way to Vienna. Adam had said the journey
would be safe: he certainly had made his arrangements.

She saw that the colonel was watching her. Her muscles
tightened. Her right thumb pressed against the wedding ring
which Madame Olszak had given her as a farewell present.
("It brought me much happiness," the faded voice had said,
and the cold lips had kissed her gently.) She waited tensely.

"Going on maneuvers," the colonel said, and Sheila relaxed once more. He nodded towards the neat, double line of
soldiers waiting patiently on the platform. They carried skis
and other winter equipment. "Fine body of men," he added.
"Eh, Lilienkron?"

Lilienkron agreed. Sheila found herself watching the platform too. So many uniforms, she thought bitterly, so many.
The colonel looked with satisfaction at the numerous officers
who paced about the station to keep warm in the cold wind.

It was then that she saw the two officers who were strid-
ing along the length of the train. The taller of them had
turned his face boldly towards the carriages. He was looking
for someone, his eyes keen, his face intent. For a moment,
as he drew level with her, his brown eyes looked deeply
into hers. Sheila's thumb tightened again on her ring. Her
right hand clenched. She felt she had turned to stone. Then
the officers' steady pace carried them out of sight. She began to breathe again. Adam, dear God in Heaven, Adam. . . .
How could you? How could you do anything so wild, so
mad? She didn't know whether she wanted to laugh or to cry.

The colonel's voice was saying, "We build good soldiers.
No doubt about that. Eh, Lilienkron?"

Again Lilienkron agreed.

Sheila was smiling now, her hands smoothing her gloves on
her lap, her eyes watching the colonel. He took the smile as
one of approval, and nodded graciously.

"Leaving at last," Dr. Lilienkron said in relief, as the
train's wheels groaned and strained. "Any more delays on
this line, and I shall never reach Vienna in time for that
meeting."

The faces in the station seemed to be moving past the
window. Sheila saw Adam and his companion salute another
officer smartly as they were about to leave the station. Above
them, the giant swastika, taut in the cold afternoon wind,
stretched it crooked arms. Sheila, her eyes on Adam as he
paused for a moment to look at the departing train, kept

her face expressionless. The imposing colonel couldn't hear her heart singing.

Lilienkron had looked at her sharply. Then he was searching for some report in his hideously bright brief case to interest the colonel. The two men read and talked intermittently until it was time for dinner. Rather surprisingly, it was the colonel who insisted that they should have the pleasure of her company.

The journey became stereotyped. It was like any journey in an express train across Europe on any winter holiday. Except that everyone spoke German. Except that all the younger men were in uniform, and all the newspapers and menus and notices were in a thick black script.

At Brno, the colonel departed. To the very end, Sheila was glad to note, he had never got her name correctly once. Dr. Lilienkron's introduction had been a masterly study in ambiguity.

At Vienna, the silent doctor made his farewell.

"Someone is meeting you?" he asked politely, as they joined the straggling stream of weary travelers.

Sheila noticed the tall, thin man with a green tie who had marked down the doctor and his companion and was now waiting for them to separate. "Yes," she said. "My brother-in-law."

Dr. Lilienkron left her as vaguely as he had met her. The tall, thin man's choice of welcoming phrase was what she had expected. She answered as she had been taught. His handshake was firm, friendly, comforting. The second stage of the journey was over.

Three days later, two nuns left Vienna. They traveled south towards Italy. In the manner of nuns, they were quiet, gently sad, and yet somehow contented. In comparison, their fellow travelers seemed overexcited, rudely energetic, violently unhappy. At the frontier, their few earthly belongings were easily examined. Their papers were in correct order.

"Sometimes it seems a waste," the younger customs official remarked as his eyes followed the two nuns departing from his table. "That young one . . ."

The older official shook his head. "Sometimes, I think they are the lucky ones," he said wearily, and turned his attention to an argumentative Rumanian.

In the local Italian train, the two nuns sat silently amid the general uproar of a third-class carriage. Children clambered over the wooden seats. Peasants hugged their large bundles on their knees. A young man played disjointed tunes on a concertina. A girl with heavy black hair, a black shawl and long jet earrings sang in a harsh sharp voice. A baby cried on one high sustained note. A fat goose waddled down the center passage. Hens clucked noisily from wicker baskets. The carriage smelled of human bodies, sounded with high exclamations and denunciations. Scolding and laughter, garlic and sour red wine filled the air.

The older nun smiled tolerantly. But the younger nun seemed oblivious to everything around her. Only her eyes were alive in her face, and the thoughts that filled them were far removed from these surroundings. Once the older nun had touched the scarred left hand beside her, and pointed to the neatly husbanded field with its row of cypress trees, black in the faint winter sunlight. "A country at peace," she said comfortingly.

The younger nun roused herself politely. Obediently, she looked. Peace, she was thinking, and yet only the pretense of peace. There was no real peace, anywhere, until there was peace everywhere. How long until then? She wondered, her eyes fixed on the cold blue winter sky. How long? Never too long, Adam had said. Sheila smiled sadly: she was going to learn the meaning of patience. She had learned fear, and sorrow, and hatred, and love. Patience was still to be learned. At least, she had already discovered that there was no use in trying to avoid these realities. Life was a hard school: the sooner you accepted that, the sooner you learned.

The older nun beside her shook her head. They were all like that, those who got out ... silent, brooding, unseeing. Poor things, it was as if they had left their hearts and minds in the hell from which their bodies had escaped. It was as if they were ashamed that they had escaped, at all.

She pointed to the sunset, deepening suddenly, "Eh! *Com'é bella!*" she said.

## CHAPTER XLI

### *Never Too Long*

UNCLE MATTHEWS pushed aside the forgotten cup of coffee and rested his elbows on the tablecloth which he had liberally sprinkled with cigarette ash. Sheila's voice had ended, and her hands played with the rose petal in the finger bowl. Even if Uncle Matthews' housekeeper could only give them a carefully rationed menu, at least the candles and the best crystal and all the other table trimmings had been set forth for the prodigal's return.

"Well," Uncle Matthews said at last. "Interesting story."

Sheila looked at the serious face opposite her, always grim in repose in spite of the pink cheeks, blue eyes, and white hair. "You don't quite believe it," she said with a smile.

"Why not? It's interesting, but not unusual. I've heard more incredible tales than that in the last four weeks."

Sheila raised an eyebrow, and her uncle laughed suddenly at the expression on her face. "You don't quite believe that," he challenged.

She remembered Mr. Olszak and his friends. "Why not?" she echoed, imitating her uncle's voice.

"I don't want to hurry you, but there's a couple of chaps I'd like you to meet. Tomorrow. While the details you've given me are still fresh in your head. Do you feel up to seeing them?"

"Of course. Are they British?"

"One is. The other is Polish."

Suddenly Sheila felt pleased. "Do you think what I have to tell could possibly be of some use?" she asked eagerly.

Uncle Matthews suppressed a smile. "Possibly," he said, and lit another cigarette.

"I wish," she said abruptly, "I do wish I could really have been of some use."

He took a long time to extinguish the match.

"I mean," she went on, "when I had a chance to do something...In Warsaw. Just when I was getting into that Gestapo circle...If I hadn't gone to Korytów to warn the village, if I hadn't met Reymont and his men, if—"

"Too many ifs," said Uncle Matthews quietly. "You wouldn't have lasted very long in that Gestapo circle, as you call it. You'd need a couple of years' training first, for that kind of work. Personally, I don't think you did so badly. Olszak doesn't think so, anyway. I had a message from him yesterday."

"Yes?" Sheila's eyes widened impatiently.

"He sent you his love."

"He didn't!"

"Well, words to that effect. He thinks you saved him."

"Oh...if I hadn't found out about Dittmar...then I suppose someone else would have."

"Would they?" Uncle Matthews was smiling openly now. "By the way, I like that fellow Stevens. Good man. Works hard."

Sheila smiled. "Yes," she said warmly.

"He's engaged to be married, you know."

"Steve?" Sheila studied the woven water-lily on the white tablecloth. What right had she to be so surprised? She smiled, and then laughed at herself. "I'm so glad," she said. "I hope she's as nice as Steve deserves."

"Pretty girl. American. Writes for some newspaper."

There was a pause. "Any other news?" Sheila hoped her voice sounded disinterested.

"We made a short advance yesterday against the Siegfried Line."

"Uncle Matthews!"

"Be careful of that finger bowl. It spills quite easily." And then he relented. "Your husband is well. He has gone further east now. Madame Aleksander is well. Mr. Hofmeyer is well; and doing remarkably good business. In fact, so far things have been going nicely for all of them. Olszak's organization is building up slowly and surely. He isn't trying for any spectacular successes just now. He's preparing for the future. Clever fellow, Olszak."

"Yes." Sheila could agree about that. Farther east, she was thinking. She must get hold of a map, a nice detailed map. She waited patiently, hoping for some more crumbs of good news. But that was all she was to be allowed.

"One point we'd better discuss before you start seeing people again. You know, of course, that no one must learn how you lived, or what you've been doing, or how you traveled out of Poland to Italy."

"Of course."

"Also, Sheila, I think it better for you to keep your old name, Matthews. Wisniewski is on the German records as having been killed in Warsaw towards the end of the siege. We want to keep him officially dead. So, until the war ends, you had just better remain Miss Matthews. Agreed?"

Sheila looked strangely at him. She seemed to be trying to say something, without succeeding very well.

"Couldn't we invent a name?" she suggested at last.

"What's wrong with Matthews?" said her uncle in amusement. "It was good enough for you for more than twenty years."

"It isn't the Matthews part that worries me." She half-smiled. "Unless, of course, you don't mind introducing us to your friends as Miss Matthews and son."

Uncle Matthews stared at her. All his amusement had gone.

"Or Miss Matthews and daughter," Sheila added quietly. "You never can tell about such things, I believe."

Uncle Matthews still said nothing. It was the only time in her life, Sheila thought, that she had ever succeeded in surprising him.

He recovered quickly. "And that," he was saying as if to himself, "was the real reason why we managed to get you out of Poland."

Sheila didn't deny it.

Uncle Matthews suddenly laughed. "I thought it was because of my pressure on Olszak. Olszak thought it was all a matter of security. Your husband thought it was to ensure your safety. You weren't thinking anywhere along our lines, were you?"

"No," Sheila answered.

Uncle Matthews laughed again. There is no joke which a Scotsman enjoys more than a pleasant one against himself.

Sheila smiled. "Well, that's a relief, Uncle Matthews. I wasn't quite sure whether you'd rage like a bull or roar like a lion."

He looked slightly startled at the idea. "Come now," he said, "apart from a natural resentment at being kicked upstairs into the great-uncle class, I'm delighted." He was keeping his voice especially mild, to prove to himself the exaggeration of her description.

Sheila rose and came round to where he sat, and laid a hand on his shoulder. She wondered what he would say if she planted a kiss on his cheek. He'd probably like it, although he'd never admit it. She tried it. She was right.

"Picking up Polish customs, I see," he said as she left him to cross over to the window.

"If we put out the lights," she called over her shoulder, "we could draw back the curtains and I could see my first London blackout."

"What's so wonderful about that?" he grumbled; but he extinguished the candles one by one.

The frost gleamed on the sloping slate roofs. The gray stone was whitened by the moon. The soot-marks became black shadows. The stars seemed brighter over the darkened city, like the stars over the sea, or the stars above silent mountains. The same moon and the same stars would be fading now as the dawn began in the Carpathians.

Unexpectedly he had come over to stand beside her at the window. Together they looked at the bright stars.

"It may be a long time," he said gently. "You know that, Sheila? The war hasn't really begun for us over here. Not yet."

"I know." Her voice was even. "It will be long," she was saying. She turned abruptly away from the window. "Never too long," she added quietly; so quietly that he wondered if he had really caught the whole phrase. He puzzled over that for a moment; never too long to wait, if . . . ? If what you waited for was really worth while? That, he decided, must be the implication. He felt a sudden relief. At least she wasn't going to lament or complain, she wasn't going to dramatize. Tonight she had talked about Kortyów and Madame Aleksander, of Barbara and Uncle Edward and Olszak, of Reymont, and Jan, of Casimir and his dog Volterscot, of Kati and Zygmunt, of Andrew and Stefan and little Teresa, of Madame Olszak, of the men in the forest and Adam Wisniewski. He knew, now that once their story had been told she wasn't going to keep on talking about them. She had her own thoughts about the past. She had her own beliefs about the future. She wanted no one to invade them.

She faced him again, and she was smiling as she looked up at the night sky.

He had a strange feeling that, for the moment, he didn't exist.

# About the Author

HELEN MacINNES was born in Scotland, grew up there, was graduated from the University of Glasgow, and later studied at University College in London. After her marriage to the late Gilbert Highet, they lived in Oxford, where he was a don at St. John's College. In 1937 Mr. Highet was invited to lecture at Columbia University and, except during his distinguished war service as a high-level member of British Intelligence, the Highets made their home in New York. They became United States citizens in 1951.

Miss MacInnes started to write for publication in 1939. Her first novel, *Above Suspicion*, was an immediate success and launched her on a spectacular writing career that has made her an international favorite. Her previous nineteen novels have sold well over twenty million copies in America alone and have been translated into twenty-two languages. Each of her novels has been a best seller and a book-club selection. Several have been adapted as films.

Miss MacInnes died in 1985.